CITIES IN FLIGHT

JAMES BLISH

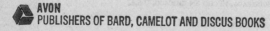

AVON
PUBLISHERS OF BARD, CAMELOT AND DISCUS BOOKS

AVON BOOKS
A division of
The Hearst Corporation
959 Eighth Avenue
New York, New York 10019

THE NOVELS
OF THE
CITIES IN FLIGHT

They Shall Have Stars

The cycle begins — in the farthest reaches of
the Solar System, on the raging, frozen, gaseous
hell-planet of Jupiter.

A Life for the Stars

The cities of Earth become galactic wanderers,
deserting the wornout home planet for the
vast reaches of deep space.

Earthman, Come Home

As foretold by cyclic theories of sociohistorians,
colonies of space traveling cities revert to barbarism
and turn on their native planet to obliterate
their ancient birthplace.

The Triumph of Time

History comes full circle as the cities journey
into inter-galactic space and glimpse the birthplace
of continuous creation — wherein mankind's
Judgment Day is contained.

Other Avon books by
James Blish

AND ALL THE STARS A STAGE   41186 $1.50

THEY
SHALL
HAVE
STARS

And death shall have no dominion
Dead men naked they shall be one
With the man in the wind and the west moon;
When their bones are picked clean and the
  clean bones gone,
They shall have stars at elbow and foot ...
DYLAN THOMAS

" ... While Vegan civilization was undergoing this peculiar decline in influence, while at the height of its political and military power, the culture which was eventually to replace it was beginning to unfold. The reader should bear in mind that at that time nobody had ever heard of the Earth, and the planet's sun, Sol, was known only as an undistinguished type G_0 star in the Draco sector. It is possible—although highly unlikely—that Vega knew that the Earth had developed space flight some time before the events we have just reviewed here. It was, however, only local interplanetary flight; up to this period, Earth had taken no part in Galactic history. It was inevitable, however, that Earth should make the two crucial discoveries which would bring it on to that starry stage. We may be very sure that Vega, had she known that Earth was to be her successor, would have exerted all of her enormous might to prevent it. That Vega failed to do so is evidence enough that she had no real idea of what was happening on Earth at this time. ..."
—ACREFF-MONALES: The Milky Way:
Five Cultural Portraits

BOOK ONE

PRELUDE: Washington

We do not believe any group of men adequate enough or wise enough to operate without scrutiny or without criticism. We know that the only way to avoid error is to detect it, that the only way to detect it is to be free to inquire. We know that in secrecy error undetected will flourish and subvert.

— J. ROBERT OPPENHEIMER

THE SHADOWS flickered on the walls to his left and right, just inside the edges of his vision, like shapes stepping quickly back into invisible doorways. Despite his bone-deep weariness, they made him nervous, almost made him wish that Dr. Corsi would put out the fire. Nevertheless, he remained staring into the leaping orange light, feeling the heat tightening his cheeks and the skin around his eyes, and soaking into his chest.

Corsi stirred a little beside him, but Senator Wagoner's own weight on the sofa seemed to have been increasing ever since he had first sat down. He felt drained, lethargic, as old and heavy as a stone despite his forty-eight years; it had been a bad day in a long succession of bad days. Good days in Washington were the ones you slept through.

Next to him Corsi, for all that he was twenty years older, formerly Director of the Bureau of Standards, formerly Director of the World Health Organization, and presently head man of the American Association for the Advancement of Science (usually referred to in Washington as "the left-wing Triple A-S"), felt as light and restless and quick as a chameleon.

"I suppose you know what a chance you're taking, coming to see me," Corsi said in his dry, whispery voice. "I wouldn't be in Washington at all if I didn't think the

interests of the AAAS required it. Not after the drubbing
I've taken at MacHinery's hands. Even outside the govern-
ment, it's like living in an aquarium—in a tank labeled
'Piranha.' But you know about all that."

"I know," the senator agreed. The shadows jumped
forward and retreated. "I was followed here myself. Mac-
Hinery's gumshoes have been trying to get something on
me for a long time. But I had to talk to you, Seppi. I've
done my best to understand everything I've found in the
committee's files since I was made chairman—but a non-
scientist has inherent limitations. And I didn't want to ask
revealing questions of any of the boys on my staff. That
would be a sure way to a leak—probably straight to
MacHinery."

"That's the definition of a government expert these
days," Corsi said, even more dryly. "A man of whom you
don't dare ask an important question."

"Or who'll give you only the answer he thinks you want
to hear," Wagoner said heavily. "I've hit that too. Working for the government isn't a pink tea for a senator,
either. Don't think I haven't wanted to be back in Alaska
more than once; I've got a cabin on Kodiak where I can
enjoy an open fire, without wondering if the shadows it
throws carry notebooks. But that's enough self-pity. I ran
for the office, and I mean to be good at it, as good as I
can be, anyhow."

"Which is good enough," Corsi said unexpectedly, taking the brandy snifter out of Wagoner's lax hand and
replenishing the little amber lake at the bottom of it. The
vapors came welling up over his cupped hand, heavy and
rich. "Bliss, when I first heard that the Joint Congressional
Committee on Space Flight was going to fall into the
hands of a freshman senator, one who'd been nothing but
a press agent before his election—"

"Please," Wagoner said, wincing with mock tenderness.
"A public relations counsel."

"As you like. Still and all, I turned the air blue. I knew
it wouldn't have happened if any senator with seniority
had wanted the committee, and the fact that none of them
did seemed to me to be the worst indictment of the
present Congress anyone could ask for. Every word I said
was taken down, of course, and will be used against you,
sooner or later. It's already been used against me, and
thank God *that's* over. But I was wrong about you.
You've done a whale of a good job; you've learned like

magic. So if you want to cut your political throat by asking me for advice, then by God I'll give it to you."

Corsi thrust the snifter back into Wagoner's hand with something more than mock fury. "That goes for you, and for nobody else," he added. "I wouldn't tell anybody else in government the best way to pound sand—not unless the AAAS asked me to."

"I know you wouldn't, Seppi. That's part of our trouble. Thanks, anyhow." He swirled the brandy reflectively. "All right, then, tell me this: what's the matter with space flight?"

"The army," Corsi said promptly.

"Yes, but that's not all. Not by a long shot. Sure, the Army Space Service is graft-ridden, shot through with jealousy and gone rigid in the brains. But it was far worse back in the days when a half-dozen branches of government were working on space flight at the same time—the weather bureau, the navy, your bureau, the air force and so on. I've seen some documents dating back that far. The Earth Satellite Program was announced in 1944 by Stuart Symington; we didn't actually get a manned vehicle up there until 1962, after the army was given full jurisdiction. They couldn't even get the damned thing off the drawing boards; every rear admiral insisted that the plans include a parking place for his pet launch. At least now we *have* space flight.

"But there's something far more radically wrong now. If space flight were still a live proposition, by now some of it would have been taken away from the army again. There'd be some merchant shipping maybe; or even small passenger lines for a luxury trade, for the kind of people who'll go in uncomfortable ways to unliveable places just because it's horribly expensive." He chuckled heavily. "Like fox-hunting in England a hundred years ago; wasn't it Oscar Wilde who called it 'the pursuit of the inedible by the unspeakable'?"

"Isn't it still a little early for that?" Corsi said.

"In 2013? I don't think so. But if I'm rushing us on that one point, I can mention others. Why have there been no major exploratory expeditions for the past fifteen years? I should have thought that as soon as the tenth planet, Proserpine, was discovered some university or foundation would have wanted to go there. It has a big fat moon that would make a fine base—no weather exists at those temperatures—there's no sun in the sky out there to louse up photographic plates—it's only another zero-magnitude star—and so on. That kind of thing used to be meat and drink to private explorers. Given a millionaire with a thirst for science, like old Hale, and a sturdy organizer with a little grandstand in him—a Byrd-type—and we should have had a Proserpine Two station long ago. Yet space has been dead since Titan Station was set up in 1981. Why?"

He watched the flames for a moment.

"Then," he said, "there's the whole question of invention in the field. It's stopped, Seppi. Stopped cold."

Corsi said: "I seem to remember a paper from the boys on Titan not so long ago—"

"On xenobacteriology. Sure. That's not space flight, Seppi; space flight only made it possible; their results don't update space flight itself, don't improve it, make it more attractive. Those guys aren't even interested in it. *Nobody* is any more. That's why it's stopped changing.

"For instance: we're still using ion-rockets, driven by an atomic pile. It works, and there are a thousand minor variations on the principle; but the principle itself was described by Coupling in 1954! Think of it, Seppi—not one single new, basic engine design in *fifty years!* And what about hull design? That's still based on von Braun's work—older even than Coupling's. Is it really possible that there's nothing better than those frameworks of hitched onions? Or those powered gliders that act as ferries for them? Yet I can't find anything in the committee's files that looks any better."

"Are you sure you'd know a minor change from a major one?"

"You be the judge," Wagoner said grimly. "The hottest thing in current spaceship design is a new elliptically wound spring for acceleration couches. It drags like a leaf-spring with gravity, and pushes like a coil-spring against it. The design wastes energy in one direction, stores it in the other. At last reports, couches made with it feel like sacks stuffed with green tomatoes, but we think we'll have the bugs out of it soon. Tomato bugs, I suppose. Top Secret."

"There's one more Top Secret I'm not supposed to know," Corsi said. "Luckily it'll be no trouble to forget."

"All right, try this one. We have a new water-bottle for ships' stores. It's made of aluminum foil, to be collapsed from the bottom like a toothpaste tube to feed the water into the man's mouth."

"But a plastic membrane collapsed by air pressure is handier, weighs less—"

"Sure it does. And this foil tube is already standard for paste rations. All that's new about this thing is the proposal that we use it for water too. The proposal came to us from a lobbyist for CanAm Metals, with strong endorsements by a couple of senators from the Pacific Northwest. You can guess what we did with it."

"I am beginning to see your drift."

"Then I'll wind it up as fast as I can," Wagoner said. "What it all comes to is that the whole structure of space flight as it stands now is creaking, obsolescent, overelaborate, decaying. The field is static; no, worse than that, it's losing ground. By this time, our ships ought to be sleeker and faster, and able to carry bigger payloads. We ought to have done away with this dichotomy between ships that can land on a planet, and ships that can fly from one planet to another.

"The whole question of *using* the planets for something—something, that is, besides research—ought to be within sight of settlement. Instead, nobody even discusses it any more. And our chances to settle it grow worse every year. Our appropriations are dwindling, as it gets harder and harder to convince the Congress that space flight is really good for anything. You can't sell the Congress on the long-range rewards of basic research, anyhow; representatives have to stand for election every two years, senators every six years; that's just about as far ahead as most of them are prepared to look. And suppose we tried to explain to them the basic research we're doing? We couldn't; it's classified!

"And above all, Seppi—this may be only my personal ignorance speaking, but if so, I'm stuck with it—above all, I think that by now we ought to have some slight clue toward an inter*stellar* drive. We ought even to have a model, no matter how crude—as crude as a Fourth of July rocket compared to a Coupling engine, but with the principle visible. But we don't. As a matter of fact, we've written off the stars. Nobody I can talk to thinks we'll ever reach them."

Corsi got up and walked lightly to the window, where he stood with his back to the room, as though trying to look through the light-tight blind down on to the deserted street.

To Wagoner's fire-dazed eyes, he was scarcely more than a shadow himself. The senator found himself thinking, for perhaps the twentieth time in the past six months, that Corsi might even be glad to be out of it all, branded unreliable though he was. Then, again for at least the twentieth time, Wagoner remembered the repeated clearance hearings, the oceans of dubious testimony and gossip from witnesses with no faces or names, the clamor in the press when Corsi was found to have roomed in college with a man suspected of being an ex-YPSL member, the denunciation on the senate floor by one of MacHinery's captive solons, more hearings, the endless barrage of vilification and hatred, the letters beginning "Dear Doctor Corsets, You bum," and signed "True American." To get out of it that way was worse than enduring it, no matter how stoutly most of your fellow scholars stood by you afterwards.

"I shan't be the first to say so to you," the physicist said, turning at last. "I don't think we'll ever reach the stars either, Bliss. And I am not very conservative, as physicists go. We just don't live long enough for us to become a star-traveling race. A mortal man limited to speeds below that of light is as unsuited to interstellar travel as a moth would be to crossing the Atlantic. I'm sorry to believe that, certainly; but I do believe it."

Wagoner nodded and filed the speech away. On that subject he had expected even less than Corsi had given him.

"But," Corsi said, lifting his snifter from the table, "it isn't impossible that inter*planetary* flight could be bettered. I agree with you that it's rotting away now. I'd suspected that it might be, and your showing tonight is conclusive."

"Then why is it happening?" Wagoner demanded.

"Because scientific method doesn't work any more."

"*What!* Excuse me, Seppi, but that's sort of like hearing an archbishop say that Christianity doesn't work any more. What do you mean?"

Corsi smiled sourly. "Perhaps I was overdramatic. But it's true that, under present conditions, scientific method is a blind alley. It depends on freedom of information, and we deliberately killed that. In my bureau, when it was mine, we seldom knew who was working on what project

at any given time; we seldom knew whether or not somebody else in the bureau was duplicating it; we never knew
whether or not some other department might be duplicating it. All we could be sure of was that many men,
working in similar fields, were stamping their results
Secret because that was the easy way—not only to keep
the work out of Russian hands, but to keep the workers in
the clear if their own government should investigate them.
How can you apply scientific method to a problem when
you're forbidden to see the data?

"Then there's the caliber of scientist we have working
for the government now. The few first-rate men we have
are so harassed by the security set-up—and by the constant suspicion that's focused on them because they *are*
top men in their fields, and hence anything they might
leak would be particularly valuable—that it takes them
years to solve what used to be very simple problems. As
for the rest—well, our staff at Standards consisted almost
entirely of third-raters: some of them were very dogged
and patient men indeed, but low on courage and even lower
on imagination. They spent all their time operating
mechanically by the cook-book—the routine of scientific
method—and had less to show for it every year."

"Everything you've said could be applied to the spaceflight research that's going on now, without changing a
comma," Wagoner said. "But, Seppi, if scientific method
used to be sound, it should still be sound. It ought to work
for anybody, even third-raters. Why has it suddenly turned
sour now—after centuries of unbroken successes?"

"The time lapse," Corsi said somberly, "is of the first
importance. Remember, Bliss, that scientific method is *not*
a natural law. It doesn't exist in nature, but only in our
heads; in short, it's a way of thinking about things—a way
of sifting evidence. It was bound to become obsolescent
sooner or later, just as sorites and paradigms and syllo-
gisms became obsolete before it. Scientific method works
fine while there are thousands of obvious facts lying about
for the taking—facts as obvious and measurable as how
fast a stone falls, or what the order of the colors is in a
rainbow. But the more subtle the facts to be discovered
become—the more they retreat into the realms of the
invisible, the intangible, the unweighable, the sub-
microscopic, the abstract—the more expensive and time-
consuming it is to investigate them by scientific method.

"And when you reach a stage where the *only* research

worth doing costs millions of dollars *per experiment*, then those experiments can be paid for only by government. Governments can make the best use only of third-rate men, men who can't leaven the instructions in the cookbook with the flashes of insight you need to make basic discoveries. The result is what you see: sterility, stasis, dry rot."

"Then what's left?" Wagoner said. "What are we going to do now? I know you well enough to suspect that you're not going to give up all hope."

"No," Corsi said, "I haven't given up, but I'm quite helpless to change the situation you're complaining about. After all, I'm on the outside. Which is probably good for me." He paused, and then said suddenly: "There's no hope of getting the government to drop the security system completely?"

"Completely?"

"Nothing else would do."

"No," Wagoner said. "Not even partially, I'm afraid. Not any longer."

Corsi sat down and leaned forward, his elbows on his knobby knees, staring into the dying coals. "Then I have two pieces of advice to give you, Bliss. Actually they're two sides of the same coin. First of all, begin by abandoning these multi-million-dollar, Manhattan-District approaches. We don't need a newer, still finer measurement of electron resonance one-tenth so badly as we need new pathways, new categories of knowledge. The colossal research project is defunct; what we need now is pure skullwork."

"From *my* staff?"

"From wherever you can get it. That's the other half of my recommendation. If I were you, I would go to the crackpots."

Wagoner waited. Corsi said these things for effect; he liked drama in small doses. He would explain in a moment.

"Of course I don't mean total crackpots," Corsi said. "But you'll have to draw the line yourself. You need marginal contributors, scientists of good reputation generally whose obsessions don't strike fire with other members of their profession. Like the Crehore atom, or old Ehrenhaft's theory of magnetic currents, or the Milne cosmology—you'll have to find the fruitful one yourself. Look for discards, and then find out whether or not the idea deserved to be *totally* discarded. And—don't accept the first 'expert' opinion that you get."

"Winnow chaff, in other words."

"What else is there to winnow?" Corsi said. "Of course it's a long chance, but you can't turn to scientists of real stature now; it's too late for that. Now you'll have to use sports, freaks, near-misses."

"Starting where?"

"Oh," said Corsi, "how about gravity? I don't know any other subject that's attracted a greater quota of idiot speculations. Yet the acceptable theories of what gravity is are of no practical use to us. They can't be put to work to help lift a spaceship. We can't manipulate gravity as a field; we don't even have a set of equations for it that we can agree upon. No more will we find such a set by spending fortunes and decades on the project. The law of diminishing returns has washed that approach out."

Wagoner got up. "You don't leave me much," he said glumly.

"No," Corsi agreed. "I leave you only what you started with. That's more than most of us are left with, Bliss."

Wagoner grinned tightly at him and the two men shook hands. As Wagoner left, he saw Corsi silhouetted against the fire, his back to the door, his shoulders bent. While he stood there, a shot blatted not far away, and the echoes bounded back from the face of the embassy across the street. It was not a common sound in Washington, but neither was it unusual: it was almost surely one of the city's thousands of anonymous snoopers firing at a counter-agent, a cop, or a shadow.

Corsi made no responding movement. The senator closed the door quietly.

He was shadowed all the way back to his own apartment, but this time he hardly noticed. He was thinking about an immortal man who flew from star to star faster than light.

CHAPTER ONE: New York

In the newer media of communication ... the populariza-
tion of science is confounded by rituals of mass entertain-
ment. One standard routine dramatizes science through
the biography of a hero scientist: at the denouement, he is
discovered in a lonely laboratory crying 'Eureka' at a
murky test tube held up to a bare light bulb.

          —GERARD PIEL

THE PARADE of celebrities, notorieties, and just plain brass
that passed through the reception room of Jno. Pfitzner &
Sons was marvelous to behold. During the hour and a half
that Colonel Paige Russell had been cooling his heels, he
had identified the following publicity-saints: Senator Bliss
Wagoner (Dem., Alaska), chairman of the Joint Congressional Committee on Space Flight; Dr. Guiseppi Corsi,
president of the American Association for the Advancement of Science, and a former Director of the World
Health Organization; and Francis Xavier MacHinery,
hereditary head of the FBI.

He had seen also a number of other notables, of lesser
caliber, but whose business at a firm which made biologicals was an equally improper subject for guessing games.
He fidgeted.

At the present moment, the girl at the desk was talking
softly with a seven-star general, which was a rank nearly
as high as a man could rise in the army. The general was
so preoccupied that he had failed completely to recognize
Paige's salute. He was passed through swiftly. One of the
two swinging doors with the glass ports let into them
moved outward behind the desk, and Paige caught a
glimpse of a stocky, dark-haired, pleasant-faced man in a
conservative grosse-pointilliste suit.

"Gen. Horsefield, glad to see you. Come in."

The door closed, leaving Paige once more with nothing
to look at but the motto written over the entrance in
German black-letter:

Wider den Tod ist kein Kräutlein gewachsen!

Since he did not know the language, he had already translated this by the If-only-it-were-English system, which made it come out, "The fatter toad is waxing on the kine's cole-slaw." This did not seem to fit what little he knew about the eating habits of either animal, and it was certainly no fit admonition for workers.

Of course, Paige could always look at the receptionist— but after an hour and a half he had about plumbed the uttermost depths of that ecstasy. The girl was pretty in a way, but hardly striking, even to a recently returned spaceman. Perhaps if someone would yank those black-rimmed pixie glasses away from her and undo that bun at the back of her head, she might pass, at least in the light of a whale-oil lamp in an igloo during a record blizzard.

This too was odd now that he thought about it. A firm as large as Pfitzner could have its pick of the glossiest of office girls, especially these days. Then again, the whole of Pfitzner might well be pretty small potatoes to the parent organization, A. O. LeFevre et Cie. Certainly at least Le Fevre's Consolidated Warfare Service operation was bigger than the Pfitzner division, and Peacock Camera and Chemicals probably was too; Pfitzner, which was the pharmaceuticals side of the cartel, was a recent acquisition, bought after some truly remarkable broken-field running around the diversification amendments to the anti-trust laws.

All in all, Paige was thoroughly well past mere mild annoyance with being stalled. He was, after all, here at these people's specific request, doing them a small favor which they had asked of him—and soaking up good leave-time in the process. Abruptly he got up and strode to the desk.

"Excuse me, miss," he said, "but I think you're being goddamned impolite. As a matter of fact, I'm beginning to think you people are making a fool of me. Do you want these, or don't you?"

He unbuttoned his right breast pocket and pulled out three little pliofilm packets, heat-sealed to plastic mailing tags. Each packet contained a small spoonful of dirt. The tags were addressed to Jno. Pfitzner & Sons, div. A. O. LeFevre et Cie, the Bronx 153, WPO 249920, Earth; and each card carried a $25 rocket-mail stamp for which Pfitzner had paid, still uncancelled.

"Colonel Russell, I agree with you," the girl said, looking up at him seriously. She looked even less glamorous than she had at a distance, but she did have a pert and interesting nose, and the current royal-purple lip-shade suited her better than it did most of the starlets to be seen on 3-V these days. "It's just that you've caught us on a very bad day. We do want the samples, of course. They're very important to us, otherwise we wouldn't have put you to the trouble of collecting them for us."

"Then why can't I give them to someone?"

"You could give them to me," the girl suggested gently. "I'll pass them along faithfully, I promise you."

Paige shook his head. "Not after this run-around. I did just what your firm asked me to do, and I'm here to see the results. I picked up soils from every one of my ports of call, even when it was a nuisance to do it. I mailed in a lot of them; these are only the last of a series. Do you know where these bits of dirt came from?"

"I'm sorry, it's slipped my mind. It's been a very busy day."

"Two of them are from Ganymede; and the other one is from Jupiter V, right in the shadow of the Bridge gang's shack. The normal temperature on both satellites is about two hundred degrees below zero Fahrenheit. Ever try to swing a pick against ground frozen that solid—working inside a spacesuit? But I got the dirt for you. Now I want to see why Pfitzner wants dirt."

The girl shrugged. "I'm sure you were told why before you even left Earth."

"Supposing I was? I know that you people get drugs out of dirt. But aren't the guys who bring in the samples entitled to see how the process works? What if Pfitzner gets some new wonder-drug out of one of my samples— couldn't I have a sentence or two of explanation to pass on to my kids?"

The swinging doors bobbed open, and the affable face of the stocky man was thrust into the room.

"Dr. Abbott not here yet, Anne?" he said.

"Not yet, Mr. Gunn. I'll call you the minute he arrives."

"But you'll keep me sitting at least another ninety minutes," Paige said flatly. Gunn looked him over, staring

at the colonel's eagle on his collar and stopping at the
winged crescent pinned over his pocket.

"Apologies, Colonel, but we're having ourselves a small
crisis today," he said, smiling tentatively. "I gather you've
brought us some samples from space. If you could possibly
come back tomorrow, I'd be happy to give you all the time
in the world. But right now——"

Gunn ducked his head in apology and pulled it in, as
though he had just cuckooed 2400 and had to go somewhere and lie down until 0100. Just before the door came
to rest behind him, a faint but unmistakable sound slipped
through it.

Somewhere in the laboratories of Jno. Pfitzner & Sons a
baby was crying.

Paige listened, blinking, until the sound was damped off.
When he looked back down at the desk again, the expression of the girl behind it seemed distinctly warier.

"Look," he said. "I'm not asking a great favor of you. I
don't want to know anything I shouldn't know. All I want
to know is how you plan to process my packets of soil. It's
just simple curiosity—backed up by a trip that covered a
few hundred millions of miles. Am I entitled to know for
my trouble, or not?"

"You are and you aren't" the girl said steadily. "We
want your samples, and we'll agree that they're unusually
interesting to us because they came from the Jovian system—the first such we've ever gotten. But that's no
guarantee that we'll find anything useful in them."

"It isn't?"

"No. Colonel Russell, you're not the first man to come
here with soil samples, believe me. Granted that you're the
first man to bring anything back from outside the orbit of
Mars; in fact, you're only the sixth man to deliver samples
from any place farther away than the Moon. But evidently you have no idea of the volume of samples we get here,
routinely. We've asked virtually every space pilot, every
Believer missionary, every commercial traveler, every ex-
plorer, every foreign correspondent to scoop up soil samples for us, wherever they may go. Before we discovered
ascomycin, we had to screen *one hundred thousand* soil
samples, including several hundred from Mars and nearly
five thousand from the Moon. And do you know where
we found the organism that produces ascomycin? On an
over-ripe peach one of our detail men picked up from a
peddler's stall in Baltimore!"

"I see the point," Paige said reluctantly. "What's ascomycin, by the way?"

The girl looked down at her desk and moved a piece of paper from *here* to *there*. "It's a new antibiotic," she said. "We'll be marketing it soon. But I could tell you the same kind of story about other such drugs."

"I see." Paige was not quite sure he did see, however, after all. He had heard the name Pfitzner fall from some very unlikely lips during his many months in space. As far as he had been able to determine after he had become sensitized to the sound, about every third person on the planets was either collecting samples for the firm or knew somebody who was. The grapevine, which among spacemen was the only trusted medium of communication, had it that the company was doing important government work. That, of course, was nothing unusual in the Age of Defense, but Paige had heard enough to suspect that Pfitzner was something special—something as big, perhaps, as the historic Manhattan District and at least twice as secret.

The door opened and emitted Gunn for the second time hand-running, this time all the way.

"Not yet?" he said to the girl. "Evidently he isn't going to make it. Unfortunate. But I've some spare time now, Colonel—"

"Russell, Paige Russell, Army Space Corps."

"Thank you. If you'll accept my apologies for our preoccupation, Colonel Russell, I'll be glad to show you around our little establishment. My name, by the way, is Harold Gunn, vice-president in charge of exports for the Pfitzner division."

"I'm importing at the moment," Paige said, holding out the soil samples. Gunn took them reverently and dropped them in a pocket of his jacket. "But I'd enjoy seeing the labs."

He nodded to the girl and the doors closed between them. He was inside.

The place was at least as fascinating as he had expected it to be. Gunn showed him, first, the rooms where the incoming samples were classified and then distributed to the laboratories proper. In the first of these, a measured fraction of a sample was dropped into a one-litre flask of sterile distilled water, swirled to distribute it evenly, and then passed through a series of dilutions. The final suspensions were then used to inoculate test-tube slants and petri plates, containing a wide variety of nutrient media, which went into the incubator.

"In the next lab here—Dr. Aquino isn't in at the moment, so we mustn't touch anything, but you can see through the glass quite clearly—we transfer from the plates and agar slants to a new set of media," Gunn explained. "But here each organism found in the sample has a set of cultures of its own, so that if it secretes anything into one of the media, that something won't be contaminated."

"If it does, the amount must be very tiny," Paige said "How do you detect it?"

"Directly, by its action. Do you see the rows of plates with the white paper discs in their centers, and the four furrows in the agar radiating from the discs? Well, each one of those furrows is impregnated with culture medium from one of the pure cultures. If all four streaks grow thriving bacterial colonies, then the medium on the paper disc contains no antibiotic against those four germs. If one or more of the streaks fails to grow, or is retarded compared to the others, then we have hope."

In the succeeding laboratory, antibiotics which had been found by the disc method were pitted against a whole spectrum of dangerous organisms. About 90 per cent of the discoveries were eliminated here, Gunn explained, either because they were insufficiently active or because they duplicated the antibiotic spectra of already known drugs. "What we call 'insufficiently active' varies with the circumstances, however," he added. "An antibiotic which shows *any* activity against tuberculosis or against Hansen's disease—leprosy—is always of interest to us, even if it attacks no other germ at all."

A few antibiotics which passed their spectrum tests went on to a miniature pilot plant, where the organisms that produced them were set to work in a deep-aerated fermentation tank. From this bubbling liquor, comparatively large amounts of the crude drug were extracted, purified, and sent to the pharmacology lab for tests on animals.

"We lose a lot of otherwise promising antibiotics here, too," Gunn said. "Most of them turn out to be too toxic to be used in—or even on—the human body. We've had Hansen's bacillus knocked out a thousand times in the test-tube only to find here that the antibiotic is much more quickly fatal *in vivo* than is leprosy itself. But once we're sure that the drug isn't toxic, or that its toxicity is out-weighed by its therapeutic efficacy, it goes out of our shop entirely, to hospitals and to individual doctors for clinical trial. We also have a virology lab in Vermont where we test our new drugs against virus diseases like the 'flu and the common cold—it isn't safe to operate such a lab in a heavily populated area like the Bronx."

"It's much more elaborate than I would have imagined," Paige said. "But I can see that it's well worth the trouble. Did you work out this sample-screening technique here?"

"Oh, my, no," Gunn said, smiling indulgently. "Waksman, the discoverer of streptomycin, laid down the essential procedure decades ago. We aren't even the first firm to use it on a large scale; one of our competitors did that and found a broad-spectrum antibiotic called chlor-amphenicol with it, scarcely a year after they'd begun. That was what convinced the rest of us that we'd better adopt the technique before we got shut out of the market entirely. A good thing, too; otherwise none of us would have discovered tetracycline, which turned out to be the most versatile antibiotic ever tested."

Farther down the corridor a door opened. The squall of a baby came out of it, much louder than before. It was not the sustained crying of a child who had had a year or so to practice, but the short-breathed "ah-la, ah-la, ah-la," of a newborn infant.

Paige raised his eyebrows. "Is that one of your experi-mental animals?"

"Ha, ha," Gunn said. "We're enthusiasts in this business, Colonel, but we must draw the line somewhere. No, one of our technicians has a baby-sitting problem, and so we've given her permission to bring the child to work with her, until she's worked out a better solution."

Paige had to admit that Gunn thought fast on his feet. That story had come reeling out of him like so much ticker tape without the slightest sign of a preliminary double-take. It was not Gunn's fault that Paige, who had been through a marriage which had lasted five years before he had taken to space, could distinguish the cry of a baby old enough to be out of a hospital nursery from that of one only days old.

"Isn't this," Paige said, "a rather dangerous place to park an infant—with so many disease germs, poisonous disinfectants, and such things all around?"

"Oh, we take all proper precautions. I daresay our staff has a lower yearly sickness rate than you'll find in industrial plants of comparable size, simply because we're more aware of the problem. Now if we go through this door, Colonel Russell, we'll see the final step, the main plant where we turn out drugs in quantity after they've proved themselves."

"Yes, I'd like that. Do you have ascomycin in production now?"

This time, Gunn looked at him sharply and without any attempt to disguise his interest. "No," he said, "that's still out on clinical trial. May I ask you, Colonel Russell, just how you happened to—"

The question, which Paige realized belatedly would have been rather sticky to answer, never did get all the way asked. Over Harold Gunn's head, a squawk-box said, "Mr. Gunn, Dr. Abbott has just arrived."

Gunn turned away from the door that, he had said, led out to the main plant, with just the proper modicum of polite regret. "There's my man," he said. "I'm afraid I'm going to have to cut this tour short, Colonel Russell. You may have seen what a collection of important people we have in the plant today; we've been waiting only for Dr. Abbott to begin a very important meeting. If you'll oblige me—"

Paige could say nothing but "Certainly." After what seemed only a few seconds, Gunn deposited him smoothly in the reception room from which he had started.

"Did you see what you wanted to see?" the receptionist said.

"I think so," Paige said thoughtfully. "Except that what I wanted to see sort of changed in mid-flight. Miss Anne, I have a petition to put before you. Would you be kind enough to have dinner with me this evening?"

"No," the girl said. "I've seen quite a few spacemen, Colonel Russell, and I'm no longer impressed. Furthermore, I shan't tell you anything you haven't heard from Mr. Gunn, so there's no need for you to spend your money or your leave-time on me. Good-by."

"Not so fast," Paige said. "I mean business—or, if you like, I mean to make trouble. If you've met spacemen before, you know that they like to be independent—not much like the conformists who never leave the ground. I'm not after your maidenly laughter, either. I'm after information."

"Not interested," the girl said. "Save your breath."

"MacHinéry is here," Paige said quietly. "So is Senator Wagoner, and some other people who have influence. Suppose I should collar any one of those people and accuse Pfitzner of conducting human vivisection?"

That told: Paige could see the girl's knuckles whitening. "You don't know what you're talking about," she said.

"That's my complaint. And I take it seriously. There were some things Mr. Gunn wasn't able to conceal from me, though he tried very hard. Now, I am going to put my suspicions through channels—and get Pfitzner investigated—or would you rather be sociable over a fine flounder broiled in paprika butter?"

The look she gave him back was one of almost pure hatred. She seemed able to muster no other answer. The expression did not at all suit her; as a matter of fact, she looked less like someone he would want to date than any other girl he could remember. Why *should* he spend his money or his leave-time on her? There were, after all, about five million surplus women in the United States by the Census of 2010, and at least 4,999,950 of them must be prettier and less recalcitrant than this one.

"All right," she said abruptly. "Your natural charm has swept me off my feet, Colonel. For the record, there's no other reason for my acceptance. It would be even funnier to call your bluff and see how far you'd get with that vivisection tale, but I don't care to tie my company up in a personal joke."

"Good enough," Paige said, uncomfortably aware that his bluff in fact *had* been called. "Suppose I pick you up—"

He broke off, suddenly noticing that voices were rising behind the double doors. An instant later, General Horsefield bulled into the reception room, closely followed by Gunn.

"I want it clearly understood, once and for all," Horsefield was rumbling, "that this entire project is going to wind up under military control unless we can show results before it's time to ask for a new appropriation. There's still a lot going on here that the Pentagon will regard as piddling inefficiency and highbrow theorizing. And if that's what the Pentagon reports, you know what the Treasury will do—or Congress will do it for them. We're going to have to cut back, Gunn. Understand? Cut right back to basics!"

"General, we're as far back to basics as we possibly can get," Harold Gunn said, placatingly enough, but with considerable firmness as well. "We're not going to put a gram of that drug into production until we're satisfied with it on all counts. Any other course would be suicide."

"You know I'm on your side," Horsefield said, his voice becoming somewhat less threatening. "So is General Alsos, for that matter. But this is a war we're fighting, whether the public understands it or not. And on as sensitive a matter as these death-dopes, we can't afford—"

Gunn, who had spotted Paige belatedly at the conclusion of his own speech, had been signaling Horsefield ever since with his eyebrows, and suddenly it took. The general swung around and glared at Paige, who, since he was uncovered now, was relieved of the necessity for saluting. Despite the sudden freezing silence, it was evident that Gunn was trying to retain in his manner toward Paige some shreds of professional cordiality—a courtesy which Paige was not too sure he merited, considering the course his conversation with the girl had taken.

As for Horsefield, he relegated Paige to the ghetto of "unauthorized persons" with a single look. Paige had no intention of remaining in that classification for a second longer than it would take him to get out of it, preferably without having been asked his name; it was deadly dangerous. With a mumbled "—at eight, then," to the girl, Paige sidled ingloriously out of the Pfitzner reception room and beat it.

He was, he reflected later in the afternoon before his shaving mirror, subjecting himself to an extraordinary series of small humiliations, to get close to a matter which was none of his business. Worse: it was obviously Top Secret, which made it potentially lethal even for everyone authorized to know about it, let alone for rank snoopers. In the Age of Defense, to know was to be suspect, in the West as in the USSR; the two great nation-complexes had been becoming more and more alike in their treatment of "security" for the past fifty years. It had even been a mistake to mention the Bridge on Jupiter to the girl—for despite the fact that everyone knew that the Bridge existed, anyone who spoke of it with familiarity could quickly earn the label of being dangerously flap-jawed. Especially if the speaker, like Paige, had actually been stationed in the Jovian system for a while, whether he had had access to information about the Bridge or not.

And especially if the talker, like Paige, had actually spoken to the Bridge gang, worked with them on marginal projects, was known to have talked to Charity Dillon, the Bridge foreman. More especially if he held military rank, making it possible for him to sell security files to Congressmen, the traditional way of advancing a military career ahead of normal promotion schedules.

And most especially if the man was discovered nosing about a new and different classified project, one to which he hadn't even been assigned.

Why, after all, was he taking the risk? He didn't even know the substance of the matter; he was no biologist. To all outside eyes the Pfitzner project was simply another piece of research in antibiotics, and a rather routine research project at that. Why should a spaceman like Paige find himself flying so close to the candle already?

He wiped the depilatory cream off his face into a paper towel and saw his own eyes looking back at him from the concave mirror, as magnified as an owl's. The image, however, was only his own, despite the distortion. It gave him back no answer.

CHAPTER TWO: Jupiter V

. . . it is the plunge through the forbidden zones that catches the heart with its sheer audacity. In the history of life there have been few such episodes. It is that which makes us lonely. We have entered a new corridor, the cultural corridor. There has been nothing here before us. In it we are utterly alone. In it we are appallingly unique. We look at each other and say, "It can never be done again."
                                          —LOREN C. EISELEY

A SCREECHING tornado was rocking the Bridge when the alarm sounded; the whole structure shuddered and swayed. This was normal, and Robert Helmuth on Jupiter V barely noticed it. There was always a tornado shaking the Bridge. The whole planet was enswathed in tornadoes and worse.

The scanner on the foreman's board was given 114 as the sector where the trouble was. That was at the north-western end of the Bridge, where it broke off, leaving nothing but the raging clouds of ammonia crystals and methane, and a sheer drop thirty miles down to the invisi-ble surface. There were no ultra-phone "eyes" at that end to show a general view of the area—in so far as any general view was possible—because both ends of the Bridge were incomplete.

With a sigh, Helmuth put the beetle into motion. The little car, as flat-bottomed and thin through as a bedbug, got slowly under way on its ball-bearing races, guided and held firmly to the surface of the Bridge by ten close-set flanged rails. Even so, the hydrogen gales made a terrific siren-like shrieking between the edge of the vehicle and the deck, and the impact of the falling drops of ammonia upon the curved roof was as heavy and deafening as a rain of cannon balls. In fact, the drops weighed almost as much as cannon balls there under Jupiter's two-and-a-half-fold gravity, although they were not much bigger than ordinary raindrops. Every so often, too, there was a blast, accompanied by a dull orange glare, which made the car, the deck, and the Bridge itself buck savagely; even a small shock wave traveled through the incredibly dense atmo-sphere of the planet like the armor-plate of a bursting battleship.

These blasts were below, however, on the surface. While they shook the structure of the Bridge heavily, they almost never interfered with its functioning. And they could not, in the very nature of things, do Helmuth any harm.

Helmuth, after all, was *not* on Jupiter—though that was becoming harder and harder for him to bear in mind. Nobody was on Jupiter; had any real damage ever been done to the Bridge, it probably would never have been repaired. There was nobody on Jupiter to repair it; only the machines which were themselves part of the Bridge.

The Bridge was building itself. Massive, alone, and lifeless, it grew in the black deeps of Jupiter.

It had been well planned. From Helmuth's point of view—that of the scanners on the beetle—almost nothing could be seen of it, for the beetle tracks ran down the center of the deck, and in the darkness and perpetual storm even ultrawave-assisted vision could not penetrate more than a few hundred yards at the most. The width of the Bridge, which no one would ever see, was eleven miles; its height, as incomprehensible to the Bridge gang as a skyscraper to an ant, thirty miles; its length, deliberately unspecified in the plans, fifty-four miles at the moment and still increasing—a squat, colossal structure, built with engineering principles, methods, materials and tools never touched before now. . . .

For the very good reason that they would have been impossible anywhere else. Most of the Bridge, for instance, was made of ice: a marvelous structural material under a pressure of a million atmospheres, at a temperature of 94° below zero Fahrenheit. Under such conditions, the best structural steel is a friable, talc-like powder, and aluminum becomes a peculiar transparent substance that splits at a tap; water, on the other hand, becomes Ice IV, a dense, opaque white medium which will deform to a heavy stress, but will break only under impacts huge enough to lay whole Earthly cities waste. Never mind that it took millions of megawatts of power to keep the Bridge up and growing every hour of the day; the winds on Jupiter blow at velocities up to twenty-five thousand miles per hour, and will never stop blowing, as they may have been blowing for more than four billion years; there is power enough.

Back home, Helmuth remembered, there had been talk of starting another Bridge on Saturn, and perhaps later still on Uranus too. But that had been politicians' talk. The Bridge was almost five thousand miles below the visible surface of Jupiter's atmosphere—luckily in a way, for at the top of that atmosphere the temperature was 76° Fahrenheit colder than it was down by the Bridge, but even with that differential the Bridge's mechanisms were just barely manageable. The bottom of Saturn's atmosphere, if the radiosonde readings could be trusted, was just 16,878 miles below the top of the Saturnian clouds one could see through the telescope, and the temperature down there was below —238° F. Under those conditions, even pressure-ice would be immovable, and could not be worked with anything softer than itself.

And as for a Bridge on Uranus. . . .

As far as Helmuth was concerned, Jupiter was quite bad enough.

The beetle crept within sight of the end of the Bridge

and stopped automatically. Helmuth set the vehicle's
"eyes" for highest penetration, and examined the nearby
I-beams.

The great bars were as close-set as screening. They had
to be, in order to support even their own weight, let alone
the weight of the components of the Bridge. The gravity
down here was two and a half times as great as Earth's.

Even under that load, the whole webwork of girders
was flexing and fluctuating to the harpist-fingered gale. It
had been designed to do that, but Helmuth could never
help being alarmed by the movement. Habit alone assured
him that he had nothing to fear from it.

He took the automatic cut-out of the circuit and inched
the beetle forward on manual control. This was only
Sector 113, and the Bridge's own Wheatstone scanning
system—there was no electronic device anywhere on the
Bridge, since it was impossible to maintain a vacuum on
Jupiter—said that the trouble was in Sector 114. The
boundary of that sector was still fully fifty feet away.

It was a bad sign. Helmuth scratched nervously in his
red beard. Evidently there was cause for alarm—real
alarm, not just the deep grinding depression which he
always felt while working on the Bridge. Any damage
serious enough to halt the beetle a full sector short of the
trouble area was bound to be major.

It might even turn out to be the disaster which he had
felt lurking ahead of him ever since he had been made
foreman of the Bridge—that disaster which the Bridge
itself could not repair, sending a man reeling home from
Jupiter in defeat.

The secondaries cut in, and the beetle hunkered down
once more against the deck, the ball-bearings on which it
rode frozen magnetically to the rails. Grimly, Helmuth cut
the power to the magnet windings and urged the flat craft
inch by inch across the danger line.

Almost at once, the car tilted just perceptibly to the
left, and the screaming of the winds between its edges and
the deck shot up the scale, sirening in and out of the
soundless-dogwhistle range with an eeriness which set
Helmuth's teeth on edge. The beetle itself fluttered and
chattered like an alarm-clock hammer between the surface
of the deck and the flanges of the tracks.

Ahead there was still nothing to be seen but the hori-
zontal driving of the clouds and the hail, roaring along the
length of the Bridge, out of the blackness into the beetle's

fanlights, and onward into darkness again toward the horizon which, like the Bridge itself, no eye would ever see.

Thirty miles below, the fusillade of hydrogen explosions continued. Evidently something really wild was going on down on the surface. Helmuth could not remember having heard so much vulcanism in years.

There was a flat, especially heavy crash, and a long line of fuming orange fire came pouring down the seething air into the depths, feathering horizontally like the mane of a Lipizzan stallion, directly in front of Helmuth. Instinctively, he winced and drew back from the board, although that stream of flame actually was only a little less cold than the rest of the storming, streaming gases, and far too cold to injure the Bridge.

In the momentary glare, however, he saw something: an upward twisting of shadows, patterned but obviously unfinished, fluttering in silhouette against the lurid light of the hydrogen cataract.

The end of the Bridge.

Wrecked.

Helmuth grunted involuntarily and backed the beetle away. The flare dimmed; the light poured down the sky and fell away into the raging sea of liquid hydrogen thirty miles below. The scanner clucked with satisfaction as the beetle recrossed the danger line into Sector 113.

Helmuth turned the body of the vehicle 180 degrees on its chassis, presenting its back to the dying orange torrent. There was nothing further that he could do at the moment for the Bridge. He searched his control board—a ghost image of which was cast on the screen across the scene on the Bridge—for the blue button marked *Garage,* punched it savagely, and tore off his fireman's helmet.

Obediently, the Bridge vanished.

CHAPTER THREE: New York

Does it not appear as if one who lived habitually on one side of the pain threshold might need a different sort of religion from one who habitually lives on the other?
                                        —WILLIAM JAMES

THE GIRL—whose full name, Paige found, was Anne Abbott—looked moderately acceptable in her summer suit, on the left lapel of which she wore a model of the tetracycline molecule with the atoms picked out in tiny synthetic gems. But she was even less inclined to talk when he picked her up than she had been in Pfitzner's reception room. Paige himself had never been expert at making small talk, and in the face of her obvious, continuing resentment, his parched spring of social invention went underground completely.

Five minutes later, all talk became impossible anyhow. The route to the restaurant Paige had chosen lay across Foley Square, where there turned out to be a Believer Mission going. The Caddy that Paige had hired—at nearly a quarter of his leave-pay, for commercial kerosene-fueled taxis were strictly a rich man's occasional luxury—was bogged down almost at once in the groaning, swaying crowd.

The main noise came from the big plastic proscenium, where one of the lay preachers was exhorting the crowd in a voice so heavily amplified as to be nearly unintelligible. Believers with portable tape recorders, bags of tracts and magazines, sandwich-boards lettered with fluorescent inks, confessions for sinners to sign, and green baize pokes for collections were well scattered among the pedestrians, and the streets were crossed about every fifteen feet with the straight black snakes of compressed-air triggers.

As the Caddy pulled up for the second time, a nozzle was thrust into the rear window and a stream of iridescent bubbles poured across the back seat directly under Paige's and Anne's noses. As each bubble burst, there was a wave of perfume—evidently it was the "Celestial Joy" the Believers were using this year—and a sweet voice said:

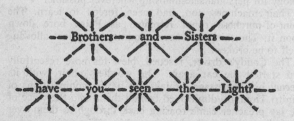

Paige fought at the bubbles with futile windmillings, while Anne Abbott leaned back against the cushions of the Caddy and watched him with a faint smile of contemptuous amusement. The last bubble contained no word, but only an overpowering burst of perfume. Despite herself, the girl's smile deepened: the perfume, in addition to being powerfully euphoric, was slightly aphrodisiac as well. This year, apparently, the Believers were readier than ever to use any means that came to hand.

The driver lurched the Caddy ahead. Then, before Paige could begin to grasp what was happening, the car stopped, the door next to the steering wheel was wrenched open, and four spidery, many-fingered arms plucked the driver neatly from his seat and deposited him on his knees on the asphalt outside.

"SHAME! SHAME!" the popai-robot thundered. "YOUR SINS HAVE FOUND YOU OUT! REPENT, AND FIND FORGIVENESS!"

A thin glass globe of some gas, evidently a narcosynthetic, broke beside the car, and not only the unfortunate chauffeur but also the part of the crowd which had begun to collect about him—mostly women, of course—began to weep convulsively.

"REPENT!" the robot intoned, over a sneaked-in-choir now singing "Ah-ah-ah-ah-ah-h-h-h-h" somewhere in the warm evening air. "REPENT, FOR THE TIME IS AT HAND!"

Paige, astonished to find himself choking with sourceless, maudlin self-pity, flung himself out of the Caddy in search of a nose to break. But there were no live Believers in sight. The members of the order, all of whom were charged with spreading the good word by whatever means seemed good to them, had learned decades ago that their proselytizing was often resented, and had substituted technology for personal salesmanship wherever possible.

Their machines, too, had been forced to learn. The point-of-purchase robot retreated as Paige bore down upon it. The thing had been conditioned against allowing itself to be broken.

The Caddy's driver, rescued, blew his nose resentfully and started the car again. The wordless choir, with its eternal bridge-passage straight out of the compositions of Dmitri Tiomkin, diminished behind them, and the voice of the lay preacher came roaring back through to them over the fading, characterless music.

"I say to you," the P.A. system was moaning unctuous-ly, like a lady hippopotamus reading A. E. Housman, "I say to you, the world, and the things which are the world's come to an end and a quick end. In his overweening pride, man has sought even to wrest the stars from their courses, but the stars are not man's, and he shall rue that day. Ah, vanity of vanities, all is vanity (Preacher v: 796). Even on mighty Jove man dared to erect a great Bridge, as once in Babel he sought to build a tower to heaven. But this also is vanity, it is vicious pride and defiance, and it too shall bring calamity upon men. Pull down thy vanity, I say pull down! (Ezra lxxxi: 99). Let there be an end to pride, and there shall be peace. Let there be love, and there shall be understanding. I say to you—"

At this point, the Believers' over-enthusiastic booby-trapping of the square cut off whatever the preacher was going to say next as far as the occupants of the Caddy were concerned. The car passed over another trigger, and there was a blinding, rose-colored flash. When Paige could see again, the car seemed to be floating in mid-air, and there were actual angels flapping solemnly around it. The *vox humana* of a Hammond organ sobbed among the clouds.

Paige supposed that the Believers had managed to crys-talize temporarily, perhaps with a supersonic pulse, the glass of the windows, which he had rolled up to prevent another intromission of bubbles, and to project a 3-V tape against the glass crystals with polarized ultra-violet light. The random distribution of fluorescent trace compounds in ordinary window glass would account for the odd way the "angels" changed color as they moved.

Understanding the vision's probable *modus operandi* left Paige no less furious at the new delay, but luckily the thing turned out to be a trick, left over from last year's Revival, for which the Caddy was prepared. The driver touched something on the dash and the saccharine scene vanished, hymns and all. The car lunged abruptly through an opening in the crowd, and a moment later the square was behind them.

"Whew!" Paige said, leaning back at last. "Now I un-derstand why taxi depots have vending machines for trip-insurance policies. The Believers weren't much in evidence the last time I was on Earth."

"Every tenth person you meet is a Believer now," Anne

said. "And eight of the other nine claim that they've given
up religion as a bad job. While you're caught in the middle
of one of those Revivals, though, it's hard to believe the
complaints you read about our times—that people have no
faith and so on."

"I don't find it so," Paige said reflectively. This certainly
did not strike him as light social conversation, but since it
was instead a kind of talk he much more enjoyed—talk
which was about something—he could only be delighted
that the ice was broken. "I've no religion of my own, but I
think that when the experts talk about 'faith' they mean
something different than the shouting kind, the kind the
Believers have. Shouting religions always strike me as
essentially like pep-meetings among salesmen; their ceremonies and their manners are so aggressive because they
don't really believe the code themselves. Real faith is so
much a part of the world you live in that you seldom
notice it, and it isn't always religious in the formal sense.
Mathematics is based on faith, for instance, for those who
know it."

"I should have said that it was based on the antithesis
of faith," Anne said, turning a little cooler. "Have you had
any experience in the field, Colonel?"

"Some," he said, without rancor. "I'd never have been
allowed to pilot a ship outside the orbit of the Moon
without knowing tensors, and if I expect to get my next
promotion, I'm going to have to know spinor calculus as
well—which I do."

"Oh," the girl said. She sounded faintly dashed. "Go on;
I'm sorry I interrupted."

"You were right to interrupt; I made my point badly. I
meant to say that the mathematician's belief that there is
some relationship between maths and the real world is a
faith; it can't be proven, but he feels it very strongly. For
that matter, the totally irreligious man's belief that there
even *is* a real world, corresponding to what his senses show
him, can't be proven. John Doe and the most brilliant of
physicists both have to take that on faith."

"And they don't conduct ceremonies symbolizing the
belief," Anne added, "and train specialists to reassure
them of it every seven days."

"That's right. In the same way, John Doe used to feel
that the basic religions of the West had some relationship
to the real world which was valid even though it couldn't
be proven. And that includes Communism, which was

born in the West, after all. John Doe doesn't feel that way
any more—and by my guess, neither do the Believers or
they wouldn't be shouting so loud. In that sense, there's
not much faith lying around loose these days anywhere, as
far as I can see. None for me to pick up, that much I've
found out the hard way."

"Here you are," the chauffeur said.

Paige helped the girl out of the car, trying not to notice
how much fare he had to pay, and the two were shown to
a table in the restaurant. Anne was silent again for a while
after they were seated. Paige had about decided that she
had chosen to freeze up once more and had begun to
wonder if he could arrange to have the place invaded by
Believers to start the conversation again when she said,
"You seem to have been thinking about faith quite a bit.
You talk as though the problem meant something to you.
Could you tell me why?"

"I'd be glad to try," he said slowly. "The standard
answer would be that while you're out in space you have
lots of time to think—but people use thinking time differently. I suppose I've been looking for some frame of
reference that could be mine ever since I was four, when
my father and mother split up. She was a Christian Scientist and he was a Dianeticist, so they had a lot to fight
about. There was a court battle over custody that lasted
for nearly five years.

"I joined the army when I was seventeen, and it didn't
take me very long to find out that the army is no substitute for a family, let alone a church. Then I volunteered
for space service school. That was no church either. The
army got jurisdiction over space travel when the whole
field was just a baby, because it had a long tradition of
grafting off land-grants, and it didn't want the navy or the
air force to grab off the gravy from any such grants that
might be made on the planets. That's one of the army's
historic prerogatives; the idea is that anything that's found
on an army site—diamonds, uranium, anything of value—
is found money, to be lived off during peacetime when the
Congress gets stingy with appropriations. I spent more
time helping the army space-travel department fight unifi-
cation with the space arms of the other services than I did
doing real work in space. That was what I was ordered to
do—but it didn't help me to think of space as the ultimate
cathedral. . . .

"Somewhere along in there, I got married and we had

one son; he was born the same day I entered space school. Two years later, the marriage was annulled. That sounds funny, I know, but the circumstances were unusual.

"When Pfitzner approached me and asked me to pick up soil samples for them, I suppose I saw another church with which I could identify myself—something humanitarian, long-range, impersonal. And when I found this afternoon that the new church wasn't going to welcome the convert with glad cries—well, the result is that I'm now weeping on your shoulder." He smiled. "That's hardly flattering, I know. But you've already helped me to talk myself into a spot where the only next step is to apologize, which I hereby do. I hope you'll accept it."

"I think I will," she said, and then, tentatively, she smiled back. The result made him tingle as though the air-pressure had dropped suddenly by five pounds per square inch. Anne Abbott was one of those exceedingly rare plain girls whose smiles completely transform them, as abruptly as the bursting of a star-shell. When she wore her normal, rather sullen expression, no one would ever notice her—but a man who had seen her smile might well be willing to kill himself working to make her smile again, as often as possible. A woman who was beautiful all the time, Paige thought, probably never could know the devotion Anne Abbott would be given when she found that man.

"Thank you," Paige said, rather inadequately. "Let's order, and then I'd like to hear you talk. I dumped The Story of My Life into your lap rather early in the game, I'm afraid."

"You order," she said. "You talked about flounder this afternoon, so you must know the menu here—and you handed me out of the Caddy so nicely that I'd like to preserve the illusion."

"Illusion?"

"Don't make me explain," she said, coloring faintly. "But. . . . Well, the illusion of there being one or two cavaliers in the world still. Since you haven't been a surplus woman on a planet full of lazy males, you wouldn't understand the value of a small courtesy or two. Most men I meet want to be shown my mole before they'll bother to learn my last name."

Paige's surprised shout of laughter made heads turn all over the restaurant. He throttled it hurriedly, afraid that it would embarrass the girl, but she was smiling again, making him feel instead as though he had just had three whiskies in quick succession.

"That's a quick tranformation for me," he said. "This afternoon I was a blackmailer, and by my own intention, too. Very well, then, let's have the flounder; it's a specialty of the house. I had visions of it while I was on Ganymede munching my concentrates."

"I think you had the right idea about Pfitzner," Anne said slowly when the waiter had gone. "I can't tell you any secrets about it, but maybe I can tell you some bits of common knowledge that you evidently don't know. The project the plant is working on now seems to me to fit your description exactly: it's humanitarian, impersonal, and just about as long-range as any project I can imagine. I feel rather religious about it, in your sense. It's something to tie to, and it's better for me than being a Believer or a WAC. And I think you could understand why I feel that way—better than either Hal Gunn or I thought you could."

It was his turn to be embarrassed. He covered by dosing his Blue Points with Worcestershire until they flinched visibly. "I'd like to know."

"It goes like this," she said. "In between 1940 and 1960, a big change took place in Western medicine. Before 1940—in the early part of the century—the infectious diseases were major killers. By 1960 they were all but knocked out of the running. The change started with the sulfa drugs; then came Fleming and Florey and mass production of penicillin during World War II. After that war we found a whole arsenal of new drugs against tuberculosis, which had really never been treated successfully before—streptomycin, PAS, isoniazid, viomycin, and so on, right up to Bloch's isolation of the TB toxins and the development of the metabolic blocking agents.

"Then came the broad-spectrum antibiotics, like terramycin, which attacked some virus diseases, protozoan diseases, even worm diseases; that gave us a huge clue to a whole set of tough problems. The last major infectious disease—bilharzia, or schistosomiasis—was reduced to the status of a nuisance by 1966."

"But we still have infectious diseases," Paige objected.

"Of course we do," the girl said, the little atom points in her brooch picking up the candle-light as she leaned forward. "No drug ever wipes out a disease, because it's impossible to kill all the dangerous organisms in the world just by treating the patients they invade. But you can reduce the danger. In the 1950's, for instance, malaria was the world's greatest killer. Now it's as rare as diphtheria. We still have both diseases with us—but how long has it been since you heard of a case of either?"

"You're asking the wrong man—germ diseases aren't common on space vessels. We bump any crewman who shows up with as much as a head-cold. But you win the point, all the same. Go on. What happened then?"

"Something kind of ominous. Life insurance companies, and other people who kept records, began to be alarmed at the way the degenerative diseases were coming to the fore. Those are such ailments as hardening of the arteries, coronary heart disease, embolisms, and almost all the many forms of cancer—diseases where one or another body mechanism suddenly goes haywire, without any visible cause."

"Isn't old age the cause?"

"*No,*" the girl said forcefully. "Old age is just the *age;* it's not a thing in itself, it's just the time of life when most degenerative diseases strike. Some of them prefer children—leukemia or cancer of the bone marrow, for instance. When the actuaries first began to notice that the degenerative diseases were on the rise, they thought that it was just a sort of side-effect of the decline of the infectious diseases. They thought that cancer was increasing because more people were living long enough to come down with it. Also, the reporting of the degenerative diseases was improving, and so part of the rise in incidence really was an illusion—it just meant that more cases than before were being detected.

"But that wasn't all there was to it. Lung cancer and stomach cancer in particular continued to creep up the statistical tables, far beyond the point which could have been accounted for by better reporting, or by the increase in the average life-span, either. Then the same thing took place in malignant hypertension, in Parkinsonism and other failures of the central nervous system, in muscular dystrophy, and so on, and so on. It began to look very much as though we'd exchanged a devil we knew for a devil we didn't.

"So there was quite a long search for a possible infectious origin for each of the degenerative diseases. Because some animal tumors, like poultry sarcoma, are caused by viruses, a lot of people set to work hunting like mad for all kinds of cancer viruses. There was a concerted attempt to implicate a group called the pleuropneumonia-like organisms as the cause of the arthritic diseases. The vascular diseases, like hypertension and thrombosis, got blamed on everything from your diet to your grandmother.

"And it all came to very little. Oh, we did find that *some* viruses did cause *some* types of cancer, leukemia among them. The PPLO group does cause *a* type of arthritis, too, but only the type associated with a venereal disease called essential urethritis. And we found that the commonest of the three types of lung cancer was being caused by the radio-potassium content of tobacco smoke; it was the lip and mouth cancers that were caused by the tars. But for the most part, we found out just what we had known before—that the degenerative diseases weren't infectious. We'd already been down *that* dead end.

"About there was when Pfitzner got into the picture. The NHS, the National Health Service, got alarmed enough about the rising incidence-curves to call the first really major world congress on the degenerative diseases. The U.S. paid part of the bill because the armed services were getting nervous about the rising rate of draft rejections."

"I heard some talk about that part of it," Paige said. "It started right in my own service. A spaceman only has about ten years of active life; after that he's given garrison duty somewhere—so we like to catch 'em young. And even then we were turning back a huge proportion of young volunteers for 'diseases of old age'—incipient circulatory disease in most cases. The kids were shocked; most of them had never suspected any such thing, they felt as healthy as bulls, and in the usual sense I suppose they were—but not for space flight."

"Then you saw one of the key factors very early," Anne said. "But it's no longer a special problem of the Space Service alone. It's old stuff to all the armed services' medical departments now; at the time the NHS stepped in, the overall draft rejection rate for 'diseases of old age' was about 10 per cent for men in their early twenties. Anyhow, the result of the congress was that the U.S. Department of Health, Welfare and Security somehow got a billion-dollar appropriation for a real mass attack on the degenerative diseases. In case you drop zeros as easily as I do, that was about half what had been spent to produce the first atomic bomb. Since then, the appropriation has been added to once, and it's due for renewal again now.

"Pfitzner holds the major contract on that project, and we're well enough staffed and equipped to handle it so that we've had to do very little sub-contracting. We simply share the appropriation with three other producers of biologicals, two of whom are producers only and so have no hand in the research; the third firm has done as much research as we have, but we know—because this is supposed to be a co-ordinated effort with sharing of knowledge among the contractors—that they're far gone down another blind alley. We would have told them so, but after one look at what *we'd* found, the government decided that the fewer people who know about it, the better. We didn't mind; after all, we're in business to make a profit, too. But that's one reason why you saw so many government people on our necks this afternoon."

The girl broke off abruptly and delved into her pocketbook, producing a flat compact which she opened and inspected intently. Since she wore almost no make-up, it was hard to imagine the reason for the sudden examination; but after a brief, odd smile at one corner of her mouth, she tucked the compact away again.

"The other reason," she said, "is even simpler, now that you have the background. *We've just found what we think may be a major key to the whole problem.*"

"Wow," Paige said, inelegantly but *affetuoso*.

"Or zowie, or biff-bam-krunk," Anne agreed calmly, "or maybe God-help-us-every-one. But so far the thing's held up. It's passed every test. If it keeps up that performance, Pfitzner will get the whole of the new appropriation—and if it doesn't, there may not be any appropriation at all, not only for Pfitzner, but for the other firms that have been helping on the project.

"The whole question of whether or not we lick the degenerative diseases hangs on those two things: the validity of the solution we've found and the money. If one goes, the other goes. And we'll have to tell Horsefield and MacHinery and the others what we've found some time this month, because the old appropriation lapses after that."

The girl leaned back and seemed to notice for the first time that she had finished her dinner. "And that," she said, pushing regretfully at the sprig of parsley with her fork, "isn't exactly public knowledge yet! I think I'd better shut up."

"Thank you," Paige said gravely. "It's obviously more than I deserve to know."

"Well," Anne said, "you can tell *me* something, if you will. It's about this Bridge that's being built on Jupiter. Is it worth all the money that they're pouring into it? Nobody seems to be able to explain what it's good for. And now there's talk that another Bridge'll be started on Saturn, when this one's finished!"

"You needn't worry," Paige said. "Understand, I've no connection with the Bridge, though I do know some people on the Bridge gang, so I haven't any inside information. I do have some public knowledge, just like yours—meaning knowledge that anyone can have, if he has the training to know where to look for it. As I understand it, the Bridge on Jupiter is a research project, designed to answer some questions—just what questions, nobody's bothered to tell me, and I've been careful not to ask; you can see Francis X. MacHinery's face in the constellations if you look carefully enough. But this much I know: the conditions of the research demand the use of the largest planet in the system. That's Jupiter, so it would be senseless to build another Bridge on a smaller planet, like Saturn. The Bridge gang will keep the present structure going until they've found out what they want to know. Then the project will almost surely be discontinued—not because the bridge is 'finished,' but because it will have served its purpose."

"I suppose I'm showing my ignorance," Anne said, "but it sounds idiotic to me. All those millions and millions of dollars—that *we* could be saving lives with!"

"If the choice were mine," Paige agreed, "I'd award the money to you, not to Charity Dillon and his crew. But then, I know almost as little about the Bridge as you do, so perhaps it's just as well that I'm not allowed to route the check. Is it my turn to ask a question? I still have a small one."

"Your witness," Anne said, smiling her altogether lovely smile.

"This afternoon, while I was in the labs, I twice heard a baby crying—and I think it was actually two different babies. I asked your Mr. Gunn about it, and he told me an obvious fairy story." He paused. Anne's eyes had already begun to glitter.

"You're on dangerous ground, Colonel Russell," she said.
"I can tell. But I mean to ask my question anyhow.
When I pulled my absurd vivisection threat on you later, I
was out-and-out flabbergasted that it worked, but it set me
to thinking. Can you explain—and if so, would you?"

Anne got out her compact again and seemed to consult
it warily. At last she said: "I suppose I've forgiven you,
more or less. Anyhow, I'll answer. It's very simple: the
babies *are* being used as experimental animals. We have a
pipeline to a local foundling home. It's all only technically
legal, and had you actually brought charges of human
vivisection against us, you probably could have made them
stick."

His coffee cup clattered into its saucer. "Great God,
Anne. Isn't it dangerous to make such a joke these days—
especially with a man you've known only half a day? Or
are you trying to startle me into admitting I'm a
stoolie?"

"I'm not joking and I don't think you're a stoolie," she
said calmly. "What I said was perfectly true—oh, I souped
up the way I put it just a little, maybe because I haven't
entirely forgiven you for that bit of successful blackmail,
and I wanted to see you jump. And for other reasons. But
it's true."

"But Anne—why?"

"Look, Paige," she said. "It was fifty years ago that we
found that if we added minute amounts of certain antibiotics, really just traces, to animal feeds, the addition brought
the critters to market months ahead of normally-fed animals. For that matter, it even provokes growth spurts in
plants under special conditions; and it works for poultry,
baby pigs, calves, mink cubs, a whole spectrum of animals. It was logical to suspect that it might work in
newborn humans too."

"And you're trying that?" Paige leaned back and poured
himself another glass of Chilean Rhine. "I'd say you
souped up your revelation quite a bit, all right."

"Don't be so ready to accept the obvious, and listen to
me. We are *not* doing that. It was done decades ago,
regularly and above the board, by students of Paul
György and half a hundred other nutrition experts. Those
people used only very widely known and tested antibiotics,
drugs that had already been used on literally millions of
farm animals, dosages worked out to the milligram of
drug per kilogram of body weight, and so on. But this

particular growth-stimulating effect of antibiotics happens to be a major clue to whether or not a given drug has the kind of biological activity *we* want—and we have to know whether or not it shows that activity *in human beings*. So we screen new drugs on the kids, as fast as they're found and pass certain other tests. We have to."

"I see," Paige said. "I see."

"The children are 'volunteered' by the foundling home, and we could make a show of legality if it came to a court fight," Anne said. "The precedent was established in 1952, when Pearl River Labs used children of its own workers to test its live-virus polio vaccine—which worked, by the way. But it isn't the legality of it that's important. It's the question of how soon and how thoroughly we're going to lick the degenerative diseases."

"You seem to be defending it to me," Paige said slowly, "as though you cared what I thought about it. So I'll tell you what I think: it seems mighty damned cold-blooded to me. It's the kind of thing of which ugly myths are made. If ten years from now there's a pogrom against biologists because people think they eat babies, I'll know why."

"Nonsense," Anne said. "It takes centuries to build up that kind of myth. You're over-reacting."

"On the contrary. I'm being as honest with you as you were with me. I'm astonished and somewhat repelled by what you've told me. That's all."

The girl, her lips slightly thinned, dipped and dried her fingertips and began to draw on her gloves. "Then we'll say no more about it," she said. "I think we'd better leave now."

"Certainly, as soon as I pay the check. Which reminds me: do you have any interest in Pfitzner, Anne—a personal interest, I mean?"

"No. No more interest than any human being with a moment's understanding of the implications would have. And I think that's a rather ugly sort of question."

"I thought you might take it that way, but I really wasn't accusing you of being a profiteer. I just wondered whether or not you were related to the Dr. Abbott that Gunn and the rest were waiting for this afternoon."

She got out the compact again and looked carefully into it. "Abbott's a common enough name."

"Sure. Still, *some* Abbotts are related. And it seems to make sense."

"Let's hear you do that. I'd be interested."

"All right," he said, beginning to become angry himself. "The receptionist at Pfitzner, ideally, should know exactly what is going on in the plant at all times, so as to be able to assess accurately the intentions of every visitor—just as you did with me. But at the same time, she has to be an absolutely flawless security risk, or otherwise she couldn't be trusted with enough knowledge to be that kind of a receptionist. The best way to make sure of the security angle is to hire someone with a blood tie to another person on the project. That adds up to *two* people who are being careful. A classical Soviet form of blackmail, as I recall.

"That much is theory. There's fact, too. You certainly explained the Pfitzner project to me this evening from a broad base of knowledge that nobody could expect to find in an ordinary receptionist. On top of that, you took policy risks that, properly, only an officer of Pfitzner should be empowered to take. I conclude that you're not *only* a receptionist; your name is Abbott; and ... there we have it, it seems to me."

"Do we?" the girl said, standing abruptly in a white fury. "Not quite! Also, I'm not pretty, and a receptionist for a firm as big as Pfitzner is usually pretty striking. Striking enough to resist being pumped by the first man to notice her, at least. Go ahead, complete the list! Tell the whole truth!"

"How can I?" Paige said, rising also and looking squarely at her, his fingers closing slowly, "If I told you honestly just what I think of your looks—and by God I will, I think the most beautiful woman in the world would bathe every day in fuming nitric acid just to duplicate your smile—you'd hate me more than ever. You'd think I was mocking you. Now you tell me the rest of the truth. You *are* related to Dr. Abbott."

"Patly enough," the girl said, each word cut out of smoking-dry ice, "Dr. Abbott is my father. And I insist upon being allowed to go home now, Colonel Russell. Not ten seconds from now, but *now*."

CHAPTER FOUR: Jupiter V

The firm determination to submit to experiment is not enough; there are still dangerous hypotheses; first, and above all, those which are tacit and unconscious. Since we make them without knowing it, we are powerless to abandon them.

—HENRI POINCARÉ

THE BRIDGE vanished as the connection was broken. The continuous ultronic pulses from the Jovian satellites to the selsyns and servos of the Bridge never stopped, of course; and the Bridge sent back information ceaselessly on the same sub-etheric channels to the ever-vigilant eyes and ears and hands of the Bridge gang on Jupiter V. But for the moment, the vast structure's guiding intelligence, the Bridge gang foreman, had quitted it.

Helmuth set the heavy helmet carefully in its niche and felt of his temples, feeling the blood passing under his fingertips. Then he turned.

Dillon was looking at him.

"Well?" the civil engineer said. "What's the matter, Bob? Is it bad—?"

Helmuth did not reply for a moment. The abrupt transition from the storm-ravaged deck of the Bridge to the quiet, placid air of the operations shack on Jupiter's fifth moon was always a shock. He had never been able to anticipate it, let alone become accustomed to it; it was worse each time, not better.

He pulled the jacks from the foreman's board and let them flick back into the desk on their alive, elastic cables, and then got up from the bucket seat, moving carefully upon shaky legs, feeling implicit in his own body the enormous weights and pressures his guiding intelligence had just quitted. The fact that the gravity on the foreman's deck was as weak as that of most of the habitable asteroids only made the contrast greater, and his need for caution in walking more extreme.

He went to the big porthole and looked out. The unworn, tumbled, monotonous surface of airless Jupiter V looked almost homey after the perpetual holocaust of Jupiter itself. But there was an overpowering reminder of that holocaust—for through the thick quartz of the port-hole, the face of the giant planet stared at Helmuth across only 112,600 miles, less than half the distance between Earth's moon and Earth; a sphere-section occupying almost all of the sky, except the near horizon, where one could see a few first-magnitude stars. The rest of the sky was crawling with color, striped and blotched with the eternal, frigid, poisonous storming of Jupiter's atmosphere, spotted with the deep-black, planet-sized shadows of moons closer to the sun than Jupiter V.

Somewhere down there, six thousand miles below the clouds that boiled in Helmuth's face, was the Bridge. The Bridge was thirty miles high and eleven miles wide and fifty-four miles long—but it was only a sliver, an intricate and fragile arrangement of ice-crystals beneath the bulging, racing tornadoes.

On Earth, even in the West, the Bridge would have been the mightiest engineering achievement of all history, could the Earth have borne its weight at all. But on Jupiter, the Bridge was as precarious and perishable as a snowflake.

"Bob?" Dillon's voice asked. "What is it? You seem more upset than usual. Is it serious?"

Helmuth looked up. His superior's worn, young face, lantern-jawed and crowned by black hair already beginning to gray at the temples, was alight both with love for the Bridge and with the consuming ardor of the responsibility he had to bear. As always, it touched Helmuth and reminded him that the implacable universe had, after all, provided one warm corner in which human beings might huddle together.

"Serious enough," he said, forming the words with difficulty against the frozen inarticulateness Jupiter had forced upon him. "But not fatal, as far as I could see. There's a lot of hydrogen vulcanism on the surface, especially at the northwest end, and it looks like there must have been a big blast under the cliffs. I saw what looked like the last of a series of fire-falls."

Dillon's face relaxed while Helmuth was talking, slowly, line by engraved line. "Oh. It was just a flying chunk then."

"I'm almost sure that was what it was. The cross-draughts are heavy now. The Spot and the STD are due to pass each other some time next month, aren't they? I haven't checked, but I can feel the difference in the storms."

"So the chunk got picked up and thrown through the end of the Bridge. A big piece?"

Helmuth shrugged. "That end is all twisted away to the left, and the deck is burst into matchwood. The scaffolding is all gone, too, of course. A pretty big piece, all right, Charity—two miles through at a minimum."

Dillon sighed. He, too, went to the window, and looked out. Helmuth did not need to be a mind reader to know what he was looking at. Out there, across the stony waste of Jupiter V plus 112,600 miles of space, the South Tropical Disturbance was streaming toward the great Red Spot, and would soon overtake it. When the whirling funnel of the STD—more than big enough to suck three Earths into deep-freeze—passed the planetary island of sodium-tainted ice which was the Red Spot, the Spot would follow it for a few thousand miles, at the same time rising closer to the surface of the atmosphere.

Then the Spot would sink again, drifting back toward the incredible jet of stress-fluid which kept it in being—a jet fed by no one knew what forces at Jupiter's hot, rocky, 22,000-mile core, compacted down there under 16,000 miles of eternal ice. During the entire passage, the storms all over Jupiter became especially violent; and the Bridge had been forced to locate in anything but the calmest spot on the planet, thanks to the uneven distribution of the few "permanent" land-masses.

But—"permanent"? The quote-marks Helmuth's thinking always put around that word were there for a very good reason, he knew, but he could not quite remember the reason. It was the damned conditioning showing itself again, creating another of the thousand small irreconcilables which contributed to the tension.

Helmuth watched Dillon with a certain compassion, tempered with mild envy. Charity Dillon's unfortunate given name betrayed him as the son of a hangover, the only male child of a Believer family which dated back long before the current resurgence of the Believers. He was one of the hundreds of government-drafted experts who had planned the Bridge, and he was as obsessed by the Bridge as Helmuth was—but for different reasons. It was widely believed among the Bridge gang that Dillon, alone among them, had not been given the conditioning, but there was no way to test that.

Helmuth moved back to the port, dropping his hand gently on Dillon's shoulders. Together they looked at the screaming straw yellows, brick reds, pinks, oranges, browns, even blues and greens that Jupiter threw across the ruined stone of its innermost satellite. On Jupiter V, even the shadows had color.

Dillon did not move. He said at last: "Are you pleased, Bob?"

"Pleased?" Helmuth said in astonishment. "No. It scares me white; you know that. I'm just glad that the whole Bridge didn't go."

"You're quite sure?" Dillon said quietly.

Helmuth took his hand from Dillon's shoulder and returned to his seat at the central desk. "You've no right to needle me for something I can't help," he said, his voice even lower than Dillon's. "I work on Jupiter four hours a day—not actually, because we can't keep a man alive for more than a split second down there—but my eyes and ears and my mind are there on the Bridge, four hours a day. Jupiter is not a nice place. I don't like it. I won't pretend I do.

"Spending four hours a day in an environment like that over a period of years—well, the human mind instinctively tries to adapt, even to the unthinkable. Sometimes I wonder how I'll behave when I'm put back in Chicago again. Sometimes I can't remember anything about Chicago except vague generalities, sometimes I can't even believe there is such a place as Earth—how could there be when the rest of the universe is like Jupiter or worse?"

"I know," Dillon said. "I've tried several times to show you that isn't a very reasonable frame of mind."

"I know it isn't. But I can't help how I feel. For all I know it isn't even my own frame of mind—though the part of my mind that keeps saying 'The Bridge *must* stand' is more likely to be the conditioned part. No, I don't think the bridge will last. It can't last; it's all wrong. But I don't *want* to see it go. I've just got sense enough to know that one of these days Jupiter is going to sweep it away."

He wiped an open palm across the control boards, snapping all the toggles to "Off" with a sound like the fall of a double-handful of marbles on a pane of glass. "Like that, Charity! And I work four hours a day, every day, on the Bridge. One of these days, Jupiter is going to destroy the Bridge. It'll go flying away in little flinders, into the storms. My mind will be there, supervising some puny job, and my mind will go flying away along with my mechanical eyes and ears and hands—still trying to adapt to the unthinkable, tumbling away into the winds and the flames and the rains and the darkness and the pressure and the cold—"

"Bob, you're deliberately running away with yourself. Cut it out. Cut it out, I say!"

Helmuth shrugged, putting a trembling hand on the edge of the board to steady himself. "All right, I'm all right, Charity. I'm here, aren't I? Right here on Jupiter V, in no danger, in no danger at all. The Bridge is one hundred and twelve thousand six hundred miles away from here, and I'll never be an inch closer to it. But when the day comes that the Bridge is swept away—"

"Charity, sometimes I imagine you ferrying my body back to the cosy nook it came from, while my soul goes tumbling and tumbling through millions of cubic miles of poison. . . . All right, Charity, I'll be good. I won't think about it out loud, but you can't expect me to forget it. It's on my mind; I can't help it, and you should know that."

"I do," Dillon said, with a kind of eagerness. "I do, Bob. I'm only trying to help make you see the problem as it is. The Bridge isn't really that awful, it isn't worth a single nightmare."

"Oh, it isn't the Bridge that makes me yell out when I'm sleeping," Helmuth said, smiling bitterly. "I'm not that ridden by it yet. It's while I'm awake that I'm afraid the Bridge will be swept away. What I sleep with is a fear of myself."

"That's a sane fear. You're as sane as any of us," Dillon insisted, fiercely solemn. "Look, Bob. The Bridge isn't a monster. It's a way we've developed for studying the behavior of materials under specific conditions of pressure, temperature and gravity. Jupiter isn't Hell, either; it's a set of conditions. The Bridge is the laboratory we set up to work with those conditions."

"It isn't going anywhere. It's a bridge to noplace."

"There aren't many *places* on Jupiter," Dillon said, missing Helmuth's meaning entirely. "We put the Bridge on an island in the local sea because we needed solid ice we could sink the foundation in. Otherwise, it wouldn't have mattered where we put it. We could have floated the caissons on the sea itself, if we hadn't wanted a fixed point from which to measure storm velocities and such things."

"I know that," Helmuth said.

"But, Bob, you don't show any signs of understanding it. Why, for instance, should the Bridge *go* any place? It isn't even, properly speaking, a bridge at all. We only call it that because we used some bridge engineering principles in building it. Actually, it's much more like a traveling crane—an extremely heavy-duty overhead rail line. It isn't going anywhere because it hasn't any place interesting to go to, that's all. We're extending it to cover as much territory as possible, and to increase its stability, not to span the distance between places. There's no point to reproaching it because it doesn't span a real gap—between, say, Dover and Calais. It's a bridge to knowledge, and that's far more important. Why can't you see that?"

"I can see that; that's what I was talking about," Helmuth said, trying to control his impatience. "I have at present as much common sense as the average child. What I am trying to point out is that meeting colossalness with colossalness—out here—is a mug's game. It's a game Jupiter will always win without the slightest effort. What if the engineers who built the Dover-Calais bridge had been limited to broom-straws for their structural members? They could have got the bridge up somehow, sure, and made it strong enough to carry light traffic on a fair day. But what would you have had left of it after the first winter storm came down the Channel from the North Sea? The whole approach is idiotic!"

"All right," Dillon said reasonably. "You have a point. Now you're being reasonable. What better approach have you to suggest? Should we abandon Jupiter entirely because it's too big for us?"

"No," Helmuth said. "Or maybe, yes. I don't know. I don't have any easy answer. I just know that this one is no answer at all—it's just a cumbersome evasion."

Dillon smiled. "You're depressed, and no wonder. Sleep it off, Bob, if you can—you might even come up with that answer. In the meantime—well, when you stop to think about it, the surface of Jupiter isn't any more hostile, inherently, than the surface of Jupiter V, except in degree. If you stepped out of this building naked, you'd die just as fast as you would on Jupiter. Try to look at it that way."

Helmuth, looking forward into another night of dreams, said: "That's the way I look at it now."

BOOK TWO

INTERMEZZO: Washington

Finally, in semantic aphasia, the full significance of words and phrases is lost. Separately, each word or each detail of a drawing can be understood, but the general significance escapes; an act is executed on command, though the purpose of it is not understood. . . . A general conception cannot be formulated, but details can be enumerated.
—HENRI PIÉRON

We often think that when we have completed our study of one we know all about two, because 'two' is 'one and one.' We forget that we have still to make a study of 'and.'
—A. S. EDDINGTON

THE REPORT of the investigating sub-committee of the Senate Finance Committee on the Jupiter Project was a massive document, especially so in the mimeographed, uncorrected form in which it had been rushed to Wagoner's desk. In its printed form—not due for another two weeks—the report would be considerably less bulky, but it would probably be more unreadable. In addition, it would be tempered in spots by the cautious second thoughts of its seven authors; Wagoner needed to see their opinions in the raw "for colleagues only" version.

Not that the printed version would get a much wider circulation. Even the mimeographed document was stamped "Top Secret." It had been years since anything about the government's security system had amused Wagoner in the slightest, but he could not repress a wry grin now. Of course the Bridge itself was Top Secret; but had the sub-committee's report been ready only a little over a year ago, everybody in the country would have heard about it, and selected passages would have been printed in the newspapers. He could think offhand of at least ten opposition senators, and two or three more inside his own party, who had been determined to use the report to prevent his reelection—or any parts of the report that might have been turned to that purpose. Unhappily for them, the report had been still only a third finished when election day had come, and Alaska had sent Wagoner back to Washington by a very comfortable plurality.

And, as he turned the stiff legal-length pages slowly, with the pleasant, smoky odor of duplicator ink rising from them as he turned, it became clear that the report would have made pretty poor campaign material anyhow. Much of it was highly technical and had obviously been written by staff advisers, not by the investigating senators themselves. The public might be impressed by, but it could not read and would not read, such a show of erudition. Besides, it was only a show; nearly all the technical discussions of the Bridge's problems petered out into meaningless generalities. In most such instances Wagoner was able to put a mental finger on the missing fact, the ignorance or the withholding of which had left the chain of reasoning suspended in mid-air.

Against the actual operation of the Bridge the senators had been able to find nothing of substance to say. Given in advance the fact that the taxpayers had wanted to spend so much money to build a Bridge on Jupiter—which is to say, somebody (Wagoner himself) had decided that for them, without confusing them by bringing the proposition to their attention—then even the opposition senators had had to agree that it had been built as economically as possible and was still being built that way.

Of course, there had been small grafts waiting to be discovered, and the investigators had discovered them. One of the supply-ship captains had been selling cakes of soap to the crew on Ganymede at incredible prices with the co-operation of the store clerk there. But that was nothing more than a bookkeeper's crime on a project the size of the Bridge. Wagoner a little admired the supply-captain's ingenuity—or had it been the store clerk's?—in discovering an item wanted badly enough on Ganymede, and small enough and light enough to be worth smuggling. The men on the Bridge gang banked most of their salaries automatically on Earth without ever seeing them; there was very little worth buying or selling on the moons of Jupiter.

Of major graft, however, there had been no trace. No steel company had sold the Bridge any sub-standard castings, because there was no steel in the Bridge. A Jovian might have made a good thing of selling the Bridge sub-standard Ice IV—but as far as anyone could know there were no Jovians, so the Bridge got its Ice IV for nothing but the cost of cutting it. Wagoner's office had been very strict about the handling of the lesser contracts— for pre-fabricated moon huts, for supply ferry fuel, for equipment—and had policed not only its own deals, but all the Army Space Service sub-contracts connected with the Bridge.

As for Charity Dillon and his foreman, they were rigidly efficient—partly because it was in their natures to work that way, and partly because of the intensive conditioning they had all been given before being shipped to the Jovian system. There was no waste to be found in anything that they supervised, and if they had occasionally been guilty of bad engineering judgment, no outside engineer would be likely to detect it. The engineering principles by which the Bridge operated did not hold true anywhere but on Jupiter.

The hugest loss of money the whole Jupiter Project had yet sustained had been accompanied by such carnage that it fell—in the senators' minds—in the category of warfare. When a soldier is killed by enemy action, nobody asks how much money his death cost the government through the loss of his gear. The part of the report which described the placing of the Bridge's foundation mentioned reverently the heroism of the lost two hundred and thirty-one crewmen; it said nothing about the cost of the nine specially-designed space tugs which now floated in silhouette, as flat as so many tin cut-outs under six million pounds per square inch of pressure, somewhere at the bottom of Jupiter's atmosphere—floated with eight thousand vertical miles of eternally roaring poisons between them and the eyes of the living.

Had those crewmen been heroes? They had been enlisted men and officers of the Army Space Service, acting under orders. While doing what they had been ordered to do, they had been killed. Wagoner could not remember whether or not the survivors of that operation had also been called heroes. Oh, they had certainly been decorated—the Army liked its men to wear as much fruit salad on their chests as it could possibly spoon out to them, because it was good public relations—but they were not mentioned in the report.

This much was certain: the dead men had died because of Wagoner. He had known, generally at least, that many of them would die, but he had gone ahead anyhow. He knew that there might be worse to come. Nevertheless, he would proceed, because he thought that—in the long run—it would be worth it. He knew well enough that the end cannot justify the means; but if there are *no* other means, and the end is necessary. . . .

But from time to time he thought of Dostoevski and the Grand Inquisitor. Would the Millennium be worth having, if it could be ushered in only by the torturing to death of a single child? What Wagoner foresaw and planned for was by no means the Millennium; and while the children at Jno. Pfitzner & Sons were certainly not being tortured or even harmed, their experiences there were at least not normal for children. And there were two hundred and thirty-one men frozen solid somewhere in the bottomless hell of Jupiter, men who had had to obey their orders even more helplessly than children.

Wagoner had not been cut out to be a general.

The report praised the lost men's heroism. Wagoner lifted the heavy pages one after another, looking for a word from the investigating senators about the cause those deaths had served. There was nothing but the conventional phrases, "for their country," "for the cause of peace," "for the future." High-order abstractions—blabs. The senators had no notion of what the Bridge was for. They had looked, but they hadn't seen. Even with a total of four years to think back on the experience, they hadn't seen. The very size of the Bridge evidently had convinced them that it was a form of weapons research—so much "for the cause of peace"—and that it would be better for them not to know the nature of the weapon until an official announcement was circulated to them.

They were right. The Bridge was assuredly a weapon. But in neglecting to wonder what kind of a weapon it might be, the senators had also neglected to wonder at whom it was pointed. Wagoner was glad that they had.

The report did not even touch upon those two years of exploration, of search for some project which might be worth attacking, which had preceded even the notion of the Bridge. Wagoner had had a special staff of four devoted men at work during every minute of those two years, checking patents that had been granted but not sequestered, published scientific papers containing suggestions other scientists had decided not to explore, articles in the lay press about incipient miracles which hadn't come off, science-fiction stories by practicing scientists, anything and everything that might lead somewhere. The four men had worked under orders to avoid telling anybody what they were looking for, and to stay strictly away from the main currents of modern scientific thought on the subject; but no secret is ever truly safe; no face in nature is ever truly a secret.

Somewhere, for instance, in the files of the FBI, was a tape recording of the conversation he had had with the chief of the four-man team, in his office, the day the break came. The man had said, not only to Wagoner, but to the attentive FBI microphones no senator dared to seek out and muffle: "This looks like a real line, Bliss. On Subject G." (Something on gravity, chief.)

"Keep it to the point." (A reminder: Keep it too technical to interest a casual eavesdropper—if you *have* to talk about it here, with all these bugs to pick it up.)

"Sure. It's a thing called the Blackett equation. Deals with a possible relationship between electron-spin and magnetic moment. I understand Dirac did some work on that, too. There's a G in the equation, and with one simple algebraic manipulation you can isolate the G on one side of the equals-sign, and all the other elements on the other." (Not a crackpot notion this time. Real scientists have been interested in it. There's math to go with it.)

"Status?" (Why was it never followed, then?)

"The original equation is about status seven, but there's no way anybody knows that it could be subjected to an operational test. The manipulated equation is called the Locke Derivation, and our boys say that a little dimensional analysis will show that it's wrong; but they're not entirely sure. However, it *is* subject to an operational test if we want to pay for it, where the original Blackett formula isn't." (Nobody's sure what it means yet. It may mean nothing. It would cost a hell of a lot to find out.)

"Do we have the facilities?" (Just how much?)

"Only the beginnings." (About four billion dollars, Bliss.)

"Conservatively?" (Why so much?)

"Yes. Field strength again."

(That was shorthand for the only problem that mattered, in the long run, if you wanted to work with gravity. Whether you thought of it, like Newton, as a force, or like Faraday as a field, or like Einstein as a condition in space, gravity was incredibly weak. It was so weak that, although theoretically it was a property of every bit of matter in the universe no matter how small, it could not be worked with in the laboratory. Two magnetized needles will rush toward each other over a distance as great as an inch; so will two balls of pith as small as peas if they bear opposite electrical charges. Two ceramet magnets no bigger than doughnuts can be so strongly charged that it is impossible to push them together by hand when their like poles are opposed, and impossible for a strong man to hold them apart when their unlike poles approach each other. Two spheres of metal of any size, if they bear opposite electrical charges, will mate in a fat spark across the insulating air, if there is no other way that they can neutralize each other.

(But gravity—theoretically one in kind with electricity and magnetism—cannot be charged on to any object. It produces no sparks. There is no such thing as an insulation against it—a di-gravitic. It remains beyond detection as a force, between bodies as small as peas or doughnuts. Two objects as huge as skyscrapers and as massive as lead will take centuries to crawl into the same bed over a foot of distance, if nothing but their mutual gravitational attraction is drawing them together; even love is faster than that. Even a ball of rock eight thousand miles in diameter— the Earth—has a gravitational field too weak to prevent one single man from pole-vaulting away from it to more than four times his own height, driven by no opposing force but that of his spasming muscles.)

"Well, give me a report when you can. If necessary, we can expand." (Is it worth it?)

"I'll give you the report this week." (Yes!)

And that was how the Bridge had been born, though nobody had known it then, not even Wagoner. The senators who had investigated the Bridge still didn't know it. MacHinery's staff at the FBI evidently had been unable to penetrate the jargon on their recording of that conversation far enough to connect the conversation with the Bridge; otherwise MacHinery would have given the transcript to the investigators. MacHinery did not exactly love Wagoner; he had been unable thus far to find any handle by which he might grasp and use the Alaskan senator.

All well and good.

And yet the investigators had come perilously close, just once. They had subpoenaed Guiseppi Corsi for the preliminary questioning.

Committee Counsel: Now then, Dr. Corsi, according to our records, your last interview with Senator Wagoner was in the winter of 2013. Did you discuss the Jupiter Project with him at that time?

Corsi: How could I have? It didn't exist then.

Counsel: But was it mentioned to you in any way? Did Senator Wagoner say anything about plans to start such a project?

Corsi: No.

Counsel: You didn't yourself suggest it to Senator Wagoner?

Corsi: Certainly not. It was a total surprise to me, when it was announced afterwards.

Counsel: But I suppose you know what it is.

Corsi: I know only what the general public has been told. We're building a Bridge on Jupiter. It's very costly and ambitious. What it's for is a secret. That's all.

Counsel: You're sure you don't know what it's for?

Corsi: For research.

Counsel: Yes, but research for what? Surely you have some clues.

Corsi: I don't have any clues, and Senator Wagoner didn't give me any. The only facts I have are those I read in the press. Naturally I have some conjectures. But all I *know* is what is indicated, or hinted at, in the official announcements. Those seem to convey the impression that the Bridge is for weapons research.

Counsel: But you think that maybe it isn't?

Corsi: I—I'm not in a position to discuss government projects about which I know nothing.

Counsel: You could give us your opinion.

Corsi: If you want my opinion as an expert, I'll have my office go into the subject and let you know later what such an opinion would cost.

Senator Billings: Dr. Corsi, do we understand that you

refuse to answer the question? It seems to me that in view of your past record you might be better advised—

Corsi: I haven't refused an answer, Senator. I make part of my living by consultation. If the government wishes to use me in that capacity, it's my right to ask to be paid. You have no right to deprive me of my livelihood, or any part of it.

Senator Croft: The government made up its mind about employing you some time back, Dr. Corsi. And rightly, in my opinion.

Corsi: That is the government's privilege.

Senator Croft:—but you are being questioned now by the Senate of the United States. If you refuse to answer, you may be held in contempt.

Corsi: For refusing to state an opinion?

Counsel: If you will pardon me, Senator Croft, the witness may refuse to offer an opinion—or withhold such an opinion, pending payment. He can be held in contempt only for declining to state the facts as he knows them.

Senator Croft: All right, let's get some facts, and stop the pussyfooting.

Counsel: Dr. Corsi, was anything said during your last meeting with Senator Wagoner which might have had any bearing on the Jupiter Project?

Corsi: Well, yes. But only negatively. I did counsel him against any such project. Rather emphatically, as I recall.

Counsel: I thought you said that the Bridge hadn't been mentioned.

Corsi: It hadn't. Senator Wagoner and I were discussing research methods in general. I told him that I thought research projects of the Bridge's order of magnitude were no longer fruitful.

Senator Billings: Did you charge Senator Wagoner for that opinion, Dr. Corsi?

Corsi: No, Senator. Sometimes I don't.

Senator Billings: Perhaps you should have. Wagoner didn't follow your free advice.

Senator Croft: It looks like he considered the source.

Corsi: There's nothing compulsory about advice. I gave him my best opinion at the time. What he did with it was up to him.

Counsel: Would you tell us if that is your best opinion now? That research projects the size of the Bridge are— I believe your phrase was, "no longer fruitful"?

Corsi: That is still my opinion.

Senator Billings: Which you will give us free of charge . . . ?

Corsi: It is the opinion of every scientist I know. You could get it free from those who work for you. I have better sense than to charge fees for common knowledge.

It had been a near thing. Perhaps, Wagoner thought, Corsi had after all remembered the really crucial part of that interview and had decided not to reveal it to the sub-committee. It was more likely, however, that those few words that Corsi had thrown off while standing at the blinded windows of his apartment would not have stuck in his memory as they had stuck in Wagoner's.

Yet surely Corsi knew, at least in part, what the Bridge was for. He must have remembered the part of that conversation which dealt with gravity. By now he would have reasoned his way from those words all the difficult way to the Bridge—after all, the Bridge was not a difficult object for an understanding like Corsi's.

But he had said nothing about it. That had been a crucial silence.

Wagoner wondered if it would ever be possible for him to show his gratitude to the aging physicist. Not now. Possibly never. The pain and the puzzlement in Corsi's mind stood forth in what he had said, even through the coldness of the official transcript. Wagoner badly wanted to assuage both. But he couldn't. He could only hope that Corsi would see it whole, and understand it whole, when the time came.

The page turned on Corsi. Now there was another question which had to be answered. Was there a single hint, anywhere in the sixteen hundred mimeographed pages of the report, that the Bridge was incomplete without what was going on at Jno. Pfitzner & Sons? . . .

No, there was not. Wagoner let the report fall, with a sigh of relief of which he was hardly conscious. That was that.

He filed the report, and reached into his "In" basket for the dossier on Paige Russell, Colonel, Army Space Corps, which had come in from the Pfitzner plant only a week ago. He was tired, and he did not want to perform an act of judgment on another man for the rest of his life—but he had asked for the job, and now he had to work at it.

Bliss Wagoner had not been cut out to be a general. As a god he was even more inept.

CHAPTER FIVE: New York

The original phenomena which the soul-hypothesis attempted to explain still remain. Homo sapiens *does have some differences from other animal species. But when his biological distinctions and their consequences are clearly described, man's 'morality,' his 'soul,' and his 'immortality' all become accessible to a purely naturalistic formulation and understanding, . . . Man's 'immortality' (in so far as it differs from the immortality of the germ plasm of any other animal species) consists in his time-transcending inter-individually shared values, symbol-systems, languages, and cultures—and in nothing else.*
                                        —WESTON LA BARRE

IT TOOK Paige no more than Anne's mandatory ten seconds, during breakfast of the next day in his snuggery at the spaceman's Haven, to decide that he was going back to the Pfitzner plant and apologize. He didn't quite understand why the date had ended as catastrophically as it had, but of one thing he was nearly certain: the fiasco had had something to do with his space-rusty manners, and if it were to be mended, he had to be the one to tool up for it.

And now that he came to think of it over his cold egg, it seemed obvious in essence. By his last line of questioning, Paige had broken the delicate shell of the evening and spilled the contents all over the restaurant table. He had left the more or less safe womb of technicalities, and had begun, by implication at least, to call Anne's ethics into question—first by making clear his first reaction to the business about the experimental infants, and then by pressing home her irregular marriage to her firm.

In this world called Earth of disintegrating faiths, one didn't call personal ethical codes into question without getting into trouble. Such codes, where they could be found at all, obviously had cost their adherents too much pain to be open for any new probing. Faith had once been self-evident; now it was desperate. Those who still had it—or had made it, chunk by fragment by shard—wanted nothing but to be allowed to hold it.

As for why he wanted to set matters right with Anne Abbott, Paige was less clear. His leave was passing him by rapidly, and thus far he had done little more than stroll while it passed—especially if he measured it against the desperate meter-stick established by his last two leaves, the two after his marriage had shattered and he had been alone again. After the present leave was over, there was a good chance that he would be assigned to the Proserpine station, which was now about finished and which had no competitors for the title of the most forsaken outpost of the solar system. None, at least, until somebody should discover an 11th planet.

Nevertheless, he was going to go out to the Pfitzner plant again, out to the scenic Bronx, to revel among research scientists, business executives, government brass, and a frozen-voiced girl with a figure like an ironing-board, to kick up his heels on a reception-room rug in the sight of gay steel engravings of the founders, cheered on by a motto which might or might not be Dionysiac, if he could only read it. Great. Just great. If he played his cards right, he could go on duty at the Proserpine station with fine memories: perhaps the vice-president in charge of export would let Paige call him "Hal," or maybe even "Bubbles."

Maybe it was a matter of religion, after all. Like everyone else in the world, Paige thought, he was still looking for something bigger than himself, bigger than family, army, marriage, fatherhood, space itself, or the pub-crawls and tyrannically meaningless sexual spasms of a spaceman's leave. Quite obviously the project at Pfitzner, with its air of mystery and selflessness, had touched that very vulnerable nerve in him once more. Anne Abbott's own dedication was merely the touchstone, the key. . . . No, he hadn't the right word for it yet, but her attitude somehow fitted into an empty, jagged-edge blemish in his own soul like—like . . . yes, that was it: like a jigsaw-puzzle piece.

And besides, he wanted to see that sunburst smile again.

Because of the way her desk was placed, she was the first thing he saw as he came into Pfitzner's reception room. Her expression was even stranger than he had expected; and she seemed to be making some kind of covert gesture, as though she were flicking dust off the top of her desk toward him with the tips of all her fingers. He took several slower and slower steps into the room and stopped, finally baffled.

Someone rose from a chair which he had not been able to see from the door, and quartered down on him. The pad of the steps on the carpet and the odd crouch of the shape in the corner of Paige's eye were unpleasantly stealthy. Paige turned, unconsciously closing his hands.

"Haven't we seen this officer before, Miss Abbott? What's his business here—or has he any?"

The man in the eager semi-crouch was Francis X. MacHinery.

When he was not bent over in that absurd position, which was only his prosecutor's stance, Francis X. MacHinery looked every inch the inheritor of an unbroken line of Boston aristocrats, as in fact he was. Though he was not tall, he was very spare, and his hair had been white since he was 26 years old, giving him a look of cold wisdom which was complemented by his hawk-like nose and high cheekbones. The FBI had come down to him from his grandfather, who had somehow persuaded the then incumbent president—a stunningly popular Man-on-Horseback who dripped *charisma* but had no brains worth mentioning—that so important a directorship should not be hazarded to the appointments of his successors, but instead ought to be handed on from father to son like a corporate office.

Hereditary posts tend to become nominal with the passage of time, since it takes only one weak scion to destroy the importance of the office; but that had not happened yet to the MacHinery family. The current incumbent could, in fact, have taught his grandfather a thing or two. MacHinery was as full of cunning as a wolverine, and he had managed times without number to land on his feet regardless of what political disasters had been planned for him. And he was, as Paige was now discovering, the man for whom the metaphor "gimlet-eyed" had all unknowingly been invented.

"Well, Miss Abbott?"

"Colonel Russell was here yesterday," Anne said. "You may have seen him then."

The swinging doors opened and Horsefield and Gunn

came in. MacHinery paid no attention to them. He said, "What's your name, soldier?"

"I'm a spaceman," Paige said stiffly. "Colonel Paige Russell, Army Space Corps."

"What are you doing here?"

"I'm on leave."

"Will you answer the question?" MacHinery said. He was, Paige noticed, not looking at Paige at all, but over his shoulder, as though he were actually paying no real heed to the conversation. "What are you doing at the Pfitzner plant?"

"I happen to be in love with Miss Abbott," Paige said sharply to his own black and utter astonishment. "I came here to see her. We had a quarrel last night and I wanted to apologize. That's all."

Anne straightened behind her desk as though a curtain rod had been driven up her spine, turning toward Paige a pair of blindly blazing eyes and a rigidly unreadable expression. Even Gunn's mouth sagged slightly to one side; he looked first at Anne, then at Paige, as if he were abruptly uncertain that he had ever seen either of them before.

MacHinery, however, shot only one quick look at Anne, and his eyes seemed to turn into bottle-glass. "I'm not interested in your personal life," he said in a tone which, indeed, suggested active boredom. "I will put the question another way, so that there'll be no excuse for evading it. Why did you come to the plant in the first place? What is your *business* at Pfitzner, soldier?"

Paige tried to pick his next words carefully. Actually it would hardly matter what he said, once MacHinery developed a real interest in him; an accusation from the FBI had nearly the force of law. Everything depended upon so conducting himself as to be of no interest to MacHinery to begin with—an exercise at which, fortunately up to now, Paige had had no more practice than had any other spaceman.

He said: "I brought in some soil samples from the Jovian system. Pfitzner asked me to do it as part of their research program."

"And you brought these samples in yesterday, you told me."

"No, I didn't tell you. But as a matter of fact I did bring them in yesterday."

"And you're still bringing them in today, I see." Mac-

Hinery perked his chin over his shoulder toward Horsefield, whose face had frozen into complete tetany as soon as he had shown signs of realizing what was going on. "What about this, Horsefield? Is this one of your men that you haven't told me about?"

"No," Horsefield said, but putting a sort of a question mark into the way he spoke the word, as though he did not mean to deny anything which he might later be expected to affirm. "Saw the man yesterday, I think. For the first time to the best of my knowledge."

"I see. Would you say, General, that this man is no part of the Army's assigned complement on the project?"

"I can't say that for sure," Horsefield said, his voice sounding more positive now that he was voicing a doubt. "I'd have to consult my T.O. Perhaps he's somebody new in Alsos' group. He's not part of my staff, though—doesn't claim that he is, does he?"

"Gunn, what about this man? Did you people take him on without checking with me? Does he have security clearance?"

"Well, we did in a way, but he didn't need to be cleared," Gunn said. "He's just a field collector, hasn't any real part in the research work, no official connection. These field people are all volunteers; you know that."

MacHinery's brows were drawing closer and closer together. With only a few more of these questions, Paige knew even from the few newspapers which had reached him in space, he would have material enough for an arrest and a sensation—the kind of sensation which would pillory Pfitzner, destroy every civilian working for Pfitzner, trigger a long chain of courts martial among the military assignees, ruin the politicians who had sponsored the research, and thicken MacHinery's scrapbook of headlines about himself by at least three inches. That last outcome was the only one in which MacHinery was really interested; that the project itself would die was a side-effect which, though nearly inevitable, could hardly have interested him less.

"Excuse me, Mr. Gunn," Anne said quietly. "I don't think you're quite as familiar with Colonel Russell's status as I am. He's just come in from deep space, and his security record has been in the 'Clean and Routine' file for years; he's not one of our ordinary field collectors."

"Ah," Gunn said. "I'd forgotten, but that's quite true." Since it was both true and perfectly irrelevant, Paige could not understand why Gunn was quite so hearty about agreeing to it. Did he think Anne was stalling?

"As a matter of fact," Anne proceeded steadily, "Colonel Russell is a planetary ecologist specializing in the satellites; he's been doing important work for us. He's quite well known in space, and has many friends on the Bridge team and elsewhere. That's correct, isn't it, Colonel Russell?"

"I know most of the Bridge gang," Paige agreed, but he barely managed to make his assent audible. What the girl was saying added up to something very like a big, black lie. And lying to MacHinery was a short cut to ruin; only MacHinery had the privilege of lying, never his witnesses.

"The samples Colonel Russell brought us yesterday contained crucial material," Anne said. "That's why I asked him to come back; we needed his advice. And if his samples turn out to be as important as they seem, they'll save the taxpayers quite a lot of money—they may help us close out the project a long time in advance of the projected closing date. If that's to be possible, Colonel Russell will have to guide the last steps of the work personally; he's the only one who knows the microflora of the Jovian satellites well enough to interpret the results."

MacHinery looked dubiously over Paige's shoulder. It was hard to tell whether or not he had heard a word. Nevertheless, it was evident that Anne had chosen her final approach with great care, for if MacHinery had any weakness at all, it was the enormous cost of his continual, overlapping investigations. Lately he had begun to be nearly as sure death on "waste in government" as he was traditionally on "subversives." He said at last:

"There's obviously something irregular here. If all that's so, why did the man say what he said in the beginning?"

"Perhaps because it's also true," Paige said sharply.

MacHinery ignored him. "We'll check the records and call anyone we need. Horsefield, let's go."

The general trailed him out, his back very stiff, after a glare at Paige which failed to be in the least convincing, and an outrageously stagey wink at Anne. The moment the outer door closed behind the two, the reception-room seemed to explode. Gunn swung on Anne with a motion astonishingly tiger-like for so mild-faced a man. Anne was already rising from behind her desk, her face twisted with fear and fury. Both of them were shouting at once.

"Now see what you've done with your damned nosiness
—"

"What in the world did you want to tell MacHinery a
tale like that for—"

"—even a spaceman should know better than to hang
around a defense area—"

"—you know as well as I do that those Ganymede
samples are trash—"

"—you've probably cost us our whole appropriation
with your snooping—"

"—we've never hired a 'Clean and Routine' man since
the project began—"

"—I hope you're satisfied—"

"—I would have thought you'd have better sense by
now—"

"*Quiet!*" Paige shouted over them with the authentic
parade-ground blare. He had never found any use for it in
deep space, but it worked now. Both of them looked at
him, their mouths still incongruously half-opened, their
faces white as milk. "You act like a pair of hysterical
chickens, both of you! I'm sorry if I got you into trouble—
but I didn't ask Anne to lie in my behalf—and I didn't ask
you to go along with it, either, Gunn! Maybe you'd best
stop yelling accusations and try to think the thing through.
I'll try to help for whatever that's worth—but not if
you're going to scream and weep at each other and at
me!"

The girl bared her teeth at him in a real snarl, the first
time he had ever seen a human being mount such an
expression and mean it. She sat down, however, swiping at
her patchily red cheeks with a piece of cleansing tissue.
Gunn looked down at the carpet and just breathed noisily
for a moment, putting the palms of his hands together
solemnly before his white lips.

"I quite agree," Gunn said after a moment, as calmly as
if nothing had happened. "We'll have to get to work and
work fast. Anne, please tell me: why was it necessary for
you to say that Colonel Paige was essential to the project? I'm not accusing you of anything, but we need to
know the facts."

"I went to dinner with Colonel Russell last night," Anne
said. "I was somewhat indiscreet about the project. At the
end of the evening we had a quarrel which was probably
overheard by at least two of MacHinery's amateur in-

formers in the restaurant. I had to lie for my own protection as well as Colonel Russell's."

"But you have an Eavesdropper! If you knew that you might be overheard—"

"I knew it well enough. But I lost my temper. You know how these things go."

It all came out as emotionless as a tape recording. Told in these terms, the incident sounded to Paige like something that had happened to someone whom he had never met, whose name he could not even pronounce with certainty. Only the fact that Anne's eyes were reddened with furious tears offered any bridge between the cold narrative and the charged memory.

"Yes; nasty," Gunn said reflectively. "Colonel Russell, *do* you know the Bridge team?"

"I know some of them quite well, Charity Dillon in particular; after all, I was stationed in the Jovian system for a while. MacHinery's check will show that I've no official connection with the Bridge, however."

"Good, good," Gunn said, beginning to brighten. "That widens MacHinery's check to include the Bridge too, and dilutes it from Pfitzner's point of view—gives us more time, though I'm sorry for the Bridge men. The Bridge and the Pfitzner project both suspect—yes, that's a big mouthful even for MacHinery; it will take him months. And the Bridge is Senator Wagoner's pet project, so he'll have to go slowly; he can't assassinate Wagoner's reputation as rapidly as he could some other senator's. Hmm. The question now is, just how are we going to use the time?"

"When you calm down, you calm right down to the bottom," Paige said, grinning wryly.

"I'm a salesman," Gunn said. "Maybe more creative than some, but at heart a salesman. In that profession you have to suit the mood to the occasion, just like actors do. Now about those samples—"

"I shouldn't have thrown that in," Anne said. "I'm afraid it was one good touch too many."

"On the contrary, it may be the only out we have. MacHinery is a 'practical' man. Results are what counts with him. So suppose we take Colonel Russell's samples out of the regular testing order and run them through right now, issuing special orders to the staff that they are to find something in them—anything that looks at all decent."

"The staff won't fake," Anne said, frowning.

"My dear Anne, who said anything about faking? Nearly every batch of samples contains some organism of interest, even if it isn't good enough to wind up among our choicest cultures. You see? MacHinery will be contented by results if we can show them to him, even though the results may have been made possible by an unauthorized person; otherwise he'd have to assemble a committee of experts to assess the evidence, and that costs money. All this, of course, is predicated on whether or not we have any results by the time MacHinery finds out Colonel Russell *is* an unauthorized person."

"There's just one other thing," Anne said. "To make good on what I told MacHinery, we're going to have to turn Colonel Russell into a convincing planetary ecologist—*and* tell him just what the Pfitzner project is."

Gunn's face fell momentarily. "Anne," he said, "I want you to observe what a nasty situation that strong-arm man has gotten us into. In order to protect our legitimate interests from our own government, we're about to commit a real, serious breach of security—which would never have happened if MacHinery hadn't thrown his weight around."

"Quite true," Anne said. She looked, however, rather poker-faced, Paige thought. Possibly she was enjoying Gunn's discomfiture; he was not exactly the first man one would suspect of disloyalty or of being a security risk.

"Colonel Russell, there is no faint chance, I suppose, that you *are* a planetary ecologist? Most spacemen with ranks as high as yours are scientists of some kind."

"No, sorry," Paige said. "Ballistics is my field."

"Well, you do have to know something about the planets, at least. Anne, I suggest that you take charge now. I'll have to do some fast covering. Your father would probably be the best man to brief Colonel Russell. And, Colonel, would you bear in mind that from now on, every piece of information that you're given in our plant might have the giver jailed or even shot, if MacHinery were to find out about it?"

"I'll keep my mouth shut," Paige said. "I'm enough at fault in this mess to be willing to do all I can to help—and my curiosity has been killing me anyhow. But there's something you'd better know, too, Mr. Gunn."

"And that is—"

"That the time you're counting on just doesn't exist. My

leave expires in ten days. If you think you can make a planetary ecologist out of me in that length of time, I'll do my part."

"Ulp," Gunn said. "Anne, get to work." He bolted through the swinging doors.

The two looked at each other for a starchy moment, and then Anne smiled. Paige felt like another man at once.

"Is it really true—what you said?" Anne said, almost shyly.

"Yes. I didn't know it until I said it, but it's true. I'm really sorry that I had to say it at such a spectacularly bad moment; I only came over to apologize for my part in last night's quarrel. Now it seems that I've a bigger hassle to account for."

"Your curiosity is really your major talent, do you know?" she said, smiling again. "It took you only two days to find out just what you wanted to know—even though it's about the most closely guarded secret in the world."

"But I don't know it yet. Can you tell me here—or is the place wired?"

The girl laughed. "Do you think Hal and I would have cussed each other out like that if the place were wired? No, it's clean, we inspect it daily. I'll tell you the central fact, and then my father can give you the details. The truth is that the Pfitzner project isn't out to conquer the degenerative diseases alone. It's aimed at the end-product of those diseases, too. *We're looking for the answer to death itself.*"

Paige sat down slowly in the nearest chair. "I don't believe it can be done," he whispered at last.

"That's what we all used to think, Paige. That's what that says." She pointed to the motto in German above the swinging doors. *"Wider den Tod ist kein Krautlein gewachsen."* " 'Against Death doth no simple grow.' That was a law of nature, the old German herbalists thought. But now it's only a challenge. Somewhere in nature there *are* herbs and simples against death—and we're going to find them."

Anne's father seemed both preoccupied and a little worried to be talking to Paige at all, but it nevertheless took him only one day to explain the basic reasoning behind the project vividly enough so that Paige could understand it. In another day of simple helping around the part of the Pfitzner labs which was running his soil sam-

ples—help which consisted mostly of bottle-washing and
making dilutions—Paige learned the reasoning well
enough to put forward a version of it himself. He practiced it on Anne over dinner.

"It all rests on our way of thinking about why antibiotics work," he said, while the girl listened with an atten-
tiveness just this side of mockery. "What good are they to
the organisms that produce them? We assumed that the
organism secretes the antibiotic to kill or inhibit compet-
ing organisms, even though we were never able to show
that enough antibiotic for the purpose is actually produced
in the organism's natural medium, that is, the soil. In
other words, we figured, the wider the range of the antibiotic, the less competition the producer had."

"Watch out for teleology," Anne warned. "That's not
why the organism secretes it. It's just the result. Function,
not purpose."

"Fair enough. But right there is the borderline in our
thinking about antibiosis. What is an antibiotic to the
organisim it *kills?* Obviously, it's poison, a toxin. But
some bacteria always are naturally resistant to a given
antibiotic, and through—what did your father call it?—
through clone-variation and selection, the resistant cells
may take over a whole colony. Equally obviously, those
resistant cells would seem to produce an antitoxin. An
example would be the bacteria that secrete penicillinase,
which is an enzyme that destroys penicillin. To those
bacteria, penicillin is a toxin, and penicillinase is an antitoxin—isn't that right?"

"Right as rain. Go on, Paige."

"So now we add to that still another fact: that both
penicillin and tetracycline are not only antibiotics—which
makes them toxic to many bacteria—but *antitoxins* as
well. Both of them neutralize the placental toxin that
causes the eclampsia of pregnancy. Now, tetracycline is a
broad-range antibiotic; is there such a thing as a broad-
range antitoxin, too? Is the resistance to tetracycline that
many different kinds of bacteria can develop all derived
from a single counteracting substance? The answer, we
know now, is Yes. We've also found another kind of
broad-range antitoxin—one which protects the organism
against many different kinds of antibiotics. I'm told that
it's a whole new field of research and that we've just
begun to scratch the surface.

"Ergo: Find the broad-range antitoxin that acts against

the toxins of the human body which accumulate after growth stops—as penicillin and tetracycline act against the pregnancy toxin—and you've got your magic machine-gun against degenerative disease. Pfitzner already has found that antitoxin: its name is ascomycin. . . . How'd I do?" he added anxiously, getting his breath back.

"Beautifully. It's perhaps a little too condensed for MacHinery to follow, but maybe that's all to the good—it wouldn't sound authoritative to him if he could understand it all the way through. Still it might pay to be just a little more roundabout when you talk to him." The girl had the compact out again and was peering into it intently. "But you covered only the degenerative diseases, and that's just background material. Now tell me about the direct attack on death."

Paige looked at the compact and then at the girl, but her expression was too studied to convey much. He said slowly: "I'll go into that if you like. But your father told me that the element of the work was secret even from the government. Should I discuss it in a restaurant?"

Anne turned the small, compact-like object around, so that he could see that it was in fact a meter of some sort. Its needle was in uncertain motion, but near the zero-point. "There's no mike close enough to pick you up," Anne said, snapping the device shut and restoring it to her purse. "Go ahead."

"All right. Some day you're going to have to explain to me why you allowed yourself to get into that first fight with me here, when you had that Eavesdropper with you all the time. Right at the moment I'm too busy being a phony ecologist.

"The death end of the research began back in 1952, with an anatomist named Lansing. He was the first man to show that complex animals—it was rotifers he used—produce a definite aging toxin as a normal part of their growth, and that it gets passed on to the offspring. He bred something like fifty generations of rotifers from adolescent mothers, and got an increase in the life-span in every new generation. He ran 'em up from a natural average span of 24 days to one of 104 days. Then he reversed the process, by breeding consistently from old mothers, and cut the life-span of the final generation way *below* the natural average."

"And now," Anne said, "you know more about the

babies in our labs than I told you before—or you should. The foundling home that supplies them specializes in the illegitimates of juvenile delinquents—the younger, for our purposes, the better."

"Sorry, but you can't needle me with that any longer, Anne. I know now that it's a blind alley. Breeding for longevity in humans isn't practicable; all that those infants can supply to the project is a set of comparative readings on their death-toxin blood-levels. What we want now is something much more direct: an antitoxin against the aging toxin of humans. We know that the aging toxin exists in all complex animals. We know that it's a single, specific substance, quite distinct from the poisons that cause the degenerative diseases. And we know that it can be neutralized. When your lab animals were given ascomycin, they didn't develop a single degenerative disease— but they died anyhow, at about the usual time, as if they'd been set, like a clock at birth. Which, in effect, they had, by the amount of aging toxin passed on to them by their mothers.

"So what we're looking for now is not an antibiotic—an anti-life drug—but an anti-agathic, an anti-death drug. We're running on borrowed time, because ascomycin already satisfies the condition of our development contract with the government. As soon as we get ascomycin into production, our government money will be cut down to a trickle. But if we can hold back on ascomycin long enough to keep the money coming in, we'll have our anti-agathic too."

"Bravo," Anne said. "You sound just like father. I wanted you to raise that last point in particular, Paige, because it's the most important single thing you should remember. If there's the slightest suspicion that we're systematically dragging our feet on releasing ascomycin— that we're taking money from the government to do something the government has no idea can be done— there'll be hell to pay. We're so close to running down our anti-agathic now that it would be heartbreaking to have to stop, not only heartbreaking for us, but for humanity at large."

"The end justifies the means," Paige murmured.

"It does in this case. I know secrecy's a fetish in our society these days—but here secrecy will serve everyone in the long run, and it's *got* to be maintained."

"I'll maintain it," Paige said. He had been referring, not

to secrecy, but to cheating on government money; but he saw no point in bringing that up. As for secrecy, he had no practical faith in it—especially now that he had seen how well it worked.

For in the two days that he had been working inside Pfitzner, he had already found an inarguable spy at the very heart of the project.

CHAPTER SIX: Jupiter V

Yet the barbarians, who are not divided by rival traditions, fight all the more incessantly for food and space. Peoples cannot love one another unless they love the same ideas.

—GEORGE SANTAYANA

THERE WERE three yellow "Critical" signals lit on the long gangboard when Helmuth passed through the gang deck on the way back to duty. All of them, as usual, were concentrated on Panel 9, where Eva Chavez worked.

Eva, despite her Latin name—such once-valid tickets no longer meant anything among the West's uniformly mixed-race population—was a big girl, vaguely blonde, who cherished a passion for the Bridge. Unfortunately, she was apt to become enthralled by the sheer Cosmicness of It All, precisely at the moment when cold analysis and split-second decisions were most crucial.

Helmuth reached over her shoulder, cut her out of the circuit except as an observer, and donned the co-operator's helmet. The incomplete new shoals caisson sprang into being around him. Breakers of boiling hydrogen seethed seven hundred feet up along its slanted sides—breakers that never subsided, but simply were torn away into flying spray.

There was a spot of dull orange near the top of the north face of the caisson, crawling slowly toward the pediment of the nearest truss. Catalysis—

Or cancer, as Helmuth could not help but think of it. On this bitter, violent monster of a planet, even tiny specks of calcium carbide were deadly, that same calcium carbide which had produced acetylene gas for buggy lamps two centuries ago on Earth. At these wind velocities, such specks imbedded themselves deeply in anything they struck; and at fifteen million p.s.i. of pressure, under the catalysis of sodium, pressure-ice took up ammonia and carbon dioxide, building protein-like compounds in a rapid, voracious chain of decay:

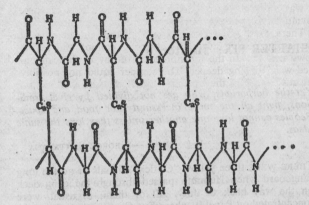

For a moment, Helmuth watched it grow. It was, after all, one of the incredible possibilities the Bridge had been built to study. On Earth, such a compound, had it occurred at all, might have grown porous, hard, and as strong as rhinoceros-horn. Here, under nearly three times Earth's gravity, the molecules were forced to assemble in strict aliphatic order, but in cross section their arrangement was hexagonal, as though the stuff would become an aromatic compound if only it could. Even here it was moderately strong in cross section—but along the long axis it smeared like graphite, the calcium and sulphur atoms readily changing their minds as to which was to act as the metal of the pair, surrendering their pressure-driven holds on one carbon atom to grab hopefully for the next one in line, or giving up altogether to become incorporated instead in a radical with a self-contained double sulphur bond, rather like cystine. . . .

It was not too far from the truth to call it a form of cancer. The compound seemed to be as close as Jupiter came to an indigenous form of life. It grew, fed, reproduced itself, and showed something of the characteristic structure of an Earthly virus, such as tobacco-mosaic. Of course it grew from outside by accretion like any non-living crystal, rather than from the inside, by intus-susception, like a cell; but viruses grew that way too, at least in *vitro*.

It was no stuff to hold up the piers of humanity's greatest engineering project, that much was sure. Perhaps it was a suitable ground-substance for the ribs of some Jovian jellyfish; but in a Bridge-caisson, it was cancer.

There was a scraper mechanism working on the edge of the lesion, flaking away the shearing aminos and laying down new ice. In the meantime, the decay in the caisson-face was working deeper. The scraper could not possibly get at the core of the trouble—which was not the calcium carbide dust, with which the atmosphere was charged beyond redemption, but was instead one imbedded speck of metallic sodium which was taking no part in the reaction—fast enough to extirpate it. It could barely keep pace with the surface spread of the disease.

And laying new ice over the surface of the wound was worthless, as Eva should have known. At this rate, the whole caisson would slough away and melt like butter, within an hour, under the weight of the Bridge above it.

Helmuth sent the futile scraper aloft. Drill for the speck of metal? No—it was far too deeply buried already, and its location was unknown.

Quickly he called two borers up from the shoals below, where constant blasting was taking the foundation of the caisson deeper and deeper into Jupiter's dubious "soil." He drove both blind, fire-snouted machines down into the lesion.

The bottom of that sore turned out to be a hundred feet within the immense block of ice. Helmuth pushed the red button all the same.

The borers blew up, with a heavy, quite invisible blast, as they had been designed to do. A pit appeared on the face of the caisson.

The nearest truss bent upward in the wind. It fluttered for a moment, trying to resist. It bent farther.

Deprived of its major attachment, it tore free suddenly, and went whirling away into the blackness. A sudden flash of lightning picked it out for a moment, and Helmuth saw it dwindlling like a bat with torn wings being borne away by a cyclone.

The scraper scuttled down into the pit and began to fill it with ice from the bottom. Helmuth ordered down a new truss and a squad of scaffolders. Damage of this order of magnitude took time to repair. He watched the tornado tearing ragged chunks from the edges of the pit until he was sure that the catalysis-cancer had been stopped. Then—suddenly, prematurely, dismally tired—he took off the helmet.

He was astounded by the white fury that masked Eva's big-boned, mildly pretty face.

"You'll blow the Bridge up yet, won't you?" she said, evenly, without preamble. "Any pretext will do!"

Baffled, Helmuth turned his head helplessly away; but that was no better. The suffused face of Jupiter peered swollenly through the picture-port, just as it did on the foreman's deck.

He and Eva and Charity and the gang and the whole of satellite V were falling forward toward Jupiter; their uneventful, cooped-up lives on Jupiter V were utterly unreal compared to the four hours of each changeless day spent on Jupiter's ever-changing surface. Every new day brought their minds, like ships out of control, closer and closer to that gaudy inferno.

There was no other way for a man—or a woman—on Jupiter V to look at the giant planet. It was simple experience, shared by all of them, that planets do not occupy four-fifths of the whole sky, unless the observer is himself up there in that planet's sky, falling toward it, falling faster and faster—

"I have no intention," he said tiredly, "of blowing up the Bridge. I wish you could get it through your head that I want the Bridge to stay up—even though I'm not starry-eyed to the point of incompetence about the project. Did you think that that rotten spot was going to go away by itself after you'd painted it over? Didn't you know that—"

Several helmeted, masked heads nearby turned blindly toward the sound of his voice. Helmuth shut up. Any distracting conversation or other activity was taboo down here on the gang deck. He motioned Eva back to duty.

The girl donned her helmet obediently enough, but it was plain from the way that her normally full lips were thinned that she thought Helmuth had ended the argument only in order to have the last word.

Helmuth strode to the thick pillar which ran down the central axis of the operations shack, and mounted the spiraling cleats toward his own foreman's cubicle. Already he felt in anticipation the weight of the helmet upon his own head.

Charity Dillon, however, was already wearing the helmet. He was sitting in Helmuth's chair.

Charity was characteristically oblivious of Helmuth's entrance. The Bridge operator must learn to ignore, to be utterly unconscious of, anything happening about his body except the inhuman sounds of signals; must learn to heed only those senses which report something going on thousands and hundreds of thousands of miles away.

Helmuth knew better than to interrupt him. Instead, he watched Dillon's white, blade-like fingers roving with blind sureness over the controls.

Dillon, evidently, was making a complete tour of the Bridge—not only from end to end, but up and down, too. The tally board showed that he had already activated nearly two-thirds of the ultraphone eyes. That meant that he had been up all night at the job; had begun it immediately after he had last relieved Helmuth.

Why?

With a thrill of unfocused apprehension, Helmuth looked at the foreman's jack, which allowed the operator here in the cubicle to communicate with the gang when necessary, and which kept him aware of anything said or done on the gang boards.

It was plugged in.

Dillon sighed suddenly, took the helmet off, and turned.

"Hello, Bob," he said. "It's funny about this job. You can't see, you can't hear, but when somebody's watching you, you feel a sort of pressure on the back of your neck. Extra-sensory perception, maybe. Ever felt it?"

"Pretty often, lately. Why the grand tour, Charity?"

"There's to be an inspection," Dillon said. His eyes met Helmuth's. They were frank and transparent. "A couple of Senate sub-committee chairmen, coming to see that their eight billion dollars isn't being wasted. Naturally, I'm a little anxious to see to it that they find everything in order."

"I see," Helmuth said. "First time in five years, isn't it?"

"Just about. What was that dust-up down below just now? Somebody—you, I'm sure, from the drastic handiwork involved—bailed Eva out of a mess, and then I heard her talk about your wanting to blow up the Bridge. I checked the area when I heard the fracas start, and it did seem as if she had let things go rather far, but—What was it all about?"

Dillon ordinarily hadn't the guile for cat-and-mouse games, and he had never looked less guileful than now. Helmuth said carefully: "Eva was upset, I suppose. On the subject of Jupiter we're all of us cracked by now, in our different ways. The way she was dealing with the catalysis didn't look to me to be suitable—a difference of opinion, resolved in my favor because I had the authority. Eva didn't. That's all."

"Kind of an expensive difference, Bob. I'm not niggling by nature, you know that. But an incident like that while the sub-committees are here—"

"The point is," said Helmuth, "are we going to spend an extra ten thousand, or whatever it costs to replace a truss and reinforce a caisson, or are we to lose the whole caisson—and as much as a third of the whole Bridge along with it?"

"Yes, you're right there, of course. That could be explained, even to a pack of senators. But—it would be difficult to have to explain it very often. Well, the board's yours, Bob; you could continue my spotcheck, if you've time."

Dillon got up. Then he added suddenly, as though it were forced out of him:

"Bob, I'm trying to understand your state of mind. From what Eva said, I gather that you've made it fairly public. I . . . I don't think it's a good idea to infect your fellow workers with your own pessimism. It leads to sloppy work. I know. I know that you won't countenance sloppy work, regardless of your own feelings, but one foreman can do only so much. And you're making extra work for yourself—not for me, but for yourself—by being openly gloomy about the Bridge.

"It strikes me that maybe you could use a breather, maybe a week's junket to Ganymede or something like that. You're the best man on the Bridge, Bob, for all your grousing about the job and your assorted misgivings. I'd hate to see you replaced."

"A threat, Charity?" Helmuth said softly.

"*No.* I wouldn't replace you unless you actually went nuts, and I firmly believe that your fears in that respect are groundless. It's a commonplace that only sane men suspect their own sanity, isn't it?"

"It's a common misconception. Most psychopathic obsessions begin with a mild worry—one that can't be shaken."

Dillon made as if to brush that subject away. "Anyhow, I'm not threatening; I'd fight to keep you here. But my say-so only covers Jupiter V and the Bridge; there are people higher up on Ganymede, and people higher yet back in Washington—and in this inspecting commission.

"Why don't you try to look on the bright side for a change? Obviously the Bridge isn't ever going to inspire you. But you might at least try thinking about all those dollars piling up in your account back home, every hour you're on this job. And about the bridges and ships and who knows what-all that you'll be building, at any fee you ask, when you get back down to Earth. All under the magic words: 'One of the men who built the Bridge on Jupiter!' "

Charity was bright red with embarrassment and enthusiasm. Helmuth smiled.

"I'll try to bear it in mind, Charity," he said. "And I think I'll pass up a vacation for the time being. When is this gaggle of senators due to arrive?"

"That's hard to say. They'll be coming to Ganymede directly from Washington, without any routing, and they'll stop there for a while. I suppose they'll also make a stop at Callisto before they come here. They've got something new on their ship, I'm told, that lets them flit about more freely than the usual uphill transport can."

An icy lizard suddenly was nesting in Helmuth's stomach, coiling and coiling but never settling itself. The persistent nightmare began to seep back into his blood; it was almost engulfing him—already.

"Something . . . new?" he echoed, his voice as flat and non-committal as he could make it. "Do you know what it is?"

"Well, yes. But I think I'd better keep quiet about it until—"

"Charity, nobody on this deserted rock-heap could possibly be a Soviet spy. The whole habit of 'security' is idiotic out here. Tell me now and save me the trouble of dealing with senators; or tell me at least that you know I know. *They have antigravity!* Isn't that it?"

One word from Dillon, and the nightmare would be real.

"Yes," Dillon said. "How did you know? Of course, it couldn't be a complete gravity screen by any means. But it seems to be a good long step toward it. We've waited a long time to see that dream come true—

"But you're the last man in the world to take pride in the achievement, so there's no sense in exulting about it to you. I'll let you know when I get a definite arrival date. In the meantime, will you think about what I said before?"

"Yes, I will." Helmuth took the seat before the board.

"Good. With you, I have to be grateful for small victories. Good trick, Bob."

"Good trick, Charity."

CHAPTER SEVEN: New York

When Nietzsche wrote down the phrase 'transvaluation of all values' for the first time, the spiritual movement of the centuries in which we are living found at last its formula. Transvaluation of all values is the most fundamental character of every civilization; for it is the beginning of a Civilization that remoulds all the forms of the Culture that went before, understands them otherwise, practises them in a different way.

—OSWALD SPENGLER

PAIGE'S GIFT for putting two and two together and getting 22 was in part responsible for the discovery of the spy, but the almost incredible clumsiness of the man made the chief contribution to it. Paige could hardly believe that nobody had spotted the agent before. True, he was only one of some two dozen technicians in the processing lab where Paige had been working; but his almost open habit of slipping notes inside his lab apron, and his painful furtiveness every time he left the Pfitzner laboratory building for the night, should have aroused someone's suspicions long before this.

It was a fine example, Paige thought, of the way the blunderbuss investigation methods currently popular in Washington allowed the really dangerous man a thousand opportunities to slip away unnoticed. As was usual among groups of scientists, too, there was an unspoken covenant among Pfitzner's technicians—against informing on each other. It protected the guilty as well as the innocent, but it would never have arisen at all under any fair system of juridical defense.

Paige had not the smallest idea what to do with his fish once he had hooked it. He took an evening—which he greatly begrudged—away from seeing Anne, in order to trace the man's movements after a day which had produced two exciting advances in the research, on the hunch that the spy would want to ferry the information out at once.

This hunch proved out beautifully, at least at first. Nor was the man difficult to follow; his habit of glancing continually over first one shoulder and then the other, evidently to make sure that he was not being followed, made him easy to spot over long distances, even in a crowd. He left the city by train to Hoboken, where he rented a motor scooter and drove directly to the cross-roads town of Secaucus. It was a long pull, but not at all difficult otherwise.

Outside Secaucus, however, Paige nearly lost his man for the first and last time. The cross-roads, which lay across U.S. 46 to the Lincoln Tunnel, turned out also to be the site of the temporary trailer city of the Believers—nearly 300,000 of them, or almost half of the 700,000 who had been pouring into town for two weeks now for the Revival. Among the trailers Paige saw license plates from as far away as Eritrea.

The trailer city was far bigger than any nearby town except Passaic. It included a score of supermarkets, all going full blast even in the middle of the night, and about as many coin-in-slot laundries, equally wide open. There were at least a hundred public baths, and close to 360 public toilets. Paige counted ten cafeterias, and twice that many hamburger stands and one-arm joints, each of the stands no less than a hundred feet long; at one of these he stopped long enough to buy a "Texas wiener" nearly as long as his forearm, covered with mustard, meat sauce, sauerkraut, corn relish, and piccalilli. There were ten highly conspicuous hospital tents, too—and after eating the Texas wiener Paige thought he knew why—the smallest of them perfectly capable of housing a one-ring circus.

And, of course, there were the trailers, of which Paige guessed the number at sixty thousand, from two-wheeled jobs to Packards, in all stages of repair and shininess. Luckily, the city was well lit, and since everyone living in it was a Believer, there were no booby-traps or other forms of proselytizing. Paige's man, after a little thoroughly elementary doubling on his tracks and setting up false trails, ducked into a trailer with a Latvian license plate. After half an hour—at exactly 0200—the trailer ran up a stubby VHF radio antenna as thick through as Paige's wrist.

And the rest, Paige thought grimly, climbing back on his own rented scooter, is up to the FBI—if I tell them.

But what would he say? He had every good reason of his own to stay as far out of sight of the FBI as possible. Furthermore, if he informed on the man now, it would mean immediate curtains on the search for the anti-agathic, and a gross betrayal of the trust, enforced though it had been, that Anne and Gunn had placed in him. On the other hand, to remain silent would give the Soviets the drug at the same time that Pfitzner found it—in other words, before the West had it as a government. And it would mean, too, that he himself would have to forego an important chance to prove that he was loyal, when the inevitable showdown with MacHinery came around.

By the next day, however, he had hit upon what should have been the obvious course in the beginning. He took a second evening to rifle his fish's laboratory bench—the incredible idiot had stuffed it to bulging with incriminating photomicrograph negatives, and with bits of paper bearing the symbols of a simple substitution code once circulated to Tom Mix's Square Shooters on behalf of Shredded Ralston—and a third to take step-by-step photos of the hegira to the Believer trailer city, and the radio-transmitter-equipped trailer with the buffer-state license. Assembling everything into a neat dossier, Paige cornered Gunn in his office and dropped the whole mess squarely in the vice-president's lap.

"My goodness," Gunn said, blinking. "Curiosity is a disease with you, isn't it, Colonel Russell? And I really doubt that even Pfitzner will ever find the antidote for that."

"Curiosity has very little to do with it. As you'll see in the folder, the man's an amateur—evidently a volunteer from the Party, Rosenberg, rather than a paid expert. He practically led me by the nose."

"Yes, I see he's clumsy," Gunn agreed. "And he's been reported to us before, Colonel Russell. As a matter of fact, on several occasions we've had to protect him from his own clumsiness."

"But why?" Paige demanded. "Why haven't you cracked down on him?"

"Because we can't afford to," Gunn said. "A spy scandal in the plant now would kill the work just where it stands. Oh, we'll report him sooner or later, and the work you've done here on him will be very useful then—to all of us, yourself included. But there's no hurry."

"No hurry!"

"No," Gunn said. "The material he's ferrying out now is of no particular consequence. When we actually have the drug—"

"But he'll already know the production method by that time. Identifying the drug is a routine job for any team of chemists—your Dr. Agnew taught me that much."

"I suppose that's so," Gunn said. "Well, I'll think it over, Colonel. Don't worry about it, we'll deal with it when the time seems ripe."

And that was every bit of satisfaction that Paige could extract from Gunn. It was small recompense for his lost sleep, his lost dates, the care he had taken to inform Pfitzner first, or the soul-searching it had cost him to put the interests of the project ahead of his officer's oath and of his own safety. That evening he said as much to Anne Abbott and with considerable force.

"Calm down," Anne said. "If you're going to mix into the politics of this work, Paige, you're going to get burned right up to the armpits. When we do find what we're looking for, it's going to create the biggest political explosion in history. I'd advise you to stand well back."

"I've been burned already," Paige said hotly. "How the hell can I stand back now? And tolerating a spy isn't just politics. It's treason, not only by rumor, but in fact. Are you deliberately putting everyone's head in the noose?"

"Quite deliberately. Paige, this project is for everyone— every man, woman and child on the Earth and in space. The fact that the West is putting up the money is incidental. What we're doing here is in every respect just as anti-West as it is anti-Soviet. We're out to lick death for human beings, not just for the armed forces of some one military coalition. What do we care who gets it first? We want everyone to have it."

"Does Gunn agree with that?"

"It's company policy. It may even have been Hal's own idea, though he has different reasons, different justifications. Have you any idea what will happen when a death-curing drug hits a totalitarian society—a drug available in limited quantities only? It won't prove fatal to the Soviets, of course, but it ought to make the struggle for succession over there considerably bloodier than it is already. That's essentially the way Hal seems to look at it."

"And you don't," Paige said grimly.

"No, Paige, I don't. I can see well enough what's going to happen right here at home when this thing gets out. Think for a moment of what it will do to the religious people alone. What happens to the after-life if you never need to leave this one? Look at the Believers. They believe in the literal truth of everything in the Bible—that's why they revise the book every year. And this story is going to break before their Jubilee year is over. Did you know that their motto is: 'Millions now living will never die'? They mean themselves, but what if it turns out to be *everybody?*

"And that's only the beginning. Think of what the insurance companies are going to say. And what's going to happen to the whole structure of compound interest. Wells's old yarn about the man who lived so long that his savings came to dominate the world's whole financial structure—*When the Sleeper Wakes,* wasn't it?—well, that's going to be theoretically possible for *everybody* with the patience and the capital to let his money sit still. Or think of the whole corpus of the inheritance laws. It's going to be the biggest, blackest social explosion the West ever had to take. We'll be much too busy digging in to care about what's happening to the Central Committee in Moscow."

"You seem to care enough to be protecting the Central Committee's interests, or at least that they probably think of as their interests," Paige said slowly. "After all, there is a possibility of keeping the secret, instead of letting it leak."

"There is no such possibility," Anne said. "Natural laws can't be kept secret. Once you give a scientist the idea that a certain goal can be reached, you've given him more than half of the information he needs. Once he gets the idea that the conquest of death is possible, no power on Earth can stop him from finding out how it's done—the 'know-how' we make so many fatuous noises about is the most minor part of research; it's even a matter of total indifference to the essence of the question."

"I don't see that."

"Then let's go back to the fission bomb again for a moment. The only way we could have kept that a secret was to have failed to drop it at all, or even test-fire it. Once the secret was out that the bomb existed—and you'll remember that we announced that before hundreds of thousands of people in Hiroshima—we had no secrets in that field worth protecting. The biggest mystery in the Smyth report was the specific method by which uranium slugs were 'canned' in a protective jacket; it was one of the toughest problems the project had to lick, but at the same time it's exactly the kind of problem you'd assign to an engineer, and confidently expect a solution within a year.

"The fact of the matter, Paige, is that you can't keep scientific matters a secret from yourself. A scientific secret is something that some other scientist can't *contribute to,* any more than he can profit by it. Contrariwise, if you arm yourself through discoveries in natural law, you also arm the other guy. Either you give him the information, or you cut your own throat; there aren't any other courses possible.

"And let me ask you this, Paige: should we give the USSR the advantage—temporary though it'll be—of having to get along *without* the anti-agathics for a while? By their very nature, the drugs will do more damage to the West than they will to the USSR. After all, in the Soviet Union one isn't permitted to inherit money, or to exercise any real control over economic forces just because one's lived a long time. If both major powers are given control over death at the same time, the West will be at a natural disadvantage. If we give control over death to the West alone, we'll be sabotaging our own civilization without putting the USSR under any comparable handicap. Is that sensible?"

The picture was staggering, to say the least. It gave Paige an impression of Gunn decidedly at variance with the mask of salesman-turned-executive which the man himself wore. But it was otherwise self-consistent; that, he knew, was supposed to be enough for him.

"How could I tell?" he said coldly. "All I can see is that every day I stick with you, I get in deeper. First I pose for the FBI as something that I'm not. Next I'm given possession of information that it's unlawful for me to have. And now I'm helping you conceal the evidence of a high crime. It looks more and more to me as though I was supposed to be involved in this thing from the beginning. I don't see how you could have done so thorough a job on me without planning it."

"You needn't deny that you asked for it, Paige."

"I don't deny that," he said. "You don't deny deliberately involving me, either, I notice."

"No. It was deliberate, all right. I thought you'd have suspected it before. And if you're planning to ask me why, save your breath. I'm not permitted to tell you. You'll find out in due course."

"You two—"

"No. Hal had nothing to do with involving you. That was my idea. He only agreed to it—and he had to be convinced from considerably higher up."

"You two," Paige said through almost motionless lips, "don't hesitate to trample on the bystanders, do you? If I didn't know before that Pfitzner was run by a pack of idealists, I'd know it now. You've got the characteristic ruthlessness."

"That," Anne said in a level voice, "is what it takes."

CHAPTER EIGHT: Jupiter V

When new turns in behaviour cease to appear in the life of the individual its behaviour ceases to be intelligent.
                                        —C. E. COGHILL

INSTEAD OF sleeping after his trick—for now Helmuth knew that he was really afraid—he sat up in the reading chair in his cabin. The illuminated microfilmed pages of a book flicked by across the surface of the wall opposite him, timed precisely to the reading rate most comfortable for him, and he had several weeks' worry-conserved alcohol and smoke rations for ready consumption.

But Helmuth let his mix go flat and did not notice the book, which had turned itself on, at the page where he had abandoned it last, when he had fitted himself into the chair. Instead, he listened to the radio.

There was always a great deal of ham radio activity in the Jovian system. The conditions were good for it, since there was plenty of power available, few impeding atmosphere layers and those thin, no Heaviside layers, and few official and no commercial channels with which the hams could interfere.

And there were plenty of people scattered about the satellites who needed the sound of a voice.

" . . . anybody know whether or not the senators are coming here? Doc Barth put in a report a while back on a fossil plant he found here, at least he thinks it was a plant. Maybe they'd like a look at it."

"It's the Bridge team they're coming to see." A strong voice, and the impression of a strong transmitter wavering in and out to the currents of an atmosphere; that would be Sweeney, on Ganymede. "Sorry to throw the wet blanket, boys, but I don't think the senators'll be interested in our rock-balls for their own lumpy selves. They're only scheduled to stay here three days."

Helmuth thought grayly: *Then they'll stay on Callisto only one.*

"Is that you, Sweeney? Where's the Bridge tonight?"

"Dillon's on duty," a very distant transmitter said. "Try to raise Helmuth, Sweeney."

"Helmuth, Helmuth, you gloomy beetle-gooser! Come in, Helmuth!"

"Sure, Bob, come in and dampen us a little. We're feeling cheerful."

Sluggishly, Helmuth reached out to take the mike, from where it lay clipped to one arm of the chair. But before he had completed the gesture, the door to his room swung open.

Eva came in.

She said: "Bob, I want to tell you something."

"His voice is changing!" the voice of the Callisto operator said. "Sweeney, ask him what he's drinking!"

Helmuth cut the radio out. The girl was freshly dressed— in so far as anybody dressed in anything on Jupiter V—

and Helmuth wondered why she was prowling the decks at this hour, half-way between her sleep period and her trick. Her hair was hazy against the light from the corridor, and she looked less mannish than usual. She reminded him a little of the way she had looked when they had been lovers, before the Bridge had come to bestride his bed instead. He put the memory aside.

"All right," he said. "I owe you a mix, I guess. Citric, sugar and the other stuff are in the locker ... you know where it is. Shot-cans are there, too."

The girl shut the door and sat down on the bunk, with a free litheness that was almost grace, but with a determination which, Helmuth knew, meant that she had just decided to do something silly for all the right reasons.

"I don't need a drink," she said. "As a matter of fact, I've been turning my lux-R's back to the common pool. I suppose you did that for me—by showing me what a mind looks like that's hiding from itself."

"Evita, stop sounding like a tract. Obviously you're advanced to a higher, more Jovian plane of existence, but won't you still need your metabolism? Or have you decided that vitamins are all-in-the-mind?"

"Now you're being superior. Anyhow, alcohol isn't a vitamin. And I didn't come to talk about that. I came to tell you something I think you ought to know."

"Which is—?"

She said: "Bob, I mean to have a child here."

A bark of laughter, part sheer hysteria and part exasperation, jack-knifed Helmuth into a sitting position. A red arrow bloomed on the far wall, obediently marking the paragraph which, supposedly, he had reached in his reading. Eva twisted to look at it, but the page was already dimming and vanishing.

"*Women!*" Helmuth said, when he could get his breath back. "Really, Evita, you make me feel much better. No environment can change a human being much, after all."

"Why should it?" she said suspiciously, looking back at him. "I don't see the joke. Shouldn't a woman want to have a child?"

"Of course she should," he said, settling back. The pages began to flip across the wall again. "It's quite ordinary. All women want to have children. All women dream of the day they can turn a child out to play in an airless rock garden like Jupiter V, to pluck fossils and make dust-castles and get quaintly starburned. How cosy to tuck the blue little body back into its corner that night, and give it its oxygen bottle, promptly as the sound of the trick-change bell! Why it's as natural as Jupiter-light—as Western as freeze-dried apple pie."

He turned his head casually away. "Congratulations. As for me, though, Eva, I'd much prefer that you take your ghostly little pretext out of here."

Eva surged to her feet in one furious motion. Her fingers grasped him by the beard and jerked his head painfully around again.

"You reedy male platitude!" she said, in a low grinding voice. "How you could see almost the whole point, and make so little of it—*Women*, is it? So you think I came creeping in here, full of humbleness, to settle our technical differences in bed!"

He closed his hand on her wrist and twisted it away. "What else?" he demanded, trying to imagine how it would feel to stay reasonable for five minutes at a time with these Bridge-robots. "None of us need bother with games and excuses. We're here, we're isolated, we were all chosen because, among other things, we were quite incapable of forming permanent emotional attachments and capable of any alliances we liked without going unbalanced when the attraction died and the alliance came unstuck. None of us have to pretend that our living arrangements would keep us out of jail in Boston, or that they have to involve any Earth-normal excuses."

She said nothing. After a while he asked, gently: "Isn't that so?"

"Of course it's not so," Eva said. She was frowning at him; he had the absurd impression that she was pitying him. "If we were really incapable of making any permanent attachment, we'd never have been chosen. A cast of mind like that is a mental disease, Bob; it's anti-survival from the ground up. It's the conditioning that made us this way. Didn't you know?"

Helmuth hadn't known; or if he had, he had been conditioned to forget it. He gripped the arms of the chair tighter.

"Anyhow," he said, "that's the way we are."

"Yes, it is. Also it has nothing to do with the matter."

"It doesn't? How stupid do you think I am? *I* don't care whether or not you've decided to have a child here, if you really mean what you say."

She, too, seemed to be trembling. "You really don't, either. The decision means nothing to you."

"Well, if I liked children, I'd be sorry for the child. But as it happens, I can't stand children—and if that's the conditioning, too, I can't do a thing about it. In short, Eva, as far as I'm concerned you can have as many kids as you want, and to me you'll *still* be the worst operator on the Bridge."

"I'll bear that in mind," she said. At this moment she seemed to have been cut from pressure-ice. "I'll leave you something to charge your mind with, too, Robert Helmuth. I'll leave you sprawled here under your precious book ... what is Madame Bovary to you, anyhow, you unadventurous turtle? ... to think about a man who believes that children must always be born into warm cradles—a man who thinks that men have to huddle on warm worlds, or they won't survive. A man with no ears, no eyes, scarcely any head. A man in terror, a man crying: Mamma! *Mamma!* all the stellar days and nights long!"

"Parlor diagnosis."

"Parlor labeling! Good trick, Bob. Draw your warm woolly blanket in tight around your brains, or some little sneeze of sense might creep in, and impair your—efficiency!"

The door closed sharply after her.

A million pounds of fatigue crashed down without warning on the back of Helmuth's neck, and he fell back into the reading chair with a gasp. The roots of his beard ached, and Jupiters bloomed and wavered away before his closed eyes.

He struggled once, and fell asleep.

Instantly he was in the grip of the dream.

It started, as always, with commonplaces, almost realistic enough to be a documentary film-strip—except for the appalling sense of pressure, and the distorted emotional significance with which the least word, the smallest movement was invested.

It was the sinking of the first caisson of the Bridge. The actual event had been bad enough. The job demanded enough exactness of placement to require that manned ships enter Jupiter's atmosphere itself; a squadron of twenty of the most powerful ships ever built, with the five-million-ton asteroid, trimmed and shaped in space, slung beneath them in an immense cat's-cradle.

Four times that squadron had disappeared beneath the

racing clouds; four times the tense voices of pilots and engineers had muttered in Helmuth's ears, and he had whispered back, trying to guide them by what he could see of the conflicting trade-blasts from Jupiter V; four times there were shouts and futile orders and the snapping of cables and men screaming endlessly against the eternal howl of the Jovian sky.

It had cost, altogether, nine ships, and two hundred thirty-one men, to get one of five laboriously-shaped asteroids planted in the shifting slush that was Jupiter's surface. Until that had been accomplished, the Bridge could never have been more than a dream. While the Great Red Spot had shown astronomers that some structures on Jupiter could last for long periods of time—long enough, at least, to be seen by many generations of human beings—it had been equally well known that nothing on Jupiter could be really permanent. The planet did not even have a "surface" in the usual sense; instead, the bottom of the atmosphere merged more or less smoothly into a high-pressure sludge, which in turn thickened as it went deeper into solid pressure-ice. At no point on the way down was there any interface between one layer and another, except in the rare areas where a part of the deeper, more "solid" medium had been thrust far up out of its normal level to form a continent which might last as long as two years or two hundred. It was on to one of these great ribs of bulging ice that the ships had tried to plant their asteroid—and, after four tries, had succeeded.

Helmuth had helped to supervise all five operations, counting the successful one, from his desk on Jupiter V. But in the dream he was not in the control shack, but instead on shipboard, in one of the ships that was never to come back—

Then, without transition, but without any sense of discontinuity either, he was on the Bridge itself. Not *in absentia,* as the remote guiding intelligence of a beetle but in person, in an ovular, tank-like suit the details of which would never come clear. The high brass had discovered antigravity and had asked for volunteers to man the Bridge. Helmuth had volunteered.

Looking back on it in the dream, he did not understand why he had volunteered. It had simply seemed expected of him, and he had not been able to help it, even though he had known to begin with what it would be like. He belonged on the Bridge, though he hated it—he had been doomed to go there from the first.

And there was ... something wrong ... with the antigravity. The high brass had asked for its volunteers before the research work had been completed. The present antigravity fields were weak, and there was some basic flaw in the theory. Generators broke down after only short periods of use; burned out, unpredictably, sometimes only moments after having passed their production tests with perfect scores. In waking life, vacuum tubes behaved in the unpredictable way; there were no vacuum tubes anywhere on Jupiter, but machines on Jupiter burned out all the same, burned out at temperatures which would freeze Helmuth solid in an instant.

That was what Helmuth's antigravity set was about to do. He crouched inside his personal womb, above the boiling sea, the clouds raging by him in little scouring crystals which wore at the chorion protecting him, lit by a plume of hydrogen flame—and waited to feel his weight suddenly become three times greater than normal, the pressure on his body go from sixteen pounds per square inch to fifteen million, the air around him take on the searing stink of poisons, the whole of Jupiter come pressing its burden upon him.

He knew what would happen to him then.

It happened.

Helmuth greeted "morning" on Jupiter V with his customary scream.

BOOK THREE

ENTR'ACTE: Washington

The layman, the "practical" man, the man in the street, says, What is that to me? The answer is positive and weighty. Our life is entirely dependent on the established doctrines of ethics, sociology, political economy, government, law, medical science, etc. This affects everyone

*consciously or unconsciously, the man in the street in the
first place, because he is the most defenseless.*
                                        —ALFRED KORZYBSKI

                                        4th January 2020
Dear Seppi,
   Lord knows I have better sense than to mail this, send
it to you by messenger, or leave it anywhere in the
files—or indeed on the premises—of the Joint Committee;
but if one is sensible about such matters these days, one
never puts anything on paper at all, and then burns the
carbons. As a bad compromise, I am filing this among my
personal papers, where it will be found, opened and sent
to you only after I will be beyond reprisals.
   That's not meant to sound as ominous as, upon reread-
ing, I see it does. By the time you have this letter,
abundant details of what I've been up to should be available to you, not only through the usual press garble, but
through verbatim testimony. You will have worked out,
by now, a rational explanation of my conduct since my
re-election (and before it, for that matter). At the very
least, I hope you now know why I authorized such a
monstrosity as the Bridge, even against your very good
advice.
   All that is water over the dam (or ether over the
Bridge, if you boys are following Dirac's lead back to the
ether these days. How do I know about that? You'll see in
a moment.). I don't mean to rehash it here. What I want
to do in this letter is to leave you a more specialized
memo, telling you in detail just how well the research
system you suggested to me worked out for us.
   Despite my surface appearance of ignoring that advice,
we were following your suggestion, and very closely. I
took a particular interest in your hunch that there might
be "crackpot" ideas on gravity which needed investigation.
Frankly, I had no hope of finding anything, but that would
have left me no worse off than I had been before I talked
to you. And actually it wasn't very long before my research chief came up with the Locke Derivation.
   The research papers which finally emerged from this
particular investigation are still in the Graveyard file, and
I have no hope that they'll be released to non-government
physicists within the foreseeable future. If you don't get
the story from me, you'll never get it from anyone; and
I've enough on my conscience now to be indifferent to a

small crime like breaking Security. Besides, as usual, this particular "secret" has been available for the taking for years. A man named Schuster—you may know more about him than I do—wondered out loud about it as far back as 1891, before anybody had thought of trying to keep scientific matters a secret. He wanted to know whether or no every large rotating mass, like the Sun for instance, was a natural magnet (That was before the sun's magnetic field had been discovered, too.) And by the 1940's it was clearly established for *small* rotating bodies like electrons—a thing called the Lande factor with which I'm sure you're familiar. I myself don't understand Word One of it. (Dirac was associated with much of that part of the work.) Finally, a man named W. H. Babcock, of Mount Wilson, pointed out in the 1940's that the Lande factor for the Earth, the Sun, and a star named 78 Virginius was identical, or damned close to it.

Now all this seemed to me to have nothing to do at all with gravity, and I said so to my team chief, who brought the thing to my attention. But I was wrong (I suppose you're already ahead of me by now). Another man, Prof. P. M. S. Blackett, whose name was even familiar to *me*, had pointed out the relationship. Suppose, Blackett said (I am copying from my notes now), we let P be magnetic moment, or what I have to think of as the leverage effect of a magnet—the product of the strength of the charge times the distance between the poles. Let U be angular momentum—rotation to a slob like me; angular speed times moment of inertia to you. Then if C is the velocity of light, and G is the acceleration of gravity (and they always are in equations like this, I'm told), then:

$$P = \frac{BG^{1/2}U}{2C}$$

(B is supposed to be a constant amounting to about 0·25. Don't ask me why.) Admittedly this was all speculative; there would be no way to test it, except on another planet with a stronger magnetic field than Earth's—preferably about a hundred₄ times as strong. The closest we could come to that would be Jupiter, where the speed of rotation is about 25,000 miles an hour at the equator—and that was obviously out of the question.

Or was it? I confess that I never thought of using

Jupiter, except in wish-fulfillment daydreams, until this matter of the Locke Derivation came up. It seems that by a simple algebraic manipulation, you can stick G on one side of the equation, and all the other terms on the other, and come up with this:

$$G=\left(\frac{2PC}{BU}\right)^2$$

To test that, you need a gravitational field little more than twice the strength of Earth's. And there, of course, is Jupiter again. None of my experts would give the notion a nickel—they said, among other things, that nobody even knew who Locke was, which is true, and that his algebraic trick wouldn't stand up under dimensional analysis, which turned out to be true—but irrelevant. (We *did* have to monkey with it a little after the experimental results were in.) What counted was that we could make a practical use of this relationship.

Once we tried that, I should add, we were astonished at the accompanying effects: the abolition of the Lorentz-Fitzgerald relationship inside the field, the intolerance of the field itself to matter outside its influence, and so on; not only at their occurring at all—the formula doesn't predict them—but at their order of magnitude. I'm told that when this thing gets out, dimensional analysis isn't the only scholium that's going to have to be revamped. It's going to be the greatest headache for physicists since the Einstein theory; I don't know whether you'll relish this premonitory twinge or not.

Pretty good going for a "crackpot" notion, though.

After that, the Bridge was inevitable. As soon as it became clear that we could perform the necessary tests only on the surface of Jupiter itself, we had to have the Bridge. It also became clear that the Bridge would have to be a dynamic structure. It couldn't be built to a certain size and stopped there. The moment it was stopped, Jupiter would tear it to shreds. We had to build it to grow—to do more than just resist Jupiter—to push back against Jupiter, instead. It's double the size that it needed to be to test the Locke Derivation, now, and I still don't know how much longer we're going to have to keep it growing. Not long, I hope; the thing's a monster already.

But Seppi, let me ask you this: Does the Bridge really

fall under the interdict you uttered against the gigantic research projects? It's gigantic, all right. But—is it gigantic *on Jupiter?* I say it isn't. It's peanuts. A piece of attic gadgetry and nothing more. And we couldn't have performed the necessary experiments on any other planet.

Not all the wealth of Ormus or of Ind, or of all the world down the ages, could have paid for a Manhattan District scaled to Jupiter's size.

In addition—though this was incidental—the apparent giganticism involved was a useful piece of misdirection. Elephantine research projects may be just about played out, but government budgetary agencies are used to them and think them normal. Getting the Joint Committee involved in one helped to revive the committeemen from their comatose state, as nothing else could have. It got us appropriations we never could have corralled otherwise, because people associate such projects with weapons research. And—forgive me, but there is a sort of science to politics too—it seemed to show graphically that I was *not* following the suspect advice of the suspect Dr. Corsi. I owed you that, though it's hardly as large a payment as I would like to make.

But I don't mean to talk about the politics of crackpot-mining here; only about the concrete results. You should be warned, too, that the method has its pitfalls.

You will know by now about the anti-agathic research, and what we got out of it. I talked to people who might know what the chances were, and got general agreement from them as to how we should proceed. This straight-line approach looked good to me from the beginning.

I set the Pfitzner people to work on it at once, since they already had that HWS appropriation for similar research, and HWS wouldn't be alert enough to detect the moment when Pfitzner's target changed from just plain old age to death itself. But we didn't overlook the crackpots—and before long we found a real dilly.

This was a man named Lyons, who insisted that the standard Lansing hypothesis, which postulates the existence of an aging-toxin, was exactly the opposite of the truth. (I go into this subject with a certain relish, because I suspect that you know as little about it as I do; it's not often that I find myself in that situation.) Instead, he said, what happens is that it's the *young* mothers who pass on to their offspring some substance which makes them long-lived. Lansing's notion that the old mothers were the ones who did the passing along, and that the substance passed along speeding up ageing, was unproven, Lyons said.

Well, that threw us into something of a spiral. Lansing's Law—"Senescence begins when growth ends"—had been regarded as gospel in gerontology for decades. But Lyons had a good hypothetical case. He pointed out that, among other things, all of Lansing's long-lived rotifers showed characteristics in common with polyploid individuals. In addition to being hardy and long-lived, they were of unusually large size, and they were less fertile than normal rotifers. Suppose that the substance which was passed along from one generation to another was a chromosome-doubler, like colchicine?

We put that question to Lansing's only surviving student, a living crotchet named MacDougal. He wouldn't hear of it; to him it was like questioning the Word of God. Besides, he said, if Lyons is right, how do you propose to test it? Rotifers are microscopic animals. Except for their eggs, their body cells are invisible even under the microscope. Technically speaking, in fact, they don't seem to have any body-cells as adults—just a sort of generalized protoplasmic continuum in which the nuclei are scattered at random, rather like the plasmodium of a slime-mold. It would be quite a few months of Sundays before we ever got a look at a rotifer chromosome.

Lyons thought he had an answer for that. He proposed to develop a technique of microtome preparation which would make, not one, but several different slices through a rotifer's egg. With any sort of luck, he said, we might be able to extend the technique to rotifer spores, and maybe even to the adult critters.

We thought we ought to try it. Without telling Pfitzner about it, we gave Pearl River Labs that headache. We put Lyons himself in charge and assigned MacDougal to act as a consultant (which he did by sniping and scoffing every minute of the day, until not only Lyons, but everybody else in the plant hated him). It was awful. Rotifers, it turns out, are incredibly delicate animals, just about impossible to preserve after they're dead, no matter what stage of their development you catch them in. Time and time again, Lyons came up with microscope slides which, he said, *proved* that the long-lived rotifers were at least triploid—three labeled chromosomes per body-cell instead of two—and maybe even tetraploid. Every other expert in the Pearl River plant looked at them, and saw nothing but a blur which might have been rotifer chromosomes, and might equally well have been a newspaper halftone of a grey cat walking over a fur rug in a thick fog. The comparative tests—producing polyploid rotifers and other critters with drugs like colchicine, and comparing them with the critters produced by Lansing's and MacDougal's classical breeding methods—were just as indecisive. Lyons finally decided that what he needed to prove his case was the world's biggest and most expensive X-ray microscope, and right then we shut him down.

MacDougal had been right all the time. Lyons was a crackpot with a plausible line of chatter, enough of a technique at microdissection to compel respect, and a real and commendable eagerness to explore his idea right down to the bottom. MacDougal was a frozen-brained old man with far too much reverence for his teacher, a man far too ready to say that a respected notion was right because it was respected, and a man who had performed no actual experiments himself since his student days. But he had been right—purely intuitively—in predicting that Lyons' inversion of Lansing's Law would come to nothing. I gather that victory in the sciences doesn't always go to the most personable man, any more than it does in any other field. I'm glad to know it; I'm always glad to find some small area of human endeavor which resists the con-man and the sales-talk.

When Pftizner discovered ascomycin, we had HWS close Pearl River out entirely.

Negative results of this kind are valuable for scientists too, I'm told. How you will evaluate your proposed research method in the light of these two experiences is unknown to me; I can only tell you what I think *I* learned. I am convinced that we must be much slower, in the future, to ignore the fringe notion and the marginal theorist. One of the virtues of these crackpots—if that is what they are—is that they tend to cling to ideas which can be tested. That's worth hanging on to, in a world where scientific ideas have become so abstract that even their originators can't suggest ways to test them. Whoever Locke was, I suppose he hadn't put a thousandth as much time into thinking about gravity as Blackett had; yet Blackett couldn't suggest a way to test his equation, whereas the Locke Derivation was testable (on Jupiter) and turned out to be right. As for Lyons, his notion was wrong; but it too fell down because it failed the operational test, the very test it proposed to pass; until we performed that test, we had no real assessment of Lansing's Law, which had been traveling for years on prestige because of the "impossibility" of weighing any contrary hypothesis. Lyons forced us to do that, and enlarged our knowledge.

And so, take it from there; I've tried to give back as good as I have gotten. I'm not going to discuss the politics of this whole conspiracy with you, nor do I want you to concern yourself with them. Politics is death. Above all, I beg you—if you're at all pleased with this report—not to be distressed over the situation I will probably be in by the time this reaches you. I've been ruthless with your reputation to advance my purposes; I've been ruthless with the careers of other people; I've been quite ruthless in sending some men—some hundreds of men—to deaths they could surely have avoided had it not been for me; I've put many others, including a number of children, into considerable jeopardy. With all this written against my name, I'd think it a monstrous injustice to get off scot-free.

And that is all I can say; I have an appointment in a few minutes. Thank you for your friendship and your help.

BLISS WAGONER

CHAPTER NINE: New York

It is sometimes claimed that religious intolerance is the fruit of conviction. If one be absolutely certain that one's faith is right and all others wrong, it seems criminal to permit one's neighbors' obvious error and perdition. I am tempted to think, however, that religious fanaticism often is the result not of conviction but rather of doubt and insecurity.

—GEORGE SARTON

RUTHLESSNESS, ANNE had said, is what it takes. But—Paige thought afterwards—is it?

Does faith add up to its own flat violation? It was all well enough to have something in which you could believe.

But when a faith in humanity-in-general automatically results in casual inhumanity toward individual people, something must have gone awry. Should the temple bell be struck so continually that it has to shatter—make all its worshippers ill with terror until it is silenced?

Silence. The usual answer. Or was the fault not in faith itself, but in the faithful? The faithful were usually pretty frightening as people, Believers and humanitarians alike.

Paige's time to debate the point with himself had already almost run out—and with it, his time to protect himself, if he could. Nothing had emerged from his soil samples. Evidently bacterial life on the Jovian moons had never at any time been profuse and consisted now only of a few hardy spores of common species, like *Bacillus subtilis*, which occurred on every Earth-like world and sometimes even in meteors. The samples plated out sparsely and yielded nothing which had not been known for decades—as, indeed, the statistics of this kind of research had predicted from the beginning.

It was now known around the Bronx plant that some sort of investigation of the Pfitzner project was rolling, and was already moving too fast to be derailed by any method the company's executives could work out. Daily reports from Pfitzner's Washington office—actually the Washington branch of Interplanet Press, the public relations agency Pfitzner maintained—were filed in the plant, but they were apparently not very informative. Paige gathered that there was some mystery about the investigation at the source, though neither Gunn nor Anne would say so in so many words.

And, finally, Paige's leave was to be over, day after tomorrow. After that, the Proserpine station—and probably an order to follow, emerging out of the investigation, which would maroon him there for the rest of his life in the service.

And it wasn't worth it.

That realization had been staring him in the eyes all along. For Anne and Gunn, perhaps, the price was worth paying, the tricks were worth playing, the lying and the cheating and the risking of the lives of others were necessary and just to the end in view. But when the last card was down, Paige knew that he himself lacked the necessary dedication. Like every other road toward dedication that he had assayed, this one had turned out to have been paved with pure lead—and had left him with no better emblem of conduct than the miserable one which had kept him going all the same: self-preservation.

He knew then, with cold disgust toward himself, that he was going to use what he knew to clear himself, as soon as the investigation hit the plant. Senator Wagoner, the grapevine said, would be conducting it—oddly enough, for Wagoner and MacHinery were deadly political enemies; had MacHinery gotten the jump on him at last?—and would arrive tomorrow. If Paige timed himself very carefully, he could lay down the facts, leave the plant forever, and be out in space without having to face Hal Gunn or Anne Abbott at all. What would happen to the Pfitzner project thereafter would be old news by the time he landed at the Proserpine station—more than three months old.

And by that time, he told himself, he would no longer care.

Nevertheless, when the quick morrow came, he marched into Gunn's office—which Wagoner had taken over—like a man going before a firing squad.

A moment later, he felt as though he had been shot down while still crossing the door-sill. Even before he realized that Anne was already in the room, he heard Wagoner say:

"Colonel Russell, sit down. I'm glad to see you. I have a security clearance for you, and a new set of orders; you can forget Proserpine. You and Miss Abbott and I are leaving for Jupiter. Tonight."

It was like a dream after that. In the Caddy on the way to the spaceport, Wagoner said nothing. As for Anne, she seemed to be in a state of slight shock. From what little Paige thought he had learned about her—and it was very little—he deduced that she had expected this as little as he had. Her face as he had entered Gunn's office had been guarded, eager, and slightly smug all at once, as though she had thought she'd known what Wagoner would say. But when Wagoner had mentioned Jupiter, she'd turned to look at him as though he'd been turned from a senator into a boxing kangaroo, in the plain sight of the Pfitzner Founders. Something was wrong. After the long catalog of things already visibly wrong, the statement didn't mean very much. But something had clearly gone wrong.

There were fireworks in the sky to the south, visible from the right side of the Caddy where Paige sat as the car turned east on to the parkway. They were big and spectacular, and seemed to be going up from the heart of Manhattan. Paige was puzzled until he remembered, like a fact recalled from the heart of an absurd dream, that this was the last night of the Believer Revival, being held in the stadium on Randalls Island. The fireworks celebrated the Second Coming, which the Believers were confident could not now be long delayed.

> *Gewiss, gewiss, es naht noch heut'*
> *und kann nicht lang mehr säumen ...*

Paige could remember having heard his father, an ardent Wagnerian, singing that; it was from *Tristan.* But he thought instead of those frightening medieval paintings of the Second Coming, in which Christ stands ignored in a corner of the canvas while the people flock reverently to the feet of the Anti-Christ, whose face, in the dim composite of Paige's memory, was a curious mixture of Francis X. MacHinery and Bliss Wagoner.

Words began to bloom along the black sky at the hearts of starshells:

— Millions — now — living — will — never — die! —

No doubt, Paige thought bleakly. The Believers also believed that the Earth was flat; but Paige was on his way to Jupiter—not exactly a round planet, but rounder than the Believers' Earth. In quest, if you please, of immortality, in which he too had believed. Tasting bile, he thought, *It takes all kinds.*

A final starshell, so brilliant even at this distance that the word inside it was almost dazzled out, burst soundlessly into blue-white fire above the city. It said:

— TOMORROW —

Paige swung his head abruptly and looked at Anne. Her face, a ghostly blur in the dying light of the shell, was turned raptly toward the window; she had been watching, too. He leaned forward and kissed her slightly parted lips, gently, forgetting all about Wagoner. After a frozen moment he could feel her mouth smiling against his, the smile which had astonished him so when he had seen it first, but softened, transformed, giving. The world went away for a while.

Then she touched his cheeks with her fingertips and sank back against the cushions; the Caddy swung sharply north off the parkway; and the spark of radiance which was the last retinal image of the shell vanished into drifting purple blotches, like after-visions of the sun—or of Jupiter seen close-on. Anne had no way of knowing, of course, that he had been running away from her, toward the Proserpine station, when he had been cornered in this Caddy instead. *Anne, Anne, I believe; help me in mine unbelief.*

The Caddy was passed through the spaceport gates after a brief, whispered consultation between the chauffeur and the guards. Instead of driving directly for the Administration Building, however, it turned craftily to the left and ran along the inside of the wire fence, back toward the city and into the dark reaches of the emergency landing pits. It was not totally dark there, however; there was a pool of light on an apron some distance ahead, with a needle of glare pointing straight up from its center.

Paige leaned forward and peered through the double glass barrier—one pane between himself and the driver, the other between the driver and the world. The needle of light was a ship, but it was not one he recognized. It was a single-stage job: a ferry, designed to take them out no farther than to Satellite Vehicle One, where they would be transferred to a proper interplanetary vessel. But it was small, even for a ferry.

"How do you like her, Colonel?" Wagoner's voice said, unexpectedly, from the black corner where he sat.

"All right," Paige said. "She's a little small, isn't she?"

Wagoner chuckled. "Pretty damn small," he said, and fell silent again. Alarmed, Paige began to wonder if the senator was feeling entirely well. He turned to look at Anne, but he could not even see her face now. He groped for her hand; she responded with a feverish, rigid grip.

The Caddy shot abruptly from the fence. It bore down on the pool of light. Paige could see several marines standing on the apron at the tail of the ship. Absurdly, the vessel looked even smaller as it came closer.

"All right," Wagoner said. "Out of here, both of you. We'll be taking off in ten minutes. The crewmen will show you your quarters."

"Crewmen?" Paige said. "Senator, that ship won't hold more than four people, and one of them has to be the tube-man. That leaves nobody to pilot her but me."

"Not this trip," Wagoner said, following him out of the car. "We're only passengers, you and I and Miss Abbott, and of course the marines. The *Per Aspera* has a separate crew of five. Let's not waste time, please."

It was impossible. On the cleats, Paige felt as though he were trying to climb into a .22 calibre long-rifle cartridge. To get ten people into this tiny shell, you'd have to turn them into some sort of human concentrate and pour them, like powdered coffee.

Nevertheless, one of the marines met him in the airlock, and within another minute he was strapping himself down inside a windowless cabin as big as any he'd ever seen on board a standard interplanetary vessel—far bigger than any ferry could accommodate. The intercom box at the head of his hammock was already calling the clearance routine.

"Dog down and make all fast. Airlock will cycle in one minute."

What had happened to Anne? She had come up the cleats after him, of that he was sure—

"All fast. Take-off in one minute. Passengers 'ware G's."

—but he'd been hustled down to this nonsensical cabin too fast to look back. There was something very wrong. Was Wagoner—

"Thirty seconds. 'Ware G's."

—making some sort of a getaway? But from what? And why did he want to take Paige and Anne with him? As hostages they were—

"Twenty seconds."

—worthless, since they were of no value to the government, had no money, knew nothing damning about Wagoner—

"Fifteen seconds."

But wait a minute. Anne knew something about Wagoner, or thought she did.

"Ten seconds. Stand by."

The call made him relax instinctively. There would be time to think about that later. At take-off—

"Five seconds."

—it didn't pay—

"Four."

—to concentrate—

"Three."

—on anything—

"Two."

—else but—

"One."

—actual—

"Zero."

—*takeoff* hit him with the abrupt, bone-cracking, gut-wrenching impact of all ferry take-offs. There was nothing you could do to ameliorate it but let the strong muscles of the arms and legs and back bear it as best they could, with the automatic tetanus of the Seyle GA reaction, and concentrate on keeping your head and your abdomen in exact neutral with the acceleration thrust. The muscles you used for that were seldom called upon on the ground, even by weight-lifters, but you learned to use them or were invalided out of the service; a trained spaceman's abdominal muscles will bounce a heavy rock, and no strong man can make him turn his head if his neck muscles say *no*.

Also, it helped a little to yell. Theoretically, the yell collapses the lungs—acceleration pneumothorax, the books call it—and keeps them collapsed until the surge of powered flight is over. By that time, the carbon dioxide level of the blood has risen so high that the breathing reflex will reassert itself with an enormous gasp, even if crucial chest muscles have been torn. The yell makes sure that when next you breathe, you *breathe*.

But more importantly for Paige and every other spaceman, the yell was the only protest he could form against that murderous nine seconds of pressure; it makes you *feel* better. Paige yelled with vigor.

He was still yelling when the ship went into free fall.

Instantly, while the yell was still dying incredulously in his throat, he was clawing at his harness. All his spaceman's reflexes had gone off at once. The powered-flight period had been too short. Even the shortest possible take-off acceleration outlasts the yell. Yet the ion-rockets were obviously silenced. The little ship's power had failed—she was falling back to the Earth—

"Attention, please," the intercom box said mildly. "We are now under way. Free fall will last only a few seconds. Stand by for restoration of normal gravity."

And then. . . . And then the hammock against which Paige was struggling was *down* again, as though the ship were still resting quietly on Earth. Impossible; she couldn't even be out of the atmosphere yet. Even if she were, free fall should last all the rest of the trip. Gravity in an interplanetary vessel—let alone a ferry—could be re-established only by rotating the ship around its long axis; few captains bothered with the fuel-expensive maneuvre, since hardly anybody but old hands flew between the planets. Besides, this ship—the *Per Aspera*—hadn't gone through any such maneuvre, or Paige would have detected it.

Yet his body continued to press down against the hammock with an acceleration of one Earth gravity.

"Attention, please. We will be passing the Moon in one point two minutes. The observation blister is now open to passengers. Senator Wagoner requests the presence of Miss Abbott and Colonel Russell in the blister."

There was no further sound from the ion-rockets, which had inexplicably been shut off when the *Per Aspera* could have been no more than 250 miles above the surface of the Earth. Yet she was passing the Moon now, without the slightest sensation of movement, though she must still be accelerating. What was driving her? Paige could hear nothing but the small hum of the ship's electrical generator, no louder than it would have been on the ground, unburdened of the job of RF-heating the electron-ion plasma which the rockets used. Grimly, he unsnapped the last gripper from his harness, conscious of what a baby he evidently was on board this ship, and got up.

The deck felt solid and abnormal under his feet, pressing against the soles of his shoes with a smug terrestrial pressure of one unvarying gravity. Only the habits of caution of a service lifetime prevented him from running forward up the companionway to the observation blister.

Anne and Senator Wagoner were there, the dimming

moonlight bathing their backs as they looked ahead into deep space. They had been more than a little shaken up by the take-off, that was obvious, but they were already almost recovered; compared to the effects of the normal ferry take-off, this could only have ruffled them; and of course the sudden transformation to the impossible one-gravity field would not have bollixed their untrained reflexes with anything like the thoroughness that it had scrambled Paige's long-conditioned reactions. Looked at this way, space-flight like this might well be easier for civilians than it would be for spacemen, at least for some years to come.

He padded cautiously toward them, feeling disastrously humbled. Shining between them was a brilliant, hard spot of yellow-white light, glaring into the blister through the thick, cosmics-proof glass. The spot was fixed and steady, as were all the stars looking into the blister; proof positive that the ship's gravity was not being produced by axial spin. The yellow spot itself, shining between Wagoner's elbow and Anne's upper arm, was—

Jupiter.

On either side of the planet were two smaller bright dots; the four Galilean satellites, as widely separated to Paige's naked eye as they would have looked on Earth through a telescope the size of Galileo's.

While Paige hesitated in the doorway to the blister, the little spots that were Jupiter's largest moons visibly drew apart from each other a little, until one of them went into occulation behind Anne's right shoulder. The *Per Aspera* was still accelerating; it was driving toward Jupiter at a speed nothing in Paige's experience could have prepared him for. Stunned, he made a very rough estimate in his head of the increase in parallax and tried to calculate the ship's rate of approach from that.

The little lunar ferry, humming scarcely louder than a transformer for carrying five people—let alone ten—as far as SV-1, was now hurtling toward Jupiter at about a quarter of the speed of light.

At least forty thousand miles per second.

And the deepening color of Jupiter showed that the *Per Aspera* was still picking up speed.

"Come in, Colonel Russell," Wagoner's voice said, echoing slightly in the blister. "Come watch the show. We've been waiting for you."

CHAPTER TEN: Jupiter V

That is precisely what common sense is for, to be jarred into uncommon sense. One of the chief services which mathematics has rendered the human race in the past century is to put 'common sense' where it belongs, on the topmost shelf next to the dusty canister labeled 'discarded nonsense.'

—ERIC TEMPLE BELL

THE SHIP that landed as Helmuth was going on duty did nothing to lighten the load on his heart. In shape it was not distinguishable from any of the short-range ferries which covered the Jovian satellary circuit, carrying supplies from the regular SV-1-Mars-Belt-Jupiter X cruiser to the inner moons—and, sometimes, some years-old mail; but it was considerably bigger than the usual Jovian ferry, and it grounded its outsize mass on Jupiter V with only the briefest cough of rockets.

That landing told Helmuth that his dream was well on its way to coming true. If the high brass had a real anti-gravity, there would have been no reason why the ion-streams should have been necessary at all. Obviously, what had been discovered was some sort of partial gravity screen, which allowed a ship to operate with far less rocket thrust than was usual, but which still left it subject to a sizable fraction of the universal G, the inherent stress of space.

Nothing less than a complete, and completely controllable gravity screen would do, on Jupiter.

And theory said that a complete gravity screen was impossible. Once you set one up—even supposing that you could—you would be unable to enter it or leave it. Crossing a boundary-line between a one G field and a no-G field would be precisely as difficult as surmounting a high-jump with the bar set at infinity, and for the same reasons. If you crossed it from the other direction, you would hit the ground on the other side of the line as hard as though you had fallen there from the Moon; a little harder, in fact.

Helmuth worked mechanically at the gang board, thinking. Charity was not in evidence, but there was no special reason why the foreman's board had to be manned on this trick. The work could be as easily supervised from here, and obviously Charity had expected Helmuth to do it that way, or he would have left notice. Probably Charity was already conferring with the senators, receiving what would be for him the glad news.

Helmuth realized suddenly that there was nothing left for him to do now, once this trick was over, but to cut and run.

There could be no real reason why he should be required to re-enact the entire nightmare, helplessly, event for event, like an actor committed to a role. He was awake now, in full control of his own senses, and still at least partially sane. The man in the dream had volunteered—but that man would not be Robert Helmuth. Not any longer.

While the senators were here on Jupiter V, he would turn in his resignation. Direct—over Charity's head.

The wave of relief came washing over him just as he finished resetting the circuits which would enable him to supervise from the gang board, and left him so startlingly weak that he had to put the helmet down on the ledge before he had raised it half-way to his head. So *that* had been what he had been waiting for: to quit, nothing more.

He owed it to Charity to finish the Grand Tour of the Bridge. After that, he'd be free. He would never have to see the Bridge again, not even inside a viewing helmet. A farewell tour, and then back to Chicago, if there was still such a place.

He waited until his breathing had quieted a little, scooped the helmet up on to his shoulders, and the Bridge . . .

. . . came falling into existence all around him, a Pandemonium beyond broaching and beyond hope, sealed on all sides. The drumfire of rain against his beetle's hull was so loud that it hurt his ears, even with the gain knob of his helmet backed all the way down to the thumb-stop. It was impossible to cut the audio circuit out altogether; much of his assessment of how the Bridge was responding to stress depended on sound; human eyesight on the Bridge was almost as useless as a snail's.

And the bridge was responding now, as always, with its medley of dissonance and cacophony: *crang ... crang ... spungg ... skreek ... crang ... ungg ... oingg ... skreek ... skreek ....* These structural noises were the only ones that counted; they were the polyphony of the Bridge, everything else was decorative and to be ignored by the Bridge operator—the fioritura shrieking of the winds, the battery of the rain, the pedal diapason of thunder, the distant grumbling roll of the stage-hand volcanoes pushing continents back and forth on castors down below.

This time, however, at long last, it was impossible to ignore any part of this great orchestra. Its composite uproar was enormous, implacable, incredible even for Jupiter, overwhelming even in this season. The moment he heard it, Helmuth knew that he had waited too long.

The Bridge was not going to last much longer. Not unless every man and woman on Jupiter V fought without sleep to keep it up, throughout this passage of the Red Spot and the South Tropical Disturbance—

—if even that would serve. The great groans that were rising through the tornado-riven mists from the caissons were becoming steadily, spasmodically deeper; their hinges were already overloaded. And the deck of the Bridge was beginning to rise and fall a little, as though slow, frozen waves were passing along it from one unfinished end to the other. The queasy, lazy tidal swell made the beetle tip first its nose into the winds, then its tail, then back again, so that it took almost all of the current Helmuth could feed into the magnet windings to keep the craft stuck to the rails on the deck at all. Cruising the deck seemed to be out of the question; there was not enough power left over for the engines—almost every available erg had to be devoted to staying put.

But there was still the rest of the Grand Tour to be made. And still one direction which Helmuth had yet to explore:

Straight down.

Down to the ice; down to the Ninth Circle, where everything stops, and never starts again.

There was a set of tracks leading down one of the Bridge's great buttresses, on to which Helmuth could switch the beetle in nearby sector 94. It took him only a few moments to set the small craft to creeping, head downward, toward the surface.

The meters on the ghost board had already told him that the wind velocity fell off abruptly at twenty-one miles—that is, eleven miles down from the deck—in this sector, which was in the lee of The Glacier, a long rib of mountain-range which terminated nearby. He was unprepared, however, for the near-calm itself. There was some wind, of course, as there was everywhere on Jupiter, especially at this season; but the worst gusts were little more than a few hundred miles per hour, and occasionally the meter fell as low as seventy-five.

The lull was dream-like. The beetle crawled downward through it, like a skin-diver who has already passed the safety-knot on his line, but is too drugged by the ecstasy of the depths to care. At fifteen miles, something white flashed in the fan-lights, and was gone. Then another; three more. And then, suddenly, a whole stream of them.

Belatedly, Helmuth stopped the beetle and peered ahead, but the white things were gone now. No, there were more of them, drifting quite slowly through the lights. As the wind died momentarily, they almost seemed to hover, pulsating slowly—

Helmuth heard himself grunt with astonishment. Once, in a moment of fancy, he had thought of Jovian jellyfish. That was what these looked like—jellyfish, not of the sea, but of the air. They were ten-ribbed, translucent, ranging in size from that of a closed fist to one as big as a football. They were beautiful—and looked incredibly delicate for this furious planet.

Helmuth reached forward to turn up the lights, but the wind rose just as his hand closed on the knob, and the creatures were gone. In the increased glare, Helmuth saw instead that there was a large platform jutting out from the buttress not far below him, just to one side of the rails. It was enclosed and roofed, but the material was transparent. And there was motion inside it.

He had no idea what the structure could be; evidently it was recent. Although he had never been below the deck in this sector before, he knew the plans well enough to recall that they had specified no such excrescence.

For a wild instant he had thought that there was a man on Jupiter already; but as he pulled up just above the platform's roof, he realized that the moving thing inside was—of course—a robot: a misshapen, many-tentacled thing about twice the size of a man. It was working busily with bottles and flasks, of which it seemed to have thousands on benches and shelves all around it. The whole enclosure was a litter of what Helmuth took to be chemical apparatus, and off to one side was an object which might have been a microscope.

The robot looked up at him and gesticulated with two or three tentacles. At first Helmuth failed to understand; then he saw that the machine was pointing to the fanlights, and obediently turned them almost all the way down. In the resulting Jovian gloom he could see that the laboratory—for that was obviously what it was—had plenty of artificial light of its own.

There was, of course, no way that he could talk to the robot, nor it to him. If he wanted to, he could talk to the person operating it; but he knew the assignment of every man and woman on Jupiter V, and running this thing was no part of any of their duties. There was not even any provision for it on the boards—

A white light began to wink on the ghost board. That would be the incoming line for Europa. Was somebody on that snowball in charge of this many-tentacled experimenter, using Jupiter V's booster station to amplify the signals that guided it? Curiously, he plugged the jack in.

"Hello, the Bridge! Who's on duty there?"

"Hello, Europa. This is Bob Helmuth. Is this your robot I'm looking at, in sector ninety-four?"

"That's me," the voice said. It was impossible to avoid thinking of it as coming from the robot itself. "This is Doc Barth. How do you like my laboratory?"

"Very cosy," Helmuth said. "I didn't even know it existed. What do you do in it?"

"We just got it installed this year. It's to study the Jovian life-forms. You've seen them?"

"You mean the jellyfish? Are they really alive?"

"Yes," the robot said. "We are keeping it under our hats until we had more data, but we knew that sooner or later one of you beetle-goosers would see them. They're alive, all right. They've got a colloidal continuum-discontinuum exactly like protoplasm—except that it uses liquid ammonia as a sol substrate, instead of water."

"But what do they live on?" Helmuth said.

"Ah, that's the question. Some form of aerial plankton that's certain; we've found the digested remnants inside

them, but haven't captured any live specimens of it yet.
The digested fragments don't offer us much to go on. And
what does the plankton live on? I only wish I knew."

Helmuth thought about it. Life on Jupiter. It did not
matter that it was simple in structure, and virtually helpless in the winds. It was life all the same, even down here
in the frozen pits of a hell no living man would ever visit.
And who could know, if jellyfish rode the Jovian air, what
Leviathans might not swim the Jovian seas?

"You don't seem to be much impressed," the robot said.
"Jellyfish and plankton probably aren't very exciting to a
layman. But the implications are tremendous. It's going to
cause quite a stir among biologists, let me tell you."

"I can believe that," Helmuth said. "I was just taken
aback, that's all. We've always thought of Jupiter as lifeless—"

"That's right. But now we know better. Well, back to
work; I'll be talking to you." The robot flourished its
tentacles and bent over a workbench.

Abstractedly, Helmuth backed the beetle off and turned
it upward again. Barth, he remembered, was the man who
had found a fossil on Europa. Earlier, there had been an
officer doing a tour of duty in the Jovian system who had
spent some of his spare time cutting soil samples, in search
of bacteria. Probably he had found some; scientists of the
age before space-flight had even found them in meteors.
The Earth and Mars were not the only places in the
universe that would harbor life, after all; perhaps it was—
everywhere. If it could exist in a place like Jupiter, there
was no logical reason to rule it out even on the Sun—
some animated flame no one would recognize as life. . . .

He regained the deck and sent the beetle rumbling for
the switchyard; he would need to transfer to another track
before he could return the car to its garage. It had
occurred to him during the ghostly proxy-conversation
that he had never met Doc Barth, or many of the other
men with whom he had talked so often by ham radio.
Except for the Bridge operators themselves, the Jovian
system was a community of disembodied voices to him.
And now, he would never meet them. . . .

"Wake up, Helmuth," a voice from the gang deck
snapped abruptly. "If it hadn't been for me, you'd have
run yourself off the end of the Bridge. You had all the
automatic stops on that beetle cut out."

Helmuth reached guiltily and more than a little too late

for the controls. Eva had already run his beetle back beyond the danger line.

"Sorry," he mumbled, taking the helmet off. "Thanks, Eva."

"Don't thank me. If you'd actually been in it, I'd have let it go. Less reading and more sleep is what I recommend for you, Helmuth."

"Keep your recommendations to yourself," he growled.

The incident started a new and even more disturbing chain of thought. If he were to resign now, it would be nearly a year before he could get back to Chicago. Antigravity or no antigravity, the senators' ship would have no room for unexpected extra passengers. Shipping a man back home had to be arranged far in advance. Living space had to be provided, and a cargo equivalent of the weight and space requirements he would take up on the return trip had to be dead-headed out to Jupiter V.

A year of living in the station on Jupiter V without any function—as a man whose drain on the station's supplies no longer could be justified in terms of what he did. A year of living under the eyes of Eva Chavez and Charity Dillon and the other men and women who still remained Bridge operators, men and women who would not hesitate to let him know what they thought of his quitting.

A year of living as a bystander in the feverish excitement of direct, personal exploration of Jupiter. A year of watching and hearing the inevitable deaths—while he alone stood aloof, privileged and useless. A year during which Robert Helmuth would become the most hated living entity in the Jovian system.

And, when he got back to Chicago and went looking for a job—for his resignation from the Bridge gang would automatically take him out of government service—he would be asked why he had left the Bridge at the moment when work on the Bridge was just reaching its culmination.

He began to understand why the man in the dream had volunteered.

When the trick-change bell rang, he was still determined to resign, but he had already concluded bitterly that there were after all, other kinds of hells besides the one on Jupiter.

He was returning the board to neutral as Charity came up the cleats. Charity's eyes were snapping like a skyful of comets. Helmuth had known that they would be.

"Senator Wagoner wants to speak to you if you're not too tired, Bob," he said. "Go ahead; I'll finish up there."

"He does?" Helmuth frowned. The dream surged back upon him. *No.* They would not rush him any faster than he wanted to go. "What about, Charity? Am I suspected of unwestern activities? I suppose you've told them how I feel."

"I have," Dillon said, unruffled. 'But we've agreed that you may not feel the same way after you've talked to Wagoner. He's in the ship, of course. I've put out a suit for you at the lock."

Charity put the helmet over his head, effectively cutting himself off from further conversation or from any further consciousness of Helmuth at all.

Helmuth stood looking at the blind, featureless bubble on Charity's shoulders for a moment. Then, with a convulsive shrug, he went down the cleats.

Three minutes later, he was plodding in a spacesuit across the surface of Jupiter V with the vivid bulk of the mother planet splashing his shoulders with color.

A courteous marine let him through the ship's airlock and deftly peeled him out of the suit. Despite a grim determination to be uninterested in the new antigravity and any possible consequence of it, he looked curiously about as he was conducted up toward the bow.

But the ship on the inside was like the ones that had brought him from Chicago to Jupiter V—it was like any spaceship: there was nothing in it to see but corridor walls and cleatwalls, until you arrived at the cabin where you were needed.

Senator Wagoner was a surprise. He was a young man, no more than sixty at most, not at all portly, and he had the keenest pair of blue eyes that Helmuth had ever seen. The cabin in which he received Helmuth was obviously his own, a comfortable cabin as spaceship accommodations go, but neither roomy nor luxurious. The senator was hard to match up with the stories Helmuth had been hearing about the current Senate, which had been involved in scandal after scandal of more than Roman proportions.

There were only two people with him: a rather plain girl who was possibly his secretary, and a tall man wearing the uniform of the Army Space Corps and the eagles of a colonel. Helmuth realized, with a second shock of surprise, that he knew the officer: he was Paige Russell, a ballistics expert who had been stationed in the Jovian

system not too long ago. The dirt-collector. He smiled
rather wryly as Helmuth's eyebrows went up.

Helmuth looked back at the senator. "I thought there
was a whole sub-committee here," he said.

"There is, but we left them where we found them, on
Ganymede. I didn't want to give you the idea that you
were facing a grand jury," Wagoner said, smiling. "I've
been forced to sit in on most of these endless loyalty
investigations back home, but I can't see any point in
exporting such religious ceremonies to deep space. Do sit
down, Mr. Helmuth. There are drinks coming. We have a
lot to talk about."

Stiffly, Helmuth sat down.

"You know Colonel Russell, of course," Wagoner said,
leaning back comfortably in his own chair. "This young
lady is Anne Abbott, about whom you'll hear more shortly. Now then: Dillon tells me that your usefulness to the
Bridge is about at an end. In a way, I'm sorry to hear
that, for you've been one of the best men we've had on
any of our planetary projects. But, in another way, I'm
glad. It makes you available for something much bigger,
where we need you much more."

"What do you mean by that?"

"You'll have to let me explain it in my own way. First,
I'd like to talk a little about the Bridge. Please don't feel
that I'm quizzing you, by the way. You're at perfect
liberty to say that any given question is none of my
business, and I'll take no offense and hold no grudge.
Also, 'I hereby disavow the authenticity of any tape or
other tapping of which this statement may be a part.' In
short, our conversation is unofficial, highly so."

"Thank you."

"It's to my interest; I'm hoping that you'll talk freely to
me. Of course, my disavowal means nothing, since such
formal statements can always be excised from a tape; but
later on I'm going to tell you some things you're not
supposed to know, and you'll be able to judge by what I
say that anything you say to me is privileged. Paige and
Anne are your witnesses. Okay?"

A steward came in silently with the drinks and left
again. Helmuth tasted his. As far as he could tell, it was
exactly like many he had mixed for himself back in the
control shack from standard space rations. The only difference was that it was cold, which Helmuth found star-

tling but not unpleasant after the first sip. He tried to relax. "I'll do my best," he said.

"Good enough. Now: Dillon says that you regard the Bridge as a monster. I've examined your dossier pretty closely—as a matter of fact I've been studying both you and Paige far more intensively than you can imagine—and I think perhaps Dillon hasn't quite the gist of your meaning. I'd like to hear it straight from you."

"I don't think the Bridge is a monster," Helmuth said slowly. "You see, Charity is on the defensive. He takes the Bridge to be conclusive evidence that no possible set of adverse conditions will ever stop man for long, and there I'm in agreement with him. But he also thinks of it as Progress, personified. He can't admit—you asked me to speak my mind, Senator—he can't admit that the West is a decadent and dying culture. All the other evidence that's available shows that it is. Charity likes to think of the Bridge as giving the lie to that evidence."

"The West hasn't many more years," Wagoner agreed, astonishingly.

Paige Russell mopped his forehead. "I still can't hear you say that," the spaceman said, "without wanting to duck under the rug. After all, MacHinery's with that pack on Ganymede—"

"MacHinery," Wagoner said calmly, "is probably going to die of apoplexy when we spring this thing on him, and I for one won't miss him. Anyhow, it's perfectly true; the dominoes have been falling for some time now, and the explosion Anne's outfit has cooked up is going to be the final blow. Still and all, Mr. Helmuth, the West has been responsible for some really towering achievements in time. Perhaps the Bridge could be considered as the last and mightiest of them all."

"Not by me," Helmuth said. "The building of gigantic projects for ritual purposes—doing a thing for the sake of doing it—is the last act of an already dead culture. Look at the pyramids in Egypt for an example. Or at an even more enormous and more idiotic example, bigger than anything human beings have accomplished yet—the laying out of the 'Diagram of Power' over the whole face of Mars. If the Martians had put all that energy into survival instead, they'd probably be alive yet."

"Agreed," Wagoner said, "with reservations. You're right about Mars, but the pyramids were built during the springtime of the Egyptian culture. And 'doing a thing for the sake of doing it' is not a definition of ritual; it's a definition of science."

"All right. That doesn't greatly alter my argument. Maybe you'll also agree that the essence of a vital culture is its ability to defend itself. The West has beaten the Soviets for half a century now—but as far as I can see, the Bridge is the West's 'Diagram of Power,' its pyramids, or what have you. It shows that we're mighty, but mighty in a non-survival sort of way. All the money and the resources that went into the Bridge are going to be badly needed, *and won't be there,* when the next Soviet attack comes."

"Correction: it has already come," Wagoner said. "And it has already won. The USSR played the greatest of all von Neumann games far better than we did, because they didn't assume as we did that each side would always choose the best strategy; they played also to wear down the players. In fifty years of unrelenting pressure, they succeeded in converting the West into a system so like the Soviets' as to make direct military action unnecessary; we Sovietized ourselves, and our moves are now exactly predictable.

"So in part I agree with you. What we needed was to sink the energy and the money into the game—into social research, since the menace was social. Instead, typically, we put it into a physical research project of unprecedented size. Which was, of course, just what the theory of games said we would do. For a man who's been cut off from Earth for years, Helmuth, you seem to know more about what's going on down there than most of the general populace does."

"Nothing promotes an interest in Earth like being off it," Helmuth said. "And there's plenty of time to read out here." Either the drink was stronger than he had expected—which was reasonable, considering that he had been off the stuff for some time now—or the senator's calm concurrence in the collapse of Helmuth's entire world had given him another shove toward the abyss; his head was spinning.

Wagoner saw it. He leaned forward suddenly, catching Helmuth flat-footed. *"However,"* he said, "it's difficult for me to agree that the Bridge serves, or ever did serve, a ritual purpose. The Bridge served several huge practical purposes which are now fulfilled. As a matter of fact, the Bridge, as such, is now a defunct project."

"Defunct?" Helmuth said faintly.

"Quite. Of course, we'll continue to operate it for a while. You can't stop a process of that size on a dime. Besides, one of the reasons why we built the Bridge was because the USSR expected us to; the game said that we should launch another Manhattan District or Project Lincoln at this point, and we hated to disappoint them. One thing we are *not* going to do this time, however, is to tell them the problem that the project was supposed to solve—let alone that it *can* be solved, and has been.

"So we'll keep the Bridge going, physically and publicly. That'll be just as well, too, for people like Dillon who are emotionally tied up in it, above and beyond their conditioning to it. You're the only person in authority in the whole station who's already lost enough interest in the bridge to make it safe for me to tell you that it's being abandoned."

"But why?"

"Because," Wagoner went on quietly, "the Bridge has now given us confirmation of a theory of stupendous importance—so important, in my opinion, that the imminent fall of the West seems like a puny event in comparison. A confirmation, incidentally, which contains in it the seeds of ultimate destruction for the Soviets, whatever they may win for themselves in the next hundred years or so."

"I suppose," Helmuth said, puzzled, "that you mean antigravity?"

For the first time, it was Wagoner's turn to be taken aback. "Man," he said at last, "do you know *everything* I want to tell you? I hope not, or my conclusions will be mighty unwelcome to both of us. Do you also know what an anti-agathic is?"

"No," Helmuth said. "I don't even recognize the root of the word."

"Well, that's a relief. But surely Charity didn't tell you we had antigravity. I strictly enjoined him not to mention it."

"No. The subject's been on my mind," Helmuth said. "But I certainly don't see why it should be so world-shaking, any more than I see how the Bridge helped to bring it about. I thought it would be developed independently, for the further exploitation of the Bridge. In other words, to put men down there, and short-circuit this remote control operation we have on Jupiter V. And I thought it would step up Bridge operation, not discontinue it."

"Not at all. Nobody in his right mind would want to put men on Jupiter, and besides, gravity isn't the main problem down there. Even eight gravities is perfectly tolerable for short periods of time—and anyhow a man in a pressure suit couldn't get five hundred miles down through that atmosphere before he'd be as buoyed up and weightless as a fish—and even more thoroughly at the mercy of the currents."

"And you can't screen out the pressure?"

"We can," Wagoner said, "but only at ruinous cost. Besides, there'd be no point in trying. The Bridge is finished. It's given us information in thousands of different categories, much of it very valuable indeed. But the one job that *only* the Bridge could do was that of confirming, or throwing out, the Blackett-Dirac equations."

"Which are—?"

"They show a relationship between magnetism and the spinning of a massive body—that much is the Dirac part of it. The Blackett Equation seemed to show that the same formula also applied to gravity; it says G equals $(2CP/BU^2)$, where C is the velocity of light, P is magnetic moment, and U is angular momentum. B is an uncertainty correction, a constant which amounts to 0.25.

"If the figures we collected on the magnetic field strength of Jupiter forced us to retire the equations, then none of the rest of the information we've gotten from the Bridge would have been worth the money we spent to get it. On the other hand, Jupiter was the only body in the solar system available to us which was big enough in all relevant respects to make it possible for us to test those equations at all. They involve quantities of infinitesimal orders of magnitudes.

"And the figures showed that Dirac was right. *They also show that Blackett was right.* Both magnetism *and* gravity are phenomena of rotation.

"I won't bother to trace the succeeding steps, because I think you can work them out for yourself. It's enough to say that there's a drive-generator on board this ship which is the complete and final justification of all the hell you people on the Bridge have been put through. The gadget has a long technical name—The Dillon-Wagoner gravitron polarity generator, a name which I loathe for obvious reasons—but the technies who tend it have already nicknamed it the spindizzy, because of what it does to the magnetic moment of any atom—*any* atom—within its field.

"While it's in operation, it absolutely refuses to notice any atom outside its own influence. Furthermore, it will notice no other strain or influence which holds good beyond the borders of that field. It's so snooty that it has to be stopped down to almost nothing when it's brought close to a planet, or it won't let you land. But in deep space . . . well, it's impervious to meteors and such trash, of course; it's impervious to gravity; and—it hasn't the faintest interest in any legislation about top speed limits. It moves in its own continuum, not in the general frame."

"You're kidding." Helmuth said.

"Am I, now? This ship came to Ganymede directly from Earth. It did it in a little under two hours, counting maneuvring time. That means that most of the way we made about 55,000 miles per second—with the spindizzy drawing less than five watts of power out of three ordinary No. 6 dry cells."

Helmuth took a defiant pull at his drink. "This thing really has no top speed at all?" he said. "How can you be sure of that?"

"Well, we can't," Wagoner admitted. After all, one of the unfortunate things about general mathematical formulae is that they don't contain cut-off points to warn you of areas where they don't apply. Even quantum mechanics is somewhat subject to that criticism. However, we expect to know pretty soon just how fast the spindizzy can drive an object. We expect you to tell us."

"I?"

"Yes, you, and Colonel Russell, and Miss Abbott too, I hope." Helmuth looked at the other two; both of them looked at least as stunned as he felt. He could not imagine why. "The coming débâcle on Earth makes it absolutely imperative for us—the West—to get inter-stellar expeditions started at once. Richardson Observatory, on the Moon, has two likely-looking systems mapped already—one at Wolf 359, the other at 61 Cygni—and there are sure to be others, hundreds of others, where Earth-like planets are highly probable.

"What we're doing, in a nutshell, is evacuating the West—not physically, of course, but in essence, in idea. We want to scatter adventurous people, people with a thoroughly indoctrinated love of being free, all over this part of the galaxy, if it can be done.

"Once they're out there, they'll be free to flourish, with no interference from Earth. The Soviets haven't the spin-dizzy yet, and even after they get it, they won't dare allow it to be used. It's too good and too final an escape route for disaffected comrades.

"What we want you to do, Helmuth . . . now I'm getting to the point, you see . . . is to direct this exodus, with Colonel Russell's help. You've the intelligence and the cast of mind for it. Your analysis of the situation on Earth confirms that, if any more confirmation were needed. And—there's no future for you on Earth now."

"You'll have to excuse me for a while," Helmuth said firmly. "I'm in no condition to be reasonable now; it's been more than I could digest in a few moments. And the decision doesn't entirely rest with me, either. If I could give you an answer in . . . let me see . . . about three hours. Will that be soon enough?"

"That'll be fine," the senator said.

For a moment after the door closed behind Helmuth there was silence in the senator's cabin. At last Paige said:

"So it was long life for spacemen you were after, all the time. Long life, by God, for *me*, and for the likes of me."

Wagoner nodded. "This was the one part of this affair that I couldn't explain to you back in Hal Gunn's office," he said. "Until you had ridden in this ship, and understood as a spaceman just what kind of a thing we have in it, you wouldn't have believed me; Helmuth does, you see, be-cause he already has the background. In the same way, I didn't go into the question of the anti-agathic with Hel-muth, because that's something he's going to have to experi-ence; you two have the background to understand that part of it through explanation alone.

"Now you see why I didn't give a whistle about your spy, Paige. The Soviets can have the Earth. As a matter of fact they will take it before very long, whether we give into them or not. But we are going to scatter the West throughout the stars, scatter it with immortal people car-rying immortal ideas. People like you, and Miss Abbott."

Paige looked back to Anne. She was aloofly regarding the empty space just above Wagoner's head, as though still looking at the bewhiskered picture of the Pfitzner founder which hung in Gunn's office. There was something in her face, however, that Paige could read. He smothered a grin and said: "Why me?"

"Because you're just what we need for the job. I don't mind telling you that your blundering into the Pfitzner project in the first place was an act of Providence from my point of view. When Anne first called your qualifications to my attention, I was almost prepared to believe that they'd been faked. You're going to be liason-man between the Pfitzner side of the project and the Bridge side. We've got the total output to date of both ascomycin and the new anti-agathic salted away in the cargo-hold, and Anne's already shown you how to take the stuff and how to administer it to others. After that—just as soon as you and Helmuth can work out the details—the stars are yours."

"Anne," Paige said. She turned her head slowly toward him. "Are you with this thing?"

"I'm here," she said. "And I'd had a few inklings of what was up before. You were the one who had to be brought in, not I."

Paige thought about it a moment more. Then something both very new and very old occurred to him.

"Senator," he said, "you've gone to an immense amount of trouble to make this whole thing possible—but I don't think you plan to go with us."

"No, Paige, I don't. For one thing, MacHinery and his crew will regard the whole project as treasonous. If it's to be carried out nevertheless, someone has to stay behind and be the goat—and after all, the idea *was* mine, so I'm the logical candidate." He fell silent for a moment. Then he added ruminatively: "The government boys have nobody but themselves to thank for this. The whole project would never have been possible so long as the West had a government of laws and not of men, and stuck to it. It was a long while ago that some people—MacHinery's grandfather among them—set themselves up to be their own judges of whether or not a law ought to be obeyed. They had precedents. And now here we are, on the brink of the most enormous breach of our social contract the West has ever had to suffer—and the West can't stop it." He smiled suddenly. "I'll have good use for that argument in the court."

Anne was on her feet, her eyes suddenly wet, her lower lip just barely trembling. Evidently, over whatever time she had known Wagoner and had known what he had planned, it had never occurred to her that the young-old senator might stay behind.

"That's no good!" she said in a low voice. "They won't listen, and you know it. They might easily hang you for it. If they find you guilty of treason, they'll seal you up in the pile-waste dump—that's the current penalty, isn't it? You can't go back!"

"It's a phony terror. Pile wastes are quick chemical poisons; you don't last long enough to notice that they're also hot," Wagoner said. "And what difference does it make, anyhow? Nothing and nobody can harm me now. The job is done."

Anne put her hands to her face.

"Besides, Anne," Wagoner said, with gentle insistence, "the stars are for young people—eternally young people. An eternal oldster would be an anachronism."

"Why—did you do it, then?" Paige said. His own voice was none too steady.

"Why?" Wagoner said. "You know the answer to that, Paige. You've known it all your life. I could see it in your face, as soon as I told Helmuth that we were going out to the stars. Supposing you tell *me* what it is."

Anne swung her blurred eyes on Paige. He thought he knew what she expected to hear him say; they had talked about it often enough, and it was what he once would have said himself. But now another force seemed to him to be the stronger: a special thing, bearing the name of no established dogma, but nevertheless and unmistakably the force to which he had borne allegiance all his life. He in turn could see it in Wagoner's face now, and he knew he had seen it before in Anne's.

"It's the thing that lures monkeys into cages," he said slowly. "And lures cats into open drawers and up telephone poles. It's driven men to conquer death, and put the stars into our hands. I suppose that I'd call it Curiosity."

Wagoner looked startled. "Is that really what you want to call it?" he said. "Somehow it seems insufficient; I should have given it another name. Perhaps you'll amend it later, somewhere, some day out by Aldebaran."

He stood up and looked at the two for a moment in silence. Then he smiled.

"And now," he said gently, "*nunc dimittis . . .* suffer thy servant to depart in peace."

CHAPTER ELEVEN: Jupiter V

*. . . the social and economic rewards for such scientific
activities do not primarily accrue to the scientist or to the
intellectual. Still, that has perhaps been his own moral
speciation, a choice of one properly humane activity: to
have knowledge of things, not to have things. If he loves
and has knowledge, all is well.*

—WESTON LA BARRE

"AND SO, that's the story," Helmuth said.

Eva remained silent in her chair for a long time.

"One thing I don't understand," she said at last. "Why
did you come to me? I'd have thought that you'd find the
whole thing terrifying."

"Oh, it's terrifying, all right," Helmuth said, with quiet
exultation. "But terror and fright are two different things
as I've just discovered. We were both wrong, Evita. I was
wrong in thinking that the Bridge was a dead end. You
were wrong in thinking of it as an end in itself."

"I don't understand you."

"I didn't understand myself. My fears of working in
person on the Bridge were irrational; they came from
dreams. That should have tipped me off right away. There
was really never any chance of anyone's working in person
on Jupiter; but I *wanted to*. It was a death wish, and it
came directly out of the goddamned conditioning. I knew,
we all knew, that the Bridge couldn't stand forever, but we
were conditioned to believe that it had to. Nothing else
could justify the awful ordeal of keeping it going even one
day. The result: the classical dilemma that leads to madness. It affected you, too, and your response was just as
insane as mine: you wanted to have a child there.

"Now all that's changed. The work the Bridge was
doing was worth while after all. I was wrong in calling it a
bridge to nowhere. And Eva, you no more saw where it
was going than I did, or you'd never have made it the
be-all and end-all of your existence.

"Now, there's a place to go to. In fact, there are places—hundreds of places. They'll be Earthlike places. Since the Soviets are about to win the Earth, those places will be more Earthlike than Earth itself, at least for the next century or so!"

She said: "Why are you telling me this? Just to make peace between us?"

"I'm going to take on this job, Evita ... if you'll go along."

She turned swiftly, rising out of the chair with a marvelous fluidity of motion. At the same instant, all the alarm bells in the station went off at once, filling every metal cranny with a jangle of pure horror.

"Posts!" the loudspeaker above Eva's bed roared, in a distorted, gigantic caricature of Charity Dillon's voice. *"Peak storm overload! The STD is now passing the Spot. Wind velocity has already topped all previous records, and part of the land mass has begun to settle. This is an A-1 overload emergency."*

Behind Charity's bellow, they could hear what he was hearing, the winds of Jupiter, a spectrum of continuous, insane shrieking. The Bridge was responding with monstrous groans of agony. There was another sound, too, an almost musical cacophony of sharp, percussive tones, such as a dinosaur might make pushing its way through a forest of huge steel tuning-forks. Helmuth had never heard the sound before, but he knew what it was.

The deck of the Bridge was splitting up the middle.

After a moment more, the uproar dimmed, and the speaker said, in Charity's normal voice: "Eva, you too, please. Acknowledge, please. This is it—unless everybody comes on duty at once, the Bridge may go down within the next hour."

"Let it," Eva responded quietly.

There was a brief, startled silence, and then a ghost of a human sound. The voice was Senator Wagoner's, and the sound just might have been a chuckle.

Charity's circuit clicked out.

The mighty death of the Bridge continued to resound in the little room.

After a while, the man and the woman went to the window, and looked past the discarded bulk of Jupiter at the near horizon, where there had always been visible a few stars.

CODA: Brookhaven National Laboratories
(the pile-dump)

*But I say unto you, Love your enemies, bless them that
curse you, do good to them that hate you, and pray for
them which despitefully use you, and persecute you; That
ye may be the children of your Father which is in heaven:
for he maketh his sun to rise on the evil and on the good,
and sendeth rain on the just and on the unjust. For if ye
love them which love you, what reward have ye? do not
even the publicans the same? And if ye salute your breth-
ren only, what do ye more? do not even the publicans so?*

"EVERY END," Wagoner wrote on the wall of his cell on
the last day, "is a new beginning. Perhaps in a thousand
years my Earthmen will come home again. Or in two
thousand, or four, if they still remember home then.
They'll come back, yes; but I hope they won't stay. I pray
they will not stay."

He looked at what he had written and thought of
signing his name. While he debated that, he made the
mark for the last day on his calendar, and the point on his
stub of pencil struck stone under the calcimine and
snapped, leaving nothing behind it but a little coronet of
frayed, dirty blond wood. He could wear that away against
the window-ledge, at least enough to expose a little graphite, but instead he dropped the stub in the waste can.

There was writing enough in the stars that he could see,
because he had written it there. There was a constellation
called Wagoner, and every star in the sky belonged to it.
That was surely enough.

Later that day, a man named MacHinery said: "Bliss
Wagoner is dead."

As usual, MacHinery was wrong.

A
LIFE
FOR
THE
STARS

CHAPTER ONE: Press Gang

From the embankment of the long-abandoned Erie-Lackawanna-Pennsylvania Railroad, Chris sat silently watching the city of Scranton, Pennsylvania, preparing to take off, and sucked meditatively upon the red and white clover around him.

It was a first time for each of them. Chris had known since he had been a boy—he was sixteen now—that the cities were deserting the Earth, but he had never seen one in flight. Few people had, for the nomad cities, once gone, were gone for good.

Nor was it a very happy occasion, interesting though it was. Scranton was the only city Chris had ever seen, let alone visited, and the only one he was ever likely to see. It represented what small livelihood his father and his older brother had been able to scratch out of this valley; it was where the money was made, and where it was spent, somehow always managing to go out faster than it came in.

Scranton had become steadily greedier as the money to be made dwindled, but somehow never greedy enough. Now, as it had for so many other towns, the hour of the city's desperation had struck. It was going into space, to become a migrant worker among the stars.

The valley sweltered in the mercilessly hot July sunlight, and the smoke from the plant chimneys rose straight up. There were only a few smokestacks going, though, and those would be shut down shortly, until the city should find another planet on which to work. Nothing would be allowed to smoke in the confined air of a star-cruising vessel, even as big a one as a city—not so much as a cigarette.

Down at the bottom of the railroad embankment, where the tar-paper shacks huddled, a red-necked man in

an undershirt and levis scratched at a kitchen garden with
a hoe. Chris wondered if he knew what was about to
happen. Certainly he was paying no attention; maybe he
just didn't care. Chris's own father had reached the
gloomy state of mind long ago. But all the same, it was
odd that there were no sight-seers other than Chris himself.

A circular belt of cleared land, nothing but raw, red,
dry earth, ran around the city, separating it from the
shacks, from the battered and flaking suburbs, and from
all the rest of the world. Inside it, the city looked the
same as always, even to the yellow and orange glare of
the slag heaps. Scranton was going to leave half its homes
behind, but it was taking the slag heaps along; they were
part of its stock in trade. Somewhere, out among the
stars, there would be a frontier planet with iron ore to
process; somewhere else, a planet with a use for slag, or
something that might be extracted from slag—a use still
beyond speculation, but not to be foreclosed by shortsight-
edness. People, on the other hand, were largely useless;
weight for weight, the slag would be worth more.

At least, that was the hope. What was certain was that
there was no more iron ore on Earth worth processing.
The voracious Second Millennium—the books called it the
"Age of Waste"—had used it all up, except for such
artificial mines as used-car dumps and other deposits of
scrap and rust. There was still native iron on Mars, of
course, but none of that was available for Scranton. Pittsburgh was already on Mars, as well equipped with guns as
with blast furnaces. Besides Mars was too small a planet to
support more than one steel town, not because the red
world was short of iron, but because it was short of
oxygen, which was also essential for the making of steel.

Any work Scranton might find to do now would have to
lie beyond the reaches of the solar system. There was no
iron on Venus or Mercury that a steel town could afford
to process—and no iron at all on the other six planets, the
five gas giants and the remote ice ball that was Pluto.

The man in the kitchen garden straightened, leaned his
hoe against the back of his shack, and went inside. Now
the valley outside the raw-earth circle looked deserted
indeed, and it suddenly occurred to Chris that this might
be more than an appearance. Was there something dangerous about being too close to a city under a spindizzy
field? Were he and the lone gardener being foolhardy?

At the moment, the whole world was silent except for the distant grumbling of Scranton itself. He knew he had nothing to fear from the rail bed behind him, for the tracks had been torn up long ago to feed the furnaces. There was a legend in the valley that on quiet nights one could still hear the Phoebe Snow going by, but Chris scoffed at such fairy tales. (Besides, his father had told him, that had been a daytime train.) Even the ties were gone, burned as firewood by the shack dwellers through generations of harsh Pennsylvania winters.

He racked his memory for what little he knew about the behavior of spindizzies, but could come up with nothing but that they were machines and that they lifted things. Though his schooling had been poor and spasmodic, he was a compulsive reader, devouring even the labels on cans if there was nothing else available; but the physics of interstellar flight is an impossible discipline to grasp even for an advanced student without a first-rate teacher to help, and the closest Chris had even come to a good teacher was Scranton's public librarian. She had tried hard; but she did not know the subject.

As a result, Chris stayed where he was. He would probably have done so even had he known positively that there was some danger; for in the valley, anything new was a change—even the fact, disastrous though it was, that Scranton was about to go as permanently out of his life and world as Betelgeuse. His own life thus far had held little but squirrel trapping; stealing eggs from neighbors as badly off as his own family; hunting scrap to sell to the mills; helping Bob nurse their father through repeated bouts of an illness which, but for the fact that there was no one in thirty-second-century America to diagnose it, would have been recognized as the ancient African scourge of *kwashiorkor* or malignant malnutrition; keeping the little girls out of the berry patch; fishing for fingerlings; and watching the rockets of the rich howl remotely through the highest reaches of the indifferent sky.

He had often thought of leaving, though he had no trade to practice and knew of no place in the world where his considerable but utterly untrained brute strength could be sold at any price. But there was loyalty and love in the motherless family, and it had often before sustained them when there had been nothing to eat but fried dough and green tomatoes, and no warmth against the Christmas snows but huddling with the little kids under a heap of the old rags that were their clothes; and in the end, Chris stuck by it as stubbornly and devotedly as Bob always had. In all the depopulated Earth there was no place to which he owed more loyalty, and no place which could offer him more in return—the worst possible substratum for dreams of escape, even for a temperament as naturally sunny and sanguine as Chris's. In a world where a Ph.D. in economics could find no one to teach, nor use his knowledge of how the economy wagged to find any other niche in it—a world in which a thousand penny-ante jobs left him no time even to tend his wife's grave, yet all the same paid him less and less every year—what hope could his boys reasonably cherish for any better future? The answer, alas, was all too obvious; and for the little girls, the foreseeable future was even more grim.

The nomad cities offered no better way of escape. More often than not, Chris had read, star roving was simply another form of starvation, without even the company of a blue sky, a scrub forest or a patch of ground to grow turnips in. Otherwise, why did almost every city which had ever left the Earth fail to come back home? Pittsburgh had made its fortune on Mars, to be sure—but it was a poor sort of fortune that kept you sitting in a city all your life, with nothing to see beyond the city limits but an ochre desert, a desert with no air you could breath, a desert that would freeze you solid only a few minutes after the tiny sun went down. Sooner or later, too, his father said, Pittsburgh would have to leave the solar system as all the other cities had—not, this time, because it had exhausted the iron and the oxygen, but because there would be too few people left on the Earth to buy steel. There were already too few to justify Pittsburgh's coming back to the once-golden triangle of rivers it had abandoned thirty years ago; Pittsburgh had wealth, but was finding it increasingly hard to spend on the Earth, even for necessities. The nomad cities seemed, like everything else, to be a dead end.

Nevertheless Chris sat on the embankment and watched, for only a single, simple reason: Something was going on. If he envied the city its decision to leave the valley, he was unaware of it. He was there simply to see something happen, for a change.

A brief rustle of shrubbery behind him made him turn. A dog's head peered across the roadbed at him from the

foot of the mountainside, surrounded incongruously by the
trumpets of tiger lilies; it looked a little as if it were being
served up on a platter. Chris grinned.

"Hello, Kelly. Look out for bees."

The dog whuffed and came trotting to him, looking
foolishly proud of itself—as it probably was, for Kelly was
usually not very good at finding anything, even his own
way home. Bob, whose dog Kelly officially was, said that
Kelly was a combination of Kerry blue and collie—hence
the name—but Chris had never seen a pure sample of
either breed, and Kelly did not look anything like the
pictures of either. He looked, in point of fact, like a
shaggy mutt, which was fortunate for him, since that was
what he was.

"What do you make of it, handsome? Think they'll ever
get that thing off the ground?"

Kelly gave an imitation of a dog trying to think, regis-
tered pain, wagged his tail twice, woofed at a butterfly and
sat down, panting. It had obviously always been his
impression that he belonged to Chris, an impression Bob
had wisely never tried to discourage. Explaining something
that abstract to Kelly was (a) a long and complicated
task, and (b) utterly hopeless anyhow. Kelly earned his
own keep—he caught rabbits—which made up for the
nuisance he was when he caught a porcupine; so nobody
in the family but Chris much cared whom he thought he
belonged to.

There was at last some activity around the parching
city. Small groups of men, made so tiny by distance that
they were almost invisible except for their bright yellow
steelworkers' helmets, were patrolling the bare perimeter.
There was probably a law about that, Chris reflected.
Equally probably it would be the last Earth law Scranton
would ever be *obliged* to observe—no matter how many
of them the city fathers took into space of their own free
will. No doubt the patrol was looking for rubbernecks
who might be standing too close for safety.

He imagined it so vividly that for a moment he had the
illusion of hearing their voices. Then he realized with a
start that it was not an illusion. A flash of yellow hard
hats revealed another group of patrollers working their
way through the shacks at the foot of the embankment
and coming in his direction.

With the ingrained prudence of the lifelong poacher, he
took at once to the bushes on the other side of the

roadbed. Not only would he be invisible from there, but, of course, he could no longer see the patrol; however, he could still hear it.

". . . anybody in these shacks. Ask me, it's a waste of time."

"The boss says look, so we look, that's all. Myself, I think we'd make out better in Nixonville."

"Them tramps? They can smell work ten miles away. People on this side of town, they used to *look* for work. Not that there ever was any."

Chris cautiously parted the shrubbery and peered out. The gang was still out of sight, but there was another group coming toward him from the other direction, walking along the old roadbed. He let the bushes swing closed hastily, wishing that he had retreated farther up the mountainside. It was too late for that now, though. The new patrol was close enough to hear the brush rustle, and would probably see him too if he was in motion.

Down in the valley there was a sudden, slight hum, like bee-buzz, but infinitely gentler, and deeper in tone. Chris had never heard anything exactly like it before, but there could be no doubt in his mind about what it was: Scranton's spindizzies were being tuned. Was he going to have to hide right through the take-off, and miss seeing it? But surely the city wouldn't leave until its patrols were back on board!

The voices came closer, and beside him Kelly growled softly. The boy grasped the dog firmly by the scruff and shook him gently, not daring to speak. Kelly shut up, but all his muscles were tensed.

"Hey! Look what we got here!"

Chris froze as completely as a rabbit smelling fox; but another voice struck in at once.

"You guys get outa here. This here's my place. You got no business with me."

"Yeah? You didn't hear anything about getting out of the valley by noon today? There's a poster on your own front door that says so. Can't read, huh, Jack?"

"I don't do everything any piece of paper says. I live here, see? It's a lousy dump, but it's mine, and I'm staying, that's all. Now blow, will you?"

"Well, now, I don't know if that's all, Jack. It's the law that you're supposed to be vacated. *We* don't want your shack, but it's the law, see?"

"It's the law that I got a right to my own property, too."

A new voice chimed in from the embankment, not fifteen feet from where Chris and Kelly crouched. "Trouble down there, Barney?"

"Squatter. Won't move. Says he owns the place."

"That's a laugh. Get him to show you his deed."

"Ah, why bother with that? We ain't got the time. Let's impress him and get moving."

"No you don't—"

There was the meaty sound of a blow landing, and a grunt of surprise. "Hey, he wants to play rough! All right, mister—"

More impacts, and then the sound of something smashing—glass or crockery, Chris guessed, but it might have been furniture. Before Chris could do more than grab at him convulsively, Kelly burst into a volley of high, howling yelps, broke free, crashed out of the bushes and went charging across the embankment toward the fracas.

"Look out! Hey—Where'd that mutt come from?"

"Out of the bushes there. Somebody's in there still. Red hair, I can see it. All right, Red, out in the open—on the double!"

Chris rose slowly, ready to run or fight at the drop of a hard hat. Kelly, on the far side of the embankment, gave up his idiot barking for a moment, his attention divided between the struggle in the shack and the group now surrounding Chris.

"Well, Red, you're a husky customer. I suppose you didn't hear about any vacate order, either."

"No, I didn't," Chris said defiantly. "I live in Lakebranch. I only came over to watch."

"Lakebranch?" the leader said, looking at another of his leathery-faced patrolmates.

"Hick town, way out back some place. Used to be a resort. Nothing out there now but poachers and scratchers."

"That's nice," the other man said, tipping back his yellow helmet and grinning. "Nobody'll miss you, I guess, Red. Come along."

"What do you mean, come along?" Chris said, his fists clenching. "I have to be home by five."

"Watch it—the kid's got some beef on him."

The other man, now clearly in charge, laughed scornfully. "You scared? He's a kid, isn't he? Come on, Red, I got no time to argue. You're here past noon, we got a legal right to impress you."

"I told you, I'm due home."

"You should have thought of that before you came here. Move along. You give us a hard time, we give you one, get it?"

Below, three men came out of the shack, holding hard to the gardener Chris had seen earlier. All looked considerably battered, but the sullen red-neck was secured all the same.

"We got this one—no thanks to you guys. Thought you was going to be right down. Big help you was!"

"Got another one, Barney. Let's go, Red."

The press-gang leader took Chris by the elbow. He was not unnecessarily violent about it, but the movement was sudden enough to settle matters in Kelly's slow brain. Kelly was unusually stupid, even for a dog, but he now knew which fight interested him most. With a snarl which made even Chris's hackles rise—he had never in his life before heard a dog make such a noise, let alone Kelly— the animal streaked back across the embankment and leaped for the big man's legs.

In the next thirty seconds of confusion Chris might easily have gotten away—there were a hundred paths through the undergrowth that he might have taken that these steel puddlers would have found it impossible to follow—but he couldn't abandon Kelly. And with an instinct a hundred thousand years old, the patrol fell on the animal enemy first, turning their backs on the boy without even stopping to think.

Chris was anything but a trained in-fighter, but he had instincts of his own. The man with Kelly's teeth in him was obviously busy enough. Chris lobbed a knob-kerrie fist at the man next to him. When the target looked stunned but failed to fall, Chris threw the other fist. It didn't land where Chris had meant it to land, exactly, but the man staggered away anyhow, which was good enough. Then Chris was in the middle of the melee and no longer had any chance even to try to call his shots.

After a while, he was on the broken granite of the old roadbed, and no longer cared about Scranton, Kelly or even himself. His head was ringing. Over him, considerable swearing was going on.

"—more trouble than he's worth. Give him a shoe in the head and let's get back!"

"No. No killing. We can impress 'em, but we can't bump 'em off. One of you guys see if you can slap Huggins awake."

"What are you—chicken all of a sudden?"

The press-gang leader was breathing hard, and as Chris's sight cleared, he saw that the big man was sitting on the ground wrapping a bloody leg in a length of torn shirt. Nevertheless he said evenly: "You want to kill a kid because he gave you a fight? That's the lousiest excuse for killing a man I ever heard, let alone a kid. You give me any more of that, I'll take a poke at you myself."

"Ah, shaddup, will you?" the other voice said surlily. "Anyhow we got the dog—"

"You loud-mouthed—*look out!*"

Two men grabbed Chris, one from each side, as he surged to his feet. He struggled fiercely, but all the fight left in him was in his soul, not any in his muscles.

"What a bunch of flap-jaws. No wonder you can't hold your own with a kid. Huggins, put your hat on. Red, don't you listen to that slob, he's been all mouth all his life. Your dog ran away, that's all."

The lie was kindly meant, no matter how clumsy it was, but it was useless. Chris could see Kelly, not far away. Kelly had done the best he could; he would never have another chance.

The youngster the press-gang dragged stumbling toward Scranton had a heart made of stone.

CHAPTER TWO: A Line of Boiling Dust

The city inside the perimeter of raw earth was wavery and unreal. It did not hum any more, but it gave a puzzling impression of being slightly in shadow, though the July sun was still blazing over it. Even in his grief and anger, Chris was curious enough to wonder at the effect, and finally he thought he saw what caused it: The heat waves climbing the air around the town seemed to be detouring it, as though the city itself were inside a dome. No, not a dome, but a bubble, only a part of which was underground; it met the earth precisely at the cleared perimeter.

The spindizzy field was up. It was invisible in itself, but it was no longer admitting the air of the Earth.

Scranton was ready.

Thanks to the scrapping, the patrol was far behind schedule; the leader drove them all through the scabrous, deserted suburbs without any mercy for his own torn leg. Chris grimly enjoyed watching him wince at every other step, but the man did not allow the wound to hold him up, nor did he let any of the lesser bruises and black eyes in the party serve as excuses for foot dragging.

There was no way to tell, by the normal human senses, when the party passed through the spindizzy screen. Midway across the perimeter, which was a good five hundred feet wide, the leader unshipped from his belt a device about as big as an avocado, turned it in his hands until it whined urgently, and then directed the group on ahead of him in single file, along a line which he traced in the dry red ground with the toe of his boot.

As his two guards left his side, Chris crouched instinctively. He was not afraid of them, and the leader apparently was going to stay behind. But the big man saw the slight motion.

"Red, I wouldn't if I were you," he said quietly. "If you try to run back this way after I turn off this gadget—or if you try to go around me—you'll go straight up in the air. Look back and see the dust rising. You're a lot heavier than a dust speck, and you'll go up a lot farther. Better relax. Take it from me."

Chris looked again at the dubious boundary line he had just crossed. Sure enough, there was a hair-thin ruling there, curving away to both sides as far as he could see, where the inert friable earth seemed to be turning over restlessly. It was as though he were standing inside a huge circle of boiling dust.

"That's right, that's what I meant. Now look here." The press-gang leader bent and picked up a stone just about as big as his fist—which was extraordinarily big—and shied it back the way they had come. As the rock started to cross the line above the seething dust, it leaped skyward with an audible screech, like a bullet ricocheting. In less than a second, Chris had lost sight of it.

"Fast, huh? And it'd throw you much farther, Red. In a few minutes, it'll be lifting a whole city. So don't go by how things look. Right where you stand, you're not even on the Earth any more."

Chris looked at the mountains for a moment, and then back at the line of boiling dust. Then he turned away and resumed marching toward Scranton.

And yet they were now on a street Chris had traveled a score of times before, carrying fifty cents for the Sunday paper's Help Wanted ads, or rolling a wheel-barrow not quite full of rusty scrap, or bringing back a flat package of low-grade ground horsemeat. The difference lay only in the fact that just beyond the familiar corner the city stopped, giving place to the new desert of the perimeter—and all in the overarching shadow which was not a shadow at all.

The patrol leader stopped and looked back. "We'll never make it from here," he said finally. "Take cover. Barney, watch that red-neck. I'll take the kid with me; he looks sensible."

Barney started to answer, but his reply was drowned out by a prolonged fifty-decibel honking which made the very walls howl back. The noise was horrifying; Chris had never before heard anything even a fraction so loud, and it seemed to go on forever. The press-gang boss herded him into a doorway.

"There's the alert. Duck, you guys. Stand still, Red. There's probably no danger—we just don't know. But something might just shake down and fall—so keep your head in."

The honking stopped; but in its place Chris could again hear the humming, now so pervasive that it made his teeth itch in their sockets. The shadow deepened, and out in the bare belt of earth the seething dust began to leap into the air in feathery plumes almost as tall as ferns.

Then the doorway lurched and went askew. Chris grabbed for the frame; and just in time, for a second later, the door jerked the other way; and then, back again. Gradually, the quakes became periodic, spacing themselves farther apart in time, and slowly weakening in violence.

After the first quake, however, Chris's alarm began to dwindle into amazement, for the movements of the ground were puny compared to what was going on before his eyes. The whole city seemed to be rocking heavily, like a ship in a storm. At one instant, the street ended in nothing but sky; at the next, Chris was staring at a wall of sheared earth, its rim looming clifflike, fifty feet or more above the new margin of the city; and then the blank sky was back again—

These huge pitching movements should have brought the whole city down in a roaring avalanche of steel and stone. Instead, only these vague twitchings and shudderings of the ground came through, and even those seemed to be fading away. Now the city was level again, amidst an immense cloud of dust, through which Chris could see the landscape begin to move solemnly past him. The city had stopped rocking, and was now turning slowly. There was no longer even the slightest sensation of movement; the illusion that it was the valley that was revolving around the city was irresistible and more than a little dizzying.

I can see where the spindizzy got its name, Chris thought. *Wonder if we go around like a top all the time we're in space? How'll we see where we're going, then?*

But now the high rim of the valley was sinking. In a breath, the distant roadbed of the railroad embankment was level with the end of the street; then the lip of the street was at the brow of the mountain; then with the treetops ... and then there was nothing but blue sky, becoming rapidly darker.

The big press-gang leader released an explosive sigh. "By thunder," he said, "we got her up." He seemed a little dazed. "I guess I never really believed it till now."

"Not so sure I believe it yet," the man called Barney said. "But I don't see any cornices falling—we don't have to hang around here any longer. The boss'll have our necks for being even this late."

"Yeah, let's move. Red, use your head and don't give us any more trouble, huh? You can see for yourself, there's no place to run to now."

There was no doubt about that. The sky at the end of the street, and overhead too, was now totally black; and even as Chris looked up, the stars became visible—at first only a few of the brightest, but the others came out steadily in their glorious hundreds. From their familiar fixity Chris could also deduce that the city was no longer rotating on its axis, which was vaguely reassuring, somehow. Even the humming had faded away again; if it was still present, it was now inaudible in the general noise of the city.

Oddly, the sunlight was still as intense as ever. From now on, "day" and "night" would be wholly arbitrary terms aboard the city: Scranton had emerged into the realm of Eternal Daylight-Saving Time.

The party walked two blocks and then stopped while the

big man located a cab post and pulled the phone from it. Barney objected at once.

"It'll take a fleet of cabs to get us all to the Hall," he complained. "And we can't get enough guys into a hack to handle a prisoner, if he gets rough."

"The kid won't get rough. Go ahead and march your man over. I'm not going to walk another foot on this leg."

Barney hesitated, but obviously the big man's marked limp was an unanswerable argument. Finally he shrugged and herded the rest of his party around the corner. His boss grinned at Chris; but the boy looked away.

The cab came floating down out of the sky at the intersection and maneuvered itself to rest at the curb next to them with a finicky precision. There was, of course, nobody in it; like everything else in the world requiring an I.Q. of less than 150, it was computer-controlled. The world-wide dominance of such machines, Chris's father had often said, had been one of the chief contributors to the present and apparently permanent depression: the coming of semi-intelligent machines into business and technology had created a second Industrial Revolution, in which only the most highly creative human beings, and those most gifted at administration, found themselves with any skills to sell which were worth the world's money to buy.

Chris studied the cab with the liveliest interest, for though he had often seen them before from a distance, he had of course never ridden in one. But there was very little to see. The cab was an egg-shaped bubble of light metals and plastics, painted with large red-and-white checkers, with a row of windows running all around it. Inside, there were two seats for four people, a speaker grille, and that was all; no controls, and no instruments. There was not even any visible place for the passenger to deposit his fare.

The big press-gang leader gestured Chris into the front seat, and himself climbed into the back. The doors slid shut simultaneously from the ceiling and floor, rather like a mouth closing, and the cab lifted gently until it hovered about six feet above street level.

"Destination?" the Tin Cabby said cheerily, making Chris jump.

"City Hall."

"Social Security number?"

"One five six one one dash zero nine seven five dash zero six nine eight two one seven."

"Thank you."

"Shaddup."

"You're welcome, sir."

The cab lifted vertically, and the gang captain settled back into his seat. He seemed content for the moment to allow Chris to sight-see out the windows at the passing stubby towers of the flying city; he looked relaxed and a little indulgent, but a little wary, too. Finally he said:

"I need to dutch-uncle you a little, Red. I didn't call a cab because of the leg—I've walked farther on worse. Feel up to listening?"

Chris felt himself freezing. Distracted though he was by all this enormous budget of new experience and the vast reaches of the unknown which stretched before him, the press-gang leader's remark reminded him instantly of Kelly, and as instantly made him ashamed that he had forgotten. In the same rush of anger he remembered that he had been kidnapped, and that now there was no one left to take care of his father and the little kids but Bob. That had been hard enough to do when there had been two of them. It was bad enough that he would never see Annie and Kate and Bob and his father again, but far worse that they should be deprived of his hands and his back and his love; and worst of all, they would never know what had happened.

The little girls would only think that he and Kelly had run away, and wonder why, and mourn a little until they forgot about it. But Bob and his father might well think that he'd deserted them . . . most likely of all, that he had gone off with Scranton on his own hook, leaving them all to scrounge for themselves.

There was a well-known ugly term for that among the peasantry of the Earth, expressing all the contempt it felt for any man who abandoned his land, no matter how unrewarding it was, to tread the alien streets and star lanes of a nomad city: it was called, "going Okie."

Chris had gone Okie. He had not done it of his own free will, but his father and Bob and the little girls would never know that. For that matter, it would never have happened had it not been for his own useless curiosity; and neither would the death of poor Kelly, who, Chris now remembered too, had been Bob's dog.

The big man in the hard hat saw his expression close down, and made an impatient gesture. "Listen, Red, I know what you're thinking. What good would it do now if

I said I was sorry? What's done is done; you're on board, and you're going to stay on board. We didn't put the snatch on you either. If you didn't know about the impressment laws, you've got your own ignorance to blame."

"You killed my brother's dog."

"No, I didn't. I've got a bad rip or two under that rag to prove I had reasons to kill him; but I wasn't the guy who did it, and I couldn't have done it, either. But that's done too, and can't be undone. Right now I'm trying to help you, and I've got about three minutes left to do it in, so if you don't shut up and listen it'll be too late. You *need* help, Red; can't you understand that?"

"Why do you bother?" Chris said bitterly.

"Because you're a bright kid and a fighter, and I like that. But that's not going to be enough aboard an Okie city, believe me. You're in a situation now that's totally new to you, and if you've got any skills you can make a career on here, I'll be darned surprised, I can tell you that. And Scranton isn't going to start educating you this far along in your life. Are you smart enough to take some advice, or aren't you? If you aren't, there's no sense in my bothering. You've got about a minute left to think it over."

What the big man said made a bitter dose to have to swallow, but it did seem to make sense. And it did seem likely, too, that the man's intentions were good—otherwise, why would he be taking the trouble? Nevertheless Chris's emotions were in too much of a turmoil for him to trust himself to speak; instead, he merely nodded mutely.

"Good for you. First of all, I'm taking you to see the boss—not the mayor, he doesn't count for much, but Frank Lutz, the city manager. One of the things he'll ask you is what you do, or what you know about. Between now and when we get there, you ought to be thinking up an answer. I don't care what you tell him, but tell him *something*. And it had better be the thing you know the most about, because he'll ask you questions."

"I don't know anything—except gardening, and hunting," Chris said grimly.

"No, no, that's not what I mean! Don't you have any book subjects? Something that might be useful in space? If you don't, he'll put you to work pitching slag—and you won't have much of a lifetime as an Okie."

The cab slowed, and then began to settle.

"And if he doesn't seem interested in what you tell him, *don't* try to satisfy him by switching to something else. No true specialist really knows more than one subject, especially at your age. Stick to the one you picked and try to make it sound useful. Understand?"

"Yes, but—"

"No time left for 'buts.' One other thing: If you ever get into a jam on board this burg, you'll need to know somebody to turn to, and it'd better not be Frank Lutz. My name is Frad Haskins—not Fred but Frad, F-R-A-D."

The cab hovered for a moment, and then its hull grated against the cobblestones and the doors slid open. Chris was thinking so hard and in so many directions that for a long moment he did not understand what the press-gang chief was trying to convey by introducing himself. Then the realization hit home, and Chris was struggling unsuccessfully to blurt out his thanks and give his own name at the same time.

"Destination, gentlemen," the Tin Cabby said primly.

"Shaddup. Come along, Red."

Frank Lutz, the city manager of Scranton-in-flight, reminded Chris instantly of a skunk—but by this Chris meant not at all what a city boy would have meant by a skunk. Lutz was small, sleek, handsome, and plump, and even sitting behind his desk, he gave an appearance of slight clumsiness. As he listened to Haskins' account of the two impressments, even his expression had something of the nearsighted amiability of the woods pussy; but as Haskins finished, the city manager looked up suddenly—and Chris knew, if he had ever been in any doubt about it before, that this animal was also dangerous . . . and never more so than when it seemed to be turning its back.

"That impressment law was a nuisance. But I suppose we'll have to make a show of maintaining our pickups until we get to some part of space where the police aren't so thick."

"We've got no drug for them, that's for sure," Haskins agreed obscurely.

"That's not a public subject," Lutz said, with such deadly coldness that Chris was instantly convinced that the slip, whatever its meaning, had been intended by Haskins for his own ears. The big man was a lot more devious than his size or his bluffness suggested. That much was becoming clearer every minute. "As for these samples, I don't suppose they can do anything. They never can."

The deceptively mild hazel eyes, watery and inoffensive, swung suddenly to bear on the red-neck. "What's your name?"

"Who wants to know? That's what I want to know. You got no right—"

"Don't buck me, bum, I haven't got the time. So you've got no name. Have you a trade?"

"I'm no bum, 'm a puddler," the red-neck said indignantly. "A *steel* puddler."

"Same thing. Anything else?"

"I been a puddler twenty years. 'M a Master Puddler, fair an' square. I got seniority, see? I don' need to be anything else, see? I got a trade. Nobody knows it like I do."

"Been working lately?" the city manager said quietly.

"No. But I got seniority. And a card. 'M no bum, 'm a craftsman, see?"

"If you were a Genius Puddler I couldn't use you, buddy . . . not even if, as and when we ever see any steel again. This is a Bessemer-process town, and it was one even back when you were an apprentice. You didn't notice? Tough. Barney, Huggins, this one's for the slag heaps."

This order was not executed without a good deal of renewed shouting and struggling, during which Lutz looked back down at his papers, as obviously harmless a critter as a skunk which had just happened upon a bird's egg and was wondering if it might bite, his small hands moving tentatively. When the noise was over, he said:

"I hope your luck was better, Frad. How about it, sonny? Have you got a trade?"

"Yes," Chris said instantly. "Astronomy."

"What? At your age?" The city manager stared at Haskins. "What's this, Frad—another one of your mercy projects? Your judgment gets worse every day."

"It's all news to me, boss," Haskins said with complete and obvious honesty. "I thought he was just a scratcher. He never said anything else to me."

The city manager drummed delicately on the top of his desk. Chris held his breath. His claim was ridiculous and he knew it, but he had been able to think of nothing else to answer which would have had a prayer of interesting the boss of a nomad city. Insofar as he had been able to stay awake past dusk, Chris had read a little of everything, and of his reading he had retained best the facts and theories of history; but Haskins had cautioned him to espouse something which might be useful aboard an Okie city, and plainly it didn't qualify. The fragments of economics he had picked up from his father might possibly have been more useful had there been more of them, and those better integrated into *recent* history, but his father had never been well enough to do that job since Chris had reached the age of curiosity. He was left with nothing but his smattering of astronomy, derived from books, most of which had been published before he was born, and from many nights spent lying on his back in the fields, breathing clover and counting meteors.

But he had no hope that it would work. A nomad city would need astronomy for navigation, primarily, a subject about which he knew nothing—indeed he lacked even the rudimentary trigonometry necessary to approach it. His knowledge of the parent subject, astronomy, was purely descriptive, and would become obsolete the minute Scranton was far enough away from the Sun to make the constellations hard to recognize—which in fact had probably happened already.

Nevertheless, Frank Lutz seemed to be a little bit baffled, for the first time. He said slowly:

"A Lakebranch kid who claims he's an astronomer! Well, at least it's new. Frad, you've let the kid sell you a hobby. If he ever got through grammar school I'll eat your tin hat, paint and all."

"Boss, I swear I never heard a word of all this until now."

"Hmm. All right, sonny. Name the planets, going outward from the Sun."

That was easy, but the next ones would surely be harder. "Mercury, Venus, Earth, Mars, Jupiter, Saturn, Uranus, Neptune, Pluto, Proserpina."

"You left out a few didn't you?"

"I left out about five thousand," Chris said, as steadily as he could manage. "You said planets—not asteroids or satellites."

"All right, what's the biggest satellite? And the biggest asteroid?"

"Titan, and Ceres."

"What's the nearest fixed star?"

"The Sun."

The city manager grinned, but he did not seem to be much amused. "Oho. Well, it won't be, not much longer. How many months in a light-year?"

"Twelve, just like any other year. A light-year isn't a measure of time, it's a measure of distance—the distance light travels in a year. Months don't have anything to do with it. You might as well ask how many weeks there are in an inch."

"There are fifty-two weeks to the inch—or it'll seem like that, once you're as old as I am." Lutz drummed on the desk again. "Where'd you get all this stuff? You won't pretend you had any schooling in Lakebranch, I hope?"

"My father taught almost all his life at the University, till it was shut down," Chris said. "He was the best there was. I got most of it from him. The rest I read about, or got from observation, and paper and pencil."

Here Chris was on firm ground, provided only that he be allowed one lie: the substitution of astronomy for economics. The next question did not bother him in the least, for it was thoroughly expectable:

"What's your name?"

"Crispin deFord," he said reluctantly.

There was a surprised guffaw from the remainder of the audience, but Chris did his best to ignore it. His ridiculous name had been a burden to him through so many childhood fights with the neighbors that he was now able to carry it with patience, though still not very gladly. He was surprised, however, to see Haskins raising his bushy bleached eyebrows at him with every evidence of renewed interest. What that meant, Chris had no idea; the part of his brain that did his guessing was almost worn out already.

"Check that, somebody," the city manager said. "We've got a couple of people left over from the S. U. faculty, at least. By Hoffa, Boyle Warner was a Scranton prof, wasn't he? Get him up here, and let's close this thing out."

"What's the matter, boss?" Haskins said, with a broad grin. "Running out of trick questions?"

The city manager smiled back, but again the smile was more than a little frosty. "You could call it that," he said, with surprising frankness. "But we'll see if the kid can fool Warner."

"The ole bassar must be good for something," somebody behind Chris mumbled. The voice was quiet, but the city manager heard it; his chin jerked up, and his fist struck a sudden, terrible blow on the top of his desk.

"He's good for getting us where we're going, and don't you forget it! Steel is one thing, but stars are another—we may never see another lie or another ingot without Boyle. Next to him we're *all* puddlers, just like that red-neck. And that may go for the kid here, too."

"Ah, boss, don't lay it on. What can *he* know?"

"That's what I'm trying to find out," Lutz said, in a white fury. "What do you know about it? Anybody here know what a geodesic is?"

Nobody answered.

"Red, do you know?"

Chris swallowed. He knew the answer, but he found it impossible to understand why the city manager considered it worth all this noise.

"Yes, sir. It's the shortest distance between two points."

"Is that all?" somebody said incredulously.

"It's all there is between us and starvation," Lutz said. "Frad, take the kid below and see what Boyle says about him; on second thought, I don't want to pull Boyle out of the observatory, he must be up to his eyebrows in course-corrections. Get to Boyle as soon as he's got some free time. Find out if there ever was any Professor deFord at S. U.; and then get Boyle to ask the kid some hard questions. *Real* hard. If he makes it, he can be an apprentice. If he doesn't, there are always the slag heaps; this has taken too long already."

CHAPTER THREE:
"Like a Barrel of Scrap"

Even a city which has sloughed off its slums to go space flying has hidey holes, and Chris had lost no time in finding one of his own. He had located it with the simple instinct of a hunted animal going to ground.

Not that anybody was hunting for him—not yet. But something told him that it would be only a matter of time. Dr. Boyle Warner, the city's astronomer, had been more than kind to him, but he had asked hard questions all the same; and these had revealed quickly enough that

Chris's knowledge of astronomy, while extraordinary in a youngster with no formal education worth mentioning, was too meager to be of any help to Dr. Warner or of any use to the city.

Dr. Warner signed him on as an apprentice anyhow, and so reported to the city manager's office, but not without carefully veiled misgivings, and an open warning:

"I can think of very little for you to do around the observatory that would be useful, Crispin, I'm sorry to say. If I so much as set you to work sweeping the place, one of Frank Lutz's henchmen would find out about it sooner or later; and Frank would point out quite legitimately that I don't need so big a fellow as you for so light a task as that. While you're with me, you'll have to appear to be studying all the time."

"I will be studying," Chris said. "That's just what I'd like."

"I appreciate that," Dr. Warner said sadly. "And I sympathize. But Crispin, it can't last forever. Neither I nor anyone else in Scranton can give you in two years the ten years of study that you've missed, let alone any part of what it took me thirty more years to absorb. I'll do my best, but that best can only be a pretense—and sooner or later they'll catch us at it."

After that, Chris already knew, would come the slag heaps—hence the hidey hole. He wondered if they would send Dr. Warner to the slag heaps too. It didn't seem very likely, for the frail, pot-bellied little astrophysicist could hardly last long at the wrong end of a shovel, and besides he was the only navigator the city had. Chris mentioned this guardedly to Frad Haskins.

"Don't you believe it," Frad said grimly. "The fact is that we've got no navigator at all. Expecting an astronomer to navigate is about like asking a chicken to fry an egg. Doc Warner ought to be a navigator's assistant himself, not a navigator-in-chief, and Frank Lutz knows it. If we ever run across another city with a spare *real* navigator to trade, Frank could send Boyle Warner to the slag heaps without blinking an eye. I don't say that he would, but he might."

It could hardly be argued that Haskins knew his boss, and after only one look of his own at Lutz, Chris was more than ready to agree. Officially, Chris continued to occupy the single tiny room at the university dormitory to which he had been assigned as Dr. Warner's apprentice, but he kept nothing there but the books that Dr. Warner lent him, the mathematical instruments from the same source, and the papers and charts that he was supposed to be working on; plus about a quarter of the rough clothing and the even rougher food which the city had issued him as soon as he had been given an official status. The other three-quarters of both went into the hole, for Chris had no intention of letting himself be caught at an official address when the henchmen of Frank Lutz finally came looking for him.

He studied as hard in the hole as he did in the dormitory and at the observatory, all the same. He was firmly determined that Dr. Warner should not suffer for his dangerous kindness if there was anything that Chris could possibly do to avoid it. Frad Haskins, though his visits were rare—he had no real business at the university—detected this almost at once; but he said only:

"I knew you were a fighter."

For almost a year Chris was quite certain that he was making progress. Thanks to his father, for example, he found it relatively easy to understand the economy of the city—probably better than most of its citizens did, and almost certainly better than either Frad Haskins or Dr. Warner. Once aloft, Scranton had adopted the standard economy of all tribes of highly isolated nomad herdsmen, to whom the only real form of wealth is grass: a commune, within which everyone helped himself to what he needed, subject only to the rules which established the status of his job in the community. If Frad Haskins needed to ride in a cab, for instance, he boarded it, and gave the Tin Cabby his social security number—but if, at the end of the fiscal year, his account showed more cab charges than was reasonable for his job, he would hear about it. And if he or anyone else took to hoarding physical goods—no matter whether they were loaves of bread or lock washers, they could not by definition be in anything but short supply on board an Okie city—he would do more than hear about it: The penalties for hoarding of any kind were immediate and drastic.

There was money aboard the city, but no ordinary citizen ever saw it or needed it. It was there to be used exclusively for foreign trade—that is, to bargain for grazing rights, or other privileges and supplies which the city did not and could not carry within the little universe bounded by its spindizzy field. The ancient herdsmen had accumulated gold and jewels for the same reason. Aboard Scranton, the equivalent metal was germanium, but there was actually very little of it in the city's vaults; since germanium had been the universal metal base for money throughout this part of the galaxy ever since space flight had become practical most of the city's currency was paper—the same "Oc dollar" everyone used in trading with the colonies.

All this was new to Chris in the specific situation in which he now found himself, but it was far from new to him in principle. As yet, however, he was too lowly an object in Scranton to be able to make use of his understanding; and remembering the penury into which his father had been driven, back on Earth, he was far from sure that he would ever have a use for it.

As the year passed, so also did the stars. The city manager, according to Haskins, had decided not to cruise anywhere inside "the local group"—an arbitrary sphere fifty light-years in diameter, with Sol at its center. The planetary systems of the local group had been heavily settled during the great colonial Exodus of 2375—2400, mostly by people from Earth's fallen Western culture who were fleeing the then world-wide Bureaucratic State. It was Lutz's guess—quickly confirmed by challenges received by Scranton's radio station—that the density of older Okie cities would be too high to let a newcomer into competition.

During this passage, Chris busied himself with trying to identify the stars involved by their spectra. This was the only possible way to do it under the circumstances, for of course their positions among the constellations changed rapidly as the city overtook them. So did the constellations themselves, although far more slowly.

It was hard work, and Chris was often far from sure his identifications were correct. All the same, it was impressive to know that those moving points of light all around him were the almost legendary stars of colonial times, and even more impressive to find that he had one of those storied suns in the small telescope. Their very names echoed with past adventure: Alpha Centauri, Wolf 359, RD—4°4048', Altair, 61 Cygni, Sirius, Kruger 60, Procyon, 40 Eridani. Only a very few of these, of course, lay anywhere near the city's direct line of flight—indeed, many of them were scattered "astern" (that is, under the keel of the city), in the imaginary hemisphere on the

other side of his home Sun. But most of them were at
least visible from here, and the rest could be photo-
graphed. The city, whatever Chris thought of it as a home,
had to be given credit for being a first-class observatory
platform.

How he saw the stars was another matter, and one that
was a complete mystery to him. He knew that Scranton
was now traveling at a velocity many times that of light,
and it seemed to him that under these circumstances there
should have been no stars at all still visible in the city's
wake, and those to the side and even straight ahead should
be suffering considerable distortion. Yet in fact he could
see no essential change in the aspect of the skies. To
understand how this could be so would require at least
some notion of how the spindizzies worked, and on this
theory Dr. Warner's explanations were even more unclear
than usual . . . so much so that Chris suspected him of not
understanding it any too well himself.

Lacking the theory, Chris's only clue was that the stars
from Scranton-in-flight looked to him much as they always
had from a field in the Pennsylvania backwoods, where
the surrounding Appalachians had screened him from the
sky glare of Scranton-on-the-ground. From this he deduct-
ed that the spindizzy screen, though itself invisible, cut
down the apparent brightness of the stars by about three
magnitudes, as had the atmosphere of the Earth in the
region where Chris had lived. Again he didn't know the
reason why, but he could see that the effect had some
advantages. For instance, it blanked out many of the
fainter stars completely to the naked eye, thus greatly
reducing the confusing multitudes of stars which would
otherwise have been visible in space. Was that really an
unavoidable effect of the spindizzy field—or was it instead
something imposed deliberately, as an aid to navigation?

"I'm going to ask Lutz that question myself," Dr. Warner said, when Chris proposed it. "It's no help to me; in
fact, it takes all the fun out of being an astronomer in free
space. And there's no time like the present. Come along,
Crispin—I can't very well leave you in charge, and the
only other logical place for Lutz to see an apprentice of
mine is with me."

It seemed to Chris that nobody aboard Scranton ever
said anything officially to him but "Come along," but he
went. He did not relish the prospect of seeing the city
manager again, but it was probably true that he would be

safer under the astronomer's wing than he would be any-place else; in fact, he was both surprised by, and a little admiring of, Dr. Warner's boldness.

But if Boyle Warner ever asked the question, Chris never heard the answer.

Frank Lutz did not believe in making people who came to see him on official business wait in ante-chambers. It wasted his time as well as theirs, and he at least had none to waste—and they had better not have. Nor were there many details of his administration that he thought he needed to keep secret, not now that those who might oppose him no longer had any place to run to. To remind his people who was boss, he occasionally kept the mayor waiting out of earshot, but everyone else came and went quite freely when he held court.

Dr. Warner and Chris sat in the rearmost benches— for Lutz's "court" was actually held in what once had been a courtroom—and waited patiently to work their way for-ward to the foot of the city manager's desk. In the process, the astronomer fell into a light doze; Frank Lutz's other business was nothing to him, and in addition his hearing was no better than usual for a man his age. Both Chris's curiosity and his senses, on the other hand, shared the acuity of his youth, and the latter had been sharpened by almost a lifetime of listening and watching for the rustle of small animals in the brush; and the feeling of personal danger with which Frank Lutz had filled him on their first encounter was back again, putting a razor edge upon hearing and curiosity alike.

"We're in no position to temporize," the city manager was saying. "This outfit is big—the biggest there is—and it's offering us a fair deal, The next time we meet it, it may not be so polite, especially if we give it any sass this time around. I'm going to talk turkey with them."

"But what do they want?" someone said. Chris craned his neck, but he did not know the man who had spoken. Most of Lutz's advisers were nonentities, in any event—except for those like Huggins, who were outright thugs.

"They want us to veer off. They've analyzed our course and say we're headed for a region of space that they'd had staked out long before we showed up. Now this, let me point out, is actually all to the good. They have a prelimi-nary survey of the area, and we don't—everything ahead of *us* is all alike, until we've had some experience of it. Furthermore, one of the things they offer in payment is a new course which they say will take us into an iron-bearing star cluster, very recently settled, where there's likely to be plenty of work for us."

"So *they* say."

"And I believe them," Lutz said sharply. "Everything they've said to me, they've also said on the open air, by Dirac transmitter. The cops have heard every word, not only locally, but wherever in the whole universe that there's a Dirac transceiver. Big as they are, they're not going to attempt to phony an open contract. The only question in my mind is, what ought to be the price?"

He looked down at the top of his desk. Nobody seemed to have any suggestions. Finally he looked up again and smiled coldly.

"I've thought of several, but the one I like best is this: They can help us run up our supplies. We haven't got the food to reach the cluster that they've designated—I'd hoped we'd make a planetfall long before we had to go that far—but that's something that they can't know, and that I'm not going to tell them."

"They'll know when you ask for the food, Frank—"

"I'm not such an idiot. Do you think any Okie city would ever sell food at *any* price? You might as well try to buy oxygen, or money. *I'm* going to ask them to throw in some minor piece of machinery or other, it doesn't matter what, and two or three technicians to man and service it; and as an evidence of good faith, I'll offer back for these oh-so-valuable technicians a big batch of our people—people that are of no use to us. There won't be so many of them that a town *that* size would have any difficulty in absorbing them—but to us, they'll represent just the number of extra mouths to feed that would prevent us from reaching the iron-bearing cluster that Amalfi's offered to guide us to. Food will never be mentioned. It'll be just a standard swap of personnel, under the usual Okie 'rule of discretion.' "

There was a long minute of respectful silence. Even Chris was forced to admire the ingenuity of the scheme, insofar as he understood it. Frank Lutz smiled again and added:

"And this way we get rid of every single one of those useless bums and red-necks we had to take aboard under the impressment laws. The cops will never know it; and neither will Amalfi; he has to carry enough food and, ah, medicines to maintain a crew of well over a million. He'll swallow another three hundred yokels without as much effort as you'd swallow an aspirin, and probably think it a fair trade for two technies and a machine that are useless to him. The most beautiful part of it all is, it might even *be* a fair trade—which brings me to my next point—"

But Chris did not stay to hear the next point. After a last, quick, regretful glance at the drowsing astronomer who had befriended him, he stole out of the court as silently as any poacher, and went to ground.

The hole was structurally an accident. Located in a warehouse at the edge of the city nearest the university, it was in the midst of an immense stack of heavy crates which evidently had shifted during the first few moments of take-off, thus forming a huge and unpredictable three-dimensional maze which no map of the city would ever show. By worrying a hole in the side of one crate with a pocketknife, Chris had found that it contained mining machinery (and, evidently, so did all the others, since they all bore the same stenciled code number). The chances were good, he thought, that the crates would not be unstacked until Scranton made its first planetfall; the city in flight would have nothing to dig into.

Nor did Chris have any reason to leave the hole, at least for now. The warehouse itself had a toilet he could visit, and seemed to be unfrequented; and of course it didn't need a watchman—Who would bother to steal heavy machinery, and where would they run with it? If he was careful not to set any fires with his candles—for the hole, although fairly well ventilated through the labyrinth, was always pitch dark—he would probably be safe until his food ran out. After that, he would have to take his chances . . . but he had been a poacher before.

But nothing in his plans had allowed for a visitor.

He heard the sounds of the approach from some dist and blew out his candle at once. Maybe it was on casual prowler; maybe even only a strayed child—may at the worst, another refugee from Lutz's flesh-tradi deal, looking for a hole. There were plenty of holes amid the piled-up crates, and the way to this one was so complex that two of them could live in the heap for weeks without encountering each other.

But his heart sank as he realized how quietly the footsteps were approaching. The newcomer was negotiating

the maze with scarcely a false turn, let alone a noisy
blunder.

Someone knew where he was—or at least knew where
his hole was.

The footsteps became louder, slowed, and stopped. Now
he could distinctly hear someone breathing.

Then the beam of a hand torch caught him full in the
face.

"Hell, Chris. Make a light, huh?"

The voice was that of Frad Haskins. Anger and relief
flooded through Chris at the same time. The big man had
been his first friend, and almost his name-brother—for
after all, Fradley O. Haskins is not much more ridiculous
a name than Crispin deFord—but that blow of light in the
face had been like a betrayal.

"I've only got candles. If you'd set the flashlight on end,
it'd be just as good—maybe better."

"Okay." Haskins sat down on the floor, placing the
torch on the small crate Chris used for a table, so that it
made a round spot of light on the boards overhead. "Now
tell me something. Just what do you think you're doing?"

"Hiding," Chris said, a little sullenly.

"I can see that. I knew what this place was from the
day I saw you toting books into it. I have to keep in
practice on this press-gang dodge; I'll need it some day on
some other planet. But in your case, what's the sense?
Don't you *want* to be transferred to a bigger city?"

"No, I don't. Oh, I can't say that Scranton's been like
home to me. I hate it. I wish I could really go home. But
Frad, at least I'm getting to know the place. I already
knew part of it, back while it was on the ground. I don't
want to be kidnapped twice, and go through it all again—
ard some city where I don't know even as much about
reets as I knew about Scranton—and maybe find out
I hate it even worse. And I don't like being swapped,
—like a barrel of scrap."

Vell, maybe I can't blame you for that—though it's
ndard Okie procedure, not anything that Lutz thought
p in his own head. Do you know where the 'rule of
discretion' came from?"

"No."

"From the trading of players between baseball teams.
It's that old—more than a thousand years. The contract law
that sanctions it is supposed to be a whale of a lot older,
even."

"All right," Chris said. "It could even be Roman, I suppose. But Frad, I'm not a barrel of scrap and I still don't want to be swapped."

"Now that part of it," the big man said patiently, "is just plain silly. You've got no future in Scranton, and you ought to know it by now. On a really big town you could probably find something to do—and the least you'll get is some schooling. All our schools are closed, for good and forever. And another thing: We've only been aloft a year, and it's a cinch we've got some hard times ahead of us. An older town would be a darn sight safer—not absolutely safe, no Okie ever is; but safer."

"Are you going, too?"

Haskins laughed. "Not a chance. Amalfi must have ten thousand of the likes of me. Besides, Lutz needs me. He doesn't know it, but he does."

"Well . . . then . . . I'd rather stay with you."

Haskins smote one fist into the other palm in exasperation. "Look, Red . . . Cripes, what do you say to this kid? Thanks, Chris; I—I'll remember that. But if I'm lucky, I'll have a boy of my own some day. This isn't the day. If you don't face facts right now, you aren't going to get a second chance. Listen, I'm the only guy who knows where you are, yet, but how long can that last? Do you know what Frank will do when he roots you out of a hole full of cached food? *Think*, please, will you?"

Chris's stomach felt as though he had just been thrown out of a window.

"I guess I never thought of that."

"You need practice. I don't blame you for that. But I'll tell you what Frank will do: *He'll have you shot*. And nobody else in town'll even raise an eyebrow. In the Okie lawbook, hoarding food comes under the head of endangering the survival of the city. Any such crime is a capital crime—and not only in Scranton, either."

There was a long silence. At last, Chris said quietly:

"All right. Maybe it is better this way. I'll go."

"That's using your head," Haskins said gruffly. "Come on, then. We'll tell Frank you were sick. You *look* sick, right enough. But we'll have to hustle—the gigs leave in two hours."

"Can I take my books?"

"They're not yours, they're Boyle Warner's," Fred said impatiently. "I'll get 'em back to him later. Pick up the torch and let's go—you'll find plenty of books where you're going." He stopped suddenly and glared at Chris through the dim light. "Not that you care where you're going! You haven't even asked the name of the town."

This was true; he had not asked, and now that he came to think about it, he didn't care. But his curiosity came forward even through the gloom of the maze, and even through his despair. He said, "So I haven't. What is it?"

"New York."

CHAPTER FOUR: Schoolroom in the Sky

The sight from the gig was marvelous beyond all imagination: an island of towers, as tall as mountains, floating in a surfaceless, bottomless sea of stars. The gig was rocket-powered, so that Chris was also seeing the stars from space in all their jeweled majesty for the first time in his life; but the silent pride of the great human city, aloof in its spindizzy bubble—which was faintly visible from the outside—completely took precedence. Behind the gig, Scranton looked in comparison like a scuttleful of old stove bolts.

The immigrants were met at the perimeter by a broad-shouldered, crew-cut man of about forty, in a uniform which made all of Chris's hackles rise; cops were natural enemies, here as everywhere. But the perimeter sergeant, who gave his name as Anderson, did no more than herd them all into separate cubicles for interviews.

There was nobody in Chris's cubicle but Chris himself. He was seated before a small ledge or banquette, facing a speaker grille which was set into the wall. From this there issued the questions, and into this he spoke his answers. Most of the questions were simple matters of vital statistics—his name, his age, point of origin, date of boarding Scranton and so on—but he rather enjoyed answering them; the fact was that never before in his life had anyone been interested enough in him to ask them. In fact he himself did not know the answers to some of them.

It was also interesting to speculate on the identity of the questioner. It was a machine, Chris was almost sure, and one speaking not from any vocabulary of prerecorded

words sounded by a human voice, but instead from some
store of basic speech sounds which it combined and
recombined as it went along. The result was perfectly
understandable and nonmechanical, carrying many of the
stigmata of real human speech—for example, the sentences emerged in natural speech rhythms, and with
enough inflection so that key words and even punctuation
could be distinguished—yet all the same he would never
have mistaken it for a human voice. Whatever the difference was, he thought of it as though the device were
speaking all in capital letters.

Even in an age long dominated by computers, to the
exclusion, in many cases, of human beings, Chris had
never heard of a machine with intelligence enough to be
able to construct its speech in this fashion, let alone one
intelligent enough to be given the wide discretionary lati-
tude implied by the conduct of this interview. He had
never before heard of a machine which referred to itself
as "we," either.

"How much schooling had you had before you
were impressed, Mr. deFord?"

"Almost none."

"Did you receive any schooling aboard Scranton?"

"A little. Actually it was only just tutoring—the kind of
thing I used to get from my father, when he felt up to it."

"It is rather late to start, but we can arrange
schooling for you if you wish—"

"Boy, do I!"

"That is the question. An accelerated secondary
education is physically very trying. It is possible
that you would have no need of it here, depending
upon your goals. Do you wish to be a passenger, or a
citizen?"

On the surface, this was a perfectly easy question. What
Chris most wanted to do was to go home and back to
being a citizen of nothing more complicated than the
Commonwealth of Pennsylvania, Western Common Market, Terran Confederation. He had had many bad nights
spent wondering how his family was doing without him,
and what they had thought of his disappearance, and he
was sure that he would have many more. Yet by the same
token, by now they had doubtless made whatever adjustment was possible for them to the fact of his being gone;
and an even more brutal fact was that he was now sitting
on a metropolis of well over a million people which was

floating in empty space a good twenty light-years away from Sol, bound for some destination he could not even guess. This monstrous and wonderful construct was not going to turn itself into his personal Tin Cabby simply because he said he wanted to go home, or for any other reason.

So if Chris was stuck with the city, he reasoned, he might as well be a citizen. There was no point in being a passenger when he had no idea where he was going, or whether it would be worth the fare when he got there. Being a citizen, on the other hand, sounded as though it conferred some privileges; it would be worth while knowing what they were. It would also be worth knowing whether or not the two terms the machine had used carried some special technical meaning of which he ought to be wary.

"Who'm I talking to?"

"THE CITY FATHERS."

This reply nearly threw him completely off course; he tabled the baker's dozen of questions it raised only by a firm exercise of will. What was important about it right now was that it told him that he was talking to a responsible person—whatever the meaning of "Person" might be when one is dealing with a machine with a collective personality.

"Am I entitled to ask questions too?"

"YES, WITHIN LIMITS IT WOULD TAKE TOO LONG TO DEFINE FOR THE PURPOSE OF THIS INTERVIEW. IF YOU ASK US QUESTIONS, WE WILL AT PRESENT EITHER ANSWER OR NOT ANSWER."

Chris thought hard. The City Fathers, despite their mention of time limitations, waited him out without any evidence of impatience. Finally he said:

"What's the most important single difference between a passenger and a citizen."

"A CITIZEN LIVES AN INDEFINITELY PROLONGED LIFE."

Nothing they could have said could have been farther from any answer that Chris might have expected. It was so remote from anything he had ever thought or read about that it was almost meaningless to him. Finally he managed to ask cautiously: "How long is indefinitely?"

"INDEFINITELY LONG. OUR PRESENT MAYOR WAS BORN IN 2998. THE AGE OF THE OLDEST CITY MAN OF WHOM WE HAVE ANY RECORD IS FIVE HUNDRED AND THIRTEEN YEARS, BUT IT IS STATISTICALLY DEFENSIBLE TO ASSUME THAT

THERE ARE SEVERAL OLDER SPECIMENS, SINCE THE FIRST OF
THE ANTIDEATH DRUGS WAS DISCOVERED IN THE YEAR
2018."

Antideath drugs! The dose was now entirely too big to
swallow. It was all Chris could do to cling to the one
microgram of it that seemed to have some meaning for
him right now: that were he to live a long time—a very
long time—he might some day find his way back home, no
matter how far he had wandered in the meantime. All the
rest would have to be thought through later. He said:

"I want to be a citizen."

"IT IS REQUIRED THAT WE INFORM YOU THAT YOU ARE PER-
MITTED TO CHANGE YOUR MIND UNTIL YOUR EIGHTEENTH
BIRTHDAY, BUT THAT A DECISION TO BECOME A PASSENGER
MAY NOT THEREAFTER BE RESCINDED, EXCEPT BY SPECIAL
ORDER OF THE MAYOR." A thin slot which Chris had not
noticed until now suddenly spat out upon the banquette a
long white card. "THIS IS YOUR CITY REGISTRATION, WHICH
IS USED TO OBTAIN FOOD, CLOTHING, HOUSING AND OTHER
NECESSITIES. WHEN IT IS REJECTED ON PRESENTATION, YOU
WILL KNOW THAT THE GOODS OR SERVICES YOU HAVE
CLAIMED HAVE BEEN DISALLOWED. THE CARD IS INDESTRUC-
TIBLE EXCEPT BY CERTAIN SPECIAL TECHNIQUES, BUT WE
ADVISE YOU NOT TO LOSE IT, SINCE FOUR TO SIX HOURS
WILL ELAPSE BEFORE IT CAN BE RETURNED TO YOU. IT IS
PRESENTLY VALIDATED FOR ACCELERATED SCHOOLING. IF
YOU HAVE NO FURTHER QUESTIONS, YOU MAY LEAVE."

The accelerated schooling to which the City Fathers
had remanded Chris did not at first seem physically stren-
uous at all. In fact it seemed initially to be no more
demanding than sleeping all day might be. (This to Chris
was a Utopian notion; he had never had the opportunity
to try sleeping as a career, and so had no idea how
intolerably exhausting it is.)

The "schoolroom" was a large, gray, featureless chamber devoid of blackboard or desk; its only furniture consisted of a number of couches scattered about the floor.
Nor were there any teachers; the only adults present were
called monitors, and their duties appeared to be partly
those of an usher, and partly those of a nurse, but none
pertinent to teaching in any sense of the term Chris had
ever encountered. They conducted you to your couch and
helped you to fit over your head a bright metal helmet
which had inside it what seemed to be hundreds of tiny,

extremely sharp points which bit into your scalp just
enough to make you nervous, but without enough pressure
to break the skin. Once this gadget, which was called a
toposcope, was adjusted to their satisfaction, the monitors
left, and the room began to fill with the gray gas.

The gas was like a fog, except that it was dry and
faintly aromatic, smelling rather like the dried leaves of
mountain laurel that Bob had liked to add sparingly to
rabbit stews. But like a thick fog, it made it impossible to
see the rest of the room until the session was over, when it
was sucked out with a subdued roar of blowers.

Thus Chris could never decide whether or not he actually slept while class was in session. The teaching technique, to be sure, was called hypnopaedia, an ancient word
from still more ancient Greek roots which when translated
literally meant "sleep-teaching." And, to be sure, it filled
your head with strange voices and strange visions which
were remarkably like dreams. Chris also suspected that
the gray gas not only cut off his vision, but also his other
senses; otherwise he should surely have heard such random sounds as the coughing of other students, the movements of the monitors, the whir of the ventilators, the
occasional deep sounds of the city's drivers, and even the
beating of his own heart; but none of these came through,
or if they did, he did not afterwards have any memory of
them. Yet the end result of all this was almost surely not
true sleep, but simply a divorcing of his mind from every
possible bodily distraction which might have come between him and his fullest attention to the visions and
voices which were poured directly into his mind through
the shining helmet of the toposcope.

It was easy to understand why no such distraction could
be tolerated, for the torrent of facts that came from the
memory cells of the City Fathers into the prickly helmet
was overwhelming and merciless. More than once, Chris
saw ex-Scrantonites, all of them older than he was, being
supported by monitors out of the classroom at the end of
a session in a state closely resembling the kind of epileptic
fit called "petit mal" ... nor were they ever allowed back
on their couches again. He himself left the sessions in a
curious state of wobbly, washed-out detachment which
became more and more marked every day, despite the
tumbler of restorative drink which was the standard antidote for the gray gas: a feeling of weakness which no
amount of sleep seemed to make up for.

The drink tasted funny, furthermore, and besides, it made him sneeze. But on the day after he had refused it for the first time, the memory banks decanted a double dose of projective Riemannian geometry, and he awoke to find four monitors holding him down on the couch during the last throes of a classical Jacksonian seizure.

His education nearly stopped right there. Luckily, he had the sense to admit that he had skipped drinking the anticonvulsant drug the day before; and the records of the patterns of electrical activity of his brain which the toposcope had been taking continued to adjudge him a good risk. He was allowed back into the hall—and after that he was no longer in any doubt that learning can be harder physical labor than heaving a shovel.

The voices and the visions resumed swarming gleefully inside his aching head.

In retrospect, Chris found Okie history the least difficult subject to absorb, because the part of it dealing with the early years of the cities, and in particular with what had happened on Earth before the first of the cities had left the ground, was already familiar to him. Nevertheless he was now hearing it for the first time from the Okie point of view, which omitted great swatches which an Earthman would have considered important, and instead brought to the fore for study many events of which Chris had never heard but which obviously were essential for the understanding of how the cities had gone into space and prospered in it. It was, perhaps predictably, like seeing the past life of the Earth through the wrong end of a telescope.

As the memory banks told the story (without the pictures and sounds and other sensations, which, though they were so vivid as to become at once a part of Chris's immediate experience, could not possibly be reproduced in print), it went like this:

"The exploration of the solar system was at first primarily the province of the military, who alone could demand the enormous sums of money necessary for space travel under rocket power, which is essentially a bruteforce method of propulsion directly dependent upon how much power is thrown away. The highest achievement of this phase was the construction of a research and observation station upon Proserpina II, the second satellite of the most remote of all the planets from Sol. Proserpina Station was begun in 2016; it was, however, still not completed when it was abandoned temporarily twenty-eight years later.

"The reasons for the abandonment of Proserpina Station and all other solar system colonies at this time may be found in the course of contemporary Terrestrial politics. Under the relentless pressure of competition from the USSR and its associated states, the Earth's Western culture had undertaken to support a permanent war economy, under the burden of which its traditional libertarian political institutions were steadily eroded away. By the beginning of the twenty-first century it was no longer realistically possible to see any difference between the rival cultures, although their outward forms of government continued to be called by different names. Both were police states in which the individual citizen had lost all right to juridical defense, and both operated under a totally controlled economy. In the West, the official term for this form of public policy was "anti-Communism"; in the East it was called "anti-Fascism," and both terms were heavily laden with mob emotion. The facts of the matter, however, were that neither state was economically either fascist or communist, and that as economic systems neither fascism nor communism has ever been tried in recorded Terrestrial history.

"It was during this period that two Western research projects under the direction of the Alaskan senator Bliss Wagoner discovered the basic inventions upon which the second phase of space flight was to be based. The first of these was the Dillon-Wagoner gravitronpolarity generator, now known as the spindizzy, which was almost immediately developed into an interstellar drive. The second was ascomycin, the first of the anti-agathics, or death-postponing drugs. The first interstellar expedition was launched from the Jovian satellary system in 2021 under Wagoner's personal direction, although Wagoner himself was arrested and executed for his complicity in this 'treasonable' event. Though no record exists of the fate of this expedition, it is certain that it survived, since the second expedition, more than three hundred and fifty years later, found the planets of the stars of the local group well scattered with human beings speaking recognizable Terrestrial languages.

"At this time an attempt was made to settle the rivalry between the two power blocs by still another personal pact between their respective leaders, President MacHinery of the Western Common Market and Premier Erdsenov of the USSR. This took place in 2022, and the subsequent Cold Peace provided little incentive for space flight. In 2027 MacHinery was assassinated, and Erdsenov proclaimed himself premier and president of a United Earth; however, Erdsenov was himself assassinated in 2032. During this same year, an underground Western group calling itself the Hamiltonians succeeded in escaping from the solar system in a large number of small spindizzy-powered craft which they had built from funds collected secretly to finance a supposed new American revolution, thus leaving behind the vast majority of their followers. No survivors of the Hamiltonian exodus have thus far been found; they succeeded, however, in escaping the Terror, the worldwide program by which a United Earth government was actually established for the first time.

"One of the first acts of this government, now called the Bureaucratic State, was the banning in 2039 of spaceflight and all associated sciences. The existing colonies on the planets and satellites of the solar system were not evacuated home, but were simply cut off and abandoned. The consolidation of the State proceeded rapidly, and historians generally agree that the fall of the West must be dated no later than the year 2105. Thus began a period of systematic oppression and exploitation unmatched on Earth even by the worst decades of the Roman Empire.

"In the meantime the interstellar exiles continued to consolidate new planets and to jump from star to star. In 2289, one such expedition made its first contact with what proved to be a planet of the Vegan Tyranny, an interstellar culture which, we now know, had ruled most of this quadrant of the galaxy for eight to ten thousand years, and was still in the process of expanding. The Vegans were quick to see potential rivals even in these unorganized and badly supplied colonists, and made a concerted attempt to stamp out all the colonies. However, the distances involved were so vast that the first real engagement of the Vegan War, the battle of Altair, did not occur until 2310. The colonial forces were defeated and scattered, but not before inflicting sufficient damage to set back the Vegans' timetable for razing the colonial planets—permanently, as it turned out.

"In 2375, the spindizzy was independently rediscovered on Earth and the Thorium Trust's Plant Number Eight used it to wrench its entire installation from off the ground and leave the Earth, using the plant as a self-contained spaceship. Other plants followed, and shortly thereafter, whole cities. Many of these were driven to leave as much by the permanent depression which had settled over the Earth as by the long-established political repressions of the Bureaucratic State. These escaping cities quickly found the earlier Earth colonies among the nearby stars, to which they provided badly needed industrial strength, and with whom they joined forces against Vega. The outcome was both triumphant and shameful. In 2394 one of the escaping cities, Gravitogorsk-Mars, now calling itself the Interstellar Master Traders, was responsible for the sacking of the new Earth colony on Thor V; this act of ferocity earned for them the nickname of 'the Mad Dogs,' but it gradually became a model for dealing with Vegan planets. The capital world of the Tyranny, Vega II, was invested in 2413 by a number of armed cities, including IMT, whose task it was to destroy the many orbital forts surrounding the planet, and by the Third Colonial Navy under Admiral Alois Hrunta, who was charged with occupying Vega II in the event of its surrender. Instead, Admiral Hrunta scorched the planet completely, and led the Third Navy off into an uncharted quadrant with the intention of founding his own interstellar empire. In 2451 the colonial court found him guilty *in absentia* of atrocities and attempted genocide, and an attempt to bring him to justice culminated in 2464 in the battle of BD 40° 4048′, which was destructive but completely indecisive for both sides. The same year Alois Hrunta declared himself Emperor of Space.

"The Exodus of Earth's industrial power had by now become so marked that the Bureaucratic State no longer had a productive base upon which to rest, and it is generally agreed that it collapsed in 2522. In the same year there began the police interregnum, a limited government deriving its powers from a loose confederation based roughly upon the ancient United Nations, but without sufficient popular base or industrial support to control the economy. Realizing, however, that the only hope for the restoration of economic health to Earth lay in the colonists and the free cities, the confederation proclaimed an amnesty for everyone in space, and at the same time instituted a limited but systematic program for the policing of those nomad cities which had begun to prey upon colony planets or upon each other.

"The confederation is still the only operative government in this arm of the galaxy. The poisoning of Alois Hrunta in 3089 was followed by the rapid Balkanization of the Hruntan Empire, which was never even at its best highly cohesive, and although there is a present self-styled Emperor of Space, Arpad Hrunta, his realm does not appear to be of any importance. Effectively, today, law and order in Arm II are provided by the Earth police, and its economy is supported by the migrant cities. Both systems are haphazard and inefficient, and often operate at cross purposes.

"It is impossible to predict when better methods will emerge, or what they will be."

CHAPTER FIVE: "Boy, You Are Dumb!"

While the memory cells chattered and called up dreams, the immense city soared outward among the stars, at what seemed like a breakneck pace after the tentative first explorations of Scranton within the local group. The streets were thronged 24 hours a day with myriads of people hurrying on unimaginable errands; and in addition to the constant flitting of Tin Cabs, there was often the distant but edgy roar of subway trains coursing through tunnels bored through the very granite keel of the city. All of this activity seemed purposeful and even cheerful, but it was also extremely bewildering.

Chris's schooling left him very little time to explore it. Not all of his education was machine education, either, for, as he slowly realized, no one really *learns* anything through hypnopaedia; machine teaching at its best enables the student to accumulate nothing better than facts; it does not show how to tie them together, let alone how to do something with them. To train the intelligence—not just the memory—a real human tutor is required.

The one assigned to Chris, a stocky, fierce, white-haired woman named Dr. Helena Braziller, was far and away the best teacher Chris had ever encountered in his life—and

far and away the worst taskmaster. The City Fathers wore
him out only by taxing his memory; whereas Dr. Braziller
made him *work*.

"The fundamental equation of the Blackett-Dirac
scholium reads as follows:

$$P = \frac{BG^{1/2}U}{2C}$$

where P is magnetic moment, U is angular momentum, C
and G have their usual values, and B is a constant with
the value 0.25 approximately. A first transform of this
identity gives:

$$G = \left(\frac{2PC}{BU}\right)^2$$

which is the usual shorthand form of the primary spindizzy equation, called the Locke Derivation. Blackett, Dirac
and Locke all assumed that it would hold true for large
bodies, such as gas-giant planets and suns. Show on the
blackboard by dimensional analysis why this assumption is
invalid."

As far as Chris was concerned, the answer could have
been much more simply arrived at; Dr. Braziller could just
have told him that this relationship between gravitation
and the spin of a body applied only to electrons and other
submicroscopic objects, and disappeared, for all practical
purposes, in the world of the macrocosm; but that was not
her way. Had she only told him that, it would have come
into his mind as a fact like any other fact—for instance,
like the facts that the memory cells of the City Fathers
were constantly pouring into his ears and eyes—but by her
lights he would not have understood it. She wanted him to
repeat not only the original reasoning of Blackett, Dirac
and Locke, but to see for himself, not just because she
told him so, where they had gone astray, and hence why a
natural law which had first been proposed in the gas-lit,
almost prehistoric year of 1891, and was precisely formulated as the Lande Factor in 1940, nevertheless failed to
lift so much as a grain of sand off the Earth until the year
2019.

"But Dr. Braziller, why isn't it enough to see that they made a mistake? We know that now. Why repeat it?"

"Because that's what all these great men have labored toward: so that you could do it right, yourself. Up until about the thirteenth century, nobody in the world except a few dedicated scholars could do long division; then Fibonacci introduced the Arabic numbers to the West. Now, any idiot can do what it took a great mind to do in those days. Are you going to complain that because Fibonacci found a better way to do long division, you shouldn't be required to learn why it's better? Or that because a great inventor like Locke didn't understand dimensional analysis, you should be allowed to be just as ignorant, after all these years? They spent their lives making things simple for you that were enormously difficult for them, and until you understand the difficulties, you can't possibly understand the simplifications. Go back to the blackboard and try again."

Being in a "live" class had its compensations, though; and one of these was Piggy Kingston-Throop. Piggy—his real name was George, but nobody ever called him that, not even Dr. Braziller—was not much of a prize as a friend and companion, but he was the only member of the small class who was exactly Chris's age; all the others were much younger. From this Chris deduced that Piggy was not a student, which turned out to be true.

Piggy seemed glad enough to encounter someone who was as retarded as he was, whatever the reasons, and who knew less than he did about a great many subjects which were commonplaces to him. And in many ways he was quite a pleasant sort of fellow; blond, plump and affable, with a ready wit and a tendency to be unimpressed by almost everything that other people considered important. In this last, he made a particularly good foil for Chris, who in his ignorance and in the strangeness of his situation often could not help but be earnest to the point of grimness over what later turned out to be trivia.

Not that Chris allowed these differences over value judgments always to be resolved in Piggy's favor; they quarreled over them almost from the beginning. The first of these tangles, which soon proved to be a model for the others, involved the subject of the antiagathic drugs.

"You're going to be a citizen, aren't you, Piggy?"

"Oh, sure. I'm all set."

"I wish I were. My trouble is, I don't even know what I want to do—let alone what I'm good at."

Piggy turned and stared at him. They had paused on the way from school on the Tudor Tower Place bridge leading over 42nd Street. Long ago, the view from here across First Avenue to the East River had been blocked by the UN Building, but that had been demolished during the Terror, and there was nothing to mark where it had stood but a plaza; and on the far side of that, starry space itself.

"What do you mean, *do?*" Piggy said. "Oh, maybe you'll have a little trouble, what with not having been born here. But there's ways around that. Don't believe everything they tell you."

Like many of the things Piggy said, fully 80 per cent of this speech meant nothing to Chris. In self-defense, he could do nothing but answer the question. "You know all this better than I do. But the laws do say pretty clearly that a man has to be good for something before he's allowed to become a citizen and be started on the drug treatments. Let's see; there are supposed to be three ways to go about it; and I ought to have them straight, because I just had them put into my head a few days ago."

He concentrated a moment. He had discovered a useful trick for dredging up the information which had been implanted in his mind from the memory cells: If he half closed his eyes and imagined the gray gas, in a moment he would begin to feel, at least in retrospect, the same somnolence under which the original facts had been imparted, and they would come back in very much the same words. It worked equally well this time; almost at once, he heard his own voice saying, in a curious monotone imitation of the City Fathers:

" 'There are three general qualifications for citizenship. They are: (1) Display of some obviously useful talent, such as computer programming, administration, or another gift worth retaining, as opposed to depending upon the accidents of birth to provide new such men for each succeeding generation; (2) a demonstrable bent toward any intellectual field, including scientific research, the arts and philosophy, since in these fields one lifetime is seldom enough to attain masterhood, let alone put it to the best use; and (3) passage of the Citizenship Tests, which are designed to reveal reserves and potentials in the late-maturing eighteen-year-old whose achievement record is unimpressive. No matter how you slice it, it doesn't sound easy!"

That's only what the City Fathers say, Piggy said scornfully. "What do they know about it? They're only a bunch of machines. They don't know anything about people. Those rules don't even make sense."

"They make sense to me," Chris objected. "It's a cinch the antiagathics can't be given to everybody—from what I hear, they're scarcer than germanium. On Scranton, the big boss wouldn't even allow them to be mentioned in public. So there's got to be *some* way of picking who gets them and who doesn't."

"Why?"

"Why? Well, to begin with, because a city is like an island—an island in the middle of the biggest ocean you can think of, and then some. Nobody can get on, and nobody can get off, except for a couple of guys now and then. If everybody gets this drug and lives forever, pretty soon the place is going to be so crowded that we'll all be standing on each other's feet.

"Ah, cut it out. Look around you. Are *we* all standing on each other's feet?"

"No, but that's because the drugs are restricted, and because not everybody's allowed to have children, either. For that matter, look at you, Piggy—your father and your mother are both big wheels on this town, but you're an only child, and furthermore, the first one they've been allowed to have in a hundred and fifty years."

"Leave them out of this," Piggy growled. "They didn't play their cards right, I'll tell you that. But that's none of your business."

"All right. Take me, then. Unless I turn out to be good for something before I'm eighteen—and I can't think what it would be—I won't be a citizen and I won't get the drugs. Or even if I do get to be a citizen, say by passing the Tests, I'll still have to prove myself useful stock before I'm allowed to have even one kid of my own. That's just the way it has to be when the population has to be kept stable; it's simple economics, Piggy, and there's a subject I think I know something about."

Piggy spat reflectively over the railing, though it was hard to tell whether or not he was expressing an opinion, and if so, whether it referred to economics alone or to the entire argument. "All right, then," he said. "Suppose you get the drugs, and they let you have a kid. Why shouldn't they give the kid the drugs too?"

"Why should they, unless he qualifies?"

"Boy, you *are* dumb! That's what the Citizenship Tests are for, can't you see that? They're an out—an escape hatch, a dodge—and that's all they are. If you don't get in any other way, you get in that way. At least you do if you've got any sort of connections. If you're a nobody, maybe the City Fathers rig the Tests against you—that's likely enough. But if you're a somebody, they're not going to be too tough. If they are, my father can fix their wagon—he programs 'em. But either way, there's no way to study for the Tests, so they're obviously a sell."

Chris was shaken, but he said doggedly: "But they're not supposed to be that kind of test at all. I mean, they're not supposed to show whether or not you're good at dimensional analysis, or history, or some other subject. They're supposed to show up gifts that you were born with, not anything that you got through schooling or training."

"Spindizzy whistle. A test you can't study for is a test you can't pass unless it's rigged—otherwise it doesn't make any sense at all. Listen, Red, if you're so sold on this idea that everybody who gets to take the drugs has to be a big brain, what about the guardain they handed you over to? He's got no kids of his own, and he's nothing but a cop . . . but he's almost as old as the Mayor!"

Up to now, Chris had felt vaguely that he had been holding his own; but this was like a blow in the face.

Chris had originally been alarmed to find that his ID card assigned him lodgings with a family, and horrified when the assignment number turned out to belong to Sgt. Anderson. His first few weeks in the Andersons' apartment—it was in the part of the city once called Chelsea—were prickly with suspicion, disguised poorly by as much formality as his social inexperience would allow.

It soon became impossible, however, to continue believing that the perimeter sergeant was an ogre; and his wife, Carla, was as warm and gracious a woman as Chris had ever met. They were childless, and could not have welcomed Chris more whole-heartedly had he been one of their own. Furthermore, as the City Fathers had of course calculated, Anderson was the ideal guardian for a brand-new young passenger, for few people, even the Mayor, knew the city better.

He was, in fact, considerably more than a cop, for the city's police force was also its defense force—and its Marines, should the need for a raid or a boarding party ever arise. Technically, there were many men on the force who were superior to the perimeter sergeant, but Anderson and one counterpart, a dark taciturn man named Dulany, headed picked squads and were nearly independent of the rest of the police, reporting directly to Mayor Amalfi.

It was this fact which opened the first line of friendly communication between Chris and his guardian. He had not yet even seen Amalfi with his own eyes. Although everyone in the city spoke of him as if they knew him personally, here at last was one man who really did, and saw him several times a week. Chris was unable to restrain his curiosity.

"Well, that's just the way people talk, Chris. Actually hardly anyone sees much of Amalfi, he's got too much to do. But he's been in charge here a long time and he's good at his job; people feel that he's their friend because they trust him."

"But what is he *like?*"

"He's complicated—but then most people are complicated. I guess the word I'm groping for is 'devious.' He sees connections between events that nobody else sees. He sizes up a situation like a man looking at a coat for the one thread that'll make the whole thing unravel. He has to—he's too burdened to deal with things on a stitch-by-stitch basis. In my opinion he's killing himself with overwork as it is."

It was to this point that Chris returned after his upsetting argument with Piggy. "Sergeant, the other day you said that the Mayor was killing himself with overwork. But the City Fathers told me he's several centuries old. On the drugs, he ought to live forever, isn't that so?"

"Absolutely not," Anderson said emphatically: "*Nobody* can live forever. Sooner or later, there'd be an accident, for one thing. And strictly speaking, the drugs aren't a 'cure' for death anyhow. Do you know how they work?"

"No," Chris admitted. "School hasn't covered them yet."

"Well, the memory banks can give you the details—I've probably forgotten most of them. But generally, there are several antiagathics, and each one does a different job. The main one, ascomycin, stirs up a kind of tissue in the body called the reticulo-endothelial system—the white blood corpuscles are a part of it—to give you what's called 'nonspecific immunity.' What that means is that for about the next seventy years, you can't catch any infectious disease. At the end of that time you get another shot, and so on. The stuff isn't an antibiotic, as the name suggests, but an endotoxin fraction—a complex organic sugar called a mannose; it got its name from the fact that it's produced by fermentation, as antibiotics are.

"Another is TATP—triacetyltriparanol. What this does is inhibit the synthesis in the body of a fatty stuff called cholesterol; otherwise it collects in the arteries and causes strokes, apoplexy, high blood pressure and so on. This drug has to be taken every day, because the body goes right on trying to make cholesterol every day."

"Doesn't that mean that it's good for something?" Chris objected tentatively.

"Cholesterol? Sure it is. It's absolutely essential in the development of a fetus, so women have to lay off TATP while they're carrying a child. But it's of no use to men—and men are far more susceptible to circulatory diseases than women.

"There are still two more antiagathics in use now, but they're minor; one, for instance, blocks the synthesis of the hormone of sleep, which again is essential in pregnancy but a thundering nuisance otherwise; that one was originally found in the blood of ruminant animals like cows, whose plumbing is so defective that they'd die if they lay down."

"You mean you *never sleep?*"

"Haven't got the time for it," Anderson said gravely. "Or the need any longer, thank goodness. But ascomycin and TATP between them prevent the two underlying major causes of death: heart diseases and infections. If you prevent those alone, you extend the average lifetime by at least two centuries.

"But death is still inevitable, Chris. If there isn't an accident, there may be cancer, which we can't prevent yet—oh, ascomycin attacks tumors so strongly that cancer doesn't kill people any longer, in fact the drug even offers quite a lot of protection against hard radiation; but cancer can still make life so agonizing that death is the only humane treatment. Or a man can die of starvation, of being unable to get the antiagathics. Or he can die of a bullet—or of overwork. We live long lives in the cities, sure; *but there is no such thing as immortality*. It's as mythical as the unicorn. Not even the universe itself is going to last forever."

This, at last, was the opportunity Chris had been hoping for, though he still hardly knew how to grasp it.

"Are—are the drugs ever stopped, once a man's been made a citizen?"

"Deliberately? I've never heard of such a case," Anderson said, frowning. "Not on our town. If the City Fathers want a man dead, they shoot him. Why let him linger for the rest of his seventy-year stanza? That would be outrageously cruel. What would be the reason for such a procedure?"

"Well, no tests are foolproof. I mean, supposing they make a man a citizen, and then discover that he really isn't—uh—as big a genius as they thought he was?"

The perimeter sergeant looked at Chris narrowly, and there was quite a long silence, during which Chris could clearly hear the pulsing of his own blood in his temples. At last Anderson said slowly:

"I see. It sounds to me like somebody's been feeding you spindizzy whistle. Chris, if only geniuses could become citizens, how long do you think a city could last? The place'd be depopulated in one crossing. That isn't how it works at all. The whole reason for the drugs is to save skills—and it doesn't matter one bit what the skills are. All that matters is whether or not it would be logical to keep a man on, rather than training a new one every four or five decades.

"Take me for an example, Chris. I'm nobody's genius; I'm only a boss cop. But I'm good at my job, good enough so that the City Fathers didn't see any reason to bother raising and training another one from the next generation; they kept this one, which is me; but a cop is, all the same, all I am. Why not? It suits me, I like the work, and when Amalfi needs a boss cop he calls me or Dulany—not any officer on the force, because none of them have the scores of years of experience at this particular job that we do under their belts. When the Mayor wants a perimeter sergeant he calls me; when he wants a boarding squad he calls Dulany; and when he wants a specific genius, he calls a genius. There's one of everything on board this town— partly because it's so big—and so long as the system works, no need for more than one. Or more than X, X being whatever number you need."

Chris grinned. "You seemed to remember the details all right."

"I remembered them all," Anderson admitted. "Or all that they gave me. Once the City Fathers put a thing into your head, it's hard to get rid of."

As he spoke, there was a pure fluting sound, like a brief tune, somewhere in the apartment. The perimeter sergeant's heavy head tipped up; then he, too, grinned.

"We're about to have a demonstration," he said. He was obviously pleased. He touched a button on the arm of his chair.

"Anderson?" a heavy voice said. Chris thought instantly that the father bear in the ancient myth of Goldilocks must have sounded much like that.

"Yes—Here, sir."

"We're coming up on a contract. It looks fairly good to me and the City Fathers, and I'm about to sign it. Better come up here and familiarize yourself with the terms, just in case: This'll be a rough one, Joel."

"Right away." Anderson touched the button, and his grin became broader and more boyish than ever.

"The Mayor!" Chris burst out.

"Yep."

"But what did he mean?"

"That he's found some work for us to do. Unless there's a hitch, we should be landing in just a few days."

CHAPTER SIX: A Planet Called Heaven

Nothing could be seen of Heaven from the air. As the city descended cautiously, the spindizzy field became completely outlined as a bubble of boiling black clouds, glaring with blue-green sheets and slashes of lightning, and awash with streams of sleet and rain. At lower altitude the sleet disappeared, but the rain increased.

After so many months of starlit skies and passing suns, the grumbling, closed-in darkness was oppressive, even alarming. Sitting with Piggy on an old pier at the foot of

Gansevoort Street, from which Herman Melville had
sailed into the distant South Sea marvels of *Typee, Omoo*
and *Mardi,* Chris stared at the globe of thunder around
the city as nervously as though he had never seen weather
before. Piggy, for once, was in no better shape, for he
never *had* seen weather before; this was New York's first
planetfall since he had been born.

How Amalfi could see where he was going was hard to
imagine; but the city continued to go down anyhow; it had
a contract with Heaven, and work was work. Besides,
there would have been no point in waiting for the storms
to clear away. It was always and everywhere like this on
Heaven, except when it was worse. The settlers said so.

"Wow!" Chris said, for the twelfth or thirteenth time.
"What a blitzkrieg of a storm! Look at *that!* How far up
are we still, Piggy?"

"How should I know?"

"D'you think Amalfi knows? I mean really knows?"

"Sure, he knows," Piggy said miserably. "He always
does the tough landings. He never misses."

WHAM!

For a second the whole sphere of the spindizzy field
seemed to be crawling with electric fire. The noise was
enormous and bounded back again and again from the
concrete sides of the towers behind them. It had never
occurred to Chris that a field which could protect a whole
city from the hard radiation, the hard stones and the hard
vacuum of space might pass noise when there was air
outside it as well as inside—but it surely did. The descent
already seemed to have been going on forever.

After a while, Chris found that he was beginning to
enjoy it. Between thunder rolls, he shouted maliciously:

"He must be flying sidewise this time. But he's lost."

"What do you know about it? Shut up."

"*I've* seen thunderstorms. You know what? We're going
to be up here forever. Sailing under a curse, like IMT."
The sky lit. *WHAM!* "Hey, what a beauty!"

"If you don't shut up," Piggy said with desperate grimness, "I'm going to poke you right in the snoot."

This was hardly a very grave threat, for although Piggy
outweighed Chris by some twenty pounds, most of it was
blubber. Amid the excitement of the storm Chris almost
made the mistake of laughing at him; but at the same
instant, he felt the boards of the ancient pier begin to
shudder beneath them to the tramp of steel boots. Star-

tled, he looked back over his shoulder, and then jumped up.

Twenty men in full space armor were behind them, faceless and bristling, like a phalanx of giant robots. One of them came forward, making the planks of the pier groan and squeal under the weight, and suddenly spoke to him.

The voice was blarey and metallic, as though the gain had been turned up in order to shout across acres of ground and through cannonades of thunder, but Chris had no difficulty in recognizing it. The man in the armor was his guardian.

"CHRIS!" The volume of sound suddenly went down a little. "Chris, what are you doing here? And Kingston-Throop's kid! Piggy, you ought to know better than this. We're landing in twenty minutes—and this is a sally port. Beat it—both of you."

"We were only looking," Piggy said defiantly. "We can look if we want."

"I've got no time to argue. Are you going or not?"

Chris pulled at Piggy's elbow. "Come on, Piggy. What's the sense of being in the way?"

"Let go. I'm not in the way. They can walk right by me. I don't have to go just because he says so. He's not *my* guardian—he's only a cop."

A steel arm reached out, and steel pincers opened at the end of it. "Give me your card," Anderson's voice said harshly. "I'll let you know later what you're charged with. If you won't move now, I'll assign two men to move you—though I can't spare the men, and when that winds up on your card you may spend the rest of one lifetime wishing it hadn't."

"Oh, all right. Don't throw your weight around. I'm going."

The bulbous steel arm remained stiffly extended, the pincers menacingly open. "I want the card."

"I said I was going!"

"Then go."

Piggy broke and ran. After a puzzled look at the armored figure of his guardian, Chris followed, dodging around and through the massive blue-steel statues standing impassively along almost the whole length of the pier.

Piggy had already vanished. As Chris ran for home, his mind full of bewilderment, the city grounded in a fanfare of lightning bolts.

Unfortunately, so far as Chris was concerned the City Fathers took no notice of the landing: his schooling went on regardless, so that he got only the most confused picture of what was going on. Though the municipal pipeline, WNYC, had five-minute news bulletins on tap every hour for anyone who wanted to dial into them, decades of the uneventfulness of interstellar travel had reduced the WNYC news bureau to a state of vestigial ineptitude—the pipeline's only remaining real function was the broadcasting of the city's inexhaustible library of music and drama; Chris suspected that most of the citizens found the newscasts almost as dim-witted and uninformative as he did. What little meaningful information he was able to garner, he got from Sgt. Anderson, and that was not very much, for the perimeter sergeant was hardly ever home now; he was too busy consolidating the beachhead on Heaven. Nevertheless, Chris picked up a few fragments, mostly from conversations between the sergeant and Carla:

"What they want us to do is to help them industrialize the planet. It sounds easy, but the kicker is that their social setup is feudal—the sixty-six thousand people they call the Elect are actually only free landholders or franklins, and below *them* there's a huge number of serfs—nobody's ever bothered to count them. The Archangels want it to stay that way even after they've got their heavy industries established."

"It sounds impossible," Carla said.

"It is impossible, as they'll find out when we've finished the job. But that's exactly the trouble. We're not allowed to change planets' social systems, but we can't complete this contract without starting a revolution—a long, slow one, sure, but a revolution all the same. And when the cops come here afterward and find that out, we'll have a Violation to answer for."

Carla laughed musically. "The cops! My dear, is that still a three-letter word for you? What else are you? How many more centuries is it going to take you to get used to it?"

"You know what I mean," Anderson said, frowning. "So all right, I'm a cop. But I'm not an Earth cop, I'm a *city* cop, and that makes all the difference. Well, we'll see. What's for lunch? I've got to go in half an hour."

The storm, as predicted, went on all the time. When he

had the chance, Chris watched the machinery being uncrated and readied, and followed it to the docks at the working perimeter of the city, beyond which always bobbed and crawled a swarm of the glowing swamp vehicles of the colonists of Heaven. Though these came in all sizes, they were all essentially of the same design: a fat cylinder of some transparent cladding, ribbed with metal, provided on both sides with caterpillar treads bearing cleats so large that they could also serve as paddles where the going underfoot became especially sloppy. The shell was airtight, for buoyancy, but Chris was sure that the vessel could make little or no headway afloat, even if it were equipped somewhere with a screw propeller; under those circumstances it probably could do no more than try to maintain its position as best it could while it radioed for help. It was certainly well studded with antennae. Mainly, it seemed to be designed to shed water, rather than to swim in it.

How could any sort of industry be possible under these soggy conditions? He could not imagine how even an agricultural society could survive amidst these perpetual torrents, especially since there was very little land area above water on the planet. But then he recalled a little of the history of the colonization of Venus, which had presented somewhat similar problems. There, farming eventually had been taken beneath the sea; but even that needed an abundance of energy, and besides, the people of Heaven hadn't even gotten that far—they seemed to be living mostly on fish and mudweed.

He listened as closely as possible to the conversations of the colonists on the docks—not the conversations in English with the Okies, which were technical and unrevealing, but what the colonists said to each other in their own language. This was a gluey variant of Russian, the now dead Universal language of deep space, which the memory cells had been cramming into Chris's head at a cruel rate almost since the beginning of his city education. It was a brute of a language to master, especially on board a town where it was very seldom used, and perhaps for this reason the colonists, though mostly they were circumspect even in their private conversations, did not really seem to believe that the Okies spoke it; their very possession of it assured them that their history was safely pre-Okie. Quite certainly it never occurred to them that it might be understood, however imperfectly, by a teen-age boy standing about the quaysides gawping at their power-boats.

Between these eavesdroppings and the increasingly rare visits home of his guardian, Chris gradually built up a fuzzy picture of what the colonists seemed to want. As a citizen, he could have asked the City Fathers directly for the text of the contract, but access to this was denied to passengers. In general, however, he gathered that the Archangels proposed to establish an economy like that of Venus, complete with undersea farming and herding, with the aid of broadcast power of the kind that kept the city's Tin Cabs in the air. The Okies were to do the excavating in the shifting, soaking terrain, and were to build the generator-transmitter station involved. They were also to use city facilities to refine the necessary power metals, chiefly thorium, of which Heaven had an abundance beyond its ability to process. After the economy was revamped, the Archangels hoped to have their own refin-eries, and to sell the pure stuffs to other planets. Curious-ly, they also had enough germanium to be willing to pay for the job in this metal, although it too was notoriously difficult to refine; this was fortunate for them, since with-out any present interstellar trade, they were woefully short of Oc Dollars.

Once the whole operation had rumbled and sloshed out into the field and was swallowed up in the enveloping, eternal storm, Sgt. Anderson's absences became pro-longed, and the number of colonists to be found on the docks also diminished sharply. Now there were only a few of the swamp vehicles—inexplicably called swan boats—to be seen at the end of each day, when Chris was released from school, and these were mostly small craft whose owners were engaged in dickering with individual Okies for off-planet curios to give to their ladies. This commerce also was bogging down rather rapidly, for the single citi-zen had no use for money, and the lords and franklins of Heaven had few goods to barter. Soon the flow of in-formation available to Chris had almost stopped, frustrat-ing him intensely.

In this extremity he had an inspiration. He still carried with him a small, cheap clasp knife with a tiny compass embedded in its handle, the last of the exceedingly few gifts his father had ever been able to give him; perhaps it would have status here as an off-planet curio. When the notion first occurred to him, he rejected it with distress at even having thought of it—but when first Sgt. Dulany, and then his own guardian, were officially posted on the "Missing" list, he hesitated no longer. His only remaining doubt was whether or not the compass would work here, amid so much electrical activity (but then it had never worked very well on Earth, either).

He waited until he saw the lord of a six-man swan boat stalking disappointedly away from a deal he had been unable to close, and then approached him with the knife outstretched on his palm.

"Gospodin—"

The man, a huge burly fellow with a face like one of the eternal thunderclouds of his planet, stopped in his tracks and looked down. "Boy? Did you speak?"

"Yes sir. With your permission, I have here useful tool, earthly in origin. Would my lord care to examine?"

"But you speak our language," the man said, still frowning. He took the knife abstractedly; it was plain that he was interested, but Chris's stumbling Russian seemed to interest him more. "How is that?"

"By listening, lord. It is very hard, but I am trying. Please see object, it is from Earth, from *kolkhoz* of Pennsylvania. Genuine antique, touched once by human hands in factory."

"Well, well. How does it work?"

Chris showed him how to pry out the two blades, but his attempts to explain the compass were dismissed with a brusque gesture. Either his command of the language was insufficient to make the matter clear, or the lord already had recognized that such a thing would be useless in the lightning-stitched ether of Heaven.

"Hmm. Sleazy, to be sure, but perhaps my lady would like it for her charm-necklace. What do you ask for it?"

"Lord, I would like to drive your swan boat one time, one distance. I ask no more."

The colonist stared at him for a long moment, and then burst into deep guffaws of laughter. "Come along, come along," he said when he had recovered a little. "Sharp traders, you tramps, but this is the best story yet—I'll be telling it for years! Come along—you have a bargain."

Still chortling, he led the way to the dock, where they were both stopped by a perimeter cop who recognized Chris. Between them, the boy and the lord explained the bargain, and the Okie guard dubiously allowed Chris to board the swan boat.

In the forward cabin of the bobbing cylinder, two other colonists confronted them at once, wearing expressions at once nervous and angry, but the owner shushed them with a swift slash of one hand. He still seemed to be highly amused.

"It's only an infant. It traded me a bangle to learn how to mush the boat about. There's nothing to that. Go on aft; I'll join you in a minute."

To judge by their expressions, the other two still disapproved, but they took orders. The big man sat Chris down in a bucket seat before the broad front window and showed him how to grasp the two handles, one on each side of the half-circle of the control wheel, which were the throttles of the vehicle.

"It's not enough simply to turn the wheel, because you must also deliver power to one tread or the other. To do that, you push the handle forward or back, to speed the treads or slow them down. Past the red mark here, the tread will reverse. If you're not getting any traction, tilt the whole wheel forward on its column; that blows the tanks and allows the boat to settle in the mud. When the ground gets harder, the boat will of course climb up by itself and that will start the pumps; as the pressure in the tanks rises, the steering column tilts back to its original position automatically. Understand me so far?"

"But can I try?"

"Well, I suppose so. Yes. I have some talking to do abaft. Let me back the craft away from the pier, and then you can try crawling in a circle just outside the perimeter. Make sure you can always see your city beacon there."

"Let me back it up, lord?" Chris said urgently.

"All right," the big man said with amused indulgence. "But don't be rough with it. Gently back of the red line on both throttles. That's it. Not so fast. Gently! Now into neutral on the left. That's it; see how it turns around?"

There was a shout from somewhere in the rear of the vessel, to which the big man responded with a tremendously rapid burst of speech, only a few words of which were intelligible to Chris. "I have to leave for a few minutes," he added. "Remember, don't try anything tricky, and don't lose sight of the beacon."

"No, lord."

As the boat's owner left the cabin, Chris caught a few more words, amusedly beginning to relate the story of the dock boy who had picked up a few stammering words of

the language and immediately had decided that he was a
pilot; then the voices dwindled to a blurred murmur. Chris
spent the next few minutes testing the controls of the boat
in small jerks and spurts, being as inexpert about it as he
could manage, although the machine was really not difficult to master. Then, as directed, he set it to crawling in a
fixed circle, counter-clockwise, left the bucket seat, and
edged his way back to the door leading to the next
chamber.

He had no idea what it was that he expected to overhear—he was simply avid for more information, to relieve
the recent famine. He was certainly unprepared for what
he got.

The men were talking in a rapid patois which differed
sharply from the form of the Universal Language which
the memory cells had been teaching him, but many
phrases were clear and distinct:

". . . can't be done without keeping the city, that's all
there is to it."

". . . Disable it? . . . Don't even have a blueprint of the
machinery, let alone a map."

"That can come later, after we've occupied . . . We've
got thousands of commoners to throw away, but the
defenses—It's essential first to immobilize their Huacu, or
whatever they call it here. We can't afford to fight on their
terms."

"Then what's the problem? We've got their two chief
generals for hostages. We can hold them forever if necessary . . . Don't even know the name of Castle Wolfwhip,
let alone where it—"

There the conversation ended abruptly. With a grinding
thump, the swan boat hit something and began clumsily to
try to climb it. Chris was thrown to the deck, and on the
other side of the doorway there was the sound of scrambling and of angry shouting. Then that too was cut off as
the bulkhead swung to, of its own inertia.

Fighting to regain his balance against the blind lurching
of the boat, Chris scrambled up, and dogged the bulkhead
tightly closed all the way around. Was there any way to
lock it, too? Yes, there was a big bolt that could be
thrown which would hold the whole series of dogs in
place, provided that it could not be unbolted from the
other side. Well, he'd have to take his chances on that,
though a fat padlock to complete the job would have

made him feel more comfortable. Then, he clambered up the tilted, pitching deck to the control seat.

The boat had been doing its best to travel in a circle, but Chris had failed to realize that mud is a shifting, inexact sort of medium in which to turn a machine loose. The circle had been precessing, and the boat had run head-on into a dock. Okie cops were running toward it.

Chris reversed both engines, backing away from the city as rapidly as the boat would go, but that was not half as fast as he would have liked. Then he switched the vehicle around, end for end, and set it to whining and sliding squarely into the teeth of the storm, aiming it for the pip on the cross hairs which showed on the control board as its homing signal.

Where that might wind him up, he had no idea. He could only hope that it might be Castle Wolfwhip, and that he would find Anderson and Dulany there—and that the six furious colonists in back of the locked bulkhead would not be able to burn their way out before he got there.

CHAPTER SEVEN: Why Not to
Keep Demons

Before the swan boat had been on its slobbering way outward for more than five minutes, the sodium-yellow glare of the city's dockside beacon dimmed and vanished as swiftly as if it had been snuffed out. Except for his prisoners, whom he was trying to ignore, Chris was alone in the shell of the boat, like a chick in an egg, with nothing for company but the unfamiliar instruments, the grunting of the engines, and the flash and crash of the eternal storm.

He studied the control board intently, but it told him very little that he did not already know. All the lettering on and around the instruments were in the Cyrillic alphabet—and although the City Fathers expected citizens to be able to speak the Universal Language, up to now they had given Chris not even a first lesson in how to read it. Even so obvious a device as the swan boat's radio set was incomprehensible to him in detail; after a brief study, he gave up all hope of finding the city's master frequency and calling for pursuit and aid. He could not even decide whether it was a AFM or a PM tuner, let alone read the calibrations on the dial.

Nevertheless he urgently needed to signal. Above all, he needed to let the city know the details, fragmentary though they were, of the plotting that he had overheard. Running away with the plotters in their own swan boat had been an impulse of desperation, which he was already beginning more and more to regret. If only he had managed somehow to get back on shore, and told somebody in Amalfi's office what he had learned, pronto!

But the question was, would they have listened, or believed him if they had? Nobody who was anybody aboard the city seemed to want to bother with youngsters until they had become citizens; the adults were all too old, somehow, to be even approachable—and for that matter citizens paid very little attention to passengers of any age.

Of course, Chris could have told the City Fathers what he knew, easily enough—but everything that was told the City Fathers went into the memory cells, which was the equivalent of putting it in dead storage. The City Fathers never took action on what they knew, or even volunteered information, unless directed; otherwise they only held it until it was asked for, which might take centuries.

In any event the die was cast. Now he also needed someone in the city to know where he was going, and to follow him. But among the glittering, enigmatic instruments before him he could find no way to bring that about, nor did he in fact know even vaguely how the city might chase after him if it did know what his situation was. The Tin Cabs operated upon broadcast power which faded out at the city's perimeter, and to the best of Chris's knowledge, the city had no ground vehicles capable of coping with shifting, ambiguous, invisible terrain of this kind. Somewhere in storage, true, it did have a limited number of larger military aircraft, but how could you fly one of them in this region of perpetual storm? And even if you could, what would you look for, in a world where even the largest villages and castles produced and consumed so little power that detecting instruments would be unable to differentiate a city from a random splatter of lightning bolts?

The swan boat churned onward single-mindedly. After a while, Chris noticed that it had been at least several minutes since he had had to apply corrections in order to keep the green pip on the cross hairs. Experimentally, he let go of the controls entirely. The pip stayed centered. Some signal—perhaps simply his keeping the pip centered for a given length of time—had cut in an automatic pilot.

That was a help, in a way, but it deprived him of anything to do but worry, and added a new worry to the list: How could he cut the autopilot *out* of the circuit if he needed to? The pertinent switch was doubtless in plain sight and clearly marked, but again, he couldn't read the markings. As for his prisoners, they were being disturbingly quiet. In the back of his mind he had been anticipating some attempt to burn through the door—surely they had some sort of hand weapon back there which might serve the purpose—but they hadn't so much as pounded on it.

He hoped fervently that they were just being fatalistic about their captivity. If their silence meant that they were satisfied with it, that was bad news. The news was bad enough already, for he had no idea what he was going to do with them, or with the boat, when he got to Castle Wolfwhip—

And no time left to invent any plan, for in the next flash of lightning he saw the castle.

It was still several miles away, but even at this distance its massiveness was awe-inspiring. There were many towers in the city that were smaller; despite the lack of any adjacent structure with which to compare it, Chris guessed that the black, windowless pile could not be less than thirty stories high.

At first, he thought it was surrounded by a moat, but that was only an effect of foreshortening brought on by distance. Actually, it stood in the middle of a huge lake, so storm-lashed that Chris could not imagine how the clumsy swan boat could survive on it, let alone make any headway.

He pulled back on the throttles; but as he had suspected, the boat no longer answered to the manual controls. It plowed doggedly forward into the water. A moment later, the compressed air tanks blew with a bubbling roar, and the lake closed over the boat completely. It was now traveling on the bottom.

Now he no longer had even the lightning flashes to see by—nothing but the lights inside the boat, which did not penetrate the murky water at all. It was as though the transparent shell had abruptly gone opaque.

After what seemed a long while—though it was probably no more than ten minutes—the treads made a grinding noise, as if they had struck stone, and the vehicle came gradually to a halt. On a hunch, Chris tried the manuals again, but there was still no response.

Then the outside lights came on.

The swan boat was sitting snugly in a berth within a sizable cavern. Through the rills of yellow water draining down its sides, Chris saw that it had a reception committee: four men, with rifles. They looked down into the boat at him, grinning unpleasantly. While he stared helplessly back, the engines quit—

—and the outside door swung open.

They put him in the same cell with Anderson and Dulany. His guardian was appalled to see him—"Gods of all stars, Irish, now they're snatching children!"—and then, after he had heard the story, thoroughly disgusted. Dulany, as usual, said very little, but he did not look exactly pleased.

"There's probably a standard recognition signal you should have sent, except that you wouldn't have known what it was," Anderson said. "These petty barons did a lot of fighting among themselves before we got here—fleecing us is probably the first project they've been together on since this mudball was colonized."

"Bluster," Dulany commented.

"Yes, it's part of the feudal *mores*. Chris, those men in the boat are going to take a lot of ribbing from their peers, regardless of the fact that they were never in any danger and they had sense enough to let you spin your own noose. They'll be likely to take it out on you when you're taken out for questioning."

"I've already been interviewed," Chris said grimly. "And they did."

"You have? Murder! There goes that one up the flue, Irish."

"Complication," Dulany agreed.

Anderson fell silent, leaving Chris to wonder what they had been talking about. Evidently they had been planning something which his news had torpedoed—though it was hard to imagine even the beginnings of such a plan, for their captors, out of a respect for the two Okies which Chris knew to be more than justified, had left them nothing but their underwear. At last the boy said hesitantly:

"What could I have done if my interview were still coming up?"

"Located our space suits," Anderson said gloomily. "Not that they'd have let you search the place, that's for sure, but you might have gotten a hint, or tricked them into dropping one. Even wary men sometimes underestimate youngsters. Now we'll just have to think of something else."

"There are dozens of space suits standing around the wall of that big audience chamber," Chris said. "If you could only get there, maybe one of them would fit one of you."

Dulany only smiled slightly. Anderson said: "Those aren't suits, Chris; they're armor—plate armor. Useless here, but they have some kind of heraldic significance; I think the Barons used to collect them from each other, like scalps."

"That may be," Chris said stubbornly, "but there were at least two real suits there. I'm sure of that."

The two sergeants looked at each other. "Is it possible —?" Anderson said. "They've got the bravado for it, all right."

"Could be."

"By Sirius, there's a bluff we've got to call! Get busy on that lock, Irish!"

"In my underwear? Nix."

"What difference does that—oh, I see." Anderson grimaced impatiently. "We'll have to wait for lights out. Happily it won't be long."

"How are you going to bust the lock, Sergeant Dulany?" Chris asked. "It's almost as big as my head!"

"Those are the easy kinds," Dulany said loquaciously.

Chris in fact never did find out what Dulany did with the lock, for the operation was performed in the dark. Standing as instructed all the way to the back of the cell, he did not even hear anything until the huge, heavy door was thrown back with a thunderous crash.

The crash neatly drowned out the only yell the guard outside managed to get off. In this thunder-ridden fortress, nobody would think anything of such a noise. Then there was a jangle of keys, and two loud clicks as the

unfortunate man was manacled with his own handcuffs.
The Okies rolled him into the cell.

"What'll I do if he comes to?" Chris whispered hoarsely.

"Won't for hours," Dulany's voice said. "Shut the door.
We'll be back."

From the boarding-squad sergeant, nine words all in
one speech had the reassuring force of an oration. Chris
grinned and shut the door.

Nothing seemed to happen thereafter for hours, except
that the thunder got louder. That was certainly no novelty
on Heaven. But was it possible for even the heaviest
thunderclap to shake a pile of stone as squat and massive
as Castle Wolfwhip? Surely it couldn't last long if that
were the case—and yet it was obviously at least a century
old, probably more.

The fourth such blast answered his question. It was an
explosion, and it was *inside* the building. In response, all
the lights came on; and Chris saw that the door had been
jarred open.

When he went over to close it again, he found himself
looking down a small precipice. The corridor floor had
collapsed. Several stunned figures were sitting amid the
rubble it had made on the story below it. Considering the
size of the blocks of which it had been made, they were
lucky that it hadn't killed them.

Still another explosion, and this time the lights went
back out. Quite evidently, the suits Chris had seen in the
audience hall had indeed been Anderson's and Dulany's
battle dress. Well, this ought to cure the baron of Castle
Wolfwhip of the habit of exhibiting his scalps. It ought to
cure him of the habit of kidnapping Okies, too. It occurred to Chris that the whole plan of using Anderson and
Dulany as hostages, even in their underwear, was about as
safe an operation as trying to imprison two demons in a
corncrib.

Then they were back. Seeing them hovering in the
collapsed corridor, their helmet lamps making a shifting,
confusing pattern of shadows, Chris realized, too, what
kind of vehicle the city would have sent out after him if
he had managed to get word back.

"You all right?" Anderson's PA speaker demanded.
"Good. Didn't occur to me that the floor might go."

They came into the cell. The guard, who had just
recovered his senses, took one look and crawled into the
corner farthest from the two steel figures.

"Now we've got a problem. We've got a safe-conduct out of the castle, but we can't carry you through that storm, and we don't dare risk putting you in one of their suits."

"Boat," Dulany said, pointing at Chris.

"That's right, I forgot, he knows how to drive one. Okay, boy, stick your elbows out and we'll fly you out to where there's a floor you can walk on. Irish, let's go."

"One minute." Dulany unhooked a bunch of keys from his waist and tossed them into the corner where the guard was cowering. "Right."

Only Anderson joined him in the swan boat, still in his armor; Dulany stayed airborne, in radio communication with Anderson, in case the colonials should have the notion of making the boat turn around and return home on autopilot. After he saw the holes the two cops had torn through the great walls of Castle Wolfwhip, Chris doubted that they'd even entertain such a notion, but obviously it was sensible not to take chances where it wasn't necessary.

The moment the boat was crawling across the bottom of the lake, Anderson took his helmet off and turned promptly to studying the control board. Finally he nodded and snapped three switches.

"That should do it."

"Do what?"

"Prevent them from putting this tub under remote control. In fact from this point on they won't even be able to locate her. Now Irish can shoot on ahead of us and get the word to the Mayor." He put the helmet back on and spoke briefly, then doffed it.

"Now, Chris," he said grimly, "comes the riot act."

CHAPTER EIGHT: The Ghosts of Space

The "riot act" was every bit as unpleasant as he had foreseen it would be, but somehow he managed to live through it—mostly by bearing in mind as firmly as possible that he had it coming. He was never likely to become

a real Okie by stealing the property of people who had
hired the city on to do a job, no matter how good he
thought his reasons were.

And in this first disastrous instance he had simply been
in the way. The city would have known soon enough in
any event of the fact that Anderson and Dulany were being
held prisoner, since the colonists of Heaven could not have
used them effectively as hostages without notifying Amalfi
of the fact; and there was no doubt in Chris's mind that
the two cops could have gotten out of Castle Wolfwhip
without his intervention, and perhaps a good deal faster,
too. Aboue all, they might have been gotten out by
Amalfi *without violence,* and thus saved the contract in-
tact. The appearance of Chris as a third prisoner had been
totally unwelcomed to *both* sides, and had turned what
had been merely a tense situation into an explosion.

In the end, they gave him full marks for imagination
and boldness, as well as for coolness under fire, but by that
time Chris had learned enough about the situation to feel
that his chances of ever becoming a citizen were not
worth an Oc dollar. The new contract was considerably
more limited than the old, and called for reparations for
the damage the two sergeants had done to Castle
Wolfwhip; under it, the city stood to gain considerably less
than before.

Chris was astonished that there was any new contract at
all, and said so, rather hesitantly. Anderson explained:

"Violence between employer and employee is as old as
man, Chris, but the work has to be done all the same. The
colonists as a corporate entity disown the kidnapper and
claim the right to deal with him according to their own
system of justice, which we're bound to respect. Damage
to real property, on the other hand, has to be paid
for—and the city can't disown Irish and me because we're
officers and agents of the city."

"But what about the scheme to ground the city and
take it over?"

"We know nohing about that except what you overheard. That would have no status in a colonial court, and
probably wouldn't even if you were a citizen—in this case,
if you were of legal age."

And there it was again. "Well, there's something else
I've been wondering about," Chris said. "Why is the age to
start the drugs fixed at eighteen? Wouldn't they work at
any age? Suppose we took aboard a man forty years old

who also happened to be a red-hot expert at something we needed. Couldn't you start him on the drugs anyhow?"

"We could and we would," Anderson assured him. "Eighteen is only the *optimum* age, the earliest age at which we can be sure the specimen is physically mature. You see the drugs can't set the clock back. They just arrest aging from the moment when they're first given. Tell me, have you ever heard of the legend of Tithonus?"

"No, I'm afraid not."

"I don't know it very well myself; ask the City Fathers. But briefly, he got himself in the good books of the goddess of dawn, Eos, and asked for the gift of immortality. She gave it to him, but he was pretty old at the time. When he realized that he was just going to stay that way forever, he asked Eos to take the gift back. So she changed him into a grasshopper, and you know how long *they* live."

"Hmm. A man who was going to be a permanent seventy-five wouldn't be much good to himself, I guess. Or to the city either."

"That's the theory," the perimeter sergeant agreed. "But of course we have to take 'em as we find 'em. Amalfi went on the drugs at fifty—which, for him, happened to be his prime."

Thus his education went on, much as before, except that he stayed scrupulously away from the docks. Since the new contract was limited to three months, there probably wouldn't have been much to see down there anyhow—or so he told himself, not without a suspicion that there were a few holes in his logic. In addition, he got some sympathy and support from a wholly unexpected source: Piggy Kingston-Throop.

"It just goes to show you how much truth there is in all this jabber about citizenship," he said fiercely, at their usual after-class meeting. "Here you go and do them a big fat favor, and all they can think of to do is lecture you for getting in their way. They even go right on doing business with these guys who were going to grab the city if they could."

"Well, we do have to eat."

"Yeah, but it's dirty money all the same. Come to think of it, though, if I'd have been in your shoes I'd have handled it differently."

"I know," Chris said, "that's what they all keep telling me. I should never have gotten into the boat in the first place."

"Pooh, that part's all right," Piggy said scornfully. "If you hadn't gotten into the boat they'd never have known about the plot to take the city—that's the favor you did them, and don't you forget it. They're on their guard now. No, I mean what happened after you locked the guys up in the back cabin. You said that the boat had bumped into the dock and was trying to climb it, right?"

"Yes."

"And a lot of cops came running?"

"I don't know about a lot," Chris said cautiously. "There were three or four, I think."

"Okay. Now if it had been me, I would have just stopped the boat right there, and gotten out. and told the cops what I'd heard. Let *them* drag it out of the guys you'd locked up. You know how the City Fathers cram all that junk into our heads in class—well, they can take stuff out the same way. Dad says it's darned unpleasant for the victim, but they get it."

Chris could only shrug helplessly. "You're right. That would have been the sensible thing to do. And it seems obvious the way you tell it. But all I can say is it didn't occur to me." He thought a moment, and then added: "But in a way I'm not too sorry, Piggy. That way, I never would have gotten to Castle Wolfwhip at all—sure, it would have been better if I hadn't—but it sure was exciting while I was there."

"Boy, I'll bet it was! I wish I'd been there!" Piggy began to shadowbox awkwardly. "I wouldn't have hidden in any cell, believe you me. I'd have showed 'em!"

Chris did his best not to laugh. "Going by what I heard, if you'd gone along with the sergeants—if they'd let you— you'd have been killed by your own friends. Those weren't just rotten eggs they were throwing around."

"All the same, I'll bet—Hullo, we're lifting."

The city had not lifted yet, but Chris knew what Piggy meant; he too could hear the deepening hum of the spindizzies. "So we are. That three months sure went by in a hurry."

"Three months isn't much in space. We'll be eighteen before we know it."

"That," Chris said gloomily, "is exactly what I'm afraid of."

"Well, *I* don't give a darn. This whole deal about your running off with the boat proves that they don't mean what they say about earning citizenship. Like I say, the whole thing's just a scheme to keep kids in line, so they won't have to be watched so much. The minute you actually *do* something for the survival of the city, bingo! the roof falls on you. Never mind that, it was a good thing to do and shows you've got guts—you've caused them trouble, and that's what the system's supposed to prevent."

There was, Chris saw, something to be said for the theory, no matter how exaggerated Piggy's way of putting it was. In Chris's present state of discouragement, it would be a dangerously easy point of view to adopt.

"Well, Piggy, what I want to know is, what are you going to do if you're wrong? I mean, supposing the City Fathers decide not to make you a citizen, and it turns out that they can't be fixed? Then you'll be stuck with being a passenger for the rest of your life—and it'd only be a normal lifetime, too."

"Passengers aren't as helpless as they think," Piggy said darkly. "Some one of these days the Lost City is going to come back, and when that happens, all of a sudden the passengers are going to be top dog."

"The Lost City? I never heard of it."

"Of course you haven't. And the City Fathers won't ever tell you about it, either. But word gets around."

"Okay, don't be mysterious," Chris said. "What's it all about?"

Piggy's voice dropped to a hoarse whisper. "Do you swear not to tell anybody else, except another passenger?"

"Sure."

Piggy looked elaborately over both shoulders before going on. As usual, they were the only youngsters on the street, and none of the adults were paying the slightest attention to them.

"Well," he said in the same tone of voice, "it's like this. One of the first cities ever to take off was a big one. Nobody knows its name, but *I* think it was Los Angeles. Anyhow, it got lost, and ran out of drugs, and then out of food, way off in some part of space that was never colonized, so it couldn't find any work either. But then they made a planetfall on a new world, something nobody had ever seen before. It was like Earth—bigger, but the same gravity, and a little more oxygen in the air, and a perfect climate—like spring all year round, even at the poles. If you planted seeds there, you had to jump back in a hurry or the plant would hit you under the chin, they grew so fast.

"But that wasn't the half of it."

"It sounds like plenty," Chris said.

"That was all good, but they found something else even better. There was a kind of grain growing wild there, and when they analyzed it to see whether or not it was good to eat, *they found it contained an antideath drug*—not any of ours, but better than all of ours rolled into one. They didn't even have to extract it—all they had to do was make bread out of the plant."

"Wow. Piggy, is this just a story?"

"Well, I can't give you an affidavit," Piggy said, offended. "Do you want to hear the rest or don't you?"

"Go ahead," Chris said hastily.

"So then the question was, what were they going to do with their city? They didn't need it. Everything they needed came right up out of the ground while their backs were turned. So they decided to stock it up and send it out into space again, to look for other cities. Whenever they make contact with a new Okie town, they take all the passengers off—nobody else—and take them back to this planet where *everybody* can have the drugs, because there's never any shortage."

"Suppose the other city doesn't want to give up its passengers?"

"Why wouldn't it want to? If it had any use for them, they'd be citizens, wouldn't they?"

"Yes, but just suppose."

"They'd give them up anyhow. Like I said, the Lost City is *big*."

Unfortunately for the half-million other questions Chris wanted to ask, at that point the city moaned softly to the sound of the take-cover siren. The boys parted hurriedly; but Chris, after a moment's thought, did not go home. Instead, he holed up in a public information booth, where he fed his car into the slot and asked for the Librarian.

He had promised not to mention the Lost City to anyone but another passenger, which ruled out questioning his guardian, or the City Fathers directly; but he had thought of a way to ask an indirect question. The Librarian was that one of the 134 machines comprising the City Fathers which had prime charge of the memory banks, and was additionally charged with teaching; it did not collect information, but only catalogued and dispensed it. Interpretation was not one of its functions.

"CARD ACCEPTED. PROCEED."

"Question: Do any antiagathics grow naturally—I mean, do they occur in plants that could be raised as crops?"

A brief pause. "A PRECURSOR OF THE ANTISLEEP DRUG IS A STEROID SUBSTANCE OCCURRING NATURALLY IN A NUMBER OF YAMLIKE PLANTS FOUND ON EARTH, LARGELY IN CENTRAL AND SOUTH AMERICA. THIS SAPOGENIN IS NOT, HOWEVER, IN ITSELF AN ANTIAGATHIC, AND MUST BE CONVERTED; HUNDREDS OF DIFFERENT STEROIDS ARE PRODUCED FROM THE SAME STARTING MATERIAL.

"ASCOMYCIN IS PRODUCED BY DEEP-TANK FERMENTATION OF A MICROORGANISM AND HARVESTED FROM THE BEER. THIS PROCEDURE MIGHT BROADLY BE DEFINED AS CROPRAISING.

"ALL OTHER KNOWN ANTIAGATHICS ARE WHOLLY SYNTHETIC DRUGS."

Chris sat back, scratching his head in exasperation. He had hoped for a clear-cut, yes-or-no answer, but what he had gotten stood squarely in the middle. No antiagathics were harvested from real crops; but if a crop plant could produce something at least enough like an antiagathic to be converted into one, then that part of Piggy's astounding story was at least possible. Unhappily, he could think of no further questions sufficiently indirect to keep his main point of interest hidden.

Then he noticed that the booth had not returned his card to him. This was quite usual; it meant only that the Librarian, which spent its whole mechanical life substituting free association for thinking, had a related subject it would talk about if he liked. Usually it wasn't worth while exploring them, for the Librarian could go on forever if so encouraged; all he needed to do now was to say "Return," and he could take his card and go. But the take-cover alert wasn't over yet; so, instead, he said, "Proceed."

"SUBJECT, ANTIAGATHICS AS BY-PRODUCTS OF AGRICULTURE. SUB-SUBJECT, LEGENDARY IDYLLIC PLANETS." Chris sat bolt upright. "ANTIAGATHICS AS BY-PRODUCTS OF AGRICULTURE, USUALLY IN THE DAILY BREAD, IS ONE OF THE COMMON FEATURES OR DIAGNOSTIC SIGNS OF THE LEGENDARY PLANETS OF NOMAD-CITY MYTHOLOGY. OTHERS INCLUDE: EARTHLIKE GRAVITY BUT GREATER LAND AREA; EARTHLIKE ATMOSPHERE BUT MORE ABUNDANT OXYGEN; EARTHLIKE WEATHER BUT WITH UNIFORM CLIMATE, AND

COMPLETE ISOLATION FROM EXISTING TRADE LANES. NO PLANET MATCHING THIS DESCRIPTION IN ANY PARTICULAR HAS YET BEEN FOUND. NAMES OFTEN GIVEN TO SUCH WORLDS INCLUDE: ARCADY, BRADBURY, CELEPHAIS . . ."

Chris was so stunned that the Librarian had worked its way all the way through "ZIMIAMVIA" and had begun another alphabetical catalogue before he thought to ask for his card back. His question had not been very crafty, after all.

By the time he emerged from the booth, the storms of Heaven had vanished and the city was once more soaring amid the stars. Furthermore, he was late for dinner.

So, after all, there had been no secret to keep. Chris told the Andersons the story of his failure to outwit the Librarian; it made the best possible excuse for his lateness, since it was true, and it reduced Carla to tears of helpless laughter. The perimeter sergeant was amused, too, but there was an undercurrent of seriousness beneath his amusement.

"You're learning, Chris. It's easy to think that because the City Fathers are dead, they're also stupid; but you see that that isn't the case. Otherwise they would never have been given the power that they wield—and in some departments their power is absolute."

"Even over the Mayor?"

"Yes and no. They can't forbid the Mayor anything. But if he goes against their judgment more often than they're set to tolerate, they can revoke his office. That's never happened here, but if it does, we'll have to sit still for it. If we don't, they'll stop the machinery."

"Wow. Isn't it dangerous to give machines so much power? Suppose they had a breakdown?"

"If there were only a few of them, that would be a real danger; but there are more than a hundred, and they monitor and repair each other, so in fact it will never happen. Sanity and logic is their stock in trade—which is why they can accept or reject the results of any election we may run. The popular will is sometimes an idiot, but no human being can be given the power to overrule it; not safely. But the machines can.

"Of course, there are stories about towns whose City Fathers ran amok with them. They're just stories, like Piggy's 'Lost City'—but they're important even when they're not true. Whenever a new way of living appears in the universe, the people who adopt it see quickly enough that it isn't perfect. They try to make it better, sure; but there are always some things about it that can't be changed. And the hopes and fears that are centered on those points get turned into stories.

"Piggy's myth, for instance. We live long lives in the cities, but not everybody can have the gift. It's impossible that everyone should have it—the whole universe isn't big enough to contain the sheer mass of flesh that would accumulate if we all lived and bred as long as we each wanted to. Piggy's myth says it is possible, which is untrue; but what *is* true about it is that it points to one of the real dissatisfactions with our way of living, real because nothing can be done about it.

"The story of the runaway City Fathers is another. No such thing has ever happened as far as I know, and it doesn't seem to be possible. but no live man *likes* to take orders from a bunch of machines, or to think that he may lose his life if they say so—but he might. because the City Fathers are the jury aboard most cities. So he invents a cautionary tale about City Fathers running amok, though actually he's talking not about the machines at all—he's warning that *he* may run amok if he's pushed too far.

"The universe of the cities is full of these ghosts. Sooner or later somebody is going to tell you that some cities go bindlestiff."

"Somebody has," Chris admitted. "But I didn't know what he meant."

"It's an old Earth term. A hobo was an honest migratory worker, who lived that way because he liked it. A tramp was the same kind of fellow, except that he wouldn't work—he lived by stealing or begging from settled people. In hobo society both kinds were more or less respectable. But the bindlestiff was a migrant who stole from other migrants—he robbed their bindles, the bags they carried their few belongings in. That man was an outcast from both worlds.

"It's common talk that some cities in trouble have gone bindlestiff—taken to preying on other cities. Again, there are no specific instances. IMT is the town that's most often mentioned, but the last we heard of IMT. she wasn't a bindlestiff—she'd been outlawed for a horrible crime on a colony planet, but technically that makes her only a tramp. A mean one, but still only a tramp."

"I see," Chris said slowly. "It's like the story about City

Fathers going crazy. Cities do starve, I know that; and the bindlestiff story says, 'How will *we* behave when the pinch comes?' "

Anderson looked gratified. "Look at that," he said to Carla. "Maybe I should have been a teacher!"

"Nothing to do with you," Carla said composedly. "Chris is doing all the thinking. Besides, I like you better as a cop."

The perimeter sergeant sighed, a little ruefully. "Oh, well, all right. Then I'll give you only one more story. You've heard of the Vegan orbital fort?"

"Oh, sure. That was in the history, way back."

"'Good. Well, for once, that's a real thing. There was a Vegan orbital fort, and it did get away, and nobody knows where it is now. The City Fathers say that it probably died when it ran out of supplies, but it was a pretty big job and might well have survived under circumstances no ordinary city could live through. If you ask the City Fathers for the probabilities, they tell you that they can't give you any figures—which is a bad sign in itself.

"Now, that's as far as the facts go. But there's a legend to go with them. The legend says that the fort is foraging through the trade lanes, devouring cities—just the way a dragonfly catches mosquitoes, on the wing. Nobody has actually seen the fort since the scorching of Vega, but the legend persists; every time a city disappears, the word goes around, first, that a bindlestiff got it, and next, that the fort got it.

"What's it all about, Chris? Tell me."

Chris thought for a long time. At last he said:

"I'm kind of confused. It ought to be the same kind of story as the others—something people are afraid of. Like meeting up some day with a planet, like the Vegan system, where the people have more on the ball than we do and will gobble us up the way we did Vega—"

Anderson's big fist crashed down on the dinner table, making all the plates jump. "Precisely!" he crowed. "Look there, Carla—"

Carla's own hands reached out and covered the sergeant's fist gently. "Dear, Chris isn't through yet. You didn't give him a chance to finish."

"I didn't? But—sorry, Chris. Go ahead."

"I don't know whether I'm through or not," Chris said, embarrassed and floundering. "This one story just confuses me. It's not as simple as the others; I think I'm sure of that."

"Go ahead."

"Well, it's sensible to be afraid of meeting somebody stronger than yourself. It might well happen. And there is a real Vegan orbital fort, or at least there was one. The other stories don't have that much going for them that's real—except the things people are actually afraid of, the things the stories *actually* are about. Does this make sense?"

"Yes. The things the stories symbolize."

"That's the word. To be afraid of the fort is to be afraid of a real thing. But what does the story symbolize? It's got to be the same kind of thing in the end—the fear people have of themselves. The story says, 'I'm tired of working to be a citizen, and obeying the Earth cops, and protecting the city, and living a thousand years with machines bossing me, and taking sass from colonists, and I don't know what all else. If I had a great big city that I could run all by myself, I'd spend the next thousand years smashing things up!' "

There was a long, long silence, during which Chris became more and more convinced that he had again talked out of turn, and far too much. Carla did not seem to be upset, but her husband looked stunned and wrathful.

"There *is* something wrong with the apprenticeship system," he growled at last, though he did not appear to be speaking to either of them. "First the Kingston-Throop kid—and now this. Carla! You're the brains in the family. Did it ever occur to you that that fort legend had anything to do with education?"

"Yes, dear. Long ago."

"Why didn't you say so?"

"I would have said so as soon as we had a child; until then, it wasn't any of my business. Now Chris has said it for me."

The perimeter sergeant turned a lowering face on Chris. "You," he said, "are a holy terror. I set out to teach you, as I was charged to do, and you wind up teaching me. Not even Amalfi knows this side of the fort story, I'll swear to that—and when he hears it, there's going to be a real upheaval in the schools."

"I'm sorry," Chris said miserably. He did not know what else to say.

"Don't be sorry!" Anderson roared, surging to his feet.

"Stick to your guns! Let the other guy be afraid of ghosts—you know the one thing about ghosts that you need to know, no matter what kind of ghosts they are: They have nothing to do with the dead. It's *always* themselves that people are afraid of."

He looked about distractedly. "I've got to go topside. Here's my hurry—where's my hat?" He roared out, banging one hand against the side of the door, leaving Chris frozen with alarm.

Then Carla began to laugh all over again.

CHAPTER NINE: **The Tramp**

But if the errand on behalf of which Sgt. Anderson had undertaken his rhinoceros-charge exit had really had anything to do with education, Chris had yet to see it reflected in his own. That got steadily harder, as the City Fathers, blindly and impersonally assuming that he had comprehended what they had already stuffed into his head, began to build his store of knowledge toward some threshold where it would start to be useful for the survival of the city. As this process went forward, Chris's old headaches dwindled into the category of passing twinges; these days, he sometimes felt actively, physically sick from sheer inability to make sense of what was being thrust upon him. In a moment of revulsion, he told the City Fathers so.

"IT WILL PASS. THE NORMAL HUMAN BEING FEELS AN AVERAGE OF TWENTY SMALL PAINS PER HOUR. IF ANY PERSIST, REPORT TO MEDICAL."

No, he was not going to do that; he was not going to be invalided out of his citizenship if he could help it. Yet it seemed to him that what he was suffering couldn't fairly be called "small pains." What to do, since he feared that Medical's cure would be worse than the disease? He didn't want to worry the Andersons, either—he had repaid their kindnesses with enough trouble already.

That left nobody to talk to but Dr. Braziller, that fearsome old harpy who seldom spoke in any language but logarithms and symbolic logic. Chris stood off from this next-but-worst choice for weeks; but in the end he had to do it. Though there was nothing physically wrong with him even now, he had the crazy notion that the City Fathers were about to kill him; one more stone of fact on his head and his neck would break.

"And well it might," Dr. Braziller told him, in her office after class. "Chris, the City Fathers are not interested in your welfare; I suppose you know that. They're interested in only one thing: the survival of the city. That's their prime directive. Otherwise they have no interest in people at all; after all, they're only machines."

"All right," Chris said, blotting his brow with a trembling hand. "But Dr. Braziller, what good will it do the city for them to blow all my fuses? I've been trying, really I have. But it isn't good enough for them. They keep right on piling the stuff in, and it makes no *sense* to me!"

"Yes, I've noticed that. But there's reason behind what they're doing, Chris. You're almost eighteen; and they're probing for some entrance point into your talents—some spark that will take fire, some bent of yours that might some day turn into a valuable specialty."

"I don't think I have any," Chris said dully.

"Maybe not. That remains to be seen. If you have one, they'll find it; the City Fathers never miss on this kind of thing. But Chris, my dear, you can't expect it to be easy on you. Real knowledge is always hard to come by—and now that the machines think you might actually be of some use to the city—"

"But they can't think that! They haven't found anything!"

"I can't read their minds, because they haven't any," Dr. Braziller said quietly. "But I've seen them do this before. They wouldn't be driving you in this way if they didn't suspect that you're good for something. They're trying to find out what it is, and unless you want to give up right now, you're going to have to sit still while they look. It doesn't surprise me that it makes you ill. It made me ill, too; I feel a little queasy just remembering it, and that was eighty years ago."

She fell silent suddenly, and in that moment, she looked even older than she had ever seemed before . . . old, and frail, and deeply sad, and—could it be possible?—beautiful.

"Now and then I wonder if they were right," Dr. Braziller told the heaped papers on her desk. "I wanted to be a composer. But the City Fathers had never heard of a successful woman composer, and it's hard to argue with that kind of charge. No, Chris, once the machines have fingered you, you have to be what they want you to be; the only alternative is to be a passenger—which means, to be nothing at all. I don't wonder that it makes you ill. But, Chris—fight back, fight back! Don't let those cabinet-heads lick you! Stick them out. They're only probing, and the minute we find out what they want, we can bear down on it. I'll help wherever I can—*I hate those things*. But first, we have to find out what they want. Have you got the guts, Chris?"

"I don't know. I'll try. But I don't know."

"Nobody knows, yet. They don't know themselves—that's your only hope. They want to know what you can do. You have to show them. As soon as they find out, you will be a citizen—but until then, it's going to be rough, and there will be nothing that anybody can do to help you. It will be up to you, and you alone."

It was heartening to have another ally, but Chris would have found Dr. Braziller's whole case more convincing had he been able to see the faintest sign of a talent—any talent at all—emerging under the ungentle ministrations of the machines. True, lately they had been bearing down heavily on his interest in history—but what good was that aboard a Okie city? The City Fathers themselves were the city's historians, just as they were its library, its accounting department, its schools and much of its government. No live person was needed to teach the subject or to write about it, and at best, as far as Chris could see, it could never be more than a hobby for an Okie citizen.

Even in the present instance, Chris was not being called upon to *do* anything with history but pass almost incredibly hard tests in it—tests which consisted largely of showing that he had retained all of the vast mass of facts that the City Fathers were determinedly shoving into him. And this was no longer just history from the Okie point of view. Whole systems of world and interstellar history—Machiavelli, Plutarch, Thucydides, Gibbon, Marx, Pareto, Spengler, Sarton, Toynbee, Durant and a score of others—came marching through the gray gas into his head, without mercy and with apparent indifference to the fact that they all contradicted each other fatally at crucial points.

There was no punishment for failures, since the City Fathers' pedagogy made failure of memory impossible, and it was only his memory that they seemed to be exploiting here. Instead, punishment was continuous: It lay in the certainty that though today's dose had been fiendish, tomorrow's would be worse.

"Now there you're wrong," Dr. Braziller told him. "Dead though they are, the machines aren't ignorant of human psychology—far from it. They know very well that some students respond better to reward than to punishment, and that others have to be driven by fear. The second kind is usually the less intelligent, and they know that too; how could they *not* know it after so many generations of experience? You're lucky that they've put you in the first category."

"You mean they're *rewarding* me?" Chris squeaked indignantly.

"Certainly."

"But how?"

"By letting you go on studying even when they're not satisfied with your progress. That's quite a concession, Chris."

"Maybe so," Chris said glumly. "But I'd get the point faster if they handed out lollipops instead."

Dr. Braziller had never heard of lollipops; she was an Okie. She only responded, a little primly: "You'd get it fast enough if they decided on a punishment system for you instead. They're rigidly just, but know nothing about mercy; and leniency with children is utterly foreign to them—which is one reason why I'm here."

The city hummed onward, and so did the days—and the months. Only Chris seemed to be making no progress in any visible direction.

No, that wasn't quite true. Piggy was going nowhere, either, as far as Chris could see. But there the situation was even more puzzling and full of complications. To begin with, ever since Chris had first met him, Piggy had been denying that he cared about what happened to him when he turned eighteen; so it was odd—though not entirely surprising—to discover that he did care, after all. In fact, though his situation appeared to be now quite hopeless, Piggy was full of loud self-confidence, belied in the next breath by dark hints of mysterious plans to cinch what was supposed to be cinched already, and even darker hints of awful things to come if it didn't turn out to be cinched. It was all more than Chris could manage to sort out, especially considering his inability to see more than half a minute into his own future. Some days he felt as though Piggy's old accusation—"Boy, you *are* dumb!"—were written on his forehead in letters of fire.

Although Piggy said almost nothing about it, Chris gathered that he had already approached his father on the subject of biasing the City Fathers in his favor on the Citizenship Tests, and had been rebuffed with a loud roar, only slightly tempered by the intervention of his mother. There was of course no way to study for the Tests, since they measured nothing but potentials, not achievements; which meant, in turn, that there was no such thing as a pony or a crib for them.

Now, it was obvious, Piggy was thinking back to Chris's adventure on Heaven. Judging by the questions he asked about it, Chris deduced that Piggy was searching for something heroic to do, in order to do it much better than Chris had. Chris was human enough to doubt that Piggy could make a much better showing, but in any event the city was still in space, so no opportunity offered itself.

Occasionally, too, he would disappear after class for several days running. On his return, his story was that he had been prowling around the city eavesdropping on the adult passengers. They were, Piggy said, up to something— just possibly, the building of a secret Dirac transmitter with which to call the Lost City. Chris did not believe a word of this, nor did he think Piggy did either.

The simple, granite-keel facts were that time was running out for both of them, and that desperation was setting in: for Piggy because he had never tried, and for Chris because nothing he tried seemed to get him anywhere. All around them their younger schoolmates seemed to be opening into talents with the violence and unpredictability of popcorn, turning everything the memory cells fed them into salt and savor no matter how high the heat was turned up. In comparison, Chris felt as retarded as a dinosaur, and just as clumsy and gigantic.

It was in this atmosphere of pervasive, incipient failure that Sgt. Anderson one evening said calmly:

"Chris, the Mayor wants to talk to you."

From anyone else, Chris would have taken such an announcement as a practical joke, too absurd to be even upsetting. From Sgt. Anderson he did not know how to take it; he simply stared.

"Relax—it isn't going to be an ordeal, and besides I

didn't say he wanted to *see* you. Sit back down and I'll explain."

Numbly, Chris did so.

"What's happened is this: We're approaching another job of work. From the first contacts we had with these people, it sounded simple and straightforward, but of course nothing ever is. (Amalfi says the biggest lie it's possible to tell in the English language is, 'It was as simple as that.') Supposedly we were going to be hired on to do a straightforward piece of local geology and mining—nothing so tricky as changing the whole setup of a planet; just a standard piece of work. You've seen the motto on City Hall?"

Chris had. It read: MOW YOUR LAWN, LADY? It had never seemed very dignified to him, but he was beginning to understand what it implied. He nodded.

"Well, that's the way it's always supposed to be: We come in, we do a job, we go out again. Local feuds don't count; we take no part in them.

"But as we got closer to signing a contract with this place—it's called Argus Three—we began to get hints that we were second comers. Apparently there'd already been one city on Argus, hired to do the job, but hadn't done it well.

"We tried to find out more about this, naturally, to be sure the Argidae were telling a straight story; we didn't want to be poaching on any other city's contract. But the colonists were very vague about the whole thing. Finally, though, they let it slip that the other city was still sitting on their planet, and still claimed to be working on the job, even though the contract deadline had passed. Tell me— what would you do in a case like that, if you were Amalfi?"

Chris frowned. "I don't know any other answer but the one in the books. If the planet has an overstayed city, it's supposed to call the cops. All other cities should stay clear, otherwise they might get involved in the shooting, if there is any."

"Right; and this appears to be a classic case. The colonists can't be too explicit because they know that every word they broadcast to us is going to be overheard; but the City Fathers have analyzed what Argus Three *has* sent us, and the chances are a hundred to one that that other city has settled on Argus Three for good ... in short, that it means to take over the planet. The Argidae don't want to call the cops, for reasons we don't know. Instead, they seem to be trying to hire us to take on this tramp city and clear him out. If we tackle that, there *will* be shooting, that's for sure—and the cops will probably show up anyhow before it's over.

"Obviously, as you say, the thing to do is get out of the vicinity, fast. Cities ought not to fight with each other, let alone get involved in anything like a Violation. But Argus Three's offering us sixty-three million dollars in metal to slough them of the tramp before the cops arrive, and the Mayor thinks we can do it. Also, he hates tramps—I think he might even have taken on the job for nothing. The fact, anyhow, is that he *has* taken it."

The perimeter sergeant paused and eyed Chris, seemingly waiting for comments. At last Chris said: "What did the City Fathers say?"

"They said NO in a loud voice until the money was mentioned. After that they ran an accounting of the treasury, and gave Amalfi his head. They had a few additional facts to work from that I haven't told you yet, most of which seem to indicate that we can dispossess this tramp without too much damage to our own city, and very possibly before the cops even hear that anything's happening. All the same, bear in mind that they think of nothing but the city as a whole. If some of us get killed in the process they won't care, as long as the city itself gets off cleanly. They're not sentimental."

"I already know that," Chris said, with feeling. "But— how do I come into all this? Why does the Mayor want to talk to me? I don't know anything but what you've told me—and besides, he's already made up his mind."

"He's made up his mind," Anderson agreed, "but you know a lot that he doesn't know. As we get closer to Argus Three, he wants you to listen to the broadcasts from the Argidae, and anything we may pick up from the tramp, and fill him in on any clues you hear."

"But why?"

"Because you're the only person on board who knows the tramp at first hand," the perimeter sergeant said, with slow, deliberate emphasis. "It's your old friend Scranton."

"But—that can't be so! There were hundreds of us put on board from Scranton—all adults but me—"

"Press-gang sweepings," Anderson said with cold disgust. "Oh, there were one or two specialists we found a use for, but none of them ever paid any attention to city politics. The rest were bulgy-muscled misfits, a large proportion of them psychotics. We cured them, but we couldn't raise their IQ's; without something to sell, or the Interplanetary Grand Prix, or heavy labor to keep their minds off their minds, they're just so many vegetables. We—Irish and I—couldn't find even one worth taking into our squads. We've made citizens of the three good specialists, but the rest will be passengers till they die.

"But you're the happy accident of that crew right now, Chris. The City Fathers say that your history aboard Scranton shows that you *know* something about the town. Amalfii wants to mine that knowledge. Want to tackle it?"

"I—I'll try."

"Good." The perimeter sergeant turned to the miniature tape recorder at his elbow. "Here's a complete transcript of everything we've heard from Argus Three so far. After you've heard it and made any comments that occur to you, Amalfii will begin to feed us the live messages, from the bridge. Ready?"

"No," Chris said, more desperately than he could ever have imagined possible for him. "Not yet. My head is about to bust already. Do I get off from school while this is going on? I couldn't take it, otherwise."

"No," Anderson said, "you don't. If a live message comes through while you're in class, we'll pull you out. But you'll go right back in again. Otherwise your schooling will go right on just as before, and if you can't take the new burden, well, that'll be too bad. You'd better get that straight right away, Chris. This isn't a vacation, and it isn't a prize. It's a job, *for the survival of the city.* Either you take it or you don't; either way, you get no special treatment. Well?"

For what seemed to him to be a long time, Chris sat and listened to his echoing Okie headache. At last, however, he said resignedly:

"I'll take it."

Anderson snapped the switch, and the tape began to run on the spools.

The earliest messages, as Anderson had noted, were vague and brief. The later ones were longer, but even more cryptic. Chris was able to worry very little more information out of them than Amalfi and the City Fathers already had. As promised, he spoke to Amalfi—but from

the Andersons' apartment, through a hookup which fed
what he had to say to the mayor and to the machines
simultaneously.

The machines asked questions about population, energy
resources, degree of automation and other vital matters,
not a one of which Chris could answer. The Mayor mostly
just listened; on the few occasions when his heavy voice
cut in, Chris was unable to figure out what he was getting
at.

"Chris, this railroad you mentioned; how long before
you were born had it been pulled up?"

"About a century, sir, I think. You know Earth went
back to the railroads in the middle two thousands, when
all the fossil fuels ran out and they had to give up the
highways to farmland."

"No, I didn't know that. All right, go ahead."

Now the City Fathers were asking him about armament. He had no answer for that one, either.

There came a day, however, when this pattern changed
suddenly and completely. He was, indeed, pulled out of
class for the purpose, and hurried into a small anteroom
containing little but a chair and two television screens.
One of the screens showed Sgt. Anderson; the other, nothing but a testing pattern.

"Hello, Chris. Sit down and pay attention; this is important. We're getting a transmission from the tramp city. We
don't know whether it's just a beacon or whether they
want to talk to us. Amalfi thinks it's unlikely that they'd
be putting out a beacon in their situation, regardless of the
law—they've broken too many others already. He's going
to try to raise them, now that you're here; he wants you
to listen."

"Right, sir."

Chris could not hear his own city calling, but after only
a few minutes—for they were quite close to Argus Three
now—the test pattern on the other screen vanished, and
Chris saw an odiously familiar face.

"Hullo. This here's Argus Three."

" 'This here' is *not* Argus Three," Amalfi's deep voice
said promptly. " 'This here' is the city of Scranton, Pennsylvania, and there's no point in your hiding it. Get me
your boss."

"Now wait a minute. Just who do you think—"

"This *here* is New York, New York, calling, and I said,
'Get me your boss.' Go do it."

The face by now was both sullen and confused. After a moment's hesitation, it vanished. The screen flickered, the test pattern came back briefly, and then a second familiar face was looking directly at Chris. It was impossible to believe that the man couldn't see him, and the idea was outright frightening.

"Hello, New York," he said, affably enough. "So you've got us figured out. Well, we've got you figured out, too. This planet is under contract to us; be notified."

"Recorded," Amalfi said. "We also have it a matter of record that you are in Violation. Argus Three has made a new contract with us. It'd be the wisest course to clear ground and spin."

The man's eyes did not waver. Chris realized suddenly that it was an image of Amalfi he was staring at, not at Chris himself. "Spin yourself," he said evenly. "Our argument is with the colonists, not with you. We don't spin without a Vacate order from the cops. Once you mix into this, you may find it hard to mix out again. Be notified."

"Your self-confidence," Amalfi said, "is misplaced. Recorded."

The image from Scranton contracted to a bright point and vanished. The Mayor said once:

"Chris, do you know either of those guys?"

"Both of them, sir. The first one's a small-time thug named Barney. I think he was the one who killed my brother's dog when I was impressed, but I didn't see who did it."

"I know the type. Go ahead."

"The other one is Frank Lutz. He was the city manager when I was aboard. It looks as if he still is."

"What's a city manager? Never mind, I'll ask the machines. All right. He looks dangerous; is he?"

"Yes, sir, he is. He's smart and he's tricky—and he has no more feeling than a snake."

"Sociopath," Amalfi said. "Thought so. One more question: Does he know you?"

Chris thought hard before answering. Lutz had seen him only once, and had never had to think about him as an individual again—thanks to the lifesaving intervention of Frad Haskins. "Sir, he just might, but I'd say not."

"Okay. Give the details to the City Fathers and let them calculate the probabilities. Meanwhile we'll take no chances. Thanks, Chris. Joel, come topside, will you?"

"Yes, sir." Anderson waited until he heard the Mayor's

circuit cut out. Then his image, too, seemed to be staring directly at Chris. In fact, it was.

"Chris, did you understand what Amalfi meant about taking no chances?"

"Uh—no, not exactly."

"He meant that we're to keep you out of this Lutz's sight. In other words, *no deFord expeditions on this job*. Is that clear?"

It was all too clear.

CHAPTER TEN: Argus Asleep

The Argus system was well named: It was not far inside a crowded and beautiful cluster of relatively young stars, so that the nights on its planet had indeed a hundred eyes, like the Argus of the myth. The youth of the cluster went far toward explaining the presence of Scranton, for like all third-generation stars, the sun of Argus was very rich in metals. and so were its planets.

Of these there were only a few—just seven, to be exact, of which only the three habitable ones had been given numbers, and only Argus III actually colonized; II was suitable only for Arabs, and IV for Eskimos. The other four planets were technically of the gas giant class. but they were rather undernourished giants: the largest of them was about the size of Sol's Neptune. The closeness of the stars in the cluster to each other had swept up much of the primordial gas before planet formation had gotten a good start the Argus system was in fact the largest yet to be encountered in the cluster.

Argus III. as the city droned down over it, looked heart-stoppingly like Pennsy'vania Chris began to feel a little sorry for the coming dispossession of Scranton—of which he had no doubts whatsoever—for surely the planet must have provided an intolerable temptation. It was mountainous over most of its land area, which was considerable; water was confined to many thousands of lakes, and a few small and intensely salty seas It was also heavily wooded—almost entirely with conifers, or plants much like them, for evolution here had not yet gotten as far as a flowering plant. The firlike trees had thick boles and reared up hundreds of feet, noble monsters with their many shoulders hunched, as they had to be to bear their own weight in the two-G gravitation of this metal-heavy planet. The first sound Chris heard on Argus III after the city grounded was the explosion of a nearby seed cone, as loud as a crack of thunder. One of the seeds broke a window on the thirtieth floor of the McGraw-Hill Greenhouse, and the startled staff there had had to hack it to bits with fire axes to stop its germinating on the rug.

Under these circumstances it hardly mattered where the city settled; there was iron everywhere· and conversely there was no place on the planet which would be out of eavesdropping or of missile range of Scranton, to the mutual inconvenience of both parties. Nevertheless, Amalfi chose a site with great care. one just over the horizon from the great scar in the ground Scranton had made during its fumbled mining attempt and with the highest points of an Allegheny-like range reared up between the two Okies. Only then did the machinery begin to rumble out into the forests.

Chris was beginning to practice thinking like Amalfi— not very confidently to be sure, since he had never seen the man, but at least it made a good game. The landing, Chris concluded tentatively, had been chosen mostly to prevent Scranton from seeing what the city was doing without sending over planes: and secondly to prevent foot traffic between the two cities. Probably it would never come to warfare between the two cities, anyhow, for nothing would be more likely to bring the cops to the scene in a hurry: and besides, it was already quite clear from New York's history that Amalfi actively hated anything that did the city damage, whether it was bombs or only rust.

In the past, his most usual strategy had been to outsit the enemy. If that failed, he tried to outperform them. As a last resort, he tried to bring them into conflict with themselves. There were no pure cases of any of these policies on record—every example was a mixture, and a complicated one—but these three flavorings were the strongest, and usually one was far more powerful than the other two. When Amalfi salted his dish, you could hardly taste the pepper or the mustard.

Not everyone could eat it thereafter, either: there were, Chris suspected, more subtle schools of Okie cookery. But that was how Amalfi did it, and he was the only chef the city had. Thus far, the city had survived him, which was the only test that counted with the citizens and the City Fathers.

On Argus III, it seemed, Amalfi's hope was to starve Scranton out by outperforming it. The city had the contract; Scranton had lost it. The city could do the job; Scranton had made a mess of it, and left behind a huge yellow scar around its planetfall which might not heal for a century. And while New York worked and Scranton starved—here was where a faint pinch of outsittery was added to the broth—Scranton couldn't carry through on its desperate hope of seizing Argus III as a new home planet; though the Argidae could not yell for the cops at the first sign—or the last—of such a piracy, New York could and would. Okie solidarity was strong, and included a firm hatred of the cops ... but it did not extend to encouraging another incident like Thor V, or bucking the cops against another city like IMT. Even the outlaw must protect himself against the criminally insane, especially if they seem to be on his side.

Okay; if that was what Amalfi planned, so be it. There was nothing that Chris could say about it, anyhow. Amalfi was the mayor, and he had the citizens and the City Fathers behind him. Chris was only a youngster and a passenger.

But he knew one thing about the plan that neither Amalfi nor any other New Yorker could know, except himself:

It was not going to work.

He knew Scranton; the city didn't. If this was how Amalfi planned to proceed against Frank Lutz, it would fail.

But was he reading Amalfi's mind aright? That was probably the first question. After several days of worrying—which worsened his school record drastically—he took the question to the only person he knew who had ever seen Amalfi: his guardian.

"I can't tell you what Amalfi's set us up to do, you aren't authorized to know," the perimeter sergeant said gently. "But you've done a lot of good guessing. As far as you've guessed, Chris, you're pretty close."

Carla banged a coffee cup angrily into a saucer. "Pretty close? Joel, all this male expertise is a pain in the neck.

Chris is right and you know it. Give him a break and tell him so."

"I'm not authorized," Anderson said doggedly, but from him that was tantamount to an admission. "Besides, Chris is wrong on one point. We can't sit there forever, just to prevent this tramp from taking over Argus Three. Sooner or later we'll have to be on our own way. and we can't overstay our contract, either—we've got Violations of our own on our docket that we care about, whether Scranton cares about Violations or not. We have a closing date that we mean to observe—and that makes the problem *much* stiffer."

"'I see it does," Chris said diffidently. "But at least I understood part of it. And it seems to me that there are two big holes in it—and I just hope I'm wrong about those."

"Holes?" the perimeter sergeant said. "Where? What are they?"

"Well, first of all, they're probably pretty desperate over there, or if they aren't now, they soon will be. The fact that they're in this part of space at all, instead of wherever it was the Mayor directed them, back when I came on board here, shows that something went wrong with their first job, too."

Anderson snapped a switch on his chair. "Probability?" he said to the surrounding air.

"SEVENTY-TWO PER CENT." the air said back, making Chris start. He still had not gotten used to the idea that the City Fathers overheard everything one said, everywhere and all the time; among many other things, the city was their laboratory in human psychology, which in turn enabled them to answer such questions as Anderson had just asked.

"Well, score another for you," the sergeant said in a troubled voice.

"But I hadn't quite gotten to my point yet, sir. The thing is, now *this* job has gone sour on them too, so they must be awfully low on supplies. No matter how good our strategy is, it has to assume that the other side is going to react logically. But desperate men almost never behave logically: look at German strategy in the last year of World War Two. for instance."

"Never heard of it," Anderson admitted. "But it seems to make sense. What's the other hole?"

"The other one is really only a guess," Chris said. "It's

based on what I know about Frank Lutz, and I only saw him twice, and heard one of his aides talk about him. But I don't think he'd ever allow anybody to outbluff him; he'd always fight first. He has to prove he's the toughest guy in any situation, or his goose is cooked—somebody else'll take over. It's always like that in a thug society—look at the history of the Kingdom of Naples, or Machiavelli's Florence."

"I'm beginning to suspect you're just inventing these examples," Anderson said, frowning blackly. "But again, it does make a certain amount of sense—and nobody but you knows even a little about this man Lutz. Supposing you're right; what could we do about it that we're not doing now?"

"You could use the desperation," Chris said eagerly. "If Lutz and his gang are desperate, then the ordinary citizen must be on the edge of smashing things up. And I'm sure they don't have any 'citizens' in our sense of the word, because the aide I mentioned before let slip that they were short on the drugs. I think he meant me to overhear him, but it didn't mean anything to me at the time. The man on the street must hate the gang even in good times. We could use them to turn Lutz out."

"How?" Anderson said, with the air of a man posing a question he knows to be unanswerable.

"I don't know exactly. It'd have to be done more or less by feel. But I used to have at least two friends over there, one of them with constant access to Lutz. If he's still around and I could sneak over there and get in touch with him—"

Anderson held up a hand and sighed. "I was kind of afraid you were going to trot out something like that. Chris, when are we going to cure you of this urge to go junketing? You know what Amalfi said about that."

"Circumstances alter cases," Carla put in.

"Yes, but—oh, all right, all right, I'll go one step farther, at least." Once more he snapped the switch, and said to the air: "Comments?"

"WE ADVISE AGAINST SUCH A VENTURE, SERGEANT ANDERSON. THE CHANCE THAT MISTER DEFORD WOULD BE RECOGNIZED IS PROHIBITIVELY HIGH."

"There, you see?" Anderson said. "Amalfi would ask them the same question. He ignores their advice more often than not, but in this case what they say is just what he's already decided himself."

"Okay," Chris said, not very much surprised. "It's a pretty fuzzy sort of idea, I'll admit. But it was the only one I had."

"There's a lot to it. I'll tell the Mayor your two points, and suggest that we try to do something to stir up the animals over there. Maybe he'll think of another way of tackling that. Cheer up, Chris; it's a darned good thing you told me all this, so you shouldn't feel bad if a small part of what you said gets rejected. You can't win them all, you know."

"I know," Chris said. "But you can try."

If Amalfi thought of any better idea for "stirring up the animals" in Scranton, Chris did not hear of it; and if he tried it, obviously it had no significant effect. While the city worked, Scranton sat sullenly where it was, ominously silent, while New York's contract termination date drew closer and closer. Poor and starving though it must have been, Scranton had no intention of being outsat at the game of playing for so rich a planet as Argus III; if Amalfi wanted Scranton off the planet, he was going to have to throw it off—or call for the cops. Frank Lutz was behaving pretty much as Chris had predicted, at least so far.

Then, in the last week of the contract, the roof fell in.

Chris got the news, as usual, from his guardian. "It's your friend Piggy," he said wrathfully. "He had the notion that he could pretend to turn his coat, worm his way into Scranton's government, and then pull off some sort of coup. Of course Lutz didn't believe him, and now we're all in the soup."

Chris was torn between shock and laughter. "But how'd he get there?"

"That's one of the worst parts of it. Somehow he sold two women on the idea of being deadly female spies, concubine type, as if a thug government ever had any shortage of women, especially in a famine! One of them is a sixteen-year-old girl whose family is spitting flames, for every good reason. The other is a thirty-year-old passenger who's the sister of a citizen, and *he's* one of Irish Dulany's fighter pilots. The sister, the City Fathers tell us now, is a borderline psychotic, which is why she never made citizenship herself; but they authorized the brother to teach her to fly because it seemed to help her clinically. She stole the boarding-squad plane for the purpose, and by the time we got the whole story from the machines, it was all over."

"You mean that the City Fathers heard Piggy and the others planning all this?"

"Sure they did. They hear everything—you know that."

"But why didn't they tell somebody?" Chris demanded.

"They're under orders never to volunteer information. And a good thing too, almost all the time; without such an order they'd be jabbering away on all channels every minute of the day—they have no judgment. Now Lutz is demanding ransom. We'd pay any reasonable sum, but what he wants is the planet—you were right again, Chris, logic has gone out the window over there—and we can't give him what we don't own, and we wouldn't if we could. Piggy has gotten us into a war, and not even the machines can see what the consequences will be."

Chris blew out his breath in a long gust. "What are we going to do?"

"Can't tell you."

"No, I don't want to know about tactics or anything like that. Just a general idea. Piggy *is* a friend of mine—it sounds silly right now, but I really like him."

"If you don't like a man when he's in trouble, you probably never liked him at all," the perimeter sergeant agreed reflectively. "Well, I can't tell you very much more, all the same. In general terms, Amalfi is stalling in a way he hopes will give Lutz the idea that he's going to give in, but won't give the Argidae the same impression; the machines have run him up a set of key words that should convey the one thing to the colonists and the other to Scranton. Contact termination is only a week away, and if we can stall Lutz until the day before that—well, I can't say what we'll do. But generally, again, we'll move in there and deprive him of his marbles. That'll give us a day to get out of this system before the cops come running, and when they do catch us, at least they'll find that we have a fulfilled contract. Incidentally, it also gives us a day to collect our pay—"

"OVERRIDE," the City Fathers said suddenly, without being asked anything at all.

"Woof! Sorry. Either I've already said one word too many, or I was going to. Can't say anything else, Chris."

"But I thought they never volunteered information!"

"They don't," Anderson said. "That wasn't volunteered. They are under orders from Amalfi to monitor talk about this situation and shut it up when it begins to get too loose. That's all I can say—and it's none of it the best news I ever spread."

Only a week to go—and the contract date, Chris realized for the first time, was exactly one day before his birthday. Everything was going to be gained or lost within the same three days: for himself, for Piggy and his two victims, for Scranton, for Argus III, for the city.

And again he knew, as surely as he knew his left hand from his right, that Amalfi's present plan was not going to work.

And again the rock upon which it was sure to founder was Frank Lutz.

Chris did not doubt that Amalfi could outsmart Lutz hands down in any face-to-face situation, but that was not what this was. He did doubt, and doubted most thoroughly, that any list of trigger words the City Fathers could prepare could fool Lutz for long, no matter how well they lulled the hundred eyes of Argus to sleep; the city manager of Scranton was educated, shrewd, experienced in the ways of politics and power—and by now, on top of all that, he would be almost insanely suspicious. Suspicion of everyone had been normal for him even in good times; if he suspected his friends when things were going right, he would hardly be more trustful of his enemies in the very last days of a disaster.

Chris knew very little yet about the politics of Okie cities, but he knew his history. Also, he knew skunks; he had often marveled at the obduracy with which poor Kelly had failed to profit by his tangles with them. Maybe the dog had liked them; they are affectionate pets for a cautious master. But the human variety was not worth the risk. One look at Frank Lutz had taught Chris that.

And even supposing that Lutz did not shoot from the hip while New York was still trying to stall, bringing down upon the city a rain of missiles or whatever other bombardment Scranton was able to mount; even supposing that Lutz was totally taken in by Amalfi's strategy, so that New York took his city away from him at the very last minute, without firing a shot or losing a man; even supposing all this—and it was an impossible budget of suppositions—Piggy and the two women prisoners would not survive it. In New York only Chris could know with what contempt Lutz treated the useless people aboard his own town; and only Chris could guess what short shrift he would give three putative refugees from a great city that did tolerate passengers.

Piggy's pitiful expedition was probably heaving slag right now. If Lutz allowed them to live, more or less, through the next week, he would certainly have them executed the instant he saw his realm toppling, no matter how fast Amalfi moved upon Scranton when the H-hour arrived—it takes no more than five seconds to order that hostages be sacrificed. That was the whole and only reason why the many wars of medieval Earth had gone on so many years after all the participants had forgotten why they had been started or, if they remembered, no longer cared: there was still ransom money to be made.

His guardian was already impatient of that kind of example, however. As for Amalfi and the City Fathers, they had made their position too clear to be worth appealing to now. Were Chris to go back to them, they would give him more than another No; such an approach would give them all the reasons they could possibly need to put Chris under a 24-hour watch.

Yet this time he *knew* they were wrong; and this time he planned very carefully, fighting off the constant conviction that these ancient men and machines could not possibly have made a mistake . . . and would snap the switch on him at any moment.

If they knew what he was up to, they remained inactive, and kept their own counsel. He trudged out of the city the next night. Nobody tried to stop him. Nobody even seemed to see him go.

That was exactly what he had hoped for; but it made him feel miserably in the wrong, and on his own.

CHAPTER ELEVEN: The Hidey Hole

Ordinarily Chris would not have ventured into a strange wilderness at night; even under present circumstances, he would have left perhaps an hour before sunrise, leaving himself only enough darkness to put distance between himself and any possible pursuit. But on Argus III, he had several advantages going for him.

One of these was a homing compass, a commonplace Okie object the needle of which always pointed toward the strongest nearby spindizzy field. On most planets, cities tended to keep a fractional field going to prevent the local air from mixing with that of the city itself—and when the city was on a war footing, the generators would be kept running as a matter of course in case a quick getaway should be needed. The gadget would point him away from New York for half his trip, and an ordinary magnetic compass would serve to show which way; thereafter, the homing compass would be pointing steadily toward Scranton.

The second advantage was light. Argus had no moon—but it had the hundred eyes of the nearby blue-white giant suns of the cluster, and beyond them the diffuse light of the rest of the cluster, throughout this half of the year. The aggregate sky glow was almost twice as bright as Earthly moonlight—more than good enough to read by, and to cast sharp shadows, though not quite enough to trigger the color sensitivity of the human eye.

Most important of all, Chris knew pine woods and mountains. He had grown up among them.

He traveled light, carrying with him only a small pack containing two tins of field rations, a canteen and a change of clothing. The "fresh" clothes were those he had been wearing when he had first been transferred to New York; it had taken considerable courage to ask the City Fathers if they were still in storage, despite his knowledge that the machines never told what they knew unless asked. The request left behind a clue, but that really didn't matter; once Sgt. Anderson realized Chris was missing, he could be in little doubt about where he had gone.

By dawn he was almost over the crest of the range. By noon he had found himself a cave on the other side from which a small, ice-cold stream issued. He went very cautiously in this, as deep as he could go on his hands and knees, looking for old bones, droppings, bedding or any other sign that some local animal lived there. He found none, as he had expected; few animals care to make a home directly beside running water—it is too damp at night, and it attracts too many potential enemies. Then he ate for the first time and went to sleep.

He awoke at dusk, refilled his canteen from the stream,

and began the long scramble down the other side of the range. The route he took was necessarily more than a little devious, but thanks to the two compasses he was never in any doubt about his bearings, for more than a few minutes at a time. Long before midnight, he caught his first glimpse of Scranton, glowing dully in the valley like a scatter of dewdrops in a spider's web. By dawn, he had buried his pack along with the New York clothes—by now more than a little dirty and torn—and was shambling cheerfully across the cleared perimeter of Scranton, toward the same street by which he had boarded the town willy-nilly so long ago. There were many differences this time, not the least of which was his possession of the necessary device for getting through the edge of the spin-dizzy field.

He was spotted at once, of course, and two guards came trotting out to meet him, red-eyed and yawning; obviously, it was near the end of their trick.

"Whatcha doin' out here?"

"Went to pick mushrooms," Chris said, with what he hoped was an idiotic grin. "Didn't find any. Funny kind of woods they got here."

One of the sleepy guards looked him over, but apparently saw nothing but the issue clothing and Chris's obvious youth. He cussed Chris out more or less routinely and said:

"Where ya work?"

"Soaking pits."

The two guards exchanged glances. The soaking pits were deep, electrically heated holes in which steel ingots were cooled, gently and slowly. Occasionally they had to be cleaned, but it wasn't economical to turn the heat off. The men who did the job were lowered into the pits in asbestos suits for four minutes at a time, which was the period it took for their insulating wooden shoes to burst into flame; then they were hauled out, given new shoes, and lowered into the pit again—and this went on for a full working day. Nobody but the mentally deficient could safely be assigned to such an inferno.

"Awright, feeb, get back on the job. And don't come out here no more, get me? You're lucky we didn't shoot you."

Chris ducked his head, grinned, and ran. A minute later, he was twisting and dodging through the shabby streets. Despite his confidence, he was a little surprised at how well he remembered them.

The hidey hole among the crates was still there, too, exactly as he and Frad had last left it, even to the stub of candle. Chris ate his other tin of field rations, and sat down in the darkness to wait.

He did not have to wait long, though the time *seemed* endless. About an hour after the end of the work day, he heard the sounds of someone threading the labyrinth with sure steps; and then the light of the flash came darting in upon him.

"Hi, Frad," he said. "I'm glad to see you. Or I will be, once you get that light out of my eyes."

The spoor of the flashlight beam swung toward the ceiling. "It that you, Chris?" Frad's voice said. "Yep, I see it is. But you must have grown a foot."

"I guess I have. I'm sorry I didn't get here sooner."

The big man sat down with a grunt. "Never thought you'd make it at all—it was just a hunch, once I heard who it was we were up against. I hope you're not trying to switch sides, like those other three idiots."

"Are they still alive?" Chris said with sudden fear.

"Yep. As of an hour ago. But I wouldn't put any money on them lasting. Frank is getting wilder by the day—I used to think I understood him, but not any more. Is that what you're here for—to try and sneak those kids out? You can't do it."

"No," Chris said. "Or, anyhow, not exactly. And I'm not trying to switch sides, either. But we were wondering why you let your city manager get you into this mess. Our City Fathers say he's gone off his rocker, and if the machines can see it, you ought to be able to. In fact, you just said you did."

"I've heard about those machines of yours," Frad said slowly. "Do they really run the city, the way the stories say?"

"They run most of it. They don't boss it, though; the Mayor does that."

"Amalfi. Hmm. To tell you the truth, Chris, everybody knows that Frank's lost control. But there's nothing we can do about it. Suppose we threw him out—not that it'd be easy—where'd we go from there? We'd still be in the same mess."

"You wouldn't be at war with my town any more," Chris suggested.

"No, and that'd be a gain, as far as it went. But we'd still be in the rest of the hole. Just changing a set of names won't put any money in the till, or any bread in our mouths." He paused for a moment and then added bitterly, "I suppose you know we're starving. Not me, personally—Frank feeds his own—but I don't eat very well either when I have to look at the faces I meet on the streets. Frank's big play against Amalfi is crazy, sure—but except for that we've got *no* hope."

Chris was silent. It was what he had expected to find, but that made the problem no easier.

"But you haven't answered my question," Frad said. "What are you up to? Just collecting information? Maybe I should have kept my mouth shut."

"I'm trying to promote a revolution," Chris said. It sounded embarrassingly pompous, but he couldn't think of any other way to put it. He was also trying to avoid saying anything which would be an outright lie, but from this point onward that was going to be increasingly difficult. "The Mayor says you must have flunked your contracts because you don't have any machines to judge them. Evidently that happens a lot of times to small cities that don't have computer control. And the City Fathers say you *could* have done this job."

"Now wait a minute. Let's take this one step at a time. Suppose we got rid of Frank and patched things up with Amalfi. Could we get some help from your City Fathers on reorganizing the job?"

Now the guesswork had to begin, to be followed rapidly by the outright lying. "Sure you could. But we'd have to have our people back first—Piggy Kingston-Throop and the two women."

Frad made a quick gesture of dismissal in the dim light. "I'd do that for a starter, not as part of a deal. But look, Chris, this is a complicated business. Your city landed here to do the job we defaulted on. If we do it after all, then somebody doesn't get paid. Not a likely deal for Amalfi to make."

"Mayor Amalfi isn't offering any deal yet. But Frad, you know what our contract with Argus is like. Half of it is to do the job you didn't do, sure. But the other half of it is to get rid of Scranton. If you turn into a decent town instead of a bindlestiff, we'll get that part of the money—

and it's the bigger part, now. Naturally the Mayor'd rather do it by finagling than by fighting—if we fight, we'll need all the money and more just to pay for the damages, both of us. Isn't that logical?"

"Hmm. I guess it is. But if you want to keep *me* reasonable, you'd better lay off that word 'bindlestiff.' It's true enough, but it makes me mad all the same. Either we treat as equals, or we don't treat."

"I'm sorry," Chris said. "I don't know a lot about this kind of thing. The Mayor would have sent somebody else if he'd had anybody who could have gotten in. But there wasn't anyone but me."

"Okay. I'm edgy, that's all. But there's one thing more, and that's the colonists. They're not going to trust us just because we've gotten rid of Frank. *They* don't know that he's the problem, and they'll have no better reason to trust the next city manager. If we're going to get back the mining part of the contract, Amalfi will have to guarantee it. Would he do that?"

Chris was already in far deeper waters than his conscience could possibly justify. He knew abruptly that he could push no farther into the untrue and the unknown.

"I don't know, Frad. I never asked, and he didn't say. I suppose he'd have to ask the City Fathers for an opinion first—and *nobody* knows what they might say."

Frad squatted and thought about it, smacking one fist repeatedly into the other palm. After a moment, he seemed about to ask another question, but it never got out.

"Well," he muttered finally, "every deal has one carrot in it. I guess we take the chance. You'll have to stay here, Chris. I can knock Barney's and Huggins' heads together easy enough, but Frank's something else again. When the shooting really starts, he might turn out to be a lot faster than I am—and besides, he won't care what else he hits. If I manage to dump him I'll come back for you soon enough—but you'd better stay out of sight until it's over."

Chris had expected nothing else, but the prospect of again missing all the excitement, while he simply sat and waited, disappointed him all the same. However, it also reminded him of something.

"I'll stay here. But, Frad, if it doesn't look as if it's working, don't wait till it's hopeless. Let me know and I'll try to get help."

"Well . . . all right. But better not to have any outsiders

visible if it's going to stick. If anybody in this town sees
New York's finger in this even people who hate Frank'll
be on his side again. We're all a little crazy around here
lately."

He stood up, his face somber, and picked up the flashlight.

"I hope you've got the straight goods," he said. "I
don't like to do this. Frank trusts me—I guess I'm the last
man he does trust. And for some reason I always liked
him, even though I knew he was a louse from the very
beginning. Some guys hit you that way. It's not going to
be fun, stabbing him in the back. He's got it coming sure—
but all the same I wouldn't do it if I didn't trust you
more."

He swung to the exit into the labyrinth. Chris swallowed
and said: "Thanks, Frad. Good luck."

"Sit tight. I'll see you."

Of necessity, Chris did not stay in the hole every minute
of the day, but even so he found that he quickly lost track
of the passage of time. He ate when he seemed to need
to—though most of the food had been removed from the
hide-out, Frad had missed one compact cache—and slept as
much as possible. That was not very much, however, for
now that he was inactive he found himself a prey to more
and more anxiety and tension, made worse by his total
ignorance of what was going on outside.

Finally he was convinced that the deadline had passed.
After all, all possibility of sleep vanished; from minute to
minute he awaited the noises of battle joined, or the
deepening drone which would mean that Scranton was
carrying him off again. The close confines of the hole
made the tension even more nightmarish. At the first faint
sound in the labyrinth, he jumped convulsively, and would
have started like a hare had there been any place to run to.

In the uncertain light of the flash, Frad looked ghastly:
he had several days' growth of beard and was haggard
with sleeplessness. In addition, he had a beautiful black
eye.

"Come on out," he said tersely. "The job's mostly
done."

Chris followed Frad out into the half-light of the warehouse, which seemed brilliant after the stuffy inkiness of
the hole, and thence into the intolerable brilliance of
late-afternoon sunlight.

"What happened to Frank Lutz?" he said breathlessly.

Frad stared straight ahead, and when he replied, his voice was totally devoid of expression.

"We got rid of him. The subject is closed."

Chris shied off from it hastily. "What happens now?"

"There's still a little mopping up to do, and we could use some help. If you called your friends now, we could let them in—as long as Amalfi doesn't send a whole boarding squad."

"No, just two men."

Frad nodded. "Two good men in full armor should flatten things out in a day or so at the most." He hailed a passing Tin Cab. As it settled obediently beside them, Chris saw that there were several inarguable bullet holes in it. How old they were was of course impossible to know, but it was Chris's guess that they hadn't been there for as much as a week. "I'll get you to the radio and you can take it from there. Then it'll be time to get the deal drawn up."

And that would be the moment that Chris had been dreading above all others—the moment when he would have to talk to Anderson and Amalfi, and tell them what he had done, what he had started, what he had committed them to.

There was no doubt in his mind as to how he felt about it. He was scared.

"Come on, hop in," Frad said. "What are you waiting for?"

CHAPTER TWELVE: An Interview
                   With Amalfi

The city was still administered, with due regard for tradition, from City Hall, but its control room was in the mast of the Empire State Building. It was here that Amalfi received them all—Chris, Frad, and Sgts. Anderson and Dulany—for he had been occupying it around the clock while the alert had been on, as officially it still was.

It was a marvelous place, jammed to the ceilings with screens, lights, meters, automatic charts, and scores of devices Chris could not even put a name to; but Chris was more interested in the Mayor. Since he was at the moment talking to Frad, Chris had plenty of opportunity to study him.

The fabulous Amalfi had turned out to be a complete surprise. Chris could not say any more just what kind of man he had pictured in his mind. Something more stalwart, lean and conventionally heroic, perhaps—but certainly not a short barrel-shaped man with a bull neck, a totally bald head and hands so huge that they looked as though they could crush rocks. The oddest touch of all was the cigar, held in the powerful fingers with almost feminine delicacy, and drawn on with invariable relish. Nobody else in the city smoked—*nobody* else—because there was no place in it to grow tobacco. The cigar, then, was more than a badge of office; it was a symbol of the wealth of the city, like the snow imported from the mountains by the Roman emperors, and Amalfi treated it like a treasure, not a habit. When he was thinking, he had an odd way of holding it up and looking at it, as though everything that was going on in his head was concentrated in its glowing coal.

He was saying to Frad: "The arrangements with the machinery are cumbersome, but not difficult in principle. We can lend you our Brood assembly until she replicates herself; then you reset the daughter machine, feed her scrap, and out come City Fathers to the number that you'll need—probably about a third as many as we carry, and it'll take maybe ten years. You can use the time feeding them data, because in the beginning they'll be idiots except for the computation function.

"In the meantime we'll refigure your job problem on our own machines. Since we'll trust the answer, and since Chris says you're a man of your word, that means that of course we'll underwrite your contract with Argidae."

"Many thanks," Frad said.

"Not necessary," Amalfi rumbled. "For value received. In fact we got more than we're paying for—we learned something from you. Which brings us to our drastic friend Mr. deFord." He swung on Chris, who tried unsuccessfully to swallow his heart. "I suppose you're aware, Chris, that this is D-day for you: your eighteenth birthday."

"Yes. sir. I sure am."

"Well, I've got a job for you if you want it. I've been studying it ever since it was first mentioned to me, and all I can say is, it serves you right."

Chris swallowed again. The Mayor studied the cigar judiciously.

"It calls for a very odd combination of skills and character traits. Taking the latter first, it needs initiative, boldness, imagination, a willingness to improvise and take short-cuts, and an ability to see the whole of a complex situation at a glance. But at the same time, it needs conservative instincts, so that even the boldest ideas and acts tend to be those that save men, materials, time, money. What class of jobs does that make you think of so far?"

"MILITARY GENERAL OFFICERS," the City Fathers promptly announced.

"I wasn't talking to you," Amalfi growled. He was plainly irritated, but it seemed to Chris an old irritation, almost a routine one. "Chris?"

"Well, sir, they're right, of course. I might even have thought of it myself, though I can't swear to it. At least all the great generals follow that pattern."

"Okay. As for the skills, a lot of them are required, but only one is cardinal. The man has got to be a first-class cultural morphologist."

Chris recognized the term, from his force feeding in Spengler. It denoted a scholar who could look at any culture at any stage in its development, relate to it all other cultures at similar stages, and come up with specific predictions of how these people would react to a given proposal or event. It surely wouldn't be a skill a general would ever be likely to have a use for, even if he had the time to develop it.

"You've got the character traits, that's plain to see— including the predisposition toward the skill. Most Okies have that, but in nowhere near the degree you seem to. The skill itself, of course, can only emerge with time and practice . . . but you'll have lots of time. The City Fathers say five years' probation.

"As for the city, we never had such a job on the roster before, but a study of Scranton and some more successful towns convinces us that we need it. Will you take it?"

Chris's head was whirling with a wild, humming mixture of pride and bafflement. "Excuse me, Mr. Mayor—but just what is it?"

"City manager."

Chris stared at Sgt. Anderson, but his guardian looked as stunned as Chris felt. After a moment, however, he winked solemnly. Chris could not speak; but at last he managed to nod his head. It was all the management he was capable of, right now.

"Good. The City Fathers predicted you would, so you were started on the drugs in your first meal of today. Welcome to citizenship, Mr. deFord."

Even at this moment, however, a part of Chris's mind seemed curiously detached. He was thinking of the original reason he had wanted long life: in the hope that some day, somehow, he might yet get back home. It had never occurred to him that by the time that happened, there would be nothing left back there that he could call his own. Even now, Earth was unthinkably remote, not only in space, but in his heart.

His definition of "home" had changed. He had won long life; but with it, new ties and new obligations; not an eternal childhood on Earth, but a life for the stars.

He wrenched his attention back to the control room. "What about Piggy?" he said curiously. "I talked to him on the way back. He seems to have learned a lot."

"Too late," Amalfi said, his voice inflexibly stern. "He wrote his own ticket. It's a passenger ticket. He's got boldness and initiative, all right—all of it of the wrong kind, totally untempered by judgment or imagination. The same kind of pitfall will always lie ahead of you, Chris; that, too, is an aspect of the job. It'd be wise not to forget it."

Chris nodded again, but the warning could not dampen his spirits now; for this was for some reason the highest moment of them all—the moment when Frad Haskins, the new city manager of Scranton, shook his hand and said huskily:

"Colleague, let's talk business."

EARTHMAN,
COME
HOME

PROLOGUE

SPACE flight got its start as a war weapon amid the collapse of the great Western culture of Earth. The invention of Muir's tape-mass engine carried early explorers out as far as Jupiter; and gravity was discovered—though it had been postulated centuries before—by the 2018 Jovian expedition, the last space flight with Muir engines which was completed on behalf of the West before that culture's final extinction. The building, by remote control, of the Bridge on the face of Jupiter itself, easily the most enormous (and in most other respects the most useless) engineering project ever undertaken by man, had made possible direct, close measurements of Jupiter's magnetic field. The measurements provided final confirmation of the Blackett-Dirac equations, which as early as 1948 had proposed a direct relationship between magnetism, gravitation, and the rate of spin of any mass.

Up to that time, nothing had been done with the Blackett-Dirac hypothesis, which remained a toy of pure mathematicians. Then, abruptly, the hypothesis and the mathematicians had their first innings. From the many pages of symbols and the mumbled discussions of the possible field-strength of a single electronic pole in rotation, the Dillon-Wagonner gravitron polarity generator—almost immediately dubbed the "spindizzy" in honor of what it did to electron rotation—sprang as if full-born. The overdrive, the meteor screen, and antigravity had all arrived in one compact package labeled "$G = 2(PC/BU)^2$."

Every culture has its characteristic mathematic, in which its toriographers can see its inevitable social form. This expression, couched in the algebra of the Magian culture, pointing toward the matrix mechanics of the new Nomad Era, remained essentially a Western discovery. At first its major significance seemed to lie in the fact that it was rooted in a variation of the value of *C*, the velocity of light, as a limit. The West used the spindizzy to scatter the nearby stars with colonists during the last fifty years of its existence; but even then, it did not realize the power of the weapon that it held in its faltering hands. Essentially, the West never found out that the spindizzy could lift *anything,* as well as protect it and drive it faster than light.

In the succeeding centuries, the whole concept of space flight was almost forgotten. The new culture on Earth, that narrow planar despotism called by historiographers the Bureaucratic State, did not think that way. Space flight had been a natural, if late, outcome of Western thought patterns, which had always been ambitious for the infinite. The Soviets, however, were opposed so bitterly to the very idea that they would not even allow their fiction writers to mention it. Where the West had soared from the rock of Earth like a sequoia, the Soviets spread like lichens over the planet, tightening their grip, satisfied to be at the bases of the pillars of sunlight the West had sought to ascend.

This was the way the Bureaucratic State had been born and had triumphed, and it was the way it meant to maintain its holdings. There had never been any direct military conquest of the West by the Soviets. Indeed, by 2105, the date usually assigned to the fall of the West, any such battle would have depopulated the Earth almost overnight. Instead, the West helped conquer itself, a long and painful process which many people foresaw but no one was able to halt. In its anxiety to prevent infiltration by the enemy, the West developed thought controls of its own, which grew ever tighter. In the end, the two opposing cultures could no longer be told apart—and since the Soviets had had far more practice at running this kind of monolithic government than had the West, Soviet leadership became a bloodless fact.

The ban on thinking about space flight extended even to the speculations of physicists. The omnipresent thought police were instructed in the formulae of ballistics and other disciplines of astronautics, and could detect such work—Unearthly Activities, it was called—long before it might have reached the proving-stand stage.

The thought police, however, could not ban atomic

research because the new state's power rested upon it. It had been from study of the magnetic moment of the electron that the Blackett equation had emerged. The new state had suppressed the spindizzy—it was too good an escape route—and the thought police had never been told that the original equation was one of those in the "sensitive area." The Soviets did not dare let even that much be known about it.

Thus, despite all of the minority groups purged or "reeducated" by the Bureaucratic State, the pure mathematicians went unsuspected about the destruction of that state, innocent even in their own minds of revolutionary motives. The spindizzy was rediscovered, quite inadvertently, in the nuclear physics laboratories of the Thorium Trust.

The discovery spelled the doom of the flat culture, as the leveling menace of the nuclear reactor and the Solar Phoenix had cut down the soaring West. Space flight returned. For a while, cautiously, the spindizzy was installed only in new spaceships, and there was another period—comically brief—of interplanetary exploration. The tottering edifice fought to retain its traditional balance. But the center of gravity had shifted. The waste inherent in using the spindizzy only in a ship could not be disguised. There was no longer any reason why a man-carrying vehicle to cross space needed to be small, cramped, organized fore-and-aft, penurious of weight. Once antigravity was an engineering reality, it was no longer necessary to design ships specially for space travel, for neither mass nor aerodynamic lines meant anything any more. The most massive and awkward object could be lifted and hurled off the Earth, and carried almost any distance. Whole cities, if necessary, could be moved.

Many were. The factories went first; they toured Earth, from one valuable mineral lie to another, and then went farther aloft. The exodus began. Nothing could be done to prevent it, for by that time the whole trend was obviously in the best interests of the State. The mobile factories changed Mars into the Pittsburgh of the solar system; the spindizzy had lifted the mining equipment and the refining plants bodily to bring life back to that lichen-scabbed ball of rust. The blank where Pittsburgh itself had been was a valley of slag and ashes. The great plants of the Steel

Trust gulped meteors and chewed into the vitals of satellites. The Aluminum Trust, the Germanium Trust, and the Thorium Trust put their plants aloft to mine the planets.

But the Thorium Trust's Plant No. 8 never came back. The revolution against the planar culture began with that simple fact. The first of the Okie cities soared away from the solar system, looking for work among the colonists left stranded by the ebb tide of Western civilization. The new culture began among these nomad cities; and when it was all over, the Bureaucratic State, against its own will, had done what it had long promised to do "when the people were ready"—it had withered away. The Earth that it once had owned, right down to the last grain of sand, was almost deserted. Earth's nomad cities—migratory workers, hobos, Okies—had become her inheritors.

Primarily the spindizzy had made this possible; but it could not have maintained it without heavy contributions from two other social factors. One of these was longevity. The conquest of so-called "natural" death had been virtually complete by the time the technicians on the Jovian Bridge had confirmed the spindizzy principle, and the two went together like hand in spacemitt. Despite the fact that the spindizzy would drive a ship—or a city—at speeds enormously faster than that of light, interstellar flight still consumed finite time. The vastness of the galaxy was sufficient to make long flights consume lifetimes, even at top spindizzy speed.

But when death yielded to the anti-agathic drugs, there was no longer any such thing as a "lifetime" in the old sense.

The other factor was economic: The rise of the metal germanium as the jinn of solid-state physics. Long before flight into deep space became a fact, the metal had assumed a fantastic value on Earth. The opening of the interstellar frontier drove its price down to a manageable level, and gradually it emerged as the basic, stable monetary standard of space trade. Nothing else could have kept the nomads in business.

And so the Bureaucratic State had fallen; but the social structure did not collapse entirely. Earth laws, though much changed, survived, and not entirely to the disadvantage of the Okies. The migrant cities found worlds that refused them landing permits. Others allowed them to land, but exploited them mercilessly. The cities fought back, but they were not efficient fighting machines. Steam shovels, by and large, had been more characteristic of the West than tanks, but in a fight between the two, the outcome was predictable; that situation never changed. It was, of course, a waste to bottle a spindizzy in so small an object as a spaceship, but a war vessel is meant to waste power—the more, the more deadly. The Earth police put the rebel cities down; and then, in self-protection, because the cities were needed, Earth passed laws protecting the cities.

Thus the Earth police held their jurisdiction, but the hegemony of Earth was weak, for the most part. There were many corners of the galaxy which knew Earth only as a legend, a green myth floating unknown thousands of parsecs away in space, known and ineluctable thousands of years away in history. Some of them remembered much more vividly the now-broken tyranny of Vega, and did not know—some of them never had known—even the name of the little planet that had broken that tyranny.

Earth itself became a garden planet, bearing only one city worth noticing, the sleepy capitol of a galaxy. Pittsburgh valley bloomed, and rich honeymooners went there to frolic. Old bureaucrats went to Earth to die.

Nobody else went there at all.

————ACREFF-MONALES: *The Milky Way*:
Five Cultural Portraits

CHAPTER ONE: Utopia

AS John Amalfi emerged onto the narrow, worn granite ledge with its gritty balustrade, his memory encountered one of those brief boggles over the meaning of a word which had once annoyed him constantly, like a bubble in an otherwise smoothly blown French horn solo. Such moments of confusion were very rare now, but they were still a nuisance.

This time he found himself unable to decide on a name

for where he was going at the moment. Was it a belfry, or was it a bridge?

It was, of course, only a matter of simple semantics, depending, as the oldest saying goes, on the point of view. The ledge ran around the belfry of City Hall. The city, however, was a spaceship, much of which was sometimes operated from this spot, and from which Amalfi was accustomed to assess the star-seas that the city sailed. That made it a bridge. But the ship was a city, a city of jails and playgrounds, alleys and alley cats, and there was even one bell still in the belfry, though it no longer had a clapper. The city was still called New York, N.Y., too, but that, the old maps showed, was misleading; the city aloft was only Manhattan, or New York County.

Amalfi's step across the threshold struck the granite without perceptible interruption. The minute dilemma was familiar: he had been through others of its kind often in the years immediately after the city had taken to the skies. It was hard to decide the terms in which one thought about customary things and places after they had become utterly transformed by space flight. The difficulty was that, although the belfry of City Hall still looked much as it had in 1850, it was now the bridge of a spaceship, so that neither term could quite express what the composite had become.

Amalfi looked up. The skies, too, looked about as they must have in 1850 on a very clear night. The spindizzy screen which completely englobed the flying city was itself invisible, but it would pass only elliptically polarized light, so that it blurred the points which were stars seen from space, and took them down in brilliance about three magnitudes to boot. Except for the distant, residual hum of the spindizzies themselves—certainly a much softer noise than the composite traffic roar which had been the city's characteristic tone back in the days before cities could fly—there was no real indication that the city was whirling through the emptiness between stars, a migrant among migrants.

If he chose, Amalfi could remember those days, since he had been mayor of the city—although only for a short time—when the City Fathers had decided that it was time to go aloft. That had been in 3111, decades after every other major city had already left the Earth; Amalfi had been just 117 years old at the time. His first city manager

had been a man named deFord, who for a while had
shared Amalfi's amused puzzlement about what to call all
the familiar things now that they had turned strange—but
deFord had been shot by the City Fathers around 3300
for engineering an egregious violation of the city's contract with a planet called Epoch, which had put a black
mark on the city's police record which the cops still had
not forgotten.

The new city manager was a youngster less than 400
years old named Mark Hazleton, who was already as little
loved by the City Fathers as deFord had been and for
about the same reasons, but who had been born after the
city had gone aloft and hence had no difficulty in finding
the appropriate words for things. Amalfi was prepared to
believe that he was the last living man on board the flying
city who still had occasional bubbles blown into his stream
of consciousness by old Earthbound habits of thinking.

In a way, Amalfi's clinging to City Hall as the center of
operations for the city betrayed the mayor's ancient ties to
Earth. City Hall was the oldest building on board, and so
only a few of the other structures could be seen from it. It
wasn't tall enough, and there were too many newer buildings around it. Amalfi didn't care. From the belfry—or
bridge, if that was what he had to call it now—he never
looked in any direction but straight up, his head tilted all
the way back on his bull neck. He had no reason to look
at the buildings around Battery Park, after all. He had
already seen them.

Straight up, however, was a sun, surrounded by starry
sable. It was close enough to show a perceptible disc, and
becoming slowly larger. While Amalfi watched it, the
microphone in his hand began to emit intermittent
squawks.

"It looks good enough to me," Amalfi said, lowering his
bald head grudgingly a centimeter or two toward the
mike. "It's a type G star, or near to it, and Jake in
Astronomy says two of the planets are Earthlike. And
Records says that both of 'em are inhabited. Where there's
people, there's work."

The phone quacked anxiously, each syllable evenly
weighted, but without any over-all sense of conviction.
Amalfi listened impatiently. Then he said, "Politics."

The way he said it made it sound fit only to be scrawled
on sidewalks. The phone was silenced; Amalfi hung it on

its hook on the railing and thudded back down the archaic stone steps which led from the belfry/bridge.

Hazleton was waiting for him in the mayor's office, drumming slim fingers upon the desk top. The current city manager was an excessively tall, slender, disjointed sort of man. Something in the way his limbs were distributed over Amalfi's chair made him also look lazy. If taking devious pains was a sign of laziness, Amalfi was quite willing to call Hazleton the laziest man in the city.

Whether he was lazier than anybody outside the city didn't matter. Nothing that went on outside the city was of real importance any more.

Hazleton said, "Well?"

"Well enough." Amalfi grunted. "It's a nice yellow dwarf star, with all the fixings."

"Sure," Hazleton said with a wry smile. "I don't see why you insist on taking a personal look at every star we go by. There are screens right here in the office, and the City Fathers have all the data. We knew even before we could see this sun what it was like."

"I like a personal look," said Amalfi. "I haven't been mayor here for five hundred years for nothing. I can't really tell about a sun until I see it with my own eyes. Then I know. Images don't mean a thing—no *feel* to 'em."

"Nonsense," Hazleton said, without malice. "And what does your feelership say about this one?"

"It's a good sun; I like it. We'll land."

"All right, suppose I tell you what's going on out there?"

"I know, I know," Amalfi said. His heavy voice took on a finicky, nervous tone, his own exaggerated version of the mechanical speech of the City Fathers. " 'THE PO-LITICAL SIT-UATION IS *VER*-Y DISTURBING.' It's the food situation that I'm worried about."

"Oh? Is it so bad, then?"

"It's not bad yet. It will be, unless we land. There's been another mutation in the *Chlorella* tanks; must have started when we passed through that radiation field near Sigma Draconis. We're getting a yield of about twenty-two hundred kilograms per acre in terms of fats."

"That's not bad."

"Not bad, but it's dropping steadily, and the rate of decrease is accelerating. If it's not arrested, we won't have any algae crops at all in a year or so. And there's not enough crude-oil reserve to tide us over to the next nearest star. We'd hit there eating each other."

Hazleton shrugged. "That's a big *if*, boss," he said. "We've never had a mutation we couldn't get under control before. And it's very nasty on those two planets."

"So they're having a war. We've been through that kind of situation before. We don't have to take sides. We land on the planet best suited——"

"If it were an ordinary interplanetary squabble, okay. But as it happens, one of those worlds—the third from the sun—is a sort of free-living polyp of the old Hruntan Empire, and the inner one is a survivor of the Hamiltonians. They've been fighting for a century, on and off, without any contact with Earth. Now—the Earth's found them."

"And?" Amalfi said.

"And it's cleaning them both out," Hazleton said grimly. "We've just received an official police warning to get the hell out of here."

Above the city the yellow sun was now very much smaller. The Okie metropolis, skulking out from the two warm warring worlds under one-quarter drive, crept steadily into hiding within the freezing blue-green shadow of one of the ruined giant planets of the system. Tiny moons, a quartet of them, circled in a gelid minuet against the chevrons of ammonia-storms that banded the gas giant.

Amalfi watched the vision screens tensely. This kind of close maneuvering, involving the balancing of the city against a whole series of conflicting gravitational fields, was very delicate, and not the kind of thing to which he was accustomed; the city generally gave gas giants a wide berth. His own preternatural "feel" for the spatial conditions in which he spent his life must here be abetted by every electronic resource at his command.

"Too heavy, Twenty-third Street," he said into the mike. "You've got close to a two-degree bulge on your arc of the screen. Trim it."

"Trim, boss."

Amalfi watched the image of the giant planet and its chill hand-maidens. A needle tipped gently.

"Cut!"

The whole city throbbed once and went silent. The

silence was a little frightening: the distant hum of the
spindizzies was a part of the expected environment, and
when it was damped, one felt a strange shortness of
breath, as if the air had gone bad. Amalfi yawned involuntarily, his diaphragm sucking against an illusory shortage
of oxygen.

Hazleton yawned, too, but his eyes were glittering.
Amalfi knew that the city manager was enjoying himself
now; the plan had been his, and so he no longer cared
that the city might be in serious danger from here on out.
He was taking lazy folks' pains.

Amalfi only hoped that Hazleton was not outsmarting
himself and the city at the same time. They had had some
narrow squeaks with Hazleton's plans before. There had
been, for instance, that episode on Thor V. Of all the
planets in the inhabited galaxy on which an Okie might
choose to throw his weight around, Thor V was easily the
worst. The first Okie city Thor V ever saw had been an
outfit which had dropped its city name and taken to
calling itself the Interstellar Master Traders. By the time it
had left Thor V again, it had earned itself still another
appellation: the Mad Dogs. On Thor V, hatred of Okies
was downright hereditary, and for good reason . . .

"Now we'll sit tight for a week," Hazleton said, his
spatulate fingers shooting the courser of his slide rule back
and forth. "Our food will hold out that long. And that was
a very convincing orbit Jake gave us. The cops will be
sure we're well on our way out of this system by now—
and there aren't enough of them to take care of the two
warring planets and to comb space for us at the same
time, anyhow."

"You hope."

"It stands to reason, doesn't it?" Hazleton said, his eyes
gleaming. "Sooner or later, within a matter of weeks,
they'll find out that one of those two planets is stronger
than the other, and concentrate their forces on that one.
When that happens, we'll hightail for the planet with the
weaker police investiture. The cops'll be too busy to prevent our landing there, or to block our laying on supplies
once we're grounded."

"That's fine as far as it goes. But it also involves us
directly with the weaker planet. The cops won't need any
better excuse for dispersing the city."

"Not necessarily," Hazleton insisted. "They can't break

us up just for violating a Vacate order. They know that as well as we do. If necessary, we can call for a court ruling and show that the Vacate order was inhumane—and in the meantime, they can't enforce the order while we're under the aegis of an enemy of theirs. Which reminds me—we've got an 'I want off' from a man named Webster, a pile engineer. He's one of the city's original complement, and as good as they come; I hate to see him leave."

"If he wants off, he gets it," Amalfi said. "What does he opt?"

"Next port of call."

"Well, this looks like it. Well——"

The intercom on the flight board emitted a self-deprecatory burp. Amalfi pressed the stud.

"Mr. Mayor?"

"Yep."

"This is Sergeant Anderson at the Cathedral Parkway lookout. There's a whopping big ship just come into view around the bulge of the gas giant. We're trying to contact her now. A warship."

"Thanks," Amalfi said, shooting a glance at Hazleton. "Put her through to here when you do make contact." He dialed the 'visor until he could see the limb of the giant planet opposite the one into which the city was swinging. Sure enough, there was a tiny sliver of light there. The strange ship was still in direct sunlight, but even so, she must have been a whopper to be visible at all so far away. The mayor stepped up the magnification, and was rewarded with a look at a tube about the size of his thumb.

"Not making any attempt to hide," he murmured, "but then you couldn't very well hide a thing that size. She must be all of a thousand feet long. Looks like we didn't fool 'em."

Hazleton leaned forward and studied the innocuous-looking cylinder intently. "I don't think that's a police craft," he said. "The police battleships on the clean-up squad are more or less pear-shaped, and have plenty of bumps. This boat only has four turrets, and they're faired into the hull—what the ancients used to call 'streamlining.' See?"

Amalfi nodded, thrusting out his lower lip speculatively. "Local stuff, then. Designed for fast atmosphere transit. Archaic equipment—Muir engines, maybe."

The intercom burped again. "Ready with the visiting craft, sir," Sergeant Anderson said.

The view of the ship and the blue-green planet was wiped away, and a pleasant-faced young man looked out at them from the screen. "How do you do?" he said formally. The question didn't seem to mean anything, but his tone indicated that he didn't expect an answer to it anyhow. "I am speaking to the commanding officer of the . . . the flying fortress?"

"In effect," Amalfi said. "I'm the mayor here, and this gentleman is the city manager; we're responsible for different aspects of command. Who are you?"

"Captain Savage of the Federal Navy of Utopia," the young man said. He did not smile. "May we have permission to approach your fort or city or whatever it is? We'd like to land a representative.'

Amalfi snapped the audio switch and looked at Hazleton. "What do you think?" he said. The Utopian officer politely and pointedly did not watch the movements of his lips.

"It should be safe enough. Still, that's a big ship, even if it is a museum piece. They could as easily send their man in a life craft."

Amalfi opened the circuit again. "Under the circumstances, we'd just as soon you stayed where you are," he said. "You'll understand, I'm sure, Captain. However, you may send a gig if you like; your representative is welcome here. Or we will exchange hostages——"

Savage's hand moved across the screen as if brushing the suggestion away. "Quite unnecessary, sir. We heard the interstellar craft warn you away. Any enemy of theirs must be a friend of ours. We are hoping that you can shed some light on what is at best a confused situation."

"That's possible," Amalfi said. "If that is all for now ——"

"Yes sir. End of transmission."

"Out."

Hazleton arose. "Suppose I meet this emissary. Your office?"

"Okay."

The city manager went out, and Amalfi, after a few moments, followed him, locking up the control tower. The city was in an orbit and would be stable until the time came to put it in flight again. On the street, Amalfi flagged a cab.

It was a fairly long haul from the control tower, which was on Thirty-fourth Street and The Avenue, down to Bowling Green, where City Hall was; and Amalfi lengthened it a bit more by giving the Tin Cabby a route that would have put folding money into the pocket of a live one of another, forgotten age. He settled back, bit the end off a hydroponic cigar, and tried to remember what he had heard about the Hamiltonians. Some sort of a republican sect, they'd been, back in the very earliest days of space travel. There'd been a public furor . . . recruiting . . . government disapproval and then suppression . . . hm-m-m. It was all very dim, and Amalfi was not at all sure that he hadn't mixed it up with some other event in Terrestrial history.

But there *had* been an exodus of some sort. Shiploads of Hamiltonians going out to colonize, to set up model planets. Come to think of it, one of the nations then current in the West on Earth had had a sort of Hamiltonianism of its own, something called a timocracy. It had all died down after a while, but it had left traces. Nearly every major political wave after space flight had its vestige somewhere in the inhabited part of the galaxy.

Utopia must have been colonized very early. The Hruntan Imperials, had *they* arrived first, would have garrisoned both habitable planets as a matter of course.

It was a little easier to remember the Hruntan Empire, since it was of much more recent vintage than the Hamiltonians; but there was less to remember. The outer margins of exploration had spawned gimcrack empires by the dozen in the days when Earth seemed to be losing her grip. Alois Hrunta had merely been the most successful of the would-be emperors of space. His territory had expanded as far as the limits of communication would allow an absolute autocracy to spread, and then had been destroyed almost before he was assassinated, broken into duchies by his squabbling sons. Eventually the duchies fell in their turn to the nominal but irresistible authority of Earth, leaving, as the Hamiltonians had left, a legacy of a few remote colonies—worlds where a dead dream was served with meaningless pomp.

The cab began to settle, and the façade of City Hall drifted past Amalfi's cab window. The once-golden motto—

MOW YOUR LAWN, LADY?—looked greener than ever in
the light of the giant planet. Amalfi sighed. These political
squabbles were dull, and they were guaranteed to make a
major project out of the simple matter of earning a square
meal.

The first thing that Amalfi noticed upon entering his
office was that Hazleton looked uncomfortable. This was
practically a millennial event. Nothing had ever disturbed
Hazleton before; he was very nearly the perfect citizen of
space: resilient, resourceful, and almost impossible to surprise—or bluff. There was nobody else in the office but a
girl whom Amalfi did not recognize; probably one of the
parliamentary secretaries who handled many of the in-
tramural affairs of the city.

"What's the matter, Mark? Where's the Utopian contact
man?"

"There," Hazleton said. He didn't exactly point, but
there was no doubt about his meaning. Amalfi felt his
eyebrows tobogganing over his broad skull. He turned and
studied the girl.

She was quite pretty: black hair, with blue lights in it;
gray eyes, very frank, and a little amused; a small body,
well made, somewhat on the sturdy side. She was dressed
in the most curious garment Amalfi had ever seen—she
had a sort of sack over her head, with holes for her arms
and neck, and the cloth was pulled in tightly above her
waist. Her hips and her legs down to just below her knees
were covered by a big tube of black fabric, belted at the
top. Her legs were sheathed into token stockings of some
sleazily woven, quite transparent stuff. Little flecks of
color spotted the sack, and around her neck she had a sort
of scarf—no, it wasn't a scarf, it was a ribbon—what *was*
it, anyhow? Amalfi wondered if even deFord could have
named it.

After a moment the girl began to seem impatient of his
inspection, and he turned his head away and continued
walking toward his desk. Behind him, her voice said gently, "I didn't mean to cause a sensation, sir. Evidently you
didn't expect a woman . . . ?"

Her accent was as archaic as her clothes; it was almost
Eliotian. Amalfi sat down and collected his scattered impressions.

"No, we didn't," he said. "However, we have women in
positions of authority here. I suppose we were misled by

Earth custom, which doesn't allow women much hand in the affairs of the military. You're welcome, anyhow. What can we do for you?"

"May I sit down? Thank you. First of all, you can tell us where all these vicious fighting ships come from. Evidently they know you."

"Not personally," Amalfi said. "They know the Okie cities as a class, that's all. They're the Earth police."

The Utopian girl's piquant face dimmed subtly, as though she had expected the answer and had been fighting to believe it would not be given.

"That's what they told us," she said. "We . . . we couldn't accept it. Why are they attacking us then?"

"It was bound to happen sooner or later," Amalfi said as gently as possible. "Earth is incorporating the independent planets as a matter of policy. Your enemies the Hruntans will be taken in, too. I don't suppose we can explain why very convincingly. We aren't exactly in the confidence of Earth's government."

"Oh," the girl said. "Then perhaps you will help us? This immense fortress of yours——"

"I beg your pardon," Hazleton said, smiling ruefully. "The city is no fortress, I assure you. We are only lightly armed. However, we may be able to help you in other ways—frankly, we're anxious to make a deal."

Amalfi looked at him under his eyelids. It was incautious, and unlike Hazleton, to discuss the city's armament or lack of it with an officer who had just come on board from a strange battleship.

The girl said, "What do you want? If you can teach us how those—those police ships fly, and how you keep your city aloft——"

"You don't have the spindizzy?" Amalfi said. "But you must have had it once, otherwise you'd never have got way out here from Earth."

"The secret of interstellar flight has been lost for nearly a century. We still have the first ship our ancestors flew in our museum; but the motor is a mystery. It doesn't seem to *do* anything."

Amalfi found himself thinking: Nearly a century? Is that supposed to be a *long* time? Or do the Utopians lack the anti-agathic drugs, too? But ascomycin was supposed to have been discovered more than half a century before the Hamiltonian Exodus. Curiouser and curiouser.

Hazleton was smiling again. "We can show you what the spindizzy does," he said. "It is too simple to yield its secret lightly. As for us—we need supplies, raw materials. Oil, most of all. Have you that?"

The girl nodded. "Utopia is very rich in oil, and we haven't needed it in quantity for nearly twenty-five years—ever since we rediscovered molar valence." Amalfi pricked up his ears again. The Utopians lacked the spindizzy and the anti-agathics—but they had something called molar valence. The term told its own story: anyone who could modify molecular bonding beyond the usual adhesion effects would have no need for mechanical lubricants like oil. And if the Utopians thought they had only *re*discovered such a technique, so much the better.

"As for us, we can use anything you can give us," the girl went on. Abruptly she looked very weary in spite of her healthy youth. "All our lives we have been fighting these Hruntan barbarians and waiting for the day when help would arrive from Earth. Now Earth has come—and its hand is against *both* worlds! Things must have changed a great deal."

"The fault doesn't lie in change," Hazleton said quietly, "but in that you people have failed to change. Traveling away from Earth for us is very like traveling in time: different distances from the home planet have different year-dates. Stars remote from Earth, like yours, are historical backwaters. And the situation becomes complicated when the historical periods interpenetrate, as your Hamiltonian era and the Hruntan Empire have interpenetrated. The two cultures freeze each other the moment they come in conflict, and when history catches up with them—well, naturally it's a shock."

"On a more practical subject," Amalfi said, "we'd prefer to pick our own landing area. If we can send technicians to your planet in advance, they'll find a lie for us."

"A lie?"

"A mining site. That's to be permitted, I presume?"

"I don't know," the girl said uncertainly. "We're very short on metals, steel especially. We have to salvage all our scrap——"

"We use almost no iron or steel," Amalfi assured her. "We reclaim what we need, as you do—steel's nearly indestructible, after all. What we're after is germanium and some other rare-earth metals for instruments. You ought

to have plenty of those to spare." Amalfi saw no point in
adding that germanium was the base of the present universal coinage. What he had said was true as far as it
went, and in dealing with these backward planets, there
were always five or six facts best suppressed until after the
city had left.

"May I use your phone?"

Amalfi moved away from the desk, then had to come
back again as the girl dabbed helplessly at the 'visor
controls. In a moment she was outlining the conversation
to the Utopian captain. Amalfi wondered if the Hruntans
understood English; not that he was worried about the
present interchange being overheard—the giant planet
would block that most effectively, since the Utopians used
ordinary radio rather than ultraphones or Dirac communi-
cators—but it was of the utmost importance, if Hazleton's
scheme was to be made workable, that the Hruntans
should have heard and understood the warning the Earth
police had issued to the city. It was a point that would
have to be checked as unobtrusively as possible.

It might also be just as well to restrict sharply the
technical information the city passed out in this star system. If the Hamiltonians—or the Hruntans—suddenly
blossomed out with Bethé blasters, field bombs, and the
rest of the modern arsenal (or what had been modern the
last time the city had been able to update its files, not
quite a century ago), the police would be unhappy. They
would also know whom to blame. It was comforting to
know that nobody in the city knew how to build a Canceller, at least. Amalfi had a sudden disquieting mental picture of a mob of Hruntan barbarians swarming out of this
system in spindizzy-powered ships, hijacking their way
back to an anachronistic triumph, snuffing out stars like
candle flames as they went.

"It is agreed," the girl said. "Captain Savage suggests
that I take your technicians back with me in the gig to
save time. And is there also someone who understands the
interstellar drive———"

"I'll go along," Hazleton said. "I know spindizzies as
well as the next man."

"Nothing doing, Mark. I need you here. We've plenty
of grease monkeys for that purpose. We can send them
your man Webster; here's his chance to get off the city
before we even touch ground." Amalfi spoke rapidly into

the vacated 'visor. "There. You'll find the proper people waiting at your gig, young lady. If Captain Savage will phone us exactly one week from today and tell us where on Utopia we're to land, we'll be out of occultation with this gas planet, and will get the message."

There was a long silence after the Utopian girl had left. At last Amalfi said slowly, "Mark, there is no shortage of women in the city."

Hazleton flushed. "I'm sorry, boss. I knew it was impossible directly the words were out of my mouth. Still, I think we may be able to do something for them; the Hruntan Empire was a pretty nauseating sort of state, if I remember correctly."

"That's none of our business," Amalfi said sharply. He disliked having to turn the full force of his authority upon Hazleton; the city manager was for Amalfi the next best thing to that son his position had never permitted him to father—for the laws of all Okie cities include elaborate safeguards against the founding of any possible dynasty. Only Amalfi knew how many times this youngster's elusive, amoral intelligence had brought him close to being deposed and shot by the City Fathers; and a situation like this one was crucial to the survival of the city.

"Look, Mark. We can't afford to have sympathies. We're Okies. What are the Hamiltonians to us? What are they to themselves, for that matter? I was thinking a minute ago of what a disaster it'd be if the Hruntans got a Canceller or some such weapon and blackmailed their way back to a real empire again. But can you see a rebirth of Hamiltonianism any better—in *this* age? Superficially it would be easier to take, I'll admit, than another Hruntan tyranny—but historically, it'd be just as disastrous. These two planets have been fighting each other over two causes that played themselves out half a millennium ago. They aren't either of them *relevant* any more."

Amalfi stopped for a breath, taking the mangled cigar out of his mouth and eyeing it with mild surprise. "I knew that the girl was disturbing your judgment the moment I realized that I'd have to read you the riot act like this. Ordinarily you're the best cultural morphologist I've ever had, and every city manager has to be a good one. If you weren't in a sexual uproar, you'd see that these people are the victims of a pseudomorphosis—dead cultures both of 'em, going through the pangs of decay, even though they both do think it's rebirth."

"The cops don't see it that way," Hazleton said abstractedly.

"How could they? They haven't our point of view. I'm not talking to you as a cop. I'm trying to talk like an Okie. What good does it do you to be an Okie if you're going to mix in on some petty border feud? Mark, you might as well be dead—or back on Earth, it's the same thing in the end."

He stopped again. Eloquence was unnatural to him; it embarrassed him a little. He looked sharply at the city manager, and what he saw choked off the springs of his rare volubility. He felt, not for the first time, the essential loneliness that went with perspective.

Hazleton wasn't listening any more.

There was a battle in progress when the city made its run to Utopia. It was rather spectacular. The Hruntan planet, military in organization and spirit down to the smallest detail of daily living, had not waited for the Earth police to englobe it. The Hruntan ships, though they were nearly of the same vintage as those flown by the Utopians, were being fought to the limit, fought by experienced officers who were unencumbered by any sniveling notions about the intrinsic value of human life. There was not much doubt as to the outcome, but for the time being, the police were unhappy.

The battle was not directly visible from the city; the Hruntan planet was nearly forty degrees away from Utopia now. It was the steady widening of the distance between the two planets that had first given Hazleton his idea for a sneak landing. It had also been Hazleton who had dispatched the proxies—guided missiles less than five meters long—which hung invisibly upon the outskirts of the conflict and watched it with avid television eyes.

It was an instructive dogfight. The police craft, collectively, had not engaged in a major battle for decades; and individually, few of the Earthmen had ever been involved in anything more dangerous than a pushover. The Hruntans, vastly inferior in equipment, were rich in experience, and their tactics were masterly. They had forced the engagement in a heavily mined area, which was equivalent to picking a fight in the heart of a furnace—except that the Hruntans, having sown the mines, knew where the fire was hottest. Their losses, of course, were terrific—nearly five to one. But they had the numbers to waste, and it was obvious that officers who did not value their own lives would be unlikely to value those of their crews.

After a while, even Hazleton had to turn the screen off and order O'Brien to recall the proxies. The carnage was frightening, not just per se, but in the mental attitude behind it. Even a hardened killer, after a certain amount of watching men trying to snuff out a fire by leaping into it, might have felt his brains cracking.

The city settled toward Utopia. Outlying police scouts reported the fact—the reports were plainly audible in the city's Communications Room—and those reports would be exhumed later and acted upon. But now, in the midst of the battle, the cops had no time to care about what the city did. When they began to care again, the city hoped to be gone—or invulnerable.

The question of how Utopia had resisted the Hruntan onslaught for nearly a century remained a riddle. It became more of a riddle after the city landed on Utopia. The planet was a death trap of radioactivity. There were no cities; there were seething white-hot pools that would never cool within the lifetime of humanity to show where cities once had stood. One of the continental land masses was not habitable at all. The very air disturbed counters slightly. In the daytime, the radioactivity was just below the dangerous limit; at night, when the drop in temperature released the normal microscopic increase in the radon content—a phenomenon common to the atmospheres of all Earthlike planets—the air was unbreathable.

Utopia had been bombarded with fission bombs and dust canisters at every opposition with the Hruntan planet for the past seventy Utopian years. The favorable oppositions occurred only once every twelve years—otherwise even the underground life of Utopia would have been impossible.

"How have you kept them off?" Amalfi asked. "Those boys are soldiers. If they can put up this much of a battle against the police, they should be able to wipe up the floor with you folks."

Captain Savage, perched uncomfortably in the belfry, blinking at the sun, managed a thin smile. "We know all their tricks. They are very fine strategists—I will grant you that. But in some respects they are unimaginative.

Necessarily, I suppose; initiative is not encouraged among them." He stirred uneasily. "Are you going to leave your city out here in plain sight? And at night, too?"

"Yes. I doubt that the Hruntans will attack us; they're busy, and besides, they probably know that the police don't love us, and will be too puzzled to call us an enemy of theirs right off the bat. As for the air—we're maintaining a point naught two per cent spindizzy field. Not enough to be noticeable, but it changes the moment of inertia of our own atmosphere enough to prevent much of your air from getting in."

"I don't think I understand that," Savage said. "But doubtless you know your own resources. I confess, Mayor Amalfi, that your city is a complete mystery to us. What does it do? Why are the police against you? Are you exiled?"

"No," Amalfi said. "And the police aren't against us exactly. We're just rather low in the social scale; we're migratory workers, interstellar hobos, Okies. The police are as obligated to protect us as they are to protect any other citizen—but our mobility makes us possible criminals by their figuring, so we have to be watched."

Savage's summary of his reaction to this was the woeful sentence Amalfi had come to think of as the motto of Utopia. "Things have changed so much," the officer said.

"You should set that to music. I can't say that I understand yet how you've held out so long, either. Haven't you ever been invaded?"

"Frequently," Savage said. His voice was half gloomy and half charged with pride. "But you have seen how we live. At best, we have beaten them off; at worst, we cannot be found. And the Hruntans themselves have made this planet a difficult place to live. Many of their landing parties succumbed to the results of their own bombing."

"Still——"

"Mob psychology," Savage said, "is something of a science with us—as it is with them, but we have developed it in a different direction. Combined with the subsidiary art of camouflage, it is a powerful weapon. By dummy installations, faked weather conditions, false high-radioactivity areas, we have thus far been able to make the Hruntans erect their invasion camps exactly on the spots we have previously chosen for them. It is a form of chess: one persuades, or lures, the enemy into entering an

area where one can dispose of him in perfect safety and
with a minimum of effort."

He blinked up at the sun, nibbling at his lower lip. After
a while he added, "There is another important factor. It is
freedom. We have it. The Hruntans do not. They are
defending a system which is ascetic in character—that is,
it offers few rewards to the individual, even once it has
triumphed. We on Utopia are fighting for a system which
has personal rewards for us—the rewards of freedom. It
makes a difference. The incentive is greater."

"Oh, freedom," Amalfi said. "Yes, that's a great thing, I
suppose. Still, it's the old problem. Nobody is ever free.
Our city is vaguely republican, it might even be Hamiltonian in one sense. But we aren't free of the requirements
of our situation, and never can be. As for efficiency in
warfare being increased by freedom—I question that.
Your people are not free now. A wartime political economy has to tend toward dictatorship; that's what killed off
the West back on Earth. Your people are fighting for
steak tomorrow, not steak today. Well—so are the Hruntans. The difference between you exists as a potential,
but—a difference which makes no difference is no difference."

"You are subtle," Savage said, standing up. "I think I
can see why you would not understand that part of our
history. You have no ties, no faith. You will have to
excuse us ours. We cannot afford to be logic-choppers."

He went down the stairs, his shoulders thrown back
unnaturally. Amalfi watched him go with a rueful grin.
The young man was a character; talking with him was like
being brought face to face with a person from a historical
play. Except, of course, that a character in a play is
ordinarily understandable even at his queerest; Savage had
the misfortune to be real, not the product of an artificer
with an ax to gind.

Amalfi was reminded abruptly of Hazleton. Where was
Hazleton, anyhow? He had gone off hours ago with that
girl upon some patently trumped-up errand. If he didn't
hurry, he'd be trapped underground overnight. Amalfi did
not mind working alone, but there were managerial jobs in
the city which the mayor simply could not handle effi-
ciently—and besides, Hazleton might be committing the
city to something inconvenient. Amalfi went down to his
office and called the Communications Room.

Hazleton had not reported in. Grumbling, Amalfi went about the business of organizing the work of the city—the work for which it had gone aloft, but which it found so seldom. It disturbed him that there was no official work contract between the city and Utopia; it was not customary, and if Utopia should turn out, as so many ideals-ridden planets had turned out, to be willing to cheat on an astronomical scale for the sake of its obsession, there would be no recourse under the Earth laws. People with Ends in view were quick to justify all kinds of Means, and the city, which was nothing but Means made concrete and visible, had learned to beware of short cuts.

Hazleton, it appeared, was off somewhere on a short cut. Amalfi could only hope that he—and the city—would survive it.

The Earth police did not wait for Hazleton, either. Amalfi was mildy appalled to see how rapidly the Earth forces reformed and were reinforced. Their logistics had been much improved since the city had last seen them in action. The sky sparkled with ships driving in on the Hruntan planet.

That was bad. Amalfi had expected to have several months at least to build up a food reserve on Utopia before making the run to the Hruntan planet that Hazleton's strategy called for. Evidently, however, the Hruntan world would be completely blockaded by that time.

The mayor sent out an emergency warning at once. The thin resistance which the spindizzy field had offered to Utopia's atmosphere became a solid, hard-driven wall. The spindizzies screamed into the highest level of activity they could maintain without snapping the gravitational thread between the city and Utopia. Around the perimeter of that once-invisible field, a flicker of polarization thickened to translucence. Drive-fields were building, and only a few light rays, most of them those to which the human eye was least sensitive, got through the fields and out again. To Utopian onlookers the city went dark blood-color and became frighteningly indistinct.

Calls began to come in at once. Amalfi ignored them; his flight board, a compressed analog of the banks in the control tower, was alive with alarm signals, and all the speakers were chattering at once.

"Mr. Mayor, we've just made a strike in that old till; it's lousy with oil-bearing shale—"

"Stow what you have and make it tight."

"Amalfi! How can we get any thorium out of——"

"More where we're going. Damp your stock on the double."

"Com Room. Still no word from Mr. Hazleton——"

"Keep trying."

"Calling the flying city! Is there something wrong? Calling the flying——"

Amalfi cut them all off with a brutal swipe at the toggles. "Did you think we'd stay here forever? Stand by!"

The spindizzies screamed. The sparkling of the ships coming to invest the Hruntan planet became brighter by the minute. It would be a near thing.

"Whoop it up there on Forty-second Street! What d'you think you're doing, warming up tea? You've got ninety seconds to get that machine to take-off pitch!"

"Take-off? Mr. Mayor, it'll take at least four minutes——"

"You're kidding me. I can tell. Dead men don't kid. *Move!*"

"Calling the flying city——"

The sparks spread over the sky like a Catherine wheel whirling into life. The watery quivering of the single point of light that was the Hruntan planet dimmed among them, shivered, blended into the general glitter. From Astronomy, Jake added his voice to the general complaint.

"Thirty seconds," Amalfi said.

From the speaker which had been broadcasting the puzzled, fearful inquiries of the Utopians, Hazleton's voice said calmly, "Amalfi, are you out of your mind?"

"No," Amalfi said. "It's your plan, Mark. I'm just following through. *Twenty-five seconds.*"

"I'm not pleading for myself. I like it here, I think. I've found something here that the city doesn't have. The city needs it—"

"Do you want off, too?"

"No, hell no," Hazleton said. "I'm not asking for it. But if I had to take it anyhow, I'd take it here——"

A brief constriction made Amalfi's big frame knot up tightly. Nothing emotional—no, nothing to do with Hazleton; probably some spindizzy operator was hurrying things. He staggered to his feet and threw up in the little washstand. Hazleton went on talking, but Amalfi could hardly hear him. The clock grinned and rushed on.

"Ten seconds," Amalfi gasped, a little late.

"Amalfi, listen to me!"

"Mark," Amalfi said, choking, "Mark, I haven't time. You made your choice. I . . . *five seconds* . . . I can't do anything about that. If you like it there, go ahead and stay. I wish you, I wish you everything, Mark, believe me. But I have to think of——"

The clock brought its thin palms together piously.

". . . the city——"

"Amalfi——"

"Spin!"

The city vaulted skyward. The sparks whirled in around it.

CHAPTER TWO: Gort

THE flying of the city normally was in Hazleton's hands. In his absence—though it had never happened before—a youngster named Carrel took charge. Amalfi's own hand rarely touched the stick except in spots where even the instruments could not be trusted.

Running the Earth blockade to the Hruntan planet was no easy job, especially for a green pilot like Carrel, but Amalfi did not greatly care. He huddled in his office and watched the screens through a gray mist, wondering if he would ever be warm again. The baseboards of the room were pouring out radiant heat, but it didn't seem to do any good. He felt cold and empty.

"Ahoy the Okie city," the ultraphone barked savagely. "You've had one warning. Pay up and clear out of here, or we'll break you up."

Reluctantly Amalfi tripped the toggle. "We can't," he said uninterestedly.

"What?" the cop said. "Don't give me that. You're in a combat area, and you've already landed on Utopia in defiance of a Vacate order. Pay your fine and beat it, or you'll get hurt."

"Can't," Amalfi said.

"We'll see about that. What's to prevent you?"

"We have a contract with the Hruntans."

There was a long and very dead silence. At last the police vessel said, "You're pretty sharp. All right, proof your contract over on the tape. I suppose you know that we're about to blow the Hruntans to a thin haze."

"Yep."

"All right. Go ahead and land if you've got a contract. The more fools you. Make sure you stay for the full contract period. If you do get off before we reduce the planet, make sure you can pay your fine. If you don't— good riddance, Okie!"

Amalfi managed a ghost of a grin. "Thanks," he said. "We love you, too, flatfoot."

The ultraphone growled and stopped transmitting. There was a world of frustration in that final growl. The Earth police accepted officially the Okie cities' status as hobos—migratory workers—but unofficially and openly the cities were called tramps in the wardrooms of the police cruisers. Opportunities to break up a city did not come very often, and were met with relish; it must have been quite a blow to the cop to find the vanadium-clad, never-varying Contract in his way.

But now there were the Hruntans to cope with. This was the penultimate and most delicate stage of Hazleton's plan—and Hazleton wasn't on deck to administer it. As a matter of fact, if his Utopian friends had heard Amalfi admit to a contract with the Hruntans, he was probably in the hottest water of his career right now. Amalfi tried not to think about it.

The plan originally had not included signing any contracts with either planet; so long as the city was not committed legally, it could refuse jobs, leave them when it pleased, and generally exercise the freedom of the unemployed. But it hadn't worked out that way. The speed with which the police had been reinforced had made it impossible even to approach the Hruntan planet without uncrackable legal protection.

At least the city's stay on Utopia had accomplished some part of its purposes. The oil tanks were a little over half full, and the city's treasury was comfortable, though still not exactly bulging. That left the rare-earth and the power metals still to be attended to; collecting and refining them was unavoidably time-consuming, and would take even longer on the Hruntan planet than on Utopia—the Imperial world, farther out from its sun than Utopia, had been given a correspondingly smaller allowance of heavy elements.

But there was no help for it. To stay on Utopia while the Hruntans were being conquered—or "consolidated," as it was officially called on Earth—would have left the city completely at the mercy of the Earth forces. Even at best, it would have been impossible to leave the system without paying the fine for violating the Vacate order, and Amalfi was constitutionally unwilling to part with the money for which the city had labored. Even at the present state of the treasury, it might easily have bankrupted them, for work had been very scarce lately.

The intercom had been modestly calling attention to itself for several minutes. Answered, it said, "Sergeant Anderson, sir. We've got another visitor."

"Yes," Amalfi said. "That would be the Hruntan delegation. Send 'em up."

While he waited, chewing morosely on a dead cigar, he checked the contract briefly. It was standard, requiring payment in germanium "or equivalent"—the give-away clause which had prevented its use on Utopia. It had been signed by ultraphone—the possession of that tight-beam device alone "placed" the Hruntans as to century—and the work the city was to do was left unspecified. Amalfi hoped devoutly that the Hruntans would in turn give themselves away when it came to being specific on that count.

The buzzer sounded once more, and Amalfi pushed the button that released the door. The next instant he was not sure it had been a wise move. The Hruntan delegation bore an unmistakable resemblance to a boarding party. First of all, there were an even dozen soldiers, clad in tight-fitting red leather breeches, gleaming breastplates, and scarlet-plumed casques; the breastplates, too, were emblazoned with a huge scarlet sun. The men snapped to attention in two files of six on each side of the door, bringing to "present arms" weapons which might have been copies of Kammerman's original mesotron rifle.

Between the files, flanked by two lesser lights as gorgeously and unfunctionally clad as macaws, came a giant carved out of gold. His clothing was interwoven with golden threads; his breastplate and helmet were gilded; even his complexion was tanned to a deep golden tone; and he sported a luxuriant golden-blond beard and flowing mustache. He was altogether a most unlikely-looking figure.

He spoke two harsh-sounding words, and boot heels and weapons slammed against the floor. Amalfi winced and stood up.

"We," the golden giant said, "are the Margraf Hazca, Vice Regent of the Duchy of Gort under his Eternal Eminence, Arpad Hrunta. Emperor of Space."

"Oh," Amalfi said, blinking. "My name's Amalfi; I'm the mayor here. Do you sit down?"

The Margraf said he sat down, and did. The soldiers remained stiffly "at ease," and the two subsidiary nobles posed themselves behind the Margraf's chair. Amalfi subsided behind his desk with a muffled sigh of relief.

"I presume you're here to discuss the contract."

"We are. We are told that you have been among the rabble of the second planet."

"An emergency landing only," Amalfi said.

"No doubt," the Margraf said dryly. "We do not concern ourselves with the doings of the Hamiltonians: we will add them to our serfs in due time, after we have driven off these upstarts from decadent Earth. In the meantime, we have use for you; any enemy of Earth must be friends with us."

"That's logical," Amalfi said. "Just what can we do for you? We have quite a variety of equipment here——"

"The matter of payment comes first," said the Margraf. He got up and began pacing slowly up and down with enormous strides, his golden cloak streaming out behind him. "We are not prepared to make any payment in germanium; we need all we have for transistors. The contract speaks of equivalents. What counts as equivalent?"

It was remarkable how the regal manner was snuffed out when it got down to honest haggling. Amalfi said cautiously, "Well, you could allow us to mine for germanium ourselves——"

"Do you think this planet's resources will last forever?

Give us the equivalent, not some roundabout scheme for being paid in the metal itself!"

"Equipment, then," Amalfi said, "or skills, at a mutually agreed valuation. For instance, what are you using for lubrication?"

The big count's eyes glittered. "Ah," he said softly. "You have the secret of the friction-fields, then. That we have long sought, but the generators of the rabble melt when we touch them. Does Earth know this process?"

"No."

"You got it from the Hamiltonians? Excellent." The two minor nobles were beginning to grin wickedly. "We need babble no further of 'mutually agreed valuations,' then." He gestured. Amalfi found himself looking down a dozen rifle barrels.

"What's the idea?"

"You are within our defensive envelope," Hazca said with wolfish gusto. "And you are not likely to survive long among the Earthmen, should you by some miracle break free of us. You may call your technicians and tell them to prepare a demonstration of the friction-field generator; also, prepare to land. Graf Nandór here will give you explicit instructions."

He strode toward the door; the soldiers parted deferentially. As Amalfi's hand reached for the button to let him out, the big man whirled. "And you need not attempt to trip any hidden alarms," he growled. "Your city has already been boarded in a dozen places and is under the guns of four cruisers."

"Do you think you can win technical information by force?" Amalfi said.

"Oh yes," said the Margraf, his eyes shining dangerously. "We are—experts."

Carrel, Hazleton's protégé, was a very plausible lecturer, and seemed completely at home in the echoing, barbaric gorgeousness of the Margraf's Council Chamber. He had attached his charts to the nearest tapestry and had propped his blackboard on the arms of the great chair in which, Amalfi supposed, the Margraf usually sat; his chalk traced swift symbols on the slate and squeaked deafeningly in the groined vault of the room.

The Margraf himself had left; five minutes of Carrel's talk had been enough to arouse his impatience. The Graf

Nandór was still there, wearing the suffering expression of
a man delegated to do the dirty work. So were four or
five other nobles. Three of these were chattering in the
back of the room with muffled sniggers, and a raucous
laugh broke in upon Carrel's dissertation every so often.
The remaining peacocks, evidently of subordinate ranks,
were seated, listening with painful, brow-furrowing concentration, like ham actors overregistering Deep Thought.
"This will be enough to show the analogy between
atomic and molecular binding energies," Carrel said
smoothly. "The Hamiltonians"—he had seen that the word
annoyed the peacocks and used it often—"the Hamiltonians have shown, not only that this binding energy is
responsible for the phenomena of cohesion, adhesion, and
friction, but also that it is subject to a relationship analogous to valence."

The appearance of concentration of the nobles became
so grave as to be outright grotesque. "This phenomenon of
molar valence, as the Hamiltonians have aptly named it, is
intensified by the friction-fields which they have designed
into a condition analogous to ionization. The surface layers of molecules of two contiguous surfaces come into
dynamic equilibrium in the field; they change places con-
tinuously and rapidly, but without altering the *status quo*,
so that a shear-plane is readily established between the
roughest surfaces. It is evident that this equilibrium does
not in any sense do away with the binding forces in
question, and that a certain amount of drag, or friction,
still remains—but only about a tenth of the resistance
which obtains even with the best systems of gross lubrication."

The nobles nodded together. Amalfi gave over watching
them; the Hruntan technicians worried him most. There
were an even dozen of them, a number of which the
Margraf seemed fond. Four were humble, frightened-
looking creatures who seemed to regard Carrel with more
than a little awe. They scribbled frantically, fighting to
take down every word, even material which was of no
conceivable importance, such as Carrel's frequent pats on
the back of the Hamiltonians.

All but one of the rest were well-dressed, hard-faced
men who treated the nobles with only perfunctory deference, and who took no notes at all. This type was also
quite familiar in a barbarian milieu: head scientists, direc-

tors, entirely committed to the regime, entirely aware of
how crucial they were to its successes, and already infected with the aristocratic virus of letting lesser men dirty
their hands with actual messy laboratory experiments.
Probably some of them owed their positions as much to a
ruthless skill at court intrigue as to any great scientific
ability.

But the twelfth man was of a different order altogether.
He was tall, spare, and sparse-haired, and his face as he
listened to Carrel was alive with excitement. An active
brain, this one, doubtless politically unconscious, hardly
caring who ruled it as long as it had equipment and a free
hand. The man would be tolerated by the regime for his
productivity, but would be under constant suspicion. And
he was, by Amalfi's judgment, the only man capable of
going beyond what Carrel was saying to what Carrel was
leaving unsaid.

"Are there any questions?" Carrel said.

There were some, mostly dim-witted, from the technies—
how do you build this, and how do you wire that; no one
with any initiative would have wanted to be led by the
nose in such a fashion. Carrel answered in detail. The
hardfaced men left without a word, as did the nobles, who
lingered only long enough to save face. The scientist—he
was *the* scientist for Amalfi's money—was left alone to
launch into an ardent stammering dispute over Carrel's
math. He seemed to consider Carrel as an equal as a
matter of course, and Carrel was beginning to look
uncomfortable by the time Amalfi summoned him to the
back of the hall.

The scientist left, pocketing his few notes and pulling
thoughtfully at his nose. Carrel watched him go.

"I can't hide the kicker from that boy long, sir," he
said. "Believe me, he's got *brains*. Give him about two
days and he'll have the whole thing worked out for himself. He won't get any sleep tonight for thinking about it; I
know the type."

"So do I," Amalfi said. "I also know barbarian council
halls—the arrases have ears. Just pray you weren't overheard, that's all. Come on."

Amalfi was silent until they were safe within the city
and in a cab. Then he said, "You have to be careful,
Carrel, in dealing with outsiders. You take to it well, but
you're inexperienced. *Never* say anything outside the city,

even to me, that doesn't fit your part. Now then—I agree with you about that scientist; I was watching him. And now he knows you, so I can't use you against him. Is there someone in your organization who's done undercover work for Mark who hasn't been out of the city since we hit Gort? An experienced hand?"

"Sure, four or five, at least. I can put my finger on any of 'em."

"Good. Find a fairly husky one, a man that could pass for a thug with a minimum of make-up, and send him to Indoctrination for hypnopaedia. In the meantime, you'll have to see that scientist again. Get a picture of him somewhere, a tri-di if they have them here. When you talk to him, answer any questions he asks you."

Carrel looked puzzled. "Any questions?"

"Any technical questions, yes. It won't matter what he knows very shortly. Here's another lesson in practical public relations for you, Carrel. When on a strange planet, you have to use its social system to the best advantage possible. On a world like this one, where the struggle for power is plenty raw, assassination must be very common—and nine chances to one there's a regular Assassins' Guild, or, at least, plenty of free-lance killers for hire."

"You're going to—have Doctor Schloss assassinated?"

The shocked expression on Carrel's face made Amalfi abruptly sodden with weariness. Training a new city manager up to the point where his election would be endorsed by the City Fathers was a long and heartbreaking task, for so much of the training had to be absorbed the hard way. He felt too old for such a job now, and much too aware of some failure in his methods, the failure which alone had made the job necessary now.

"Yes," he said. "It's a shame, but it has to be done. In other circumstances we'd take the man into the city—he doesn't care who he works for—but the Hruntans would look for him, and find him, too. There has to be an inarguable corpse, and if possible, a local culprit. Your operative, after a suitable course in this Balkanese they speak here, will scout the rivalries among the scientific clique and try to pin the killing on one of those hawk-nosed laboratory chieftains. But the man must be killed—for the survival of the city."

Carrel did not protest, for the final formulation was the be-all and end-all of Okie logic; but it was plain that the waste of intelligence the plot necessitated upset him. Amalfi decided silently to keep Carrel exceptionally busy in the city for a while—at least until the Hruntans had their anti-friction installation well under way.

Now, anyhow, was the time to put another needle into the cops; Hazleton's timetable called for it, and although Amalfi had already been forced to abandon much of Hazleton's strategy—Hazleton's timetable, for instance, had called for a treacherous Utopian landing on Gort, with the full force of the Hamiltonians thrown behind delivering the Hruntan planet into the hands of the Earth police—the notion of bargaining with the cops for the planet still seemed to have merit.

Dismissing Carrel, Amalfi went to his office, where he took the flexible plastic dust cover off a little-used instrument: the Dirac transmitter. It was the only form of communication which the Hruntans—and, of course, the Hamiltonians—did not have; the want of it had cost them an empire, for it operated instantaneously over any distance. Amalfi thrust a cigar absently between his teeth and sent out a call for the captain of police.

The obsolete model had no screen, but the captain's voice conveyed his feelings graphically. "If you're going to rub my nose in the fact that we're obliged to protect you because the Hruntans have violated the contract," he snarled, "you can save your breath. I've half a mind to blow up the planet anyhow. Some one of these years the Okie laws are going to be changed, and then——"

"You wouldn't have blown up the planet in any case," Amalfi said tranquilly. "The shock wave would have detonated the local sun and destroyed the whole system, and your superiors would have had your scalp. What I'm trying to do is save you some trouble. If you're interested, make me an offer."

The cop laughed.

"All right," Amalfi said. "Laugh, you jackass. In about ten months you'll be yanked back to patrolling a stratosphere beat on Earth that sees a plane once every two years, and braying about how unjust it all is. As soon as the home office hears that you let the Hruntans and the Hamiltonians join forces, and that the war is going to cost Earth two or three hundred billion Oc dollars and last maybe twenty-five years——"

"You're a bum liar, Okie," the cop said. The bravado

behind the pun seemed a little strained, however. "They been fighting each other a century now."

"Times change," Amalfi said. "In any event, the merger will be forcible, because if you don't want the Duchy of Gort, I'm going to offer it to Utopia. The combined arsenal will be impresive—each side has some stuff the other hasn't, and we couldn't prevent either of them from learning a few tricks from us. However——"

"Wait a minute," the cop said cautiously. He was quite aware, Amalfi was more than certain, that this conversation was inevitably being overheard by hundreds and perhaps thousands of Dirac receivers throughout the inhabited galaxy, including those in police headquarters on Earth. That was one of the major characteristics of Dirac transmission—whether you called it a flaw or an advantage depended largely on what use you made of it. "You mean you got the upper hand there already? How do I know you can hold it?"

"You don't risk a thing. Either I deliver the planet to you, or I don't. All I want is for you to rescind the fine against the city, wipe the tape of the earlier Vacate order, and give us a safe-conduct out of this system. If we don't deliver, you don't pay."

"Hm-mm." There was a muttering in the background, as though somebody were talking softly over the cop's shoulder. "How'd you pull it off?"

"That," Amalfi said dryly, "would be telling. If you want to play, proof over the agreement."

"No saop. You violated the Vacate order and you'll have to pay the fine—that's flat."

That was good enough for Amalfi. The cop certainly was not going to promise to wipe his tape of evidence of a tort while he was talking on the Dirac; that he had picked this particular point to stick on indicated general agreement, however.

"Just send me a safe-conduct under seal, then. I'll put the whole thing in the Margraf Hazca's strong room; you get it back when you get the planet."

After a short silence, the cop said, "Well . . . all right." The tape began to whir at Amalfi's elbow. Satisfied, he broke the contact.

If this coup came off on schedule, it would become legendary—the police would be mighty tight-lipped about it, but the Okie cities would spread the tale all over the galaxy.

Somehow, the desertion of Hazleton made the prospect savorless.

Someone was shaking him. He wanted very badly to awaken, but his sleep was as deep as death, and it seemed that no possible struggle could bring him up to the rim of the pit. Shapes and faces whirled about him, and in the blackness he felt the approach of great steel teeth.

"Amalfi! Wake up, man! Amalfi, it's Mark—wake up——"

The steel jaws came together with a terrible snapping report, and the wheeling faces vanished. Bluish light spilled into his eyes.

"Who? What is it?"

"It's me," Hazleton said. Amalfi blinked up at him uncomprehendingly. "Quick, quick. There's only a little time."

Amalfi sat up slowly and looked at the city manager. He was too stunned to know whether he was pleased or not, and the oppression of his nightmare was still with him, a persistent emotion lingering after dreamed events he could no longer remember.

"I'm glad to see you," he said. Oddly, the statement seemed untrue; he could only hope it would become true later. "How'd you get through the police cordon? I'd have said it couldn't be done."

"By force, and fraud, the old combination. I'll explain later."

"You nearly didn't make it," Amalfi said, feeling a sudden influx of energy. "Is it still night here? Yes. The big blowup isn't due much before noon, otherwise I wouldn't have been asleep. After that, you'd have found no city here."

"Before noon? That isn't according to the timetable. But that can wait. Get up, boss, there's work waiting."

The door to Amalfi's room slid aside suddenly, and the Utopian girl stood at the sill, her face pinched with anxiety. Amalfi reached hastily for his jacket.

"Mark, we must hurry. Captain Savage says he won't wait but fifteen minutes more. And he won't—he hates you underneath, I can tell, and he'd love to leave us here with the barbarians!"

"Right away, Dee," Hazleton said, without turning.

The girl disappeared. Amalfi stared at the prodigal city manager. "Wait a minute," he said. "What *is* all this, anyhow? Mark, you haven't sold yourself on some idiotic personal rescue mission?"

"Personal? No." Hazleton grinned. "We're getting the whole city out of here, right on the timetable. I wanted to get word to you that we were following through as planned, but the Utopians have no Diracs, and I didn't want to tip off the cops. Get dressed, that's a good fellow, and I'll explain as we go. These Hamiltonians have been working like demons, installing spindizzies in every available ship. They'd about decided to surrender to the cops— after all, they've more in common with Earth than with the Hruntans—but when I told them what we planned, and showed them how the spindizzy works, it was like giving them all new hearts."

"They believed you as quickly as that?"

Hazleton shrugged. "No, of course not. To be on the safe side, they made up an escape fleet of twenty-five ships—reconverted light cruisers—and sent them out on this mission. They're upstairs now."

"Over the city?"

"Yes. I heard the hijacking of the city—I gather you had the radio on for the benefit of the cops, but it came through pretty clearly on Utopia, too. So I sold them on combining their escape project with a sneak raid to escort the city out. It took some selling, but I convinced them that they'd get out of this system easier if the cops had two things to think about at once. And so here we are, right on the timetable." Hazleton grinned again. "The cops had no notion that there were any Utopian ships anywhere near this planet, and they keep a sloppy watch. They know now, of course, but it'll take them a little while to mass here—and by that time, we'll be gone."

"Mark, you're a romantic ass," Amalfi said. "Twenty-five light cruisers—archaic ones at that, spindizzies or not!"

"There's nothing archaic about Savage's plans," Hazleton said. "He hates my guts for swiping Dee from him, but he knows space combat. This is a survival fleet, for Hamiltonianism, not just people. As soon as we're attacked, all twenty-five of them are going to take off in different directions, putting up a stiff battle and doing their best to turn the affair into a series of individual dogfights.

That insures the survival of some of them, of their ideology—and of the city."

"I expected something more from you than a gesture out of a bad stereo," Amalfi said. "Napoleonism! Heedless of danger, young hero leads devoted band into enemy stronghold, snatching beloved sovereign from enraged infidel! Pah! The city's staying where it is. If you want to go off with this suicide squadron, go ahead."

"Amalfi, you don't understand——"

"You underestimate me," Amalfi said harshly. He strode across the room to the balcony, Hazleton at his heels. "Sensible Hamiltonians stayed home, that's a cinch. Giving them the spindizzy was a smart idea—it made them fight longer and kept the cops busy when we needed the time. But these people who are trying to escape toward the edge of the galaxy—they're the incurables, the fanatics. Do you know how they'll wind up? You should, and you would if there wasn't a woman in your head addling your brains with a long-handled spoon. After a few generations on the rim, none of 'em will remember Hamiltonianism. Making a new planet livable is a job for a carefully prepared, fully manned expedition. These people are the tatters of a military debacle—and you want us to help set up the debacle! No thanks."

He threw the door to the balcony open so hard that Hazleton had to jump to avoid being hit, and went out. It was a clear night, bitterly cold as always on Gort, and hundreds of stars glared through the glow the city cast upon the sky. The Utopian ships, of course, could not be seen: they were too high, and probably were as well near to invisible and undetectable, even close up, as Utopian science could make them.

"I'll have a job explaining this to the Hruntans," he said, his voice charged with suppressed rage. "The best I'll be able to do is to claim the Hamiltonians were trying to destroy us before we could finish giving away the friction-field plans. And to do that, I'll have to yell to the Hruntans for help right away."

"You gave the Hruntans——"

"Certainly!" Amalfi said. "It was the only weapon we had left after we had to sign a contract with them. The possibility of a Utopian landing in force here vanished the moment the police beat us to the punch. And here you are still trying to use the blunted tool!"

"Mark!" the girl's voice drifted out from the room, frantic with anxiety. "Mark! Where are you?"

"Go along," Amalfi said, without turning his head. "After a while they'll have no time to cherish their ritual beliefs, and you can have a nice frontier home, on the ox-bone plow level. The city is staying there. By noon tomorrow, the Utopians who stayed will be put in an excellent position to bargain with Earth for rights, the Hruntans will be horn-swoggled, and we'll be on our way."

The girl, evidently having noticed the open door, came through it in time to hear the last two sentences. "Mark!" she cried "What does he mean? Savage says——"

Hazleton sighed. "Savage is an idiot and so am I. Amalfi's right; I've been acting like a child. You'd better get aloft while you have the chance, Dee."

She came forward to the railing and took his arm, looking up at him. Her face was so full of puzzlement and hurt that Amalfi had to look away; that look reminded him of too many things best forgotten—some of them not exactly remote. He heard her say, "Do you—do you want me to go, Mark? You're staying with the city?"

"Yes," Hazleton muttered. "I mean, no. I've made a terrific mess of things, it appears. Maybe I can help now—maybe not. But I've got to stay. You'd be better off with your own people——"

"Mayor Amalfi," the girl said. Amalfi turned unwillingly. "You said when I first met you that there was a place for women in this city. Do you remember?"

"I remember," Amalfi said. "But you wouldn't like our politics, I'm sure. This is not a Hamiltonian state. It's stable, self-sufficient, static—a beachcomber by the seas of history. We're Okies. Not a nice name."

The girl said, "It may not always be so."

"I'm afraid it will. Even the people don't change much, Dee. I suspect that you haven't been told this before, but the great majority of them are well over a century old. I myself am nearly seven hundred. And you would live as long if you joined us."

Dee's face was a study in mixed shock and incredulity, but she said doggedly, "I'll stay."

The sky began to pale slightly. No one spoke. Aloft, the stars were dimming, and there was no sign to show that a tiny fleet of ships was dwindling away into the boundless universe.

Hazleton cleared his throat. "What's for me to do, boss?" he said hoarsely.

"Plenty. I've been making do with Carrel, but though he's willing, he lacks experience. First of all, make us ready to take off at the very first notice. Then cudgel your brains to think up something to tell the Hruntans about this Utopian fleet. You can fancy up my excuse, or think up one of your own—I don't care which. You're better at that kind of thing than I ever was."

"So what's supposed to happen at noon?"

Amalfi grinned. He realized with a subdued shock that he felt good. Getting Hazleton back was like finding a flawed diamond that you'd thought you'd lost—the flaw was still there and would never go away, but still the diamond had been the cleanest-cutting tool in the house, and had had a certain sentimental value.

"It goes like this. Carrel sold the Hruntans on building a master friction-field generator for the whole planet—said it would make their machines consume less power, or some such nonsense. The plans he gave them call for a generator at least twice as powerful as the Hruntans think it is, and with nearly all the controls left off. It will run only one way: full positive. Tomorrow at noon they're scheduled to give it a trial run.

"In the meantime, there's a Hruntan named Schloss who probably has the machine tabbed for what it actually is, and we've set up the old double-knife trick to get him out of the picture. It's my guess that this should start a big enough rhubarb among the scientists to keep them from prying until it's too late. Since this whole deal looked as though it would work out the same way that the Utopian landing would have, I also called the cops according to your timetable and got a safe-conduct. Simple?"

Halfway through the explanation, Hazleton was far enough back to normal to begin looking amused. When it was over, he was chuckling.

"That's a honey," he said. "Still, I can see why you weren't too satisfied with Carrel. Amalfi, you're a prime bluffer. Telling me to go off with Savage in that dramatic fashion! Do you know that your fancy plot isn't going to come off?"

"Why, Mark?" Dee said. "It sounds perfect to me."

"It's clever, but it's full of loose ends. You have to look at these things like a dramatist; a climax that *almost* comes off is no climax. We'd better———"

In the bedroom, Amalfi's private phone chimed melodiously, and a neon bulb went on over the balcony doorway. Amalfi frowned and flicked a switch on the railing.

"Mr. Mayor?" a concealed speaker said nervously. "Sorry to wake you up, but there's trouble. First of all, at least twenty ships were over here a while back; we were going to call you for that, but they went away on their own. But now we've got a sort of a refugee, a Hruntan who calls himself Doctor Schloss. He claims the other Hruntans are all out to get him and he wants to work for us. Shall I send him to Psych or what? It might just be true."

"Of course it's true," Hazleton said. "There's your first loose end, Amalfi."

The affair of Dr. Schloss proved difficult to untangle; Amalfi had not studied his man closely enough. Carrel's agent had done a thorough job of counterfeiting local politics. It was always preferable, when the city needed a man's death, to so arrange matters that the actual killing was done by an outsider, and in this case that had proven absurdly easy to arrange. There were four separate cliques within the scientific hierarchy of Gort, all of them undercutting each other with fanatical perseverance, like shipmates trying to do for each other by boring holes in the hull. In addition, the court itself did not trust Dr. Schloss, and took sides sporadically when the throat-cutting became overt.

It had been simple enough to set currents in motion which would sweep Dr. Schloss away, but Schloss had declined to be swept. The moment he became aware of any threat, he had come with disconcerting directness to the city.

"The trouble is," Carrel reported, "that he didn't realize what was flying until it was almost too late. He's a peculiarly sane character and would never dream that anybody was 'out to get him' until the knife actually pricked him."

Hazelton nodded. "It's my bet that it was the court itself that finally alarmed him—they wouldn't bother trying to sneak up on him."

"That's correct, sir."

"Which means that we'll have Bathless Hazca and his dandies here looking for him," Amalfi growled. "I don't suppose he bothered to cover his tracks. What are you going to do, Mark? We can't count on their starting the anti-friction fields early enough to get us out of this."

"No," Hazleton agreed. "Carrel, does your man still have contact with the group that was going to punch Schloss's ticket?"

"Sure."

"Have him rub out the top man in that group, then. The time is past for delicate measures."

"What do you propose to gain by that?" Amalfi asked.

"Time. Schloss has disappeared. Hazca may guess that he's come here, but most of the cliques will think he's been killed. This will look like a vengeance killing by some member of Schloss's group—he has no real clique of his own, of course, but there must be several men who thought they stood to gain by keeping him alive. We'll start a vendetta. Confusion is what counts in a fight like this."

"Perhaps so," Amalfi said. "In that case I'd better tackle Graf Nandór right away with a fistful of accusations and complaints. The more confusion, the more delay—and it's less than four hours to noon now. In the meantime, we'll have to hide Schloss as best we can, before he's spotted by one of Hazca's guards here. That invisibility machine in the old West Side subway tunnel seems like the best place . . . do you remember the one? The Lyrans sold it to us, and it just whirled and blinked and buzzed and didn't do a thing."

"That was what my predecessor got shot for," Hazleton said. "Or was it for that fiasco on Epoch? But I know where the machine is, yes. I'll arrange to have the gadget do a little whirling and blinking—Hazca's soldiery is afraid of machinery and would never think of looking inside one that's working, even if they did suspect a fugitive inside it. Which they won't, I'm sure. And . . . gods of all stars, what was *that*?"

The long, terrifying metallic roar died away into a mutter. Amalfi was grinning.

"Thunder," he said. "Planets have a phenomenon called weather, Mark; a nasty habit of theirs. I think we're due for a storm."

Hazleton shuddered. "It makes me want to hide under the bed. Well, let's get to work."

He went out, with Dee trailing. Amalfi, reflecting on the merits of attack as a defensive measure, waved a cab up to the balcony and had himself ferried to the first setback of the mid-town RCA building. He would have liked to have landed at the top, where the penthouse was, but the cornices of the building now bristled with pompoms and mesotron rifles; Graf Nandór was taking no chances.

The elevator operator was not allowed to take Amalfi beyond the seventieth floor. Swearing, he climbed the last five flights of steps; the blue rage he was working up was not going to be counterfeit by the time he reached the penthouse. At every landing he was inspected with insolent suspicion by lounging groups of soldiers.

There was music in the penthouse, and it reeked of the combination of perfume and unwashed bodies which was the personal trademark of Hruntan nobility. Nandór was sprawled in a chair, surrounded by women, listening to a harpist sing a ballad of unspeakable obscenity in a quavering, emotionless voice. In one jeweled hand he held a heavy goblet half full of fuming Rigellian wine—it must have come from the city's stores, for the Hruntans had had no contact with Rigel for centuries—which he passed back and forth underneath his substantial nose, inhaling the vapors delicately.

He lifted his eyes over the rim of the goblet as Amalfi came in, but did not otherwise bother to acknowledge him. Amalfi felt his blood pressure mounting and his wrists growing cold and numb, and tried to control himself. It was all very well to be properly angry, but he needed some mastery over what he said and did.

"Well?" Nandór said at last.

"Are you aware of the fact that you've just escaped being blown into a rarified gas?" Amalfi demanded.

"Oh, my dear fellow, don't tell me you've just circumvented an assassination attempt on my behalf," Nandór said. His English seemed to have been picked up from a Liverpudlian—only the men of that Okie city spoke through their adenoids in that strange fashion. "Really, that's a bit thick."

"There were twenty-five Hamiltonian ships over the city," Amalfi said grimly. "We beat 'em off, but it was a close shave. Evidently the whole business didn't even wake you or your bosses up. What good are we going to be to you if you can't even protect us?"

Nandór looked alarmed. He pulled a mike from among the pillows and spoke into it for a moment in his own tongue. The answer was inaudible to Amalfi, but after it came, the Hruntan looked less anxious, though his face was still clouded.

"What are you selling me, my man?" he said querulously. "There was no battle. The ships dropped no bombs, did no damage; they have been pursued out as far as the police englobement."

"Does a deaf man recognize an argument?" Amalfi said. "And how do you dazzle a blind man? You people think that all weapons have to go 'bang!' to be deadly. If you'll look at our power boards, you'll see records of a million megawatt drain over one half hour at dawn—and we don't chew up energy at that rate making soup!"

"That's of no moment," the Graf murmured. "Such records can be faked, and there are a good many ways of consuming energy anyhow—or wasting it. Let us suppose instead that these ships who 'attacked' you landed a spy— eh? And that subsequently a Hruntan scientist, a traitor to his emperor, was taken from your city, perhaps in the hope of carrying him back to Utopia?"

His face darkened suddenly. "You interstellar tramps are childishly stupid. Obviously the Hamiltonian rabble hoped to rescue your city, and were frightened off by our warriors. Schloss may have gone with them—or he may be hiding in the city somewhere. We will have our answer directly."

He waved at the silent women, who crowded hastily out through the curtained doorway. "Do you care to tell me now where he is?"

"I keep no tabs on Hruntans," Amalfi said evenly. "Sorting garbage is no part of my duties."

Coolly Nandór threw the remainder of his wine in Amalfi's face. The fuming stuff turned his eye sockets into fire. With a roar he stumbled forward, groping for the Hruntan's throat. The man's laughter retreated from him mockingly; then he felt heavy hands dragging his arms behind his back.

"Enough," the Graf said. "Hazca's chief questioner will make some underling babble, if we have to hang them all up by their noses." A blast of thunder interrupted him; outside the penthouse, rain roared along the walls like surf, the first such shower the city had experienced in more than thirty years. Through a haze of pain, Amalfi found that he could see the lights again, although the rest of the world was a red blur. "But I think we'd best shoot this one at once—he talks rather *more* freely than pleases me. Give me your pistol, you there with the lance-corporal's collar."

Something moved across Amalfi's clearing vision, a long shadow with a knot at the end of it—an arm with a pistol. "Any last words?" Nandór said pleasantly. "No? *Tsk.* Well, then——"

A thousand bumblebees took flight in the room. Amalfi felt his whole body jerk upward. Oddly, there was no pain, and he could still see—things continued to take on definition all around him. The clear sight of the dying? . . .

"Proszáchá!" Nandór roared. *"Egz prá strasticzek Maria, dó*——"

The thunder cut him off again. Somewhere in the room one of the soldiers was whimpering with fright. To Amalfi's fire-racked sight, everyone and everything seemed to be floating in mid-air. Nandór sprawled rigidly, half-erect, his body an inch or so off the cushions, his clothing standing away from him. The pistol was still pointed at Amalfi, but Nandór was not holding it; it hung immobile above the carpet, an inch away from his frozen fingers. The carpet itself was not on the floor but above it, a sea of fur, every filament of which bristled straight up. Pictures had sprung away from the walls and were suspended. The cushions had risen from the chair and moved away from each other a little, then stopped, as if caught by a stroboscopic camera in the first stages of an explosion; the chair itself was an inch above the rug. At the far side of the room, a bookshelf had burst, and the cans of microfilm were ranked neatly in front of the case, evenly spaced, supported by nothing but the empty air.

Amalfi took a cautious breath. His jacket, which, like Nandór's, had ballooned away from his chest, creaked a little, but the fabric was elastic enough to stretch. Nandór saw the movement and made a frantic snatch for the pistol. His left forearm was glued to its position above the chair and could not be moved at all. The gun retreated from his free hand, then followed it back obediently as Nandór pulled back for another try.

The second try was an even greater fiasco. Nandór's arm brushed one of the arms of the chair, and then it, too, was held firmly, an inch away from the wood. Amalfi chuckled.

"I would advise you not to move any more than you can help," he said. "If you should bring your head too close to some other object, for instance, you would have to spend the rest of your time looking at the ceiling."

"What . . . have you done?" Nandór said, choking. "When I get free——"

"You can't, not as long as your friends have their friction-field in operation," Amalfi said. "The plans we gave you were accurate enough, except in one respect: your generator can be operated only in reverse. Instead of allowing molecular valence full play, it freezes molecular relationships as they stand, and creates adherence between *all* surfaces. If you had been able to put full power into that generator, you would have stopped molecular movement in place, and frozen all of us to death in a split second—but your power sources are rather puny."

He realized suddenly that his feet were aching violently; the plastic membrances of his shoes were trying to stand away from his flesh, and pressing heavily against his skin. His jaw muscles were aching, too; only the fact that the field traveled over surfaces had protected him from having his teeth jammed away from each other, and even at that it was an effort to part his lips to talk against the pressure.

He inhaled slowly. The jacket creaked again. His ribs ground against his sternum. Then, suddenly, the fabric gave way, and the silver belt which had been stitched into it snapped into a tense hoop around his body. His soles hit the straining carpet heavily, and the air puffed out of his shoes.

He swung his arms experimentally, brushing his hands past his thighs. They moved freely. Only the silver belt maintained its implausible position, girdling the keg of his chest like a stave, soaking up the field.

"Good-by," he said. "Remember not to move. The cops will let you go in a little while."

Nandór was not listening. He was watching with bulging eyes the slow amputation of six of his fingers by the rings he was wearing.

There was now, Amalfi knew, no longer than fifteen minutes before the overdriven friction-field would begin to have more serious effects. Normal molecular cohesion could not be disturbed; homogeneous objects—stones, girders, planks—would remain as they were, but things which were made up of fitted parts would soon begin to yield to the pressure driving them away from each other. After that, structures joined by binders of smaller coherence than the coherence of their parts would begin to give way; older buildings, such as City Hall, would become taller and of greater volume as the ancient bricks pulled away from each other—and would collapse the moment the influence of the friction-field was removed. More modern constructions and machines would last only a little longer. By the time the cops inherited Gort, the planet would be a mass of rubble.

And eventually the human body, assembled of a thousand tubes, tunnels, caverns, and pockets, would strain, and swell, and burst—and only a few city men had the silver belt; there had not been time.

Puffing, Amalfi threw himself down the stairs, dodging among the paralyzed, floating guards. The bumblebee sound was very hard on the nerves. At the seventieth floor he found an unexpected problem; the lights on the elevator board told him that the car had been sealed in the shaft, probably by the action of the safety mechanisms when it had been derailed by the friction-field.

Going down by the stairs was out of the question. Even under normal conditions he could never have traveled seventy flights of stairs, and in the influence of the field, his feet moved as if in thick mud, for the belt could not entirely protect his extremities. Tentatively he touched the wall. The same nauseous sucking sensation enfolded his hand, and he pulled it away.

Gravity . . . the quickest way down . . .

He entered the nearest office, threading his way among the four suspended, moaning figures who belonged there, and kicked the window out. It was impossible to open it against the field, which had sprung it an inch from its lands; only the amazing lateral strength of glass had preserved the pane, but against a cross-sectional blow, it shattered at once. He climbed out.

It was twenty stories down to the next setback. He planted his feet against the metal, and then his hands. As

an afterthought, he also laid his forehead against the wall.
He began to slide.

The air whispered in his ears, and windows blinked past
him. His palms were beginning to feel warm; they were
not actually touching the metal, but the reluctant binding
energies were exacting a toll. It was the penalty he had to
pay for the heightened pull of friction.

As the setback rushed up to him, he flattened his whole
body against the side of the building. The impact of the
deck was heavy, but it did not seem to break any bones.
He staggered to the parapet and climbed over, without
allowing a split second for second thoughts. The long,
whistling slide began again.

For a moment after he fell against the concrete of the
sidewalk, he was ready to get up and throw himself over
still another cliff. His hands and his forehead were as
seared as if they had been dipped in boiling oil, and inside
his teflon shoes his feet seemed to be bubbling like lumps
of fat in a rendering vat. On the solid ground, a belated
vertigo knotted him helplessly for long, valuable minutes.

The building whose flank he had traversed began to
groan.

All along the street, men stood in contorted attitudes. It
was like the lowest circle of hell. Amalfi got up, retching,
and lurched toward the control tower. The bumblebee
sound filled the universe.

"Amalfi! Gods of all stars, what happened to you——"

Someone took Amalfi's arm. Serum from the enormous
blister which was his forehead flooded his eyes.

"Mark——"

"Yes, yes. What's the matter—how did you——"

"Get aloft. Get——"

Pain wrenched him into a ringing darkness.

After a while he felt his head and his hands being laved
with something cool. The touch was very delicate and
soothing. He swallowed and tried to breathe.

"Easy, John. Easy."

John. No one called him that. A woman's voice. A
woman's hands.

"Easy."

He managed a croaking sound, and then a word or two.
The hands stroked the coolness across his forehead, gently, monotonously. "Easy, John. It's all right."

"Aloft?"

"Yes."

"Who's . . . that? Mark——"

"No," said the voice. It laughed, surprisingly, a musical sound. "This is Dee, John. Hazleton's girl."

"The Hamiltonian girl." He allowed himself to be silent for a while, savoring the coolness. But there were too many things that needed to be done. "The cops. They should have the planet."

"They have it. They almost had us. They don't keep their bargains very well. They charged us with aiding Utopia; that was treason, they said."

"What happened?"

"Doctor Schloss made the invisibility machine work. Mark says the machine must have been damaged in transit, so the Lyrans didn't cheat you after all. He hid Doctor Schloss in it—that was your idea, wasn't it?—and Schloss got bored and amused himself trying to figure out what the machine was for; nobody had told him. He found out. He made the whole city invisible for nearly half an hour before his patchwork connections burned out."

"Invisible? Not just opaque?" Amalfi tried to think about it. And he had nearly had Schloss killed! "If we can use that——"

"We did. We sailed right through the police ring, and they looked right through us. We're on our way to the next star system."

"Not far enough," Amalfi said, stirring uneasily. "Not if we're charged with technical treason. Cops will detect us, follow us. Tell Mark to head for the Rift."

"What is the Rift, John?"

At the word, the bottom seemed to fall out of things, and Amalfi was again sinking into that same pit in which he had been floundering in dream the night that Hazleton had come back to the city. How do you tell a planetbound colonial girl what the Rift is? How do you teach her, in just a few words, that there is a place in the universe so empty and lightless that even an Okie dreams about it? Let it go.

"The Rift is a hole. It's a place where there aren't any stars. I can't explain it any better. Tell Mark we have to go there, Dee."

There was a long silence. She was frightened, that much was plain. But at last she said, "The Rift. I'll tell him."

"He'll argue. Say it's an order."

"Yes, John. The Rift; it's an order."

And then she was silent. Somehow she had accepted it. Amalfi was surprised; but the steady, uneventful passage of the cool hands was putting him to sleep. Yet there was still something more . . .

"Dee?"

"Yes, John."

"You said—*we're* on our way."

"Yes, John."

"You, too? Even to the Rift?"

The girl made her fingertips trace a smile upon his forehead. "Me, too," she said. "Even to the Rift. The Hamiltonian girl."

"No," Amalfi said. He sighed. "Not any more, Dee. Now you're an Okie."

There was no answer, but the movement of the cool fingers did not hesitate. Under Amalfi the city soared outward, humming like a bee, into the raw night.

CHAPTER THREE: The Rift

EVEN to the men of the flying city, the Rift was awesome beyond all human experience. Loneliness was natural between the stars, and starmen of all kinds were used to it—the star-density of the average cluster was more than enough to give a veteran Okie claustrophobia. But the enormous empty loneliness of the Rift was unique.

To the best of Amalfi's knowledge, no human being, let alone a city, had ever crossed the Rift before. The City Fathers, who knew everything, agreed. Amalfi was none too sure that it was wise, for once, to be a pioneer.

Ahead and behind, the walls of the Rift shimmered, a haze of stars too far away to resolve into individual points of light. The walls curved gently toward a starry floor, so many parsecs "beneath" the granite keel of the city that it seemed to be hidden in a rising haze of star dust.

"Above" there was nothing; a nothing as final as the

slamming of a door. It was the empty ocean of space that washes between galaxies.

The Rift was, in effect, a valley cut in the face of the galaxy. A few stars swam in it, light millennia apart—stars which the tide of human colonization could never have reached. Only on the far side was there likely to be any inhabited planet, and, consequently, work for the city.

On the near side there was still the police. It was not, of course, the same contingent which had consolidated Utopia and the Duchy of Gort; such persistence by a single squadron of cops, over a trail which had spanned nearly three centuries, would have been incredible for so small a series of offenses on the city's part. Nevertheless, there was a violation of a Vacate order still on the books, and a little matter of a trick . . . and the word had been passed. To turn back was out of the question for the city.

Whether or not the police would follow the city even as far as the Rift, Amalfi did not know. It was, however, a good gamble. Crossing a desert of this size would probably be impossible for so small an object as a ship, out of a sheer inability to carry enough supplies; only a city which could grow its own had much chance of surviving such a crossing.

Soberly Amalfi contemplated the oppressive chasm which the screens showed him. The picture came in from a string of proxies, the leader of which was already parsecs out across the gap. And still the far wall was featureless, just beginning to show a faintly granular texture which gave promise of resolution into individual stars at top magnification.

"I hope the food holds out," he muttered. "If we make this one, it'll make the most colossal story any Okie ever had to tell. They'll be calling us the Rifters from one end of the galaxy to the other."

Beside him, Hazleton drummed delicately upon the arm of his chair. "And if we don't," he said, "they'll be calling us the biggest damned fools that ever got off the ground— but we won't be in a position to care. Still, we do seem to be in good shape for it, boss. The oil tanks are almost full, and the *Chlorella* crops are flourishing. Both breeders are running, so there'll be no fuel problem. And I doubt that we'll have any mutation trouble in the crops out here— isn't free-field incidence supposed to vary directly with star-density?"

"Sure," Amalfi said, irritated. "We won't starve if everything goes right." He paused; there had been a stir behind him, and he turned around. Then he smiled.

There was something about Dee Hazleton that relaxed him. She had not yet seen enough actual space cruising to acquire the characteristic deep Okie star-burn, nor yet to lose the wonder of being now, by Utopian standards, virtually immortal, and so she seemed still very pink and young and unharried.

Someday, perhaps, the constant strain of wandering from star to star, from crisis to crisis, would tell on her, as it did upon all Okies. She would not lose the wanderlust, but the wanderlust would take its toll.

Or perhaps her resiliency was too great even for that. Amalfi hoped so.

"Go ahead," she said, "I'm only kibitzing."

The word, like a great part of Dee's vocabulary, was a mystery to Amalfi. He grinned and turned back to Hazleton. "If we hadn't been sound enough to risk crossing," he went on, "I'd have let us be captured; we could have paid the fine on the Vacate violation, just barely, and with luck we could have gotten a show-cause injunction against breaking us up slapped on the cops for that 'treason' charge. But just look at that damned canyon, Mark. We've never been as long as fifty years without a planet-fall before, and this crossing is going to take all of the hundred and four the Fathers predicted. The slightest accident, and we'll be beyond help—we'll be out where no ship could reach us."

"There'll be no accident," Hazleton said confidently.

"There's fuel decomposition—we've never had a flash fire before, but there's always a first time. And if that Twenty-third Street spindizzy conks out again, it'll damn near double the time of the crossing——"

He stopped abruptly. Through the corner of his eye, a minute pinprick of brightness poked insistently into his brain. When he looked directly at the screen, it was still there, though somewhat dimmed as its image moved off the fovea centralis of his retina. He pointed.

"Look—is that a cluster? No, it's too small and sharp. If that's a single free-floating star, it's close."

He snatched up a phone. "Give me Astronomy. Hello, Jake. Can you figure me the distance of a star from the source of an ultraphone videocast?"

"Why, yes," the voice on the phone said. "Wait, and I'll pick up your image. Ah—I see what you're after: something at ten o'clock, can't tell what yet. Dinwiddlie pickups on your proxies? Intensity will tell the tale." The astronomer chuckled like a parrot on the rim of a cracker barrel. "Now if you'll just tell me how many proxies you have ahead, and how far they——"

"Five. Full interval."

"Hm-m. A big correction, then." There was a long, itching silence. Amalfi knew that there would be no hurrying Jake. He was not the city's original astronomer; that man had fallen victim to a native of a planet called St. Rita's after he had insisted once too often to said native that St. Rita's was not the center of the universe. Jake had been swapped from another city for an atomic-pile engineer and two minor protosynthetics technicians under the traditional "rule of discretion," and he had turned out to be interested only in the behavior of the more remote galaxies. Persuading him to think about the immediate astronomical situation of the city was usually a hopeless struggle; he seemed to feel that problems of so local a nature were nearly beneath notice.

The "rule of discretion" was an Okie tradition which Amalfi had never before invoked, and never since, for it seemed to him to smell suspiciously of peonage. It had evolved, the City Fathers said, from the trading of baseball players, a term which meant nothing to Amalfi. The results of his one violation of his own attitude toward the rule sometimes seemed to him to smack of divine retribution.

"Amalfi?"

"Yeah."

"About ten parsecs, give or take four-tenths. That's from the proxies, not from us. I'd say you've found a floater, my boy."

"Thanks." Amalfi put the phone back and drew a deep breath. "Just a few years' travel. What a relief."

"You won't find any colonists on a star that isolated," Hazleton reminded him.

"I don't care. It's a landing point, possibly a fuel or even a food source. Most stars have planets; a freak like this might not, or it might have dozens. Just cross your fingers."

He stared at the tiny sun, his eyes aching from sympathetic strain. A star in the middle of the Rift—almost certainly a wild star, moving at four hundred or five hundred kilometers per second, but not, as such stars usually were, a white dwarf; by eye alone, Amalfi estimated it to be an F star like Canopus. It occurred to him that a people living on a planet of that star might remember the moment when it burst through the near wall of the Rift and embarked upon its journey into the emptiness.

"There might be people there," he said. "The Rift was swept clean of stars once, somehow. Jake claims that this is an overdramatic way of putting it, that the mean motions of the stars probably opened the gap naturally. But either way, that sun must be a recent arrival, going at quite a clip, since it's moving counter to the general tendency. It could have been colonized while it was still passing through a populated area. Runaway stars tend to collect hunted criminals as they go by, Mark."

"Possibly," Hazleton admitted. "Though I'll bet that if that star ever was among the others, it was way back before space flight. By the way, that image is coming in from your lead proxy, out across the valley. Don't you have any outriggers? I ordered them sent."

"Sure. But I don't use them except for routine. Cruising the Rift lengthwise would *really* be suicide."

"I know. But where there's one isolated star, there may be another. Maybe a nearer one."

Amalfi shrugged. "We'll take a look if you like."

He touched the board. On the screen, the far wall of the Rift was wiped away. Nothing was left but what looked like a thin haze; down at that end, the Rift turned and eventually faded out into a rill of emptiness, soaking into the sands of the stars.

"Nothing on that side. Lots of nothing."

Amalfi moved the switch again.

On the screen, apparently almost within hallooing distance, a city was burning.

It was all over in a few minutes. The city bucked and toppled in a maelstrom of lightning. Feeble flickers of resistance spat around its edges—and then it no longer had any edges. Sections of it broke off and melted like wraiths. From its ardent center, a few hopeless life craft shot out into the gap; whatever was causing the destruction let them go. No conceivable life ship could live long enough to get out of the Rift.

Dee cried out. Amalfi cut in the audio circuit, filling the control room with a howl of static. Far behind the wild blasts of sound, a tiny voice was shouting desperately, "Rebroadcast if anyone hears us. Repeat: We have the fuelless drive. We're destroying our model and evacuating our passenger. Pick him up if you can. We're being blown up by a bindlestiff. Rebroadcast if——"

Then there was nothing left but the skeleton of the city, glowing whitely, evaporating in the blackness. The pale, innocent light of the guide beam for a Bethé blaster played over it, but it was still impossible to see who was wielding the weapon. The Dinwiddie circuits in the proxies were compensating for the glare, so that nothing was coming through to the screen that did not shine with its own light.

The terrible fire died slowly, and the stars brightened. As the last spark flared and went out, a shadow loomed against the distant star-wall. Hazleton drew his breath in sharply.

"*Another* city! So some outfits really do go bindlestiff! And we thought we were the first ones out here!"

"Mark," Dee said in a small voice. "Mark, what is a bindlestiff?"

"A tramp," Hazleton said, his eyes still on the screen. "The kind of outfit that gives all Okies a bad name. Most Okies are true hobos, Dee; they work for their living wherever they can find work. The bindlestiff lives by robbery—and murder."

His voice was bitter. Amalfi himself felt a little sick. That one city should destroy another was bad enough; but it was even more of a wrench to realize that the whole scene was virtually ancient history. Ultrawave transmission was somewhat faster than light, but only by about 25 per cent; unlike the Dirac transmitter, the ultraphone was by no means an instantaneous communicator. The dark city had destroyed its counterpart years ago, and must now be beyond pursuit. It was even beyond identification, for no orders could be sent now to the lead proxy which would result in any action until still more years had passed.

"Some outfits go bindlestiff, all right," he said. "And I think the number must have been increasing lately. Why that should be, I don't know, but evidently it's happening.

We've been losing a lot of legitimate, honest cities lately—getting no answer to Dirac casts, missing them at rendezvous, and so on. Maybe now we know why."

"I've noticed," Hazleton said. "But I don't see how there could be enough piracy to account for all the losses. For all we know, the Vegan orbital fort may be out here, picking off anybody who's venturesome enough to leave the usual commerce lanes."

"I didn't know the Vegans flew cities," Dee said.

"They don't," Amalfi said abstractedly. He considered describing the legendary fort, then rejected the idea. "But they dominated the galaxy once, before Earth took to space flight. At their peak they owned more planets than Earth does right now, but they were knocked out a hell of a long time ago. . . . I'm still worried about that bindlestiff, Mark. You'd think that some heavy thinker on Earth would have figured out a way to make Diracs compact enough to be mounted in a proxy. They haven't got anything better to do back there."

Hazleton had no difficulty in penetrating to the real core of Amalfi's grumbling. He said, "Maybe we can still smoke 'em out, boss."

"Not a chance. We can't afford a side jaunt."

"Well, I'll send out a general warning on the Dirac," Hazleton said. "It's barely possible that the cops will be able to invest this part of the Rift before the 'stiff gets out of it."

"That'll trap us neatly, won't it? Besides, that bindlestiff isn't going to leave the Rift, at least not until it's picked up those life craft."

"Eh? How do you know?"

"Did you hear what the SOS said about a fuelless drive?"

"Sure," Hazleton said uneasily, "but the man who knows how to build it must be dead by now, even if he escaped when his city was blasted."

"We can't be sure of that—and that's the one thing that the 'stiff has to make sure of. If the 'stiffs get ahold of that drive, there'll be all hell to pay. After that, 'stiffs won't be a rarity any more. If there isn't widespread piracy in the galaxy now, there will be—if we let the 'stiffs get that no-fuel drive."

"Why?" Dee said.

"I wish you knew more history, Dee. I don't suppose

there were ever any pirates on Utopia, but Earth once had
plenty of them. They eventually died out, thousands of
years ago, when sailing ships were replaced by fueled
ships. The fueled ships were faster than sailing vessels—
but they couldn't themselves become pirates because they
had to touch civilized ports regularly to coal up. They
could always get food off some uninhabited island, but for
coal they had to visit a real port. The Okie cities are in
the same position now; they're fueled ships. But if that
bindlestiff can actually get its hands on a no-fuel drive—so
he can sail space without having to touch civilized planets
for power metals—well, we just can't allow it to happen,
that's all. *We've got to get that drive away from them.*"

Hazleton stood up, kneading his hands nervously.
"That's perfectly true—and that's why the 'stiff will knock
itself out to recapture those lifeships. You're right, Amalfi.
Well, there's only one place in the Rift where a lifeship
could go, and that's to the wild star. So the 'stiff is
probably there, too, by now—or on the way there." He
looked thoughtfully at the screen, once more glittering
only with anonymous stars. "That changes things. Shall I
send out the Dirac warning, or not?"

"Yes, send it out. It's the law. But I think it's up to us
to deal with the 'stiff; we're familiar with ways of manipulating strange cultures, and we know how Okies think—
even 'stiffs. Whereas the cops would just smash things up if
they did manage to get here in time."

"Check. Our course as before, then."

"Necessarily."

Still the city manager did not go. "Boss," he said at last,
"the outfit is heavily armed. They could muscle in on us
with no trouble."

"Mark, I'd call you yellow if I didn't know you were
just lazy," Amalfi growled. He stopped suddenly and
peered up the length of Hazleton's figure to his sardonic,
horselike face. "Or are you leading up to something?"

Hazleton grinned like a small boy caught stealing jam.
"Well, I did have something in mind. I don't like 'stiffs,
especially killers. Are you willing to entertain a small
scheme?"

"Ah," Amalfi said, relaxing. "That's better. Let's hear
it."

"It centers on women. Women are the best possible
bindlestiff bait."

"I grant you that," Amalfi said. "But what women would you use? Ours? Nix."

"No, no," Hazleton said. "This is predicated on there being an inhabited planet going around that star. Are you still with me?"

"I think," Amalfi said slowly, "that I may even be a meter or so ahead of you."

The wild star, hurling itself through the Rift on a course that would not bring it to the far wall for another ten thousand Earth years, carried with it six planets, of which only one was even remotely Earthlike. That planet shone deep chlorophyll green on the screens long before it had grown enough to assume a recognizable disc shape. The proxies, called in now, arrived one by one, circling the new world like a swarm of five-meter footballs, eyeing it avidly.

It was everywhere the same: savagely tropical, in the throes of a geological period roughly comparable to Earth's Carboniferous Era. Plainly, the only habitable planet would be nothing but a way station; there would be no work for pay there.

Then the proxies began to pick up weak radio signals.

Nothing, of course, could be made of the language; Amalfi turned that problem over to the City Fathers at once. Nevertheless, he continued to listen to the strange gabble while he warped the city into an orbit. The voices sounded ritualistic, somehow.

The City Fathers said:

"THIS LANGUAGE IS A VARIANT OF HUMANOID PATTERN *G*, BUT THE SITUATION IS AMBIGUOUS. GENERALLY WE WOULD SAY THAT THE RACE WHICH SPEAKS IT IS INDIGENOUS TO THE PLANET, A RARE OCCURRENCE, BUT BY NO MEANS UNHEARD OF. THERE ARE TRACES OF FORMS WHICH MIGHT BE DEGENERATES OF ENGLISH, HOWEVER, AS WELL AS STRONG EVIDENCES OF DIALECT MIXTURES SUGGESTING A TRIBAL SOCIETY. THIS LATTER FACT IS NOT CONSONANT WITH THE POSSESSION OF RADIO NOR WITH THE UNDERLYING SAMENESS OF THE PATTERN. UNDER

THE CIRCUMSTANCES, WE MUST POSITIVELY
FORBID ANY MACHINATION BY MR. HAZLETON
ON THIS VENTURE."

"I didn't ask them for advice," Amalfi said. "And what
good is a lesson in etymology at this point? Still, Mark,
watch your step——"

" 'Remember Thor Five,' " Hazleton said, mimicking
the mayor's father-bear voice to perfection. "All right. Do
we land?"

For answer, Amalfi grasped the space stick, and the city
began to settle. Nothing that appeared to answer as a
ready-made landing area offered itself, and the mayor had
already decided that nothing would. He sidled the city
downward gently, guiding himself mainly by the increasingly loud chanting in his earphones.

At four thousand meters there was a brief glitter from
amid the dark green waves of the treetops. The proxies
converged on it slowly, cautious of their prim electronic
lives, and on the screens a turreted roof showed—then
two, four, a dozen. There was a city there—not an Okie,
but a homebody, grown from the earth. Closer views
showed it to be walled, the wall standing just inside a clear
ring where nothing grew; the greenery between the towers
was camouflage.

At three thousand, a flight of small ships burst from the
native city like frightened birds, molting feathers of flame.
"Gunners!" Hazleton snapped into his mike. "Posts!"

Amalfi shook his head, and continued to bring his city
closer to the ground. The fire-tailed birds wheeled around
them, weaving a pattern in smoky plumes; yet an Earthman would have thought, not of birds, but of the nuptial
flight of drone bees.

Amalfi, who had not seen an Earthly bird or bee for
nearly a millennium now, nevertheless sensed the ceremo-
ny in the darting cortege. With fitting solemnity, he
brought the city to a stop not far from its jungle counterpart, hovering just above the tops of the giant cycads.
Then, instead of clearing a landing area with the usual
quick scythe of the mesotron rifles, he polarized the spindizzy screen.

The base and apex of the Okie city grew dim. What
happened to the giant ferns and horsetails directly beneath
it could not be seen—they were flattened into synthetic

fossils in the muck in a split second—but those just beyond the rim of the city were stripped of their fronds and splintered, and farther out, in a vast circle, the whole forest bowed low away from the city to a clap of sunlit thunder.

Unfortunately, the Twenty-third Street spindizzy blew out under the strain at the last minute, and the city dropped the last 150 meters in free fall. It arrived on the surface of the planet rather more cataclysmically than Amalfi had intended. Hazleton hung on to his bucket seat until the control tower had stopped swaying, and then wiped blood from his nose with a judicious handkerchief.

"That," he said, "was one dramatic touch too many. I'd best go have that spindizzy fixed again, just in case. Someday that machine is going to sour for good and all, boss."

Amalfi shut off the controls with a contented gesture. "If that bindlestiff should show now," he said, "they'll have a tough time amassing any prestige *here* for a while. But go ahead, Mark, it'll keep you busy."

The major eased his barrel-shaped bulk into the lift shaft and let himself be slithered through the friction-field to the street. It was certainly a much faster and pleasanter way of traveling than elevators—or skidding down the face of a building using your forehead for a brake shoe. Outside, the face of the control tower shone with hot sunlight, reminding Amalfi that the front of City Hall faced the same way, and that on it the city's motto would be clear even under its incrustation of verdigris. He hoped that the legend could not be read by any of the local folk—it would spoil the effect of the landing.

Suddenly he was aware that the chanting he had been hearing for so long through his earphones was thrilling through the air around him. Here and there the sober workaday faces of the Okie citizens were turning to look down The Avenue, and traces of wonder, mixed with amusement and an unaccountable sadness, were in those faces. Amalfi turned.

A procession of children was coming toward him— children wound in mummylike swatches of cloth down to their hips, the strips alternately red and white. Several free-swinging panels of many-colored fabric, as heavy as silk, swirled about their legs as they moved.

Each step was followed by a low bend, hands outstretched and fluttering, heads rolling from shoulder to
shoulder, feet moving in and out, toe-heel-toe, the whole
body turning and turning again. Bracelets of objects like
dried pods rattled at wrists and bare ankles. Over it all,
the voices chanted like water flutes.

Amalfi's first wild reaction was to wonder why the City
Fathers had been puzzled about the language. *These were
human children.* Nothing about them showed any trace of
alienage.

Behind them, tall black-haired men moved in less agile
procession, sounding in chorus a single word which
boomed through the skirl and pitter of the children's
dance at widespaced intervals. The men were human, too:
their hands, stretched immovably out before them, palms
up, had five fingers, with fingernails on them; their beards
had the same topography as human beards; their chests,
bared to the sun by a symbolic rent which was torn at the
same place in each garment, and marked identically by a
symbolic wound rubbed on with red chalk, showed ribs
where ribs ought to be, and the telltale tracings of clav-
icles beneath the skin.

About the women there might have been some doubt.
They came at the end of the procession, all together in a
huge cage drawn by lizards. They were all naked and sick,
and could have been any kind of primate. They made no
sound, but only stared out of purulent eyes, as indifferent
to the Okie city and its owners as to their captors. Occasionally they scratched, reluctantly, wincing from their
own claws.

The children deployed around Amalfi, evidently picking
him out as the leader because he was the biggest. He had
expected as much; it was but one more confirmation of
their humanity. He stood still while they made a circle and
sat down, still chanting and swaying and shaking their
wrists. The men, too, made a circle, keeping their faces
toward Amalfi, their hands outstretched. At last that reek-
ing cage was drawn into the double ring, virtually to
Amalfi's feet. Two male attendants unhitched the docile
lizards and led them away.

Abruptly the chanting stopped. The tallest and most
impressive of the men came forward and bent, making that
strange gesture with fluttering hands over the asphalt of
The Avenue. Before Amalfi quite realized what was in-

tended, the stranger had straightened, placed some heavy object in his hand, and retreated, calling aloud the single word the men had been intoning before. Men and children responded together in one terrific shout, and then there was silence.

Amalfi was alone with the cage in the middle of the double circle. He looked down at the thing in his hand.

It was an ornate wrought-metal key.

CHAPTER FOUR: He

MIRAMON shifted nervously in the chair, the great black saw-toothed feather stuck into his topknot bobbing uncertainly. It was a testimonial to his confidence in Amalfi that he sat in it at all, for in the beginning he had squatted, as was customary on his planet. Chairs were the uncomfortable prerogatives of the gods.

"I myself do not believe in the gods," he explained to Amalfi, bobbing the feather. "It would be plain to a technician, you understand, that your city is simply a product of a technology superior to ours, and you yourselves are men such as we are. But on this planet, religion has a terrible force, a very immediate force. It is not expedient to run counter to public sentiment in such matters."

Amalfi nodded. "From what you tell me, I can believe that. Your situation is unique, to the best of our knowledge. What, precisely, happened when your civilization fell?"

Miramon shrugged. "We do not know. It was over eight thousand years ago, and nothing is left but legend. There was a high culture here then—the priests and the scientists agree on that. And the climate was different; it got cold regularly every year, I am told, although how men could survive such a period is difficult to understand. Besides, there were many more stars—the ancient carvings show *thousands* of them, although they fail to agree on the details."

"Naturally. You're not aware that your sun is moving at an abnormally fast relative speed?"

"Moving?" Miramon laughed shortly. "Some of our more mystical scientists are of that opinion—they maintain that if the planets move, so must the sun. It is an imperfect analogy, in my opinion; after all, planets and suns are not otherwise alike as far as we can see. And would we still be in this trough of nothingness if we were moving?"

"Yes, you would—you are. You underestimate the size of the Rift. It's impossible to detect any parallax at this distance, although in a few thousand years you'll begin to suspect it. But while you were actually among the other stars, your ancestors could see the motion very well, by the changing positions of the neighboring suns."

Miramon looked dubious. "I bow to your superior knowledge, of course. But, be that as it may—the legends have it that for some sin of our people, the gods plunged us into this starless desert, and changed our climate to perpetual heat. This is why our priests say that we are in hell, and that to be put back among the cool stars again, we must redeem our sins. We have no heaven as you have defined the term; when we die, we die damned; we must win 'salvation' right here in the mud while we are still alive. The doctrine has its attractive features under the circumstances."

Amalfi meditated. It was reasonably clear, now, what had happened, but he despaired of explaining it to Miramon—hard common sense sometimes has a way of being impenetrable. This planet's axis had a pronounced tilt, and the concomitant amount of liberation. This meant that, like Earth, it had a Draysonian cycle: every so often the top wobbled, and then resumed spinning at a new angle. The result was a disastrous climatic change. Such a thing happened on Earth roughly once every twenty-five thousand years, and the first one in recorded history had given birth to some extraordinarily silly legends and faiths—sillier than those the Hevians now entertained, on the whole.

Still, it was miserably bad luck for the Hevians that a Draysonian overturn had occurred almost at the same time that the planet had begun its journey across the Rift. It had thrown a very high civilization, a culture just entering its ripest phase, forcibly back into the Inter-destructional period without the slightest transition.

The planet of He was a strange mixture now. Politically the regression had stopped just before barbarism—a measure of the lofty summits this race had scaled before the catastrophe—and was now in reverse, clawing through the stage of warring city-states. Yet the basics of the scientific techniques of eight thousand years ago had not been forgotten; now they were exfoliating, bearing "new" fruits.

Properly, city-states should fight each other with swords, not with missile weapons, chemical explosives, and supersonics—and flying should be still in the dream stage, a dream of flapping wings at that, not already a jet-propelled fact. Astronomical and geological accident had mixed history up for fair.

"What would have happened to me if I'd unlocked that cage?" Amalfi demanded abruptly.

Miramon looked sick. "Probably you would have been killed—or they would have tried to kill you, anyhow," he said, with considerable reluctance. "That would have been releasing Evil again upon us. The priests say that it was women who brought about the sins of the Great Age. In the bandit cities, to be sure, that savage creed is no longer maintained—which is one reason why we have so many deserters to the bandit cities. You can have no idea of what it is like to do your duty to the race each year as our law requires. Madness!"

He sounded very bitter. "This is why it is hard to make our people see how suicidal the bandit cities are. Everyone on this world is weary of fighting the jungle, sick of trying to rebuild the Great Age with handfuls of mud, sick of maintaining social codes which ignore the presence of the jungle—but most of all, sick of serving in the Temple of the Future. In the bandit cities the women are clean, and do not scratch one."

"The bandit cities don't fight the jungle?" Amalfi asked.

"No. They prey on those who do. They have given up the religion entirely—the first act of a city which revolts is to slay its priests. Unfortunately, the priesthood is essential; and our beast-women must be borne, since we cannot modify one tenet without casting doubt upon all—or so they tell us. It is only the priesthood which teaches us that it is better to be men than mud-puppies. So we—the technicians—follow the rituals with great strictness, stupid though some of them are, and consider it a matter of no moment that we ourselves do not believe in the gods."

"Sense in that," Amalfi admitted. Miramon, in all conscience, was a shrewd apple. If he was representative of as large a section of Hevian thought as he believed himself to be, much might yet be done on this wild runaway world.

"It amazes me that you knew to accept the key as a trust," Miramon said. "It was precisely the proper move— but how could you have guessed that?"

Amalfi grinned. "That wasn't hard. I know how a man looks when he's dropping a hot potato. Your priest made all the gestures of a man passing on a great gift, but he could hardly wait until he'd got it over with. Incidentally, some of those women are quite presentable now that Dee's bathed 'em and Medical has taken off the under layers. Don't look so alarmed, we won't tell your priests— I gather that we're the foster fathers of He from here on out."

"You are thought to be emissaries from the Great Age," Miramon agreed gravely. "What you *actually* are, you have not said."

"True. Do you have migratory workers here? The phrase comes easily in your language, yet I can't quite see how——"

"Surely, surely. The singers, the soldiers, the fruit-pickers—all go from city to city, selling their services." Then, much faster than Amalfi had expected, the Hevian reached bottom. "Do you ... do you imply ... that your resources are *for sale?* For sale to *us?*"

"Exactly, Miramon."

"But how shall we pay you?" Miramon gasped. "All of what we call wealth, all that we have, could not buy a length of the cloth in your sash!"

Amalfi thought about it, wondering principally how much of the real situation Miramon could be expected to understand. It occurred to him that he had persistently underestimated the Hevian so far. It might be profitable to try the full dose—and hope that it wouldn't prove lethal.

"It's this way," Amalfi said. "In the culture we belong to, a certain metal serves for money. You have enormous amounts of it on your planet, but it's very hard to refine, and I'm sure you've never done more than detect it. One of the things we would like is your permission to mine for that metal."

Miramon's pop-eyed skepticism was close to comical. "Permission?" he repeated. "Please, Mayor Amalfi—is your ethical code as foolish as ours? Why do you not mine this metal without permission and be done with it?"

"Our law-enforcement agencies would not allow it. Mining your planet would make us rich—almost unbelievably rich. Our assays show, not only fabulous amounts of germanium on He, but also the presence of certain drugs in your jungle—drugs which are known to be antiagathics."

"Sir?"

"Sorry. I mean that, used properly, these drugs indefinitely postpone death."

Miramon rose with great dignity.

"You are mocking me," he said. "I will return at a later date, and perhaps we may talk again."

"Sit down, please," Amalfi said contritely. "I had forgotten that aging is not everywhere known to be an anomaly, a decrease in the cell-building efficiency of the body which can be circumvented if you know how. It was conquered a long time ago—before interstellar flight, in fact. But the pharmaceuticals involved have always been in very short supply, shorter and shorter as man spread through the galaxy. Less than a two-thousandth of one per cent of our present population can get the treatment now, and most of the legitimate trade goes to the people who need life-extension the most—in other words, to people who make their living by traveling long distances in space. The result is that an ampul of any anti-agathic, even the least efficient ones, that a spaceman thinks he can spare can be sold for the price the seller asks. Not a one of the anti-agathics has ever been synthesized, so if we could harvest here——"

"That is enough; it is not necessary that I understand more," Miramon said. He squatted reflectively, evidently having abandoned the chair as an impediment to thought. "All this makes me wonder if you are not from the Great Age after all. Well—this is difficult to think about reasonably. Why would your culture object to your being rich?"

"It wouldn't, as long as we came by it honestly. We'll have to show that we worked for our riches—otherwise we'll be suspected of having peddled cut drugs on the black market, at the expense of the rank-and-file people on board our own city. We'll need a written agreement with you. A permission."

"That is clear," Miramon said. "You will get it, I am sure. I cannot grant it myself. But I can predict what the priests will ask you to do to earn it."

"What, then? This is just what I want to know. Let's have it."

"First of all, you will be asked for the secret of this ... this cure for death. They will want to use it on themselves, and hide it from the rest of us. Wisdom, perhaps; it would make for more desertions otherwise—but I am sure they will want it."

"They can have it, but I think we'll see to it that the secret leaks out. The City Fathers know the therapy, and you have so rich a supply of the drugs here that there's no reason why you shouldn't all get it." Privately, Amalfi had an additional reason: If He reached the other side of the Rift eventually with enough anti-agathics to extend coverage much among the galaxy's general population, there would be all kinds of economic hell to pay. "What next?"

"You will be asked to wipe out the jungle."

Amalfi sat back, stunned, and mopped his bald head. Wipe out the jungle! Oh, it would be easy enough to lay waste to almost all of it—even to give the Hevians energy weapons to keep those wastes clear—but sooner or later the jungle would come back. The weapons would short out in the eternal moisture; the Hevians would not take proper care of them, would not be able to repair them— how would the brightest Greek have repaired a shattered X-ray tube, even if he had known what steps to take? The technology didn't exist.

No, the jungle would come back. And the cops, in pursuit of the bindlestiff on the city's own Dirac alarm, would eventually come to He to see whether or not the Okies had fulfilled their contract—and would find the planet as raw as ever. Good-by to riches. This was jungle climate. There would be jungles here until the next Draysonian catastrophe, and that was that.

"Excuse me," he said, and reached for the control helmet. "Get me the City Fathers," he said into the mouthpiece.

"SPEAK," the spokesman vodeur said after a while.

"How would you go about wiping out a jungle?"

There was a moment's silence. "SODIUM FLUOSILI-

CATE DUSTING WOULD SERVE. IN A WET CLI-
MATE IT WOULD CREATE FATAL LEAF BLISTER.
HARDIER WEEDS COULD BE SPRAYED WITH 2, 4-
D. OF COURSE THE JUNGLE WOULD RETURN."

"That's what I meant. Any way to make the job stick?"

"NO, UNLESS THE PLANET EXHIBITS DRAY-
SONIANISM."

"What?"

"NO, UNLESS THE PLANET EXHIBITS DRAY-
SONIANISM. IN THAT CASE ITS AXIS MIGHT BE
REGULARIZED. IT HAS NEVER BEEN TRIED, BUT
THEORETICALLY IT IS QUITE SIMPLE; A BILL TO
REGULARIZE EARTH'S AXIS WAS DEFEATED BY
THREE VOTES IN THE EIGHTY-SECOND COUNCIL,
OWING TO THE OPPOSITION OF THE CONSERVA-
TION LOBBY."

"Could the city handle it?"

"NO. THE COST WOULD BE PROHIBITIVE. *MAY-
OR AMALFI, ARE YOU CONTEMPLATING TIP-
PING THIS PLANET? WE FORBID IT!* EVERY INDI-
CATION SHOWS——"

Amalfi tore the helmet from his head and flung it across
the room. Miramon sprang up in alarm.

"Hazleton!"

The city manager shot through the door as if he had
been kicked through it on roller skates. "Here, boss—
what's the——"

"Get down below and turn off the City Fathers—*fast*,
before they catch on and do something! Quick, man——"

Hazleton was already gone. On the other side of the
room, the phones of the helmet squawked dead data in
anxious, even syllables.

Then suddenly they went silent.

The City Fathers had been turned off, and Amalfi was
ready to move a world.

The fact that the City Fathers could not be consulted—
for the first time since the Epoch affair five centuries ago,
when the whole city had been without power for a while—
made the job more difficult than it needed to be, barring
their conservatism. Tipping the planet, the crux of the job,
was simple enough in essence; the city's spindizzies could
handle it. But the side effects of the medicine might easily
prove to be worse than the disease.

The problem was seismological. Rapidly whirling objects have a way of being stubborn about changing their positions in space. If that energy were overcome, it would have to appear somewhere else—the most likely place being multiple earthquakes.

Too, very little could be anticipated about the gravitics of the task. The planet's revolution produced, as usual, a sizable magnetic field. Amalfi did not know how well that field would take to being tipped in the space-lattice which it distorted, nor just what would happen to He when the city's spindizzies polarized the whole gravity field. During "moving day" the planet would be, in effect, without magnetic moment of its own, and since computation was a function of the City Fathers, there was no way of finding out where the energy would reappear, in what form, or at what intensity.

He broached the latter question to Hazleton. "If we were dealing with an ordinary problem, I'd say the energy would show up as velocity," he pointed out. "In which case we'd be in for an involuntary junket. But this is no ordinary case. The mass involved is . . . well, it's planetary, that's all. What do you think, Mark?"

"I don't know what to think," Hazleton admitted. "The equations only give us general solutions, and only quanticised solutions at that—and this whole problem is a classical field problem. When we move the city, we change the magnetic moment of its component electrons; but the city itself is a low-mass body with no spin of its own, and doesn't have a *gross* magnetic moment."

"That's what stuck me. I can't cross over from probability into tensors any more than poor old Einstein could. As far as I know, nobody's ever really faced up to the discontinuity between what the spindizzy does to the electron and what happens to a body of classical mass in a spindizzy field."

"Still—we could control velocity, or even ignore it out here. Suppose the energy reappears as heat, instead? There'd be nothing left of He but a cloud of gas."

Amalfi shook his head. "I think that's a bogey. The gyroscopic resistance may show up as heat, sure, but not the magnetogravitic. I think we'd be safest to assume that it'll appear as velocity, just as in ordinary flight. Use the standard transformation and see what you get."

Hazleton bent over his slide rule, the sweat standing out

along his forehead and above his mustache in great heavy droplets. Amalfi could understand the eagerness of the Hevians to get rid of the jungle and its eternal humidity. His own clothing, sparse though it was, had been sopping ever since the city had landed here.

"Well," the city manager said finally, "unless I've made a mistake somewhere, the whole kit and kaboodle, the planet itself, will go shooting away from here at about twice the speed of light. That's not too bad—just about coasting speed for us. We could always loop around and bring the planet back to its orbit."

"Ah, but could we? Remember, we don't control it! The vector appears automatically when we turn on the spindizzies. We don't even know in which direction that arrow is going to point. The planet could throw itself into the sun within the first second as far as we know. We can't predict the direction."

"Yes, we can," Hazleton objected. "Along the axis of spin, of course."

"Cant? And torque?"

"No problem—no, yes, there is. I keep forgetting that we're dealing with a planet instead of electrons." He applied the slipstick again. "No soap. Too many substitutions. Can't be answered in time without the City Fathers— and torque might hype the end-velocity substantially. But if we can figure a way to control the flight, it won't matter in the end. Of course there'll be perturbations of the other planets when this one goes massless, whether it actually moves or not—but nobody lives on them anyhow."

"All right, Mark, go figure a control system. I'll see what can be done on the geology end——"

The door slid back suddenly, and Amalfi looked back over his shoulder. It was Sergeant Anderson. The perimeter sergeant was usually blasé in the face of all possible wonders, unless they threatened the city. "What's the matter?" Amalfi said, alarmed.

"Mr. Mayor, we've gotten an ultracast from some outfit claiming to be refugees from another Okie city—they claim they hit a bindlestiff and got broken up. They've crash-landed on this planet up north, and they're being mobbed by one of the local bandit towns. They were holding 'em off and yelling for help, and then they stopped transmitting. I thought you ought to know."

Amalfi heaved himself to his feet almost instantly. "Did you get a bearing on that call?" he demanded.

"Yes sir."

"Give me the figures. Come on, Mark. That's our life craft from the city with the no-fuel drive. We need those boys."

Amalfi and Hazleton grabbed a cab to the edge of the city, and went the rest of the way to the Hevian town on foot, across the supersonics-cleared strip of bare turf which surrounded the walls. The turf felt rubbery. Amalfi suspected that some rudimentary form of friction-field was keeping the mud in a state of stiff gel. He had visions of foot soldiers sinking suddenly into slowly-folding ooze as the fields were turned off, and quickened his pace.

Inside the gates, the Hevian guards summoned a queer, malodorous vehicle which seemed to be powered by the combustion of hydrocarbons, and the Okies were roared through the streets toward Miramon. Throughout the journey, Amalfi clung to a cloth strap in an access of nervousness. Traveling right *on* a surface at any good speed was a rare experience for him, and the way things zipped past the windows made him jumpy.

"Is this bird out to smash us up?" Hazleton demanded petulantly. "He must be doing all of four hundred kilos an hour."

"I'm glad you feel the same way," Amalfi said, relaxing a little. "Actually, I'll bet he's doing less than two hundred. It's just the way the——"

The driver, who had been holding his car down to a conservative fifty out of deference to the strangers from the Great Age, wrenched the machine around a corner and halted it neatly before Miramon's door. Amalfi got out, his knees wobbly. Hazleton's face was a delicate puce.

"I'm going to figure out a way to make our cabs operate outside the city," he muttered. "Every time we make a new planetfall, we have to ride on ox carts, the backs of bull kangaroos, in hot air balloons, steam-driven air-screws, things that drag you feet first and face down through tunnels, or whatever else the natives think is classy transportation. My stomach won't stand much more."

Amalfi grinned and raised his hand to Miramon, whose

expression suggested laughter smothered with great difficulty.

"What brings you here?" the Hevian said. "Come in. I
have no chairs, but——"

"No time," Amalfi said. "Listen closely, Miramon, because this is going to be complex to explain, and I'm going
to have to give it to you fast. You already know that our
city isn't the only one of its type. Well, the fact is that we
aren't even the first Okie city to enter the Rift; there were
two others ahead of us. One of them, a criminal city that
we call a bindlestiff, attacked and destroyed the other; we
were too far away to prevent it. Do you follow me?"

"I think so," Miramon said. "This bindlestiff is like our
bandit cities——"

"Yes, precisely. And as far as we know, it's still in the
Rift, somewhere. Now the city that the 'stiff destroyed had
something that we want very badly, and that we *must* have
before the 'stiffs get it. We know that the dead city put off
some life craft, and that one of those craft has just landed
on your world—and has fallen afoul of one of your own
bandit cities. We've got to rescue them. They're the sole
survivors of the dead city as far as we know, and it's vital
for us to question them. We need to know what they
know about the thing we want—the no-fuel drive—and
what they know about where the bindlestiff is now."

"I see," Miramon said thoughtfully. "Will this—this
bindlestiff follow them to He?"

"We think it will. And it's powerful—it packs all the
stuff we have and more besides. We have to pick up these
survivors first, and work out some way to defend ourselves
and you people against the 'stiff when it gets here. And
above all, we must prevent the 'stiff from getting the secret
of that fuelless drive!"

"What would you like me to do?" Miramon said
gravely.

"Can you locate the Hevian town that's holding these
people prisoner? We have a fix on it, but only a blurred
one. If you can, we'll be able to get them out of there
ourselves."

Miramon went back into his house—actually, like all
the other living quarters in the town, it was a dormitory
housing twenty-five men of the same trade or profession—
and returned with a map. The map-making conventions of
He were anything but self-explanatory, but after a while

Hazleton was able to figure out the symbolism involved. "There's your city, and here's ours," he said to Miramon, pointing. "Right? And this peeled-orange thing is a butterfly grid. I've always claimed that it was a lot more faithful to spherical territory than our Geographic projection, boss."

"Easier still to express what you want to remember as a topological relationship," Amalfi said impatiently. "Nobody ever confuses a table of symbols with the territory. Show Miramon where the signals came from."

"Up here, on this wing of the butterfly."

Miramon frowned. "There is only one city there—Fabr-Suithe. A very bad place to approach, even in the military sense. But if you insist on trying, we will help you. Do you know what the end result will be?"

"We'll rescue our friends, I hope. What else?"

"The bandit cities will come out in force to hinder the Great Work. They oppose it; the jungle is their life."

"Then why haven't they impeded us before now?" Hazleton said. "Are they scared?"

"No. They fear nothing—we think they take drugs—but they have seen no way to attack you without huge losses, and their reasons for attacking you have not been sufficiently compelling to make them take the risk up to now. But if *you* attack one of *them*, that will give them reason enough. They learn hatred very quickly."

"I think we can handle them," Hazleton said coldly.

"I am sure you can," Miramon said. "But you should be warned that Fabr-Suithe is the leader of all the bandit cities. If Fabr-Suithe attacks you, so will they all."

Amalfi shrugged. "We'll chance it. We'll have to: we must have those men. Maybe we can make it quick enough to crush resistance before it starts. We can pick our own town up and go calling on Fabr-Suithe; if they don't want to deliver up these Okies——"

"Boss——"

"Eh?"

"How are you going to get us off the ground?"

Amalfi could feel his ears turning red, and swore. "I forgot that Twenty-third Street machine. Miramon, we'll have to have a task force of your own rockets. Hazleton, how are we going to work this? We can't fit anything really powerful into a Hevian rocket plane—a pile would go into one easily enough, but a frictionator or a naval-size mesotron rifle wouldn't, and there'd be no point in taking popguns. Do you suppose we could gas Fabr-Suithe?"

"You couldn't carry enough gas in a Hevian rocket either. Or carry enough men to make a raid in force."

"Excuse me," Miramon said, "but it is not even certain that the priests will authorize the use of our planes against Fabr-Suithe. We had best drive directly over to the temple and ask them for permission."

"Belsen and bebop!" Amalfi said. It was the oldest oath in his repertoire.

Talk, even with electronic aids, was impossible inside the little rocket. The whole machine roared like a gigantic tam-tam to the vibration of the venturis. Morosely Amalfi watched Hazleton connecting the mechanism in the nose of the plane with the power-leads from the pile—no mean balancing feat, considering the way the craft pitched in its passage through the tortured Hevian crosswinds. The pile itself, of course, was simple enough to handle; it consisted only of a tank about the size of a glass brick, filled with a fine white froth: heavy water containing uranium^{235} hexafluoride in solution, damped by bubbles of cadmium vapor. Most of its weight was shielding and the peripheral capillary network of the heat-exchanger.

There had been no difficulty with the priests about the little rocket task force itself; the priests had been delighted at the proposal that the emissaries from the Great Age should teach an apostate Hevian city the error of its ways. Amalfi suspected that the straight-faced Miramon had invented the need for priestly permission just to get the two Okies back into the smelly ground car again and watch their faces during the drive to the temple. Still the discomforts of that ride had been small compared to this one.

The pilot shifted his feet on the treadles, and the deck pitched. A metal trap rushed back under Amalfi's nose, and he found himself looking through misty air at a crazily canted jungle. Something long, thin, and angry flashed over it and was gone. At the same time there was a piercing, inhuman shriek, sharp enough to dwarf for a long instant the song of the rocket.

Then there were more of the same: *ptsouiiirrr! ptsouiiirrr! ptsouiiirrr!* The machine jerked to nearly every one and then shook itself violently, twisting and careening across the jungle top. Amalfi had never felt so helpless before in his life. He did not even know what the noise was; he could only be sure that it was ill-tempered. The coarse *blaam* of high explosive, when it began, was recognizable—the city had often had occasion to blast on jobs—but nothing in his experience went *kerchowkerchowkerchowkerchow,* like a demented vibratory drill, and the invisible thing that screamed its own pep yell as it flew—*eeeeeeeyokKRCHackackarackarackaracka*—seemed wholly impossible.

He was astonished to discover that the hull around him was stippled with small holes, real holes with the slipstream fluting over them. It took him what seemed to be three weeks to realize that the whooping and cheerleading which meant nothing to him was riddling the ship and threatening to kill him at any second.

Someone was shaking him. He lurched to his knees, trying to unfreeze his eyeballs.

"Amalfi! Amalfi!" The voice, although it was breathing on his ear, was parsecs away. "Pick your spot, quick! They'll have us shot down in a——"

Something burst outside and threw Amalfi back to the deck. Doggedly he crawled to the trap and peered down through the now-shattered glass. The bandit Hevian city swooped past, upside down. The mayor felt a sudden wave of motion sickness, and the city was lost in a web of tears. The second time it came by, he managed to see which building in it had the heaviest guard, and pointed, choking.

The rocket threw its tailfeathers over the nearest cloud and bored beak-first for the ground. Amalfi hung on to the edge of the suddenly blank trap, his own blood spraying back in a fine mist into his face from his cut fingers.

"Now!"

Nobody heard, but Hazleton saw his nod. A blast of pure light blew through the upended cabin, despite the shielding between it and the pile. Even through the top of his head, the violet-white light of that soundless blast nearly blinded Amalfi, and he could feel the irradiation of his shoulders and chest. He would develop no allergies on this planet, anyhow—every molecule of histamine in his blood must have been detoxified in that instant.

The rocket yawed wildly, and then came under control

again. The ordnance noises had already quit, cut off at the moment of the flash.

The bandit Hevian city was blind.

The sound of the jets cut off, and Amalfi understood for the first time what an "aching void" might be. The machine fell into a steep glide, the air howling dismally outside it. Another rocket, under the guidance of Carrel, dived down before it, scything a narrow runway in the jungle with portable mesotron rifles—for the bandit towns kept no supersonic no-plant's-land between themselves and the rank vegetation.

The moment the rocket stopped moving, Amalfi and a hand-picked squad of Okies and Hevians were out of it and slogging through the muck. From inside Fabr-Suithe drifted a myriad of screams—human screams now, screams of rage and grief, from men who thought themselves blinded for life. Amalfi did not doubt that many of them were. Certainly anyone who had had the misfortune to be looking at the sky during that instant when the entire output of the pile had been converted to visible light would never see again.

But the laws of chance would have protected most of the renegades, so speed was vital. The mud built up heavy pads under his shoes, and the jungle did not thin out until they hit the town's wall itself.

The gates had been rusted open years ago, and were choked with greenery. The Hevians hacked their way through it with practiced knives and cunning.

Inside, the going was still almost as thick. Fabr-Suithe proper presented a depressing face of proliferating despair. Most of the buildings were completely enshrouded in vines, and many were halfway toward ruins. Iron-hard tendrils had thrust their way between stones, into windows, under cornices, up drains and chimney funnels. Poison-green succulent leaves plastered themselves greedily upon every surface, and in shadowed places there were huge blood-colored fungi which smelled like a man six days dead; the sweetish taint hung heavily in the air. Even the paving blocks had sprouted—inevitably, since, whether by ignorance or laziness, most of the recent ones had been cut from green wood.

The screaming began to die into whimpers. Amalfi did his best to keep himself from inspecting the stricken inhabitants. A man who believes he has just been blinded

permanently is not a pretty sight, even when he is wrong.
Yet it was impossible not to notice the curious mixture of
soiled finery with gleamingly clean nakedness. It was as if
two different periods had mixed in the city, as if a gathering of Hruntan nobles had been sprinkled with Noble
Savages. Possibly the men who had given in completely to
the jungle had also slid back enough to discover the
pleasures of bathing. If so, they would shortly discover the
pleasures of the mud-wallow, too, and would not look so
noble after that.

"Amalfi, here they are——"

The mayor's suppressed sympathy for the blinded men
evaporated when he got a look at the imprisoned Okies.
They had been systematically mauled to begin with, and
after that sundry little attentions had been paid to them
which combined the best features of savagery and de-
cadence. One of them, mercifully, had been strangled by
his comrades early in the "questioning." Another, a basket
case, should have been rescued, for he could still talk
rationally, but he pleaded so persistently for death that
Amalfi had him shot in a sudden fit of sentimentality. Of
the other three men, all could walk and talk, but two were
mad. The catatonic was carried out on a stretcher, and
the manic was bound, gagged, and led gingerly away.

"How did you do it?" asked the rational man in Russian, the dead universal language of Earth. He was a
human skeleton, but he radiated an amazing personal
force. He had lost his tongue early in the "questioning,"
but had already taught himself to talk by the artificial
method—the result was weird, but it was intelligible. "The
savages were coming down to kill us as soon as they heard
your rockets. Then there was a sort of flash, and they all
started screaming—a pretty sound, let me tell you."

"I'll bet," Amalfi said. "Do you speak Interlingua?
Good, my Russian is rudimentary these days. That 'sort of
a flash' was a photon explosion. It was the only way we
could figure on being sure of getting you out alive. We
thought of trying gas, but if they had had gas masks, they
would have been able to kill you anyhow."

"I haven't actually seen any masks, but I'm sure they
have them. There are traveling volcanic gas clouds in this
part of the planet, they say; they must have evolved some
absorption device—charcoal is well known here. Lucky we

were so far underground, or we'd be blind, too, then. You people must be engineers."

"More or less," Amalfi agreed. "Strictly, we're miners and petroleum geologists, but we've developed a lot of side lines since we went aloft—like any Okie. On Earth we were a port city and did just about everything, but aloft you have to specialize. Here's our rocket—crawl in. It's rough, but it's transportation. How about you?"

"Agronomists. Our mayor thought there was a good field for it out here along the periphery—teaching the abandoned colonies and the offshoots how to work poisoned soil and manage low-yield crops without heavy machinery. Our side line was waxmans."

"What are those?" Amalfi said, adjusting the harness around the wasted body.

"Soil-source antibiotics. It was those the bindlestiff wanted—and got. The filthy swine. They can't bother to keep a reasonably sanitary city; they'd rather pirate some honest outfit for drugs when they have an epidemic. Oh, and they wanted germanium, too, of course. They blew us up when they found we didn't have any—we'd converted to a barter economy as soon as we got out of the last commerce lanes."

"What about your passenger?" Amalfi said with studied nonchalance.

"Doctor Beetle? Not that that was his name—I couldn't pronounce *that* even when I had my tongue. I don't imagine he survived. We had to keep him in a tank even in the city, and I can't quite see him living through a lifeship journey. He was a Myrdian—smart cookies all of them, too. That no-fuel drive of his——"

Outside, a shot cracked, and Amalfi winced. "We'd best take off—they're getting their eyesight back. Talk to you later. Hazleton, any incidents?"

"Nothing to speak of, boss. Everybody stowed?"

"Yep. Kick off."

There was a volley of shots, and then the rocket coughed, roared, and stood on its tail. Amalfi pulled a deep sigh loose from the acceleration and turned his head toward the rational man.

He was still securely strapped in, and looked quite relaxed. A brass-nosed slug had come through the side of the ship next to him and had neatly removed the top of his skull.

Working information out of the madmen was a painfully long, anxious process. Even after the manic case had been returned to a semblance of rationality, he could contribute very little.

The lifeship had not come to He because of Hazleton's Dirac warning, he said. The lifeship and the burned Okie had not had any Dirac equipment to the best of his knowledge. The lifeship had come to He, as Amalfi had predicted, because it was the only possible planetfall in the desert of the Rift. Even so, the refugees had had to use deep-sleep and strict starvation rationing to make it.

"Did you see the 'stiff again?"

"No, sir. If they heard your Dirac warning, they probably figured the police had spotted them and scrammed— or maybe they thought there was a military base or an advanced culture here on the planet."

"You're guessing," Amalfi said gruffly. "What happened to Doctor Beetle?"

The man looked startled. "The Myrdian in the tank? He got blown up with the city, I suppose."

"He wasn't put off in another lifeship?"

"Doesn't seem very likely. But I was only a pilot. Could be that they took him out in the mayor's gig for some reason."

"You don't know anything about his no-fuel drive?"

"First I heard of it."

Amalfi was far from satisfied; he suspected that there was still a short circuit somewhere in the man's memory. But that was all that could be gotten from him, and Amalfi had to accept the fact. All that remained to be done was to get some assessment of the weapons available to the bindlestiff; on this subject the ex-manic was ignorant, but the city's neurophysiologist said cautiously that something might be extracted from the catatonic within a month or two; thus far, he hadn't even succeeded in capturing the man's attention.

Amalfi accepted the estimate also, since it was the best he could get. With Moving Day for He coming near, he couldn't afford to worry overtime about another problem. He had already decided that the simplest answer to vulcanism, which otherwise would be inevitable when the planet's geophysical balance was changed, would be to reinforce the crust. At two hundred points on the surface of He, drilling teams were now sinking long, thin, slanting shafts, reaching toward the stress-fluid of the world's core. The shafts interlocked intricately, and thus far only one volcano had been created by the drilling. In general, the lava pockets which had been tapped had already been anticipated, and the flow had been bled off into many intersecting channels without ever reaching the surface. After the molten rock had hardened, the clogged channels were re-drilled, with mesotron rifles set to the smallest possible dispersion.

None of the shafts had yet tapped the stress-fluid; the plan was to complete them all simultaneously. At that point, specific volcanic areas, riddled with channel intersections, would give way, and immense plugs would be forced up toward the crust, plugs of iron, connected by ferrous cantilevers through the channels between. The planet of He would wear a cruel corset, permitting only the slightest flexure—it would be stitched with threads of steel, steel that had held even granite in solution for geological ages.

The heat problem was tougher, and Amalfi was not sure whether or not he had hit upon the solution. The very fact of structural resistance would create high temperatures, and any general formation of shearplanes would cut the imbedded girders at once. The method being prepared to cope with that was rather drastic, and its after-effects largely unknown.

On the whole, however, the plans were simple, and putting them into effect had seemed heavy but relatively uncomplicated labor. Some opposition, of course, had been expected from the local bandit towns.

But Amalfi had not expected to lose nearly 20 per cent of his crews during the first month after the raid on Fabr-Suithe.

It was Miramon who brought the news of the latest work camp found slaughtered. Amalfi was sitting under a tree fern on high ground overlooking the city, watching a flight of giant dragonflies and thinking about heat transfer in rock.

"You are sure they were adequately protected?" Miramon asked cautiously. "Some of our insects——"

Amalfi thought the insects, and the jungle, almost disturbingly beautiful. The thought of destroying it all occasionally upset him. "Yes, they were," he said shortly. "We sprayed out the camp areas with dicoumarins and fluorine-substituted residuals. Besides—do any of your insects use explosives?"

"Explosives! There was dynamite used? I saw no evidence——"

"No. That's what bothers me. I don't like all those felled trees you describe; that sounds more like TDX than dynamite or high explosive. We use TDX ourselves to get a cutting blast—it has the property of exploding in a flat plane."

Miramon goggled. "Impossible. An explosion had to expand evenly in all directions that are open to it."

"Not if the explosive is a piperazohexynitrate built from polarized carbon atoms. Such atoms can't move in any direction but at right angles to the gravity radius. That's what I mean. You people are up to dynamite, but not to TDX."

He paused, frowning. "Of course some of our losses have just been to bandit raids, with missile weapons and ordinary bombs—your friends from Fabr-Suithe and their allies. But these camps where there was an explosion and no crater to show for it——"

He fell silent. There was no point in mentioning the gassed corpses. It was hard even to think about them. Somebody on this planet had a gas which was a regurgitant, a sternutatory, and a vesicant all in one. The men had been forced out of their masks—which had been designed solely to protect them from volcanic gases—to vomit, had taken the stuff into their lungs by convulsive sneezing, and had blistered into great sacs of serum inside and out. That, obviously, had been the multiple-benzene-ring gas Hawkesite; it had been very popular during the days of the warring stellar "empires," when it had been called "*polybathroomfloorine*" for no discoverable reason. But what was it doing on He?

There was only one possible answer, and for a reason which he did not try to understand, it made Amalfi breathe a little easier. All around him the jungle sighed and swayed, and humming clouds of gnats made rainbows over the dew-laden pinnae of the ferns. The jungle, almost always murmurously quiet, had never seemed like the real enemy—and now Amalfi knew that his intuition had been right. The real enemy had at last declared itself, stealthily, but with a stealth which was naïveté itself in comparison with the ancient guile of the jungle.

"Miramon," Amalfi said tranquilly, "we're in a spot. That criminal city I told you about—the bindlestiff—is already here. It must have landed even before my city arrived, long enough ago to hide itself very thoroughly. Probably it came down at night in some taboo area. The tramps, in it have leagued themselves with Fabr-Suithe anyhow, that much is obvious."

A moth with a two-meter wingspread blundered across the clearing, piloted by a gray-brown nematode which had sunk its sucker above the ganglion between the glittering creature's pinions. Amalfi was in a mood to read parables into things, and the parasitism reminded him of how greatly he had underestimated the enemy. The bindlestiff evidently knew, and was skillful with, the secret of manipulating a new culture. A shrewd Okie never attempts to overwhelm a civilization by direct assault, but instead pilots it, as indetectably as possible, doing no apparent harm, adding no apparent burden, but turning history deftly and tyrannically aside at the crucial instant . . .

Amalfi snapped the belt switch of his ultraphone. "Hazleton?"

"Here, boss." Behind the city manager's voice was the indistinct rumble of heavy mining. "What's up?"

"Nothing yet. Are you having any bandit trouble out there?"

"No. We're not expecting any, either, with all this artillery."

"Famous last words," Amalfi said. "The 'stiff's here, Mark—and it's no stranger, either."

There was a short silence. In the background, Amalfi could hear the shouts of Hazleton's crew. When the city manager's voice came in again, it was moving from word to word very carefully, as if it expected each one to break under its weight. "You imply that the 'stiff was already on He when our Dirac broadcast went out. Right? I'm not sure these losses of ours can't be explained some simpler way, boss; the theory . . . uh . . . lacks elegance."

Amalfi grinned tightly. "A heuristic criticism," he said. "Go to the foot of the class, Mark, and think it over. Thus far they've out-thought us six ways for Sunday. We may be able to put your old scheme about the women into effect still, but if it's to work, we'll have to smoke the 'stiff out into the open."

"How?"

"Everybody here knows that there's going to be a drastic change in the planet when we finish what we're doing, but we're the only ones who know exactly what we're going to do. The 'stiffs will have to stop us, whether they've got Doctor Beetle or not. So I'm forcing their hand. Moving Day is hereby advanced by one thousand hours."

"What! I'm sorry, boss, but that's flatly impossible."

Amalfi felt a rare spasm of anger. "That's as may be," he growled. "Nevertheless, spread it around; let the Hevians hear it. And just to prove that I'm not kidding, Mark, I'm turning the City Fathers back on at M plus 1100. If you're not ready to spin before then, you may well swing instead."

The click of the belt switch to the *off* position was unsatisfying. Amalfi would much have preferred to have concluded the interview with something really final—a clash of cymbals, for instance. He swung suddenly on Miramon.

"What are you goggling at?"

The Hevian shut his mouth, flushing. "Your pardon," he said. "I was hoping to understand your instructions to your assistant, in the hope of being of some use. But you spoke in such incomprehensible terms that it sounded like a theological dispute. As for me, I never argue about politics or religion." He turned on his heel and stamped off through the trees.

Amalfi watched him go, cooling off gradually. This would never do. He must be getting to be an old man. All during the conversation with Hazleton he had felt his temper getting the better of his judgment, yet he had felt sudden and inert, unwilling to make the effort of opposing the momentum of his anger. At this rate, the City Fathers would soon depose him and appoint some stable character to the mayoralty—not Hazleton, certainly, but some unpoetic youngster who would play everything by empirics. Amalfi was in no position to be threatening anyone else with liquidation, even as a joke.

He walked toward the grounded city, heavy with sunlight, sunk in reflection. He was now about nine hundred years old, give or take fifty; strong as an ox, mentally alert and active, in good hormone balance, all twenty-eight senses sharp, his own special psi faculty—orientation—still as infallible as ever, and all in all as sane as a compulsively peripatetic starman could be. The anti-agathics would keep him in this shape indefinitely, as far as anyone knew—but the problem of *patience* had never been solved.

The older a man became, the more quickly he saw answers to tough questions because the more experience he had to bring to bear on them; and the less likely he was to tolerate slow thinking among his associates. If he were sane, his answers were generally right answers—if he were unsane, they were not; but what mattered was the speed of the thinking itself. In the end, both the sane and the unsane became equally dictatorial, less and less ready to explain why they picked one answer over another.

It was funny: before death had been indefinitely postponed, it had been thought that memory would turn longevity into a Greek gift, because not even the human brain could remember a practical infinity of accumulated facts. Nowadays, however, nobody bothered to remember many facts. That was what the City Fathers and like machines were for: they stored data. Living men memorized nothing but processes, throwing out obsolete ones for new ones as invention made it necessary. When they needed facts, they asked the machines.

In some cases, even processes were wiped from human memory to make more room if there were simple, indestructible machines to replace them—the slide rule, for instance. Amalfi wondered suddenly if there was a single man in the city who could multiply, divide, take square root, or figure pH in his head or on paper. The thought was so novel as to be alarming—as novel as if an ancient astrophysicist had seriously wondered how many of his colleagues could run an abacus.

No, memory was no problem. But it was hard to be patient after a thousand years.

The bottom of an airlock drifted into his field of view, plastered with brown tendrils of mud. He looked up. The lock, drilled directly into the great granite disc which was the foundation of the city, was a severed end of what had been a subway line running out of Manhattan centuries ago; this one evidently had been the Astoria line of the BMT, a lock seldom used, since it was too far from both the Empire State and City Hall, the city's two present centers of control. It was certainly a long way around the perimeter from where Amalfi had expected to go back on board. Feeling like a stranger, he went in.

Inside, the corridor rang with bloodcurdling shrieks which echoed endlessly. It was as if somebody were flaying a live dinosaur, or, better, a pack of them. Underneath the noise there was a sound like water being expelled under high pressure, and someone was laughing hysterically. Alarmed, Amalfi ran up the nearest steps; the noise got louder. He hunched his bull shoulders and burst through the door behind which the butchery seemed to be going on.

Surely there had never been such a place in the city. It was a huge, steamy chamber, walled with some ceramic substance placed in regular tiles. The tiles were slimy and stained, hence, old—very old. On the floor, smaller hexagonal white tiles made an endlessly repeating mosaic, reminding Amalfi at once of the structural formula of Hawkesite.

Hordes of nude women ran aimlessly back and forth in the chamber, screaming, battering at the wall, dodging wildly, or rolling on the mosaic floor. Every so often a thick stream of water caught one of them, bowling her howling away. Overhead, long banks of nozzles sprayed needles of mist into the air; Amalfi was soaking wet almost at once. The laughter got louder.

The mayor bent quickly, threw off his muddy shoes, and stalked the laughter, his toes gripping the slippery tiles. The heavy column of water swerved toward him, then was warped away again.

"John! Do you need a bath so badly? Come join the party!"

It was Dee Hazleton. She was as nude as any of her victims, and was gleefully plying an enormous hose. She looked lovely; Amalfi turned his mind determinedly away from that thought.

"Isn't this fun? We just got a new batch of these creatures. I got Mark to have the old fire hose connected, and I've been giving them their first wash."

It did not sound much like the old Dee. Amalfi expressed his opinion of women who lost their inhibitions with such drastic thoroughness. He went on at some length, and Dee made as if to turn the hose on him again.

"No, you don't," he growled, wresting it from her. It

proved extremely hard to manage. "What is this place, anyhow? I don't recall any such torture chamber in the plans."

"It was a public bath, Mark says. There's another one downtown, in the Baruch Houses district, and another one on Forty-first Street beside the Port Authority Terminal, and quite a few others. Mark says they must have been closed up when the city first went aloft. I've been using this one to sluice off these women before they're sent to Medical."

"With *city water?*" Even the thought of such waste made his hackles rise.

"Oh no, John, I know better than that. The water's pumped in from the river to the west."

"Water for bathing!" Amalfi said. "No wonder the ancients sometimes didn't have enough to drink. Still, I'd thought the static jet was older than that."

He surveyed the Hevian women, who, now that the water was turned off, were huddled in the warmest part of the echoing chamber. None of them shared Dee's gently curved ripeness, but, as usual, some of them showed promise. Hazelton was prescient, it had to be granted. Of course it had been expectable that the Hevians would turn out to be human. Only eleven non-human civilizations had ever been discovered, and of these, only the Lyrans and the Myrdians had any brains to speak of (unless one counted the Vegans; Earthmen did not think of them as human, but all the non-human cultures did; anyhow, they were extinct as a civilization).

But to have the Hevians turn over complete custody of their women to the Okies, without so much as a preliminary conference, at the first contact, had been a colossal break. Hazelton had advanced his proposal to use any possible women as bindlestiff-bait years before any Okie could have known that there were people on He at all.

Well, that was Hazelton's own psi gift: not true clairvoyance, but an ability to pluck workable plans out of logically insufficient data. Time after time only the seemingly miraculous working-out of some obvious flight of fancy had prevented Hazelton's being jettisoned by the blindly logical City Fathers.

"Dee, come to Astronomy with me," Amalfi said. "I've got something to show you. And for my sake, put on something, or the men will think I'm out to found a dynasty."

"All right," Dee said reluctantly. She was not yet used to the odd Okie standards of exposure, and sometimes appeared nude when it wasn't customary—a compensation, Amalfi supposed, for her Utopian upbringing, which had taught her that nudity had a deleterious effect upon the purity of one's politics. The Hevian women moaned and hid their heads while she put on her shorts. Most of them had been stoned for inadvertently covering themselves at one time or another, for in Hevian society women were not people but reminders of damnation, doubly evil for the slightest taint of secretiveness.

History, Amalfi thought, would be more instructive a teacher if it were not so stupefyingly repetitious. He led the way up the corridor, searching for a lift shaft, disturbingly conscious of Dee's wet soles padding cheerfully behind him.

In Astronomy, Jake was, as usual, peering wistfully at a galaxy somewhere out on the marches of nowhen, trying to turn spiral arms into elliptical orbits without recourse to the calculations section. He looked up as Amalfi and the girl entered.

"Hello," he said dismally. "Amalfi, I really need some help here. How can a man work without machines? If only you'd turn the City Fathers back on——"

"Shortly. How long has it been since you looked back the way we came, Jake?"

"Not since we started across the Rift. Why, should I have? The Rift is just a scratch in a saucer; you need real distance to work on basic problems."

"I know that. But let's take a look. I have an idea that we're not as alone in the Rift as we thought."

Resignedly, Jake went to his control desk and thumbed the buttons that moved his telescope. "What do you expect to find?" he demanded. "A haze of iron filings, or a stray meson? Or a fleet of police cruisers?"

"Well," Amalfi said, pointing to the screen, "those aren't wine bottles."

The police cruisers, so close that the light of He's star had begun to twinkle on their sides, shot across the screen in a brilliant stream, contrails of false photons striping the Rift behind them.

"So they aren't," Jake said, not much interested. "Now may I have my scope back, Amalfi?"

Amalfi only grinned. Cops or no cops, he felt young again.

Hazleton was mud up to the thighs. Long ribands of it trailed behind him as he hurtled up the lift shaft to the control room. Amalfi watched him coming, noting the set whiteness of the city manager's face as he looked up at Amalfi's bent head.

"What's this about cops?" Hazleton demanded while still in flight. "The message didn't get to me straight. We were raided, and all hell's broken loose everywhere. I nearly didn't get here straight myself." He sprang into the room, his boots shedding gummy clods.

"I saw some of the fighting," Amalfi said. "Looks like the Moving Day rumor reached the 'stiffs, all right."

"Sure. What's this about cops?"

"The cops are here. They're coming in from the north-west quadrant, already off overdrive, and should be ready to land day after tomorrow."

"Surely they're not still after us," Hazleton said. "And I can't see why they should come all this distance after the 'stiff. They must have had to use deep-sleep to make it. And we didn't say anything about the no-fuel drive in our alarm 'cast——"

"We didn't have to. They're after the 'stiff, all right. Someday I must tell you the parable of the diseased bee, but there isn't time now. Things are breaking too fast. We have to keep an eye on everything, and be ready to jump in any direction no matter which item on the agenda comes up first. How bad is the fighting?"

"Very bad. At least five of the local bandit towns are in on it, including Fabr-Suithe, of course. Two of them mount heavy stuff, about contemporary with the Hruntan Empire's in its heyday ... ah, I see you know that already. Well, this is supposed to be a holy war on us. We're meddling with the jungle and interfering with their chances for salvation-through-suffering, or something—I didn't stop to dispute the point."

"That's bad. It will convince some of the civilized towns, too. I doubt that Fabr-Suithe really believes this is a jihad—they've thrown their religion overboard—but it makes wonderful propaganda."

"You're right there. Only a few of the civilized towns, the ones that have been helping us from the beginning, are putting up a stiff fight. Almost everyone else, on both sides, is sitting it out waiting for us to cut each other's throats. Our own handicap is that we lack mobility. If we could persuade all the civilized towns to come in on our side, we wouldn't need it, but so many of them are scared."

"The enemy lacks mobility, too, until the bindlestiff town is ready to take a direct hand," Amalfi said thoughtfully. "Have you seen any signs that the tramps are in on the fighting?"

"Not yet. But they won't wait much longer. And we don't even know where they are!"

"They'll be forced to locate themselves for us today or tomorrow, of that I'm certain. Right now it's time to muster all the rehabilitated women you have and get ready to plant them; as far as I can see, that whole scheme is going to pay off. As soon as I get a fix on the bindlestiff, I'll report the location of the nearest bandit town, and you can follow through from there."

Hazleton's eyes, very weary until now, began to glitter with gratification. "And how about Moving Day?" he said. "I suppose you know that not one of your stress-fluid plugs is going to hold with the work thus incomplete."

"I know it," Amalfi said. "I'm counting on it. We'll spin on the hour. If the plugs spring high, wide, and tall, I won't weep; as a matter of fact, I don't know how else we could hope to get rid of all that heat."

The radar watch blipped sharply, and both men turned to look at the screen. There was a fountain of green dots on it. Hazleton took three quick steps and turned the switch which projected the new butterfly grid onto the screen.

"Well, where are they?" Amalfi demanded. "That's got to be them."

"Right smack in the middle of the southwestern continent, in that vine jungle where the little chigger snakes nest—the ones that burrow under your fingernails. There's supposed to be a lake of boiling mud on that spot."

"There probably is. They could be under it, surrounded by a medium-light screen."

"All right, then we've got them placed. But what's this

fountain effect the radar's giving us? What are the 'stiffs shooting up?"

"Mines, I suspect," Amalfi said. "On proximity fuses. Orbital."

"Mines? Isn't *that* dandy," Hazleton said. "They'll leave an escape lane for themselves, of course, but we'll never be able to find it. They've got us under a plutonium umbrella, Amalfi."

"We'll get out. And in the meantime, the cops can't land, either. Go plant your women, Mark. And—put some clothes on 'em first. They'll cause more of a stir that way."

"You bet they will," the city manager said feelingly. He stepped into the lift shaft and fell out of sight.

Amalfi went out onto the observation platform of the control tower. From there he could see all the rest of the city, including most of the perimeter, for the tower—it was still called, now and then, the Empire State Building— was the tallest structure in the city. There was plenty of battle noise rattling the garish tropical sunset along most of the northwest quadrant, and even an occasional tiny toppling figure. The city had adopted the local dodge of clearing and gelling the mud at its rim, and had returned the gel to the morass state at the first sign of attack, but the jungle men had broad skis, of some metal no Hevian could have machined so precisely, on which they slid over the muck. Discs of red fire marked bursting TDX shells, scything the air like death's own winnows. No gas was in evidence, but Amalfi knew that there would be gas before long with the bindlestiff directing the fighting.

The city's retaliatory fire was largely invisible, since it emerged below the top of the perimeter. There was a Bethé fender out, which would keep the rim from being scaled until one of the projectors was knocked out, and plenty of heavy rifles were being kept hot. But the city had never been designed for warfare, and many of its most efficient destroyers had their noses buried in the mud, since their intended function was only to clear a landing area. Using an out-and-out Bethé blaster was impossible where there was an adjacent planetary mass—fortunately, since the bindlestiff had such a blaster and Amalfi's city did not.

Amalfi sniffed the scarlet edges of the struggle appraisingly. The screen set up beside him did not show an intelligible battle pattern yet, but it seemed to be almost on the verge of making sense. Under Amalfi's fingers on the platform railing were three buttons which he had had placed there four hundred years ago, duplicating a set on the balcony of City Hall. They had set in motion different actions at different times. But each time they had represented choices of actions which he would have to make when the pinch came. He had never found any reason to have a fourth button installed on either railing.

Rockets shrilled overhead. Bombs fell from them, crepitating bursts of noise and smoke and flying metal. Amalfi did not look up. The very mild spindizzy screen would fend off anything moving that rapidly. Only slow-moving objects, like men, could sidle through a polarized gravitic field. He looked out toward the horizon, touching the three buttons very delicately.

Suddenly the sunset snuffed itself out. Amalfi, who had never seen a tropical sunset before coming to He, felt a vague alarm, but as far as he could tell, the abrupt darkness was natural, though startling. The fighting went on, the flying discs of TDX explosions much more lurid now against the blackness.

After a while there was a dogfight far aloft, identifiable mostly by the exhaust traceries of rockets and missiles. Evidently Miramon's air force was tangling with Fabr-Suithe's. The jungle jammered derision and fury at Amalfi's city without any letup.

Amalfi stood, watching the screen so intently as to cut the rest of the world almost completely out of his consciousness. Understanding the emerging pattern was hard work, for he had never tried to grasp a situation at such close quarters before, and the blue-coded trajectory of every shell, sketched across the screen in glowing segments of ellipses, tried to capture his exclusive attention, as if they were all planets.

About an hour past midnight, at the height of the heaviest air raid yet, he felt a touch at his elbow.

"Boss——"

Amalfi heard the word as though it had been uttered at the bottom of the Rift. The still-ascending fountain of space mines the bindlestiff was throwing up had just come into the margin of the screen—meaning that O'Brian, the proxy chief, had just located the 'stiff with one of his flying robot bystanders—and Amalfi was trying to extrapolate the shape of the top of the fountain. Somewhere up there in the aeropause, the fountain flattened into a shell of orbits encompassing the whole of He, and it was important to know how high up that shell began.

But the utter exhaustion of the voice touched something deeper. He said, "Yes, Mark."

"It's done. We lost almost everybody in the party. But we planted the women in a clearing right where a 'stiff outpost could see them. . . . What a riot that caused." A ghost of animation stirred in the voice for a moment. "You should have been there."

"I'm almost there now. Just getting the picture from a proxy. Good work, Mark. . . . Better . . . get some rest."

"Now? But boss——"

Something very heavy described a searing parabola across the screen, and then the whole city turned to a scramble of magnesium-white and ink. As the light of the star-shell faded, the screen showed a formless dim-yellow spreading and crawling, as if someone had spilled paint in the innards of the machine. Amalfi had been waiting for it.

"Gas alarm, Mark," he heard himself saying. "Sure to be Hawkesite. Barium suits for everybody—that stuff's pure death-by-torture."

"Yes, right. Boss, have you been up here all this time? You'll kill yourself running things this way. You need rest more than I do."

Amalfi found that he did not have time to answer. O'Brian's proxy had come upon the town where Hazleton had dropped the women. There was certainly a riot there. Amalfi snapped a switch, backing the point of view off to another proxy which was hovering a mile up, scanning the whole battle area. From here he could see the black tendrils of movement which were files of soldiers moving through the jungle. Some which had been approaching Amalfi's city were now turning back. Furthermore, new tendrils were being put out from Hevian towns which up to now had taken no part in the fighting—the on-the-fence towns. Evidently they were no longer on the fence, but which side they had jumped to still remained to be seen.

He snapped the switch again, bringing back a close look at the lake of boiling mud which lay at the base of the mine fountain. Something new was going on there, too: the hot mud was flowing slowly, thickly, away from the

center of the lake. Then there was a clear area in the
center, as if the lake had suddenly developed a vortex.
The clear area widened.

The bindlestiff city was rising to the surface. It came
cautiously; half an hour went by before its periphery
touched the lake shore. Then black tendrils stretched out
into the tangled desolation of the jungle; the bindlestiff
was at last risking its own men in the struggle. What they
were after was plain enough, for the files were all moving
in the direction of the town where Hazleton had dropped
the women.

The bindlestiff city itself sat and waited. Even against
the mass-pressure of the planet of He, Amalfi's sense of
spatial orientation could pick up the unmistakable, slightly
nauseating sensation of spindizzy field under medium
drive, doming the seething mud.

Dawn was coming now. The riot around the town
where the women had been dropped dwindled a little. Then
one of the task forces from the bindlestiff reached it, and it
flared all over again, worse than ever. The 'stiffs were
fighting their own allies.

Abruptly there was no Hevian town in the center of the
riot at all. There was only a mushrooming pillar of radio-
active gas which made the screen race with interference
patterns. The 'stiffs had bombed the town. What was left
of the riot retreated slowly toward the lake of boiling
mud; the 'stiffs had their women and were fighting a
rear-guard action. The news, Amalfi knew, would travel
fast.

Amalfi's own city was shrouded in sick orange mist, lit
with flashes of no-color. The blistering gas could not pass
the spindizzy screen in a body, but it diffused through,
molecule by heavy molecule. The mayor realized suddenly
that he had not heeded his own gas warning, and that
there was probably some harm coming to him. He started
and moved slightly, and discovered that he was completely
encased. What . . .

Barium paste. Evidently Hazleton had known that
Amalfi could not leave the platform, and instead had
plastered him with the paste in default of trying to get a
suit on him. Even his eyes were covered with a transparent visor, and a feeling of distension in his nostrils bespoke
a Kolman barium filter.

So much for the gas. The heavy tensions in and around

the bindlestiff city continued to gather; they would soon be unbearable. Above, just outside the shell of circling mines, the first few police cruisers were sidling down with great caution. The war in the jungle had already fallen apart into meaninglessness. The abduction of the women by the tramps had collapsed all Hevian rivalries. Bandits and civilized towns alike were bent now upon nothing but the destruction of Fabr-Suithe and its allies. Fabr-Suithe could hold them off for a long time, but it was clearly time for the bindlestiff to leave—time for it to make off with its pleased and wondering Hevian women, its anti-agathics, its germanium, and whatever else it had managed to garner—time for it to lose itself again in the Rift before the Earth police could invest the planet of He.

The gravitic field around the bindlestiff city knotted suddenly, painfully, in Amalfi's brain, and began to rise away from the lake of boiling mud. The 'stiff was taking off. In a moment it would be gone through the rent in the mine umbrella which only the tramps could see.

Amalfi pressed the button—the only one, this time, that had been connected to anything.

Moving Day began.

Moving Day began with six pillars of glaring white, forty miles in diameter, which burst through the soft soil at each compass point of He. Fabr-Suithe had sat directly over the site of one of them. The bandit town was nothing but a flake of ash in a split second, a curled black flake borne aloft on the top of a white-hot piston.

The pillars lunged, roaring, into the heavens, fifty, a hundred, two hundred miles, and burst at their tops like popcorn. The Hevian sky burned thermite-blue with steel meteors. Outside, the space mines, cut off from the world of which they had been satellites by the greatest spindizzy field in history, fled away into the Rift.

And when the meteors had burned away, the sun was growing.

The world of He was on spindizzy drive, its magnetic moment transformed into momentum. It was the biggest Okie "city" that had ever flown. There was no time to feel alarm. The sun flashed by and was dwindling to a point before the fact could be grasped. Then it was gone. The far wall of the Rift began to swell and separate into individual points of light.

The planet of He was crossing the Rift.

Appalled, Amalfi fought to understand the scale of speed. He failed. The planet of He was moving, that was all he could comprehend. It was moving at a proper cruising speed for a "city" of its size—a speed that gulped down light years as if they were gnats. Even to think of controlling such a flight was ridiculous.

Stars began to wink past He like fireflies. They had reached the other side of the Rift. The planet began to curve gradually away from the main cloud. Then the stars were all behind.

The surface of the saucer that was the galaxy began to come into view.

"Boss! We're going out of the galaxy! Look——"

"I know it. Get me a fix on He's old sun as soon as we're high enough above the Rift to see it again. After that it'll be too late."

Hazleton worked feverishly. It took him only half an hour, but during that time, the massed stars receded far enough to make plain the gray scar of the Rift as a long shadow on a spangled ground. At the end the Hevian sun was only a tenth-magnitude point in it.

"Got it, I think. But we can't swing the planet back. It'll take us thousands of years to cross to the next galaxy. We'll have to abandon He, boss, or we're sunk."

"All right. Get us aloft. Full drive."

"Our contract——"

"Fulfilled—take my word for it now. Spin!"

The city sprang aloft. The planet of He did not dwindle in the city's sky. It simply vanished, snuffed out in the intergalactic gap. Miramon, if he lived, would be the first of a totally new race of pioneers.

Amalfi moved then, back towards the controls, the barium casing cracking and falling off him as he came back to life. The air of the city still stank of Hawkesite, but the concentration of the gas already had been taken down below the harmful level by the city's purifiers. The mayor began to edge the city away from the vector of He's flight and the city's own, back toward the home lens.

Hazleton stirred restlessly.

"Your conscience bothering you, Mark?"

"Maybe," Hazleton said. "Is there some escape clause in our contract with Miramon that lets us desert him like this? If there is, I missed it, and I read the fine print pretty closely."

"No, there's no escape clause," Amalfi said abstractedly, shifting the space stick by a millimeter or two. "The Hevians won't be hurt. The spindizzy screen will protect them from loss of heat and atmosphere—their volcanoes will keep them warmer than they'll probably like, and their technology is up to producing all the light they'll need. But they won't be able to keep the planet well enough lit to satisfy the jungle. That will die. By the time Miramon and his friends reach the star that suits them in the Andromedan galaxy, they'll understand the spindizzy well enough to put their planet back into the proper orbit. Or maybe they'll like roaming better by that time, and will decide to be an Okie planet. Either way, we licked the jungle for them, just as we promised to do, fair and square."

"We didn't get paid," the city manager pointed out. "And it'll take a lot of fuel to get back to any part of our own galaxy. The bindlestiff got off ahead of us, and got carried way out of range of the cops in the process, right on our backs—with plenty of germanium, drugs, women, the no-fuel drive, everything."

"No, they didn't," Amalfi said. "They blew up the moment we moved He."

"All right," Hazleton said resignedly. "You could detect that where I couldn't, so I'll take your word for it. But you'd better be able to explain it!"

"It's not hard to explain. The 'stiffs had captured Doctor Beetle. I was pretty sure they had; after all, they came to He for no other reason. They needed the no-fuel drive, and they knew Doctor Beetle had it because they heard the agronomists' SOS, just as we did. So they snatched Doctor Beetle when he was landed—do you remember what a big fuss their bandit-city allies made about the *other* agronomist lifeship, to divert us? It worked, too—and in the meantime they cooked the secret out of him. Probably in his own tank."

"So?"

"So," Amalfi said, "the tramps forgot that any Okie city always has passengers like Doctor Beetle—people with big ideas only partially worked out, ideas that need the finishing touches that can only be provided by some other culture. After all, a man doesn't take passage on an Okie city unless he's a third-rater, hoping to make his everlasting fortune on some planet where the inhabitants know much less than he does."

Hazleton scratched his head ruefully. "That's right. We had the same experience with the Lyran invisibility machine. It never worked until we took Doc Schloss on board."

"Exactly. The 'stiffs were in too much of a hurry. They didn't carry their stolen no-fuel drive with them until they found some culture which could perfect it. They tried to use it right away. They were lazy. And they tried to use it inside the biggest spindizzy field ever generated. What happened? It blew up. I felt it happen—and the top of my head nearly came off then and there. If we hadn't left the 'stiffs parsecs behind in the first split second, Doctor Beetle's drive would have blown up He at the same time. It doesn't pay to be lazy, Mark."

"Who ever said it did?" Hazleton said. After a moment's more thought, he began to plot the point at which the city would probably re-enter its own galaxy. That point turned out to be a long way away from the Rift, in an area that, after a mental wrench to visualize it backwards from the usual orientation, promised a fair population.

"Look," he said, "we'll hit about where the last few waves of the Acolytes settled—remember the Night of Hadjjii?"

Amalfi didn't, since he hadn't been born then, but he remembered the history, which was what the city manager had meant. He said, "Good. I want to take us to garage and get that Twenty-third Street machine settled for good and all. I'm tired of its blowing out in the pinches, and it's going sour for fair now. Hear it?"

Hazleton cocked his head intently. In the lull, Amalfi saw suddenly that Dee was standing in the doorway, still completely enswathed in her anti-gas suit except for the faceplate.

"Is it over?" she said.

"Well, our stay on He is over. We're still on the run, if that's what you mean. The cops never give up, Dee; you'll learn that sooner or later."

"Where are we going?"

She asked the question in the same tone in which she had once said, "What is a volt, John?" For an astonishing moment Amalfi was almost overwhelmed with an urge to send Hazleton from the room on some excuse, to return almost bodily to those days of her innocence, to relive all the previous questions that she had asked—the moments when he had known the answers better.

There was, of course, no real answer to this one. Where would an Okie go? They were going, that was all. If there was a destination, no one could know what it was.

He endured the surge of emotion stoically. In the end, he only shrugged.

"By the way," he said, "what's the operational day?"

Hazleton looked at the clock. "M plus eleven twenty-five."

With a sidelong glance, Amalfi leaned forward, resumed the helmet he had cast aside on He, and turned on the City Fathers.

The helmet phones shrilled with alarm. "All right, all right," he growled. "What is it?"

"MAYOR AMALFI, HAVE YOU TIPPED THIS PLANET?"

"No," Amalfi said. "We sent it on its way as it was."

There was a short silence, humming with computation. It was probably just as well, Amalfi thought, that the machines had been turned off for a while; they had not had a rest in many centuries. They would probably emerge into consciousness a little saner for it.

"VERY WELL. WE MUST NOW SELECT THE POINT AT WHICH WE LEAVE THE RIFT. STAND BY FOR DETERMINATION."

Hazleton and Amalfi grinned at each other. Amalfi said, "We're coming in on the last Acolyte stars, and we'll need to decelerate far beyond spindizzy safety limits. We urgently need an overhaul on the Twenty-third Street driver. Give us a determination for the present social setup there, please——"

"YOU ARE MISTAKEN. THAT CLUSTER IS NOWHERE NEAR THE RIFT. FURTHERMORE, THE POPULACE THERE HAS A LONG RECORD OF MASS XENOPHOBIA AND HAD BEST BE AVOIDED. WE WILL GIVE YOU A DETERMINATION FOR THE FAR RIFT WALL. STAND BY."

Amalfi removed the headset gently.

"The Rift wall," he said, moving the microphone away from his mouth. "That was long ago—and far away."

CHAPTER FIVE: Murphy

A SPINDIZZY going sour makes the galaxy's most unnerving noise. The top range of the sound is inaudible, but it feels like a multiple toothache. Just below that, there is a screech like metal tearing, which blends smoothly into a composite cataract of plate glass, slate, and boulders; this is the middle register. After that, there is a painful gap in the sound's spectrum, and the rest of the noise comes into one's ears again with a hollow round dinosaurian sob and plummets on down into the subsonics, ending in frequencies which induce diarrhea and an almost unconquerable urge to bite one's thumbs.

The noise was coming, of course, from the Twenty-third Street spindizzy, but it permeated the whole city. It was tolerable only so long as the hold which contained the moribund driver was kept sealed. Amalfi knew better than to open that hold. He surveyed the souring machine via instruments, and kept the audio tap prudently closed. The sound fraction which was thrumming through the city's walls was bad enough, even as far up as the control chamber.

Hazleton's hand came over his left shoulder, stabbing a long finger at the recording thermocouple.

"She's beginning to smoke now. Damned if I know how she's lasted this long. The model was two hundred years old when we took it aboard—and the repair job I did on He was only an emergency rig."

"What can we do?" Amalfi said. He did not bother to look around; the city manager's moods were his own second nature. They had lived together a long time—long enough to learn what learning is, long enough to know that, just as habit is second nature, so nature—the seven steps from chance to meaning—is first habit. The hand which rested upon Amalfi's right shoulder told him all he needed to know about Hazleton at this moment. "We can't shut her down."

"If we don't, she'll blow for good and all. That hold's hot already."

"Hot and howling. . . . Let me think a minute."

Hazleton waited. After another moment, Amalfi said, "We'll keep her shoving. If the City Fathers can push this much juice through her, maybe they can push just a little more. Maybe enough to get us down to a reasonable cruising speed. Besides—we couldn't jury-rig that spindizzy again. It's radiating all up and down the line. The City Fathers could shut her down if we ordered it, but it'd take human beings to repair her and re-tune the setup stages. And it's too late for that."

"It'll be a year before anything alive can go into that hold," Hazleton agreed gloomily. "All right. How's our velocity now?"

"Negligible, with reference to the galaxy as a whole. But as far as the Acolyte stars proper are concerned— we'd shoot through the whole cluster at about eight times the city's top speed if we stopped decelerating now. It's going to be damned tight, that's for sure, Mark."

"Excuse me," Dee's voice said behind them. She was hesitating just beyond the threshold of the lift shaft. "Is there something wrong? If you're busy——"

"No busier than usual," Hazleton said. "Just wondering about our usual baby."

"The Twenty-third Street machine. I could tell by the curvature of your spines. Why don't you have it replaced and get it over with?"

Amalfi and the city manager grinned at each other, but the mayor's grin was short-lived.

"Well, why not?" he said suddenly.

"My gods, boss, the cost," Hazleton said with incredulity. "The City Fathers would impeach you for suggesting it." He donned the helmet. "Treasury check," he told the microphone.

"They've never had to run her all by themselves under max overdrive before now. I predict that they'll emerge from the experience clamoring to have her replaced, even if we don't eat for a year to pay for it. Besides, we should have the money, for once. We dug a lot of germanium while we were setting up He to be de-wobbled. Maybe the time really has come when we can afford a replacement."

Dee came forward swiftly, motes of light on the move

in her eyes. "John, can that be true?" she said. "I thought
we'd lost a lot on the Hevian contract."

"Well, we're not rich. We would have been, I'm still
convinced, if we'd been able to harvest the anti-agathics
on a decent scale."

"But we didn't," Dee said. "We had to run away."

"We ran away. But in terms of germanium alone, we
can call ourselves well off. Well enough off to buy a new
spindizzy. Right, Mark?"

Hazleton listened to the City Fathers a moment more,
and then took off the bone-mikes. "It looks that way," he
said. "Anyhow, we can easily cover the price of an overhaul, or maybe even of a reconditioned second-hand machine of a later model. Depends on whether or not the
Acolyte stars have a service planet, and what the garage
fees are there."

"The fees should be low enough to keep us solvent,"
Amalfi said, thrusting his lower lip out thoughtfully. "The
Acolyte area is a backwater, but it was settled originally
by refugees from an anti-Earth pogrom in the Malar
system—an aftermath of the collapse of Vega, as I recall.
There's a record of the pogrom in the libraries of most
planets—you reminded me of it, Mark: the Night of
Hadjjii—which means that the Acolytes aren't far enough
away from normal trading areas to be proper frontier
stars."

He paused, and his frown deepened. "Now that I come
to think of it, the Acolytes were an important minor
source of power metals for part of this limb of the galaxy
at one time. They'll have at least one garage planet, Mark,
depend on it. They may even have work for the city
to do."

"Sounds good," Hazleton said. "Too good, maybe. Actually, we've *got* to sit down in the Acolytes, boss, because
that Twenty-third Street machine won't carry us beyond
them at anything above a snail's pace. I asked the City
Fathers that while I was checking the treasury. This is the
end of the line for that gadget."

He sounded tired. Amalfi looked at him.

"That's not what's worrying you, Mark," he said.
"We've always had that problem waiting for us somewhere in the future, and it isn't one that's difficult of
solution. What's the real trouble? Cops, maybe?"

"All right, it's cops," Hazleton said, a little sullenly. "I know we're a long way away from any cops that know us by name. But have you any idea of the total amount of unpaid fines we're carrying? And I don't see how we can assume that any amount of distance is 'too great' for the cops to follow us if they really want us—and it seems that they do."

"Why, Mark?" Dee said. "After all, we've done nothing serious."

"It piles up," Hazleton said. "We haven't been called on our Violations docket in a long time. When we're finally caught, we'll have to pay in full, and if that were to happen now, we'd be bankrupt."

"Pooh," Dee said. Like anyone more or less recently naturalized, her belief in the capacities of her adopted city-state was as finite as it was unbounded. "We could find work and build up a new treasury. It might be hard going for a while, but we'd survive it. People have been broke before, and come through it whole."

"People, yes; cities, no," Amalfi said. "Mark is right on that point, Dee. According to the law, a bankrupt city must be dispersed. It's essentially a humane law, in that it prevents desperate mayors and city managers from taking bankrupt cities out again on long job-hunting trips, during which half of the Okies on board will die just because of the stubbornness of the people in charge."

"Exactly," Hazleton said.

"Even so, I think it's a bogey," Amalfi said gently. "I'll grant you your facts, Mark, but not your extrapolation. The cops can't possibly follow us from He's old star to here. We didn't know ourselves that we'd wind up among the Acolytes. I doubt that the cops were even able to plot He's course, let alone our subsequent one. Isn't that so?"

"Of course. But——"

"And if the Earth cops alerted every *local* police force in the galaxy to every petty offender," Amalfi continued with quiet implacability, "no local police force would ever be able to do any policing. They'd be too busy, recording and filing and checking new alerts coming in constantly from a million inhabited planets. Their own local criminals would mostly go free, to become a burden upon the filing systems of every other inhabited area.

"So, believe me, Mark, the cops around here have never even heard of us. We're approaching a normal situation, that's all. The Acolyte cops haven't the slightest reason to treat us as anything but just another wandering, law abiding Okie city—and after all, that's really all we are."

"Good," Hazleton said, his chest collapsing to expel a heavy sigh.

Amalfi heard neither the word nor the sigh.

At the same instant, the big master screen, which had been showing the swelling, granulating mass of the Acolyte star cluster, flashed blinding scarlet over its whole surface, and the scrannel shriek of a police whistle made the air in the control room seethe.

The cops swaggered and stomped on board the Okie city, and into Amalfi's main office in City Hall, as if the nothingness of the marches of the galaxy were their personal property. Their uniforms were not the customary dress coveralls—actually, space-suit liners—of the Earth police, however. Instead, they were flashy black affairs, trimmed with silver braid, Sam Browne belt, and shiny boots. The blue-jowled thugs who had been jammed into these tight-fitting creations reminded Amalfi of a period which considerably antedated the Night of Jadjjii—or any other event in the history of space flight.

And the thugs carried meson pistols. These heavy, cumbersome weapons could be held in one hand, but two hands were needed to fire them. They were very modern side arms to find in a border star cluster. They were only about a century out of date. This made them thoroughly up-to-date as far as the city's own armament was concerned.

The pistols told Amalfi several other things that he needed to know. Their existence here could mean only one thing: that the Acolytes had had a recent contact with one of those pollinating bees of the galaxy, an Okie city. Furthermore, the probability was not high that it had been the sole Okie contact the Acolytes had had for a long time, as Amalfi might otherwise have assumed.

It took years to build up the technology to mass produce meson pistols so that ordinary cops could pack them. It took more years still, years spent in fairly frequent contact with other technologies, to make adoption of the pistol possible at all. The pistol, then, confirmed unusually frequent contact with other Okies, which, in turn, meant that there was a garage planet here, as Amalfi had hoped.

The pistol also told Amalfi something else, which he did

not much like. The meson pistol was not a good antiper-
sonnel weapon.

It was much more suitable for demolition work.

The cops could still swagger in Amalfi's office, but they
could not stomp effectively. The floor was too thickly
carpeted. Amalfi never used the ancient, plushy office,
with its big black mahogany desk and other antiques,
except for official occasions. The control tower was his
normal on-duty habitat, but that was closed to non-
citizens.

"What's your business?" the police lieutenant barked at
Hazleton. Hazleton, standing beside the desk, said nothing,
but merely jerked his head toward where Amalfi was
seated, and resumed looking at the big screen back of the
desk.

"Are you the mayor of this burg?" the lieutenant demanded.

"I am," Amalfi said, removing a cigar from his mouth
and looking the lieutenant over with lidless eyes. He decided that he did not like the lieutenant. His rump was too
big. If a man is going to be barrel-shaped, he ought to do
a good job of it, as Amalfi had. Amalfi had no use for
top-shaped men.

"All right, answer the question, Fatty. What's your
business?"

"Petroleum geology."

"You're lying. You're not dealing with some isolated,
type Four-Q podunk now, Okie. These are the Acolyte
stars."

Hazleton looked with pointedly vague puzzlement at the
lieutenant, and then back to the screen, which showed no
stars at all within any reasonable distance.

The by-play was lost on the cop. "Petroleum geology
isn't a business with Okies," he said. "You'd all starve if
you didn't know how to mine and crack oil for food. Now
give me a straight answer before I decide you're a vagrant
and get tough."

Amalfi said evenly, "Our business is petroleum geology.
Naturally we've developed some side lines since we've
been aloft, but they're mostly natural outgrowths of petroleum geology—on which subject we happen to be experts.
We trace and develop petroleum sources for planets which
need the material." He eyed the cigar judiciously and
thrust it back between his teeth. "Incidentally, Lieutenant,

you're wasting your breath threatening us with a vagrancy charge. You know as well as we do that vagrancy laws are specifically forbidden by article one of the Constitution."

"Consitution?" the cop laughed. "If you mean the Earth Constitution, we don't have much contact with Earth out here. These are the Acolyte stars, see? Next question: have you any money?"

"Enough."

"How much is enough?"

"If you want to know whether or not we have operating capital, our City Fathers will give you the statutory *yes* or *no* answer if you can give them the data on your system that they'll need to make the calculation. The answer will almost assuredly be yes. We're not required to report our profit pool to you, of course."

"Now look," the lieutenant said. "You don't need to play the space lawyer with me. All I want to do is get off this town. If you've got dough, I can clear you—that is, if you got it through legal channels."

"We got it on a planet called He, some distance from here. We were hired by the Hevians to rub out a jungle which was bothering them. We did it by regularizing their axis."

"Yeah?" the cop said. "Regularized their axis, eh? I guess that must have been some job."

"It was," Amalfi said gravely. "We had to setacetus on He's left-hand frannistan."

"Gee. Will your City Fathers show me the contract? Okay, then. Where are you going?"

"To garage; we've a bum spindizzy. After that, out again. You people look like you're well past the stage where you've much use for oil."

"Yeah, we're pretty modernized here, not like some of these border areas you hear about. These are the Acolyte stars." Suddenly it seemed to occur to him that he had somehow lost ground; his voice turned brusque again. "So maybe you're all right, Okie. I'll give you a pass through. Just be sure you go where you say you're going, and don't make stopovers, understand? If you watch your step, maybe I can lend you a hand here and there."

Amalfi said, "That's very good of you, Lieutenant. We'll try not to have to bother you, but just in case we do have to call on you, who shall we ask for?"

"Lieutenant Lerner, Forty-fifth Border Security Group."

"Good. Oh, before you go, I collect medal ribbons—every man to his hobby, you know. And that royal violet one of yours is quite unusual—I speak as a connoisseur. Would you consent to sell it? It wouldn't be like giving up the medal itself—I'm sure your corps would issue you another ribbon."

"I don't know," Lieutenant Lerner said doubtfully. "It's against regs——"

"I realize that, and naturally I'd expect to cover any possible fine you might incur. (Mark, would you call down for a check for five hundred Oc dollars?) No sum I could offer you would really be sufficient to pay for a medal for which you risked your life, but five hundred Oc is all our City Fathers will allow me for hobbies this month. Could you do me the favor of accepting it?"

"Yeah, I guess so," the lieutenant said. He detached the bar of faded, dismal purple from over his pocket with clumsy eagerness and put it on the desk. A second later, Hazleton silently handed him the check, which he pocketed without seeming to notice it at all. "Well, be sure you keep a straight course, Okie. C'mon, you guys, let's get back to the boat."

The three thugs eased themselves tentatively into the lift shaft and slithered down out of sight through the friction-field wearing expressions of sternly repressed alarm. Amalfi grinned. Quite obviously the principle of molar valence, and frictionators and other gadgets using the principle, were still generally unknown.

Hazleton walked over to the shaft and peered down. Then he said, "Boss, that damn thing is a good-conduct ribbon. The Earth cops issued them by the tens of thousands about three centuries ago to any rookie who could get up out of bed when the whistle blew three days running. Since when is it worth five hundred Oc?"

"Never, until now," Amalfi said tranquilly. "But the lieutenant wanted to be bribed, and it's always wise to appear to be buying something when you're bribing someone. I put the price so high because he'll have to split it with his men. If I hadn't offered the bribe, I'm sure he'd have wanted to look at our Violations docket."

"I figured that; and ours is none too clean, as I've been pointing out. But I think you wasted the money, Amalfi.

The Violations docket should have been the first thing he asked to see, not the last. Since he didn't ask for it at the beginning, he wasn't interested in it."

"That's probably exactly so," Amalfi admitted. He put the cigar back and pulled on it thoughtfully. "All right, Mark, what's the pitch? Suppose you tell me."

"I don't know yet. I can't square the maintenance of an alert guard, so many parsecs out from the actual Acolyte area, with that slob's obvious indifference to whether or not we might be on the shady side of the law—or even be bindlestiff. Hell, he didn't even ask *who* we were."

"That rules out the possibility that the Acolytes have been alerted against some one bindlestiff city."

"It does," Hazleton agreed. "Lerner was far too easily bribed, for that matter. Patrols that are really looking for something specific don't bribe, even in a fairly corrupt culture. It doesn't figure."

"And somehow," Amalfi said, pushing a toggle to *off*, "I don't think the City Fathers are going to be a bit of help. I had the whole conversation up to now piped down to them, but all I'm going to get out of them is a bawling out for spending money, and a catechism about my supposed hobby. They never have been able to make anything out of voice tone. Damn! We're missing something important, Mark, something that would be obvious once it hit us. Something absolutely crucial. And here we are plunging on toward the Acolytes without the faintest idea of what it is!"

"Boss," Hazleton said.

The cold flatness of his voice brought Amalfi swiveling around in his chair in a hurry. The city manager was looking up again at the big screen, on which the Acolyte stars had now clearly separated into individual points. "What is it, Mark?"

"Look there—in the mostly dark area on the far side of the cluster. Do you see it?"

"I see quite a lot of star-free space there, yes." Amalfi looked closer. "There's also a spectroscopic double, with a red dwarf standing out some distance from the other components——"

"You're warm. Now look at the red dwarf."

There was also, Amalfi began to see, a faint smudge of green there, about as big as the far end of a pencil. The screen was keyed to show Okie cities in green, but no city could possibly be that big. The green smudge covered an area that would blank out an average Sol-type solar system.

Amalfi felt his big square front teeth beginning to bite his cigar in two. He took the dead object out of his mouth.

"Cities," he muttered. He spat, but the bitterness in his mouth did not seem to be tobacco juice after all. "Not one city. *Hundreds.*"

"Yes," Hazleton said. "There's your answer, boss, or part of it. It's a jungle."

"An Okie jungle."

Amalfi gave the jungle a wide berth, but he had O'Brian send proxies as soon as the city was safely down below top speed. Had he released the missiles earlier, they would have been left behind and lost, for they were only slightly faster than the city itself. Now they showed a fantastic and gloomy picture.

The empty area where the hobo cities had settled was well out at the edge of the Acolyte cluster, on the side toward the rest of the galaxy. The nearest star to the area, as Hazleton had pointed out, was a triple. It consisted of two type G_0 stars and a red dwarf, almost a double for the Soy-Alpha Centauri system. But there was one difference: the two G_0 stars were quite close to each other, constituting a spectroscopic doublet, separable visually only by the Dinwiddie circuits even at this relatively short distance; while the red dwarf had swung out into the empty area, and was now more than four light years away from its companions.

Around this tiny and virtually heatless fire, more than three hundred Okie cities huddled. On the screen they passed in an endless, boundaryless flood of green specks, like a river of fantastic asteroids, bobbing in space and passing and repassing each other in their orbits around the dwarf star. The concentration was heaviest near the central sun, which was so penurious of its slight radiation that it had been masked almost completely by the Dinwiddie code lights when Hazleton first spotted the jungle. But there were late comers in orbits as far out as three billion miles—spindizzy screens do not take kindly to being thrust into close contact with each other.

"It's frightening," Dee said, studying the screen intently.

"I knew there were other Okie cities, especially after we hit the bindlestiff. But so many! I could hardly have imagined three hundred in the whole galaxy."

"A gross underestimate," Hazleton said indulgently. "There were about eighteen thousand cities at the last census, weren't there, boss?"

"Yes," Amalfi said. He was as unable to look away from the screen as Dee. "But I know what Dee means. It scares the hell out of me, Mark. Something must have caused an almost complete collapse of the economy around this part of the galaxy. No other force could create a jungle of that kind. These bastardly Acolytes evidently have been exploiting it to draw Okies here, in order to hire the few they need on a competitive basis."

"At the lowest possible wages, in other words," Hazleton said. "But what for?"

"There you have me. Possibly they're trying to industrialize the whole cluster, to make themselves self-sufficient before the depression or whatever it is hits them. About all we can be sure of at this juncture is that we'd better get out of here the moment the new spindizzy gets put in. There'll be no decent work here."

"I'm not sure I agree," Hazleton said, redeploying his lanky, apparently universal-jointed limbs over his chair. "If they're industrializing here, it could mean that the depression is *here*, not anywhere else. Possibly they've overproduced themselves into a money shortage, especially if their distribution setup is as creaking, elaborate, and unjust as it usually is in these backwaters. If they're using a badly deflated dollar, we'll be sitting pretty."

Amalfi considered it. It seemed to hold up.

"We'll have to wait and see," he said. "You could well be right. But one cluster, even at its most booming stage, could never have hoped to support three hundred cities. The waste of technology involved would be terrific—and you don't attract Okies *to* a money-short area, you draw them *from* one."

"Not necessarily. Suppose there's an oversupply outside? Remember back in the Nationalist Era on Earth, artists and such low-income people used to leave the big Hamiltonian state, I've forgotten its name, to live in much smaller states where the currency was softer?"

"That was different. They had mixed coinage then——"

"Boys, may I break in on this bull session?" Dee said

hesitantly, but with a trace of mockery in her voice. "It's getting a little over my head. Suppose this whole end of this star-limb has had its economy wrecked. How, I'll leave to you two; on Utopia, our economy was frozen at a fixed rate of turnover, and had been for as long as any of us could remember; so maybe I can be forgiven for not understanding what you're talking about. But in any case, inflation or deflation, we can always leave when we have our new spindizzy."

Amalfi shook his head heavily. "That," he said, "is what scares me, Dee. There are a hell of a lot of Okies in that jungle, and they can't all be suffering from defects in their driving equipment. If there were someplace they could go where times are better, *why haven't they gone there?* Why do they congregate in a jungle in this Godforsaken star cluster, for all the universe as if there were no place else where they could find work? Okies aren't sedentary, or sociable, either."

Hazleton began drumming his fingers lightly on the arm of his chair, and his eyes closed slightly. "Money is energy," he said. "Still, I can't say that I like that any better. The more I look at it, the more I think this is one fix we won't get out of by any amount of cute tricks. Maybe we should have stuck with He."

"Maybe."

Amalfi turned his attention back to the controls. Hazleton was subtle; but one consequence of his subtlety was that he intended to expend unnecessary amounts of time speculating about situations the facts of which would soon become evident in any case.

The city was now approaching the local garage world, which bore the unlikely name of Murphy, and maneuvering among the close-packed stars of the cluster was a job delicate enough to demand the mayor's own hand upon the space stick. The City Fathers, of course, could have teetered the city through the conflicting gravitic fields to a safe landing on Murphy, but they would have taken a month at the job. Hazleton would have gone faster, but the City Fathers would have monitored his route all the way, and snatched control from him at the slightest transgression of the margins of error they had calculated. They were not equipped to respect short cuts.

Of course, they were also unequipped to appreciate the direct intuition of spatial distances and mass pressures which made Amalfi a master pilot. But over Amalfi they had no authority, except the ultimate authority of the revocation of his office.

As Murphy grew on the screen, technicians began to file into the control room, activating with personal keys desks which had been disconnected for more than three centuries—ever since the last new spindizzy had been brought on board. Readying the city's drive machinery for new equipment was a major project. Every other spindizzy on board would have to be retuned to the new machine. In the present case, the job would be further complicated by the radioactivity of the defective unit. While the garagemen should have special equipment to cope with that problem—de-gaussing, for instance, was the usual first step—no garage would know the machinery involved as well as the Okies who used it. Every city is unique.

Murphy, as Amalfi saw it on his own screen, was a commonplace enough world. It was just slightly above the size of Mars, but pleasanter to live on, since it was closer to its primary by a good distance.

But it looked deserted. As the city came closer, Amalfi could see the twenty-mile pockmarks which were the graving docks typical of a garage; but every one of those perfectly regular, machinery-ringed craters in the planet's visible hemisphere turned out to be empty.

"That's bad," he heard Hazleton murmur. It was certainly unpromising. The planet turned slowly under his eyes.

Then a city slid up over the horizon. Hazleton's breath sucked sharply through his teeth. Amalfi could also hear a soft stirring sound, and then footsteps—several of the technicians had come up behind him to peer over his shoulder.

"Posts!" he growled. The technicians scattered like leaves.

On the idle service world, the grounded city was startlingly huge. It thrust up from the ground like an invader—but a naked giant, fallen and defenseless, without its spindizzy screens. There was, of course, every good reason why the screens should not be up, but still, a city without them was a rare and disconcerting sight, like a flayed corpse in a tank. There seemed to be some activity at its perimeter. Amalfi could not resist thinking of that activity as bacterial.

"Doesn't that answer the question Dee's way?" Hazleton suggested at last. "There's an outfit that has dough for repairs, so money from outside the Acolyte area must still be good. It's having the repairs made, so it can't be quite hopeless—it thinks it has someplace to go from here. And it's a cinch to be a smart outfit, well worth consulting. It's prevented the Acolytes from fleecing it—and some form of Acolyte swindle is the only remaining explanation for the existence of the jungle. We'd best get in touch with it before we land, boss, and find out what to expect."

"No," Amalfi said. "Stick to your post, Mark."

"Why? Surely it can't do any harm."

Amalfi didn't answer. His own psi sense had already told him something that knocked Hazleton's argument into a cocked helmet, but that something showed on Hazleton's own instruments, if Hazleton cared to look. The city manager had allowed an extrapolation to carry him off into Cloud-Cuckoo-Land.

Abruptly the board began to wink with directional signals. Automatic guides from the control tower on Murphy were waving the city to a readied dock. Amalfi shifted the space stick obediently, awaiting the orange blinker that would announce some living intelligence ready with an opinion as to the desirability of Okies on Murphy.

But neither opinion nor blinker had yet asked for his attention even when Amalfi had begun to float the city for its planting in the unpromising soil below. Evidently business was so poor on Murphy that the garage had lost most of its staff to more "going" projects. In that case, no entities but the automatics in the tower would be on hand to supervise an unexpected landing.

With a shrug, Amalfi cut the City Fathers back in. There was no need for a human being to land a city as long as the landing presented no problem in policy. There were more than enough human uses for human beings; routine operations were the proper province of the City Fathers.

"First planetfall since He," Hazleton said. He seemed to be brightening a little. "It'll feel good to stretch our legs."

"No leg-stretching or any other kind of calisthenics," Amalfi said. "Not until we get more information. I haven't gotten a yeep out of this planet yet. For all we know, we may be restricted to our own premises by the local customs."

"Wouldn't the tower have said so?"

"No tower would be empowered to deliver a message like that to all comers. It might scare off an occasional legitimate customer. But it could still be so, Mark; you should know that. Let's do some snooping first."

Amalfi picked up his mike. "Get me the perimeter sergeant . . . Anderson? This is the mayor. Arm ten good men from the boarding squad, and meet the city manager and me at the Cathedral Parkway lookout. Station your men at the adjacent sally ports, well out of sight of the localities, if there are any such around. . . . Yes, that'd be just as well, too. . . . Right."

Hazleton said, "We're going out."

"Yes. And, Mark—*this star cluster may well be the last stop that we'll ever make. Will you remember that?*"

"I'll have no difficulty remembering it," Hazleton said, looking directly at Amalfi with eyes as gray as ice, "seeing that it's exactly what I told you four days ago. I have my own notions of the proper way to cope with the possibility, and they probably won't jibe with yours. Four days ago you were explaining to me that I was being excessively defeatist. Now you've expropriated my conclusion because something has forced it on you—and I know you better than to expect you to tell me what that something is—and so now you're telling me to 'Remember Thor Five' again. You can't have it both ways, Amalfi."

For a second, the two men's glances remained locked, pupil with pupil.

"You two," Dee's voice said, "might just as well be married."

From the skywalk of the graving dock in which the city rested at last, a walk level with the main deck of the city, the world of Murphy presented to Amalfi the face of a desolate mechanical wilderness.

It was an elephant's graveyard of cranes, hoists, dollies, spur lines, donkey engines, cables, scaffolding, pallets, half-tracks, camel-backs, chutes, conveyors, bins, tanks, hoppers, pipelines, waldoes, spindizzies, trompers, breeders, proxies, ehrenhafts, and half a hundred other devices of as many ages which might at some time be needed in servicing some city.

Much of the machinery was rusty, or fallen in upon itself, or whole on the surface but forever dead inside, with a spurious wholeness that so simple an instrument as the dosimeter every man wore on his left wrist could reveal as submicroscopic scandal. Much of it, too, was still quite usable. But all of it had the look of machinery which no one really expected to use.

On the near horizon, the other city, the one Amalfi had seen from aloft, stood tall and straight. Tiny mechanisms puttered about it.

And far below the skywalk, on the cluttered surface of Murphy, in the shadow of the bulge of Amalfi's city, a tiny and merely human figure danced and gesticulated.

Amalfi led the way down the tight spiral of the metal staircase, Hazleton and Sergeant Anderson behind him. Their steps were muffled in the thin air. He watched his own carefully; on a low-gravity world it was just as well to temper the use of one's muscles. The fact that one fell slower on such worlds did not much lessen the thump at the end of the fall, and Amalfi had found long ago that, away from the unvarying one-G field of the city, his bull strength often betrayed him even when he was being normally careful.

The dancing doll proved to be a short, curly-haired technie in a clean but mussed uniform. Possibly he had slept in it; at least it seemed clear that he had never done any work in it. He had a smooth, chubby face, dark of complexion, greasy and stippled with clogged pores. He glared at Amalfi truculently with eyes like beer-bottle ends.

"What the hell?" he said. "How'd you get here?"

"We swam, how else? When do we get some service?"

"I'll ask the questions, bum. And tell your sergeant to keep his hand off his gun. He makes me nervous, and when I'm nervous, there's no telling what I'll do. You're after repairs?"

"What else?"

"We're busy," the garageman said. "No charity here. Go back to your jungle."

"You're about as busy as a molecule at zero," Amalfi roared, thrusting his head forward. The garageman's shiny, bulbous nose retreated, but not by much. "We need repairs, and we mean to have 'em. We've got money to pay, and Lieutenant Lerner of your own local cops sent us here to get 'em. If those two reasons won't suit you, I'll have my sergeant put his gun hand to some use—he could probably draw and fire before you tripped over something in this junk yard."

"Who the hell are you threatening? Don't you know you're in the Acolyte stars now? We've broken up better— no, now wait a minute, sergeant, let's not be hasty. I've been dealing with bums until they're coming out of my ears. Maybe you're all right after all. You did say something about money—I heard you distinctly."

"You did," Amalfi said, remaining impassive with difficulty.

"Your City Fathers will vouch for it?"

"Sure. Hazleton—oh, hell, Anderson, what happened to the city manager?"

"He took a branching catwalk farther up," the perimeter sergeant said. "Didn't say where he was going."

It didn't, after all, pay to be too cautious, Amalfi thought wryly. If his brains hadn't been concentrating so exclusively on his feet, he would have detected the fact that only one other pair of feet was with him as soon as Hazleton had begun to catfoot it away.

"He'll be back—I hope," Amalfi said. "Look, friend, what we need is repair work. We've got a bad spindizzy in a hot hold. Can you haul it out and give us a replacement, preferably the newest model you've got?"

The garageman considered it. The problem seemed to appeal to him; his whole expression changed, so thoroughly that he looked almost friendly in his intimate ugliness.

"I've got a Six-R-Six in storage that might do, if you've got the refluxlaminated pediments to mount it on," he said slowly. "If you haven't, I've also a reconditioned B-C-Seven-Seven-Y that hums as sweetly as new. But I've never done any hot hauling before—didn't know spindizzies ever hotted up enough to notice. Anybody on board your burg that can give me a hand on decontamination?"

"Yes, it's all set up and ready to ride. Check the color of our money, and let's get on it."

"It'll take a little time to get a crew together," the garageman said. "By the way, don't let your men wander around. The cops don't like it."

"I'll do my best."

The garageman scampered away, dodging in and out among the idle, rust-tinted machines. Amalfi watched him go, marveling anew at how quickly the born technician can be gulled into forgetting who he's working for, let alone how his work is going to be used. First you mention money—since technies are usually underpaid; you then cap that with a tough and inherently interesting problem—and you have your man. Amalfi was always happy when he met a pragmatist in the enemy's camp.

"Boss——"

Amalfi spun. "Where the hell have you been? Didn't you hear me say that this planet is probably taboo to tourists? If you'd been on hand when you were needed, you'd have heard the 'probably' knocked out of that statement—to say nothing of speeding matters considerably!"

"I'm aware of that," Hazleton said evenly. "I took a calculated risk—something you seem to have forgotten how to do, Amalfi. And it paid off. I've been over to that other city, and found out something that we needed to know. Incidentally, the graving docks around here are a mess. This one, and the one the other city is in, must be the only ones in operation for hundreds of miles. All the rest are nearly full of sand and rust and flaked concrete."

"And the other city?" Amalfi said very quietly.

"It's been garnisheed; there's no doubt about it. It's shabby and deserted. Half of it is being held up by buttressing, and it's got huts pitched in the streets. It's nearly a hulk. There's a crew over there putting it in some sort of operating order, but they're in no hurry, and they aren't doing a damn thing to make the city habitable—all they want it to do is run. It's not the city's own complement, obviously. Where *they* are, I'm afraid to think."

"There's considerable thinking you haven't done," Amalfi said. "The original crew is obviously in debtor's prison. The garage is putting the city in order for some kind of dirty job that they don't expect it to outlast—and that no city still free could be hired to do at any price."

"And what would that be?"

"Setting up a planethead on a gas giant," said Amalfi. "They want to work some low-density, ammonia-methane world with an ice core, a Jupiter-type planet, that they can't conquer any other way. It's my guess that they hope to use such a planethead as an inexhaustible source of poison gas."

"That's not your only guess," Hazleton said, his lips thinned. "I expect to be disciplined for wandering off,

Amalfi, but I'm a big boy, and won't have rationalizations palmed off on me just to keep the myth of your omniscience going."

"I'm not omniscient," Amalfi said mildly. "I looked at the other city on the way in. And I looked at the instruments. You didn't. The instruments alone told me that almost nothing was going on in that city that was normal to Okie operation. They also told me that its spindizzies were being turned to produce a field which would burn them out within a year, and they told me what that field was supposed to do—what kind of conditions it was supposed to resist.

"Spindizzy fields will bounce any fast-moving large aggregate of molecules. They won't much impede the passage of gases by osmosis. If you so drive a field as to exclude the smallest possible molecular exchange, even under a pressure of more than a million atmospheres, you destroy the machine. That set of conditions occurs only in one kind of situation, a situation no Okie would ever commit himself to for an instant: setting down on a gas giant. Obviously then, since the city *was* being readied for that kind of job, it had been garnisheed—it was now state property, and nobody cares about wasting state property."

"Once again," Hazleton said, "you might have told me that in time to prevent my taking my side jaunt. However, this time it's just as well you didn't, because I still haven't come to the main thing I discovered. Do you know the identity of that city?"

"No."

"Good for you for admitting it. I do. It's *the* city we heard about when it was in the building three centuries ago; the so-called all-purpose city. Even under all the junk and decay, the lines are there. These Acolytes are letting it rot where it makes a real difference, just to hot-rod it for one job only. We could take it away from them if we tried. I studied the plans when they were first published, and——"

He stopped. Amalfi turned toward where Hazleton was looking. The garageman was coming back at a dead run. He had a meson pistol in one hand.

"I'm convinced," Amalfi said swiftly. "Can you get over there again without being observed? This looks to me like trouble."

"Yes, I can. There's a——"

" 'Yes' is enough for now. Tune our City Fathers to theirs, and set up Standard Situation N in both. Cue it to our 'spin' key—straight yes-no signal."

"Situation N? Boss, that's a——"

"I know what it is. I think we need it now. Our bum spindizzy prevents us from making any possible getaway without the combined knowledge of the two sets of City Fathers; we just aren't fast enough. Git, before it's too late."

The garageman was almost upon them, emitting screams of fury each time he hit the ground at the end of a leap, as if the sounds were jolted out of him by the impact. In the thin atmosphere of Murphy, the yells sounded like toots on a toy whistle.

Hazleton hesitated a moment more, then sprinted up the stairway. The garageman ducked around a trunnion and fired. The meson pistol howled at the sky and flew backwards out of his hand. Evidently he had never fired one before.

"Mayor Amalfi, shall I——"

"Not yet, sergeant. Cover him, that's all. Hey, you! Walk over here. Nice and slow, with your hands locked behind your head. That's it. . . . Now then: what were you firing at my city manager for?"

The dark-complected face was livid now. "You can't get away," he said thickly. "There's a dozen police squads on the way. They'll break you up for fair. It'll be fun to watch."

"Why?" Amalfi asked, in a reasonable one. "You shot at us first. We've done nothing wrong."

"Nothing but pass a bum check! Around here that's a crime worse than murder, brother. I checked you with Lerner, and he's frothing at the mouth. You'd damn well better pray that some other squad gets to you before his does!"

"A bum check?" Amalfi said. "You're blowing. Our money's better than anything you're using around here, by the looks of you. It's germanium—solid germanium."

"Germanium?" the dockman repeated incredulously.

"That's what I said. It'd pay you to clean your ears more often."

The garageman's eyebrows continued to go higher and higher, and the corners of his mouth began to quiver. Two fat, oily tears ran down his cheeks. Since he still had his hands locked behind his head, he looked remarkably like a man about to throw a fit.

Then his whole face split open.

"Germanium!" He howled. "Ho, haw, haw, haw! *Germanium!* What hole in the plenum have you been living in, Okie? Germanium—haw, *haw!*" He emitted a weak gasp and took his hands down to wipe his eyes. "Haven't you any silver, or gold, or platinum, or tin, or iron? Or something else that's worth something? Clear out, bum. You're broke. Take it from me as a friend, clear out; I'm giving you good advice."

He seemed to have calmed down a little, Amalfi said. "What's wrong with germanium?"

"Nothing," the dockman said, looking at Amalfi over his incredible nose with a mixture of compassion and vindictiveness, "It's a good, useful metal. But it just isn't money any more, Okie. I don't see how you could have missed finding that out. Germanium is trash now—well, no, it's still worth something, but only what it's *actually* worth, if you get me. You have to buy it; you can't buy other things with it.

"It's no good here as money. It's no good anywhere else, either. *Anywhere* else. The whole galaxy is broke. Dead broke.

"And so are you."

He wiped his eyes again. Overhead a siren groaned, softly but urgently.

Hazleton was ready, and had sighted the incoming cops.

Amalfi found it impossible to understand what happened when he closed the "spin" key. He did not hope to understand it at any time in the future, either; and it would do no good to ask the City Fathers, who would simply refuse to tell him—for the very good reason that they did not know. Whatever they had had in reserve for Standard Situation *N*—that ultimate situation which every Okie city must expect to face eventually, the situation wherein what is necessary to prevent total destruction is only and simply to *get away fast*—it was drastic and unprecedented. Or it had become so when the City Fathers had been given the chance to pool their knowledge with that of the City Fathers of the all-purpose city.

The city snapped from its graving dock on Murphy to a featureless coördinate-set space. The movement took no

time and involved no detectable display of energy. One
moment the city was on Murphy; Amalfi closed the key,
and Murphy had vanished, and Jake was demanding to
know where in space the city was. He was told to find
out.

The cops had come up on Murphy in fair order, but
they had not been given the chance to fire a single shot.
When Jake had managed to find Murphy again, O'Brian
sent a proxy out to watch the cops, who by that time were
shooting back and forth across the planet's sky like
belated actors looking for a crucial collar button.

An hour later, without the slightest preliminary activity,
the all-purpose city snapped out of existence on Murphy.
By the time the garagemen had recovered enough to sound
another alarm, the cops were scattered in all directions,
still hunting something that they had had no prior idea
could turn up missing: Amalfi's own town. By the time they
managed to reform their ranks sufficiently to trace the
all-purpose city, it had stopped operating, and thus had
become undetectable.

It was floating now in an orbit half a million miles away
from Amalfi's city. Its screens were down again. If there
had been any garagemen on it when it took off, they were
dead now; the city was airless.

And the City Fathers honestly did not know how all this
had been accomplished; or, rather, they no longer knew.
Standard Situation N was keyed in by a sealed and self-
blowing circuit. It had been set up that way long ago, to
prevent incompetent or lazy city administrators from calling upon it at every minor crisis. It could never be used
again.

And Amalfi knew that he had called it into use, not
only for his own city, but for the other one as well, in a
situation which had not really been the ultimate extreme,
had not really been Situation N. He had squandered the
final recourse of both cities.

He was still equally certain that neither city would ever
need that circuit again.

The two cities, linked only by an invisible ultraphone
tight-beam, were now floating free in the starless area
three light years away from the jungle, and eight parsecs
away from Murphy. The dim towers of the dead city were
not visible to Amalfi, who stood alone on the belfry of City

Hall; but they floated in his brain, waiting for him to tell them to come to life.

Whether or not his act of extreme desperation in the face of a not ultimately desperate situation had in actuality murdered that city was a question he could not decide. In the face of the galactic disaster, the question seemed very small.

He shelved it to consider what he had learned about his own bad check. Germanium never had had the enormous worth in real terms that it had had as a treasure metal. It did have properties which made it valuable in many techniques: the germanium lattice would part with an electron at the urging of a comparatively low amount of energy; the p-n boundary functioned as a crystal detector; and so on. The metal found its way into uncountable thousands of electronic devices—and, it was rare.

But not *that* rare. Like silver, platinum, and iridium before it, germanium's treasure value had been strictly artificial—an economic convention, springing from myths, jewelers' preferences, and the jealousy of statal monopolies. Sooner or later, some planet or cluster with a high technology—and a consequently high exchange rate—would capture enough of the metal to drive its competitors, or, more likely, its own treasury, off the germanium standard; or someone would learn to synthesize or transmute the element cheaply. It hardly mattered which had happened now.

What mattered was the result. The actual metallic germanium on board the city now had only an eighth of its former value at current rates of sale. Much worse, however, was the fact that most of the city's funds were not metal, but paper: Oc dollars, issued against government-held metal back on Earth and a few other administrative centers. This money, since it did not represent any metallic germanium that belonged to the city, was now unredeemable—valueless.

The new standard was a drug standard. Had the city come away from He with the expected heavy surplus of anti-agathics, it would now have been a multibillionaire. Instead, it was close to being a pauper.

Amalfi wondered how the drug standard had come about. To Okies, cut off for the most part from the main stream of history, such developments frequently seemed like the brainstorms of some unknown single genius; it was hard to think of them as evolving from a set of situations when none of the situations could now be intimately known. Still, however it had arisen, the notion had its point. Drugs can be graded exactly as to value by their therapeutic effect and their availability. Drugs that could be made synthetically in quantity at low cost would be the pennies and nickels of the new coinage—and those that could not, and were rare and always in heavier demand than the supply could meet, would be the hundred-dollar units.

Further, even expensive drugs could be diluted, which would make debt payment flexible; drugs could be as amenable to laboratory test for counterfeit as metal had been; and finally, drugs became outmoded rapidly enough to make for a high-velocity currency which could not be hoarded or cornered, even by the most predatory measures.

It was a good standard. Since it would be impossible to carry on real transactions in terms of fractions of a cubic centimeter of some chemical, just as it had been impractical to carry a ton and a half of germanium about in order to pay one's debts, there would still be a paper currency.

But on the drug standard, the city was poor. It had none of the new paper money at all, though it would, of course, sell all its metallic germanium at once to get a supply. Possibly its germanium-based paper money might also be sold, against Earth redemption, at about a fifth of the current market value of the metallic equivalent if the Acolytes cared to bother with redeeming it.

The actual drugs on board the city could not be traded against. They were necessary to maintain the life of the city. Amalfi winced to think of the size of the bite medical care was going to take out of every individual's budget under the new economy. The anti-agathics, in particular, would pose a terrifying dilemma: shall I use my anti-agathic credits now, as money, to relieve my current money miseries, or shall I continue to live in poverty in order to prolong my life? . . .

Remorselessly, Amalfi drove one consequence after another through the stony corridors of his skull, like a priest wielding the whip behind lowing sacrifices. The city was poor. It could find no work among the Acolyte stars at a rate which would make the work justifiable. It could look for work nowhere else without a new spindizzy.

That left only the jungle. There was no place else to go.

Amalfi had never set down in a jungle before, and the thought made him wipe the palms of his hands unconsciously upon his thighs. The word in his mind—it had always been there, he knew, lying next to the word "jungle"—was *never*. The city must always pay its own way, it must always come whole out of any crisis, it must always pull its own weight . . .

Those emblems of conduct were now clichés, which *never* had turned out to be a time, like any other time— one that had implicit in it the inevitable timeword: *Now*.

Amalfi picked up the phone which hung from the belfry railing.

"Hazleton?"

"Here, boss. What's the verdict?"

"None yet,' Amalfi said. "Supposedly we snitched the city next door for some purpose; now we need to know what the chances are of abandoning ship at this point and getting out of here with it. Get some men in suits over there and check on it."

Hazleton did not answer for a moment. In that moment, Amalfi knew that the question was peripheral, and that the verdict was already in. A line by the Earth poet Theodore Roethke crept across the floor of his brain like a salamander: *The edge cannot eat the center*.

"Right," Hazleton's voice said.

Half an eternal hour later, it added: "Boss, that city is worse off than we are, I'm afraid. It's got good drivers still, but of course they're all tuned wrong. Besides, the whole place seems to be structurally unsound on a close look; the garagemen really did a thorough job of burrowing around in it. Among other things, the keel's cracked—the Acolytes must have landed it, not the original crew."

It would, of course, be impossible to claim foreknowledge of any of this, with Hazleton's present state of mind teetering upon the edge of some rebellion Amalfi hoped he did not yet understand. It was possible that Hazleton, despite all the mayor's precautions, had divined the load of emotional guilt which had been accumulating steadily upon Amalfi—or perhaps that suspicion was only the guilt itself speaking. In any event, Amalfi had allowed himself to be stampeded into stealing the other city by Hazleton, even in the face of the foreknowledge, to keep peace in the family. He said instead, "What's your recommendation, Mark?"

"I'd cast loose from it, boss. I'm only sorry I advocated snitching it in the first place. We have the only thing it had to give us that we could make our own: our City Fathers now know everything their City Fathers knew. We couldn't take anything else but a new spindizzy, and that's a job for a graving dock."

"All right. Give it a point thirty-four per cent screen to clinch its present orbit, and come on back. Make sure you don't give it more than that, or those overtuned spindizzies will advertise its position to anyone coming within two parsecs of it, and interfere with our own operation to boot."

"Right."

And now there were the local cops to be considered. They had chalked up against Amalfi's city, not only the issuing of a bad check, but the theft of state property, and the deaths of Acolyte technicians on board the other city.

Only the jungle was safe, and even the jungle was safe only temporarily. In the jungle, at least for the time being, one city could lose itself among three hundred others—many of which would be better armed than Amalfi's city had ever been.

There might even be a chance, in such a salmon-pack of cities, that Amalfi would see at last with his own eyes the mythical Vegan orbital fort—the sole non-human construction ever to go Okie, and now the center of an enormous saga of exploits woven about it by the starmen. Amalfi was as fascinated by the legend as any other Okie, though he knew the meager facts well: the fort had circled Vega until the smashing of the Confederacy's home planet, and then—unexpectedly, since the Vegans had never been given to flying anything bigger than a battleship—had taken off for parts unknown, smashing its way through the englobement of police cruisers almost instantly. Nothing had ever been heard of it since, although the legend grew and grew.

The Vegans themselves had been anything but an attractive people, and it was difficult to say why the story of the orbital fort was so beloved with the Okies. Of course, Okies generally disliked the cops and said that they had no love for Earth, but this hardly explained why the legend of the fort was so popular among them. The fort was now said to be invulnerable and unlimited; it had done miracles in every limb of the galaxy; it was everywhere and nowhere; it was the Okies' Beowulf, their Cid, their Sigurd, Gawaine, Roland, Cuchulainn, Prometheus, Lemminkainen . . .

Amalfi felt a sudden chill. The thought that had just come to him was so outrageous that he had almost stopped thinking it in the middle, out of sheer instinct. The fort—probably it had been destroyed centuries ago. But if it did still exist, certain conclusions emerged implacably, and certain actions could be taken on them. . . .

Yes, it was possible. It was possible. And definitely worth trying. . . .

But if it actually worked . . .

Having made the decision, Amalfi put the idea resolutely aside. In the meantime, one thing was sure: as long as the Acolytes continued to use the jungle as a labor pool, their cops would not risk smashing things up indiscriminately only in order to search out one single "criminal" city. To the Acolyte's way of thinking, all Okies were lawbreakers, by definition.

Which, Amalfi thought, was quite correct as far as his own city was concerned. The city was not only a bum now, but a bindlestiff to boot—by definition.

The end of the line.

"Boss? I'm coming in. What's the dodge? We'll need to pull it soon, or——"

Amalfi looked up steadily at the red dwarf star above the balcony.

"There is no dodge," he said. "We're licked, Mark. We're going to the jungle."

CHAPTER SIX: The Jungle

THE cities drifted along their sterile orbits around the little red sun. Here and there, a few showed up on the screen by their riding lights, but most of them could not spare even enough power to keep riding lights going. The lights were vital in such close-packed quarters, but power to maintain spindizzy screens was more important still.

Only one city glowed—not with its riding lights, which were all out, but by street lighting. That city had power to waste, and it wanted the fact known. And it wanted it known, too, that it preferred to waste the power in sheer bragging to the maintenance of such elementary legalities as riding lights.

Amalfi looked soberly at the image of the bright city. It was not a very clear image, since the bright city was in a preferred position close to the red dwarf, where that sun's natural and unboundable gravitational field strained the structure of space markedly. The saturation of the intervening area with the smaller screens of the other Okies made the seeing still worse, since Amalfi's own city had been unable to press through the pack beyond eighteen AU's from the sun, a distance about equivalent to that from Sol to Uranus. For Amalfi, consequently, the red dwarf was visually only a star of the tenth magnitude— the G_0 star four light years away seemed much closer.

But obviously, three hundred-odd Okie cities could not all huddle close enough to a red dwarf to derive any warmth from it. Somebody had to be on the outside. It was equally obvious, and expectable, that the city with the most power available to it should be the one drawn up the most cosily to the dull stellar fire, while those who most needed to conserve every erg shivered in the outer blackness.

What *was* surprising was that the bright city should be advertising its defiance of local law and common sense alike—while police-escorted Acolyte ships were shoving their way into the heart of the jungle.

Amalfi looked up at the screen banks. For the second time within the year, he was in a chamber of City Hall which was almost never used. This one was the ancient reception hall, which had been fitted with a screen system of considerable complexity about five hundred and eighty years ago, just after the city had first taken to space. It was called into service only when the city was approaching a heavily developed, highly civilized star system, in order to carry on the multiple negotiations with various diplomatic, legal, and economic officials which had to be gone through before an Okie could hope to deal with such a system. Certainly Amalfi had never expected to have any use for the reception hall in a jungle.

There was a lot, he thought grimly, that he didn't know about living in an Okie jungle.

One of the screens came alight. It showed the full-length figure of a woman in sober clothing of an old style, utilitarian in cut, but obviously made of perishable materials. The woman inside the clothes was hard-eyed, but not hard of muscle; an Acolyte trader, evidently.

"The assignment," the trader said in a cold voice, "is a temporary development project on Hern Six, as announced previously. We can take six cities there, to be paid upon a per-job basis."

"Attention, Okies."

A third screen faded in. Even before the image had stabilized in the locally distorted space-lattice, Amalfi recognized its outlines. The general topology of a cop can seldom be blurred by distortion of any kind. He was only mildly surprised to find, when the face came through, that the police spokesman was Lieutenant Lerner, the man whose bribe had turned to worthless germanium in his hands.

"If there's any disorder, nobody gets hired," Lerner said. "Nobody. Understand? You'll present your offers to the lady in proper fashion, and she'll take or leave your bids as she sees fit. Those of you who are wanted outside the jungle will be held accountable if you leave the jungle—we're offering no immunities this trip. And if there's any damn insolence——"

Lieutenant Lerner's image drew its forefinger across its throat in a gesture that somehow had never lost its specificity. Amalfi growled and switched off the audio; Lerner was still talking, as was the trader, but now another screen was coming on, and Amalfi had to know what words were to come from it. The speeches of the trader and the cop could be predicted almost positively in advance—as a matter of fact, the City Fathers had already handed Amalfi the predictions, and he had listened to the actual speeches only long enough to check them for barely possible unknowns.

But what the bright city near the red dwarf—the jungle's boss, the king of the hobos—would say . . .

Not even Amalfi, let alone the City Fathers, could know that in advance. Lieutenant Lerner and the trader worked their mouths soundlessly while the wavering shadow on the fourth screen jelled. A slow, heavy, brutally confident voice was already in complete possession of the reception hall.

"Nobody takes any offer less than sixty," it said. "The class *A* cities will ask one hundred and twenty-four for the Hern Six job, and grade *B* cities don't get to underbid them until the goddam trader has all the *A*'s she'll take. If she picks all six from the *A*'s, that's tough. No *C*'s are to bid at all on the Hern Six deal. We'll take care of anybody that breaks ranks, either right away . . ."

The image came through. Amalfi goggled at it.

". . . or after the cops leave. That's all for now."

The image faded. The twisted, hairless man in the ancient metal-mesh cape stood in Amalfi's memory for quite a while afterwards.

The Okie King was a man made of lava. Perhaps he had been born at one time, but now he looked like a geological accident, a column of black stone sprung from a fissure and contorted roughly into the shape of a man.

And his face was shockingly disfigured and scarred by the one disease that still remained unconquered, unsolved, though it no longer killed.

Cancer.

A voice murmured inside Amalfi's head, coming from the tiny vibrator imbedded in the mastoid bone behind the mayor's right ear. "That's just what the City Fathers said he would say," Hazleton commented softly from his post uptown in the control tower. "But he can't be as naïve as all that. He's an old-timer; been aloft since back before they knew how to polarize spindizzy screens against cosmic radiation. Must be eight hundred years old at a minimum."

"You can lay up a lot of cunning in that length of time," Amalfi agreed in a similarly low voice. He was wearing throat mikes under a high military collar. As far as the screens were concerned, he was standing motionless, silent, and alone; though he was an expert at talking without moving his lips, he did not try to do so now, for the fuzziness of local transmission conditions made it unlikely that his murmuring would be detected. "It doesn't seem likely that he means what he says. But we'd best sit tight for the moment."

He glanced into the auxiliary battle tank, a three-

dimensional chart in which color-coded points of lights
moved, showing each city, the nearby sun, and the
Acolyte vessels, not to scale, but in their relative positions.
The tank was camouflaged as a desk and could be seen
into only from behind; hence it was out of sight of any
eye but Amalfi's. In it the Acolyte force showed itself to
consist of one trader's ship and four police craft; one of
the latter was a command cruiser, very probably Lerner's, and the others were light cruisers.

It was not much of a force, but then, there was no real
need for a full squadron here. With a minimum of organization, the Okies could run Lerner and his ward out of the
jungle, even at some cost to their own numbers—but
where would the Okies run to after Lerner had yelled for
navy support? The question answered itself.

A string of twenty-three small "personal" screens came
on now, high up along the curve of the far wall. Twenty-
three faces looked down at Amalfi—the mayors of all but
one of the class *A* cities in the jungle; Amalfi's own city
was the twenty-fourth. Amalfi valved the main audio gain
back up again.

"Are we ready to begin?" the Acolyte woman said.
"I've got codes here for twenty-four cities, and I see
you're all here. Small courage among Okies these days—
twenty-four out of three hundred of you for a simple job
like this! That's the attitude that made Okies of you in the
first place. You're afraid of honest work."

"We'll work," the King's voice said. His screen, however, remained gray-green. "Look over the codes and take
your pick."

The trader looked for the voice. "No insolence," she
said sharply. "Or I'll ask for volunteers from the grade
B's. It would save me money, anyhow."

There was no reply. The trader frowned and looked at
the code list in her hand. After a moment, she called off
three numbers, and then, with greater hesitation, a fourth.
Four of the screens above Amalfi went blank, and in the
tank, four green flecks began to move outward from the
red dwarf star.

"That's all we need for Hern Six except for a pressure
job," the woman said slowly. "There are eight cities listed
here as pressure specialists. You there—who are you,
anyhow?"

"Bradley-Vermont," one of the faces above Amalfi said.

"What would you ask for a pressure job?"

"One hundred and twenty-four," Bradley-Vermont's mayor said sullenly.

"O-ho! You've a high opinion of yourself, haven't you? You may as well float here and rot for a while longer, until you learn something more about the law of supply and demand. You—you're Dresden-Saxony, it says here. What's your price? Remember, I only need one."

Dresden-Saxony's mayor was a slight man with high cheekbones and glittering black eyes. He seemed to be enjoying himself, despite his obvious state of malnutrition; at least, he was smiling a little, and his eyes glittered over the dark shadows which made them look large.

"We ask one hundred and twenty-four," he said with malicious indifference.

The woman's lids slitted. "You do, eh? That's a coincidence, isn't it? And you?"

"The same," the third mayor said, though with obvious reluctance.

The trader swung around and pointed directly at Amalfi. In the very old cities, such as the one the King operated, it would be impossible to tell who she was pointing at, but probably most of the cities in the jungle had compensating tri-di. "What's your town?"

"We're not answering that question," Amalfi said. "And we're not pressure specialists anyhow."

"I know that, I can read a code. But you're the biggest Okie I've ever seen, and I'm not talking about your belly either; and you're modern enough for the purpose. The job is yours for one hundred—no more."

"Not interested."

"You're a fool as well as a fat man. You just came into this hell-hole and there are charges against——"

"Ah, you know who we are. Why did you ask?"

"Never mind that. You don't know what a jungle is like until you've lived in it. You'd be smart to take the job and get out now while you can. You'd be worth one hundred and twelve to me if you could finish the job under the estimated time."

"You've denied us immunity," Amalfi said, "and you needn't bother offering it, either. We're not interested in pressure work for any price."

The woman laughed. "You're a liar, too. You know as well as I do that nobody arrests Okies on jobs. And you

wouldn't find it difficult to leave the job once it's finished.
Here now—I'll give you one hundred and twenty. That's
my top offer, and it's only four less than the pressure
experts are asking. Fair enough?"

"It may be fair enough," Amalfi said. "But we don't do
pressure work; and we've already gotten in reports from
the proxies we sent to Hern Six as soon as Lieutenant
Lerner said that was where the job was. We don't like the
look of it. We don't want it. We won't take it at one
hundred and twenty, we won't take it at one hundred
and twenty-four—and we won't take it at all. Understand?"

"Very well," the woman said with concentrated vicious-
ness. "You'll hear from me again, Okie."

The King was looking at Amalfi with an unreadable,
but certainly unfriendly, expression. If Amalfi's guess was
right, the King thought Amalfi was somewhat overdoing
Okie solidarity. It might also be occurring to him that the
expression of so much independence might be a bid for
power within the jungle itself. Yes, Amalfi was sure that
that, at least, had occurred to the King.

The hiring of the class *B* cities was now all that remained, but nevertheless it took quite a while to get
started. The woman, it emerged, was more than a trader;
she was an entrepreneur of some importance. She wanted
the cities, twenty of them, each for the same identical
piece of dirty work: working low-grade carnotite lies on a
small planet too near a hot star. Twenty mining cities
working upon such a planet would reduce it to as small
and sculptured a lump of trash as a meteorite before very
many months. The method, obviously, was to get the work
done fast without paying more than a pittance for it.

Then, startlingly, while the woman was still making up
her mind, the voice came through. It was weak and
indistinct, and without any face to go with it.

"We'll take the job. Take us."

There was a murmuring from the screens, and across
some of the faces there the same shadow seemed to run.
Amalfi checked the tank, but it told him little. The signal
had been too weak. All that could be made certain was
that the voice belonged to some city far out on the
periphery of the jungle—a city desperate for energy.

The Acolyte woman seemed momentarily nonplussed.
Even in a jungle, Amalfi thought grimly, some crude rules
had to be observed; evidently the woman realized that to

EARTHMAN, COME HOME   367

take on the volunteer before interviewing the others might
be—resented.

"Keep out of this," the voice of the King said, so much
more slowly and heavily than before that its weight was
almost tangible upon the air. "Let the lady do her own
picking. She's got no use for a class C outfit."

*"We'll take the job. We're a mining town from way
back, and we can refine the stuff, too, by gaseous diffusion, mass spectrography, mass chromatography, whatever's asked. We can handle it. And we've got to have it."*

"So do the rest," the King said, coldly unimpressed.
"Take your turn."

"We're dying out here! Hunger, cold, thirst, disease!"

"Others are in the same state. Do you think any of us
like it here? Wait your turn!"

"All right," the woman said suddenly. "I'm sick of being
told who I do and who I don't want. Anything to get this
over with. File your coördinates, whoever that is out
there, and——"

"File your coördinates and we'll have a Dirac torpedo
there before you've stopped talking!" the King roared.
"Acolyte, what are you paying for this rock-heaving?
Nobody here works for less than sixty—that's flat."

"We'll go for fifty-five."

The woman smiled an unpleasant smile. "Apparently
somebody in this pest area is glad of a chance to do some
honest work for a change.Who's next?"

"Hell, you don't need to take a class C city," one of the
rejected class A's blurted. "We'll go for fifty-five. What
can we lose?"

"Then we'll take fifty," the outsider whispered immediately.

"You'll take a bolt in the teeth! As for you—you're
Coquilhatville-Congo, eh?—you're going to be sorry you
ever had a tongue to flap."

There was already a stir among the green dots in the
tank. Some of the larger cities were leaving their orbits.
The woman began to look vaguely alarmed.

"Hazleton!" Amalfi murmured quickly. "This is going to
get worse before it gets better. Set us up, as fast as you
can, to move into one of the vacated orbits close to the red
star the moment I give the word."

"We won't be able to put on any speed——"

"I wouldn't want us to if we could. It'll have to be done

slowly enough so that it won't be apparent in any tank that we're moving counter to the general tendency. Also, get me a fix on that outfit on the outside that broke ranks if you possibly can. If you can't do it without attracting attention, drop the project at once."

"Right."

"By Hadjjii's nightshirt you've got a lesson coming!" the woman was exclaiming. "The whole deal is off for today. No jobs, not for anybody. I'll come back in a week. Maybe by then you'll have some common sense back. Lieutenant, let's get the hell out of here."

That, however, proved to be a difficult assignment. There was a sort of wave front of heavy-duty cities between the Acolyte ships and open space, expanding outward into the darkness where the weaklings shivered. In that second frigid shell most of the class *C* cities were panicking; and, still farther out, the brilliant green sparks of the cities whose promised jobs had just been written off were plunging angrily back toward the main cloud.

The reception hall was a bedlam of voices, mostly those of mayors trying to establish that *they* had not been responsible for the break in the wage line. Somewhere several cities were still attempting to shout new bids to the Acolyte woman under cover of the confusion. Through it all the voice of the King whirled like a bull-roarer.

"Clear the sky!" Lerner shouted. "Clear it up out there, by——"

As if in response, the tank suddenly crackled with hair-thin sapphire tracers. The static of the scattered mesotron rifle fire rattled audio speakers, cross-hatched the desperate, shouting faces on the screens. Terror, the terror of a man who finds suddenly that the situation he is in has always been deadly, turned Lieutenant Lerner's features rigid. Amalfi saw him reach for something.

"All right, Hazleton, *spin!*"

The defective spindizzy sobbed, and the city moved painfully. Lerner's elbow jerked back toward his midriff, and from his ship came the pale guide light of a Bethé blaster.

Seconds later, something went up in the white agony of a fusion explosion—something so far off from the center of the riot that Amalfi first thought, with a shock of fury, that Lerner had undertaken to destroy Okie cities unselectively, simply to terrorize. Then the look on Lerner's face

told him that the shot had been fired at random. Lerner
was as taken aback as Amalfi, and seemingly for much the
same reasons, at the death of the unknown bystander.

The depth of the response surprised Amalfi anew. Perhaps there was hope for Lerner yet.

Some incredible fool of an Okie was firing on the cop
now, but the shots fell short; mesotron rifles were not
primarily military instruments, and the Acolytes had almost worked free of the jungle. For a moment Amalfi was
afraid that Lerner would fling a few vindictive Bethé
blasts back into the pack, but evidently the cop was
recovering the residue of his good sense; at least, no more
shots came from the command cruiser. It was possible that
he had realized that any further exchange of fire would
turn the incident from a minor brawl to a mob uprising
which would make it necessary to call in the Acolyte
navy.

Not even the Acolytes could want that, for it would end
in cutting off their supply of skilled labor.

The city's spindizzies cut out. Lurid, smoky scarlet light
leaked down the stone stairwell which led out of the
reception hall to the belfry.

"We're parked near the stinking little star, boss. We're
less than a million miles out from the orbit of the King's
own city."

"Good work, Mark. Break out a gig. We're going calling."

"All right. Anything special in the way of equipment?"

"Equipment?" Amalfi said, slowly. "Well—no. But
you'd best bring Sergeant Anderson along. And Mark——"

"Yes?"

"Bring Dee, too."

The center of government of the King's city was enormously impressive: ancient, stately, marmoreal. It was
surrounded on a lower level by a number of lesser structures of equally heavy-handed beauty. One of these was a
heavy, archaic cantilever bridge for which Amalfi could
postulate no use at all; it spanned an enormously broad
avenue which divided the city in two, an avenue which
was virtually untraveled; the bridge, too, carried only foot
traffic now, and not much of that.

He decided finally that the bridge had been retained only
out of respect to history. These seemed to be no other

sentiment which fitted it, since the normal mode of transportation in the King's city, as in every other Okie city,
was by aircab. Like the City Hall, the bridge was beautiful; possibly that had spoken for its retention, too.

The cab rocked slightly and grounded. "Here we are,
gentlemen," the Tin Cabby said. "Welcome to
Buda-Pesht."

Amalfi followed Dee and Hazleton out onto the plaza.
Other cabs, many of them, dotted the red sky, homing on
the palace and settling near by.

"Looks like a conclave," Hazleton said. "Guests from
outside, not just managerial people inside this one city;
otherwise, why the welcome from the cabby?"

"That's my guess, too, and I think we're none too early
for it, either. It's my theory that the King is in for a rough
time from his subjects. This shoot-up with Lerner, and the
loss of jobs for everybody, must have lowered his stock
considerably. If so, it'll give us an opening."

"Speaking of which," Hazleton said, "where's the entrance to this tomb, anyhow? Ah—that must be it."

They hurried through the shadows of the pillared porti-
co. Inside, in the foyer, hunched or striding figures moved
past them toward the broad, ancient staircase, or gathered
in small groups, murmuring urgently in the opulent dimness. This entrance hall was marvelous with chandeliers;
they did not cast much light, but they shed glamour like a
molting peacock.

Someone plucked Amalfi by the sleeve. He looked
down. A slight man with a worn Slavic face and black
eyes which looked alive with suppressed mischief stood at
his side.

"This place makes me homesick," the slight man said,
"although we don't go in for quite so much sheer mass on
my town. I believe you're the mayor who refused all offers,
on behalf of a city with no name. I'm correct, am I not?"

"You are," Amalfi said, studying the figure with difficulty in the ceremonial dimness. "And you're the mayor of
Dresden-Saxony: Franz Specht. What can we do for
you?"

"Nothing, thank you. I simply wanted to make myself
known. It may be that you will need to know someone,
inside." He nodded in the direction of the staircase. "I
admired your stand today, but there may be some who
resent it. Why is your city nameless, by the way?"

"It isn't," Amalfi said. "But we sometimes need to use our name as a weapon, or at least as a lever. We hold it in reserve as such."

"A weapon! Now that is something to ponder. I will see you later, I hope." Specht slipped away abruptly, a shadow among shadows. Hazleton looked at Amalfi with evident puzzlement.

"What's his angle, boss? Backing a longshot, maybe?"

"That would be my guess. Anyhow, as he says, we can probably use a friend in this mob. Let's go on up."

In the great hall, which had been the throne room of an empire older than any Okie, older even than space flight, there was already a meeting in progress. The King himself was standing on the dais, enormously tall, bald, scarred, terrific, as shining black as anthracite. Ancient as he was, his antiquity was that of some, featureless, eventless, an antiquity without history against the rich backdrop of his city. He was anything but an expectable mayor of Buda-Pesht; Amalfi strongly suspected that there were recent bloodstains on the city's log.

Nevertheless, the King held the rebellious Okies under control without apparent effort. His enormous gravelly voice roared down about their heads like a rockslide, overwhelming them all with its raw momentum alone. The occasional bleats of protest from the floor sounded futile and damned against it, like the voices of lambs objecting to the inevitable avalanche.

"So you're mad!" he was thundering. "You got roughed up a little and now you're looking for somebody to blame it on! Well, I'll tell you who to blame it on! I'll tell you what to do about it, too. And by God, when I'm through telling you, you'll *do* it, the whole pack of you!"

Amalfi pushed through the restive, close-packed mayors and city managers, putting his bull shoulders to good use. Hazleton and Dee, hand in hand, tailed him closely. The Okies on the floor grumbled as Amalfi shoved his way forward; but they were so bound up in the King's diatribe, and in their own fierce, unformulated resistance to the King's battering-ram leadership tactics, that they could spare nothing more than a moment's irritation for Amalfi's passage among them.

"Why are we hanging around here now, getting pushed around by these Acolyte hicks?" the King roared. "You're fed with it. All right, I'm fed with it, too. I wouldn't take it from the beginning! When I came here, you guys were bidding each other down to peanuts. When the bidding was over, the city that got the job lost money on it every time. It was me that showed you how to organize. It was me that showed you how to stand up for your rights. It was me that showed you how to form a wage line, and how to hold one. And it's going to be me that'll show you what to do when a wage line breaks up."

Amalfi reached behind him, caught Dee's hand, and drew her forward to stand beside him. They were now in the front row of the crowd, almost up against the dais. The King saw the movement; he paused and looked down. Amalfi felt Dee's hand tighten spasmodically upon his. He returned the pressure.

"All right," Amalfi said. When he was willing to let his voice out, he could fill a considerable space with it. He let it out. "Show, or shut up."

The King, who had been looking directly down at them, made a spasmodic movement—almost as if he had been about to take one step backwards. "Who the hell are you?" he shouted.

"I'm the mayor of the only city that held the line today," Amalfi said. He did not seem to be shouting, but somehow his voice was no smaller in the hall than the King's. A quick murmur went through the mob, and Amalfi could see necks craning in his direction. "We're the newest—and the biggest—city here, and this is the first sample we've seen of the way you run this wage bidding. We think it stinks. We'll see the Acolytes in hell before we take their jobs at *any* of the prices they offer, let alone the low pay levels you set."

Someone near by turned and looked at Amalfi slant-wise. "Evidently you folks can eat space," the Okie said dryly.

"We eat food. We won't eat slops," Amalfi growled. "You up there on the platform—let's hear this great plan for getting us out of this mess. It couldn't be any worse than the wage-line system—that's a cinch."

The King began to pace. He whirled as Amalfi finished speaking, arms akimbo, feet apart, his shiny bald cranium thrust forward, gleaming blankly against the faded tapestries.

"I'll let you hear it," he roared. "You bet I'll let you hear it. Let's see what your big talk comes to after you

know what it is. You can stay behind and try to work
boom-time wages out of the Acolytes if you want; but if
you've guts, you'll go with us."

"Where to?" Amalfi said calmly.

"We're going to march on Earth."

There was a brief, stunned silence. Then a composite
roar began to grow in the hall.

Amalfi grinned. The sound of the response was not
exactly friendly.

"Wait!" the King bellowed. "Wait, dammit! I ask you—
what's the sense in our fighting the Acolytes? They're just
local trash. They know just as well as we do that they
couldn't get away with their slave-market tactics and their
private militia and their shoot-ups if Earth had an eye on
'em."

"Then why don't we holler for the Earth cops?" someone demanded.

"Because they wouldn't come here. They can't. There
must be Okies all over the galaxy that are taking stuff
from local systems and clusters, stuff like what we're
taking. This depression is everywhere, and there just aren't
enough Earth cops to be all over the place at once.

"But we don't have to take it. We can go to Earth and
demand our rights. We're citizens, every one of us—unless
there are any Vegans here. You a Vegan, buddy?"

The scarred face stared down at Amalfi, smiling grue-
somely. A nervous titter went through the hall.

"The rest of us can go to Earth and demand that the
government bail us out. What else is government for,
anyhow? Who produces the money that kept the politicians fat all through the good centuries? What would the
government have to govern and tax and penalize if it
weren't for the Okies? Answer me that, you with the
orbital fort under your belt!"

The laughter was louder and sounded more assured now.
Amalfi, however, was quite used to gibes at his pod; such
thrusts were for him a sure sign that his current opponent
had run out of pertinent things to say. He returned
coldly: "More than half of us had charges against us when
we came here—not local charges, but violations of Earth
orders of one kind or another. Some of us have been
dodging being brought back on our Violations dockets for
decades. Are you going to offer yourselves to the Earth
cops on a platter?"

The King did not appear to be listening with more than half an ear. He had brought up a broad grin at the second wave of laughter, and had been looking back down at Dee for admiration.

"We'll send out a call on the Dirac," he said. "To all Okies, everywhere. 'We're all going back to Earth,' we'll say. 'We're going home to get an accounting. We've done Earth's heavy labor all over the galaxy, and Earth's paid us by turning our money into waste paper. We're going home to see that Earth does something about it'—we'll set a date—'and any Okie with starman's guts will follow us.' How does that sound, eh?"

Dee's grip on Amalfi's hand was now tighter than any pressure he would have believed she could exert. Amalfi did not speak to the King; he simply looked back at him, his eyes metallic.

From somewhere fairly far back in the throne room, a newly familiar voice called, "The mayor of the nameless city has asked a pertinent question. From the point of view of Earth, we're a dangerous collection of potential criminals at worst. At best we're discontented jobless people, and undesirable in large numbers anywhere near the home planet."

Hazleton pushed up to the front row, on the other side of Dee, and glared belligerently up at the King. The King, however, had looked away again, over Hazleton's head.

"Anybody got a better idea?" the immense black man said dryly. "Here's good old Vega down here; he's full of ideas. Let's hear his idea. I'll bet it's colossal. I'll just bet he's a genius, this Vegan."

"Get up there, boss," Hazleton hissed. "You've got 'em!"

Amalfi released Dee's hand—he had some difficulty in being gentle about it—bounded clumsily but without real effort onto the dais, and turned to face the crowd.

"Hey there, mister," someone shouted. "You're no Vegan!"

The crowd laughed uneasily.

"Never said I was," Amalfi retorted. Hazleton's face promptly fell. "Are you all a pack of children? No mythical fort is going to bail you out of this. Neither is any fool mass flight on Earth. There isn't any easy way out. There *is* one tough way out, if you've got the guts for it."

"Let's hear it."

"Speak up!"

"Let's get it over with."

"All right," Amalfi said. He walked back to the immense throne of the Hapsburgs and sat down in it, catching the King flatfooted. Standing, Amalfi, despite his bulk, was a smaller man than the King, but on the throne he made the King look not only smaller but also quite irrelevant. From the back of the dais, his voice boomed out as powerfully as before.

"Gentlemen," he said, "our germanium is worthless now. So is our paper money. Even the work we do doesn't seem to be worth while now, on any standard. That's our trouble, and there isn't much that Earth can do about it—they're caught in the collapse, too."

"A professor," the King said, his seamed lips twisting.

"Shaddap. You asked me up here. I'm staying up here until I've had my say. The commodity we all have to sell is labor. Hand labor, heavy work, isn't worth anything. Machines can do that. But brainwork can't be done with anything but brains; art and pure science are beyond the compass of any machine.

"Now, we can't sell art. We can't produce it; we aren't artists and aren't set up as such; there's an entirely different segment of galactic society that supplies that need. But brainwork in pure science is something we can sell, just as we've always sold brainwork in applied sciences. If we play our cards right, we can sell it anywhere, for any price we ask, regardless of the money system involved. It's the ultimate commodity, and in the long run it's a commodity which no one but the Okies could merchandise successfully.

"Selling that commodity, we could take over the Acolytes or any other star system. We could do it better in a general depression than we could ever have done it before, because we can now set any price on it that we choose."

"Prove it," somebody called.

"That's easy. We have here around three hundred cities. Let's integrate and use their accumulated knowledge. This is the first time in history that so many City Fathers have been gathered together in one place, just as it's the first time that so many big organizations specializing in different sciences have ever been gathered together. If we were to consult with each other, pool our intellectual resources, we'd come out technologically at least a thousand years ahead of the rest of the galaxy. Individual experts can be bought for next to nothing now, but no individual expert—*nor any individual city or planet*—could match what we'd have.

"That's the priceless coin, gentlemen, the universal coin: human knowledge. Look now: there are eighty-five million undeveloped worlds in this galaxy ready to pay for knowledge of the *current* vintage, the kind we all share right now, the kind that runs about a century behind Earth on the average. But if we were to pool our knowledge, then even the most advanced planets, even Earth itself, would see their coinages crumble in the face of their eagerness to buy what we would have to offer."

"Question!"

"You're Dresden-Saxony back there, right?" Amalfi said. "Go ahead, Mayor Specht."

"Are you sure accumulated technology *is* the answer? You yourself said that straight techniques are the province of machines. The ancient Gödel-Church theorems show that no machine or set of machines can score significant advances on human thought. The designer has to precede the machine, and has to have achieved the desired function before the machine can even be built."

"What is this, a seminar?" the King demanded. "Let's ――"

"Let's hear it," someone called.

"After that mess today――"

"Let 'em talk—they make sense!"

Amalfi waited a moment and then said, "Yes, Mayor Specht. Go ahead."

"I had about made my point. The machines can't do the job you offer as the solution to our troubles. This is why mayors have authority over City Fathers, rather than the other way around."

"That's quite true," Amalfi said. "And I don't pretend that a completely cross-connective hookup among all our City Fathers would automatically bail us out. For one thing we'd have to set the hookup pattern very carefully as a topological problem, to be sure we didn't get a degree of connectivity which would result in the disappearance of knowledge instead of its accumulation. There's an example of just the kind of thing you were talking about: machines can't handle topology because it isn't quantitative:

"I said that this was the hard way of solving the

problem, and I meant just that. After we'd pooled our machine-accumulated knowledge, furthermore, we'd have to interpret it before we could put it to some use.

"That would take time. Lots of time. Technicians will have to check the knowledge-pooling at every stage; they'll have to check the City Fathers to be sure they can take in what's being delivered to them—as far as we know, they have no storage limits, but that assumption hasn't ever been tested before on the practical level. They'll have to assess what it all adds up to in the end, run the assessments through the City Fathers for logical errors, assess the logic for supralogical bugs beyond the logics that the City Fathers use, check all the assessments for new implications needing complete rechecks—of which there will be thousands. . . .

"It'll take more than two years, and probably closer to five years, to do even a scratch job. The City Fathers will do their part of it in a few hours, and the rest of the time will be consumed by human brainwork. While that part of it's going on, we'll have it thin. But we've got it damn thin already, and when it's all over, we'll be able to write our own tickets, anywhere in the galaxy."

"A very good answer," Specht said. He spoke quietly, but each word whistled through the still, sweat-humid air like a thin missile. "Gentlemen, I believe the mayor of the nameless city is right."

"The hell he is!" the King howled, striding to the front of the dais and trying to wipe the air out of his way as he walked. "Who wants to sit for five years making like a pack of scientists while the Acolytes have us all digging ditches?"

"Who wants to be dispersed?" someone countered shrilly. "Who wants to pick a fight with Earth? Not me. I'll stay as far away from the Earth cops as I can. That's common sense for Okies."

"Cops!" the King shouted. "Cops look for single cities. What if a *thousand* cities marched on Earth? What cop would bother with one city on one disorderly conduct charge? If you were a cop and you saw a mob coming down at you, would you try to bust it up by pinching one man in it who'd run out on a Vacate order, or shaded a three per cent fruit-freezing contract? If that's common sense for Okies, I'll eat it.

"You guys are chicken, that's your trouble. You got

knocked around today and you hurt. You're tender. But you know damn well that the law exists to protect *you,* not scum like the Acolytes. It's a cinch we can't call the Earth cops here to protect us—the cops are too few for that, we're too few, and besides, we would get nabbed individually for whatever we've got written against us. But in a march of thousands of Okies—a peaceful march, to ask Earth to give you what belongs to you—you couldn't be touched individually. But you're scared! You'd rather squat in a jungle and die by pieces!"

"Not us!"

"Us neither!"

"When do we start?"

"That's more like it," the King said.

Specht's voice said, "Buda-Pesht, you're trying to drum up a stampede. The question isn't closed yet."

"All right," the King agreed. "I'm willing to be reasonable. Let's take a vote."

"We aren't ready for a vote yet. The question is still open."

"Well?" said the King. "You there on the overstuffed potty—you got anything more to say? Are you as afraid of a vote as Specht is?"

Amalfi got up with deliberate slowness.

"I've made my points, and I'll abide by the voting," he said, "if it's physically possible for us to do so—our spindizzy equipment wouldn't tolerate an immediate flight to Earth if the voting goes that way. I've made my point. A mass flight to Earth would be suicide."

"One moment," Specht's voice cut in again. "Before we vote, I for one want to know who it is that has been advising us. Buda-Pesht we know. But—*who are you?*"

There was instant dead silence in the throne room.

The question was loaded, as everyone in the hall knew. Prestige among Okies depended, in the long run, upon only two things: time aloft and coups recorded by the interstellar grapevine. Amalfi's city stood high on both tallies; he had only to identify his city, and he would stand at least an even chance of carrying the voting. Even while nameless, for that matter, the city had earned considerable kudos in the jungle.

Evidently Hazleton thought so, too, for Amalfi could see the frantic covert hand signals he was making. *Tell 'em, boss. It can't miss. Tell 'em!*

After a long, suspended heartbeat, the mayor said, "My name is John Amalfi, Mayor Specht."

A single broad comber of contempt rolled through the hall.

"Asked and answered," the King said, showing his ragged teeth. "Glad to have you aboard, Mister Amalfi. Now if you'll get the hell off the platform, we'll get on with the voting. But don't be in any hurry to leave town, Mister Amalfi. I want to talk to you, man to man. Understand?"

"Yeah," Amalfi said. He swung his huge bulk lightly to the floor of the hall, and walked back to where Dee and Hazleton were standing, hand in hand.

"Boss, why didn't you tell 'em?" Hazleton whispered, his face hard. "Or did you *want* to throw the whole show away? You had two beautiful chances, and you muffed 'em both!"

"Of course I muffed them. I came here to muff them. I came here to dynamite them, as a matter of fact. Now you and Dee had better get out of here before I have to give Dee to the King in order to get back to our city at all."

"You staged that, too, John," Dee said. It was not an accusation; it was simply a statement of fact.

"I'm afraid I did," Amalfi said. "I'm sorry, Dee; it had to be done, or I wouldn't have done it. I was also sure that I could fox the King on that point, if that's any consolation to you. Now move, or you will be sunk. Mark, make plenty of noise about getting away."

"What about you?" Dee said.

"I'll be along later. Git!"

Hazleton stared at Amalfi a moment longer. Then he turned and pushed back through the crowd, the frightened, reluctant girl at his heels. His method of being very noisy was characteristic of him: he was so completely silent that everyone within sight of him knew that he was making a getaway; even his footsteps made no sound at all. In the surging hall his noiselessness was as conspicuous as a siren in church.

Amalfi stood his ground long enough to let the King see that the principal hostage was still on hand, still obeying the letter of the King's order. Then, the moment the King's attention was distracted, he faded, moving with the local current in the crowd, bending his knees slightly to reduce his height, tipping his head back to point his conspicuous baldness away from the dias, and making only the normal amount of sound as he moved—becoming, in short, effectively invisible.

By this time the voting was in full course, and it would be five minutes at the least before the King could afford to interrupt it long enough to order the doors closed against Amalfi. After Hazleton's and Dee's ostentatiously alarmed exists, an emergency order in the middle of the voting would have made it painfully obvious what the King was after.

Of course, had the King had the foresight to equip himself with a personal transmitter before mounting the dais, the outcome might have been different. The King's failure to do so strengthened Amalfi's conviction that the King had not been mayor of Buda-Pesht long, and that he had not won the post by the usual processes.

But Dee and Hazleton would get out all right. So would Amalfi. On this limited subject, Amalfi had been six jumps ahead of the King all the way.

Amalfi drifted toward the part of the crowd from where, roughly, he estimated that the voice of the mayor of Dresden-Saxony had been coming. He found the worn, birdlike Slav without difficulty.

"You keep a tight holster-flap on your weapons," Specht said in a low voice.

"Sorry to disappoint you, Mayor Specht. You set it up beautifully. It might cheer you up a bit to know that the question *was* just the right one, all the same, and many thanks for it. In return I owe you the answer; are you good at riddles?"

"Riddles?"

"Raetseln," Amalfi translated.

"Oh—conundrums. No, but I can try."

"What city has two names twice?"

Evidently Specht did not need to be good at riddles to come up with the answer to that one. His jaw dropped. "You're N——" he began.

Amalfi held up his hand in the conventional Okie FYI sign: "For your information *only*." Specht gulped and nodded. With a grin, Amalfi drifted on out of the palace.

There was a lot of hard work still ahead, but from now on it should be all downhill. The "march" on Earth would be carried in the voting.

Nothing essential remained to be done now in the jungle but to turn the march into a stampede.

By the time he reached his own city, Amalfi found he was suddenly intensely tired. He berthed the second gig Hazleton had had the perimeter sergeant send for him and went directly to his room, where he ordered his supper sent up.

This last move, he was forced to conclude, had been a mistake. The city's stores were heavily diminished, and the table that was set for him—set, as it would have been for anyone else in the city, by the City Fathers with complete knowledge of his preferences—was meager and uninteresting. It included fuming Rigellian wine, which he despised as a drink for barbarians; such a choice could only mean that there was nothing else to drink in the city but water.

His weariness, the solitude, the direct transition from the audience hall of the Hapsburgs to his bare new room under the mast in the Empire State Building—it had been an elevator-winch housing until the city had converted to friction-fields—and the dullness of the meal combined to throw him into a rare and deep state of depression. What he thought he could see of the future of Okie cities did not exactly cheer him, either.

It was at this point that the door to his room irised open, and Hazleton stalked silently through it, hooking his chromoclav back into his belt.

They looked at each other stonily for a moment. Amalfi pointed to a chair.

"Sorry, boss," Hazleton said, without moving. "I've never used my key before except in an emergency, you know that. But I think maybe this is an emergency. We're in a bad way—and the way you're dealing with the problem strikes me as crazy. For the survival of the city, I want to be taken into your confidence."

"Sit down," Amalfi said. "Have some Rigel wine."

Hazleton made a wry face and sat down.

"You're in my confidence, as always, Mark. I don't leave you out of my plans except where I think you might shoot from the hip if I didn't. You'll agree that you've done that occasionally—and *don't* throw up the Thor Five situation again, because there I was on your side; it was the City Fathers that objected to that particular Hazleton gimmick."

"Granted."

"Good," Amalfi said. "Tell me what you want to know, then."

"Up to a point I understand what you're out to do," Hazleton said without preamble. "Your use of Dee as a safe-conduct in and out of the meeting was a shrewd trick. Considering the political threat we represented to the King, it was probably the only thing you could have done. Understand, I resent it personally and I may yet pay you off for it. But it was necessary, I agree."

"Good," the mayor said wearily. "But that's a minor point, Mark."

"Granted, except on the personal level. The main thing is that you threw away the whole chance you schemed so hard to get. The knowledge-pooling plan was a good one, and you had two major chances to put it across. First of all, the King set you up to claim we were Vegan—nobody has ever actually seen that fort, and physically you're enough unlike the normal run of humanity to pass for a Vegan without much trouble. Dee and I don't look Vegan, but we might be atypical, or maybe renegades.

"But you threw that one away. Then the mayor from Dresden-Saxony set you up to swing almost everybody our way by letting them know our name. If you'd followed through, you would have carried the voting. Hell, you'd probably have wound up king of the jungle to boot.

"And you threw that one away, too."

Hazleton took his slide rule out of his pocket and moodily pushed the slide back and forth in it. It was a gesture frequent enough with him, but ordinarily it preceded or followed some use of the rule. Tonight it was obviously just nervous play.

"But Mark, I didn't want to be king of the jungle," Amalfi said slowly. "I'd much rather let the present incumbent hold that responsibility. Every crime that's ever been committed, or will be committed in the near future, in this jungle, will be laid at his door eventually by the Earth cops. On top of that, the Okies here will hold him personally responsible for every misfortune that comes their way while they're in the jungle. I never did want that job; I only wanted the King to think that I wanted it. . . . Incidentally, did you try to raise that city out on the perimeter, the one that said it had mass chromatography?"

"Sure," Hazleton said. "They don't answer."

"Okay. Now, about this knowledge-pooling plan: it wouldn't work, Mark. First of all, you couldn't keep a pack of Okies working at it long enough to get any good out of it. Okies aren't philosophers, and they aren't scientists except in a limited way. They're engineers and merchants; in some respects they're adventurers, too, but they don't think of themselves as adventurers. They're *practical*—that's the word they use. You've heard it."

"I've used it," Hazleton said edgily.

"So have I. There's a great deal of meaning packed into it. It means, among other things, that if you get Okies involved in a major analytical project, they'll get restive. They want sets of applications of principles, not principles pure and useless. And it isn't in their natures to sit still in one place for long. If you convince them that they should, they'll try, and the whole thing will wind up in a terrific explosion.

"But that's only point one. Mark, have you any idea of the real scope of the knowledge-pooling project? I'm *not* trying to put you on the spot, believe me. I don't think anybody in that hall realized it. If they had, they'd have laughed me off the platform. There again, Okies aren't scientists, and their outlook is too impatient to let them carry a really long chain of reasoning to a conclusion."

"You're an Okie," Hazleton pointed out. "You carried it to a conclusion. You told them how long it would take."

"I'm an Okie. I told them it would take from two to five years to do even a scratch job. As an Okie, I'm an expert at half-truths. It would take from two to five years even to get the project set up! And the rest of the job, Mark, would take *centuries*."

"For a scratch job?"

"No such thing as a scratch job in this universe of discourse," Amalfi said, reaching for the fuming wine and reconsidering at the last minute. "Those cities out there represent the accumulated scientific knowledge of all the high-technical-level cultures they've ever encountered. Even allowing for the usual information gaps, that's about five thousand planets-full of data, at a minimum estimate. Sure, we could pool all that knowledge—just as I said at the meeting, the City Fathers could take it all in, and classify it, in only a little over an hour—*after we'd spent two to five years setting them up to do it*. And then we'd have to integrate it. And you've got to integrate it, Mark; you've got to know it thoroughly enough to be able to make it *do* something. You couldn't offer it for sale unless you did that. Would you like the job?"

"No," Hazleton said slowly, but at once. "But Amalfi, am I ever going to know what you're doing if you persist in proceeding like this? You didn't go to that meeting just to waste time; I can trust you that far. So I have to assume that the whole maneuver was a trick, designed to force the March on Earth, rather than to defeat it. You gave the cities a clearly defined, superficially sound, and less-attractive alternative. Once they had rejected the alternative, they had committed themselves to the King's tactics, without knowing it."

"That's quite right."

"If that's right," Hazleton said, looking up suddenly with a flat flash of almost-violet eyes, "I think it's stupid. I think it's stupid even though it was marvelously devious. There's such a thing as outsmarting yourself."

Amalfi said, "That could be. In any event, if the choice had been limited to marching on Earth versus staying in the jungle, the cities would have stayed in the jungle. Would it have been sensible to allow that?"

"We can't afford to stay in the jungle, anyhow."

"Of course we can't. And by the same token, we couldn't leave it by ourselves. The only way we could get free of this star cluster is in the middle of a mass movement. What else could I have been shooting for?"

"I don't know," Hazleton said. "But there's something else besides that in the back of your head."

"And your complaint is that you don't know about it in advance. I know why you don't know. You know, too."

"Dee?"

"Certainly," Amalfi said. "You weren't asking yourself the right question. You were emotionally driven to ask why I wanted Dee along. The question was pertinent enough, but it wasn't exactly central. If you had stood back a little further from the *whole* problem, you'd have seen why I wanted the March on Earth to go through, too."

"I'll keep trying," Hazleton said grimly. "Though I'd have preferred to be told. You and I are getting further apart every year, boss. It used to be that we thought very much alike; and it was then that you developed your habit of not telling me the whole story. It was a training device, I think now. The more I was made to worry about the total plan, the more I was required to think the thing out for myself—which meant trying to figure *you* out—the more training I got in thinking like you. And of course, to be a proper city manager, I had to think like you. You had to be sure that any decisions I made in your absence would be the decisions you would have made had you been around.

"All this hit me after our tangle with the Duchy of Gort. That incident was the first time that you and I had been out of touch with each other long enough for a situation of really major proportions to develop—a situation about which I knew very little until I could get back to the city from Utopia and get briefed.

"When I got back, I found that I was damn lucky *not* to have thought like you. My first failure to comprehend your whole plan—and your training method of leaving me to puzzle things out alone—apparently had doomed me in your mind. You had written me off, and you were training Carrel as my successor."

"All this is accurate reportage," Amalfi said. "If you mean to accuse me of keeping a hard school——"

"——a fool will learn in no other?"

"No. A fool won't learn at all. But I don't deny keeping a hard school. Go on."

"I haven't far to go, now. I learned in the Gort-Utopia system that thinking the way you think can sometimes be deadly for me. I got off Utopia by thinking *my* way, not yours. The confirmation came when we hit He; had I been thinking entirely like you in that situation, we'd still be on the planet."

"Mark, you still haven't made your point. I can tell. It's perfectly true that we often relied on your plans, and precisely because they come from a mind most unlike my own. What of it?"

"This of it. You're now out to rub out whatever trace of originality I have. You used to value it, as you say. You used to use it for the city, and defend it against the City Fathers when they had an attack of conservatism. But now you've changed, and so have I.

"These days, I seem to be tending toward thinking more and more like a human being, with human concerns. I don't feel like Hazleton the master conniver any more, except in flashes. The opposite change is taking place in you. You're becoming more and more alienated from human concerns. When you look at people, you see—machines. After a little more of this, we won't be able to tell you from the City Fathers."

Amalfi tried to think about it. He was very tired, and he felt old. It was not yet time for his anti-agathic shot, not by more than a decade, but knowing that he would probably not get it made the centuries he had already traversed weigh heavily upon his back.

"Or maybe I'm beginning to think that I'm a god," he said. "You accused me of that on Murphy. Have you ever tried to imagine, Mark, how completely crippling it is to any man's humanity to be the mayor of an Okie city for hundreds of years? I suppose you have—your own responsibilities aren't lighter than mine, only a little different. Let me ask you this, then: isn't it obvious that this change in you dates from the day when Dee first came on board?"

"Of course it's obvious," Hazleton said, looking up sharply. "It dates from the Utopia-Gort affair. That's when Dee came on board; she was a Utopian. Are you about to tell me that *she's* to blame?"

"Shouldn't it also be obvious," Amalfi continued, with weary implacability, "that the converse change in me dates from the same event? Gods of all stars, Mark, *don't you know that I love Dee, too?*"

Hazleton froze and went white. He looked rigidly with suddenly blind eyes at the remains of Amalfi's miserable supper. After a long time, he laid his slide rule on the table as delicately as if it were made of spun sugar.

"I do know," he said, at long last. "I did know. But I didn't—want to know that I knew."

Amalfi spread his big hands in a gesture of helplessness he had not had to use for more than half a century. The city manager did not seem to notice.

"That being the case," Hazleton resumed, his voice suddenly much tighter, "that being so, Amalfi, I——"

He stopped.

"You needn't rush, Mark. Actually it doesn't change things much. Take your time."

"Amalfi—*I want off.*"

Each evenly spaced word struck Amalfi like the strokes of a mallet against a gong, the strokes which, timed exactly to the gong's vibration period, drive it toward shattering. Amalfi had expected anything but those three words. They told him that he had had no real idea of how helpless he had become.

I want off was the traditional formula by which a starman renounced the stars. The Okie who spoke them cut himself off forever from the cities, and from the long swooping lines of the ingeodesics that the cities followed through space-time. The Okie who spoke them became planet-bound.

And—it was entirely final. The words were seared into Okie law. *I want off* could never be refused—nor retracted.

"You have it," Amalfi said. "Naturally. I won't tax you with being hasty, since it's too late."

"Thanks."

"Well, where do you want it? On the nearest planet, or at the city's next port of call?"

These, too, were merely the traditional alternatives, but Hazleton didn't seem to relish either of them. His lips were white, and he seemed to be trembling slightly.

"That," he said, "depends on where you're planning to go next. You haven't yet told me."

Hazleton's disturbance disturbed Amalfi, too, more than he liked to recognize. Mechanically, it would almost surely be possible for the ex-city manager to withdraw his decision; and mechanically, it would be possible to make the suggestion to Hazleton. Those three words had been neither overheard nor recorded as far as Amalfi knew, except —a small chance—by the treacher, the section of the City Fathers which handled tablewaiting. Even there, however, the City Fathers wouldn't be likely to scan the treacher's memory bank more than once every five years. The treacher had nothing interesting to remember but the eating preference patterns of the Okies, and such patterns change slowly and, for the most part, insignificantly. No, the City Fathers need not know that Hazleton had resigned, not for a while yet.

But allowing the city manager to back down did not even occur to Amalfi; the mayor was too thoroughly an Okie for that. Had it been proposed to him, Almalfi would have objected that the uttering of those three words had put Hazleton as totally under Amalfi's smallest command as was a private in the city's perimeter police; and he could have shown reasons why subservience of that kind was now required of Hazleton. He could also have shown that those three words could never be actually revoked, however closely they were kept a secret between Hazleton and himself; if pressed, he could have shown that he could never forget them, and that Hazleton couldn't either. He might have explained that, every time Amalfi decided against a plan of Hazleton's, the city manager would put it down to secret rancor against that smothered resignation. Or, being Amalfi, he might merely have noted that the conflict between the two men had already been deep-running, and that after Hazleton had said, "I want off," it would become outright pathological.

Actually, however, no one of these things entered his mind. Hazleton had said, "I want off." Amalfi was an Okie, and for an Okie, "I want off" is final.

"No," the mayor said, at once. "You've asked for off, and that's the end of it. You're no longer entitled to any knowledge of city policy or plans, except for what reaches you in the form of directives. Now's the time when you can use your training in thinking like me, Mark—obviously you'll have no difficulty in thinking like the City Fathers—because it'll be your only source of information on policy from now on."

"I understand," Hazleton said formally. He stood silent a moment longer. Amalfi waited.

"At the next port of call, then," Hazleton said.

"All right. Until then, you're outgoing city manager. Put Carrel back into training as your successor, and begin feeding the City Fathers predisposing data toward him now. I don't want any more fuss from them when the election is held than we had when you were elected."

Hazleton's expression became slightly more set. "Right."

"Secondly, get the city moving toward the perimeter to intersect the town you couldn't raise. I'll want an orbit that gives us logarithmic acceleration, with all the real drive concentrated at the far end. On the way, ready two work teams: one for a fast spindizzy assessment, the other to run up whatever's necessary on the mass chromatography equipment, whatever that may be. Include medium-heavy dismounting tools, below the graving dock size, but heavy enough to handle any job less drastic."

"Right."

"Also, ready Sergeant Anderson's squad, in case that city isn't quite as dead as it sounds."

"Right," Hazleton said again.

"That's it," Amalfi said.

Hazleton nodded stiffly, and made as if to turn. Then, astonishingly, his stiff face exploded into a torrential passion of speech.

"Boss, tell me this before I go," he said, clenching his fists. "Was all this to push me into asking for off? Couldn't you think of any way of keeping your plans to yourself but kicking me out—or making me kick myself out? I don't believe this love story of yours, damned if I do. You know I'll take Dee with me when I disembark. And the Great Renunciation is just slop, just pure fiction, especially coming from you. You aren't any more in love with Dee than I am with you——"

And then Hazleton turned so white that Amalfi thought for a moment that the man was about to faint.

"Score one for you, Mark," Amalfi said. "Evidently I'm not the only one who's staging a Great Renunciation."

"Gods of all stars, Amalfi!"

"There are none," Amalfi said. "I can't do anything more, Mark. I've said good-by to you a hell of a lot of times, but this has to be the last time—not by my election, but by yours. Go and get the jobs done."

Hazleton said, "Right." He spun and strode out. The door reached full dilation barely in time.

Amalfi sighed as deeply as a sleeping child. Then he flipped the treacher switch from *set* to *clear*. The treacher said, "Will that be all, sir?"

"What do you want to do, poison me twice at the same meal?" Amalfi growled. "Get me an ultraphone line."

The treacher's voice changed at once. "Communications," it said briskly.

"This is the mayor. Raise Lieutenant Lerner, Forty-fifth Acolyte Border Security Group. Don't give up too easily; that was his last address, but he's been upgraded since. When you get him, tell him you're speaking for me. Tell him also that the cities in the jungle are organizing for some sort of military action, and that if he can get a squadron in here fast enough, he can break it up. Got it?"

"Yes, sir." The Communications man read it back. "If you say so, Mayor Amalfi."

"Who else would say so? Be sure Lerner doesn't get a fix on us. Send it pulse-modulated if you can."

"Can't, boss. Mr. Hazleton just put us under way. But there's a powerful Acolyte AM ultraphone station somewhere near by. I can get our message into synch with it, and make the cop's detectors focus on the vector. Is that good enough?"

"Better, even," Amalfi said. "Hop to it."

"There's one other thing, boss. That big drone you ordered last year is finally finished, and the shop says that it has Dirac equipment mounted in it and ready to go. I've inspected it and it looks fine, except that it's as big as a lifeship and just as detectable."

"All right, good; but that can wait. Get the message out."

"Yes, sir."

The voice cut out entirely. The incinerator chute gaped suddenly, and the dishes rose from the table and soared toward the opening in solemn procession. The goblet of wine left behind a miasmic trail, like a miniature comet.

At the last minute, Amalfi jerked out of his reverie and made a wild grab in mid-air; but he was too late. The chute gulped down that final item and shut again with a satisfied slam.

Hazleton had left his slide rule upon the table.

The space-suited party moved cautiously and with grim faces through the black, dead streets of the city on the periphery. At the lead, Sergeant Anderson's hand torch flashed into a doorway and flicked out again at once.

No other lights whatsoever could be seen in the dark city, nor had there been any response to calls. Except for a weak spindizzy field, no power flowed in the city at all, and even the screen was too feeble to maintain the city's air pressure above four pounds per square inch—hence the space suits.

Inside Amalfi's helmet O'Brian's voice was saying, "The second phase is about to start in the jungle, Mr. Mayor. Lerner moved in on them with what looks from here like all of the Acolyte navy he dared to pull out of the cluster itself. There's an admiral's flagship in the fleet, but all the big brass is doing is relaying Lerner's suggestions in the form of orders; he seems to have no ideas of his own."

"Sensible setup," Amalfi said, peering ahead unsuccessfully in the gloom.

"As far as it goes, sir. The thing is, the squadron itself is far too big for the job. It's unwieldly, and the jungle detected it well in advance; we stood ready to give the alarm to the King as you ordered, but it didn't prove necessary. The cities are drawing up in a rough battle formation now. It's quite a sight, even through the proxies. First time in history, isn't it?"

"As far as I know. Does it look like it'll work?"

"No, sir," the proxy pilot said promptly. "Whatever organization the King's worked out, it's functioning only partially, and damn sloppily. Cities are too clumsy for this kind of work even under the best hand, and his is a long way from the best, I'd judge. But we'll soon see for ourselves."

"Right. Give me another report in an hour."

Anderson held up his hand and the party halted. Ahead was a huge pile of ultimately solid blackness, touched deceptively here and there with feeble stars where windows threw back reflections. Far aloft, however, one window glowed softly with its own light.

The boarding-squad men deployed quickly along opposite sides of the street while the technies took cover. Amalfi sidled along the near wall to where the sergeant was crouching.

"What do you think, Anderson?"

"I don't like it, Mr. Mayor. It stinks of mouse traps. Maybe everybody's dead and the last man didn't have the strength to turn out the light. On the other hand, just *one* light left burning for that reason, in the whole city?"

"I see what you mean. Dulany, take five men down that side street where the facsimile pillar is, follow it until you're tangent to the corner of this building up ahead, and stick out a probe. Don't use more than a couple of micro-volts, or you might get burned."

"Yessir." Dulany's squad—the man himself might best be described as a detector-detector—slipped away soundlessly, shadows among shadows.

"That isn't all I stopped us for, Mr. Mayor," Anderson said. "There's a grounded aircab just around the corner here. It's got a dead passenger in it. I wish you'd take a look at him."

Amalfi took the proffered torch, covered its lens with

the mitten of his suit so that only a thin shred of light leaked through and played it for half a second through the cab's window. He felt his spine going rigid.

Wherever the light touched the flesh of the hunched corpse, it—glistened.

"Communications!"

"Yes, sir!"

"Set up the return port for decontamination. Nobody gets back on board our town until he's been boiled alive—understand? I want the works."

There was a brief silence. Then: "Mr. Mayor, the city manager already has that in the works."

Amalfi grimaced wryly in the darkness. Anderson said, "Pardon me, sir, but—how did Mr. Hazleton guess?"

"Why, that's not too hard to see, at least after the fact, sergeant. This city we're on was desperately poor. And being poor under the new money system means being low on drugs. The end result, as Mr. Hazleton saw, and I should have seen, is—plague."

"The sons of bitches," the sergeant said bitterly. The epithet seemed intended to apply to every non-Okie in the universe.

At the same moment, a lurid scarlet glare splashed over his face and the front of his suit, and red lanes of light checkered the street. There was an almost-simultaneous flat crash, without weight in the thin air, but ugly-sounding.

"TDX!" Anderson shouted, involuntarily.

"Dulany? Dulany! Damn it all, I told the man to take it easy with that probe. Whoever survived on that squad, report!"

Underneath the ringing in Amalfi's ears, someone began to laugh. It was as ugly a sound as the TDX explosion had been. There was no other answer.

"All right, Anderson, surround this place. Communications, get the rest of the boarding squad and half the security police over here on the double."

The nasty laughter got louder.

"Whoever you are that's putting out that silly giggle, you're going to learn how to make another kind of noise when I get my hands on you," Amalfi added viciously. "Nobody uses TDX on my men, I don't care whether he's an Okie or a cop. Get me? Nobody!"

The laughter stopped. Then a cracked voice said, "You lousy damned vultures."

"Vultures, is it?" Amalfi snapped. "If you'd answered our calls in the first place, there'd have been no trouble. Why don't you come to your senses? Do you *want* to die of the pestilence?"

"Vultures," the voice repeated. It carried an overtone of sinister idiocy. "Eaters of carrion. The gods of all stars will boil your bones for soup." The cackling began again.

Amalfi felt a faint chill. He switched to tight-beam. "Anderson, keep your men at a respectable distance, and wait for the reinforcements. This place is obviously mined to the teeth, and I don't know what other surprises our batty friend has for us."

"I could lob a gas grenade through that window——"

"Don't you suppose they're wearing suits, too? Just ring the place and sit tight."

"Check."

Amalfi squatted down upon his hams behind the aircab, sweating. There just might be enough power left in the accumulators here to put up a Bethé fender around the building, but that wasn't the main thing on his mind. This business of boarding another Okie city was easily the hardest operation he had ever had to direct. Every move went against the grain. The madman's accusation had hit him in his most vulnerable spot.

After what seemed like a whole week, his helmet ultraphone said, "Proxy room. Mr. Mayor, the jungle beat off Lerner's first wave. I didn't think they could do it. They got in one good heavy lick at the beginning—blew two heavy cruisers right out of the sky—and the Acolytes act scared green. The admiral's launch has run out completely, and left Lerner holding the bag."

"Losses?"

"Four cities definitely wiped out. We haven't enough proxies out to estimate cities damaged with any accuracy, but Lerner had a group of about thirty towns enfiladed when the first cruiser got it."

"You haven't got the big drone out there, have you?" the mayor said in sudden alarm.

"No, sir; Communications ordered that one left berthed. I'm waiting now to see when the next Acolyte wave gets rolling; I'll call you as——"

CITIES IN FLIGHT

The proxy pilot's voice snapped off, and the stars went out.

There was a shout of alarm from some technie in the party. Amalfi got up cautiously and looked overhead. The single window in the big building which had shown a light was blacked out now, too.

"What the hell happened, Mr. Mayor?" Anderson's voice said quietly.

"A local spindizzy screen, at at least half-drive. Probably they've dropped their main screen entirely. Everybody keep to cover—there may be flares."

The laughter began again.

"Vultures," the voice said. "Little mangy vultures in a big tight cage."

Amalfi cut back in on the open radio band. "You're going to wreck your city," he said steadily. "And once you tear this section of it loose, your power will fail and your screen will go down again. You can't win, and you know it."

The street began to tremble. It was only a faint trembling now, but there was no telling how long the basic structure of the dead city could hold this one small area in place against the machine that was trying to fling it away into space. Hazleton, of course, would rush over a set of portable nutcrackers as soon as he had seen what had happened—but whether this part of the city would still be here when the nutcrackers arrived was an open question.

In the meantime, there was exactly nothing Amalfi could do about it. Even his contact with his own city was cut off.

"It isn't your city," the voice said, suddenly deceptively reasonable. "It's our city. You're hijacking us. But we won't let you."

"How were we supposed to know any of you were still alive?" Amalfi demanded angrily. "You didn't answer our calls. Is it our fault if you didn't hear them? We thought this town was open for salvage——"

His voice was abruptly obliterated by a new one, enormous yet familiar, which came slamming into his helmet as if it intended to drive him out of his suit entirely.

"EARTH POLICE AA EMERGENCY ACOLYTE CLUSTER CONDENSATION XIII ARM BETA," it thundered. "SYSTEM UNDER ATTACK BY MASS ARMY OF TRAMP CITIES. POLICE AID URGENTLY NEEDED. LERNER LIEUTENANT FORTY-FIFTH

Border Security Group acting commander cluster defense forces. Acknowledge."

Amalfi whistled soundlessly through his teeth. There was evidently a Dirac transceiver in operation somewhere inside the close-drawn spindizzy screen, or his helmet phones wouldn't have caught Lerner's yell for help; Diracs were too bulky for the usual proxy, let alone for a space suit. By the same token, everybody else in the galaxy possessing Dirac equipment had heard that yell—it had been the instantaneous propagation of Dirac pulses that had dealt the death blow to the West's hypercomplex relativity theories millennia ago.

And if a Dirac sender was open inside this bubble . . .

"Lerner Acolyte Defense Forces your message in. Squadron assigned your condensation on way. Hang on. Beta Arm Command Earth."

. . . then Amalfi could use it. He flipped the chest switch and shouted, "Hazleton, are your nutcrackers rolling?"

"Rolling, boss," Hazleton shot back instantly. "Another ninety seconds and——"

"Too late, this sector will tear loose before then. Tune up our own screen to twenty-four per cent and hold——"

He realized suddenly that he was shouting into a dead mike. The Okies here had caught on belatedly to what was happening, and had cut the power to their Dirac. Had that last, crucial, incomplete sentence gotten through, even a fragment of it? Or . . .

Deep down under Amalfi's feet an alarming sound began to rise. It was part screech, part monstrous rockslide, part prolonged and hollow groan. Amalfi's teeth began to itch in their sockets, and his bowels stirred slightly. He grinned.

The message had gotten through—or enough of it to enable Hazleton to guess the rest. The one spindizzy holding this field was going sour. Against the combined power of the nearby drivers of Amalfi's city, it could no longer maintain the clean space-lattice curvature it was set for.

"You're sunk," Amalfi told the invisible defenders quietly. "Give up now, and you'll not be hurt. I'll skip the TDX incident—Dulany was one of my best men, but maybe there was some reason on your side, too. Come on over with us, and you'll have a city to call your own again. This one isn't any good to you any more, that's obvious."

There was no answer.

Patterns began to race across the close-pressing black sky. The nutcrackers—portable generators designed to heterodyne a spindizzy field to the overload point—were being brought to bear. The single tortured spindizzy howled with anguish.

"Speak up, up there," Amalfi said. "I'm trying to be fair, but if you force me to drive you out——"

"Vultures," the cracked voice sobbed.

The window aloft lit up with a searing glare and burst outward. A long tongue of red flame winnowed out over the street. The spindizzy screen went down at once, and with it the awful noise from the city's power deck; but it was several minutes before Amalfi's dazzled eyes could see the stars again.

He stared up at the exploded scar on the side of the building, outlined in orange heat swiftly dimming. He felt a little sick.

"TDX again," he said softly. "Consistent to the last, the poor sick idiots."

"Mr. Mayor?"

"Here."

"This is the proxy room. There's a regular stampede going on in the jungle. The cities are streaming away from the red star as fast as they can tune up. No discernible order—just a mob, and a panicky mob, too. No signs of anything being done for the wounded cities; and it looks to me like they're just being left for Lerner to break up as soon as he gets up enough courage."

Amalfi nodded to himself. "All right, O'Brian, launch the big drone now. I want that drone to go with those cities and stick with them all the way. Pilot it personally; it's highly detectable, and there'll probably be several attempts to destroy it, so be ready to dodge."

"I will, sir. Mr. Hazleton just launched her a moment ago; I'm giving her the gun right now."

For some reason this did not improve Amalfi's temper in the least.

The Okies set to work rapidly, dismounting the dead city's spindizzies from their bases and shipping them into storage on board their own city. The one which had been overdriven in that last futile defense had to be left behind, of course; like the Twenty-third Street machine, it was hot and could not be approached, except by a graving dock.

The rest went over as whole units. Hazleton looked more and more puzzled as the big machines came aboard, but he seemed resolved to ask no questions.

Carrel, however, suffered under no such self-imposed restraints. "What are we going to do with all these dismounted drivers?" he said. All three men stood in a sally port at the perimeter of their city, watching the ungainly bulks being floated across.

"We're going to fly another planet," Hazleton said flatly.

"You bet we are," Amalfi agreed. "And pray to your star gods that we're in time, Mark."

Hazleton didn't answer.

Carrel said, "In time for what?"

"That I won't say until I have it right under my nose on a screen. It's a hunch, and I think it's a good one. In the meantime, take my word for it that we're in a hurry, like we've never been in a hurry before. What's the word on that mass chromatography apparatus, Hazleton?"

"It's a reverse-English on the zone-melting process for refining germanium, boss. You take a big column of metal—which metal doesn't matter, as long as it's pure—and contaminate one end of it with the stuff you want to separate out. Then you run a disc-shaped electric field up the column from the contaminated end, and the contaminants are carried along by resistance heating and separate out at various points along the bar. To get pure fractions, you cut the bar apart with a power saw."

"But does it work?"

"Nah," Hazleton said. "It's just what we've seen a thousand times before. Looks good in theory, but not even the guys who owned this city could make it go."

"Another Lyran invisibility machine—or no-fuel drive," the mayor said, nodding. "Too bad; a process like that would be useful. Is the equipment massive?"

"Enormous. The area it occupies is twelve city blocks on a side."

"Leave it there," Amalfi decided at once. "Obviously this outfit was bragging from desperation when it offered the technique for the Acolyte woman's job. If she'd taken them up on it, they wouldn't have been able to deliver—and I don't care to lead us into any such temptation."

"In this case the knowledge is as good as the equipment," Hazleton said. "Their City Fathers will have all the information we could possibly worry out of the apparatus itself."

"Would somebody give me the pitch on this exodus of cities from the jungle?" Carrel put in. "I wasn't along on your trip to the King's city, and I still think the whole idea of a March on Earth is crazy."

Amalfi remained silent. After a moment, Hazleton said, "It is and it isn't. The jungle doesn't dare stand up to a real Earth force and slug it out, and everybody knows now that there's an Earth force on its way here. The cities want to be somewhere else in a hurry. But they still have some hope of getting Earth protection from the Acolyte cops and similar local organizations if they can put their case before the authorities outside of a trouble area."

"That," Carrel said, "is just what I don't see. What hope do they have of getting a fair shuffle? And why don't they just contact Earth on the Dirac, as Lerner did, instead of making this long trip? It's sixty-three hundred or so light years from here to Earth, and they aren't organized well enough to make such a long haul without a lot of hardship."

"And they'll do all their talking with Earth over the Dirac even after they get there," Amalfi added. "Partly, of course, this march is sheer theatricalism. The King hopes that such a big display of cities will make an impression on the people he'll be talking to. Don't forget that Earth is a quiet, rather idyllic world these days—a skyful of ragged cities will create a lot of alarm there.

"As for getting a square shuffle: the King is relying on a tradition of at least moderately fair dealing that goes back many centuries. Don't forget, Carrel, that for the last thousand years the Okie cities have been the major unifying force in our entire galactic culture."

"That's news to me," Carrel said, a little dubiously.

"But it's quite true. Do you know what a bee is? Well, it's a little Earth insect that sucks nectar from flowers. While it's about it, it picks up pollen and carries it about; it's a prime factor in cross-fertilization of plants. Most habitable planets have similar insects. The bee doesn't know that he's essential to the ecology of his world—all he's out to do is collect as much honey as he can—but that doesn't make him any less essential.

"The cities have been like the bee for a long time. The governments of the advanced planets, Earth in particular, know it, even if the cities generally don't. The planets distrust the cities, but they also know that they're vital and must be protected. The planets are tough on bindlestiffs for the same reason. The bindlestiffs are diseased bees; the taint that they carry gets fastened upon innocent cities, cities that are needed to keep new techniques and other essential information on the move from planet to planet. Obviously, cities and planets alike have to protect themselves from criminal outfits, but there's the culture as a whole to be considered, as well as the safety of an individual unit; and to maintain that culture, the free passage of legitimate Okies throughout the galaxy has to be maintained."

"The King knows this?" Carrel said.

"Of course he does. He's eight hundred years old; how could he help but know it? He wouldn't put it like this, but all the same, it's the essence of what he's depending upon to carry through his March on Earth."

"It still sounds risky to me," Carrel said dubiously. "We've all been conditioned almost from birth to distrust Earth, and Earth cops especially——"

"Only because the cops distrust us. That means that the cops are conditioned to be strict with cities about the smallest violations; so, since small violations of local laws are inevitable in a nomadic life, it's smart for an Okie to steer clear of cops. But for all the real hatred that exists between Okies and cops, we're both on the same side. We always have been."

On the underside of the city, just within the cone of vision of the three men, the big doors to the main hold swung slowly shut.

"That's the last one," Hazleton said. "Now I suppose we go back to where we left the all-purpose city we stole from Murphy, and relieve it of its drivers, too."

"Yes, we do," Amalfi said. "And after that, Mark, we go on to Hern Six. Carrel, ready a couple of small fission bombs for the Acolyte garrison there—it can't be large enough to make us much trouble, but we've no time left to play patty-cake."

"Is Hern Six the planet we're going to fly?" Carrel said.

"It has to be," Amalfi said, with a trace of impatience. "It's the only one available. Furthermore, this time we're going to have to control the flight, not just let the planet scoot off anywhere its natural converted rotation wants it to go. Being carried clean out of the galaxy once is once too often for me."

"Then I'd better put a crack team to work on the control problem with the City Fathers," Hazleton said. "Since we didn't have them to consult with on He, we'll have to screen every scrap of pertinent information they have in stock. No wonder you've been so hot on this project for corralling knowledge from other cities. I only wish we could have gotten started on integrating it sooner."

"I haven't had this in mind quite that long," Amalfi said. "But, believe me, I'm not sorry now that it turned out this way."

Carrel said, "Where are we going?"

Amalfi turned away toward the airlock. He had heard the question before, from Dee, but this was the first time that he had had an answer.

"Home," he said.

CHAPTER SEVEN: Hern VI

MOUNTING Hern VI—as desolate and damned a slab of rock as Amalfi had ever set down upon—for guided spindizzy flight was incredibly tedious work. Drivers had to be spotted accurately at every major compass point, and locked solidly to the center of gravity of the planetoid; and then each and every machine had to be tuned and put into balance with every other. And there were not enough spindizzies to set up a drive for the planet as a whole which would be fully dirigible when the day of flight came. The flight of Hern VI, when all the work was finally done, promised to be giddy and erratic.

But at least it would go approximately where the master space stick directed it to go. That much responsiveness, Amalfi thought, was all that was really necessary— or all that he hoped would be necessary.

Periodically, O'Brian, the proxy pilot, reported on the progress of the March on Earth. The mob had lost quite a few stragglers along the way as it passed attractive-looking systems where work might be found, but the main body was still streaming doggedly toward the mother planet. Though the outsize drone was as obvious a body as a minor moon, so far not a single Okie had taken a pot shot at it. O'Brian had kept it darting through and about the marchers in a double-sine curve in three dimensions, at its top speed and with progressive modulations of the orbit. If the partial traces which it made on any individual city's radar screen were not mistaken for meteor tracks, predicting its course closely enough to lay a gun on it would keep any ordinary computer occupied full time.

It was a superb job of piloting. Amalfi made a mental note to see to it that the task of piloting the city itself was split off from the city manager's job when Hazleton stepped down. Carrel was not a born pilot, and O'Brian was obviously the man Carrel would need.

At the beginning of the Hern VI conversion, the City Fathers had placed E-Day—the day of arrival of the marchers within optical telescope distance of Earth—at one hundred fifty-five years, four months, twenty days. Each report which came in from the big drone's pilot cut this co-ordinate-set back toward the flying present as the migrating jungle lost its laggards and became more and more compact, more and more able to put on speed as a unit. Amalfi consumed cigars faster and drove his men and machines harder every time the new computation was delivered to his desk.

But a full year had gone by since installation had started on Hern VI before O'Brian sent up the report he had been dreading and yet counting upon to arrive sooner or later.

"The march has lost two more cities to greener pastures, Mr. Amalfi," the proxy pilot said. "But that's routine. We've gained a city, too."

"Gained one?" Amalfi said tensely. "Where'd it come from?"

"I don't know. The course I've got the drone on doesn't allow me to look in any one direction more than about twenty-five seconds at a time. I have to take a census every time I pass her through the pack. The last time I went around, there was this outfit on the screen, just as if it had been there all the time. But that isn't all. It's the damnedest looking city I've ever seen, and I can't find anything like it in the files, either."

"Describe it."

"For one thing, it's enormous. I'm not going to have to worry about anybody spotting my drone for a while. This outfit must have every detector in the jungle screaming blue bloody murder. Besides, it's closed up."

"What do you mean by that?"

"It's got a smooth hull all around, Mr. Mayor. It isn't the usual platform with buildings on it and a spindizzy screen around both. It's more like a proper spaceship, except for its size."

"Any communication between it and the pack?"

"About what you'd expect. Wants to join the march; the King gave it the okay. I think he was pleased; it's the very first answer he's had to his call for a general mobilization of Okies, and this one really looks like a top-notch city. It calls itself Lincoln-Nevada."

"It would," Amalfi said grimly. He mopped his face. "Give me a look at it, O'Brian."

The screen lit up. Amalfi mopped his face again.

"All right. Back your drone off a good distance from the march and keep that thing in sight from now on. Get 'Lincoln-Nevada' between you and the pack. It won't shoot at your drone; it doesn't know it doesn't belong there."

Without waiting for O'Brian's acknowledgment, Amalfi switched over to the City Fathers. "How much longer is this job going to take?" he demanded.

"ANOTHER SIX YEARS, MR. MAYOR."

"Cut it to four at a minimum. And give me a course from here to the Lesser Magellanic Cloud, one that crosses Earth's orbit."

"MR. MAYOR, THE LESSER MAGELLANIC CLOUD IS TWO HUNDRED AND EIGHTY THOUSAND LIGHT YEARS AWAY FROM THE ACOLYTE CLUSTER!"

"Thank you," Amalfi said sardonically. "I have no intention of going there, I assure you. All I want is a course with those three points on it."

"VERY WELL. COMPUTED."

"When would we have to spin, to cross Earth's orbit on E-Day?"

"FROM FIVE SECONDS TO FIFTEEN DAYS FROM TODAY, FIGURING FROM THE CENTER OF THE CLOUD TO EITHER EDGE."

"No good. We can't start within those limits. Give me a perfectly flat trajectory from here to there."

"THAT ARC INVOLVES NINE HUNDRED AND FIFTY-EIGHT DIRECT COLLISIONS AND FOUR HUNDRED ELEVEN THOUSAND AND TWO GRAZES AND NEAR-MISSES."

"Use it."

The City Fathers were silent. Amalfi wondered if it were possible for machinery to be stunned. He knew that the City Fathers would never use the crow-flight arc, since it conflicted with their most ineluctable basic directive: *Preserve the city first*. This was all right with the mayor. He had given that instruction with an eye to the tempo of building on Hern VI; he had a strong hunch that it would go considerably faster after that stunner.

And as a matter of fact, it was just fourteen months later when Amalfi's hand closed on the master space stick for Hern VI, and he said:

"Spin!"

The career of Hern VI from its native Acolyte cluster across the center of the galaxy made history—particularly in the field of instrumentation. Hern VI was a tiny world, considerably smaller than Mercury, but nevertheless it was the most monstrous mass ever kicked past the speed of light within the limits of the inhabited galaxy. Except for the planet of He, which had left the galaxy from its periphery and was now well on its way toward Messier 31 in Andromeda, no such body had ever before been flown under spindizzy or any other drive. Its passage left permanent scars in the recording banks of every detecting instrument within range, and the memories of it graven into the brains of sentient observers were no less drastic.

Theoretically, Hern VI was following the long arc laid out for it by Amalfi's City Fathers, an arc leading from the fringe of the Acolyte cluster all the way across the face of the galaxy to the center of the Lesser Magallanic Cloud. (Its mass center, of course; both clouds had emerged too recently from the galaxy as a whole to have developed the definite orbital dead centers characteristic of "spiral" nebulae.) The mean motion of the flying planet followed that arc scrupulously.

But at the speed at which Hern VI was traveling—a velocity which could not be expressed comfortably even in multiples of *C*, the old arbitrary velocity of light—the slightest variation from that orbit became a careening side jaunt of horrifying proportions before even the microsecond reactions of the City Fathers could effect the proper corrections.

Like other starmen, Amalfi was accustomed enough to traveling at transphotic speeds—in space, a medium ordinarily without enough landmarks to make real velocity very apparent. And, like all Okies, he had traveled on planets in creeping ground vehicles which seemed to be making dangerous speed simply because there were so many nearby reference points to make that speed seem great. Now he was finding out what it was like to move among the stars at a comparable velocity.

For at the velocity of Hern VI, the stars became almost as closely spaced as the girders beside a subway track—with the added hazard that the track frequently swerved enough to place two or three girders in a row between the rails. More than once Amalfi stood frozen on the balcony in the belfry of City Hall, watching a star that had been invisible half a second before cannoning directly at his head, swelling to fill the whole sky with glare——

Blackness.

Amalfi felt irrationally that there should have been an audible *whoosh* as Hern VI passed that star. His face still tingled with the single blast of its radiation which had bathed him, despite the planet's hard-driven and nearly cross-polarized spindizzy screen, at that momentary perihelion.

There was nothing the matter, of course, with the orbit corrections of the City Fathers. The difficulty was simply that Hern VI was not a responsive enough space craft to benefit by really quick orbital corrections. It took long seconds for the City Fathers' orders to be translated into enough vector thrust to affect the flight of the dead planet over parsecs of its shambling, paretic stride. And there was another, major reason: when all of Hern VI's axial rotation had been converted to orbital motion, all of a considerable axial libration had also been converted, and there was nothing that could be done about the kinks this put in the planet's course.

Possibly, had Amalfi spotted his own city's spindizzies over the surface of the planet, as he had those of the all-purpose city and the plague city, Hern VI might have been more sensitive to the space stick; at the very least, the libration could have been left as real libration, for it wouldn't have mattered had the planet heeled a little this way and that as long as it kept a straight course. But Amalfi had left the city's drivers undisturbed for the most cogent of all reasons: for the survival of the city. Only one of the machines was participating at all in the flight of Hern VI, that being the big pivot spindizzy at Sixtieth Street. The others, including the decrepit but now almost cool Twenty-third Street machine, rested.

"... *calling the free planet, calling the free planet ... is* there anybody alive on that thing? . . . *EPSILON CRUCIS, HAVE YOU SUCCEEDED IN RAISING THE BODY THAT JUST PASSED YOU? ... CALLING THE FREE* PLANET! YOU'RE ON COLLISION COURSE WITH US—HELL AND *DAMNATION!* . . . *CALLING ETA PALINURI, THE FREE PLANET JUST GAVE US A HAIRCUT AND IT'S HEADING* for you. It's either dead or out of control . . . Calling the free *planet, calling the free pla*——"

There was no time to answer such frantic calls, which poured into the city from outside like a chain of spring freshets as inhabited systems were by-passed, skirted, overshot, fringed, or actually penetrated. The calls could have been acknowledged but acknowledgment would demand that some explanation be offered, and Hern VI would be out of ultraphone range of the questioner before more than a few sentences could be exchanged. The most panicky inquiries might have been answered by Dirac, but that had two drawbacks: the minor one, that there were too many inquiries for the city to handle, and no real reason to handle them; the major one, that Earth and one other important party would be able to hear the answer.

Amalfi did not care too much about what the Earth heard—Earth was already hearing plenty about the flight of Hern VI; if Dirac transmission could be spoken of as jammed, even in metaphor (and it could, for an infinite number of possible electron orbits in no way presupposes a Dirac transmitter tuned to each one), then Earth Dirac boards were jampacked with the squalls of alarmed planets along Hern VI's arc.

But about the other party, Amalfi cared a great deal.

O'Brian kept that other party steadily in the center of his drone's field of vision, and a small screen mounted on the railing of the belfry showed Amalfi the shining, innocuous-looking globe whenever he cared to look at it. The newcomer to the Okie jungle—and to the March on Earth—had made no untoward or even interesting motion since it had arrived in the Okies' ken. Occasionally it exchanged chitchat with the King of the jungle; less often, it talked with other cities. Boredom had descended on the jungle, so there was now a fair amount of intercity touring; but the newcomer was not visited as far as O'Brian or Amalfi could tell, nor did any gigs leave it. This, of course, was natural: Okies are solitary by preference, and a refusal to fraternize, providing that it was not actively hostile in tone, would always be understood in any situation. The newcomer, in short, was giving a very good imitation of being just another member of the hegira—just one more Birnam tree on the way to Dunsinane. . . .

And if anyone in the jungle had recognized it for what it was, Amalfi could see no signs of it.

A fat star rocketed blue-white over the city and Dopplered away into the black, shrinking as it faded out. Amalfi spoke briefly to the City Fathers. The jungle would be within sight of Earth within days—and the uproar on the Dirac was now devoted more and more to the approach of the jungle, less and less to Hern VI. Amalfi had considerable faith in the City Fathers, but the terrifying flight of stars past his head could not fail to make him worry about overshooting E-Day, or undershooting it, however accurate the calculations seemed to be.

But the City Fathers insisted doggedly that Hern VI would cross the solar system of Earth on E-Day, and Amalfi had to be as content as he could manage with the answer. On this kind of problem, the City Fathers had never been known to be wrong. He shrugged uneasily and phoned down to Astronomy.

"Jake, this is the mayor. Ever heard of something called 'trepidation'?"

"Ask me a hard one," the astronomer said testily.

"All right. How do I go about introducing some trepidation into this orbit we're following?"

The astronomer sounded his irritating chuckle. "You don't," he said. "It's a condition of space around suns, and you haven't the mass. The bottom limit, as I recall, is one and five-tenths times ten to the thirtieth power kilograms, but ask the City Fathers to be sure. My figure is of the right order of magnitude, anyhow."

"Damn," Amalfi said. He hung up and took time out to light a cigar, a task complicated by the hurtling stars in the corner of his eye; somehow the cigar seemed to flinch every time one went by. He lit the nervous cheroot and called Hazleton next.

"Mark, you once tried to explain to me how a musician plays the beginning and the end of a piece a little bit faster than normal so that he can play the middle section a little bit slower. Is that the way it goes?"

"Yes, that's *tempo rubato*—literally, 'robbed time.' "

"What I want to do is introduce something like that into the motion of this rock pile as we go across the solar system without any loss in total transit time. Any ideas?"

There was a moment's silence. "Nothing occurs to me, boss. Controlling that kind of thing is almost purely intuitional. You could probably do it better by personal control than O'Brian could set it up in the piloting section."

"Okay. Thanks."

Another dud. Personal control was out of the question at this speed, for no human pilot, not even Amalfi, had reflexes fast enough to handle Hern VI directly. It was precisely because he wanted to be able to handle the planet directly for a second or so of its flight that he wanted the trepidation introduced; and even then he would be none too sure of his ability to make the one critical, razor-edged alteration in her course which he knew he would need.

"Carrel? Come up here, will you?"

The boy arrived almost instantly. On the balcony, he watched the hurtling passage of stars with what Amalfi suspected was sternly repressed alarm.

"Carrel, you began with us as an interpreter, didn't you? You must have had frequent occasion to use a voice-writer, then."

"Yes, sir, I did."

"Good. Then you'll remember what happens when the carriage of the machine returns and spaces for another line. It brakes a little in the middle of the return, so it won't deform the carriage stop by constantly slamming into it; isn't that right? Well, what I want to know is: How is that done?"

"On a small machine, the return cable is on a cam

instead of a pulley," Carrel said, frowning. "But the big
multiplex machines that we use at conclaves are electroni-
cally controlled by something called a klystron; how *that*
works, I've no idea."

"Find out," Amalfi said. "Thanks, Carrel, that's just
what I was looking for. I want such an apparatus cut into
our present piloting circuit, so as to give us the maximum
braking effect as we cross Earth's solar system that's
compatible with our arriving at the cloud on time. Can it
be done?"

"Yes, sir, that sounds fairly easy." He went below
without being dismissed; a second later, a swollen and
spotted red giant sun skimmed the city, seemingly by
inches.

The phone buzzed. "Mr. Mayor—O'Brian here. The
cities are coming up on Earth. Shall I put you through?"

Amalfi started. Already? The city was still megaparsecs
away from the rendezvous; it was literally impossible to
conceive of any speed which would make arrival on time
possible. The mayor suddenly began to find the subway-
pillar flashing of the stars reassuring.

"Yes, O'Brian, hook up the big helmet and stand by.
Give me full Dirac on all circuits, and have our alternate
course ready to plug in. Has Mr. Carrel gotten in touch
with you yet?"

"No, sir," the pilot said. "But there's been some activity
from the City Fathers in the piloting banks which I
assumed was by your orders or one of the city manager's.
Apparently we're to be out of computer control at opposition."

"That's right. Okay, O'Brian, put me through." Amalfi
donned the big helmet . . .

. . . and was back in the jungle.

The entire pack of cities, decelerating heavily now, was
entering the "local group"—an arbitrary sphere with a
radius of fifty light years, with Earth's sun at its center.
This was the galaxy's center of population still, despite the
outward movement which had taken place for the past
centuries, and the challenges which were now ringing
around the heads of the Okies were like voices from
history: 40 Eridani, Procyon, Kruger 60, Sirius, 61 Cygni,
Altair, RD-4°4048, Wolf 359, Alpha Centauri . . . to hear
occasionally from Earth itself was no novelty, but these

challenges were almost like being hailed by ancient Greece
or the Commonwealth of Massachusetts.

The jungle King had succeeded by now in drumming
the hobo cities into a roughly military formation: a huge
cone, eighteen million miles along its axis. The cone was
pointed by smaller towns unlikely to possess more than
purely defensive armament. Just behind the point, which
was actually rounded into a paraboloid like the head of a
comet, the largest cities rode in the body of the cone.
These included the King's own town, but did not include
the "newcomer," which, despite its size, was flying far
behind, roughly on the rim of the cone—it was this
positioning which made it possible for Amalfi's drone to
see almost the entire cone in the first place, for O'Brian's
orders were to keep the big sphere in view regardless of
how much of the jungle he had to sacrifice.

The main wall of the cone was made up mostly of
medium-sized heavy-duty cities, again unlikely to be heavily armed, but having the advantage of mounting spindizzy
equipment which could be polarized to virtual opacity to
any attack but that of a battleship.

All in all, Amalfi thought, a sensible organization of the
materials at hand. It suggested power in reserve, plus
considerable defensive ability, without at the same time
advertising any immediate intention to attack.

He settled the heavy viewing helmet more comfortably
on his shoulders and laid one hand on the balcony railing
near the space stick. Simultaneously, a voice rang in his
ears.

"Earth Security Center calling the Cities," the voice said
heavily. "You are ordered to kill your velocity and remain
where you are pending an official investigation of your
claims."

"Not bloody likely," the King's voice said.

"You are further warned that current Rulings in Council forbid any Okie city to approach Earth more closely
than ten light years. Current Rulings also forbid gatherings
of Okie cities in any numbers greater than four. However,
we are empowered to tell you that this latter Ruling will
be set aside for the duration of the investigation, provided
that the approach limit is not crossed."

"We're crossing it," the King said. "You're going to
take a good look at us. We're not going to form another
jungle out here—we didn't come this far for nothing."

"Under such circumstances," the speaker at Earth Security continued, with the implacable indifference of the desperate bureaucrat operating by the book, "the law prescribes that participating cities be broken up. The full penalty will be applied in this case as in all cases."

"No it won't, either, any more than it is in ninety-four cases out of a hundred. We're not a raiding force and we aren't threatening Earth with anything but a couple of good loud beefs. We're here because we couldn't hope for a fair deal any other way. All we want is justice."

"You've been warned."

"So have you. You can't attack us. You don't dare to. We're citizens, not crooks. We want justice done us, and we're coming on in to see that it gets done."

There was a sudden *click* as the City Fathers' Dirac scanner picked up a new frequency. The new voice said: "Attention Police Command Thirty-two, Command HQ speaking for Vice Admiral MacMillan. Blue alert; blue alert. Acknowledge."

Another click, this time to the frequency the King used to communicate with the jungle.

"Pull up, you guys," the King said. "Hold formation, but figure to make camp fifteen degrees north of the ecliptic, in the orbit of Saturn but about ten degrees ahead of the planet. I'll give you the exact coördinates later. If they won't dicker with us there, we'll move on to Mars and *really* throw a scare into them. But we'll give them a fair chance."

"How do you know they'll give *us* a fair chance?" someone asked petulantly.

"Go back to the Acolytes if you can't take it here. Damned if I care."

Click.

"Hello Command HQ. Command Thirty-two acknowledging blue alert, for Commander Eisenstein. Command Thirty-two blue alert."

Click.

"Hey, you guys at the base of the cone, pull up! You're piling up on us."

"Not in our tanks, Buda-Pesht."

"Look again, dammit. I'm getting a heavy mass-gain here——"

Click.

"Attention Police Command Eighty-three, Command

HQ speaking for Vice Admiral MacMillan. Blue alert, blue alert. Acknowledge. Attention Police Command Thirty-two, red alert, red alert. Acknowledge."

"Eisenstein, Command Thirty-two, red alert acknowledged."

Click.

"Calling Earth; Proserpine Two station calling Earth Security. We are picking up some of the cities. Instructions?"

("Where the hell is Prosperine?" Amalfi asked the City Fathers.)

("PROSERPINE IS A GAS GIANT, ELEVEN THOUSAND MILES IN DIAMETER, OUTSIDE THE ORBIT OF PLUTO AT A DISTANCE OF——"

("All right. Shut up.")

"Earth Security. Keep your nose clean, Prosperine Two. Command HQ is handling this situation. Take no action."

Click.

"Hello Command HQ. Command Eighty-three acknowledging blue alert; for Lieutenant Commander Fiorelli. Command Eighty-three blue alert."

Click.

"Buda-Pesht, they're bracketing us!"

"I know it. Make camp like I said. They don't dare lay a finger on us until we commit an actual aggression, and they know it. Don't let a show of cops bluff you now."

Click.

"Pluto station. We're picking up the vanguard of the cities."

"Sit tight, Pluto."

"You won't get them again until they've made camp—we're in opposition with Prosperine, but Neptune and Uranus are out of the line of flight entirely——"

"Sit tight."

Earth's sun grew gradually in Amalfi's view, growing only with the velocity of the drone, which was the velocity of the jungle. Earth's sun was still invisible from the city itself. In the helmet it was a yellow spark, without detectable disc, like a carbon arc through a lens-system set at infinity.

But it was, inarguably, the home sun. There was a curious thickness in Amalfi's throat as he looked at it. At this moment, Hern VI was screeching across the center of the

galaxy, that center where there was no condensation of
stars, such as other galaxies possessed, visible from Earth
because of the masking interstellar dust clouds; the hurtling planet had just left behind it a black nebula in which
every sun was an apparition, and every escape from those
a miracle. Ahead was the opposite limb of the Milky Way,
filled with new wonder.

Amalfi could not understand why the tiny, undistinguished yellow spark floating in front of him in the helmet
made his eyes sting and water so intolerably.

The jungle was almost at a halt now, already down to
interplanetary speeds, and still decelerating. In another ten
minutes, the cities were at rest with reference to the sun;
and from the drone, Amalfi could see, not very far away
as he was accustomed to think of spatial distance, something else he had seen only once before: the planet Saturn.

No Earthly amateur astronomer with a new, uncertain,
badly adjusted home reflector ever could have seen the
ringed giant with fresher eyes. Amalfi was momentarily
stupefied. What he saw was not only incredibly beautiful,
but obviously impossible. A gas giant with rigid rings!
Why had he ever left the Sol system at all, with a world so
anomalous in his very back yard? And the giant had
another planet circling it, too—a planet more than 3,000
miles through—in addition to the usual family of satellites
of Hern VI's order of size.

Click.

"Make camp," the King was saying. "We'll be here for
a while. Dammit, you guys at the base are still creeping
on us a little. We're going to have to stop here—can't I
pound that into your heads?"

"We're decelerating in good order, Buda-Pesht. It's the
new city, the big job, that's creeping. He's in some kind of
trouble, looks like."

From the drone, the diagnosis seemed accurate. The
enormous spherical object had separated markedly from
the main body of the jungle, and was now well ahead of
the trailing edge of the cone. The whole sphere was
wobbling a little as it moved, and every so often it would
go dim as if under unexpected and uncontrollable polarization.

"Call him and ask if he needs help. The rest of you,
take up orbits."

Amalfi barked, "O'Brian—time!"

"Course time, sir."

"How do I know when this space stick comes alive again?"

"It's alive now, Mr. Mayor," the pilot said. "The City Fathers cut out as soon as you touch it. You'll get a warning buzzer five seconds before our deceleration starts into the deep part of its curve, and then a beep every half second after that to the second inflection point. At the last beep, it's all yours, for about the next two and a half seconds. Then the stick will go dead and the City Fathers will be back in control."

Click.

"Admiral MacMillan, what action do you plan to take now—if any?"

Amalfi took an instant dislike to the new voice on the Dirac. It was flat, twangy, and as devoid as a vodeur of emotion, except perhaps for a certain self-righteousness tinged with *Angst.* Amalfi decided at once that in a face-to-face meeting the speaker would always look somewhere else than into the face of the man to whom he was speaking. The owner of that voice could not possibly be anywhere on the surface of the Earth, looking aloft for besiegers or going doggedly about his business; he was instead almost surely crouched in some subcellar.

"None, sir, at the moment," said the cops' Command HQ. "They've stopped, and appear to be willing to listen to reason. I have assigned Commander Eisenstein to cover their camp against any possible disturbance."

"Admiral, these cities have broken the law. They're here in defiance of our approach limits, and the very size of their gathering is illegal. Are you aware of that?"

"Yes, Mr. President," Command HQ said respectfully. "If you wish me to order individual arrests——"

"No, no, we can't jail a whole pack of flying tramps. I want action, Admiral. These people need to be taught a lesson. We can't have fleets of cities approaching Earth at will—it's a bad precedent. It indicates a decline of interstellar morality. Unless we return to the virtues of the pioneers, the lights will go out all over Earth, and grass will grow in the space lanes."

"Yes, sir," said Command HQ. "Well spoken, if you will permit me to say so. I stand ready for your orders, Mr. President."

"My orders are to do something. That camp is a festering sore on our heavens. I hold you personally responsible."

"Yes, sir." The Admiral's voice was very crisp. "Commander Eisenstein, proceed with Operation A. Command Eighty-two, red alert; red alert."

"Command Eighty-two acknowledging red alert."

"Eisenstein calling Command HQ."

"Command HQ."

"MacMillan, I'm taping my resignation over to you. The President's instructions don't specify Operation A. I won't be responsible for it."

"Follow orders, Commander," Command HQ said pleasantly. "I will accept your resignation—when the maneuver is completed."

The cities hung poised tensely in their orbits. For seconds, nothing happened.

Then pear-shaped, bumpy police battleships began springing out of nothingness around the jungle. Almost instantly, four cities raved into boiling clouds of gas.

The Dinwiddie pickup in the proxy backed itself hurriedly down the intensity scale until it could see again through the glare. The cities were still hanging there, seemingly stunned—as was Amalfi, for he had not imagined that Earth could have come to such a pass. Only an ideal combination of guilt and savagery could have produced so murderous a response; but evidently the president and MacMillan made up between them the necessary combination . . .

Click.

"Fight!" the King's voice roared. "Fight, you lunkheads! They're going to wipe us out! Fight!"

Another city went up. The cops were using Bethé blasters; the Dinwiddie circuit, stopped down to accommodate the hydrogen-helium explosions, could not pick up the pale guide beams of the weapons; it would have been decidedly difficult to follow the King's order effectively.

But the city of Buda-Pesht was already sweeping forward out of the head of the cone, arcing toward Earth. It spat murder back at the police ships, and actually caught one. The mass of incandescent, melting metal appeared as a dim blob in Amalfi's helmet, then faded out again. A few cities followed the King; then a larger number; and then, suddenly, a great wave.

Click.

"MacMillan, stop them! I'll have you shot! They're going to invade——".

New police craft sprang into being every second. A haze gradually began to define the area of the Okie encampment: a planetary nebula of gas molecules, dust, and condensations of metal and water vapor. Through it the Bethé guide beams played, just on the edge of visibility now, but the sun, too, was acting on the cloud, and the whole mass was beginning to re-radiate, casting a deepening luminous veil over the whole scene, about which the Dinwiddie circuit could do very little. The whole spectacle reminded Amalfi of NGC 1435 in Taurus, with exploding cities substituting novas for the Pleiades.

But there were more novas than the cities could account for, novas outside the cone of the encampment. The police craft, Amalfi noted with amazement, were beginning to burst almost as fast as they appeared. The swarming, disorganized cities were fighting back; but their inherent inefficiency as fighting machines ruled them out as the prime causes of such heavy police losses. Something else, something new was happening—something utterly deadly was loose among the cops . . .

"Command Eighty-two, Operation A sub *a*—on the double!"

A police monitor blew up with an impossible, soundless flare.

The cities were winning. Any police battleship could handle any three cities without even beginning to breathe hard, and there had been at least five battleships per city when the pogrom had started. The cities hadn't had a chance.

Yet they were winning. They streamed on toward Earth, boiling with rage, and the police ships, with their utterly deadly weapons, exploded all over the sky like milkweed.

And, a little bit ahead of the maddened cities, an enormous silver sphere wallowed toward Earth, apparently out of control.

Amalfi could now see Earth herself as the tiniest of blue-green dots. He did not try to see it any better, though it was growing to a disc with fantastic speed. He did not want to see it. His eyes were already fogged enough with sentimental tears at the sight of the home sun.

But his eyes kept coming back to it. At its pole he caught the shine of ice . . .

. . . *beep* . . .

The sound shocked him. The buzzer had already sounded, without his having heard it. The city would cross the solar system within the next two and a half seconds—*or less,* for he had no idea how many beeps had probed at his ears without response during his hypnotic struggle with the blue-green planet.

He could only guess, with the fullest impact of his intuition, that *now* was the time . . .

Click.

"PEOPLE OF EARTH. US THE CITY OF SPACES CALLS UPON YOU . . ."

He moved the space stick out and back in a flat loop about three millimeters long. The City Fathers instantly snatched the stick out of his hand. Earth vanished. So did Earth's sun. Hern VI began to accelerate rapidly, regaining the screeching velocity across the face of the galaxy for which two Okie cities had died.

". . . YOUR NATURAL MASTERS TO OKAY, THE MANS OF STARS, WHO THE UNIVERSE-UNDERSTANDING LONG-LIFE-UNDERSTANDING INHERITORS, THE INFERIOR HOMESTAYING DEC-ADENT EARTH PEOPLES THEREOVER, THE NEW RULERS OF, ARE ABOUT TO BE BECOMING. US INSTRUCTS YOU SOON TO PREPARE——"

The mouthy voice abruptly ceased to exist. The blue fleck of light which had been Amalfi's last sight of his ancestral planet had already been gone for long seconds.

The whole of Hern VI lurched and rang. Amalfi was thrown heavily to the floor of the balcony. The heavy helmet fell askew on his head and shoulders, cutting off his view of the battle in the jungle.

But he didn't care. That impact, and the death of that curious voice, meant the real end of the battle in the jungle. It meant the end of any real threat that might have existed for Earth. And it meant the end of the Okie cities—not just those in the jungle, but all of them, as a class, including Amalfi's own.

For that impact, transmitted to the belfry of City Hall thorough the rock of Hern VI, meant that Amalfi's instant of personal control had been fair and true. Somewhere on the leading hemisphere of Hern VI there was now an enormous white-hot crater. That crater, and the traces of metal salts which were dissolved in its molten lining, held the grave of the oldest of all Okie legends:

The Vegan orbital fort.

It would be forever impossible now to know how long the summated, distilled, and purified power of the Vegan military, conquered once only in fact, had been bowling through the galaxy, awaiting this one unrepeatable clear lane to a strike. Certainly no answer to that question could be found on the degenerate planets of Vega itself; the fort was as much a myth there as it had been anywhere else in the galaxy.

But it had been real all the same. It had been awaiting its one chance to revenge Vega upon Earth, not, certainly, in the hope of re-asserting the blue-white glory of Vega over every other star, but simply to smash the average planet of the average sun which had so inexplicably prevailed over Vega's magnificence. Not even the fort could have expected to prevail against Earth by itself—but in the confusion of the Okies' March on Earth, and under the expectation that Earth would hesitate to burn down its own citizen-cities until too late, it had foreseen a perfect triumph. It had swung in from its long, legend-blurred exile, disguised primarily as a city, secondarily as a fable, to make its last bid.

Residual tremors, T-waves, made the belfry rock gently. Amalfi got to his feet, steadying himself on the railing.

"O'Brian, cast us off. The planet goes on as she is. Switch the city to the alternate orbit."

"To the Greater Magellanic?"

"That's right. Make fast any quake damage; pass the word to Mr. Hazleton and Mr. Carrel."

"Yes, sir."

The Vegan fortress had nearly won, at that; only the passage of a forlorn and outcast-piloted little world had defeated it. But the Earth would never know more than a fraction of that, only the fraction which was the passage of Hern VI across the solar system. All the rest of the evidence was now seething and amalgamating in a cooling crater on the leading hemisphere of Hern VI; and Amalfi meant to see to it that Hern VI would be lost to Earth forever . . .

As the Earth was lost to Okies, from now on.

Everyone was in the old office of the mayor: Dee, Hazleton, Carrel, Dr. Schloss, Sergeant Anderson, Jake, O'Brian, the technies; and, by extension, the entire population of the city, through a city-wide, two-way P.A. hookup; even the City Fathers. It was the first such gathering since the last election; that election having been the one which put Hazleton into office, few present now remembered the occasion very well, except for the city Fathers —and they would be the least likely of all to be able to apply that memory fruitfully to the present meeting. Undertones were not their forte.

Amalfi began to speak. His voice was gentle, matter-of-fact, impersonal; it was addressed to everyone, to the city as an organism. But he was looking directly at Hazleton.

"First of all," he said, "it's necessary for everyone to understand our gross physical and astronomical situation. When we cut loose from Hern VI a while back, that planet was well on its way toward the Lesser Magellanic Cloud, which, for those of you who come from the northerly parts of the galaxy, is one of two small satellite galaxies moving away from the main galaxy along the southern limb. Hern Six is still on its way there, and unless something unlikely happens to it, it will go right on to the Cloud, through it, and on into deep intergalactic space.

"We left on it almost all the equipment we had accumulated from other cities while we were in the jungle because we had to. We hadn't the room to take much of it on board our own city; and we couldn't stick with Hern VI because Earth will almost certainly chase the planet, either until the planet leaves the galaxy, or until they're sure we aren't on it any longer."

"Why, sir?" several voices from the G.C. speaker said, almost simultaneously.

"For a long list of reasons. Our flying the planet across the face of the solar system—as well as our flying it through a number of other systems and across main interstellar traffic areas—was a serious violation of Earth laws. Furthermore, Earth has us chalked up as having sideswiped a city as we went by; they don't know the real nature of that 'city.' And incidentally, it's important that they never find out, even if keeping it a secret results in our being written up in the history books as murderers."

Dee stirred protestingly. "John, I don't see why we

shouldn't take the credit. Especially since it really was a pretty big thing we did for the Earth."

"Because we're not through doing it yet. To you, Dee, the Vegans are an ancient people you first heard about only three centuries ago. Before that, on Utopia, you were cut off from the main stream of galactic history. But the fact is that Vega ruled much of the galaxy before Earth did, and that the Vegans always were, and have just shown us that they still are, dangerous people to get involved with. That fort didn't just exist in a vacuum. It had to touch port now and then, just as we do. And being a military machine, it needed more service and maintenance than it could take care of by itself.

"Somewhere in the galaxy there is a colony of Vega which is still dangerous. That colony must be kept in utter ignorance of what happened to its major weapon. It must be made to live on faith; to believe that the fort failed on its first attempt but may some day be back for another try. It must not know that the fort is destroyed, or it will build another one.

"The second one will succeed where the first one failed. The first one failed because of the nature of the nomadic kind of culture on which Earth has been depending up to now; the Okies defeated it. We happened to have been the particular city to do the job, but it was no accident that we were on hand to do it.

"But for quite a while to come, Okies are not going to be effective or even welcome factors in the galaxy as a whole; and the galaxy, Earth in particular, is going to be as weak as a baby all during that period because of the depression. If the Vegans hear that their fort did strike at Earth, and came within a hair's breadth of knocking it out, they'll be building another fort the same day they get the news. After that . . .

"No, Dee, I'm afraid we'll have to keep the secret."

Dee, still a little rebellious, looked at Hazleton for support; but he shook his head.

"Our own situation, right now, is neither good nor bad," Amalfi continued. "We still have Hern VI's velocity. It's enough slower than the velocity we hit when we flew the planet of He to make us readily maneuverable, even though clumsily, especially since we're so much less massive than a planet. We will be able to make any port of call which is inside the cone our trajectory would describe if we rotated it. Finally, Earth has figures only on the path of Hern VI; it has none on the present path of the city.

"Cast up against that the fact that our equipment is old and faltering, and will never carry us anywhere again under our own steam. When we land at the next port of call, we will be landed for good. We have no money to buy new equipment; without new equipment, we can't make money. So it will pay us to pick our next stop with great care. That's why I've asked everybody to sit in on this conference."

One of the technies said, "Boss, are you sure it's as bad as all that? We should be able to make some kind of repairs——"

"THE CITY WILL NOT SURVIVE ANOTHER LANDING," the City Fathers said flatly. The technie swallowed and subsided.

"Our present orbit," Amalfi said, "would lead us eventually out into the greater of the two Magellanic clouds. At our present velocity, that's about twenty years' journey away still. If we actually want to go there, we'll have to plan on that period stretching on by another six years, since the clip at which we're traveling now is so great that we'd blow out every driver on board if we undertook normal deceleration.

"I propose that the Greater Magellanic Cloud is exactly where we want to go."

Tumult.

The whole city roared with astonishment. Amalfi raised his hand; those actually in the room quieted slowly, but elsewhere in the city the noise went on for quite a while. It did not seem to be a sound of general protest, but rather the angry buzzing of large numbers of people arguing among thmselves.

"I know how you feel," Amalfi said when he could be sure most of them could hear him again. "It's a long way to go, and though there are supposed to be one or two colonies on the near side of the Cloud, there can be no real interstellar commerce there, and certainly no commerce with the main body of the galaxy. We would have to settle down—maybe even take to dirt farming; it would be a matter of giving up being an Okie, and giving up being a starman. That's a lot to give up, I know.

"But I want you all to remember that there's no longer any work, or any hope of work, for us anywhere in the main body of the galaxy, even if by some miracle we manage to put our beat-up old city back into good order again. We have no choice. We *must* find a planet of our own to settle down on, a planet we can claim as our own."

"ESTABLISH THIS POINT," the City Fathers said.

"I'm prepared to do so. You all know what has happened to the galactic economy. It's collapsed completely. As long as the currency was stable in the main commerce lanes, there was some pay we could work for; but that doesn't exist any longer. The drug standard which Earth has rigged up now is utterly impossible for the cities, because the cities have to use those drugs *as drugs,* not as money, in order to stay alive long enough to do business at all. Entirely aside from the possibility of plague—and you'll remember, I think, what we saw of that not so long ago—there's the fact that we live, literally, on longevity. We can't trade on it, too.

"And that's only the beginning. The drug standard will collapse, and sooner and more finally than the germanium standard did. The galaxy's a huge place. There will be new monetary standards by the dozens before the economy gets back onto some stable basis. And there will be thousands of local monetary systems in operation before that happens. The interregnum will last at least a century——"

"AT LEAST THREE CENTURIES."

"Very well, three centuries. I was being optimistic. In either case, it's plain that we can't make a living in an economy which isn't at least reasonably stable, and we can't afford to sweat out the waiting period before the galaxy jells again. Especially since we don't know whether the eventual stabilization will have any corner in it for Okies or not.

"Frankly, I don't think the Okies have a prayer of surviving. Earth will be especially hard on them after this 'march,' which I took pains to encourage all the same because I was pretty sure we could suck in the Vegans with it. But even if there had been no march, the Okies would have been made obsolete by the depression. The histories of depressions show that a period of economic chaos is invariably followed by a period of extremely rigid economic controls—during which all the variables, the only partially controllable factors like commodity speculation, unlimited credit, free marketing, and competitive wages get shut out.

"Our city represents nearly the ultimate in competitive labor. Even if it lasts through the interregnum—which it can't—it will be an anachronism in the new economy. It will almost surely be *forced* to berth down on some planet selected by the government. My own proposition is simply that we select our *own* berth, long before the government gets around to enforcing its own selection; that we pick a place hundreds of parsecs away from the outermost boundary-surface that government will think to claim; a place which is retreating steadily and at good speed from the center of that government and everything it will eventually want to claim; and that once we get there, we dig in. There's a new imperialism starting where we used to be free; to stay free, we'll have to go out beyond any expectable frontier and start our own little empire.

"But let's face it. *The Okies are through.*"

Nobody said anything. Stunned faces scanned stunned faces.

Then the City Fathers said calmly, "THE POINT IS ESTABLISHED. WE ARE NOW MAKING AN ANALYSIS OF THE SELECTED AREA, AND WILL HAVE A REPORT FROM THE ASSIGNED SECTION IN FOUR TO FIVE WEEKS."

Still the silence persisted in the big chamber. The Okies were testing it—almost tasting it. No more roaming. A planet of their own. A city at rest, and a sun to come up and go down over it on a regular schedule; seasons; a quietness free of the eternal whirling of gravity fields. No fear, no fighting, no defeat, no pursuit; self-sufficiency—and the stars only points of light forever.

A planetbound man presented with a similar revolution in his habits would have rejected it at once, terrified. The Okies, however, were used to change; change was the only stable factor in their lives. It is the only stable factor in the life of a planetbound man, too, but the planetbound man has never had his nose rubbed in it.

Even so, had they not been in addition virtually immortal—had they been, like the people of the old times before space travel, pinned like insects on a spreading-board to a lifespan of less than a century—Amalfi would have been afraid of the outcome. A short lifespan leads to restlessness; somewhere within the next few years, there has to be some El Dorado for the ephemerid. But the conquest of age had almost eliminated that Faustian frenzy. After three or four centuries, people grew tired of searching for the unnamable; they learned—they began to think of the future not as holding a haven of placidity and riches, but simply as the realm of things that had not happened yet. They became interested in the budding, the unfolding present, and thought about the future only with an attitude of indifferent acceptance toward whatever catastrophe it might bring. They no longer burned out their lives seeking catastrophe, under the name of "security."

In short, they grew a little more realistic, and more than a little tired.

Amalfi waited with calm confidence. The smallest objections, he knew, would come first. He was not anxious to have to cope with them, and the silence had lasted so much longer than he had expected that he began to wonder if his argument had become too abstract toward the end. If so, a note of naïve practicality at this point should be proper. . . .

"This solution should satisfy almost everyone," he said briskly. "Hazleton has asked to be relieved of his post, and this will certainly relieve him of it most effectively. It takes us out of the jurisdiction of the cops. It leaves Carrel as city manager if he still wants the post, but it leaves him manager of a grounded city, which satisfies *me*, since I've no confidence in Carrel as a pilot. It——"

"Boss, let me interrupt a minute."

"Go ahead, Mark."

"What you say is all very well, but it's too damned extreme. I can't see any reason why we have to go so far afield. Granted that the Greater Magellanic is off the course Hern VI is following; granted that it's pretty remote, granted that even if the cops do go looking for us there, it's too big and unpopulated and complex for them to hope to find us. But couldn't we accomplish the same thing without leaving the galaxy? Why do we have to take up residence in a cloud that's moving away from the galaxy at some colossal speed——"

"THREE HUNDRED AND FORTY-FOUR MILES PER SECOND."

"Oh, shut up. All right, so that's not very fast. Still and all, the cloud is a long way away—and if you give me the

exact figures, I'll bust all your tubes—and if we ever want
to get back to the galaxy again, we'll have to fly another
planet to do it."

"All right," Amalfi said. "What's your alternative?"

"Why don't we hide out in a big cluster in our own
galaxy? Not a picayune ball of stars like the Acolyte
cluster, but one of the big jobs like the Great Cluster in
Hercules. There must be at least one such in the cone of
our present orbit; there might even be a Cepheid cluster
where spindizzy navigation would be impossible for anybody who didn't know the local space strains. We'd be just
as unlikely to be traced by the cops, but we'd still be on
hand inside our own galaxy if conditions began to look up."

Amalfi did not choose to contest the point. Logically, it
should be Carrel, who was being deprived of the effective
command of a flying city, who should be raising this
objection. The fact that the avowed retired Hazleton had
brought it up first was enough for Amalfi.

"I don't care if conditions ever do look up," Dee said,
unexpectedly. "I like the idea of our having a planet of our
own, and I'd want it to be as far away from the cops as
we could possibly make it. If that planet really does
become ours, would it make any difference to us whether
Okie cities become possible again two or three centuries
from now? We wouldn't need to be Okies any longer."

"You'd say that," Hazleton said, "because you haven't
lived more than two or three centuries yet, and because
you're still used to living on a planet. Some of the rest of
us are older; some of the rest of us like wandering. I'm
not speaking for myself, Dee, you know that. I'll be happy
to get off this junk pile. But this whole proposition has a
faint smell to me. Amalfi, are you sure you aren't forcing
us to set down simply to block a change of administration? It won't, you know."

Amalfi said, "Of course, I know. I'm submitting my
resignation along with yours the moment we touch
ground. Right now I'm still an officer of this city, and I'm
doing the job I've been assigned to do."

"No, I didn't mean that. Let it go. What I still want to
know is why we have to go all the way out to the Greater
Megellanic."

"Because it'll be ours," Carrel said abruptly. Hazleton
swung on him, obviously astonished; but Carrel's rapt eyes

did not see the older man. "Not only our planet—whichever one we choose—but our galaxy. Both the Magellanics are galaxies in little. I know; I'm a southerner, I grew up on a planet where the Magellanics went across the night sky like tornadoes of sparks. The Greater Magellanic even has its own center of rotation; I couldn't see it from my home planet because we were too close, but from Earth it has a distinct Milne spiral. And both clouds are moving away, taking on their own independence from the main galaxy. Hell, Mark, it isn't a matter of one planet. That's nothing. We won't be able to fly the city, but we can build spaceships. We can colonize. We can settle the economy to suit ourselves. Our own galaxy! What more could you want?"

"It's too easy," Hazleton said stubbornly. "I'm used to fighting for what I want. I'm used to fighting for the city. I want to use my head, not my back; your spaceships, your colonization, those things are going to be preceded by a lot of plain and simple weeding and plowing. There's the core of my objection to this scheme, Amalfi. It's wasteful. It commits us to a situation where most of what we'll have to do will be outside of our experience."

"I disagree," Amalfi said quietly. "There are already colonies in the Greater Magellanic. They weren't set up by spaceships. They were set up by cities. No other mechanism could have made the trip at all in those days."

"So?"

"So there's no chance that we'll be able to settle down placidly and get out our hoes. We'll have to fight to make any part of the Cloud our own. It's going to be the biggest fight we've ever had, because we'll be fighting Okies—Okies who probably have forgotten most of their history and their heritage, but Okies all the same, Okies who had this idea long before we did and who are going to defend their patent."

"As they have a right to do. Why should we poach on them when a giant cluster would serve us just as well? Or nearly as well?"

"Because they are poachers themselves—and worse. Why would a city go all the way to the Greater Magellanic in the old days, when cities were solid citizens of the galaxy? Why didn't *they* settle down in a giant cluster? Think, Mark! They were bindlestiffs. Cities who had to go to the Greater Magellanic because they had committed crimes that made every star in the main galaxy their enemies. You could name one such city yourself, and one you know must be out there in that cloud: the Interstellar Master Traders. And not only because Thor Five still remembers it, but because every sentient being in the galaxy burns for the blood of every last man on board it. Where else could it have gone but the Greater Magellanic, even though it starved itself for fifty years to make the trip?"

Hazleton began kneading his hands, slowly, but with great force. His knuckles went alternately white and red as his fingers ground over them.

"Gods of all stars," he said. His lips thinned. "The Mad Dogs. Yes, They went there if they went any place. Now there's an outfit I'd like to meet."

"Bear in mind that you might not, Mark. The Cloud's a big place."

"Sure, sure. And there may be a few other bindlestiffs, too. But if the Mad Dogs are out there, I'd like to meet them. I remember being taken for one of them on Thor Five; that's a taste I'd like to get out of my mouth. I don't care about the others. Except for them, the Greater Magellanic is ours, as far as I'm concerned."

"A galaxy," Dee murmured; almost soundlessly. "A galaxy with a home base, a home base that's ours."

"An Okie galaxy," Carrel said.

The silence sifted back over the city. It was not a contentious silence now. It was the silence of a crowd in which each man is thinking for and to himself.

"HAVE MESSRS. HAZLETON AND CARREL ANY FURTHER ADDITIONS TO THEIR PLATFORMS?" the City Fathers blared, their vodeur-voice penetrating flatly into every cranny of the hurtling city. As Amalfi had expected, the extended discussion of high policy had convinced the City Fathers that the election was for the office of mayor, rather than for that of city manager. "IF NOT, AND IF THERE ARE NO ADDITIONAL CANDIDATES, WE ARE READY TO PROCEED WITH THE TABULATION."

For a long instant, everyone looked very blank. Then Hazleton too recognized the mistake the City Fathers had made. He began to chuckle.

"No additions," he said. Carrel said nothing; he simply grinned, transported.

Ten seconds later, John Amalfi, Okie, was the mayor-elect of an infant galaxy.

CHAPTER EIGHT: IMT

THE city hovered, and then settled silently through the early morning darkness toward the broad expanse of heath which the planet's Proctors had designated as its landing place. At this hour, the edge of the misty acres of diamonds which were the Lesser Magellanic Cloud was just beginning to touch the western horizon; the whole cloud covered nearly 35° of the sky. The cloud would set at 0512; at 0600 the near edge of the home galaxy would rise, but during the summer, the suns rose earlier.

All of which was quite all right with Amalfi. The fact that no significant amount of the home galaxy could begin to show in the night sky for months to come was one of the reasons why he had chosen this planet to settle on. The situation confronting the dying city now, and its citizens, too, posed problems enough without its being recomplicated by an unsatisfiable homesickness.

The city grounded, and the last residual hum of the spindizzies stopped. From below there came a rapidly rising and more erratic hum of human activity, and the clank and roar of heavy equipment getting under way. The geology team was losing no time, as usual.

Amalfi, however, felt no disposition to go down at once. He remained on the balcony of City Hall looking at the thickly set night sky. The star-density in the Greater Magellanic was very high, even outside the clusters—often, the distances between stars were matters of light months rather than light years. Even should it prove impossible to move the city itself again—which was inevitable, considering that the Sixtieth Street spindizzy had just followed the Twenty-third Street machine into the junk pit—it should be possible to set interstellar commerce going here by cargo ship. The city's remaining drivers, ripped out and remounted on a one-per-hull basis, would provide the nucleus of quite a respectable little fleet.

It would not be much like cruising among the far-scattered, various civilizations of the Milky Way had been, but it would be commerce of a sort, and commerce was the Okies' oxygen.

He looked down. The brilliant starlight showed that the blasted heath extended all the way to the horizon in the west; in the east it stopped about a mile away and gave place to land regularly divided into tiny squares. Whether each of these minuscule fields represented an individual farm he could not tell, but he had his suspicions. The language the Proctors had used in giving the city permission to land had had decidedly feudal overtones.

While he watched, the black skeleton of some tall structure erected itself swiftly near by, between the city and the eastern stretch of the heath. The geology team already had its derrick in place. The phone at the balcony's rim buzzed, and Amalfi picked it up.

"Boss, we're going to drill now," the voice of Hazleton said. "Coming down?"

"Yes. What do the soundings show?"

"Nothing very hopeful, but we'll know for sure shortly. This does look like oil land, I must say."

"We've been fooled before," Amalfi grunted. "Start boring; I'll be right down."

He had barely hung up the phone when the burring roar of the molar drill violated the still summer night, echoing calamitously among the buildings of the city. It was almost certainly the first time any planet in the Greater Magellanic had heard the protest of collapsing molecules, though the technique had been a century out of date back in the Milky Way.

Amalfi was delayed by one demand and another all the way to the field, so that it was already dawn when he arrived. The test bore had been sunk and the drill was being pulled up again; the team had put up a second derrick, from the top of which Hazleton waved to him. Amalfi waved back and went up in the lift.

There was a strong, warm wind blowing at the top, which had completely tangled Hazleton's hair under the earphone clips. To Amalfi, it could make no such difference, but after years of the city's precise airconditioning, it did obscure things to his emotions.

"Anything yet, Mark?"

"You're just in time. Here she comes."

The first derrick rocked as the long core sprang from the earth and slammed into its side girders. There was no answering black fountain. Amalfi leaned over the rail and watched the sampling crew rope in the cartridge and guide it back down to the ground. The winch rattled and choked off, its motor panting.

"No soap,'" Hazleton said disgustedly. "I knew we shouldn't have trusted the damned Proctors."

"There's oil under here somewhere all the same," Amalfi said. "We'll get it out. Let's go down."

On the ground, the senior geologist had split the cartridge and was telling his way down the boring with a mass-pencil. He shot Amalfi a quick reptilian glance as the mayor's blocky shadow fell across the table.

"No dome," he said succinctly.

Amalfi thought about it. Now that the city was permanently cut off from the home galaxy, no work that it could do for money would mean a great deal to it; what was needed first of all was oil, so that the city could eat. Work that would yield good returns in the local currency would have to come much later. Right now the city would have to work for payment in drilling permits.

At the first contact that had seemed to be easy enough. This planet's natives had never been able to get below the biggest and most obvious oil-domes, so there should be plenty of oil left for the city. In turn, the city could throw up enough low-grade molybdenum and wolfram as a byproduct of drilling to satisfy the terms of the Proctors.

But if there was no oil to crack for food . . .

"Sink two more shafts," Amalfi said. "You've got an oil-bearing till down there, anyhow. We'll pressure jellied gasoline into it and split it. Ride along a Number Eleven gravel to hold the seam open. If there's no dome, we'll boil the oil out."

"Steak yesterday and steak tomorrow," Hazleton murmured. "But never steak today."

Amalfi swung upon the city manager, feeling the blood charging upward through his thick neck. "Do you think you'll get fed any other way?" he growled. "This planet is going to be home for us from now on. Would you rather take up farming like the natives? I thought you outgrew *that* notion after the raid on Gort."

"That isn't what I meant," Hazleton said quietly. His heavily space-tanned face could not pale, but it blued a little under the taut, weathered bronze. "I know just as well as you do that we're here for good. It just seemed funny to me that settling down on a planet for good should begin just like any other job."

"I'm sorry," Amalfi said, mollified. "I shouldn't be so jumpy. Well, we don't know yet how well off we are. The natives never have mined this planet to anything like paydirt depth, and they refine stuff by throwing it into a stewpot. If we can get past this food problem, we've still got a good chance of turning this whole Cloud into a tidy corporation."

He turned his back abruptly on the derricks and began to walk slowly away from the city. "I feel like a walk," he said. "Like to come along, Mark?"

"A walk?" Hazleton looked puzzled. "Why—sure. Okay, boss."

For a while they trudged in silence over the heath. The going was rough; the soil was clayey and heavily gullied, particularly deceptive in the early morning light. Very little seemed to grow on it: only an occasional bit of low, starved shrubbery, a patch of tough, nettlelike stalks, a few clinging weeds like crab grass.

"This doesn't strike me as good farming land," Hazleton said. "Not that I know a thing about it."

"There's better land farther out, as you saw from the city," Amalfi said. "But I agree about the heath. It's blasted land. I wouldn't even believe it was radiologically safe until I saw the instrument readings with my own eyes."

"A war?"

"Long ago, maybe. But I think geology did most of the damage. The land was let alone too long; the topsoil's all gone. It's odd, considering how intensively the rest of the planet seems to be farmed."

They half-slid into a deep arroyo and scrambled up the other side. "Boss, straighten me out on something," Hazleton said. "Why did we adopt this planet, even after we found that it had people of its own? We passed several others that would have done as well. Are we going to push the local population out? We're not too well set up for that, even if it were legal or just."

"Do you think there are Earth cops in the Greater Magellanic, Mark?"

"No," Hazelton said. "But there are Okies, and if I wanted justice, I'd go to Okies, not to cops. What's the answer, Amalfi?"

"We may have to do a little judicious pushing," Amalfi said, squinting ahead. The double suns were glaring directly in their faces. "It's all in knowing where to push, Mark. You heard the character some of the outlying planets gave this place when we spoke to them on the way in."

"They hate the smell of it," Hazelton said, carefully removing a burr from his ankle. "It's my guess that the Proctors made some early expeditions unwelcome. Still—"

Amalfi topped a rise and held out one hand. The city manager fell silent almost automatically, and clambered up beside him.

The cultivated land began only a few meters away. Watching them were two—creatures.

One, plainly, was a man—a naked man, the color of chocolate, with matted blue-black hair. He was standing at the handle of a single-bladed plow, which looked to be made of the bones of some large animal. The furrow that he had been opening stretched behind him beside its fellows, and farther back in the field there was a low hut. The man was standing, shading his eyes, evidently looking across the dusky heath toward the Okie city. His shoulders were enormously broad and muscular, but bowed even when he stood erect, as now.

The figure leaning into the stiff leather straps which drew the plow also was human—a woman. Her head hung down, as did her arms, and her hair, as black as the man's but somewhat longer, fell forward and hid her face.

As Hazelton froze, the man lowered his head until he was looking directly at the Okies. His eyes were blue and unexpectedly piercing. "Are you the men from the city?" he said.

Hazelton's lips moved. The serf could hear nothing; Hazelton was speaking into his throat mikes, audible only to the receiver imbedded in Amalfi's right mastoid process.

"English, by the gods of all stars! The Proctors speak

Interlingua. What's this, boss? Was the Cloud colonized *that* far back?"

Amalfi shook his head. "We're from the city," the mayor said aloud, in the same tongue. "What's your name, young fella?"

"Karst, lord."

"Don't call me 'lord.' I'm not one of your Proctors. Is this your land?"

"No, lord. Excuse—I have no other word———"

"My name is Amalfi."

"This is the Proctors' land, Amalfi. I work this land. Are you of Earth?"

Amalfi shot a swift sidelong glance at Hazleton. The city manager's face was expressionless.

"Yes," Amalfi said. "How did you know?"

"By the wonder," Karst said. "It is a great wonder, to raise a city in a single night. IMT itself took nine men of hands of thumbs of suns to build, the singers say. To raise a second city on the Barrens overnight—such a thing is beyond words."

He stepped away from the plow, walking with painful, hesitant steps, as if all his massive muscles hurt him. The woman raised her head from the traces and pulled the hair back from her face. The eyes that looked forth at the Okies were dull, but there were phosphorescent stirrings of alarm behind them. She reached out and grasped Karst by the elbow.

"It—is nothing," she said.

He shook her off. "You have built a city over one of night," he repeated. "You speak the Engh tongue, as we do on feast days. You speak to such as me, with words, not with the whips with the little tags. You have fine clothes, with patches of color of fine-woven cloth."

It was beyond doubt the longest speech he had ever made in his life. The clay on his forehead was beginning to streak with the effort.

"You are right," Amalfi said. "We are from Earth, though we left it long ago. I will tell you something else, Karst. You, too, are of Earth."

"This is not so," Karst said, retreating a step. "I was born here, and all my people. None claim Earth blood———"

"I understand," Amalfi said. "You are of this planet. But you are an Earthman. And I will tell you something else. I do not think the Proctors are Earthmen. I think they lost the right to call themselves Earthmen long ago, on another planet, a planet named Thor Five."

Karst wiped his callused palm against his thighs. "I want to understand," he said. "Teach me."

"Karst!" the woman said pleadingly. "It is nothing. Wonders pass. We are late with the planting."

"Teach me," Karst said doggedly. "All our lives we furrow the fields, and on the holidays they tell us of Earth. Now there is a marvel here, a city raised by the hands of Earthmen, there are Earthmen in it who speak to us——" He stopped. He seemed to have something in his throat.

"Go on," Amalfi said gently.

"Teach me. Now that Earth has built a city on the Barrens, the Proctors cannot hold knowledge for their own any longer. Even when you go, we will learn from your empty city before it is ruined by wind and rain. Lord Amalfi, if we are Earthmen, teach us as Earthmen are teached."

"Karst," said the woman. "It is not for us. It is a magic of the Proctors. All magics are of the Proctors. They mean to take us from our children. They mean us to die on the Barrens. They tempt us."

The serf turned to her. There was something indefinably gentle in the motion of his brutalized, crackle-skinned, thick-muscled body.

"You need not go," he said, in a slurred Interlingua patois which was obviously his usual tongue. "Go on with the plowing, does it please you. But this is no thing of the Proctors. They would not stoop to tempt slaves as mean as we are. We have obeyed the laws, given our tithes, observed the holidays. This is of Earth."

The woman clenched her horny hands under her chin and shivered. "It is forbidden to speak of Earth except on holidays. But I will finish the plowing. Otherwise our children will die."

"Come, then," Amalfi said. "There is much to learn."

To his complete consternation, the serf went down on both knees. A second later, while Amalfi was still wondering what to do next, Karst was up again, and climbing up onto the Barrens toward them. Hazleton offered him a hand, and was nearly hurled like a flat stone through the air when Karst took it; the serf was as solid and strong as a pile driver, and as sure on his stony feet.

"Karst, will you return before night?"

Karst did not answer. Amalfi began to lead the way back toward the city. Hazleton started down the far side of the rise after them, but something moved him to look back again at the little scrap of farm. The woman's head had fallen forward again, the wind stirring the tangled curtain of her hair. She was leaning heavily into the galling traces, and the plow was again beginning to cut its way painfully through the stony soil. There was now, of course, nobody to guide it.

"Boss," Hazleton said into the throat mike. "Are you listening, or are you too busy playing Messiah?"

"I'm listening."

"I don't think I want to snitch a planet from these people. As a matter of fact, I'm damned if I will!"

Amalfi didn't answer; he knew well enough that there was no answer. The Okie city would never go aloft again. This planet was home. There was no place else to go.

The voice of the woman, crooning as she plowed, dwindled behind them. Her song droned monotonously over unseen and starving children: a lullaby. Hazleton and Amalfi had fallen from the sky to rob her of everything but the stony and now unharvestable soil.

The city was old—unlike the men and women who manned it, who had merely lived a long time, which is quite a different thing. And like any old intelligence, its past sins lay very near the surface, ready for review either in nostalgia or in self-accusation at the slightest cue. It was difficult these days to get any kind of information out of the City Fathers without having to submit to a lecture, couched in as high a moral tone as was possible to machines whose highest morality was survival.

Amalfi knew well enough what he was letting himself in for when he asked the City Fathers for a review of the Violations docket. He got it, and in bells—big bells. The City Fathers gave him everything, right down to the day six hundred years ago when they had discovered that nobody had dusted the city's ancient subways since the managership of deFord. That had been the first time the younger Okies had heard that the city had ever had any subways.

But Amalfi stuck to the job, though his right ear ached with the pressure of the earphone. Out of the welter of

minor complaints and wistful recollections of missed opportunities, certain things came through clearly and urgently.

Amalfi sighed. In the end, it appeared that the Earth
cops would remember Amalfi's city for two things only.
One: The city had a long Violations docket, and still
existed to be brought to book on it. *Two*: The city had
gone out toward the Greater Magellanic, just as a far
older and blacker city had done centuries before—the city
which had perpetrated the massacre on Thor V, the city
whose memory still stank in the nostrils of cops and
surviving Okies alike.

Amalfi shut off the City Fathers in mid-reminiscence and
removed the phone from his aching ear. The control
boards of the city stretched before him, still largely useful,
but dead forever in one crucial bloc—the bank that had
once flown the city from star to new star. The city was
grounded; it had no choice now but to accept, and then
win, this one poor planet for its own.

If the cops would let it. The Magellanic Clouds were, of
course, moving steadily and with increasing velocity away
from the home galaxy. It would take the cops time to
decide that they should make that enormously long flight
in pursuit of one miserable Okie. But in the end they
would make that decision. The cleaner the home galaxy
became of Okies—and there was no doubt but that the
cops had by now broken up the majority of the space-
faring cities—the greater the urge would become to track
down the last few stragglers.

Amalfi had no faith in the ability of a satellite star
cloud to outrun human technology. By the time the cops
were ready to cross from the home lens to the Greater
Magellanic, they would have the techniques with which to
do it, and techniques far less clumsy than Amalfi's city had
used. If the cops wanted to chase the Greater Magellanic,
they would find ways to catch it. If . . .

Amalfi put the earphone on again. "Question," he said.
"Will the need to catch us be urgent enough to produce
the necessary techniques in time?"

The City Fathers hummed, drawn momentarily from
their eternal mulling over the past. At last they said:

"YES, MAYOR AMALFI. BEAR IN MIND THAT
WE ARE NOT ALONE IN THIS CLOUD. REMEM-
BER THOR FIVE."

There it was: the ancient slogan that had made Okies hated even on planets that had never seen an Okie city, and could never expect to. There was only the smallest chance that the city which had wrought that atrocity had made good its escape to this Cloud; it had all happened a long time ago. But even the narrow chance, if the City Fathers were right, would bring the cops here sooner or later, to destroy Amalfi's own city in expiation of that still-burning crime.

Remember Thor V. No city would be safe until that raped and murdered world could be forgotten. Not even out here, in the virgin satellites of the home lens.

"Boss? Sorry, we didn't know you were busy. But we've got an operating schedule set up, as soon as you're ready to look at it."

"I'm ready right now, Mark," Amalfi said, turning away from the boards. "Hello, Dee. How do you like your planet?"

The girl smiled. "It's beautiful," she said simply.

"For the most part, anyway," Hazleton agreed. "This heath is an ugly place, but the rest of the land seems to be excellent—much better than you'd think it from the way it's being farmed. The tiny little fields they break it up into here just don't do it justice, and even I know better cultivation methods than these serfs do."

"I'm not surprised," Amalfi said. "It's my theory that the Proctors maintain their power partly by preventing the spread of any knowledge about farming beyond the most rudimentary kind. That's also the most rudimentary kind of politics, as I don't need to tell you."

"On the politics," Hazleton said evenly, "we're in disagreement. While that's ironing itself out, the business of running the city has to go on."

"All right," Amalfi said. "What's on the docket?"

"I'm having a small plot on the heath, next to the city, turned over and conditioned for some experimental plantings, and extensive soil tests have already been made. That's purely a stop gap, of course. Eventually we'll have to expand onto good land. I've drawn up a tentative contract of lease between the city and the Proctors, which provides for us to rotate ownership geographically so as to keep displacement of the serfs at a minimum, and at the same time opens a complete spectrum of seasonal plantings to us—essentially it's the old Limited Colony contract, but heavily weighed in the direction of the Proctors' prejudices. There's no doubt in my mind but that they'll sign it. Then——"

"They won't sign it," Amalfi said. "They can't even be shown it. Furthermore, I want everything you've put into your experimental plot here on the heath yanked out."

Hazleton put a hand to his forehead in frank exasperation. "Oh, hell, boss," he said. "Don't tell me that we're *still* not at the end of the old squirrel-cage routine— intrigue, intrigue, and then more intrigue. I'm sick of it, I'll tell you that directly. Isn't a thousand years enough for you? I thought we had come to this planet to settle down!"

"We did. We will. But as you reminded me yourself yesterday, there are other people in possession of this planet at the moment—people we can't legally push out. As matters stand right now, we can't give them the faintest sign that we mean to settle here; they're already intensely suspicious of that very thing, and they're watching us for evidence of it every minute."

"Oh no," Dee said. She came forward swiftly and put a hand on Amalfi's shoulder. "John, you promised us after the March was over that we were going to make a home here. Not necessarily on this planet, but somewhere in the Cloud. You promised, John."

The mayor looked up at her. It was no secret to her, or to Hazleton either, that he loved her; they both knew, as well, the cruelly just Okie law—and the vein of iron loyalty in Amalfi that would have compelled him to act by that law even if it had never existed. Until the crisis in the jungle had forced Amalfi to reveal to Hazleton the existence of that love, neither of the two youngsters had more than suspected it over a period of nearly three centuries.

But Dee was comparatively new to Okie mores, and was, in addition, a woman. Only to know that she was loved had been unable to content her long. She was already beginning to put the knowledge to work.

She was certainly not old enough yet to realize that the crisis had passed, leaving behind only a residuum of devotion useless to her and to Amalfi alike. She could not know that the person who had replaced her in Amalfi's mind was Karst; that Amalfi was now hearing from the lips of the serf the innocent and vastly touching questions which Dee had once asked; that Amalfi had realized that

his thousand years of adult life had fitted him to answer
not one question, but a thousand. Had anyone suggested
to her that Amalfi was only just now coming into his full
maturity, she would not have understood; possibly, she
might have laughed. Amalfi had himself smiled when the
realization had come to him.

"Of course I promised," he said. "I've delivered on my
promises for a millennium now, and I'll continue to do so.
This planet will be our home if you'll give me just the
minimum of help in winning it. It's the best of all the
planets we passed on the way in, for a great many reasons
—including a couple that won't begin to show until you
see the winter constellations here, and a few more that
won't become evident for a century yet. But there's one
thing I certainly can't give you, and that's immediate
delivery."

"All right," Dee said. She smiled. "I trust you, John,
you know that. But it's hard to be patient."

"Is it?" Amalfi said, not much surprised. "Come to
think of it, I remember when the same thought occurred to me, back on He. In retrospect the problem
doesn't seem large."

"Boss, you'd better give us some substitute courses of
action," Hazleton cut in, a little coldly. "With the possible
exception of yourself, every man, woman, and alley cat in
the city is ready to spread out all over the surface of this
planet the moment the starting gun is fired. You gave us
every reason to think that that would be the way it would
happen. If there's going to be a delay, you have a good
many idle hands to put to work."

"Use straight work-contract procedure all the way
down the line. No exploiting of the planet that we
wouldn't normally do during the usual stopover for a job.
That means no truck gardens or any other form of local
agriculture; just refilling the oil tanks, re-breeding the
Chlorella strains from local sources for heterosis, making
up our water losses, and so on. The last I heard, we were
still using the Tx 71105 strain of *Chlorella pyrenoidosa;*
that's too high-temp an alga for a planet with a winter
season, like this one."

"That won't work," Hazleton said. "It may fool the
Proctors, Amalfi, but how can you fool your own people?
What are you going to do with the perimeter police, for
instance? Sergeant Anderson's whole crew knows that it

won't ever again have to make up a boarding squad or
defend the city or take up any other military duty. Nine-
tenths of them are itching to throw off their harness for
good and all and start dirt farming. What am I going to
tell them?"

"Send 'em out to your experimental patch on the
heath," Amalfi said, "on police detail. Tell 'em to pick up
everything that grows."

Hazleton started to turn toward the lift shaft, holding
out his hand to Dee. Then, characteristically, he had a
third thought and turned back.

"But why, boss?" he said plaintively. "What makes you
think the Proctors suspect us of squatting? And what
could they do about it if we did?"

"The Proctors have asked for the standard work contract," Amalfi said. "They knew what it was, they got it,
and they insist upon its observation, to the letter—
including the provision that the city must be off this planet
by the date of termination. As you know, that's impossible; we can't leave this planet at all. But we'll have to
pretend that we're going to leave up to the last possible
minute."

Hazleton looked stubborn. Dee took his hand reassur-
ingly, but it didn't seem to register.

"As for what the Proctors themselves can do about it,"
Amalfi said, picking up the earphones again, "I don't
know. I'm trying to find out. But this much I do know:

"The Proctors have *already* called the cops."

Under the gray, hazy light in the schoolroom, neutral
light which seemed cast like a cloak along the air rather
than to illuminate it, voices and visions came thronging
even into the conscious and prepared mind of the visitor,
pouring from the memory cells of the City Fathers.
Amalfi could feel their pressure, just below the surface of
his mind; it was vaguely unpleasant, partly because he
already knew what they sought to impart, so that the
redoubled impressions tended to shoulder forward into
the immediate attention, nearly with the vividness of
immediate experience.

He waved a hand before his eyes in annoyance and
looked for a monitor, found one standing at his elbow,
and wondered how long he had been there—or, converse-

ly, how long Amalfi himself had been lulled into the learning trance.

"Where's Karst?" he said brusquely. "The first serf we brought in? I need him."

"Yes, sir. He's in a chair toward the front of the room." The monitor—whose function combined the duties of classroom supervisor and nurse—turned away briefly to a nearby wall treacher, which opened and floated out to him a tall metal tumbler. The monitor took it, and led the way through the room, threading his way among the scattered couches. Usually most of these were unoccupied, since it took less than 500 hours to bring the average child through tensor calculus and hence to the limits of what he could be taught by passive inculcation alone. Now, however, every couch was occupied, and few of them by children.

One of the counterpointing, sub-audible voices was murmuring: "Some of the cities which turned bindlestiff did not pursue the usual policy of piracy and raiding, but settled instead upon faraway worlds and established tyrannical rules. Most of these were overthrown by the Earth police; the cities were not efficient fighting machines. Those which withstood the first assault sometimes were allowed to remain in power for various reasons of policy, but such cases were invariably barred from commerce. Some of these involuntary empires may still remain on the fringes of Earth's jurisdiction. Most notorious of these recrudescences of imperialism was the reduction of Thor Five, the work of one of the earliest of the Okies, a heavily militarized city which had already earned itself the popular nickname of 'the Mad Dogs.' The epithet, current among other Okies as well as planetary populations, of course referred primarily . . ."

"Here's your man," the monitor said in a low voice. Amalfi looked down at Karst. The serf had already undergone a considerable change. He was no longer a distorted and worn caricature of a man, chocolate colored with sun, wind, and ground-in dirt, so brutalized as to be almost beyond pity. He was, instead, rather like a fetus as he lay curled on the couch, innocent and still perfectable, as yet unmarked by any experience which counted. His past—and there could hardly have been much of it, for although he had said that his present wife, Eedit, had been his fifth, he was obviously scarcely twenty years old—had

been so completely monotonous and implacable that, giv-
en the chance, he had sloughed it off as easily and totally
as one throws away a single garment. He was, Amalfi
realized, much more essentially a child than any Okie
infant would ever be.

The monitor touched Karst's shoulder and the serf
stirred uneasily, then sat up, instantly awake, his intense
blue eyes questioning Amalfi. The monitor handed him the
anodized aluminum tumbler, now beaded with cold, and
Karst drank from it. The pungent liquid made him sneeze,
quickly and without seeming to notice that he had
sneezed, like a cat.

"How's it coming through, Karst? Amalfi said.

"It is very hard," the serf said. He took another pull at
the tumbler. "But once grasped, it seems to bring everything into flower at once. Lord Amalfi, the Proctors claim
that IMT came from the sky on a cloud. Yesterday I only
believed that. Today I think I understand it."

"I think you do," Amalfi said. "And you're not alone.
We have serfs by scores in the city now, learning—just
look around you and you'll see. And they're learning more
than just simple physics or cultural morphology. They're
learning freedom, beginning with the first one—freedom
to hate."

"I know that lesson," Karst said, with a profound and
glacial calm. "But you awakened me for something."

"I did," the mayor agreed grimly. "We've got a visitor
we think you'll be able to identify: a Proctor. And he's up
to something that smells damned funny to me and
Hazleton both, but we can't pin down what it is. Come
give us a hand, will you?"

"You'd better give him some time to rest, Mr. Mayor,"
the monitor said disapprovingly. "Being dumped out of
hypnopaedic trance is a considerable shock; he'll need at
least an hour."

Amalfi stared at the monitor incredulously. He was
about to note that neither Karst nor the city had the hour
to spare when it occurred to him that to say so would take
ten words where one was plenty. "Vanish," he said.

The monitor did his best.

Karst looked intently at the judas. The man on the
screen had his back turned; he was looking into the big
operations tank in the city manager's office. The indirect

light beamed on his shaved and oiled head. Amalfi watched over Karst's left shoulder, his teeth sunk firmly in a new cigar.

"Why, the man's as bald as I am," the mayor said. "And he can't be much past his adolescence, judging by his skull; he's forty-five at the most. Recognize him, Karst?"

"Not yet," Karst said. "All the Proctors shave their heads. If he would only turn around—ah. Yes. That's Heldon. I have seen him myself only once, but he is easy to recognize. He is young, as the Proctors go. He is the stormy petrel of the Great Nine—some think him a friend of the serfs. At least he is less quick with the whip than the others."

"What would he be wanting here?"

"Perhaps he will tell us." Karst's eyes remained fixed upon the Proctor's image.

"Your request puzzles me," Hazleton's voice said, issuing smoothly from the speaker above the judas. The city manager could not be seen, but his expression seemed to modulate the sound of his voice almost specifically: the tiger mind masked behind a pussy-cat purr as behind a pussy-cat smile. "We're glad to hear of new services we can render to a client, of course. But we certainly never suspected that antigravity mechanisms even existed in IMT."

"Don't think me stupid, Mr. Hazleton," Heldon said. "You and I know that IMT was once a wanderer, as your city is now. We also know that your city, like all Okie cities, would like a world of its own. Will you allow me this much intelligence, please?"

"For discussion, yes," Hazleton's voice said.

"Then let me say that it's quite evident to me that you're nurturing an uprising. You have been careful to stay within the letter of the contract, simply because you dare not breach it, any more than we; the Earth police protect us from each other to that extent. Your Mayor Amalfi was told that it was illegal for the serfs to speak to your people, but unfortunately it is illegal only for the serfs, not for your citizens. If we cannot keep the serfs out of your city, you are under no obligation to do it for us."

"A point you have saved me the trouble of making," Hazleton said.

"Quite so. I'll add also that when this revolution of

"And the spindizzies?" Amalfi said. "Who else would know of them among the Great Nine?"

"Asor, for one," Karst said. "He is the presiding officer, and the religious fanatic of the group. It is said that he still practices daily the full thirty yogas of the Semantic Rigor, even to chinning himself upon every rung of the Abstraction Ladder. The prophet Maalvin banned the flight of men forever, so Asor would not be likely to allow IMT to fly at this late date."

"He has his reasons," Hazleton said reflectively. "Religions rarely exist in a vacuum. They have effects on the societies they reflect. He's probably afraid of the spindizzies, in the last analysis. With such a weapon it takes only a few hundred men to make a revolution—more than enough to overthrow a feudal setup like this. IMT didn't dare keep its spindizzies working."

"Go on, Karst," Amalfi said, raising his hand impatiently at Hazleton. "How about the other Proctors?"

"There is Bemajdi, but he hardly counts," Karst said. "Let me think. Remember, I have never seen most of these men. The only one who matters, it seems to me, is Larre. He is a dour-faced old man with a pot belly. He is usually on Heldon's side, but seldom travels with Heldon all the way. He will worry less about the money the serfs are earning than will the rest. He will contrive a way to tax it away from us—perhaps by declaring a holiday, in honor of the visit of Earthmen to our planet. The collection of tithes is a duty of his."

"Would he allow Heldon to put IMT's spindizzies in shape?"

"No, probably not," Karst said. "I believe Heldon was telling the truth when he said that he would have to do that in secret."

"I don't know," Amalfi said. "I don't like it. On the surface, it looks as though the Proctors hope to scare us off the planet as soon as the contract expires, and then collect all the money we've paid the serfs—with the cops to back them up. But when you look closely at it, it's crazy. Once the cops find out the identity of IMT—and it won't take long—they'll break up both cities and be glad of the chance."

Karst said. "Is this because IMT was the Okie city that did—what was done—on Thor Five?"

Amalfi suddenly found that he was having difficulty in

keeping his Adam's apple where it belonged. "Let that pass, Karst," he growled. "We're not going to import that story into the Cloud. That should have been cut from your learning tape."

"I know it now," Karst said calmly. "And I am not surprised. The Proctors never change."

"Forget it. Forget it, do you hear? Forget everything. Karst, can you go back to being a dumb serf for a night?"

"Go back to my land?" Karst said. "It would be awkward. My wife must have a new man by now——"

"No, not back to your land. I want to go with Heldon and look at his spindizzies as soon as he says the word. I'll need to take some heavy equipment, and I'll need some help. Will you come along?"

Hazleton raised his eyebrows. "You won't fool Heldon, boss."

"I think I will. Of course he knows that we've educated some of the serfs, but that's not a thing he can actually see when he looks at it; his whole background is against it. He just isn't accustomed to thinking of serfs as intelligent. He knows we have thousands of them here, and yet he isn't really afraid of that idea. He thinks we may arm them, make a mob of them. He can't begin to imagine that a serf can learn something better than how to handle a sidearm—something better, and far more dangerous."

"How can you be sure?" Hazleton said.

"By analogue. Remember the planet of Thetis Alpha called Fitzgerald, where they used a big beast called a horse for everything—from pulling carts to racing? All right: suppose you visited a place where you had been told that a few horses had been taught to talk. While you're working there, somebody comes to give you a hand, dragging a spavined old plug with a straw hat pulled down over its ears and a pack on its back. (Excuse me, Karst, but business is business.) You aren't going to think of that horse as one of the talking ones. You aren't accustomed to thinking of horses as being able to talk at all."

"All right," Hazleton said, grinning at Karst's evident discomfiture. "What's the main strategy from here on out, boss? I gather that you've got it set up. Are you ready to give it a name yet?"

"Not quite," the mayor said. "Unless you like long

titles. It's still just another problem in political pseudo-morphism."

Amalfi caught sight of Karst's deliberately incurious face and his own grin broadened. "Or," he said, "the fine art of tricking your opponent into throwing his head at you."

CHAPTER NINE: Home

IMT was a squat city, long rooted in the stony soil, and as changeless as a forest of cenotaphs. Its quietness, too, was like the quietness of a cemetery, and the Proctors, carrying the fanlike wands of their office, the pierced fans with the jagged tops and the little jingling tags, were much like friars moving among the dead.

The quiet, of course, could be accounted for very simply. The serfs were not allowed to speak within the walls of IMT unless spoken to, and there were comparatively few Proctors in the city to speak to them. For Amalfi, there was also the imposed silence of the slaughtered millions of Thor V blanketing the air. He wondered if the Proctors themselves could still hear that raw silence.

He got his answer almost at once. The naked brown figure of a passing serf glanced furtively at the party, saw Heldon, and raised a finger to its lips in what was evidently an established gesture of respect. Heldon barely nodded. Amalfi, necessarily, took no overt notice at all, but he thought: *Shh, is it? I don't wonder. But it's too late, Heldon. The secret is out.*

Karst trudged behind them, shooting an occasional wary glance at Heldon from under his tangled eyebrows. His caution was wasted on the Proctor. They passed through a decaying public square, in the center of which was an almost-obliterated statuary group, so weather-worn as to have lost any integrity it might ever have had. Integrity, Amalfi mused, is not a common characteristic of monuments. Except to a sharp eye, the mass of stone on the old pedestal might have been nothing but a moderately large meteor, riddled with the twisting pits characteristic of siderites.

Amalfi could see, however, that the spaces sculpted out of the interior of that block of black stone, after the fashion of an ancient Earth sculptor named Moore, had once had meaning. Inside the stone there had once stood a powerful human figure, with its foot resting upon the neck of a slighter figure; both surrounded by matter, but cut into space.

Heldon, too, stopped and looked at the monument. There was some kind of struggle going on inside of him. Amalfi did not know what it was, but he had a good guess. Heldon was a young man; hence, as a Proctor, he was probably recently elected. Karst's testimony had made it clear that most of the other members of the Great Nine—Asor, Bemajdi, and the rest—had been members of the Great Nine from the beginning. They were, in short, not the descendants of the men who had ravaged Thor V, but those very same men, preserved by a jealous hoarding of anti-agathics right down to the present.

Heldon looked at the monument. The figures inside it made it clear that once upon a time IMT had actually been proud of the memory of Thor V, and the ancients of the Great Nine, while they might not still be proud, were still guilty. Heldon, who had not himself committed that crime, was choosing whether or not to associate himself with it in fact, as he had already associated himself by implication, by being a Proctor at all. . . .

"Ahead is the Temple," Heldon said suddenly, turning away from the statue. "The machinery is beneath it. There should be no one of interest in it at this hour, but I had best make sure. Wait here."

No one of interest: that meant the serfs. Heldon had decided; he was of the Proctors; he had taken Thor V into his pigeon's bosom.

"Suppose somebody notices us?" Amalfi said.

"This square is usually avoided. Also, I have men posted around it to divert any chance traffic. If you don't wander away, you'll be safe."

The Proctor gathered in his shirts and strode away toward the big domed building, where he disappeared abruptly down an alleyway. Behind Amalfi, Karst began to sing, in an exceedingly scratchy voice, but very softly—a folk tune of some kind, obviously. The melody, which once had had to do with a town named Kazan, was too many thousands of years old for Amalfi to recognize it, even had he not been tune deaf. Nevertheless, the mayor abruptly found himself listening to Karst, with the intensity of a hooded owl sonar-tracking a field mouse. Karst chanted:

> "Wild on the wind rose the righteous wrath of Maalvin,
>> Borne like a brand to the burning of the Barrens.
>> Arms of hands of rebels perished then,
>> Stars nor moons bedecked that midnight.
>> IMT made the sky
>> Fall!"

Seeing that Amalfi was listening to him, Karst stopped with an apologetic gesture. "Go ahead, Karst," Amalfi said at once. "How does the rest go?"

"There isn't time. There are hundreds of verses; every singer adds at least one of his own to the song. It is always supposed to end with this one:

> "Black with their blood was the brick of that barrow,
>> Toppled the tall towers, crushed to the clay.
>> None might live who flouted Maalvin,
>> Earth their souls spurned spaceward, wailing,
>> IMT made the sky
>> Fall!"

"That's great," Amalfi said grimly. "We really are in the soup—just about in the bottom of the bowl, I'd say. I wish I'd heard that song a week ago."

"What does it tell you?" Karst said wonderingly. "It is only an old legend."

"It tells me why Heldon wants his spindizzies fixed. I knew he wasn't telling me the straight goods, but that old Laputa gag never occurred to me—more recent cities aren't strong enough in the keel to risk it. But with all the mass this burg packs, it can squash us flat—and we'll just have to sit still for it!"

"I don't understand——"

"It's simple enough. Your prophet Maalvin used IMT like a nutcracker. He picked it up, flew it over the opposition, and let it down again. The trick was dreamed up away before space flight, as I recall. Karst, stick close to me; I may have to get a message to you under Heldon's eye, so watch for . . . Sst, here he comes."

The Proctor had been uttered by the alleyway like an untranslatable word. He came rapidly toward them across the crumbling flagstones.

"I think," Heldon said, "that we are now ready for your valuable aid, Mayor Amalfi."

Heldon put his foot on a jutting pyramidal stone and pressed down. Amalfi watched carefully, but nothing happened. He swept his flash around the featureless stone walls of the underground chamber, then back again to the floor. Impatiently, Heldon kicked the little pyramid.

This time, there was a protesting rumble. Very slowly, and with a great deal of scraping, a block of stone perhaps five feet long by two feet wide began to rise, as if pivoted or hinged at the far end. The beam of the mayor's flash darted into the opening, picking out a narrow flight of steps.

"I'm disappointed," Amalfi said. "I expected to see Jules Verne come out from under it—or Dean Swift. All right, Heldon, lead on."

The Proctor went cautiously down the steps, holding his skirts up against the dampness. Karst came last, bent low under the heavy pack, his arms hanging laxly. The steps felt cold and slimy through the thin soles of the mayor's sandals, and little trickles of moisture ran down the close-pressing walls. Amalfi felt a nearly intolerable urge to light a cigar; he could almost taste the powerful aromatic odor cutting through the humidity. But he needed his hands free.

He was almost ready to hope that the spindizzies had been ruined by all this moisture, but he discarded the idea even as it was forming in the back of his mind. That would be the easy way out, and in the end it would be disastrous. If the Okies were ever to call this planet their own, IMT had to be made to fly again.

How to keep it off his own city's back, once IMT was aloft, he still was unable to figure. He was piloting, as he invariably wound up doing in the pinches, by the seat of his pants.

The steps ended abruptly in a small chamber so small, chilly, and damp that it was little more than a cave. The flashlight's eyes roved, came to rest on an oval doorway sealed off with dull metal—almost certainly lead. So IMT's spindizzies ran "hot"? That was already bad news; it back-dated them far beyond the year to which Amalfi had tentatively assigned them.

"That it?" he said.

"That is the way," Heldon agreed. He twisted an inconspicuous handle.

Ancient fluorescents flickered into bluish life as the valve drew back, and glinted upon the humped backs of machines. The air was quite dry here—evidently the big chamber was kept sealed—and Amalfi could not repress a fugitive pang of disappointment. He scanned the huge machines, looking for control panels or homologues thereof.

"Well?" Heldon said harshly. He seemed to be under considerable strain. It occurred to Amalfi that Heldon's strategy might well be a personal flyer, not an official policy of the Great Nine; in which case it might go hard with Heldon if his colleagues found him in this particular place of all places with an Okie. "Aren't you going to make any tests?"

"Certainly," Amalfi said. "I was a little taken aback at their size, that's all."

"They are old, as you know," said the Proctor. "Doubtless they are built much larger nowadays."

That, of course, wasn't so. Modern spindizzies ran less than a tenth the size of these. The comment cast new doubt upon Heldon's exact status. Amalfi had assumed that the Proctor would not let him touch the spindizzies except to inspect; that there would be plenty of men in IMT capable of making repairs from detailed instructions; that Heldon himself, and any Proctor, would know enough physics to comprehend whatever explanations Amalfi might proffer. Now he was not so sure—and on this question hung the amount of tinkering Amalfi would be able to do without being detected.

The mayor mounted a metal stair to a catwalk which ran along the tops of the generators, then stopped and looked down at Karst. "Well, stupid, don't just stand there," he said. "Come on up, and bring the stuff."

Obediently Karst shambled up the metal steps, Heldon at his heels. Amalfi ignored them to search for an inspection port in the casing, found one, and opened it. Beneath was what appeared to be a massive rectifying circuit, plus the amplifier for some kind of monitor—probably a digital computer. The amplifier involved more vacuum tubes than Amalfi had ever before seen gathered into one circuit, and there was a separate power supply to deliver DC to their heaters. Two of the tubes were each as big as his fist.

Karst bent over and slung the pack to the deck. Amalfi drew out of it a length of slender black cable and thrust its double prongs into a nearby socket. A tiny bulb on the other end glowed neon-red.

"Your computer's still running," he reported. "Whether it's still sane or not is another matter. May I turn the main banks on, Heldon?"

"I'll turn them on," the Proctor said. He went down the stairs again and across the chamber.

Instantly Amalfi was murmuring through motionless lips into the inspection port. The result to Karst's ears must have been rather weird. The technique of speaking without moving one's lips is simply a matter of substituting consonants which do not involve lip movement, such as *y*, for those which do, such as *w*. If the resulting sound is picked up from inside the resonating chamber, as it is with a throat mike, it is not too different from ordinary speech, only a bit more blurred. Heard from outside the speaker's nasopharyngeal cavity, however, it has a tendency to sound like Japanese Pidgin.

"Yatch Heldon, Karst. See yhich syitch he kulls, an' nenorize its location. Got it? Good."

The tubes lit. Karst nodded once, very slightly. The Proctor watched from below while Amalfi inspected the lines.

"Will they work?" he called. His voice was muffled, as though he were afraid to raise it as high as he thought necessary.

"I think so. One of these tubes is gassing, and there may have been some failures here and there. Better check the whole lot before you try anything ambitious. You do have facilities for testing tubes, don't you?"

Relief spread visibly over Heldon's face, despite his obvious effort to betray nothing. Probably he could have fooled any of his own people without effort, but for Amalfi, who, like any Okie mayor, could follow the parataxic "speech" of muscle interplay and posture as readily as he could spoken dialogue, Heldon's expression was as clear as a signed confession.

"Certainly," the Proctor said. "Is that all?"

"By no means. I think you ought to rip out about half of these circuits, and install transistors wherever they can be used; we can sell you the necessary germanium at the legal rate. You've got two or three hundred tubes to a unit here, by my estimate, and if you have a tube failure in flight—well, the only word that fits what would happen then is *blooey!*"

"Will you be able to show us how?"

"Probably," the mayor said. "If you'll allow me to inspect the whole system, I can give you an exact answer."

"All right," Heldon said. "But don't delay. I can't count on more than another half-day at most."

This was better than Amalfi had expected—miles better. Given that much time, he could trace at least enough of the leads to locate the master control. That Heldon's expression failed totally to match the content of his speech disturbed Amalfi profoundly, but there was nothing that he could do that would alter that now. He pulled paper and stylus out of Karst's pack and began to make rapid sketches of the wiring before him.

After he had a fairly clear idea of the first generator's setup, it was easier to block in the main features of the second. It took time, but Heldon did not seem to tire.

The third spindizzy completed the picture, leaving Amalfi wondering what the fourth one was for. It turned out to be a booster, designed to compensate for the losses of the others wherever the main curve of their output failed to conform to the specs laid down for it by the crude, over all regenerative circuit. The booster was located on the backside of the feedback loop, behind the computer rather than ahead of it, so that all the computer's corrections had to pass through it; the result, Amalfi was sure, would be a small but serious "base surge" every time any correction was applied. The spindizzies of IMT seemed to have been wired together by Cro-Magnon Man.

But they would fly the city. That was what counted.

Amalfi finished his examination of the booster generator and straightened up painfully, stretching the muscles of his back. He had no idea how many hours he had consumed. It

seemed as though months had passed. Heldon was still
watching him, deep blue circles under his eyes, but still
wide awake and watchful.

And Amalfi had found no point anywhere in the underground chamber from which the spindizzies of IMT could
be controlled. The control point was somewhere else; the
main control cable ran into a pipe which shot straight up
through the roof of the cavern.

. . . IMT made the sky/ Fall . . .

Amalfi yawned ostentatiously and bent back to fasten
the plate over the booster-generator's observation port.
Karst squatted near him, frankly asleep, as relaxed and
comfortable as a cat drowsing on a high ledge. Heldon
watched.

"I'm going to have to do the job for you," Amalfi said.
"It's really major; might take weeks."

"I thought you would say so," Heldon said. "And I was
glad to give you the time to find out. But I don't think
we'll make any such replacements."

"You need 'em."

"Possibly. But obviously there is a big factor of safety
in the apparatus, or we would never have been able to fly
the city at all." (Not, Amalfi noticed, "our ancestors," but
"we"; Heldon had identified himself with the crime. He
would pay.) "You will understand, Mayor Amalfi, that we
cannot risk your doing something to the machines that we
can't do ourselves, on the unlikely assumption that you're
increasing their efficiency. If they will run as they are,
that will have to be good enough."

"Oh, they'll run," Amalfi said. He began, methodically,
to pack up his equipment. "For a while. I'll tell you flatly
that they're not safe to operate, all the same."

Heldon shrugged, and went down the spiral metal stairs
to the floor of the chamber. Amalfi rummaged in the pack
a moment more. Then he ostentatiously kicked Karst
awake—and kicked hard, for he knew better than to
play-act with a born overseer for an audience—and motioned the serf to pick up the bundle. They went down
after Heldon.

The Proctor was smiling, and it was not a nice smile.
"Not safe?" he said. "No, I never supposed that they
were. But I think now that the dangers are mostly political."

"Why?" Amalfi demanded, trying to moderate his

breathing. He was suddenly almost exhausted; it had taken—how many hours? He had no idea.

"Are you aware of the time, Mayor Amalfi?"

"About morning, I'd judge," Amalfi said dully, jerking the pack more firmly onto Karst's drooping left shoulder. "Damn late, anyhow."

"Very late," Heldon said. He was not disguising his expression now. He was openly crowing. "The contract between your city and mine expired at noon today. It is now nearly an hour after noon; we have been here all night and morning. And your city is still on our soil, in violation of the contract, Mayor Amalfi."

"An oversight——"

"No; a victory." Heldon drew a tiny silver tube from the folds of his robe and blew into it. "Mayor Amalfi, you may consider yourself a prisoner of war."

The little silver tube had made no audible sound, but there were already ten men in the room. The mesotron rifles they carried were of an ancient design, probably pre-Kammerman, like the spindizzies of IMT.

But, like the spindizzies, they looked as though they would work.

Karst froze; Amalfi unfroze him by jabbing him surreptitiously in the ribs with a finger, and began to unload the contents of his own small pack into Karst's.

"You've called the Earth police, I suppose?" he said.

"Long ago. That way of escape will be cut off by now. Let me say, Mayor Amalfi, that if you expected to find down here any controls that you might disable—and I was quite prepared to allow you to search for them—you expected too much stupidity from me."

Amalfi said nothing. He went on methodically repacking the equipment.

"You are making too many motions, Mayor Amalfi. Put your hands up in the air and turn around very slowly."

Amalfi put up his hands and turned. In each hand he held a small black object about the size and shape of an egg.

"I expected only as much stupidity as I got," he said conversationally. "You can see what I'm holding up there. I can and will drop one or both of them if I'm shot. I may drop them anyhow. I'm tired of your back-cluster ghost town."

Heldon snorted. "Explosives? Gas? Ridiculous; nothing so small could contain enough energy to destroy the city; and you have no masks. Do you take me for a fool?"

"Events prove you one," Amalfi said steadily. "The possibility was quite large that you would try to ambush me, once you had me in IMT. I could have forestalled that by bringing a guard with me. You haven't met my perimeter police; they're tough boys, and they've been off duty so long that they'd love the chance to tangle with your palace crew. Didn't it occur to you that I left my city without a bodyguard only because I had less cumbersome ways of protecting myself?"

"Eggs," Heldon said scornfully.

"As a matter of fact, they *are* eggs; the black color is an analine stain, put on the shells as a warning. They contain chick embryos inoculated with a two-hour alveolytic mutated Terrestrial rickettsialpox—a new airborne strain developed in our own BW lab. Free space makes a wonderful laboratory for that kind of trick; an Okie town specializing in agronomy taught us the techniques a couple of centures back. Just a couple of eggs—but if I were to drop them, you would have to crawl on your belly behind me all the way back to my city to get the antibiotic shot that's specific for the disease; we developed that ourselves, too."

There was a brief silence, made all the more empty by the hoarse breathing of the Proctor. The armed men eyed the black eggs uneasily, and the muzzles of their rifles wavered out of line. Amalfi had chosen his weapon with great care; static feudal societies classically are terrified by the threat of plague—they have seen so much of it.

"Impasse," Heldon said at last. "All right, Mayor Amalfi. You and your slave have safe-conduct from this chamber——"

"From the building. If I hear the slightest sound of pursuit up the stairs, I'll chuck these down on you. They burst hard, by the way—the virus generates a lot of gas in chick-embryo medium."

"Very well," Heldon said, through his teeth. "From the building, then. But you have won nothing, Mayor Amalfi. If you can get back to your city, you'll be just in time to be an eyewitness of the victory of IMT—the victory you helped make possible. I think you'll be surprised at how thorough we can be."

"No, I won't," Amalfi said, in a flat, cold, and quite merciless voice. "I know all about IMT, Heldon. This is the end of the line for the Mad Dogs. When you die, you and your whole crew of Interstellar Master Traders, *remember Thor Five.*"

Heldon turned the color of unsized paper, and so, surprisingly, did at least four of his riflemen. Then the color began to rise in the Proctor's plump, fungoid cheeks. "Get out," he croaked, almost inaudibly. Then, suddenly, at the top of his voice: "Get out; *Get out!*"

Juggling the eggs casually, Amalfi walked toward the lead radiation lock. Karst shambled after him, cringing as he passed Heldon. Amalfi thought that the serf might be overdoing it, but Heldon did not notice; Karst might as well have been—a horse.

The lead plug swung to, blocking out Heldon's furious, frightened face and the glint of the fluorescents on the ancient spindizzies. Amalfi plunged one hand into Karst's pack, depositing one egg in the siliconefoam nest from which he had taken it, and withdrew the hand again grasping an ugly Schmeisser acceleration pistol. This he thrust into the waistband of his breeches.

"Up the stairs, Karst. Fast. I had to shave it pretty fine. Go on, I'm right behind you. Where would the controls for those machines be, by your guess? The control lead went up through the roof of that cavern."

"On the top of the Temple," Karst said. He was mounting the narrow steps in huge bounds, but it did not seem to cost him the slightest effort. "Up there is Star Chamber, where the Great Nine meets. There isn't any way to get to it that I know."

They burst up into the cold stone antechamber. Amalfi's flash roved over the floor, found the jutting pyramid; Karst kicked it. With a prolonged groan, the tilted slab settled down over the flight of steps and became just another block in the floor. There was certainly some way to raise it again from below, but Heldon would hesitate before he used it; the slab was noisy in motion, noisy enough to tell Amalfi that he was being followed. At the first such squawk, Amalfi would lay a black egg, and Heldon knew it.

"I want you to get out of the city, and take every serf that you can find with you," Amalfi said. "But it's going to take timing. Somebody's got to pull that switch down below that I asked you to memorize, and I can't do it; I've got to get into Star Chamber. Heldon will guess that I'm going up there, and he'll follow me. After he's gone by, Karst, you have to go down there and open that switch."

Here was the low door through which Heldon had first admitted them to the Temple. More stairs ran up from it. Strong daylight poured under it.

Amalfi inched the old door open and peered out. Despite the brightness of the afternoon, the close-set, chunky buildings of IMT turned the alleyway outside into a confusing multitude of twilights. Half a dozen leaden-eyed serfs were going by, with a Proctor walking behind them, half asleep.

"Can you find your way back into that crypt?" Amalfi whispered, leaving the door ajar.

"There's only one way to go."

"Good. Go back, then. Dump the pack outside the door here; we don't need it any more. As soon as Heldon's crew goes on up these stairs, get back down there and pull that switch. Then get out of the city; you'll have about four minutes of accumulated warm-up time from all those tube stages; don't waste a second of it. Got it?"

"Yes, but——"

Something went over the Temple like an avalanche of gravel and dwindled into some distance. Amalfi closed one eye and screwed the other one skyward. "Rockets," he said. "Sometimes I don't know why I insisted on a planet as primitive as this. But maybe I'll learn to love it. Good luck, Karst."

He turned toward the stairs.

"They'll trap you up there," Karst said.

"No, they won't. Not Amalfi. But me no *buts*, Karst. Git."

Another rocket went over, and far away there was a heavy explosion. Amalfi charged like a bull up the new flight of stairs toward Star Chamber.

The staircase was long and widely curving, as well as narrow, and both its risers and its treads were infuriatingly small. Amalfi remembered that the Proctors did not themselves climb stairs; they were carried up them on the forearms of serfs. Such pussy-ant steps made for sure footing, but not for fast transit.

As far as Amalfi was able to compute, the steps rose gently along the outside curvature of the Temple's dome, following a one-and-a-half helix to the summit. Why? Presumably, the Proctors didn't require themselves to climb long flights of stairs for nothing, even with serfs to carry them. Why couldn't Star Chamber be under the dome with the spindizzies, for instance, instead of atop it?

Amalfi was not far past the first half-turn before one good reason became evident. There was a rustle of voices jostling its way through the chinks in the dome from below; a congregation, evidently, was gathering. As Amalfi continued to mount the flat spiral, the murmuring became more and more discreet, until individual voices could almost be separated out from it. Up there at what mathematically would be the bottom of the bowl, where the floor of Star Chamber was, the architect of the Temple evidently had contrived a whispering gallery—a vault to which a Proctor might put his ear and hear the thinnest syllable of conspiracy in the crowd of suppliants below.

It was ingenious, Amalfi had to admit. Conspirators on church-bearing planets generally tend to think of churches as safe places for quiet plotting. In Amalfi's universe any planet which sponsored churches probably had a revolt coming to it.

Blowing like a porpoise, he scrambled up the last arc of the long Greek-spiral staircase. A solidly-closed double door, worked all over with phony-Byzantine scrolls, stood looking down at him. He didn't bother to stop to admire it; he hit it squarely under the paired, patently synthetic sapphires just above its center, and hit it hard. It burst.

Disappointment stopped him for a moment. The chamber was an ellipse of low eccentricity, monastically bare and furnished only with a heavy wooden table and nine chairs, now drawn back against the wall. There were no controls here, nor any place where they could be concealed. The chamber was windowless.

The lack of windows told him what he wanted to know. The other, the compelling reason why Star Chamber was on top of the Temple dome was that it harbored, somewhere, the pilot's cabin of IMT. And that, in as old a city as IMT, meant that visibility would be all-important—requiring a situation atop the tallest structure in the city, and as close to 360° visibility as could be managed. Obviously, Amalfi was not yet up high enough.

He looked up at the ceiling. One of the big stone slabs had a semi-circular cup in it, not much bigger than a large coin. The flat edge was much worn.

Amalfi grinned and looked under the wooden table. Sure enough, there it was—a pole with a hooked bill at one end, rather like a halberd, slung in clips. He yanked it out, straightened, and fitted the bill into the opening in the stone.

The slab came down easily, hinged at one end as the block down below over the generator room had been. The ancestors of the Proctors had not been much given to varying their engineering principles. The free end of the slab almost touched the table top. Amalfi sprang onto the table and scrambled up the tilted face of the stone; as he neared the top, the translating center of gravity which he represented actuated a counterweighting mechanism somewhere, and the slab closed, bearing him the rest of the way.

This was the control cabin, all right. It was tiny and packed with panels, all of which were thick in dust. Bull's-eyes of thick glass looked out over the city at the four compass points, and there was one set overhead. A single green light was glowing on one of the panels. While he walked toward it, it went out.

That had been Karst, cutting the power. Amalfi hoped that the peasant would get out again. He had grown to like him. There was something in his weathered, unmovable, shockproof courage, and in the voracity of his starved intelligence, that reminded the mayor of someone he had once known. That that someone was Amalfi as he had been at the age of twenty-five, Amalfi did not know, and there was no one else alive who would be able to tell him.

Spindizzies in essence are simple; Amalfi had no difficulty in setting and locking the controls the way he wanted them, or in performing sundry small tasks of highly selective sabotage. How he was to conceal what he had done, when every move left huge smears in the heavy dust, was a tougher problem. He solved it at length in the only possible way: he took off his shirt and flailed it at all of the boards. The result made him sneeze until his eyes watered, but it worked.

Now all he had to do was get out.

There were already sounds below in Star Chamber, but he was not yet worried about a direct attack. He still had a black egg, and the Proctors knew it. Furthermore, he also had the pole with the hooked bill, so that in order to open up the control room at all, the Proctors would have to climb on each other's shoulders. They weren't in good physical shape for gymnastics, and besides, they would know that men indulging in such stunts could be defeated temporarily by nothing more complicated than a kick in the teeth.

Nevertheless, Amalfi had no intention of spending the rest of his life in the control room of IMT. He had only about six minutes to get out of the city altogether.

After thinking very rapidly for approximately four seconds, Amalfi stood on the stone slab, overbalanced it, and slid solemnly down onto the top of the table in Star Chamber.

After a stunned instant, half a dozen pairs of hands grabbed him at once. Heldon's face, completely unrecognizable with fury and fear, was thrust into his.

"What have you done? Answer, or I'll order you torn to pieces."

"Don't be a lunkhead. Tell your men to let go of me. I still have your safe-conduct—and in case you're thinking of repudiating it, I still have the same weapon I had before. Cast off, by God, or——"

Heldon's guards released him before he had finished speaking. Heldon lurched heavily up onto the table top and began to claw his way up the slab. Several other robed, bald-headed men jostled after him—evidently Heldon had been driven by a greater fear to tell some of the Great Nine what he had done. Amalfi walked backwards out of Star Chamber and down two steps. Then he bent, deposited his remaining black egg carefully on the threshold, thumbed his nose at the furious soldiery, and took off down the spiral stairs at a dead run.

It would take Heldon a while, perhaps as much as a minute after he switched on the controls, to discover that the generators had been cut out while he was chasing Amalfi; and another minute, at best, to get a flunky down into the basement to turn them on again. Then there would be a warm-up time of four minutes. After that— IMT would go aloft.

Amalfi shot out into the alleyway and thence into the street, caroming off an astounded Proctor. A shout rose behind him. He doubled over and kept running.

The street was nearly dark in the twilight of the twin suns. He kept in the shadows and made for the nearest corner. The cornice of the building ahead of him abruptly turned lava-white, then began to dim through the red. He never did hear the accompanying scream of the mesotron rifle. He was concentrating on something else.

Then he was around the corner. The quickest route to the edge of the city, as well as he could recall, was down the street he had just quitted, but that was now out of the question; he had no desire to be burned down. Whether or not he could get out of IMT in time by any alternate route remained to be seen.

Doggedly, he kept running. He was fired on once more, by a man who did not really know on whom he was firing. Here, Amalfi was just a running man who failed to fit the categories; any first shot at him would be a reflex of disorientation, and aimed accordingly badly. . . .

The ground shuddered, ever so delicately, like the hide of a monster twitching at flies in its sleep. Somehow Amalfi managed to run still faster.

The shudder came again, stronger this time. A long, protracted groan followed it, traveling in a heavy wave through the bedrock of the city. The sound brought Proctors and serfs alike boiling out of the buildings.

At the third shock, something toward the center of the city collapsed with a sullen roar. Amalfi was caught up in the aimless, terrified eddying of the crowd, and fought with hands, teeth, and bullet head. . . .

The groaning grew louder. Abruptly, the ground bucked. Amalfi pitched forward. With him went the whole milling mob, falling in wind-rows like stacked grain. There was frantic screaming everywhere, but it was worst inside the buildings. Over Amalfi's head a window shattered explosively, and a woman's body came twisting and tumbling through the shuddering air.

Amalfi heaved himself up, spitting blood, and ran again. The pavement ahead was cracked in great, irregular shards, like a madman's mosaic. Just beyond, the blocks were tilted all awry, reminding Amalfi irrelevantly of a breakwater he had seen on some other planet, in some other century. . . .

He was clambering over them before he realized that these could only mark the rim of the original city of IMT. There were still more buildings on the other side of the huge, rock-filled trench, but the trench itself showed where the perimeter of the ancient Okie city had been sunk into the soil of the planet. Fighting for air with saw-edged rales, he threw himself from stone to stone toward the far edge of the trench. This was the most dangerous ground of all; if IMT were to lift now, he would be ground as fine as mincemeat in the tumbling rocks. If he could just reach the marches of the Barrens. . . .

Behind him, the groaning rose steadily in pitch, until it sounded like the tearing of an endless sheet of metal. Ahead, across the Barrens, his own city gleamed in the last rays of the twin suns. There was fighting around it; little bright flashes were sputtering at its edge. The rockets Amalfi had heard, four of them, were arrowing across the sky, and black things dropped from them. The Okie city responded with spouts of smoke.

Then there was an unbearably bright burst. After Amalfi could see again, there were only three rockets. In another few seconds there wouldn't be any: the City Fathers never missed.

Amalfi's lungs burned. He felt sod under his sandals. A twisted runner of furze lashed across his ankle, and he fell again.

He tried to get up and could not. The seared turf, on which an ancient rebel city once had stood, rumbled threateningly. He rolled over. The squat towers of IMT were swaying, and all around the edge of the city, huge blocks and clods heaved and turned over, like surf. Impossibly, a thin line of light, intense and ruddy, appeared above the moiling rocks. The suns were shining *under the city* . . .

The line of light widened. The old city took the air with an immense bound, and the rending of the long-rooted foundations was ear-splitting. From the sides of the huge mass, human beings threw themselves desperately toward the Barrens; most of them, Amalfi saw, were serfs. The Proctors, of course, were still trying to control the flight of IMT. . . .

The city rose majestically. It was gaining speed. Amalfi's heart hammered. If Heldon and his crew could figure out in time what Amalfi had done to the controls, Karst's old ballad would be re-enacted, and the crushing rule of the Proctors made safe forever.

But Amalfi had done his work well. The city of IMT did not stop rising. With a profound, visceral shock, Amalfi realized that it was already nearly a mile up, and still accelerating. The air would be thinning up there, and the Proctors had forgotten too much to know what to do. . . .

A mile and a half.

Two miles.

It grew smaller, At five miles it was just a wavery ink blot, lit on one side. At seven miles it was a point of dim light.

A bristle-topped head and a pair of enormous shoulders lifted cautiously from a nearby gully. It was Karst. He continued to look aloft for a moment, but IMT at ten miles was invisible. He looked down to Amalfi.

"Can—can it come back?" he said huskily.

"No," Amalfi said, his breathing gradually coming under control. "Keep watching, Karst. It isn't over yet. Remember that the Proctors had called the Earth cops ——"

At that same moment, the city of IMT reappeared—in a way. A third sun flowered in the sky. It lasted for three or four seconds. Then it dimmed and died.

"The cops were warned," Amalfi said softly, "to watch for an Okie city trying to make a getaway. They found it, and they dealt with it. Of course they got the wrong city, but they don't know that. They'll go home now—and now we're home, and so are you and your fellow men. Home on Earth, for good."

Around them, there was a murmuring of voices, hushed with disaster, and with something else, too—something so old, and so new, that it hardly had a name on the planet that IMT had ruled. It was called *freedom*.

"On Earth?" Karst repeated. He and the mayor climbed painfully to their feet. "What do you mean? This is not Earth——"

Across the Barrens, the Okie city glittered—the city that had pitched camp to mow some lawns. A cloud of stars was rising behind it.

"It is now," Amalfi said. "We're all Earthmen, Karst. Earth is more than just one little planet, buried in another galaxy than this. Earth is much more important than that.

"Earth isn't a place. It's an idea."

THE
TRIUMPH
OF
TIME

To Lester and Evelyn del Rey

Bismillahi 'rrahmani 'rrahim
When the day that must come shall have come suddenly,
None shall treat that sudden coming as a lie:
Day that shall abase! Day that shall exalt!
When the earth shall be shaken with a shock,
And the mountains shall be crumbled with a crumbling,
And shall become scattered dust,
And into three bands shall ye be divided: . . .
    Before thee have we granted to a man a life that shall
        last forever:
If thou then die, shall they live forever?
    Every soul shall taste of death: . . .
    But it shall come on them suddenly and shall confound
        them; and they shall not be able to put it back,
        neither shall they be respited.

—The Koran;
Sura LVI, Sura XXI

PROLOGUE

... Thus we have seen that Earth, a planet like other civilized worlds, having a score of myriads of years of atmosphere-bound history behind her, and having begun manned local space-flight in approximately her own year 1960, did not achieve importance on a galactic scale until her independent discovery of the gravitron polarity generator in her year 2019. Her colonials made first contact with the Vegan Tyranny in 2289, and the antagonism between the two great cultures, one on its way down, the other rapidly developing, culminated in the Battle of Altair in 2310, the first engagement of what has come to be known as the Vegan War. Some 65 years later, Earth launched the first of the fleet of space-cruising cities, the "Okies," by which it was eventually to dominate the galaxy for a long period, and in 2413 the long struggle with the Vegans came to an end with the investment of Vega itself, and the Battle of the Forts. The subsequent scorching of the Vegan system by the Third Colonial Navy, under Admiral Alois Hrunta, prompted Earth proper to indict its admiral *in absentia* for atrocities and attempted genocide. The case was tried, also *in absentia,* by the Colonial Court; Hrunta was found guilty, but refused to submit to judgment. An attempt to bring him in by force brought home for the first time the fact that the Third Colonial Navy had defected to him almost *en masse* and resulted in 2464 in the Battle of BD 40°4048'. Both sides suffered heavy losses, but there was no other outcome, and Hrunta subsequently declared himself Emperor of Space—the first of many such gimcrack "empires" which were to spawn on the fringes of Earth's jurisdiction during the so-called Empty Years. This period officially began in 2522 with the collapse of local government on Earth—the Bureaucratic State, dating from

2105—which after a brief police interregnum allowed the now large numbers of Okie cities to develop in effectual anarchy, a condition very well suited to their proliferation of trade routes throughout the known and unknown galaxy.

We have already discussed the collapse under its own weight of the Hruntan Empire and the final reduction of the fragments by the recrudescent Earth police during the period 3545–3602. We have stressed this relatively minor aspect of Earth history not because it was at all unusual, but because it was typical of the balkanization of Earth's official power during the very period when its actual power was greatly on the rise. Our discussion of the history of one of the Okie cities, New York, N. Y., which began its space-flying career in 3111 and thus overlapped much of the history of the Hruntan Empire, may be compared to illustrate the difference in the treatment accorded by Earth to her two very different children, empires and Okies, and history shows the wisdom of the choice; for it was the wide-ranging Okies who were to make the galaxy an orchard for Earth for a relatively long period, as such periods go in galactic history.

Customs and cultures pronounced officially dead have, however, a way of stirring again long after their supposed interment. In some instances, of course, this is simply a reflex twitch; for example, though the grandiose collapse of the Earth culture certainly can be said to have begun during the Battle of the Jungle in the Acolyte cluster in 3905, we find only five years later the Acolyte-Regent, a Lt. Lerner, proclaiming himself Emperor of Space; but the Acolyte fleet, already considerably cut up by its encounter with the Okies in the jungle, was annihilated by the Earth police on their arrival a year later, and Emperor Lerner died that same year in a slum on a tenthrate Acolyte planet named Murphy from an overdose of wisdomweed. On a larger scale, the Battle of Earth in 3975, in which Earth found herself pitted against her own Okie cities, was marked also by an unexpected resurrection of the Vegan Tyranny, whose secretly constructed and long-wandering orbital fort chose this moment to make its last bid for galactic power. Its failure was a repetition in miniature of the failure of the entire Vegan Tyranny, despite superior force of arms, in any conflict with the Earthmen, who were far better chessmasters; the Vegans characteristically left prediction to computers, which lack the ability to make long intuitive leaps, as well as the decisiveness to act upon them.

The Okie city which had outplayed the Vegan orbital fort in the game of thinking ahead, our type-city New York, was far enough ahead of its own culture to have left the galaxy by 3978 for the Greater Magellanic Cloud. It left behind an Earth which in 3976 cut its own throat as a galactic power with the passage of the so-called anti-Okie Bill. Though the Magellanic planet which New York colonized in 3998 was in 3999 christened New Earth, the earlier date of 3976 marks the passing of Earth from the stellar stage. Already there were reaching out from one of the galaxy's largest and most beautiful star-clusters the first tentative strands of that strange culture called the Web of Hercules, which was destined to become the Milky Way's IVth great civilization. And yet once more a civilization which from every historical point of view had to be pronounced dead refused to stay entirely buried. The creeping, inexorable growth of the Web of Hercules through the heart of the galaxy was destined to be interrupted by that totally revolutionary, totally universal physical cataclysm now known as the Ginnangu-Gap; and though it is due entirely to the Web of Hercules that we still have records of galactic history before that cataclysm, and thus a continuity with the universe's past surely unprecedented in all the previous cycles, we must note, with more than a little awe, the sudden and critical reappearance of Earthmen in this timeless moment of chaos and creation, and the drastic and fruitful exeunt which they wrote for themselves into the universal drama.

—ACREFF-MONALES: *The Milky Way: Five Cultural Portraits*

CHAPTER ONE: New Earth

In these later years it occasionally startled John Amalfi to be confronted by evidence that there was anything in the universe that was older than he was, and the irrationality of his allowing himself to be startled by such a truism startled him all over again. This crushing sensation of age, of the sheer dead weight of a thousand years bearing down upon his back, was in itself a symptom of what was wrong with him—or, as he preferred to think of it, of what was wrong with New Earth.

He had been so startled while prowling disconsolately through the grounded and abandoned hulk of the city, itself an organism many millennia older than he was, but—as befitted such an antiquity—now only a corpse. It was, indeed, the corpse of a whole society; for nobody on New Earth now contemplated building any more space-cruising cities or in any other way resuming the wandering life of the Okies. Those of the original crew on New Earth, spread very thin among the natives and their own children and grandchildren, now looked back on that entire period with a sort of impersonal, remote distaste, and would certainly recoil from the very idea of returning to it, should anyone have the bad manners to broach such a notion. As for the second and third generations, they knew of the Okie days only as history, and looked upon the hulk of the flying city that had brought their parents to New Earth as a fantastically clumsy and outmoded monster, much as the pilot of an ancient atmospheric liner might have regarded a still more ancient quinquireme in a museum.

No one except Amalfi even appeared to take any interest in what might have happened to the whole of Okie society back in the home lens, the Milky Way galaxy of which the two Magellanics were satellites. To give them credit, finding out what had happened would in any event have been an almost impossible task; all kinds of broadcasts—literally millions of them—could be picked up easily from the home lens if anyone cared to listen, but so much time had elapsed since the colonization of New Earth that sorting these messages into a meaningful picture would require years of work by a team of experts, and none could be found who would take any interest in so fruitless and essentially nostalgic a chore. Amalfi had in fact come into the city with the vague notion of turning the task over to the City Fathers, that enormous bank of computing and memory-storage machines to which had been intrusted all the thousands of routine technical, operational and governmental problems of the city when it had been in flight. What Amalfi would do with the information when and if he got it he had no idea; certainly there was no possibility of interesting any of the other New Earthmen in it, except in the form of half an hour's idle chatter.

And after all, the New Earthmen were right. The Greater Magellanic Cloud was drawing steadily away from the home lens, at well over 150 miles per second—a trifling velocity in actuality, only a little greater than the diameter of the average solar system per year, but symbolic of the new attitude among the New Earthmen; people's eyes were directed outward, away from all that ancient history. There was considerably more interest in a nova which had flared into being in intergalactic space, somewhere beyond the Lesser Magellanic, than there was in the entire panoply of the home lens, visibly though the latter dominated the night sky from horizon to horizon during certain seasons of the year. There was, of course, still space flight, for trade with other planets in the little satellite galaxy was a necessity; the trade was conducted for the most part in large cargo hulls, and there were a number of larger units such as mobile processing plants which still needed to be powered by gravitron-polarity generators or "spindizzies"; but for the most part the trend was toward the development of local, self-sufficient industries.

It was while he was setting up the City Fathers for the problem in analysis of the million-fold transmission from the home lens, alone in what had once been his Mayor's Office, that Amalfi had suddenly had thrown at him the fragment from the writings of a man dead eleven centuries before Amalfi had been born. Possibly the uttering of the unexpected fragment had been simply an artifact of the warming-up process—like most computers of their age and degree of complexity, it took the City Fathers two to three hours to become completely sane after they had been out of service for a while—or perhaps Amalfi's fingers, working with sure automatism even after all these years, had been wiser than his head, and without the collusion of Amalfi's consciousness had built into the problem elements of what was really troubling him: the New Earthmen. In either event, the quotation was certainly apposite:

"If this be the whole fruit of victory, we say: if the generations of mankind suffered and laid down their lives; if prophets and martyrs sang in the fire, and all the sacred tears were shed for no other end than that a race of creatures of such unexampled insipidity should succeed, to protract *in saecula saeculorum* their contented and inoffensive lives—why, at such a rate, better lose than win the battle, or at all events better ring down the curtain before the last act of the play, so that a business that began so importantly may be saved from so singularly flat a winding-up."

"What was *that?*" Amalfi barked into the microphone.

"AN EXTRACT FROM *'THE WILL TO BELIEVE,'* BY WILLIAM JAMES, MR. MAYOR."

"Well, it's irrelevant; get your bottles and firecrackers back on the main problem. Wait a minute—is this the Librarian?"

"YES, MR. MAYOR."

"What's the date of the work you quoted?"

"1897, MR. MAYOR."

"All right. Switch out and hook into the analytical side of the loop; you've no business at the output end for this problem."

A flowmeter needle bobbed upward as the drain of the library machine on the circuit was discontinued for a moment, then dipped again. He did not proceed with the project for a while, however, but instead simply sat and thought about the fragment that the machines had offered him. There were, he supposed, a few unreconstructed Okies still alive on New Earth, though the only one that he knew personally was John Amalfi. He himself had no special nostalgia *qua* nostalgia for all the history he had outlived, for he could hardly forget that it had been by his foreplanning that New Earth had been founded. And for a period of perhaps four years there had been plenty to occupy his mind: the discovery that the planet, then unnamed, was at once the refuge and the feudal fief of a notorious pack of bindlestiffs calling itself Interstellar Master Traders—better known in the home lens simply as "the Mad Dogs"—had raised a considerable obstacle to colonization, the solution of which obviously needed to be drastic, and was. But the destruction of IMT in 3948 in the Battle of the Blasted Heath had left Amalfi at long last without problems and without function, and he had subsequently found himself utterly unable to become used to living in a stable and ordered society. The James quotation almost perfectly summarized his feelings about the Okie citizens who had once been his charges, and their descendants; he had of course to excuse the natives, who knew no better and were finding the problems of self-government an unprecedented challenge after their serfdom under "the Mad Dogs."

Local space travel, he knew very well, was no solution for him; one planet in the Cloud was very like another, and the Cloud itself was only 20,000 light years in diameter—a fact which made the Cloud extremely convenient to organize from one administrative center, but a fact of no significance whatsoever to a man who had once shepherded his city across 280,000 light years in a single flight. What he missed, after all, was not space, but instability itself, the feeling of being on the way to an unknown destination, unable to predict what outlandish surprises might be awaiting him at the next planetfall.

The fact of the matter was that longevity now hung on him like a curse. An indefinitely prolonged life span had been a prerequisite for an Okie society—indeed, until the discovery of the anti-agathic drugs early in the 21st Century, interstellar flight even with the spindizzy had been a physical impossibility; the distances involved were simply too great for a short-lived man to compass at any finite speed—but to be a virtually immortal man in a stable society was to be as uninteresting to one's self, for Amalfi at least, as an everlasting light bulb; he felt that he had simply been screwed into his socket and forgotten.

It was true that most of the other former Okies had seemed able to make the change-over—the youngsters in particular, whose experience of star wandering had been limited, were now putting their long life expectancies to

the obvious use: launching vast research or development
projects the fruition of which could not be expected in
under five centuries or more. There was, for example, an
entire research team now hard at work in New Manhattan
on the overall problem of anti-matter. The theoretical
brains of the project were being supplied largely by Dr.
Schloss, an ex-Hruntan physicist who had boarded the city
back in 3602 as a refugee during the reduction of the
Duchy of Gort, a last surviving polyp of the extinct
Hruntan Empire; administration of the project was in the
hands of a comparative youngster named Carrel, who not
so long ago had been the city's co-pilot and ranking
understudy to the City Manager. The immediate objective
of the project, according to Carrel, was the elucidation of
the theoretical molecular structures possible to anti-
material atoms, but it was no secret that most of the
young men in the group, with the active support of
Schloss himself, were hoping in a few centuries to achieve
the actual construction, not only of simple chemical compounds—that might come about in a matter of decades—
of this radical type, but a visible, macroscopic artifact
composed entirely of anti-matter. Upon the unthinkably
explosive object they would no doubt paint, Amalfi sur-
mised, had they by that time also composed an anti-
material paint and something to keep it in, the warning
Noli me tangere.

That was all very well; but it was equally impossible for
Amalfi, who was not a scientist, to participate. It was, of
course, perfectly possible for him to end his life; he was
not invulnerable, nor even truly immortal; immortality is a
meaningless word in a universe where the fundamental
laws, being stochastic in nature, allow no one to bar
accidents, and where life no matter how prolonged is at
bottom only a local and temporary discontinuity in the
Second Law of Thermodynamics. The thought, however,
did not occur to Amalfi; he was not the suicidal type. He
had never felt less tired, less used-up, less despairing than
he felt today; he was simply snarlingly bored, and too
confirmed in his millennia-old patterns of thought and
emotion to be able to settle for a single planet and a single
social order, no matter how utopian; his thousand years of
continuous translation from one culture to another had
built up in him an enormous momentum which now
seemed to be bearing him irresistibly toward an immovable inertial wall labeled, No Place To Go.

"Amalfi! So it's you. I might have guessed."

Amalfi shot the "hold" switch closed convulsively and swung around on his stool. He had, however, recognized the voice at once from centuries of familiarity. He had heard it often since somewhere around 3500, when the city had taken its owner on board as chief of the astronomy section: a testy and difficult little man with a deceptively mild manner who had never been precisely the chief astronomer that the city needed, but who had come through in the pinches often enough to prevent the City Fathers from allowing him to be swapped to another Okie city during the period when such swaps were still possible for Amalfi's town.

"Hello, Jake," Amalfi said.

"Hello, John," the astronomer said, peering curiously at the set-up board. "The Hazletons told me I might find you prowling around this old hulk, but I confess I'd forgotten about it by the time I decided to come over here. I wanted to use the computation section, but I couldn't get in—the machines were all shuttling back and forth on their tracks and coupling and uncoupling like a pack of demented two-hundred-ton ballet dancers. I thought maybe one of the kids had wandered in up here in the control room and was fooling with the boards. What are you up to?"

It was an extremely pointed question which, up to now, Amalfi had not asked himself. Even to consider answering Jake by describing the message-analysis project was to reject it; not that Jake would care one way or the other, but to Amalfi's inner self the answer would be an obvious blind. He said:

"I don't quite know. I had an urge to look around the place again. I hate to see it going to rust; I keep thinking it must still be good for something."

"It is, it is," Jake said. "After all, there are no computers quite like the City Fathers anywhere else on New Earth, let alone anywhere else in the Magellanics. I call on them pretty frequently when there's anything really complicated to be worked on; so does Schloss, I understand. After all, the City Fathers know a great deal that nobody else around here can know, and old though they are, they're still reasonably fast."

"I think there must be more to it than that," Amalfi said. "The city was powerful, is powerful still; the central pile is good for a million years yet at a minimum, and

some of the spindizzies must still be operable—providing
that we ever again find anything big enough to need all
the lifting power we've got concentrated down below in
the hold."

"Why should we?" the astronomer said, obviously not
very much interested. "That's all past and done with."

"But is it? I keep thinking that no machine of the
sophistication and complexity of the city can ever go quite
out of use. And I don't mean just marginal uses, like
occasionally consulting the City Fathers, or tapping the
pile for some fraction of its total charge. This city was
meant to fly, and by God it ought to be flying still."

"What for?"

"I don't know, exactly. Maybe for exploration, maybe
for work, the kind of work we used to do. There must be
some jobs in the Cloud for which nothing less than a
machine of this size is suitable—though obviously we
haven't hit such a job yet. Maybe it would be worth
cruising and looking for one."

"I doubt it," Jake said. "Anyhow, she's gotten pretty
tumbledown since we had our little difference with IMT,
what with all those rocket bombs they threw at us—and
letting her be rained on steadily ever since hasn't helped,
either. Besides, I seemed to remember that that old 23rd
St. spindizzy blew for good and all when we landed here. I
hardly think she'd stir at all now if you tried to lift her,
though no doubt she'd groan a good deal."

"I wasn't proposing to pick up the whole thing, anyhow," Amalfi said. "I know well enough that that couldn't
be done. But the city's *over*-sophisticated for a field of
action as small as the Cloud; there's a lot you could leave
behind. Besides, we'd have a great deal of difficulty in
scaring up anything more than a skeleton crew, but if we
could rehabilitate only a part of her, we might still get her
aloft again—"

"Part of her?" Jake said. "How do you propose to
section a city with a granite keel? Particularly one composed as a unit on that keel? You'd find that many of the
units that you most needed in your fraction would be in
the outlying districts and couldn't be either cut off or
transported inward; that's the way she was built, as a
piece."

This of course was true. Amalfi said, "But supposing it
could be done? How would you feel about it, Jake? You

were an Okie for nearly five centuries; don't you miss it, a little, now?"

"Not a bit," the astronomer said briskly. "To tell you the truth, Amalfi, I never liked it. It was just that there was no place else to go. I thought you were all crazy with your gunning around the sky, your incessant tangles with the cops, and your wars, and the periods of starvation and all the rest, but you gave me a floating platform to work from and a good close look at stars and systems I could never have seen as well from a fixed observatory with any possible telescope, and besides, I got fed. So I was reasonably satisfied. But do it again, now that I have a choice? Certainly not. In fact, I only came over here to get some computational work done on this new star that's cropped up just beyond the Lesser Cloud; it's behaving outrageously—in fact, it's the prettiest theoretical problem I've encountered in a couple of centuries. I wish you'd let me know when you're through with the boards: I really do need the City Fathers, when they're available."

"I'm through now," Amalfi said, getting off the stool. As an afterthought, he turned back to the boards and cleared the instruction circuits of the problem he had been setting up, a problem which he now knew all too well to be a dummy.

He left Jake humming contentedly as he set up his nova problem, and wandered without real intention or direction down into the main body of the city, trying to remember it as it had been as a living and vibrant organism; but the empty streets, the blank windows, the flat quiet of the very air under the blue sky of New Earth, was like an insult. Even the feeling of gravity under his feet seemed in these familiar surroundings a fleeting denial of the causes and values to which he had given most of his life; a smug gravity, so easily maintained by sheer mass, and without the constant distant sound of spindizzies which always before—since his distant, utterly unrememberable youth—had signified that gravity was a thing made by man, and maintained by man.

Depressed, Amalfi quit the streets for the holds of the city. There, at least, his memory of the city as a live entity would not be mocked by the unnaturally natural day. But that in the long run proved to be no better. The empty granaries and cold-storage bins reminded him that there was no longer any need to keep the city stocked for trips that might last as much as a century between planet-falls;

the empty crude-oil tanks rang hollowly, not to his touch, but simply to his footfall as he passed them; the empty dormitories were full of those peculiar ghosts which not the dead, but the living leave behind when they pass, still living, to another kind of life; the empty classrooms, which were, as was quite usual with Okie cities, small, were mocked by the memory of the myriads of children which the Okies were now farrowing on their own planet, New Earth, no longer bound by the need to consider how many children an Okie city needs and can comfortably provide for. And down at the threshold of the keel itself, he encountered the final sign and signal of his forthcoming defeat: the fused masses of two spindizzies ruined beyond repair by the landing of 3944 on the Blasted Heath. New spindizzies, of course, could be built and installed, the old yanked out; but the process would take a long time; there were no graving docks suitable for the job on New Earth, since the cities were extinct. As was the spirit.

Nevertheless, in the cold gloom of the spindizzy hold, Amalfi resolved to try.

"But what on earth do you expect to gain?" Hazleton said in exasperation, for at least the fifth time. "I think you're out of your mind."

There was still no one else on New Earth who would have had the temerity to speak to Amalfi quite like that; but Mark Hazleton had been Amalfi's city manager ever since 3301 and knew his former boss very well. A subtle, difficult, lazy, impulsive and sometimes dangerous man, Hazleton had survived many blunders for which the City Fathers would have had any other city manager shot—as, indeed, they had had his predecessor shot—and there had survived, too, his often unwarranted assumption that he could read Amalfi's mind.

There was surely no other ex-Okie on New Earth who might be as likely to understand Amalfi's present state of mind, but Hazleton was not at the moment giving a very good demonstration of this. For one thing, he and his wife Dee—the girl from a planet called Utopia who had boarded the city about the same time that Dr. Schloss had, during the reduction of the Duchy of Gort—had perhaps forgotten that an Okie tradition forbade the mayor of an Okie city to marry or have children, and that Amalfi as the mayor of New York since 3089 was conditioned beyond redemption to this state of mind; and in particular would not welcome being surrounded by the children and grandchildren of his city manager at any time, and particularly not when what he most urgently needed was advice from someone who remembered the traditions well enough to understand why another man might still be clinging to them.

It was one of Mark's virtues, however, that at his best he tended to react more like a symbiote than a truly separate entity. When the children made graceful exits soon after dinner, Amalfi knew that it was at Hazleton's behest. He also knew it was not because Hazleton even faintly suspected his friend's discomfiture in the presence of so many fruits of the settling-down process; it was just that the city manager had intuited Amalfi's need for a conference and had promptly set one up, scuttling Dee's social time-table without a qualm.

The children charged their unseasonably early departure to the grandchildren's impending bedtimes, although Amalfi knew that when the whole clan came to dinner they customarily made a great occasion of it, and all stayed the night in the adjoining building, a beehive of bedrooms where the Hazletons had raised their numerous family; the current Hazleton dwelling consisted mostly of the huge social room where they had just dined. Now that the meal was over, Amalfi just barely kept from fidgeting while all the procession of big and little Hazletons made their manners. Even the youngest had each to make his farewell speech to the great man, identifying his inconsiderable self; their parents had long since learned in their own childhoods that the busy Mr. Mayor would not trouble himself to remember which was which.

It never occurred to Amalfi to admire the children's concealment of their disappointment at leaving so precipitately, since he did not realize that they were disappointed. He simply listened without listening. One middle-sized boy caught his attention mainly because from the moment he had arrived Amalfi had noticed that the child had kept his eyes riveted on the guest of honor. It was disconcerting. Amalfi suspected he had forgotten to don some essential garment or to doff some trace of his party preparations. When the child who had caused him to rub his chin and smooth his eyebrows and finger his ears to see if there were still soapsuds in them spoke up, Amalfi paid attention.

"Webster Hazleton, sir, and I hope to be seeing you

again on a matter of the greatest importance," the boy said.
He said it as if he had been rehearsing it for weeks,
with a ringing conviction that almost impelled Amalfi to
fix an appointment then and there.

Instead, he growled, "Webster, eh?"

"Yes, sir. I was put on the Great List to be born when
Webster wanted off."

Amalfi was considerably jolted. So long ago as that!
Webster had been the pile engineer who had elected to
leave the city before the landing on Utopia, around 3600.
Of course it had taken a long time to fill up the gaps in
the city's roster after the murderous attempt of the bandit
cities to prevent fulfillment of their contract on He, and
the considerable losses in boarding the plague city in the
Acolyte jungle; and then there had been so many girls
born at first. Webster had been an unconscionably long
time in coming, though. He could not be more than
fourteen, from the looks of him.

Dee intervened. "Actually, John, Web arrived a long
time after the Great List was abandoned. It pleases him to
have his patron citizen, that's all, just like in the old days."

The boy turned his clear brown eyes on Dee briefly, and
then, as if dismissing her from their male universe, he
said, "Good night, sir." Amalfi bridled a little. Nobody
could write Dee off, not even Amalfi; he knew; once he
had tried.

The procession continued while he lapsed back into
inattention, and eventually he found himself closeted with
Dee and Mark—if closeted was the word in a room so
large and echoing with so many strong personalities. The
aura of furious domesticity remained behind on the
Hazleton hearth, and came between Amalfi and what he
was trying to say, so that his exposition was unwontedly
stumbling; and it was then that Hazleton had asked him
what he expected to gain.

"Gain?" Amalfi said. "I don't expect to gain anything.
I'd just like to be aloft again, that's all."

"But, John," Dee said. "Think about it a minute. Suppose you do succeed in persuading a few people from the
old days to go in with you. It all doesn't have any meaning
any more. You'll just turn yourself into a sort of Flying
Dutchman, sailing under a curse, going nowhere and doing
nothing."

"Maybe so," Amalfi said. "The picture doesn't frighten
me, Dee. As a matter of fact, it gives me a sort of

perverse satisfaction, if you must know. I shouldn't mind becoming a legend; at least that would fit me back into history again—give me a role to play comparable to roles I've played in the past. And besides, I'd be aloft again, which is the important thing. I'm beginning to believe that nothing else is important to me any more."

"Does it matter what's important to us?" Hazleton said. "For one thing, such a venture would leave the Cloud without a mayor. I don't know how important that is to you any more—I seem to remember that it was pretty important to you back when we were on our way here—but whether it matters to you any more or not, you ran for the job, you connived for it, you even rigged the election—Carrel and I were supposed to be the only candidates, and the office we were running for was city manager, but you had the City Fathers hornswoggled into believing that it was a mayoralty election, so of course they elected you."

"Do you want the job?" Amalfi said.

"Gods of all stars, no! I want you to keep it. You exercised considerable ingenuity to get it, and I'm not alone in expecting you to hold it down now that you've got it. Nobody else is bidding for the job; they expect you to handle it, as you undertook to do."

"Nobody else is running for it because they wouldn't know what to do with it after they got it," Amalfi said steadily. "I don't know what to do with it myself. The office of mayor is an anachronism in this Cloud. Nobody has asked me to do anything or to say anything or to appear anywhere or to be in any other way useful in I don't know how many years. I occupy an honorary office, and that's all. As everybody knows, you are the man that is actually running this Cloud, and that's as it should be. It's high time you took over in name, as well as in fact. I've given everything I could give to the initial organizing job, and my talents are unsuitable to the situation as it now stands; everybody on New Earth knows that. and it would be healthier if they'd put a name to it. Otherwise, Mark, how long could I be allowed to go on in the job? Apparently forever, under your present assumptions. This is a new society; suppose I should go right on being its titular leader for another thousand years, as is entirely possible? A thousand years during which a new society continues to give lip-service to the same old set of attitudes and ideas that I represented when they meant some-

CITIES IN FLIGHT

thing? That would be insane; and you know it. No, no, it's high time you took over."

Hazleton was silent for quite a long time. At last he said:

"I can see that. In fact, I've thought of it several times myself. Nevertheless, Amalfi, I have to say that this whole proposition distresses me a good deal. I suppose the matter of the mayoralty would settle itself out almost automatically; that wasn't a real objection. What bothers me is the exit you're contriving for yourself, not only because it's dangerous—which it is, but that wouldn't make any difference to you and I suppose it shouldn't make any difference to me—but because it's dangerous to no purpose."

"It suits my purposes," Amalfi said. "I don't see that there are any other purposes to be suited, at this juncture. If I did, I wouldn't go, Mark; you know that; but it seems to me that I am now, for the first time in all my life, a free agent; hence I may now do what I will do."

Hazleton shrugged convulsively. "And so you may," he said. "I can only say that I wish you wouldn't."

Dee bowed her head and said nothing.

And the rest was left unsaid. That Dee and Mark would be personally bereaved if Amalfi persisted on his present course, for their different reasons, was an obvious additional argument which they might have used, but they came no closer to it than that; it was the kind of argument which Hazleton would regard as pure emotional blackmail, precisely because it was unreasonably powerful, and Amalfi was grateful to him for not bringing it to bear. Why Dee had not was more difficult to fathom; there had been a time when she would have used it without a moment's hesitation; and Amalfi thought he knew her well enough to suspect that she had good reasons for wanting to use it now. She had been waiting for the founding of New Earth for a long time, indeed, almost since she had come on board the city, and anything that threatened it now that she had children and grandchildren should pro-voke her into using every weapon at her command; yet, she was silent. Perhaps she was old enough now to realize that not even John Amalfi could steal from her an entire satellite galaxy; at any event, if that was what was on her mind, she gave no inkling of it, and the evening in Hazleton's house ended with a stiff formality which, cold though it was, was far from the worst that Amalfi had expected.

The whole of the residential area to Amalfi's eyes swarmed with pets. Those to whom freedom to run was paramount, frisked and scuttered, in the wide lanes. Few of them ventured onto the wheelways, and those who did were run down instantly, but four-footed animals were a constant and undignified hazard to walkers. By day raffish dogs stopped just short of bowling strangers over, but leaped to brace forepaws on the shoulders of anyone they knew—and everyone, including, seemingly, all the dogs of New Manhattan, knew Amalfi. An occasional svengali from Altair IV—originally a rare specimen in the flying city's zoo, but latterly force-budded in New Earth labs during the full-fertility program of 3950, when every homesteader's bride had her option of a vial of trilby water or a gemmate svengali and frequently wound up with both among the household lares and penates; the half-plant, half-animal, even nowadays a not infrequent pet—took the breeze and hunted in the half-light of dawn or dusk. A svengali lay bonelessly in mid-lane and fixed its enormous eyes on any moving object until something small enough and gelid enough to ingest might blunder near. Nothing suitable ever did, on New Earth. The two-legged victim tended to drift helplessly into that hypnotic stare until the starer got stepped on; then the svengali turned mauve and exuded a protective spray which might have been nauseating on Altair IV, but on New Earth was only euphoric. Sudden friendships, bursts of song, even a brief and deliriously happy crying jag might ensue, after which the shaken svengali would undulate back indoors to rest up and be given, usually, a bowl of jellied soup.

By night in the walkways of New Manhattan, it was cats, catching with sudden claw at floating cloak or fashionable sandal-streamer. Through the air of the town sizable and brightly colored creatures flew and glided: singing birds, squawking birds, talkers and mutes, but pets every last one of them. Amalfi loathed them all.

When he walked anywhere—and he walked almost everywhere now that the city's aircabs were no more—he more than half-expected to have to free himself from the embraces of a burbling citizen or a barking dog before he got where he was going. The half-century old fad for household pets had arisen after the landing, and after his effectual abdication. What time-wasting quirk had moved so many pioneers' descendants to adopt the damnable svengalis as pets was beyond Amalfi.

He made it home from the Hazletons' without any such encounter; instead, it rained. He wrapped his cloak more tightly around him and hastened, muttering, for his own square uncompromising box of a dwelling before the full force of the storm should be let loose; his house and grounds were sheltered by a 0.02 per cent spindizzy field— the New Earthmen called the household device a "spindil-ly," a name which Amalfi loathed but put up with for the sake of, as Dee had once put it, "not knowing enough to come out of the rain." He had growled at her so convincingly for that that she had never brought up the subject again, but she had put her finger on it all the same.

Amalfi reached his entrance lane and laid his palm on the induction switch which softened the spindilly field just enough to let him through in a spatter of glistening drops, and noted with the grim dissatisfaction that was becoming natural to him that the storm had slacked off and would be over in minutes. Inside, he made a drink and stood, rubbing his hands, looking about him. If his house was an anachronism, well, he liked it that way, insofar as he liked anything on New Earth.

"What's wrong with me?" he thought suddenly. "People's pets are their own business, after all. If practically everybody else likes weather, what difference does it make if I don't? If Jake doesn't even take an interest, nor Mark either for that matter—"

He heard the distant, endlessly comforting murmur of the modified spindizzy under his feet alter momentarily; someone else had chosen to come in out of the rain. His visitor had never been there at that hour before, and had indeed never been there before alone, but he knew without a moment's doubt who had followed him home.

CHAPTER TWO: Nova Magellanis

"You'll have to make me more welcome than that, John," Dee said.

Amalfi said nothing. He lowered his head like a bull contemplating a charge, spread his feet slightly, and clasped his hands behind him.

"Well, John?" Dee insisted gently.

"You don't want me to go," he said baldly. "Or, you suspect that if I do go; Mark just may throw up the managership and New Earth along with it and take off with me."

Dee walked slowly all the way across the room and stood, hesitating, beside the great deep cushion. "Wrong, John, on both counts. I had something else altogether in mind. I thought—well, I'll tell you later what I thought. Right now, may I have a drink?"

Amalfi was forced to abandon his position, which by being so firm had imparted a certain strength to his desire to oppose her, in order to play host. "Did Mark send you, then?"

She laughed. "King Mark sends me on a good many errands, but this wouldn't be a very likely one for him." She added bitterly, "Besides, he's so wrapped up in Gifford Bonner's group that he ignores me for months on end."

Amalfi knew what she meant: Dr. Bonner was the teacher-leader of an informal philosophical group called the Stochastics; Amalfi hadn't bothered to inform himself in detail on Bonner's tenets, but he knew in general that Stochasticism was the most recent of many attempts to construct a complete philosophy, from esthetics to ethics, using modern physics as the metaphysical base. Logical positivism had been only the first of those; Stochasticism, Amalfi strongly suspected, would be far from the last.

"I could see something had been keeping his mind off the job lately," he said grimly. "He might do better to study the doctrines of Jorn the Apostle. The Warriors of God control no less than fifteen of the border planets right now, and the faith doesn't lack for adherents right here on New Earth. It appeals to the bumpkin type—and I'm afraid we've been turning out a lot of those lately."

If Dee recognized this as in part a shaft at the changes in New Earth's educational system which she had helped to institute, she showed no sign of it.

"Maybe so," she said. "But I couldn't persuade him, and I wonder if you could either. He doesn't believe there's any real threat; he thinks that a man simple-minded enough to be a Fundamentalist is too simple-minded to hold together an army."

"Oh? Mark had better ask Bonner to tell about Godfrey of Bouillon."

"Who was—?"

"The leader of the First Crusade."

She shrugged. Possibly only Amalfi, as the only New Earthman who had actually been born and raised on Earth, could ever have heard of the Crusades; doubtless they were unknown on Utopia.

"Anyhow, that isn't what I came here to talk about, either."

The wall treacher opened and floated the drinks out. Amalfi captured them and passed one over silently, waiting.

She took her glass from him but, instead of sinking down with it as he had half-pictured her doing, she walked nervously back to the door and took her first sip as if she might put it aside and be leaving at any moment.

He discovered that he did not want her to go. He wanted her to walk some more. There was something about the gown she was wearing—

That there were fashions again was a function of being earthbound. One simple utilitarian style had sufficed both men and women all their centuries aloft when there had been the unending demands of the city's spaceworthiness to keep all hands occupied. Now that the ex-Okies were busily fulfilling Franklin's law that people will breed to the point of overpopulating any space available to them, they were also frittering away their time with pets and flower-gardens and fashions that changed every time a man blinked. Women were floating around this year of 3995 in diaphanous creations that totaled so much yardage a man might find himself treading on their skirts. Dee, however, was wearing a simple white covering above and a clinging black tubular affair below that was completely different. The only diaphanous part of her outfit was a length of something gossamer and iridescent that circled her throat under a fold of the white garment and hung down between her still delicate, still gently rounded breasts, as girlish in appearance as the day Utopia had sent her out to New York, in a battleship, to ask for help.

He had it. "Dee, you looked just as you look now when I first saw you!"

"Indeed, John?"

"That black thing—"

"A sheath-skirt," she interpolated helpfully.

"—I noticed it particularly when you came aboard. I'd never seen anything like it. Haven't seen anything like it since." He refrained from telling her that during all the centuries he had loved her, he had pictured her in that black thing, turning to him instead of Hazleton. Would the course of history have been any different, had she done so? But how could he have done anything but reject her?

"It took you long enough to notice it tonight," she said. "I had it made up especially for this evening's dinner. I've been tired of all this float and flutter for a year. Essentially I'm still a product of Utopia, I guess. I like stern clothes and strong men and a reasonably hard life."

She was certainly trying to tell him something, but he was still adrift. The situation was impossible, on the face of it. He was not in the habit of discussing fashion with his best and oldest friend's wife at an hour when all sensible planet-bound pioneers were abed. He said, "It's very pretty."

To his astonishment, she burst into tears. "Oh, *don't* be stuffy, John!" She put the glass down and reached for her cloak.

"All right, Dee." Amalfi put the cloak out of her reach. "Your 'King Mark' sounds reasonably stern and hard. Suppose you sit down and tell me what this is all about."

"I want to go with you, John. You won't be the mayor of New York, you won't be bound by the old rules, if you take the city aloft now. I want—I want to—"

It was weeks before he got her to state that ultimate desire. They had talked without ceasing after that blundering beginning. When it finally penetrated his cautious bald head that the message all his senses had been clamoring from the moment of her arrival was not another daydream from the chilly past, but warm actuality, he had folded her in his arms and they had been silent for a time. But then the flow of words began again and could not be checked. They had reminisced endlessly and how-it-might-have-beens and even of certain ways it had been. He was amazed to discover that she had taken into her household however briefly every companion whose bed he had honored during the officially celibate years; in her position as First Lady of New Earth, during the intensive family years, she could have installed twenty nursemaids simultaneously without attracting undue notice, just as she

launched every new fashion and many of the fads that
made New Earth what it was. That Dee had been cruelly
bored had simply never occurred to him.

But she told him the full tale of that discontent, more
indeed than he wanted to hear. They quarreled like giddy
young lovers—except that their first and worst quarrel
followed a complaint he could have wept to hear wrung
from her.

"John," she said, "aren't you ever going to take me to
bed?"

He spread his hands in exasperation. "I'm not at all sure
I want to take Mark's wife to bed. Besides," he added,
knowing he was being cruel, "you've already had it.
You've pumped every woman I resorted to in half a
thousand years. I should think I would bore you in actuality as much as everything else does."

Their reconciliations were not much like those of young
love; they were more and more like the creeping home of
a rebellious daughter to her father's arms. And still he
held off. Now that he had for the taking what he had only
dreamed of wanting for so many years, he made the
Adamic discoveries all over again: there is wanting the
unobtainable, and there is the obtaining of desire, and the
greatest of these is the wanting. Especially since the object
of desire always turns out to exist only in some other
universe, to be mocked by actuality.

"You don't believe me, John," she said bitterly. "But it's
true. When you go, I want to go with you—all the way,
don't you understand? I want to—I want to bear you a
child."

She looked at him through a film of tears—somehow he
had never, in all the centuries of fancy, imagined or seen
her in tears, but the actuality wept as predictably as New
Earth's skies—and waited. She had shot her bolt, he saw.
This was the supreme thing that Dee Hazleton wanted to
give him.

"Dee, you don't know what you're saying! You can't
offer me your girlhood all over again—that's irretrievably
Mark's, and you know it. Besides, I don't want—"

He stopped. She was weeping again. He had never
wanted to hurt her, although he knew he had done so
unintentionally more times than he would ever know.

"Dee, I've *had* a child."

Now she was listening, wide-eyed, and he winced as he
saw pity take the place of resentment. He laid the en-

cysted pain bare like a surgeon before her. "When the population balance shifted after the landing and there were all those excess females—remember? Do you also remember the artificial insemination program? They asked me to contribute. The good old argument against it was supposed to be by-passed by the assurance that I'd never know which children carried my genes—only the doctors supervising the program would know. But there was an unprecedented wave of miscarriages and stillbirths—and some survivors that shouldn't have survived, all with the same set of ... disadvantages. I was told about it; as mayor, I had to decide what was to be done with them."

"John," she whispered. "No. Stop."

"We were taking over the Cloud," he continued implacably. Presenting him with a wizened, squalling, scarlet, normal baby boy was one favor she could not do him, and there was no way to tell her so but this. "We couldn't afford bad genes. I ordered the survivors ... dealt with; and I had a brief conference with the genetics team. They had planned not to tell me—they were going to keep up the farce, like good-hearted dolts. But I'd been in space too long; my germ plasm is damaged beyond hope; I am no longer a contributor. Do you understand me, Dee?"

Dee tried to draw his head down on her breast. Amalfi moved violently away. It irritated him unreasonably that she still thought she had anything to give him.

"The city was yours," she said tonelessly. "And now it's grown up and gone away and left you. I saw you grieving, John, and I couldn't bear it—oh, I don't mean that I was pretending. I love you, I think I always have. But I should have known that the time for us had gone by. There's nothing at all left for me to give you that you haven't had in full measure."

She bowed her head, and he stroked her hair awkwardly, wishing it had never begun, since it had to end like this. "And what now?" he said. "Now that life with father has turned out to be nothing more than that? Can you leave home again and go to Mark?"

"Mark? He doesn't even know I've been ... away. As his wife, I'm dead and buried," she said in a low voice. "Living seems to be a process of continually being born again. I suppose the trick is to learn how to make that crucial exit without suffering the trauma each time. Goodbye, John."

She didn't look as if she were being too successful at

mastering the trick, but he made no move to help her. She
was going to have to find her own way back; she was
beyond his aid now.

He thought that what she had said was probably the
truth—for a woman. For a man, he knew, life is a process
of dying, again and again; and the trick, he thought, is to
do it piecemeal, and ungenerously.

For the first time in weeks, he walked the streets of
New Manhattan again. He had never felt so utterly done
with the purpose he had sowed in his people. Now that it
was coming to fruition, he urgently needed to be seeking
some purpose far removed from theirs.

Inevitably, he found himself leaving cats, birds, svengalis, dogs and Dee for the dilapidated streets of the Okie
city. He was almost all the way down to the banks of the
City Fathers, when a suspicion that he was again being
followed turned into a certainty. For a panic moment he
feared it might be Dee, spoiling both her exit and his; but
it was not.

"All right, who is it?" he said. "Stop skulking and name
yourself."

"You wouldn't remember me, Mr. Mayor," a frightened
voice said in several registers at once.

"Remember you? Of course I do. You're Webster
Hazleton. Who's your friend? What are you doing here in
the old city? It's off limits for children."

The boy drew himself up to his full height.

"This is Estelle. She and I are in this together." Web
appeared to have some difficulty in going on. "There's
been talk—I mean, Estelle's father, he's Jake Freeman,
kind of hinted about it—that is, if the city's really going
up again. Mr. Mayor—"

"Maybe it is. I don't know yet. What of it?"

"If it is, *we want on*," the boy said in a rush.

Amalfi had had no further plans to try and convert
Jake, who certainly appeared to be as lost a cause as
Hazleton himself; but the Freeman-Hazleton partnership
represented by Web and Estelle meant that he would have
to broach the subject again to Jake sooner or later. Of
course it was out of the question that the children should
be allowed to go—and yet it was not within the bounds of
fairness to forbid them out of hand, without knowing

what their elders thought of it. Children had gone adventuring on Okie cities many a time before; but of course that had been back in the old days, when the cities had been as well equipped as any earthbound community to take good care of them, at least most of the time. Every thread he touched these days, it seemed to Amalfi, had knots in it.

Temporarily, however, the fates allowed him to shelve that part of the problem; for Jake was waiting for him again in the computation section, in a state of excitement so febrile that the sight of his daughter and Web tagging behind Amalfi barely raised his eyebrows.

"You're just in time," he said as though there had been some prior appointment. "You recall the nova I was talking to you about? Well, it isn't a nova at all, and at this point it's no longer an astronomical problem; in fact, it's your problem."

"What do you mean?" Amalfi said. "If it isn't a nova, what is it?"

"Just what I was asking myself," Jake said. One of his more irritating failings was his inability to get to a point by any but a pre-selected route. "I have a remarkable collection of spectrographs for this thing; if you looked at them without any clue as to what they were, you'd think they represented a stellar catalogue, rather than a single object—and a catalogue containing stars from all over the Russell diagram, too. On top of which, all of them show a blue shift in the absorption lines, particularly in the lines contributed by New Earth's own atmosphere, which made no sense whatsoever, up to now."

"It still doesn't make any sense to me," Amalfi admitted.

"All right," Jake said, "try this on for size; when the spectra turned out to be far too dim for an object of the apparent magnitude of this thing—remember, it's been getting brighter all the time—I asked Schloss and his crew to neglect anti-matter long enough to do a wave-trap analysis of the incoming light. It turns out to be about seventy-five per cent false photons; the thing must be leaving behind a tremendous contrail, if we were only in a position to see it—"

"Spindizzies!" Amalfi shouted. "And under damn near full deceleration! But how could an object that size—no, wait a minute; do you actually know the size yet?"

The astronomer chuckled, a noise which from Jake

never failed to remind Amalfi of a demented parrot. "I think we have the size, and all the rest of the answers, at least as far as astronomy is concerned," he said. "The rest, as I said, is your problem. The thing is a planetary body, roughly seventy-five hundred miles in diameter, and much closer than we thought it was—right now, in fact, it's actually inside the Greater Magellanic, and coming our way, directly for the system of New Earth. The change in spectra simply means that it's shining by the reflected light of the different suns it's passing, and the blue shift in the Frauenhofer lines strongly suggests an atmosphere very much like ours. I don't know offhand what that reminds you of, but I know what it should remind you of—and the City Fathers agree with me."

Web Hazleton could contain himself no longer. "I know, I know! It's the planet He! It's coming home! Isn't that it, Mr. Mayor?"

The boy knew his city history well; nobody from the old days could have been confronted with such a set of data as Jake had just trotted out without responding with the same wild surmise. The planet He had been one of the city's principal jobs of work, the outcome of which, for very complicated reasons, had entailed the installation on the planet itself of a number of spindizzies sufficient to rip He from her orbit around her home sun and send her careening, wholly out of control, out of the galaxy and into intergalactic space. The city had been carried a considerable distance with her, enabling it to re-enter the galaxy far away from any area where New York, N. Y., was being actively sought by the cops, but it had been a near thing. She, herself, presumably, had been hurtling toward the Andromeda galaxy ever since that moment in 3850 when she and the city had parted company, each vanishing to the other as abruptly and finally as a blown-out candle-flame.

"Let's not jump to conclusions," Amalfi said. "The tipping of He took place only a century and a half ago—and at that time the Hevians didn't have the technology or the resources to master controlled spindizzy flight; in fact, they weren't very far from being savages. Smart savages, I grant you, but still savages. Is this planet that's coming our way truly dirigible, or don't you know yet?"

"It looks that way," Jake said. "That's what first tipped me off that there was something unnatural about the object. It kept changing velocity and line of flight errati-

cally—in fact, in a totally irrational way, unless one assumed that the changes were in fact rational. Whoever
they are, they know enough to prevent that world of
theirs from zigging when they want to zag. And they're
headed our way, Amalfi."

"Have you made any attempt to get in touch with
them, whoever they are?" Amalfi said.

"No, indeed. In fact, I haven't even told anybody else
about it yet. Not even Mark. Somehow it struck me as
peculiarly your baby."

"That was just a waste of pussyfooting, Jake. Dr.
Schloss isn't an idiot; surely he can read his own figures as
well as you can and draw obvious conclusions from the
very question you asked him; he must have told Mark by
now, and a good thing, too. Mark is probably calling your
object right now; let's go directly up to the control room
and find out."

They made an oddly assorted procession through the
haunted streets of the Okie city: the bald-headed keg-
chested mayor with his teeth deeply sunk in a dead cigar,
the bird-like and slightly crestfallen astronomer, the
bright-eyed skipping youngsters now darting ahead of
them, then falling behind to wait to be shown the way.
Their eagerness moved Amalfi unexpectedly, bringing
home to him the realization that their dream of the city
back in flight had always been, like this, a very fragile
one; and that this incoming dirigible planet, whatever else
it might portend, would probably put the quietus to it,
serious business and the dull cold morning light it thrived
in being immemorially fatal to dreams.

On an impulse, he stopped at a station that he knew
and called for an aircab, partly, he assured himself, to see
whether or not the City Fathers still considered that
service worth maintaining at this stage in the city's long
death. In due course one came, to the obvious delight of
the children, leaving Amalfi with the rueful realization
that his had not been a fair test; a million years from now,
with the last ergs of energy remaining in the pile, the City
Fathers would of course still send a cab for the mayor; if
he wanted to know whether or not the entire garage was
still alive, he would have to ask the City Fathers directly.

But Web and Estelle were so delighted at soaring
through the silent canyons of the city in the metal and
crystal bubble, and in exploring the limited and very
respectful repartee of the Tin Cabby, that they fell entire-

ly off their precarious adolescent dignity with squeals of
laughter, alternating with gasps of not very real alarm as
the cab cut around corners and came close to grazing the
structures of the city which familiarity had worn smooth
to the point of contempt inside the Tin Cabby's flat little
black box of a brain. It was, in a way, a shame that the
youngsters were unable to make out, even had they known
where to look for it, the graven letters of the city's ancient
motto—MOW YOUR LAWN, LADY?—if only for the sense it
might have given them of the reason why Okie cities once
flew; but the motto had become unreadable a long time
ago, as its meaning had become obliterated soon after.
Only the memory remained to remind Amalfi that were
the city ever to go aloft again—which, suddenly, he did
not even believe—it would not be for the purpose of
mowing lawns for hire; there were no more; that was all
over and done with.

The control room in City Hall muted the children
considerably, as well it might, for no one much below the
age of a century had ever been allowed in it before, and
the many screens which lined its walls had seen events in a
history unlikely to be matched for drama (or even simple
interest) in any imaginable future saga of New Earth. In
this dim stagnant-smelling room the very man who was
with them now had watched the rise and fall of a galaxy-
dominating race—of which, to be sure, these children
were genetically a part, but whose inheritors they could
never be; history had passed them by.

"And don't touch anything," Amalfi said. "Everything in
this room is alive, more or less. We've never had the time
to disarm the city totally; I'm not even sure we'd know
how to go about it now. That's why it's off limits. You'd
better come stand behind me. Web and Estelle, and watch
what I do; it'll keep you out of reach of the boards."

"We won't touch anything," Web said fervently.

"I know you won't, intentionally. But I don't want any
accidents. Better you learn how to run the board from
scratch; come stand right here—you too, Estelle—and call
your grandfather's house for me. Touch the clear plastic
bar—that's it, now wait for it to light up. That lets the
City Fathers know that you want to talk to somebody
outside the city; that's very important; otherwise they'd
give you a long argument, believe you me. Now you see
the five little red buttons just above the bar; the one you

touch is number two; four and five are ultraphone and Dirac lines, which you don't need for a local call. One and three are inside trunk lines, which is why they're not lit up. Go ahead, push it."

Web touched the glowing red stud tentatively. Over his head, a voice said: "Communications."

"Now it's my turn," Amalfi said, picking up the microphone. "This is the mayor. Get me the city manager, crash priority." He lowered the mircrophone and added, "That requires the Communications section to scan for your grandfather along all of the channels on which he's known to be available, and send him a 'call-in' signal wherever he may be; New Earth Hospital has much the same call-in system for its doctors."

"Can we hear him being called?" Estelle said.

"Yes, if you like," Amalfi said. "Here, take the microphone, and put your finger on the two-button as Web did. There."

"Communications," the invisible speaker again said briskly.

"Say, 'Reprise, please'," Amalfi whispered.

"Reprise, please," the girl said.

Immediately the air of the ancient room was filled with a series of twittering pure tones and chords, as though every shadow hid a bird with a silver throat. Estelle almost dropped the microphone; Amalfi took it from her gently.

"Machines don't call for people by name," he explained. "Only very complicated machines, like the City Fathers, are able to speak at all; a simple computer like the Communications section finds it easier to use musical tones. If you listen a while, you'll begin to hear a kind of melody: that's the code for Web's grandfather; the harmonies represent the different places where the computer is looking for him."

"I like it," Estelle said. At the same instant the pipings of the invisible birds came to an end with a metallic snap, and Mark Hazleton's voice said in the middle of the air: "Boss, are you looking for me?"

Amalfi lifted the microphone back to his lips with a grim smile, the children instantly forgotten.

"You bet I am. Are you on top of this dirigible planet which seems to be heading for us?"

"Yes; I didn't know you were interested. In fact I didn't know that it was a planet instead of a star until yesterday,

when Schloss and Carrel came in to see me about it."
Amalfi threw Jake a meaningful glance. "I gather you're
calling me from the city; what do the City Fathers think?"

"I don't know, I haven't talked to them," Amalfi said.
"But Jake is here, and he's come to the obvious conclusion, as I'm sure you have. What I want to know is, have
you or Carrel made any attempt to communicate with this
object?"

"Yes, but I can't say that it's been very fruitful,"
Hazleton's voice said. "We've called them four or five
times on the Dirac, but if they've answered us, it's gotten
lost in the general babble of Dirac 'casts we're surrounded
with from the home galaxy. It puzzles me a little bit; they
do seem to be homing on us, without any question, but it's
hard to imagine what kind of signal from us they could
be using to guide on."

"Do you really think that this is He come back again?"
Amalfi said cautiously.

"Yes, I think I do," Hazleton said, with apparent equal
caution. "I don't see what other conclusion one could
come to with the data as they stand now."

"Then use your head," Amalfi said. "If this really is He,
you'll never be able to reach it with a Dirac 'cast. While
we were on He, we never even let the Hevians hear a
Dirac 'cast, or see a Dirac transmitter; they had no reason
to suspect that any such universal transmitter even existed, or could exist. And if by the same token this is *not*
He, but some exploring vessel coming in toward us for the
first time from another galaxy, and out of an entirely
different culture than any we know, then it's obvious that
they cannot have the Dirac, otherwise they would have
heard every one of the millions of Dirac messages which
have gone out from our galaxy since the day they found
the device. Try the ultraphone instead."

"He didn't have the ultraphone either, when last we saw
it," Hazleton's voice said amusedly. "And if we don't
know how to drive an ultraphone carrier through a spindizzy screen, I very much doubt that they do. If we're
going to go all the way back to methods of communications as primitive as that, shouldn't we first try wig-
wagging?"

"I think probably there is an ultraphone message from
that planet on its way here," Amalfi said. "It would be the
part of common sense to precede such a flight as that

planet is conducting into so densely populated an area as the Greater Magellanic Cloud with a general identification signal, which you could hardly do with a Dirac signal in any event; a signal which is received uniformly everywhere simultaneously with its being sent is not a proper beacon signal. It doesn't matter whether this is He or a visitor coming to us from the entirely unknown; they will be sending some sort of pip in advance, which they would absolutely have to do by ultraphone, there being no other way to do it, and if this requires them to work out a way to punch an ultraphone signal through a spindizzy screen, then they will have done so and you should be listening for it; and you can put a return signal through the same hole." He took a deep breath. "At the very least, Mark, stop wasting my time telling me it's impossible before you've even tried it."

"I tell *you*," Webster Hazleton said under his breath and turned a bright scarlet. Behind him, Estelle's father chortled alarmingly on the edge of his metaphorical crackerbarrel.

The riot act, however, had been becoming less and less effective with Hazleton in the past few decades, as Amalfi knew well; perhaps it dated from Hazleton's new preoccupation with the Stochastics, about which Amalfi had not known until Dee had brought it up; or perhaps—though this was a much less attractive possibility—from an awareness in Hazleton, paralleling Amalfi's own, of Amalfi's growing impotence on New Earth. "Nevertheless," Hazleton said gravely, "I will raise one further objection, boss, if I may. Even supposing that they are putting out an ultraphone beam we can tie to, they're still roughly fifty light-years away; by the time they hear anything we say to them by ultraphone and get a message back to us the same way, we'll be seventy-five years into the next millennium."

"True," Amalfi admitted. "Which means we'll have to send a ship. I'm all for taking ten years or so to make full contact, anyhow, since we really have no idea what it is we're confronted with, and we may need to lay in some armaments. But you'd better tell Carrel to stand ready to fly me out there no later than the beginning of next week, and in the meantime, try to eavesdrop on whatever transmission our visitor is broadcasting. I'll attend to the answering part later from shipboard."

"Right," Hazleton said, and switched out.

"Can we go too?" Web demanded immediately.

"What do you say to that, Jake? These kids were all for going with me on board the city, too."

The astronomer smiled and shrugged. "Wherever she gets the taste for spaceflight from, it can't be from me," he said. "But I knew she was going to ask sooner or later. It's an experience she'll have to have behind her before she's very much older, and I don't know of any commander in two galaxies that she'd be safer with. I think my wife will concur—though she's as uneasy about it as I am."

Web cheered; but Estelle only said, in a tone of utmost practicality:

"I'll go home and get my svengali."

CHAPTER THREE: The Nursery of Time

Even from half a million miles out, it was already plain to Amalfi that the planet of He had undergone a vast transformation since he had last seen it, back in 3850. The Okies had first encountered that planet six years earlier, the only fertile offspring of a wild star then swimming alone in a vast starless desert, not one of the normal starfree areas between spiral arms of the galaxy, but a temporary valley called the Rift, the mechanics of whose origin lay shrouded impenetrably in the origins of the universe itself.

Even at first sight, it had been apparent that the history of He had been more than ordinarily complicated. It had then been an emerald-green world, covered with rank jungle from pole to pole, a jungle which had almost completely swamped out what had obviously been a high civilization not many years before. The facts as they emerged after landing turned out to be complex in the extreme; it was highly probably that there was not another planet in the galaxy which had undergone so many fatal and unlikely accidents. The Hevians had fought them all doggedly, but by the time the Okies had arrived they had realized that nothing less than a miracle could help them now.

For Hevian civilization, the Okies had been that miracle, giving the Hevians mastery over their own local and considerable banditry, and killing off the planet-wide jungle, in the only way possible: by abruptly and permanently changing the climate of He. That this geological revolution had had to be accomplished by putting the whole planet into uncontrolled flight out of the galaxy was perhaps unfortunate, but Amalfi did not think so at the time. He had formed a high opinion of the shrewdness and latent technological ability underlying the Hevian ceremonial paint and feathers, and did not doubt that the Hevians would learn the necessary techniques for preserving their planet as an abode of life well before the danger point would be reached. After all, the Hevians had been great once, and even after the long battle with the jungle and each other they had still had such sophistications as radio, rockets, missile weapons and supersonics when the Okies had first encountered them; and during the brief period that the Okies had been in contact with them, they had snapped up such Middle Ages and Early Modern techniques as nuclear fission and chemotherapy. Besides, there had been the spindizzies, some from the city, some new-built, but all necessarily left behind and in full operation; studied with the eye of intelligence, they could not but provide the Hevians with clues to many potent disciplines which they would have little difficulty putting to work once the jungle was gone; in the meantime, the machines would maintain the atmosphere of the planet and its internal heat even in the most frigid depths of intergalactic space; it would be the darkness' of those gulfs, which the Hevians could mitigate but could hardly abolish, which would kill off the jungle.

Nevertheless, Amalfi had hardly expected to see the return of He, under wholly controlled spindizzy drive, in barely a century and a half, still faintly, patchily blue-green with cultivation under cloud-banks which glared a brilliant white in the light of a nearby Cepheid variable star. That the wandering body was He had been settled back home on New Earth as soon as Hazleton had been able to identify the wanderer's advance ultraphone beacon, as Amalfi had predicted; and hardly five minutes after Carrel had brought his ship out of spindizzy drive within hailing distance of the new planet, Amalfi had himself spoken to Miramon, the very same Hevian leader with whom the Okies had dealt one hundred and fifty years ago—to the mutual astonishment of each that the other was still alive.

"Not that I myself should have been surprised," Miramon said, from the head of his great council table of black, polished, oily wood. "After all, I myself am still alive, to an age beyond the age of all the patriarchs in our recorded history; which in turn is only a small fraction of the age you gave us to understand you had attained when first we met you. But old habits of thought die hard. We were able to isolate and purify only a few of the anti-agathics produced by our jungle, acting on the hints you had given us, before the jungle died off and the plants which produced those drugs did not prove cultivatable under the new conditions, so we had no choice but to search for ways to synthesize these compounds. We were forced to work very fast, and happily the search was successful by the third generation, but in the meantime the existing supply had sufficed to keep only a few of us alive beyond what we still think of as our normal lifespans. Hence to most of our population, Mayor Amalfi, you are now only a legend, and immortal man of infinite wisdom from beyond the stars, and I have been unable to prevent myself from coming to think of you in much the same way."

Though he still wore in his topknot the great black barbaric saw-toothed feather of his authority, the Miramon before Amalfi today bore little resemblance to the lithe, supple, hard-headedly practical semi-savage who had once squatted on the floor in Amalfi's presence, because chairs were the uncomfortable prerogatives of the gods. His skin was still firm and tanned, his eyes bright and darting, but, though his abundant hair was now quite white, he had settled into that period of life, neither youth nor age, characteristic of the man who goes on anti-agathics only when somewhat past "natural" middle age. His councillors—including Retma, of Fabr-Suithe, which in Amalfi's time had been a bandit town which had been utterly destroyed during the last struggle before He took flight, but which now, rebuilt in ceremonial pink marble, was the second city of all He—mostly wore this same look. There were one or two who obviously had not been allowed access to the death-curing drugs until they had been in their "natural" seventies, bringing to the council table the probably spurious appearance of sagacity conferred by many wrinkles, an obvious physical fragility, and a sexual neutrality which was both slightly repellent and covertly enviable at the same time—a somatotype which for mankind as a whole had long ago lost its patent as the physiological stamp of hard-won wisdom, but which here among these recent immortals still exerted a queer authority, even upon Amalfi.

"If you managed to synthesize even one of the anti-agathics, you've proven yourselves better chemists than anyone else in human history," Amalfi said. "They're far and away the most complicated molecules ever found in nature; certainly we've never heard of anyone who was able to synthesize even one."

"One is all we managed to synthesize," Miramon admitted. "And the synthetic form has certain small but undesirable side-effects we've never been able to eliminate. Several others turned out to be natural sapogenins which we could raise in our artificial climate, and modify into anti-agathics by two or three subsequent fermentation steps. Finally there are four others, of very broad usefulness, which we produce by fermentation alone, using micro-organisms grown in nutrient solutions in deep tanks, into which we feed comparatively simple and cheap precursors."

"We have one like that, the first, in fact, that was ever discovered: ascomycin," Amalfi said. "I think I will stick to my original judgment. As chemists you people could obviously give all the rest of us cards and spades."

"Then it is fortunate for us, and perhaps for every sentient being everywhere, that it is not as chemists that we come seeking you," Retma said, a trifle grimly.

"Which brings me to my main question," Amalfi said. "Just why did you turn back? I can't imagine that you would have been seeking me personally, you had no reason to believe that I was anywhere within thousands of parsecs of this area; we last parted company on the other side of the home galaxy. Obviously you must have looped back toward home as soon as you were sure you had centralized control over your spindizzy installation, long before you were much past half-way to the Andromeda galaxy. What I want to know is, what turned you back?"

"There you are both right and wrong," Miramon said, with a trace of what could have been pride; it was hard to tell, for his face was extremely solemn. "We obtained reasonably close control of the anti-gravity machines only about thirty years after you and I parted company, Mayor

Amalfi. When the full implications of what we had found
were borne in upon us, we were highly elated. Now we had
a real planet, in the radical meaning of the word, a real
wanderer which could go where it chose, settling in one
solar system or another and leaving it again when we so
decided. By that time we were almost self-sufficient, there
was obviously no need for us to become migrant workers,
as your city and its enemies had been. And since we were
well on the way to the second galaxy in any event, and
since there seemed to be absolutely no limit to the velocities we could mount with the huge mass of our planet on
which to operate, we chose to go on and explore."

"To the Andromeda galaxy?"

"Yes, and beyond. Of course we saw very little of that
galaxy, which is as vast as our home; we think that it is
not inhabited by any widespread, space-cruising race such
as yours and mine, but in the brief sampling of its stars
that we were able to take we might well simply have
missed hitting upon an inhabited or colonized system. By
that time, in any event, we had made the discovery which
was to become the basis of our lives and purposes from
then onward, and knew that we should have to return
home very shortly. We left the Andromeda nebula for its
satellite, the one that you identified for us as M-33 on our
old star-tapestries from the Great Age, and thence took
the million and a half light year leap to the Lesser Magellanic Cloud. It was during our transition from the Lesser
to the Greater Cloud that you detected us. That was, to
be sure, an accident; we had intended to go directly
through into the home galaxy and onward to Earth,
where, our experience with you had given us good reason
to believe, we might find a reservoir of knowledge great
enough to cope with what we had discovered. That our
own knowledge was insufficient was never for a moment
in doubt.

"But it is an accident of the greatest good omen that we
should have been found again by you as we were returning home, Mayor Amalfi. Surely the gods must have
arranged such an accident, which otherwise is impossibly
unlikely; for if there is any man not on Earth itself who
can help us, you are that man."

"You were not once such a believer in the gods, as I
recall," Amalfi said, smiling tightly.

"Opinions change with age; otherwise what is age for?"

"So does history," Amalfi said. "And, whether I can

help you or not, it is a lucky accident that you stopped here before carrying on into the home lens. Earth is no longer dominant there. We've had considerable difficulty in understanding what actually is going on, the messages that we get from there came pouring in to us in such an enormous garble; but of one thing I'm sure: there's a huge new imperialism on the rise there, on its way to becoming as powerful as Earth once was, and as Vegas was before Earth. It calls itself the Web of Hercules, and what remains of Earth's interstellar empire doesn't appear to be putting up much of a resistance against it. If you want my advice, I would suggest that you stay out of the home galaxy entirely, or you may well be gobbled down whole."

There was a long silence around the Hevian council table. At last, Miramon said:

"This leaves us with little recourse indeed. It may well be that there is no answer, as we have often suspected. Or it may be that the gods have indeed brought us back to the one source of wisdom that we need."

"We will know soon enough," Retma said quietly. "If in that instant there will be time enough to know anything. Or enough of time left thereafter to remember it."

"I shall probably be unable to advise you so long as I don't know what you're talking about," Amalfi said, impressed in spite of himself by the tone of high seriousness with which the Hevians spoke. "Just what was the discovery that turned you back? What is the forthcoming event that you seem to dread?"

"Nothing less," Retma said evenly, "than the imminent coming to an end of time itself."

For a while, even after they had explained it to him, Amalfi was so unable to believe that the Hevians had meant what they said that he was prepared to dismiss it as one of those superstitions with which He had been riddled, like many another provincial planet, when the Okies had first made contact with it. That time must have a stop was a proposition that nothing in all his long life had prepared him to accept even for an instant. Even after it became reluctantly clear to him that what Miramon and the Hevians had found in the intergalactic deeps had been a real event with real implications, and one which Amalfi's own people—particularly Schloss' group—were prepared to document, event and implication alike, he continued to be unable to do more with it than dismiss it out of hand.

He said so, at a conference on shipboard which included Miramon, Retma, Dr. Schloss, Carrel, and—by Dirac—Jake and Dr. Gifford Bonner, the latter the leader of that group of New Earth philosophers which Hazleton had recently joined, called the Stochastics. "If what you say is true," he said, "there's nothing to be done about it anyhow. Time will come to an end, and that's that. But the end of the world has been predicted often before, I seem to remember from history, and here we all are still; I can't credit that so vast a process as the whole physical universe could possibly come to an end in the flicker of an eyelash, and since I can't believe it, I'm not suddenly going to start behaving as if I did. No more do I see why anyone else should."

"Amalfi, you're quite right! You don't understand," Dr. Schloss said. "Of course the end of the universe has been predicted often before. It's one of those two-pronged choices that any philosopher has to make: either you hold that the universe will at some time come to an end, or else you arrive at the position that it never can; there are intermediate guesses that you can make, that's where we get our cyclical theories, but essentially they're simply hedges. If you decided that the universe has a limited lifetime, then you must begin to think about when that life will come to an end, on the basis of whatever data are available to you. We have been agreed for millennia that the universe cannot last forever, however we've hedged the agreement, so that leaves us nothing to quarrel about but the date at which we fixed the end. And sooner or later, too, the time was going to come when we had enough data to fix even the date without doubt. The Hevians have brought us sufficient facts to do that now; the date is fixed, whatever it proves to be, without cavil or quibble. If we are to talk about the matter intelligently at all, there is a fixed fact with which we must begin. It is not open to agreement. It is a fact.

"I think," Amalfi said in a voice of steel, "that you have gone quietly insane. You should listen to the City Fathers for a while on this subject, as I have; if you like, I can give you a Dirac line to them from right here aboard ship, and you can hear some of the memories that they have stored up—some of them dating back long before spaceflight; our city is very old. You should hear particularly the stories about the end of the world which emerge as inevitably as a plant from a seed every time someone takes it into his head to believe that he has a direct wire to the Almighty. Some of the stories, of course are just jokes like the many predictions of the end of the world which were made by a man named Voliva, who *knew* that the Earth was flat; or the predictions of Armageddon that came repeatedly from an Earthly sect called the Believers, which was riding high on Earth during the very decade when both the spindizzy and the anti-agathics were discovered. But high intelligence doesn't prevent you from falling into this kind of apocryphal madness, either; seven centuries before space flight on Earth, the greatest scientist of that time, a man named Bacon, was predicting the imminent arrival of Anti-Christ simply because he was unable to persuade his contemporaries to adopt scientific method, which he had just invented. Furthermore, I may add, in the decade just before spaceflight on Earth, all the best minds of the age saw no future for the human race, and all other air-breathing life on Earth, but complete obliteration in a world-wide thermonuclear war, which over a period of eight years could have broken out within any given twenty-minute period. And in that, Dr. Schloss, they were quite right; their world really could have ended during any one of these twenty-minute periods; the physical possibilities were there, but somehow the world managed to last until spaceflight became only a specter, burned out by starlight, as the ghosts of night-bound peoples evaporate from their mythologies as soon as they're able to produce light even at midnight simply by tripping a switch."

He looked around at the faces of the men drawn up at the ship's chart table. Few of them would meet his eyes; most of them were looking down at the table itself, or at their own hands. Their expressions were those of men who had been listening to a mass murderer attempting to enter a plea of insanity.

"Amalfi," Jake's voice said abruptly from the Dirac, "the time for forensics is past. This question does not have two sides, except for the right side and the wrong side, and we are going to have to shuck you off as a brilliant advocate for the wrong side. You have done your magnificent best, but since the right side does not need an advocate, you have been wasting your breath. Let me ask the rest of this conference: What shall we do now? Does it appear that, as the Hevians think, there is anything at all that we can do? I am inclined to doubt it."

"So am I," Dr. Schloss said, though there was nothing in his manner to suggest the gloom inherent in his conclusion; he seemed rather to be as intensely interested as Amalfi had ever seen him in his life. "For temporal creatures to hope to survive the end of time is surely as futile as a fish hoping to survive being thrown into a sun. The paradox is immediate, on the surface, and quite inescapable."

"No technical problem is ever that insoluble," Amalfi said in exasperation. "Miramon, if you will pardon me for passing such a judgment—and I don't care if you don't—I think you are suffering from the same syndrome as Dr. Freeman and Dr. Schloss: you have grown old before your time. You've lost your sense of adventure."

"Not entirely," Miramon said, regarding Amalfi with an expression of grave and hurt disappointment. "We, at least, are not yet convinced that there is no answer; if we do not find it here, we have every intention of continuing to travel in the hope of finding someone with whom we can combine forces, someone who may have some solution to suggest. If we find no one, then we shall continue to seek that solution ourselves."

"Good for you," Amalfi said fiercely. "And by God I'll go with you. We can't very well re-enter our own galaxy, but the next one is NGC 6822, that's about a million light years from here—for you, that's only a hop. And at least we'd be in motion; we wouldn't be sitting around here with folded hands waiting for the blow to fall."

"That would be motion without purpose," Miramon said solemnly. "I agree with you that it would be dangerous and unwise to risk any entanglement with the Web of Hercules, whatever that may be; but I can see no better point in cruising from one galaxy to another solely in the bare hope of encountering a high civilization which might be able to help us, and all the rest of the universe with us. We have that hope, but it cannot be the final goal of our journey; our ultimate destination must be the center of the metagalaxy, the hub of all the galaxies of space-time. It is only there, where all the forces of the universe lie in dynamic balance, that anyone can hope to take any action to escape or to modify the end which is coming. There is, after all, not much time left before that moment is due. And above all, Mayor Amalfi, it is not simply a technical problem; it is an ending which was written organically into the fundamental structure of the universe itself, written in the beginning by what hands we know not; all that we can know now is that it was foreordained."

And from this conclusion, though Amalfi's own psyche had been fighting against its acceptance since the moment that he himself had realized it was so, there was really no escape. Conceptually, the universe had been a reasonably comfortable place to live in, in primitive atomic theory which offered the assurance that everything, earth, air, fire or water, steel and oranges, man or star, was ultimately composed of submicroscopic vortices called protons and electrons leavened a little with neutrons and neutrinos which had no charge, and bound together by a disorderly but homely family of mesons. The type case was the hydrogen atom, one proton sitting cosily on the hearth, contentedly positive in charge, while about it wove one electron, surrounded by its negative field like crackling cat's fur. That was the simple case; but one was assured that even in the heaviest and most complicated atoms, even those man-made ones like plutonium, one need only add more and heavier logs to the fire, and more cats would come droning about it; it would be hard to tell one cat from another, but this is the customary penalty the owner of hundreds pays.

The first omen that there was something wrong with this chromo of sub-microscopic and universal domesticity appeared, as all good omens should, in the skies. Back on Earth, nearly half a century before space flight, some astronomer whose name is quite lost had noticed that two or three of the millions of meteors that entered Earth's atmosphere every day exploded at a height and with a violence which could not be accounted for by an eccentricity of orbit or velocity; and in one of those great flights of fancy which account in the long run for every new link in the great chain of understanding, he had a dream of something which he called "contra-terrene" matter—a matter made of fire with cat's fur, which would be circled by cats in flames: matter in which the fundamental hydrogen atom would have a nucleus which would be an antiproton, with the mass of a proton but carrying a negative charge, around which would orbit an anti-electron, with the negligible mass of an electron, but carrying a positive charge. A meteor of atoms constructed on this model, he reasoned, would explode with especial violence at the first contact with even the faintest traces of Earth's normal-matter atmosphere; and such meteors would suggest that somewhere in the universe there were whole planets, whole suns, whole galaxies composed of such matter, whose barest touch would be more than death—would be ultimate and complete annihilation, each form of matter converting the other wholly into energy in a flaming and total embrace.

Curiously, the contra-terrene meteors died out of the theory shortly thereafter, while the theory itself survived. The exploding meteors were found to be easier to explain in more conventional terms, but anti-matter survived, and by the middle of the Twentieth Century experimental physicists were even able to produce the stuff a few atoms at a time. Those topsy-turvy atoms proved to be nonviable beyond a few millionths of a micro-second, and it gradually became clear that even in this short lifetime the time in which they lived was running backwards. The particles of which they were made were born, in the great clumsy bevatrons of that age, some micro-seconds in the future, and their assembly into atoms of anti-matter in the present time of the observers was in fact the moment of their death. Obviously anti-matter was not only theoretically possible, but could exist; but it could not exist in this universe in any assemblage so gross as a meteor; if there were worlds and galaxies made of anti-matter, they existed only in some unthinkable separate continuum where time and the entropy gradient ran backwards. Such a continuum would require at least four extra dimensions, at a minimum, in addition to the conventional four of experience.

As the universe of normal matter expanded, unwound and ran down toward its inevitable heat-death, somewhere nearby and yet in a "somewhere" unimaginable by man, a duplicate universe as vast and complex was contracting, winding up, approaching the supernal concentration of mass and energy called the monobloc. As complete dispersion, darkness and silence was to be the fate of the universe in which the arrow of time pointed down the entropy gradient, so in the anti-matter universe the end was to be mass beyond mass, energy beyond energy, raw glare and fury to the ultimate power raging in a primeval "atom" no bigger across than the orbit of Saturn. And out of one universe might come the other; in the universe of normal matter the monobloc was the beginning, but in the universe of anti-matter it would be the end; in a universe of normal entropy, the monobloc is intolerable and must explode; in a universe of negative entropy, the heat-death is intolerable and must condense. In either case, the command is: *Let there be light.*

What the visible, tangible universe had been like before the monobloc was, however, agreed to be forever unknowable. The classic statement had been made many centuries earlier by St. Augustine, who, when asked what God might have been doing before He created the universe, replied that He was constructing a hell for persons who asked such questions; thus "pre-Augustinean time" came to be something that a historian could know all about, but a physicist, by definition, nothing.

Until now; for if the Hevians were right, they had lifted that curtain a little way and caught an instant's glimpse of the unknowable.

To have looked it full in the face could have been no more fatal.

During the course of their exultant drive upon the Andromeda galaxy, the Hevians had discovered that one of their spindizzies—oddly, it was one of the machines which had been new-built for the project, not one of the old and somewhat abused drivers which had been dismounted from the Okie city—was beginning to run somewhat hot. This was a problem which was then brand new to them, and rather than take chances on the to them unknown effects which might be produced by such a machine were it to run really wild, they shut down their entire spindizzy network while repairs were made, leaving behind only a 0.02 per cent screen necessary to protect the planet's atmosphere and heat budget.

And it was then and there, in the utter silences of intergalactic space, that their instruments detected for the first time in human history the whispers of continuous creation: the tiny *ping* of new atoms of hydrogen being born, one by one, out of nothing at all.

This would alone and in itself have been a sobering enough experience for any man of a thoughtful cast of mind, even one who lacked the Hevians' history of preoccupation with religious questions; no one could view the birth of the raw material from which the whole known universe was built, out of what was demonstrably nothingness, without being shaken by the conviction that there must also be a Creator, and that He must be in the immediate vicinity of where His work was proceeding. Those tiny pings and pips in the Hevians' instruments seemed at first to leave no room in the long arguments of cosmogony and cosmology for any cyclical theory of the universe, any continuous and eternal systole diastole from monobloc to heat-death and back again, with a Creator required only at the remote inception of the rhythmic process, or not at all. Here was creation in process: the invisible Finger touched nothingness, and from nothing came something; the ultimate absurdity, which, because it was ultimate, could be nothing else but divine.

Yet the Hevians were sophisticated enough to be suspicious. Historically, fundamental discoveries were dependably ambiguous; this discovery, which on the face of it seemed to provide a flat answer to 25,000 years of theological speculation, and in effect to bring God into inarguable being for the first time since He had been postulated by some Stone Age sun-worshipper or mushroom-eating mystic, could not be as simple as it seemed. It had been won too easily; too much else is implied by the continual creating existence of a present God to make it tenable that that existence should be provable by so simple and single a physical datum, arrived at by what could honestly only be described as ordinary accident.

Gifford Bonner was later to remark that it had been fortunate beyond belief that it had been the Hevians, a people only recently winning back to some degree of scientific sophistication, but which had never lost its sense of the continuity and the overwhelming complexity of theology in a scientific age, who had first been allowed to hear these tiny birth-cries in the nursery of time. The typical Earthman of the end of the Third Millennium, with his engineer's bias, philosphically webbed in about equal measure to a sentimentally hard-headed "common sense" and a raw and naive mystique of Progress (it was at about this point in Bonner's analysis that Amalfi had felt a slight impulse to squirm), might easily have taken the datum at face value and walked the plank on it directly into a morass of telepathy, the racial unconscious, personal reincarnation or any of a hundred other traps which await the scientifically oriented man who does not know that he too is as thorough-going a mystic as a fakir lying on a bed of nails.

The Hevians were suspicious; they questioned the discovery first of all only on the subject of what it said it was saying. Theology could wait. If continuous creation was a fact, then primarily that ruled out that there should ever have been a monobloc in the history of the universe, or that there should ever be a heat-death; instead, it would always go along like this, world without end. Therefore, if the discovery was as fundamentally ambiguous as all such discoveries before had proven to be, it should in the same breath be implying exactly the opposite; ask it *that* question, and see what it says.

This singularly tough-minded approach paid off at once, though the further implications which it offered for inspection proved in no way easier to digest than the first and contrary set had been. Taking a long chance with the still largely unfamiliar machines, and with the precarious life of their entire planet, the Hevians shut down their spindizzies entirely and listened more intently.

In that utmost of dead silences, the upsetting whisper of continuous creation proved to have two voices. Each pinging birth-pang was not a single note, but a duo. As each atom of hydrogen leapt into being from nowhere into the universe of experience, a sinister twin, a hydrogen atom of anti-matter, came there in that instant to die, from ... somewhere else.

And there it was. Even what had seemed to be fundamental, ineluctable proof of one-way time and continuous creation could also be regarded as inarguable evidence for a cyclical cosmology. In a way, to the Hevians, it was satisfying; this was physics as they knew it to be, an idiot standing at a crossroads shouting "God went thataway!" and managing to point down all four roads at once. Nevertheless, it left them a legacy of dread. This single many-barbed burr of a datum, which could have been obtained under no other circumstances, was also sufficient in itself to endorse the existence of an entire second universe of anti-matter, congruent point for point with the universe of experience of normal matter, but opposite to it in sign. What appeared to have been the birth of a hydrogen atom of anti-matter, simultaneous with the birth of the normal hydrogen atom, was actually its death; there was now no doubt that time ran backwards in the anti-matter universe, and so did the entropy gradient, one being demonstrably a function of the other.

The concept, of course, was old—so old, in fact, that Amalfi had difficulty in remembering just when in his lifetime it had become so familiar to him that he had forgotten about it entirely. Its revival here by the Hevians struck him at first as an exasperating anachronism, calculated only to get in the way of the real work of practical men. He was in particular rather scornful of the notion of a universe in which negative entropy could be an operating principle; under such circumstances, his rustily squeaking memory pointed out, cause and effect would not preserve even the rough statistical associations which they were allowed in the universe of experience; energy would accumulate, events would undo themselves, water would run uphill, old men would clump into existence out of the air and soil and unlearn their profitless ways back toward their mothers' wombs.

"Which is what they do in any event," Gifford Bonner had said gently. "But actually, I doubt that it's that paradoxical, Amalfi. Both of these universes can be regarded as unwinding, as running down, as losing energy with each transaction. The fact that from our point of view the anti-matter universe seems to be gaining energy is simply a bias built into the way we're forced to look at things. Actually these two universes probably are simply unwinding in opposite directions, like two millstones. Though the two arrows of time seem to be pointing in opposite directions, they probably both point downhill, like fingerboards at the crest of a single road. If the dynamics of it bother you, bear in mind that both are four dimensional continua and from that point of view both are wholly static."

"Which brings us to the crucial question of contiguity," Jake said cheerfully. "The point is, these two four-dimensional continua are intimately related, as the twin events the Hevians observed make very plain; which I suppose must mean that we must allow for a total of at least sixteen dimensions to contain the whole system. Which is no particular surprise in itself; you need at least that many to accommodate the atomic nucleus of average complexity comfortably. What is surprising is that the two continua are approaching each other; I agree with Miramon that the observations his people made can't be interpreted any other way; up to now, the fact that gravitation in the two universes is also opposite in sign seems to have kept them apart, but that repulsion or pressure or whatever you want to call it is obviously growing steadily weaker. Somewhere in the future, the near future, it will decline to zero, there will be a Pythagorean point-for-point collision between the two universes as a whole—"

"—and it's hard to imagine how any physical framework, even one that allows sixteen dimensions of elbowroom, will be able to contain the energy that's going to be released," Dr. Schloss said. "The monobloc isn't even in the running; if it ever existed, it was just a wet firecracker by comparison."

"Translation: *blooey*," Carrel said.

"It's perfectly possible that a rational cosmology is going to have to accommodate all three events," Gifford Bonner said. "I mean by that the monobloc, the heat death, and this thing—this event that seems to fall midway between the two. Curious; there are a number of myths, and ancient philosophical systems, that allow for such a break or discontinuity right in the middle of the span of existence; Giordano Bruno, Earth's first relativist, called it the period of Interdestruction, and a compatriot of his named Vico allowed for it in what was probably the first cyclical theory of ordinary human history; and in Scandanavian mythology it was called the Ginnangu-Gap. But I wonder, Dr. Schloss, if the destruction is going to be quite as total as you suggest. I am nobody's physicist, I freely confess, but it seems to me that if these two universes are opposite in sign *at every point,* as everyone at this meeting has been implying, then the result cannot be *only* a general transformation of the matter on both sides into energy. There will be energy transformed into matter, too, on just as large a scale, after which the gravitational pressure should begin to build up again and the two universes, having in effect passed through each other and exchanged hats, will begin retreating from each other once more. Or have I missed something crucial?"

"I'm not sure that the argument is as elegant as it appears on the surface," Retma said. "That awaits Dr. Schloss's mathematical analysis, of course; but in the meantime I cannot help but wonder why, for instance, if this simultaneous creation-interdestruction-destruction cycle is truly cyclical, it should have this ornamental waterspout of continuous creation attached to it? A machinery of creation which involves no less than three universal cataclysms in each cycle should not need to be powered by a sort of continuous drip; either the one is too grandiose, or the other is insufficient. Besides, continuous creation implies a steady state, which is irreconcilable."

"I don't know about that," Jake said. "It doesn't sound like anything the Milne transformations couldn't handle; it's probably just a clock function."

"Defined, as I recall, as a mathematical expression about the size of a bottle of aspirin," Carrel said ruefully.

"Well, there's one thing I'm perfectly certain of," Amalfi growled, "and that is that it's damned unlikely anybody is going to be around to care about the exact results of the collision after it happens. At least not at the rate this hassle is going. Is there actually anything useful that we can do, or would we be better off spending all this time playing poker?"

"That," Miramon said, "is exactly what we know least about. In fact it would appear that we know nothing about it whatsoever."

"Mr. Miramon—" Web Hazleton's voice spoke from the shadows and stopped. Obviously he was waiting to be told that he was breaking his promise not to interrupt, but it was as plain to Amalfi as it was to the rest of the group that he was interrupting nothing now; his voice had broken only a dead and despairing silence.

"Go ahead, Web," Amalfi said.

"Well, I was just thinking. Mr. Miramon came here looking for somebody to help him do something he doesn't know how to do himself. Now he thinks we don't know how to do it either. But what was it?"

"He's just said that he doesn't know," Amalfi said gently.

"That isn't what I mean," Web said hesitantly. "What I mean is, what would he *like* to do, even if he doesn't know how to do it? Even if it's impossible?"

Bonner's voice chuckled softly in the still shipboard air. "That's right," he said, "the ends determine the means. A hen is only an egg's device for producing another egg. Is that Hazleton's grandson? Good for you, Web."

"There are a good many experiments that ought to be performed, if only we knew how to design them," Miramon admitted thoughtfully. "First of all, we ought to have a better date for the catastrophe than we have now; 'the near future' is a huge block of time under these conditions, almost as shapeless a target as 'sometime'; we would need it defined to the millisecond just to begin with. I applaud the young Earthman's brilliant common sense, but I refuse to delude myself by asking for more than that; even that seems hopeless."

"Why?" Amalfi said. "What would you need to calculate it from? Given the data, the City Fathers can handle the calculations; they were designed to handle any mathematical operation once the parameters were filled, and in a thousand years I've never known them to fail to come through on that kind of thing, usually within two or three minutes; never as long as a day."

"I remember your City Fathers," Miramon said, with a brief ironical motion of his eyebrows which was perhaps a last vestigial tremor of his old savage awe at the things which were the city and of the city. "But the major parameter that needs to be filled here is a precise determination of the energy level of the other universe."

"Why, that shouldn't be so very difficult," Dr. Schloss said, in dawning astonishment. "That can't be anything but a transform of energy level in our own universe; the mayor's right, the City Fathers could give you that almost before you could finish stating the problem to them; t-tau transforms are the fundamental stuff of faster-than-light space travel—I'm astonished that you've been able to get along without them."

"Not so," Jake said. "No doubt the t-tau relationships are congruent on both sides of the barrier, I don't doubt that for a minute, but you're dealing in sixteen dimensions here; along what axis are you going to impose the congruency? Are you going to assume that t-time and tau-time apply uniformly and transformably along all sixteen axes? You can't do that, unless you're willing to involve the total system in such a double, which in t-time involves a monobloc for the whole apparatus; that's hopeless. At least it's hopeless for us, in the time we have left; we'd be frittering away our days in chase of endlessly retreating decimals. You might just as well set the City Fathers to work giving you a final figure for *pi*."

"I stand corrected," Dr. Schloss said, his tone halfway between wry humor and stiff embarrassment. "You're quite right, Miramon; there's a discontinuity here which we can't read from theory. How inelegant."

"Elegance can wait," Amalfi said. "In the meantime, why is it so impossible to get an energy-level reading from the other side? Dr. Schloss, your research group used to talk about their hopes of constructing an anti-matter artifact. Couldn't we use such a thing as an exploratory missile to the other side?"

"No," Dr. Schloss said promptly. "You forget that such an object would be on the other side—it would be on our side. We would have to work out some way of assembling it in the future of the experiment; by the time we were first able to see it, in the present of the experiment, it would be in an advanced state of decay, to say the least, and would then evolve only to the condition in which we assembled it. No reading that we got from it would tell us anything but how anti-matter behaves in our universe; it would tell us nothing about any universe in which anti-matter is normal."

After a moment, he added thoughtfully, "And besides, that would be a project hard to realize in anything under a century, I'd be more inclined to say it would take two; under the circumstances I too would rather be playing poker."

"Well, I wouldn't," Jake said unexpectedly. "I think Amalfi may be right in principle. Difficult though the problem is, there ought to be some sort of probe that we could extend across the discontinuity. Mind you, I agree that the anti-matter artifact is the wrong approach entirely; the thing would have to be absolutely immaterial, a construct made entirely out of what we could pick up in No Man's Land. But seeing across long distances under great odds is the discipline I was trained in. I don't think we should count this an impossible problem. Schloss, how do you feel about this? If you and your group are willing to give up your anti-matter artifact for poker, would you be willing to work with me on this a while? I'll need your background, but you'll need my point of view; between us we just might devise the instrument and get the message. Mind you, Miramon, I hold out no hope, but—"

"—except the hope you hold out." Miramon said, his eyes shining. "Now I am hearing from you what I hoped to hear. This is the voice of the Earth of memory. We will give you everything you need that is within our power to give; we give you our planet, to begin with; but the universe, the twin universes, the unthinkable meta-universe you must take for yourselves. We remember you now; you have always had that boundless ambition." His voice darkened suddenly. "And we shall be your disciples; that, too, is as it has always been. Only begin; that is all we ask."

Amalfi gathered the consensus of the present eyes around the chart table. Such agreement as he needed from the listeners on New Earth he was able to gather almost as well from the silence.

"I think," he said slowly, "that we have begun already."

CHAPTER FOUR: Fabr-Suithe

It was hot on the Hevian hillside in the post-noon glare of the great Cepheid about which the planet was now orbiting at the respectful distance of thirty-five astronomical units—thirty-five times the distance of old Earth from the Sun. At this distance the star, which had a mean absolute magnitude of plus one, was barely tolerable at the peak of its eight-day cycle; at the bottom of the cycle, when the star's radiation had dropped by a factor of 25, it got cold enough on He to nip one's ears—far from an ideal situation for a predominantly agricultural planet, but the Hevians did not expect to remain in the vicinity for as long as one growing season.

Web and Estelle lay in the long grass of the hillside under the hot regard of that swollen star and slowly got their breaths back. Web in particular was glad for the recess. The morning had begun in sober exploration of Fabr-Suithe, He's greatest monument to its own past, and He's present center of pure philosophy; thus far it was the only place they had found on He which they were allowed to explore by themselves, by both the adult Hevians and their own people. This morning, however, this freedom had had an unexpected but logical consequence: they had found that Fabr-Suithe was also one of the few cities on He where Hevian children were free to roam. Elsewhere there were far too many machines vital to the life of the planet as a whole; the Hevians could not afford the chance that children might get into the works, nor, with their sparse population, could they afford the loss of even a single life.

Web and Estelle had changed into the chiton-like Hevian costume the moment they had been told that they would be allowed to explore the city, albeit in very limited terms, but it did not take the Hevian youngsters long to penetrate this disguise, since Web and Estelle spoke their language only in a most rudimentary way. This language block was in part a nuisance—for although most adult

Hevians spoke the mixture of English, Interlingua and Russian which was the *bêche-de-mer* of deep space, learned long ago from the Okies, none of the children did—but it was also a blessing, since it precluded any extensive interrogation of Web and Estelle about their own world, culture and background. Shortly, instead, they found themselves involved in an elaborate chase game called Matrix, rather like run-sheep-run combined with checkers except that it was three-dimensional, for it was played in a twelve-story building with transparent floors so that one could always see the position of the other players, and with strategically placed spindizzy and friction-field shafts for fast transit from one floor to another. Web was the first to develop the suspicion that the building had either been designed for the game or had been totally abandoned to it, for the transparent floors were appropriately ruled, and the structure otherwise did not seem to contain anything or to be used for any other purpose.

Web had found the game itself exhilarating at first, but rather baffling too, and he was generally the first player to be eliminated. Had it not been for an impromptu change in the rules, he would have been It in nearly every new round, and even under the aegis of the new rules he did not make a very brave showing. Estelle, on the other hand, took to Matrix as though she had been born in the game, and within half an hour her lanky-legged, slender figure, as bosomless and hipless as any of the boys', was darting in and out of the kaleidoscope of running figures with inordinate grace and swiftness. When time was called for lunch, Web's laboring lungs and bruised ego more than welcomed the chance to escape from the city entirely for the hot stillness of the fallow hills.

"They're nice; I like them," Estelle said, rising to one elbow to attack, meditatively, a gourd-shaped green and silver melon which one of the Hevian boys had given her, apparently as a prize. At the first bite, there was a low but prolonged hiss, and the air around them became impregnated with a fragrance so overwhelmingly spicy that Estelle had to sneeze five times in quick succession. Web began to laugh, but the laughter ended abruptly in a paroxysmal sneeze of his own.

"They *love* us," he said, wiping his eyes. "You're so good at their game, they've given you a sneeze-gas bomb to keep you from playing it any longer."

The odor diminished gradually, carried off by what little

breeze there was. After a while Estelle cautiously put two thumbs into the wound she had made and broke the melon open. Nothing else happened; the odor was now tolerable, and then abruptly became both barely detectable and overpoweringly mouth-watering. Estelle handed him half. He bit into the crisp white pulp more deeply than he had intended. The result made him close his eyes; it tasted like quick-frozen music.

They finished it in reverent silence and, wiping their mouths on their chitons, lay back. After a while, Estelle said:

"I wish we could talk to them better."

"Miramon can talk to *us* well enough," Web said somnolently. "He didn't have to learn our language the hard way, either. They do it here by machine, like we used to do it when we were Okies. I wish we still did it that way."

"Hypnopaedia?" Estelle said. "But I thought that was all dead and done for. You didn't really *learn* anything that way: just facts."

"That's right, just facts. It didn't teach you to relate. For that you have to have a tutor. But it was good for learning things like $1 \times 1 = 10$, or the tables in the back of the book, or the 850 words you most need to know in a new language. It used to take only five hundred hours to cram all that stuff into you, by EEG feedback, flicker, oral repetition, and I don't know what all else— and the whole time, you were under hypnosis."

"It sounds too easy," Estelle said sleepily.

"The easy parts of things ought to be easy," Web said. "What's the point of having to learn them by rote? That takes too much time. You know yourself that something you can learn in ten repetitions, or five, it takes some kids thirty repetitions to learn. So you have to sit around through twenty or twenty-five repetitions that you don't need. If there's anything I hate about school, it's drill—all that time wasted that you could actually be doing something with."

Suddenly Web became conscious of a peculiar flopping sound at the crest of the hill behind him. He knew well enough that there were no dangerous animals left on He, but he realized that he had been hearing the sound for some time while he was talking; and the notion occurred to him that his definition of a dangerous animal might not necessarily make a good match with that of a Hevian.

Anyhow, he could hope; he could use a tiger to best, along
about now. He twisted quickly to his hands and knees.

"Don't be silly," Estelle said, without moving or even
opening her eyes. "It's only Ernest."

The svengali appeared over the crest of the hill and
came humping itself through the tall grass in a symphony
of desperate disorganization. It gave Web only the briefest
of glances, and then bent upon Estelle the reproachful
stare of an animal utterly betrayed, but still—it hoped you
noticed—firm in the true faith. Web stiffed his impulse to
laugh, for in fact he could hardly blame the poor creature; since it was as brainless as it was sexless—despite its
name—it had been able to contrive no better way of
keeping up with Estelle than to follow her through her
every move in the Matrix game, a discipline for which it
was so magnificently unequipped that it had only just now
finished. It was lucky that the children had not counted it
as a player; or poor Ernest would have been It to—Web
thought with unfocussed uneasiness—the end of time.

"We could sign up for it here," Web said abruptly.

"For what? Hypnopaedia? Your grandmother wouldn't
let us."

Web turned around and sat up, plucking a long hollow
blade of the bamboo-like grass and sinking his grinding
teeth thoughtfully into the woody butt end. "But she isn't
here," he said.

"No, but she will be," Estelle said. "And she's a school
officer on the New Earth. I used to hear her fighting
about it with my father when I was a child. She used to
tell him he was out of his mind. She would say, "Why do
kids need all this calculus and history now? What good is
it to somebody who's going to have to go out and hoe a
virgin planet?' She used to make poor Dad stutter something awful."

"But she isn't here." Web repeated, with a little unwilling exasperation. He had just realized that Estelle's
face with its closed eyes, so perfectly in repose in the
blue-white light of this one-day-long summer, was lovelier
than anything he had ever seen before. He found that he
could not go on.

At the same moment, the svengali felt rested enough to
take a consensus among the scattered ganglia which
served it, however badly, for a brain, and concluded that
its long soulful stare at Estelle was doing it no good at all.
Simultaneously one of its limbs, which had the whole time

been inching in the direction of one of the melon rinds, suddenly passed a threshold and telegraphed back to the rest of the animal the implications of that now faint spicy odor. All the rest of Ernest flowed eagerly into that arm and bunched itself around the rind; and then the polyp was rolling helplessly down the hill, curled into a ball, with the melon rind clutched firmly in the middle. As it rolled, it emitted a small thrilling whistle of alarm which made Web's back hairs stir—it was the first time he had ever heard a svengali make a sound—but it would not let go of its prize; it came to rest in the middle of a rivulet in the valley, and was washed gently downstream out of sight, still faintly protesting and avidly digesting.

"There goes Ernest," Web said.

"I know. I heard him. He's such a stupid. But he'll be back. Your grandmother will be here too. Once the Mayor and Miramon and Dr. Schloss and the rest decided to stay on He, because of all the work they have to do here, they had to send home for somebody to take care of us. They don't think we can take care of ourselves. They wouldn't let us go knocking all around a strange planet all by ourselves."

"Maybe not," Web said reluctantly. He tested the proposition; it seemed to hold water. "But why would it have to be grandmother?"

"Well, it wouldn't be Daddy, because he has to stay on New Earth and work on the New Earth part of the problem that we're working on here," Estelle said. "And it wouldn't be your grandfather because he has to stay home on New Earth and be mayor while Mayor Amalfi's here. It wouldn't be my mother because they're not scientists or philosophers and would just clutter up He even more than we're doing. If they're going to fly anyone out here to oversee us, it has to be your grandmother."

"I suppose so," Web said. "That'll put a crimp in us, for sure."

"It'll do more than that," Estelle said tranquilly. "She'll send us home."

"She wouldn't do that!"

"Yes she would. That's the way they think. She'll be practical about it."

"That's not being practical," Web protested. "It's treachery, that's what it is. She can't come all the way here to take care of us on He, just as an excuse to take us off He."

Estelle did not reply. After a moment Web opened his eyes, belatedly realizing that a shadow had fallen across his face. The Hevian boy who had given Estelle the melon was standing above them, deferentially, respecting their silence, but obviously poised to renew the game when they were ready. Behind him, the heads of the other Hevian children bobbed over the hill, obviously wondering what the strangers and their boneless odd-smelling pet would do next, but leaving the initiative to their spokesman.

"Hello," Estelle said, sitting up again.

"Hello," the tall boy said hesitantly. "Yes?"

For a moment he seemed baffled; then, making the best of the situation, he sat down and went on in as simple a Hevian as he could contrive.

"You are rested. Yes? Shall we play another game?"

"No more for me," Web said, almost indignantly. "Then play Matrix yesterday, tomorrow sometime day. Yes?"

"No, no," the Hevian boy said. "Not Matrix. This is another game, a resting game. You play it sitting down. We call it the lying game."

"Oh. How works it?"

"Everyone takes turns. Each tells a story. It must be a real story, without any truth in it. The other players are the jury. You gain a point for everything in the story that is clearly true. The low score wins."

"I lost about five key words in there somewhere," Estelle said to Web. "How does it go again?"

Web explained quickly. Although his spoken command of the Hevian language was limited to the tenses of past indictable, present excitable and future irredeemable, his vocabulary a thoroughly unbotanical mixture of stems and roots, and his declensions one massive disinclination to decline, he found that he was developing a fair facility at understanding the language, at least when it was being spoken this slowly. It was quite probable that he too had lost five words in the course of the Hevian boy's speech, but he had picked up their meaning from context; Estelle apparently was still trying to translate word by word, instead of striving first to catch the total import of the sentence.

"Oh, I see," Estelle said. "But how do they rate one truth over another? If in my story the sun rises in the morning, and I also say I'm wearing this whatever-it-is, this chiton, do I get docked one point for each?"

"I'll try to ask," Web said doubtfully. "I'm not sure I have all the nouns I need."

He put the question to the Hevian boy, finding it necessary to be rather more abstract than he wished; but the boy grasped not only the sense of what he was trying to say, but worked his way back to the concrete nouns with impressive insight.

"The jury will decide," the boy said. "But there are rules. A dress is only a little truth, and costs only one point. Sunrise on a captive planet, like New Earth, is a natural law, that may cost you fifty. On a free planet like He, it may be only partly true and cost you ten. Or it may be a flat lie and cost you nothing. That is why we have the jury."

Web had to have this restated to him in increasingly simpler terms before he chanced explaining it in turn to Estelle; but at last he was reasonably sure that both the New Earth players understood the rules of the game. To make assurance doubly sure, he asked the Hevians to begin, so that he and Estelle could become familiar with the kinds of lies which were most admired, and the way the jury of players penalized each inadvertent truth.

The first two stories came close to convincing him that he was being overcautious. At the very least it seemed plain, both from the terms in which the game had been described and the stories as they were told, that the Hevians as a race had little talent for fiction. The third player, however, a girl of about nine who obviously had been bursting with impatience for her turn to come around, stunned him completely. The moment she was called upon, she began:

"This morning I saw a letter, and the address on it was Four. The letter had feet, and the feet had shoes on them. It was delivered by missile, but it walked all the way. Though it is Four for four, it's triple treble trouble," she wound up triumphantly.

There was a short, embarrassed silence.

"That doesn't sound like a lie at all," Estelle said to Web, relapsing into her own language. "It sounds more like a riddle."

"That was not fair," the Hevian leader was telling the nine-year-old at the same time in a stern voice. "We hadn't explained the rules of the coup." He turned to Web and Estelle. "Another part of the game is to try to tell a story which is entirely true, but sounds like a lie. In the coup, the jury penalizes you for lying if it can catch you. If you aren't caught, you have told a perfect truth, which wins the round even over a perfect lie. But it was unfair of Pyla to try for a coup before we'd explained it to you."

"I challenge once," Web said gravely. "Is really this morning was? If, then we had had knowed; but we haven't.'"

"This morning," Pyla insisted, determinedly defending her coup in the face of the group's obvious disapproval. "You weren't there then. I saw you leave."

"How do you know about all these?" Web said.

"I hung around," the girl said. Abruptly, she giggled. "And I heard you two talking, too, behind the hill."

Since the whole of her answer was offered in a fluent, though heavily accented Okie *bêche-de-mer,* there were obviously no further questions to be asked.

Web was feeling just barely civil toward females, but he offered Pyla his politest smile. "In that case," he said formally, "you win. We thank you from our heartmost bottom. This is good news."

He never did quite make up his mind whether his imperfect knowledge of Hevian made this polite speech come out as "Pullup hellup yiz are ninety" or "Why do I am alook alike a poss of porterpease?", or whether he managed to say exactly what he thought he was saying, but to his great astonishment, Pyla burst into tears.

"Oh, oh, oh," she wailed. "That would have been my very first coup. And you beat me, you beat me."

The jury was already in a huddle. A few moments later Silvador, the leader, stroked Pyla gently on the temples and said, "Hush now. On the contrary, our Web-friend must be penalized for lying."

His eyes twinkling, he offered Estelle his arm, and she came to her feet in one sinuous unravelling of the knot she had tied herself into during the lying game.

"The penalty must include our Estelle-friend too," he added portentously. "You must both come with us, directly to the city, and be——" he struck an executioner's pose—— "put to sleep for a while."

"No," Web said. "We have to go." He clambered stiffly to his feet.

"Please," Silvador said. "We don't really mean to punish. You wanted to sleep-learn. We can take you to the sleep-learner. Is that not what you asked this morning? Pyla has two hours coming to her this afternoon. We were going to give it to you; you could learn Hevian and talk to us!"

"But how did we lie?" Estelle said, her eyes dancing.

"Web said it was good news," Silvador said solemnly, "that his Dee-friend was already here. He told a flat lie about an accomplished fact; that costs 50 points."

The two New Earth children looked at each other. "Oh, algae and gravity," Web said suddenly. "Let's go do it. We'll see Dee soon enough."

Dee blew her top.

"What on Earth were you thinking of, John?" she demanded. "How do you know what they teach in hyp-nopedia here? How could you let children run around a strange planet without knowing what these savages might do to them?"

"They didn't do anything to us—" Web said.

"They're not savages—" Amalfi said.

"I know what they are. I was here the first time, when you were. And I think it's criminally irresponsible to let savages tamper with a child's mind. Or any civilized mind."

"How would you recognize a civilized mind?" Amalfi demanded. But he knew that it was certainly a fruitless question, and possibly a spiteful one. He could see well enough that she was the same girl he had met during the Utopia-Gort affair, the same woman he had loved, the same bright physical image he would cherish to the near-ing end of time; but she was getting old, and how do you tell a woman that? The Hevians and the children alike were approaching the end of the world as a new experi-ence, but Dee, and Amalfi, and Mark, and indeed the whole of New Earth were approaching it from age, with the two forms of matter subsequent to the impact; Dee no thought but to stave off new experience, to dwell safely in accomplished fact. He himself would not accept that such a thing was to happen; Dee would not let the children learn a new language; they were exhibiting all the stigmata of the onset of old age, and so was their culture. The drugs still worked; physically they were still young; but age was with them nonetheless, and for good. In the long run there was no cheating time and the entropy gradient, nor any hope but that of putting one's hope into Hevians and other children. The cancer-scarred giant King of Buda-Pesht and the Acolyte jungle had been as old as

Amalfi was now when Amalfi had met and bested him, and he had even then settled into an *idée fixe;* he had been still physically arrested, but mentally he was already used up.

There were only two ways to go toward death; you accept that you are going to die, or you refuse to believe it. To deny that the problem is there is childish, or senile; it lacks the fluidity of adjustment which is that process called maturity; and when children and savages are more fluid at this than you are, you must see that curfew has struck for you and go gracefully. Otherwise, they will bury you, their titular leader, nominally alive.

Dee had not, of course, bothered to answer the question; she simply looked grim. The aborted argument had been conducted mostly *sotto voce* anyhow, for the rest of the Hevian council-room was deeply embroiled in an attempt to quanticize the amount of gamma radiation which would be produced when the two universes passed through each other, and its degree of convertibility into either of the two forms of matter subsequent to the impact; Dee had been forced to push her way into the meeting to find Web and Estelle, who by now had become accepted silent partners at such skull-sessions.

"I'm not content with that at all," Retma was saying. "Dr. Schloss is assuming that a substantial part of this energy will go off as sheer noise, as though the meeting of the two universes were analogous to the clashing of cymbals. To allow that, one has to assume that Planck's Constant holds true in Hilbert space, for which we haven't a shred of evidence. One can't superimpose an entropy gradient at right angles to a reaction which itself involves entropies of opposite sign on each side of the equation."

"But why can't you?" Dr. Schloss said. "That's what Hilbert space is for: to provide a choice of axes for just such an operation. If you have such a choice, the rest is only a simple exercise in projective geometry."

"I don't deny that," Retma said, somewhat stiffly. "I'm questioning its applicability. We have no data which suggest that handling the problem in this way would be anything *more* than an exercise—so whether it would be a simple exercise or a complex exercise is not to the point."

"I think we'd better go," Dee said. "Web, Estelle, please come along; we're only interrupting, and there's a lot we have to do."

Her penetrating stage whisper rasped across the discussion more effectively than any speech at normal conversational volume could have done. Dr. Schloss' face pinched with annoyance. For a moment, the faces of the Hevians went politely blank; then Miramon turned and looked first at Dee, and then at Amalfi, slightly raising one eyebrow. Amalfi nodded, a little embarrassed.

"Do we have to go, grandmother?" Web protested. "I mean, all this is what we're here for. And Estelle's good at math; now and then Retma and Dr. Schloss want her to match up Hevian names for terms with ours."

Dee thought about it. "Well," she said, "I suppose it can't do any harm."

This was exactly and expectedly the wrong answer, though Web could have had no way of anticipating it. He did not know, as Amalfi knew very well by direct memory, that women on He had once been much worse than slaves, that in fact they had been regarded as a wholly loathesome though necessary cross between a demon and a lower animal; hence he was unequipped to see that Hevian women today were still crucially subordinate to their men, and far from welcome in a situation of this kind. Nor did Amalfi see any present opportunity to explain to Web—or to Estelle, either—why both children must now go. The explanation would require more knowledge of Dee than either of the children had; they would need to know, for instance, that in Dee's eyes the women of He had been emancipated but not enfranchised, and that for Dee this abstract distinction carried a high emotional charge—all the more so because the Hevian women themselves were obviously quite content to have it that way.

Miramon settled his papers, arose and walked smoothly toward them, his face grave. Dee watched him approach with an expression of smouldering, resolute suspicion with which Amalfi could not help but sympathize, funny though he found it.

"We are delighted to have you with us, Mrs. Hazleton," Miramon said, bowing his head. "Much of what we are today, we owe to you. I hope you will allow us to express our gratitude; my wife and her ladies await to do you honor."

"Thanks, but I don't—I really mean—"

She had to stop, obviously finding it impossible to summon up in a split second the memory of what she had meant so many years ago, when she had been, whether she was yet aware of it or not, another person. Back then, she had in fact been one of the prime movers in the emancipation of the women of He, and Amalfi had been glad of her vigorous help, particularly since it had turned out to be crucial in a bloody power-struggle on the planet, and hence crucial to the survival of the city—the latter a formula which then had been as magical and beyond critical examination as the will to live itself, and now was as meaningless a slogan and one as far gone in time as "Remember the Bastille", "Mason, Dixon, Nixon and Yates", or "The Stars Must Be Ours!" Dee's first encounter with Hevian women had been in the days when they had been stinking unwashed creatures kept in ceremonial cages; something about Miramon's present mode of address to her apparently reminded her of those days, perhaps even made her feel the bars and the dirt falling into place about her own person; yet the time gap was too great, and the politeness too intensive, to permit her to take offense on those grounds, if indeed she was aware of them. She looked quickly at Amalfi, but his face remained unchanged; she knew him well enough to be able to see that there would be no help from that quarter.

"Thank you," she said helplessly. "Webb, Estelle, it's time we left."

Web turned to Estelle, as if for help, in unconscious burlesque of Dee's unspoken appeal to Amalfi, but Estelle was already rising. To Amalfi's eyes the girl looked amused and a little contemptuous. Dee was going to have trouble with that one. As for Web, anyone could see plainly that he was in love, so *he* would require no special handling.

"What I suggest is this," Estelle's father's voice said, way up in the middle of the air. "Suppose we assume that there is no thermodynamic crossover between the two universes until the moment of contact. If that's the case, there's no possibility of applying symmetry unless we assume that the crossover point is actually a moment of complete neutrality, no matter how explosive it seems to somebody on one side or the other of the equivalence sign. That's a reasonable assumption, I think, and it would enable us to get rid of Planck's Constant—I agree with Retma that in a situation like this that's only a bugger factor—and handle the opposite signs in terms of the old Schiff neutrino-antineutrino theory of gravitation. That can be quanticized equally well, after all."

"Not in terms of the Grebe numbers," Dr. Schloss said.

"But that's exactly the point, Schloss," Jake said excitedly. "Grebe numbers don't cross over; they apply in our universe, and probably they apply on the other side too, *but they don't cross*. What we need is a function that does cross, or else some assumption that fits the facts, that frees us of crossover entirely. That's what Retma was saying, if I understood him correctly, and I think he's right. If you don't have a crossover expression which is perfectly neutral anywhere in Hilbert space, then you're automatically making an assumption about a real No-Man's-Land. What we're forced to start with here is *No*."

Estelle stopped at the door and turned to look toward the invisible source of the voice.

"Daddy," she said, "that's just like translating Hevian math into New Earth math. If it's No-Man's-Land you have to deal with, why don't you start with the bullets?"

"Come, dear," Dee said. The door closed.

There was a very long silence in the room after that.

"You are letting those children go to waste, Mayor Amalfi," Miramon said at last. "Why do you do it? If only you would fill their brains with the facts that they need—and it is so easy, as you well know, you taught us how to do it—"

"It's no longer so easy with us," Amalfi said. "We are older than you are; we no longer share your preoccupation with the essences of things. It would take too long to explain how we came to that pass. We have other things to think about now."

"If that is true," Miramon said slowly, "then indeed we must hear no more about it. Otherwise I shall be tempted to feel sorry for you; and that must not happen, otherwise we all are lost."

"Not so," Amalfi said, smiling tightly. "Nothing is ever that final. Where were we? This is only the beginning of the end."

"Were the universe to last forever, Mayor Amalfi," Miramon said, "I should never understand you."

And so the betrayal was complete. Web and Estelle never heard the stiff and bitter exchange between Amalfi and Hazleton, across the trillions and trillions of miles of seethingly empty space between He and the New Earth, which resulted in Hazleton's being forced to call his wife home before she antagonized the Hevians any further; nor

did they know precisely why Dee's recall had to mean
their recall. They simply went, mute and grieving, willy-
nilly, expressing by silence—the only weapon that they
had—their revolt against the insanities of adult logic. In
their hearts they knew that they had been denied the first
real thing that they had ever wanted, except for each
other.

And time was running out.

CHAPTER FIVE: **Jehad**

That conversation had been unusually painful for Amalfi,
too, despite his many centuries of experience at having
differences of opinion with Hazleton, ending ordinarily in
enforcement of Amalfi's opinion if there was no other way
around it. There had been something about this quarrel
which had been tainted for Amalfi, and he knew very well
what it was: the abortive, passionless and fruitless autum-
nal affair with Dee. Sending her home to Mark now,
necessary though he believed it to be, was too open to
interpretation as an act of revenge upon the once-beloved
for being no longer loved. Such things happened between
lovers, as Amalfi knew very well.

But there was so much to be done that he managed to
forget about it after Dee and the children had left on the
recall ship. He was not, however, allowed to forget about
it for long—only, in fact, for three weeks.

The discussion of the forthcoming catastrophe had at
last entered the stage where it was no longer possible to
avoid coming to grips with the contrary entropy gradients,
and hence had entered an area where words alone no
longer sufficed—in fact, could seldom be called upon at
all. This had had the effect of driving those participants
who were primarily engineers or administrators or both,
like Miramon and Amalfi, or primarily philosophers, like
Gifford Bonner, into the stance of bystanders; so that the
discussions now had been shifted to Retma's study. Amalfi
stuck with them whenever he could, for he never knew
when Retma, Jake or Schloss might drop back out of the

symbolic stratosphere and say something he could comprehend and use.

It was being heavy weather in the study today, however. Retma was saying:

"The problem as I see it is that time in our experience is not retrodictable. We write a diffusion equation like this, for instance." He turned to his blackboard—the immemorial "research instrument" of theoretical physicists everywhere—and wrote:

$$\frac{d^2G}{dx^2} + \frac{d^2G}{dy^2} + \frac{d^2G}{dz^2} = a^2\frac{dG}{dt}$$

Over Retma's head, for Jake's benefit, a small proxy fixed its television eye on the precise chalkmarks. "In this situation a-squared is a real constant, so it is predictive only for a future time t, but not for an earlier time t, because the retrodictive expression diverges."

"An odd situation," Schloss agreed. "It means that in any thermodynamic situation we have better information about the future than we do about the past. In the anti-matter universe it has to be the other way around—but only from *our* point of view; a hypothetical observer living under their laws and composed of their energies, I assume, couldn't tell the difference."

"Can we write a convergent retrodictive equation?" Jake's voice said. "One which describes what their situation is as we would see it, if we could? If we can't, I don't see how we can design instruments to detect any difference."

"It can be done," Retma said. "For instance." He turned to the blackboard and the symbols flowed squeakily:

$$\frac{d^2G}{dx^2} + \frac{d^2G}{dy^2} + \frac{d^2G}{dz^2} = \frac{4\pi m}{ih}\frac{dG}{dt}$$

"Ah-*ha*," Schloss said. "Thus giving us an imaginary constant in place of a real one. But your second equation isn't a mirror of your first; parity is not conserved. Your first equation is an equalization process, but this one is oscillatory. Surely the gradient on the other side doesn't pulsate!"

"Parity is not conserved anyhow in these weak reactions," Jake said. "But I think the objection may be well taken all the same. If Equation Two describes anything at all, it can't be the other side. It has to be *both* sides—the whole vast system, providing that it is cyclical, which we don't know yet. Nor do I see any way to test it, it's as ultimately and finally unprovable as the Mach Hypothesis—"

The door opened quietly and a young Hevian beckoned silently to Amalfi. He got up without too much reluctance; the boys were giving him a hard time today, and he found that he missed Estelle. It had been her function to remind the group of possible pitfalls in Retma's notation: here, for instance, Retma was using the d which in Amalfi's experience was an increment in calculus, as simply an expression for a constant; he was using the G which to Amalfi was the gravitational constant, to express a term in thermodynamics Amalfi was accustomed to seeing written with the greek capital letter Ψ; and could Schloss be sure that Retma's i was equivalent to the square root of minus one, as it was in New Earth math? Doubtless Schloss had good reason to feel that agreement on that very simple symbol had been established between the New Earthmen and Retma long since, but without Estelle it made Amalfi feel uncomfortable. Besides, though he knew intellectually that all the important battles against a problem in physics are won in such blackboard sessions as this, he was not temperamentally fitted to them. He liked to see things happening.

They began to happen forthwith. As soon as the door was decently closed on the visible and invisible physicists, the young Hevian said:

"I am sorry to disturb you, Mr. Amalfi. But there is an urgent call for you from New Earth. It is Mayor Hazleton."

"Helleshin!" Amalfi said. The word was Vegan; no one now alive knew what it meant. "All right, let's go."

"Where is my wife?" Hazleton demanded without preamble. "And my grandson, and Jake's daughter? And where have you been these past three weeks? Why didn't you call in? I've been losing my mind, and the Hevians gave me the Force Four blowaround before they'd let me through to you at all—"

"What are you talking about, Mark?" Amalfi said.

"Stop sputtering long enough to let me know what this is all about."

"That's what *I* want to know. All right. I'll begin again. Where is Dee?"

"I don't know," Amalfi said patiently. "I sent her home three weeks ago. If you can't find her, that's your problem."

"She never got here."

"She didn't? But—"

"Yes, but. That recall ship never landed. We never heard from it at all. It just vanished, Dee, children and all. I've been phoning you frantically to find out whether or not you ever sent it; now I know that you did. Well, we know what *that* means. You'd better give up dabbling in physics, Amalfi, and get back here on the double."

"What can I do?" Amalfi said. "I don't know any more about it than you do."

"You can damn well come back here and help me out of this mess."

"What mess?"

"What have you been doing the past three weeks?" Hazleton yelled. "Do you mean to tell me that you haven't heard what's been happening?"

"No," Amalfi said. "And stop yelling. What did you mean, 'We know what *that* means'? If you think you know what's happened, why aren't you doing something about it, instead of jamming the Dirac raising me? You're the mayor; I've got work of my own to do."

"I'll be the mayor about two days longer, if my luck holds," Hazleton said in a savage voice. "And you're directly responsible, so you needn't bother trying to duck. Jorn the Apostle began to move two weeks ago. He has a navy now, though where he raised it is beyond me. His main body's nowhere near New Earth, but he's about to take New Earth all the same—the whole planet is swarming with farm kids with fanatical expressions and dismounted spindillies. As soon as they get to me, I'm going to surrender out of hand—you know as well as I do what one of those machines can do, and the farmers are using them as side-arms. I'm not going to sacrifice tens of thousands of lives just to maintain my administration; if they want me out, they can have me out."

"And this is my fault? I once told you the Warriors of God were dangerous."

"And I didn't listen. All right. But they'd never have

moved if it hadn't been for the fact that you and Miramon didn't censor what you're up to. It's given Jorn his cause; he's telling his followers that you're meddling with the pre-ordained Armageddon and jeopardizing their chances of salvation. He's proclaimed a jehad against the Hevians for instigating it, and the jehad includes New Earth because we're working with the Hevians—"

Over the phone came four loud, heavy strokes of fist upon metal.

"Gods of all stars, they're here already," Hazleton said. "I'll leave the line open as long as I can—maybe they won't notice. . . ." His voice faded. Amalfi hung on grimly, straining to hear every sound.

"Sinner Hazleton," a young and desperately frightened voice said, almost at once, "you have been found out. By the Word of Jorn, you—you are ordered to corrective discipline. Are you gone-tuh—will you submit humbly?"

"If you fire that thing in here," Hazleton's voice said, quite loudly—he was obviously projecting for the benefit of the mike—"you'll uproot half the city. What good will that do you?"

"We will die in the Warriors," the other voice said. It was still tense, but now that it spoke of dying it seemed more self-assured. "You will go to the flames."

"And all the other people—?"

"Sinner Hazleton. we do not threaten," a deeper, older voice said. "We think there is some good in everyone. Jorn commands us to redeem, and that we will do. We have hostages for your good conduct."

"Where are they?"

"They were picked up by the Warriors of God," the deep voice said. "Jorn in his blessedness was kind enough to grant us a *cordon sanitaire* for this Godless world. Will you yield, for the salvation of this woman and these two helpless children? I advise you, Sinner—hey, what the hell, that phone's open! Jody, smash that switch, and fast! What did I ever do to be saddled with a cadre of lousy yokels—"

The speaker began a thin howl and went dead before the cry was properly born.

For a moment, Amalfi sat stunned. He had gotten too much information too fast; and he was much older now than he had been on like occasions in the past. He had never expected that such an occasion would arise again—but here it was.

A jehad against He? No, not likely—at least, not directly. Jorn the Apostle would be wary of tackling a world so
completely mysterious to him, especially with forces more
mob than military. But New Earth was wholly vulnerable;
it was a logical first step to invest that planet. And now
Jorn had Dee and the children.

Move!

How to move was another matter; it needed to be done
in a vessel which no possible Warrior cordon would have
the strength to attack, but no such vessel existed on He.
The only other alternative was a very small, very fast ship
with a low detectability index; but that was equally impossible across so long a distance, since there is a minimum
size for even one spindizzy. Or was there? Carrel was on
He, and Carrel had had considerable experience in designing relatively small spindizzy-powered proxies; one such
had followed the March of Earth all the way, without
anybody's paying the slightest attention to it. Of course
the proxy had been magnificently, noisily detectable by
ordinary standards, and only Carrel's piloting of it had
kept the massed cities from distinguishing between the
traces that it made and the traces that were made adventi-
tiously by ordinary interstellar matter. . . .

"Can you do that again, Carrel? Remember that this
time you won't have a flock of massive cities to confuse
the issue. The gamut you'll have to run will be one thin
shell of orbiting warships, around one planet—and we
don't know how many of them there are, what arms they
mount, how careful a watch they keep—"

"Assume the worst," Carrel said. "They caught the
recall ship, after all, and they didn't even know we'd sent
it. I can do it, Mr. Amalfi, if you'll let me do the
maneuvering when the chips are down; otherwise I think
you'll be caught, no matter how small the ship is."

"Helleshin!" But there was no way around it; Amalfi
would have to subject himself to at least two days of
Carrel's violent evasive-confusive maneuvers, without once
touching the space-stick himself. It was going to be a
rough do for an old man, but Carrel was quite right, there
was no other available course.

"All right," he said. "Just make sure I'm alive when I
touch down."

Carrel grinned. "I've never lost a cargo," he said.

"Providing it's been properly secured. Where do you want to land?"

That was not easy question either. In the long run, Amalfi settled for a landing in Central Park, in the heart of the old Okie city. This was perhaps dangerously close to the Warriors' center of operations, but Amalfi did not want to be forced to trek across a thousand miles of New Earth just for a meeting with Hazleton; and there was a fair chance that the old city would be taboo for the bumpkins, or at least avoided instinctively. Jorn the Apostle would not have overlooked patrolling such an obvious rallying-point for the ousted, but presumably Jorn was somewhere at the other end of the Cloud with his main body.

Since there is, even with spindizzies, a limit to the amount of power that can be stored in a small hull, the trip was more than long enough for Amalfi to catch up, via ultraphone, on the Cloud events he had closeted himself away from on He. The picture Mark had given him had been accurate, if perhaps a little distorted in emphasis. Jorn the Apostle's real concerns were still far away from New Earth, and his jehad had been announced against unbelievers everywhere, not just against the Hevians. The Hevians were simply the article in the indictment which applied specifically to New Earth—that, and New Earth's unannounced but unconcealed intention of plumbing the end of time, which was blasphemy. It was Amalfi's guess that the uprising on New Earth and the seizure of the central government there had been an unplanned byproduct of the proclamation of which Jorn was unprepared to take full advantage. Had he been planning on it, or militarily able to capitalize on it, he would have rushed in his main body on the double; as matters stood he had only—and belatedly—set up a token blockade. If his followers' coup stuck, all well and good; if it did not, he would withdraw the blockade in a hurry, to save ships and men for another, more auspicious day.

Or so Amalfi reasoned; but he was uncomfortably aware that in Jorn the Apostle he was for the first time dealing with an enemy whose thought-processes might be utterly unlike his, from first to last.

The ship shifted abruptly from spindizzy to ion-blast drive. Amalfi stopped thinking entirely and just hung on.

Once in the atmosphere, the craft was back in Amalfi's

hands; back on He, Carrel had relinquished his remote
Dirac control over the space-stick. Amalfi was able to
make a thistledown nightside landing in south Central
Park, in a broad irregular depression which legend said
had once been a lake. The landing was without incident;
apparently it had been undetected. In the morning the
abandoned proxy might be spotted by a Warrior flyer, but
the old city was littered with such ambiguous mechanical
objects; one had to be a student of the city, as knowledge-
able as Schliemann was about the nine Troys, to know
which was new and which was not. Amalfi was confident
enough of this to leave the proxy behind without an
attempt to camouflage it.

Now the problem was, How to get in touch with Mark?
Presumably he was still under arrest, or the next thing to
it; "corrective discipline" was what the Warrior voice
Amalfi had overheard had said. Did that mean that they
were going to make the lazy, cerebral Hazleton make
beds, sweep floors and pray six hours a day? Not very
likely, especially the prayer part. Then what—?

Suddenly, trudging south along a moonlit, utterly
deserted Fifth Avenue toward the city's control tower,
Amalfi was sure he had it. Running a galaxy, even a small
and mostly unexplored satellite galaxy like this one, is not
simply a matter of taking papers out of the "IN" tray and
transferring them to the "OUT" tray. It requires centuries
of experience and a high degree of familiarity with the
communications, data-filing and other machines which
must do 98 per cent of the donkey-work. In the Okie
days, for instance, it sometimes happened—though not
very often—that a mayor was swapped to another city
under the "rule of discretion" after he had lost an election; and generally it took him five to ten years to get
used to running the new one, even in such a subordinate
post as assistant to the city manager. It was not an art
that a bumpkin, no matter how divinely inspired, could
master in a week.

Mark's most likely theater of "corrective discipline,"
then, would be his own office. He would be running the
Cloud for the Warriors—and no doubt doing a far worse
job of it than they would detect, even were they sensible
enough, as they surely were, to suspect such sabotage.
Amalfi, himself a master of making the wheels run backwards when necessary, would yield precedence in that art
to Hazleton at any time; Hazleton had been known to

work the trick on his friends, just to keep his hand in, or perhaps just out of habit.

Very good; then the problem of getting in touch with Mark was solved, clearing the way for the hard questions: How to discombobulate, and, if possible, oust the Warriors; and how to get Dee and the children back unharmed?

It would be difficult to decide which of these two hard questions was the harder. As Mark had pointed out, the uprooted spindillies in the hand of the rank-and-file Warriors were considerably more dangerous than muskets or pitchforks. Used with precision, the machine could degravitate a single opponent and send him shrieking skyward under the centrifugal thrust of New Earth's rotation on its axis; or the same effect could be used against a corner or a wall of a building, if one wanted to demolish a strong point. But the menace lay in the fact that in the hands of a plowboy the spindilly would *not* be used with precision. It had been designed, not as a weapon, but as an adjunct to home weather control, and was somewhat larger, heavier and more ungainly than a Twentieth-Century home oil-burner. Considering the difficulties involved in toting this object at all, especially on foot, the temptation would be almost overwhelming to set it at maximum output before it was even unbolted from its cement pedestal in the cellar, and leave it set there, so that the strained arm and back muscles of the bearer would thereafter have to do nothing with it to make it function but point it—more or less—and push the starter button. This meant that every time one of the plowboys lost his temper or detected heresy in some casual remark, or fired nervously at a shadow or a sudden unfamiliar sound or a svengali, he might level two or three city blocks before he remembered where the "kill" button was; or the machine, dropped and abandoned in panic, might go on to level two or three more blocks before it discharged its accumulators and shut itself off of its own accord.

Saving Dee and the children was certainly highly important, but disarming the Warriors would have to take precedence.

He caught himself bouncing a little as he stepped out of the spindizzy lift shaft onto the resilient concrete floor of the control room, and grinned ruefully. He felt alive again, after far too many years of grousing, browsing, vegetating. This was the kind of problem he had been formed for, the kind he approached with the confidence born of gusto. The end of time was certainly sizable enough as a problem; he would never find a bigger, and he was grateful for that; but it provided him with nobody with whom to negotiate and, if possible, swindle a little.

It *had* been a long time; he had better be on his guard against overconfidence. That had been known to trip him now and then even when he had been in practice. In particular, it was suspiciously easy to see what steps ought to be taken in the present situation; that was not the test; it was his ancient skill as a cultural historian—in short, as a diagnostician—which would stand or fall by what he did now ... and just incidentally, he might lose or save from three to a quarter of a million lives, one of them Estelle's.

Gently then, gently—but precisely and with decision, like a surgeon confronted with cardiac arrest. Waste no time debating alternate courses; you have four minutes to save the patient's life, if you are lucky; the bone-saw is whining in your hand—slash open the rib-cage, and slash it quick.

The City Fathers were already warmed up. He told them: "Communications. Get me Jorn the Apostle—for the survival of the city."

It would take a little while for the City Fathers to reach Jorn; though they would scan the possibilities in under a minute and select out only those worlds with high probability ratings for Jorn's presence, the chances of their getting him on the first call were not very high. Amalfi regretted that it would be then necessary to talk to Jorn on the Dirac communicator, since it would make anyone who was listening anywhere in the Cloud—or anywhere else in the known universe where the apparatus existed, for that matter—privy to the conversations; but over interstellar distances the ultraphone was out of the question for twoway exchanges, since its velocity of information propagation was only 125 per cent of the speed of light, and even this was achieved only by a trick called negative phase velocity, since the carrier wave was electromagnetic and moved at light speed and no faster.

While he waited, Amalfi ticked over the possibilities. This was all in all developing into a most curious affair, quite unlike anything he had ever been involved in before. It thus far consisted mostly of interludes and transitions, with only a small scatter of decision-points upon which action might be possible. In this sense even the events which most recalled to him the events of his earlier life seemed to be reshaping themselves into the pattern of his old age, not only allowing for but requiring a much greater exercise of reflection and an intensive weighing of values. Reflexive action was out of the question; it was possible only from some fixed guiding principle, such as "the survival of the city"; such an axiom, if it persists and dominates for a long time, allows many decisions to be reached via the reflex arc with almost no intervening intellection—one automatically jumped in the right direction, like a cat turning itself over in mid-air. No such situation existed now; the values to be weighed were mutually contradictory.

It had to be assumed, first of all, that Jorn did not know the situation on New Earth in detail; he had simply reacted as a good strategist should to capitalize upon an unexpected victory in an unexpected quarter, and almost surely did not know that his blockading fleet was holding three hostages, let alone who those hostages were. It would be impossible to intimidate him on this matter; it would be wiser not to give him the information at all. After all, the first intent of the call was to get the bumpkin army disbanded and the dismounted spindillies out of action; but it would not do to convince him out of hand that his coup on New Earth could not possibly stick, since that would result in his withdrawing his blockade and the hostages with it. Better to serve both ends, if it could be swung that way: to convince Jorn that the *putsch* had better be abandoned forthwith, but not so thoroughly as to alarm him into thinking he might lose part of his navy if he took his time about calling the *putsch* off.

It looked like a large order. It meant that the danger which Jorn the Apostle would have to be made to suspect would have to be as much ideological as it was military. As a military commander of considerable proven ability, Jorn could not but be familiar with the corruption of an occupying force by the standards and customs of the nation that it occupies—and jehads and crusades were particularly subject to this kind of corrosion. Whether he was wholly a believer in the brand of Fundamentalism he preached, or not, he would not want his followers to lose faith in the doctrine under which he had sailed so successfully thus far; that was the hold over them that he had chosen to exercise, so that if they lost that, he himself would have nothing left, regardless of what his personal beliefs might be.

Unhappily, there was no ideology available on New Earth which looked capable of corrupting the Warriors of God; they would doubtless indulge in a good deal of wristwatch collecting, a very ancient term for a timeless syndrome of a peasant army holding a territory relatively rich in consumer goods, but Jorn would anticipate that and discount it; but there was no idea inherent in the culture of New Earth which seemed strong enough to sway the Warriors from their simple, direct and centrally oriented point of view. One would have to be manufactured; at least there was no lack of raw materials.

One apparent pitfall in this course was that of taking Jorn the Apostle at his own public valuation and attempting to reach into and alarm that part of his mind where his real religion lived. Amalfi had no way of knowing whether this would work or not, and prudence dictated that it not be tried; he had to assume instead that a man as successful as Jorn had been in the world of affairs was a sophisticated man on most subjects, whether he was sophisticated as a theologian or not. The latter was even beside the point; wherever the truth lay, he would be quick to detect any attempt to push his religious buttons, since he had proven that he knew the art himself.

And, Amalfi thought suddenly, if Jorn were to turn out to be exactly as devout in his back-cluster superstitions as his public utterances suggested, pushing that button might well result in a genuine disaster. With such people, that button is a demolition button; if you touch it successfully, you shatter the man. Of course it would be necessary to treat Jorn *pro forma* as if every public word Jorn had uttered had been uttered in the utmost sincerity and out of the deepest kind of belief, not only because Jorn too would know that unknown numbers of others might be listening in, but to avoid attacking the man's image of himself irrelevantly and to no purpose. The forms had no bearing on the final outcome; it would be dangerous to assume that Jorn was identical personally with his public self only in the *substance* of Amalfi's approach to him. There would be no harm in acknowledging to him, implicitly, his claim to be every inch a Fundamentalist; but it would be fatal to expect him to panic if he got a Dirac-'cast claiming to be from Satan—

"READY WITH JORN THE APOSTLE, MR. MAYOR."

Amalfi suddenly found himself thinking at emergency speed; the City Fathers' excusable lapse—doubtless nobody had bothered to tell them that Amalfi had not been Mayor since the problem of the Ginnangu-Gap had arisen—reminded him that he had failed to decide whether or not to identify himself to Jorn. There was a small possibility that Jorn came of the peasant stock which the Okies had found sweating under the tyranny of the bindle-stiff city of IMT; a slightly larger possibility that he was a descendant of the rulers of IMT itself; but by far the greatest likelihood was that he was a child or grandchild of Amalfi's own people and so would know very well indeed who Amalfi was. To identify himself, then, would give Amalfi a certain leverage, but it would also present certain disadvantages—

However, the die was already cast; the City Fathers had called him the Mayor on the circuit, so Jorn had better be told at once that it was not Hazleton he was talking to. Bluff it out? Possible; but there lay the danger of using the Dirac: the instrument made it possible for any listener to tell Jorn, now or later, whatever facts Amalfi attempted for strategic reasons to withhold—

"READY, MR. MAYOR."

Well, there was no help for that now. Amalfi said into the microphone:

"Go ahead."

Immediately, the screen came alight. He *was* getting old; he had forgotten to tell the City Fathers to limit the call to audio only, so in actuality he had never had the option of withholding his identity. Well, regret was futile; and in fact he watched the face of Jorn the Apostle swimming into view before him with the keenest curiosity.

It was, startlingly, a very old face, narrow, bony and deeply lined, with bushy white eyebrows emphasizing the sunken darkness of the eyes. Jorn had been off the anti-agathics for at least fifty years, if indeed he had ever taken one. The realization was a profound and unexpected visceral shock.

"I am Jorn the Apostle," the ancient face said. "What do you want of me?"

"I think you should pull off of New Earth," Amalfi said. It was not at all what he had intended to say; it was in fact wholly contrary to the entire chain of reasoning he had just worked through. But there was something about the face that compelled him to say what was on his mind.

"I am not on New Earth," Jorn said. "But I take your meaning. And I take it there are many people on New Earth who share your opinion, Mr. Amalfi, as is only natural. This does not affect me."

"I didn't expect it to, just as a simple statement of opinion," Amalfi said. "But I can offer you good reasons."

"I will listen. But do not expect me to be reasonable."

"Why not?" Amalfi said, genuinely surprised.

"Because I am not a reasonable man," Jorn said patiently. "The uprising of my followers on New Earth took place without orders from me; it is a gift which God himself has placed in my hand. That being the case, reason does not apply."

"I see," Amalfi said. He paused. This was going to be tougher to bring off than he had dreamed; in fact, he had his first doubt as to whether it could be brought off at all. "Are you aware, sir, that this planet is a hotbed of Stochasticism?"

Jorn's bushy eyebrows lifted slightly. "I know that the Stochastics are strongest and most numerous on New Earth," he said. "I have no way of knowing how deeply the philosophy has penetrated the populace of New Earth as a whole. It is one of the things I mean to see stamped out."

"You'll find that impossible. A mob of farm boys can't eradicate a major philosophical system."

"But how major is it?" Jorn said. "In terms of influence? I admit I have the impression that much of New Earth may be corrupted by it, but I have no certain knowledge that this is so. At the distance from New Earth that I am forced to operate, I may well be magnifying it in my mind, especially since it is so completely antithetical to the Word of God; it would be natural for me to assume that the homeland of Stochasticism is also a 'hotbed' of it. But I do not know this to be true."

"So you will risk the souls of the Warriors of God on the assumption that it is not true."

"Not necessarily," Jorn said. "Considering the forces for which you speak, Mr. Amalfi, it is so plainly to your advantage to exaggerate the influence of Stochasticism; your very use of the tool suggests that, since I cannot think you mean me any advantage. I suspect that in actuality the Stochastics, like intellectuals at all times and in all places, are largely out of touch with the general assumptions of the culture in which they are operating; and that the people of New Earth are no more Stochastics than they are Warriors of God or anything else describable as a school of thought. If any label applies, they are simply a people who are *no longer* describable as Okies."

Amalfi sat there and sweated. He had met his match and he knew it.

"And if you are wrong?" he said at last. "If Stochasticism is as ingrained on this planet as I've tried to warn you it is?"

"Then," Jorn the Apostle said, "I must take the risk. My Warriors on New Earth are farm boys, as you have pointed out. I doubt that Stochasticism will make much headway with them; they will shrug it off, as contrary to common sense. They will be mistaken in that estimate, but how could they know that? Ignorance is the defense God the Father has given them, and I think it will be sufficient."

There was the cue. Amalfi could only hope that it had not come too late.

"Very well," he said, rather more grimly than he had intended. "Events will put us both to the proof; there is no more to be said."

"No," Jorn said, "there is this much more: you may actually have meant to do me a service, Mr. Amalfi. If it so proves out, then I will give the devil his due—one must be honest even with evil, there is no other good course. What do you want of me?"

And thus the verbal sparring-match had come so quickly to full circle; and this time there was no way to remain ignorant of, let alone to evade, the purport of the question. It was not political; it was personal; and it had been intended that way from the beginning.

"You could return me three hostages which your blockading fleet is holding," Amalfi said. His mouth tasted of aloes. "A woman and two children."

"Had you asked for that in the beginning," Jorn the Apostle said, "I would have given it to you." Was it actually pity in his voice? "But you have placed their lives upon the block of your own integrity, Mr. Amalfi. So be it; if I become convinced that I must lose New Earth because of Stochasticism, I will return the three before I withdraw my blockading squadron; otherwise, not. And, Mr. Amalfi—"

"Yes?" Amalfi whispered.

"Bear in mind what is at stake, and do not let your ingenuity overwhelm you. I know well that you are fabulously inventive; but human lives should not hang upon the success of a work of art. Go with God." The screen was dark.

Amalfi mopped his forehead with a trembling hand. With his last words, Jorn the Apostle had succeeded in telling the whole story of Amalfi's life, and it had not made comfortable listening.

Nevertheless, he hesitated only a moment longer. Though Jorn had probably already seen through the improvision which had occurred to Amalfi—late enough so that he had been unable to betray that, too, to Jorn over the Dirac for the universe to hear—there was no other course open but to try to carry it through. The alternative which Jorn had proposed actually came out to the same thing in the end: that of transforming a lie into the truth. If this was an art, as Amalfi had good reason to know it was, it was at the same time not a "work of art," but only a craft; it was Jorn himself now who was committing human lives to the dictates of a work of art, that elaborate fiction which was his religion.

Being careful, this time, to cut the screen out of the circuit in advance, Amalfi called the Mayor's office.

"This is the Commissioner of Public Safety," he told the robot secretary. In ordinary times the machine would know well enough that there was no such office, but the confusion over there now must be such that the pertinent memory banks must by now have been by-passed; he felt reasonably confident that the phrase, a code alarm of long standing in the Okie days would get through to Hazleton; as in fact it did in short order.

"You are late calling in," Mark's voice said guardedly. "Your report is overdue. Can't you report your findings in person?"

"The situation is too fluid to permit that, Mr. Mayor," Amalfi said. "At present I'm making rounds of the perimeter stations in the old city. Off-duty Warriors are trying to sightsee here, and of course with so much live machinery—"

"Who is that?" another voice said, farther in the background. Amalfi recognized it; it was the authoritative voice that had spotted the open phone when the Warriors had first arrested Hazleton. "We can't permit that!"

"It's the Commissioner of Public Safety, a man named

de Ford," Hazleton said. Amalfi grinned tightly. De Ford
had in actuality been Hazleton's predecessor as city manager; he had been shot seven centuries ago. "And of
course we can't permit that. Besides all the loose energy
there is about the old city, much of it is derelict. De Ford,
I thought you knew that the Warriors' own general put
the city off limits."

"I tell them that," Amalfi said, in a tone of injured
patience. "They just laugh and say they're not Warriors on
their own time."

"What!" said the heavy voice.

"That's what they say," Amalfi said doggedly. "Or else
they say that they're nobody's man but their own, and that
in the long run nobody owns anybody else. They sound
like they've been sitting with some Village Stochastic,
though they've got it pretty garbled. I suppose the philosophers don't try to teach the pure doctrine in the prov-
inces."

"That's beside the point," Mark said sternly. "Keep
them out of the city—that's imperative."

"I'm trying, Mr. Mayor," Amalfi said. "But there's a
limit to what I can do. Half of them are toting spindillies,
and you know what would happen if one of those things
were fired over here, even once. I'm not going to risk
that."

"Be sure you don't; but keep trying. I'll see what can be
done about it from this end. There'll be further instructions; where can I reach you?"

"Just leave the call in the perimeter sergeant's office,"
Amalfi said. "I'll pick it up on my next round."

"Very good," Hazleton said, and clicked out. Amalfi set
up the necessary line from the perimeter station to the
control tower and sat back, satisfied for the moment,
though with a deeper uneasiness that would not go away.
The seed had been planted, and there was no doubt that
Hazleton had understood the move and would foster it. It
was highly probable that Jorn the Apostle had already
ordered an inquiry made of his officers on Earth, questioning the substance of Amalfi's claims; they would of
course report back that they had had no trouble of that
kind, but the inquiry itself would sensitize them to the
subject.

Amalfi turned on the tower's FM receiver and tuned for
New Earth's federal station. The next step would be stiffer
off-limits orders to Warriors on leave, and he wanted to

be sure he heard the texts. Unless Jorn's officers phrased
those orders with an unlikely degree of sophistication, they
would result in some actual sightseers in the city—and of
course there were no longer any perimeter sergeants, nor
was there even a definable perimeter except in the minds
of the City Fathers. Somebody was bound to get hurt.

That would be one incident 'de Ford' would not report:
"I didn't hear about it. I'm sorry, but I can't be everywhere at once. I've been trying to fend these boys off
from the City Fathers—they want to ask them a lot of
questions about the history of ideas that would tie the
machines up for weeks. I've been telling the boys that I
don't know how to operate the City Fathers, but if one of
them points a spindilly at me and says 'Put me through, or
else'—well—"

That speech would necessarily mark the demise of the
'Commissioner of Public Safety,' since it would almost
surely result in the posting of a uniformed, on-duty Warrior patrol around or in the Okie city itself; Amalfi would
then have to go underground, and the rest would be up to
Mark. What, specifically, Hazleton would do could not be
anticipated, nor did Amalfi want to know about it when it
happened. One of the defects of the program was the fact
that it was, as Jorn had suspected, based on a lie, whereas
a good deception ought to contain some fundamental
stone of truth to stub the toes of the sane and the
suspicious. To put the matter with brutal directness, there
was *no* possibility that the local Warriors would be corrupted by Stochasticism, and there never had been. Even
if the program succeeded and Jorn withdrew his men, he
would interrogate them closely before he gave Amalfi
back his hostages; and if everything that he found out
bore Amalfi's stamp it would be too consistent to be
convincing. That was why Hazleton's improvisations had
to be his own from here on out, and as unknown to
Amalfi as possible until it was too late for Amalfi to undo
them even had he wished to.

It was indeed a poor piece of fiction upon which to
hang the lives of Dee and Web and Estelle; but he had to
make do with what he had.

It appeared to be working. Within the week, all Warrior
leaves were cancelled in favor of special 'orientation devo-
tions' at which attendance was mandatory. Though there
was no direct way to tell whether or not the Warriors
resented the cancellation of their leaves to secure their

faith, the predicated accident inside the city happened the next day, and the 'Commissioner of Public Safety' was promptly taxed by Hazleton to explain how he had allowed it to happen; Amalfi trotted forth the prepared lie, and retreated to an ancient communications sub-station deep in the bowels of the City Fathers themselves.

The Warrior patrol was roving through the Okie city the very next day, and Amalfi was isolated; the rest had to be up to Hazleton.

By the end of that week, the Warriors had been ordered to turn in their spindillies for regulation police stun-guns, and Amalfi knew that he had won. When a conquering army is disarmed by its own officers, it is through; in a while it will begin to tear itself apart, with very little help from outside. When that order of the day got back to Jorn, he would act, and act rapidly; Hazleton had evidently been a little too thorough as was his custom. But there was nothing that Amalfi could do now but wait.

The last Warrior blockade ship had barely touched down before Web and Estelle were scrambling out of the airlock and making straight for Amalfi.

"We have a message for you," Estelle said, out of breath, her eyes preternaturally wide. "From Jorn the Apostle. The ship's captain said to bring it to you right away."

"All right, there's not that much hurry," Amalfi growled, to hide his apprehension. "Are you all right? Did they take proper care of you?"

"They didn't hurt us," Web said. "They were so proper and polite, I wanted to kick them. They kept us in a stateroom and gave us tracts to read. It got pretty boring after a while, just reading tracts and playing tic-tac-toe on them with grandmother." Suddenly, he could not help grinning at Estelle; obviously he had gotten away with something in those quarters, all the same.

Amalfi felt a vague emotional twinge, though he was unable to identify just what kind of emotion it was; it passed too quickly. "All right, good," he said to Estelle. "Where's the message?"

"Here." She passed over a yellow flimsy, torn from the ship's Dirac printer. It said:

XXX CMNDR SSG GABRIEL SPG
32 JOHN AMALFI N EARTH V HSTGS RPT 32

I AM GIVING YOU BENEFIT OF DOUBT, RPT
DOUBT. YOU ALONE KNOW TRUTH. IF THIS DE-
FEAT SOLELY YOUR INVENTION BE SURE THE
END IS NOT YET. BUT IT WILL BE SOON.

JORN APOSTLE OF GOD

Amalfi crumpled the flimsy and dropped it onto the
flaked concrete of the spaceport.

"And so it will," he said.

Estelle looked down at the wad of yellow paper, and
then back at Amalfi's somber face. "Do you know what he
means?" she said.

"Yes, I know what he means, Estelle. But I hope you
never do."

CHAPTER SIX: Object 4001—Alephnull

Nor did Estelle ever know—though in the long run she
was in no doubt about it in her own mind—that the first
break in the problem of how to cross the information-
barrier of the coming Ginnangu-Gap sprang from her suggestion to her father that to know No-Man's-Land, one
must study it with bullets. Web and Estelle were, after all,
only children, and in the ensuing years nobody had any
time to spare for children; they were far too gone in the
fever of putting together the immaterial object which
would be their bullet across No-Man's-Land into the vast,
complementary, opposite infinity of the universe of anti-
matter. For the time being, speculation had been abandoned in favor of fact-finding; what was needed was some
direct assessment of the contemporary energy level of the
anti-matter universe; once that was known, one could
hope to date precisely the coming moment of catastrophe,
and know how much or how little time one had left to
make such preparations for going down into death as one
could bring oneself to think meaningful in the face of an
imminent and complete cancellation of all meaning—and
of the time of experience which alone gave meaning to the
concept of meaning.

Nobody had any time for children; and so they grew up

ignored, the last children that the universe would ever see. It was not surprising that they clung to each other; they would have done so even under other circumstances, for there was no question but that the fates which brood in the sub-microscopic coils and toils of the nucleic acids of heredity had formed them for each other.

Estelle sprouted in her world of oblivious adults, and took her place among them, without their noticing what she had become: tall, willowy, grey-eyed, black-haired, white-skinned, serene-faced and beautiful. These oldsters were as immune to beauty as they were immune to youth; they were perfectly happy to have the use of the sharp cutting edge of Estelle's gift for mathematics brought to bear upon their problems, but they did not see that she was also beautiful and would not have cared had they been able to see it. These days they saw nothing but death—or thought they saw it; Estelle was not so sure that they saw it as clearly as she did, for they had lived in contempt of it far too long.

Web did not know whether this suited him or not. He was moderately content to be the only one on New Earth with the good sense to see that Estelle was beautiful, but sometimes his pride felt the lack of an occasional glance of frank envy; and sometimes he suspected that Estelle cared as little about this in the long run as everyone else on New Earth but Web himself. In the fullness of time, the love which existed between them had been spoken and acknowledged, and they were now a couple, with all the delights and the responsibilities which coupling provides and demands; but somehow, nobody had noticed. The oldsters were too busy building their artifact to notice, let alone care much one way or the other, that a small green weed of love had pushed itself up amid the tumbled stones of the last of all debacles.

Yet it was not difficult for Web to understand why what was for him a miracle was not even a nuisance to the busy godlings and their machines with whom he had to live. There was not much time left; hardly a hiccup for Amalfi and Miramon and Schloss and Dee and even for Carrel, who seemed to be a perpetually young man yet who had lived lifetimes and lifetimes and could be cut down in the midst of his latest without any valid claim that his death would be a grievous waste of whatever (and Web was convinced that it was rather scanty) he carried in his head. What little time remained would be nothing to those people, who had lived so long already; but for Web and Estelle, it had been and would continue to be their growing-up time, which would be half of each of their lives no matter how long they lived thereafter.

Certainly Amalfi never noticed them. He had long forgotten that he had ever been anything less than what he was: an immortal. Probably—now—the suggestion that he had once been a child would have baffled him entirely; in the abstract it was a truism, and he would be unable to think back far enough to think of it otherwise. Once given the administration of Doom, in any event, he prosecuted it single-mindedly, like any other job, leading toward any other destination; if he knew that there would be no other jobs and no other destinations after these, it did not seem to bother him. He was up and doing; that was enough.

In the meantime:

"I love you," Web said.

"I love you."

Around them the potsherds did not even give back an echo.

Amalfi had an excuse, had someone suggested to him that he needed one: the building of the missile had gone badly from the moment—triggered by Estelle, though he did not remember this—they had decided to give it priority. At the outset it had looked so much simpler than trying to settle all the theoretical questions *a priori*, and it had had the immediate appeal of action; but it is impossible to design an experiment without certain fundamental assumptions as to what the experiment is intended to test; which assumptions turned out to be largely absent in the supposedly practical matter of designing the anti-matter missile.

As it eventually worked out, the inter-universal messenger had to be constructed from the sub-microscopic level on up out of fundamental nuclear particles which came as close to being nothing at all as either universe would ever be likely to provide: zero-spin particles with various charges and masses, and neutrino/anti-neutrino pairs. Even detecting that the object was present at all after it had been built was an almost impossible task, for neutrinos and anti-neutrinos have no mass and no charge, consisting instead partly of spin, partly of energy of translation; it did no good to try to visualize such particles since like all the fundamental particles they were entirely outside of experience in the macroscopic world. Matter was so completely transparent to them that stopping an average neutrino in flight would require a lead barrier fifty light years thick.

Only the fact that the spindizzies exercised a firm control over the rotation and the magnetic moment of any given atomic particle—hence their nickname—made it possible to assemble the object at all, and to detect and direct it after it was finished. As assembled, the messenger was a stable, electrically neutral, massless plasmoid, a sort of gravitational equivalent of ball lightning; it was derived theoretically, as Jake had proposed, from the Schiff theory of gravitation, which had been advanced as long ago as 1958 but had later been abandoned for its failure to satisfy three of the six fundamental tests which the then-established theory—general relativity—seemed to satisfy very well.

"Which from our point of view is a positive advantage," Jake had argued. "The objections from general relativity are one with the dodo anyhow, and in our special case an object which would be Lorenz-invariant, as a Schiff object couldn't be, would be a drawback. Another thing: one of the tests the Schiff theory did pass was that of explaining the red shift in the spectra of distant galaxies; which we now know to have been a clock effect and not a fair test of a gravitational theory at all. We'd be better off reevaluating the whole scholium in the light of our present knowledge."

The result was now before them all in the midst of the Okie city's ancient reception room in City Hall, which had once been Amalfi's communications center for complex diplomatic relations with client planets; it had been fitted out with an electronic network of considerable complexity so that multiple negotiations could be carried on at once while the city approached a highly developed, highly civilized star system; now that net had become, instead, a telemetering system for the inter-universal messenger.

Since the object itself was in effect little more than an intricately structured spherical spindizzy screen which screened nothing material, it would have been impossible to see it at all were it not for the small jet of artificial smoke which issued from the floor directly under it and was wreathed about it by convection currents, making it look a little like a huge bubble being supported in the middle of a fountain. Scattered throughout the interior of the bubble were steady hot pinpoints of colored light: concentrations of electron gas, of stripped nuclei, of thermal neutrons, of free radicals and of as many other basic test situations as the combined brains of two very different worlds had been able to contrive and to fit into so restricted a space—for the sphere was only six feet in diameter. At the very heart, in a spindizzy eddy all its own, was the greatest triumph of all: one cubical crystal of anti-sodium anti-chloride about the size of a single grain of a fine-grain photograph. This was Dr. Schloss's long-dreamt-of anti-matter artifact; here it was, a miracle which was already minus two weeks "young" and had yet a week to go in its spindizzy vacuum before it would collide with the flying instant of the present and decay; on the other side, it would be only a single crystal of common table salt, which might or might not lose its savor on the return journey—should the messenger come back to them at all.

Amalfi watched the red hand of the clock—the only hand it had—tick its quarter-seconds toward Zero. Nobody would launch the missile—exact timing was far too critical to allow that—but he had been given the privilege of holding down the key which kept the circuit closed against the moment when the red hand touched Zero and the impulse surged through the spindizzies and impelled the messenger on its way out of space, out of time, out of the humanly comprehensible entirely. No one knew what would happen then, least of all the designers. The missile would be unable to report back; once it had crossed the barrier, it would be incommunicado. It would have to come back to this great dark room before the tiny shining stars and the microscopic salt crystal inside it could report what had happened to them during the outward swing. How long that would take would depend upon the energy level on the opposite side, which was one of the things the messenger was being sent to find out; hence no transit-time could be predicted.

"We ought to give it a name," Amalfi said, fidgeting slightly. The index and middle fingers of his right hand were beginning to ache; he realized that he had been pushing down on the key for a long time with far more pressure than was necessary, as though the universe would end at once were the straining of his hand and arm to falter for an instant. Nevertheless, he did not let up; he had the good sense to realize that fatigue had already made him unable to judge how much relaxation might result, and he was not going to risk breaking the contact. "Now that we have it built, it doesn't look like anything. Let's christen it quick, before it gets away from us, it may never come back."

"I'd be afraid to give it a name," Gifford Bonner said, with a ghastly smile. "Any name we could give it would promise too much. How about a number? Back at the beginning of spaceflight, when the first unmanned satellites were going up, they numbered them like comets or other celestial objects, with the year-date and a Greek letter; the first sputnik, for instance, was called Object 1957-*a*."

"That appeals to me," Jake said. "Except for the Greek letter. This thing ought not to be indexed with any character that's ever been used before to label a known or knowable situation. How about using the trans-finite integers?"

"Very good," Gifford Bonner said. "Who will do the honors?"

"I will," Estelle said. She stepped forward. She did not dare to touch the object, but she raised her hand toward it. "I christen thee *Object 4101-Alephnull.*"

"The next one, presuming that we're so lucky," Jake said, "can be Object 4101-C, which is the power of the continuum; and the next one—"

There was a soft chime. Startled, Amalfi looked up at the clock. The red hand was just passing over the third quartile of the first second after Zero. In the center of the room, the smoke spun in a turbulent spiral; the bubble with the pinpoint lights had vanished.

Object *4101-Alephnull* had departed without anyone's seeing it go.

Some quartiles of a second later, he remembered to let go of the key. His millennium-firmed right hand continued to tremble for the next fifteen minutes.

The suspense was dreadful. Certainly nobody expected the messenger to return within a few hours, or even within a few days; were that to happen, it would mean that the Ginnangu-Gap itself would be right on its heels, leaving no time to analyze the colored stars or indeed do anything but fold one's hands and wait to be snuffed out. Yet the mere fact that that very possibility existed was enough to guarantee the maintenance of a death-watch in the huge, dark old room—a death-watch enlivened by the discovery that all the instruments which had been watching the missile while it was still there had dropped back to nothing on the instant of its departure, having recorded no phenomenon of any kind about the departure itself. Not even the spindizzies—as interpreted for by the City Fathers—were prepared to say how the surge of power with which they had launched the messenger had been applied; which should have been reassuring, at least as negative evidence that the messenger had not been shoved off in some known and hence useless direction, but which under the circumstances only added to the gloom and tension. All that power shot; and where had it gone? Apparently nowhere at all.

Ordinarily Amalfi rarely dreamed (or rather, like most Okies, he dreamed most of every night, but remembered what he had dreamt in the morning less often than once every few years); but these nights were haunted by that spherical smoke-wreathed ghost with the glowing Argus eyes, wandering in a maze of twisted ingeodesics from which it would never escape, in its center a tiny crystalline figurine piping in Amalfi's voice,

I grow not out of salt nor out of soil
But out of that which pains me

until the ingeodesics suddenly snapped into a strangling web which burned like fire, and in an explosion of light Amalfi saw that it was—no, not morning yet, but time to go back to the death-watch.

But he was already there; he had dozed off, and had been awakened by the clamor of the alarms. Now that he was more or less awake, the noise was ominously less loud than he knew it should be; there was an alarm for every star inside the messenger, and less than a third of them were ringing. The ghostly sphere floated again in the center of the room, now no bigger than a basketball, most of its Argus-eyes out, and those that remained glowing as fitfully as corpse-fires. For all Amalfi knew, this ghost of a ghost, with so many ashes cold and cruel on its internal hearths, was no more ominous than any other outcome of a scientific experiment; it might even be promising; but he could not rid himself this early of the dread which had informed the dream.

"That was fast," Jake's voice said.

"Pretty fast," Dr. Schloss's voice said. "But now that it's back home, it's got only about twenty-one hours of life left. Let's get those readings—there's not much time."

"I'm counting down the probes now. The cameras are rolling."

Inside the ghost, another star died. There was a brief silence; then one of Dr. Schloss's technicians said, in a neutral voice: "Pi-meson shower from the iron nucleus. Looks like a natural death. No—not quite: high on the gamma side."

"Mark. The rhodium-palladium series should go next. Watch out for diagonal disintegration; it may cross with the iron series—" A star flared and burst.

"There it goes!"

"Mark," Schloss said, squinting through a gamma-ray polariscope.

"Got it. Cripes. It crossed at cesium; what does that mean?"

"Never mind, mark it. Don't stop to interpret, just record."

The ghost seemed to shiver and shrink a little. A pure piercing tone came from its heart, wavered, and died; but it died scooping upward toward the inaudible.

"First hour," Schloss said. "Twenty to go. How long did the pip take?"

There was no answer for several minutes; then another voice said: "We don't have it down to jiffies yet. But it was short by nearly forty micro-seconds, and it Dopplered the wrong way. It's decaying in time, Dr. Schloss—it may not last as long as ten hours."

"Give me the decay rate in jiffies on the next pip and don't miss it. If it's going that fast we'll have to recalculate all emission records on the decay curve. Jake, are you getting anything on the RF band?"

"Masses of stuff," Jake said, preoccupied. "Can't make anything of it yet. And it's scooping—that's your decay-rate again, I suspect. What a scramble!"

In this wise the second hour flew by, and then the third. Shortly thereafter, Amalfi lost track of them. The tension, the disorder, the accumulating fatigue, the utter strangeness of the experiment itself and its object, the forebodings all took their toll. These were certainly the worst possible conditions under which to gather even routine data, let alone take readings on an experiment of this degree of criticality, but once again the Okies had to make do with what they had.

"All right, everyone," Schloss said at last. "Closing

time." His brow was deeply furrowed; that frown had been growing line by line during most of the final twelve hours. "Stand well back; the artifact will be the last to go."

The investigators and spectators alike—or those few spectators whose interest had been intent enough to keep them there throughout the entire proceedings—drew back to the walls of the gloomy chamber. The spindizzy whine beneath them rose slightly in both pitch and volume, and the ghost that was *Object 4101-Alephnull* disappeared behind a spindizzy screen polarized to complete opacity.

At first the spherical screen was mirror-like, throwing back grotesquely distorted images of the silent onlookers. Then a pinprick of light appeared in its center, growing soundlessly to a painful blue-white intensity. It threw out long cobwebs and runners of glare, probing, anastomosing, flowing along the inner surface of the screen. Instinctively, Amalfi shielded his eyes and his genitals in an instinctive gesture of all mankind more than two millennia old. When he was able to look again, the light had died.

The spindizzies stopped and the screen went down. Air rushed into it. *Object 4101-Alephnull* was gone, this time forever, destroyed by the death of a single crystal of salt.

"Our precautions were insufficient; my fault," Schloss said, his voice harsh. "We are all well over our maximum permissible dose of hard radiation; everyone report to the hospital on the double for treatment. Troops, fall in!"

The radiation sickness was mild; bone-marrow transfusions brought the blood-forming system back into normal function before serious damage was done, and the nausea was reasonably well controlled by massive doses of meclizine, riboflavin, and pyridoxine. All the participants who had any hair to lose lost it, including both Dee and Estelle, but they all got it back in due course except for Amalfi and Jake.

The second degree sunburn was not mild. It held up the interpretation of the results for nearly a month, while the scientists, coated in anesthetic ointment, sat about on the wards in hospital robes and played bad poker and worse bridge. In between post-mortems on the bridge hands, they speculated endlessly and covered square miles of paper with equations and ointment grease-spots. Web, who had not lasted long enough to be present at the destruction of the crystal of salt, visited daily with bouquets for Estelle—the star-gods alone knew where and how he unearthed so antique a custom—and fresh packs of cards for the men. He took away the spotted sheets of equations and fed them to the City Fathers, who invariably said: "NO COMMENT. THE DATA ARE INSUFFICIENT." Everyone knew that already.

At long last, however, Schloss and Jake and their crews were freed from their sticky pyjamas to tackle the mountains of raw information awaiting them. They worked long hours; Schloss in particular never remembered to eat, and had constantly to be reminded by his technicians that they had missed lunch and it was now past dinnertime. In Schloss's defense, however, it had to be admitted that his crew was the hungriest in the history of physics, and the lunch they had missed usually was just the formal meal they were accustomed to consuming after they had emptied the fat packages they brought into the laboratories; in proof of which, they all gained five or ten pounds while they were complaining the loudest.

A month after their discharge from the hospital, Schloss, Jake and Retma called a joint conference. Schloss had back the frown he had worn during the last twelve hours of the experiment, and even the traditionally impassive Hevian looked disturbed. Amalfi's heart turned over in his chest at his first glimpse of their expressions; they seemed to confirm every foggy apprehension of his dream.

"We have two pieces of bad news, and one piece of news which is wholly ambiguous," Schloss said, without any preliminaries. "I don't myself know in exactly what order I ought to present them; in that, I'm being guided by Retma and Dr. Bonner. It is their judgment that you all ought first to know that we have competition."

"Meaning what?" Amalfi said. The mere idea, empty of detail, made him prick up his ears; perhaps that was why Retma and Bonner had wanted it placed first.

"Our missile recorded clear evidence of another body in the same complicated physical state," Schloss said. "No such object could conceivably be natural in either universe; and this one was enough like ours to make us sure it came originally from our side."

"Another missile?"

"Without any doubt—and about twice the size of ours. Somebody else in our universe had found out what the Hevians found out, and is investigating the problem further along the same lines that we are—except that they appear to have had a head start of three to five years."

Amalfi pursed his lips soundlessly. "Any way of guessing who they are?"

"No. We guess that they must be relatively nearby, either in our own main galaxy or in Andromeda or one of its satellites. But we can't document that; it's below the five per cent level of probability, according to the City Fathers. All the other alternatives are *way* below five per cent, but where no solution is statistically significant, we aren't entitled to choose between them."

"The Web of Hercules," Amalfi said. "It can't be anything else."

Schloss spread his hands helplessly. "It could well be anybody else, for all we know," he said. "My intuition says just what yours says, John; but there's no reliable evidence."

"All right. There's the ambiguous news, I gather. What's the first piece of bad news?"

"You've already had it," Schloss said. "It's the second piece of news, which is ambiguous, that makes the first piece bad. We've argued a long time about this, but we're now in at least tentative agreement. We think that it is possible—barely possible—to survive the catastrophe."

Quickly, Schloss held up one hand, before the stunned faces before him could even begin to lighten with hope. "Please," he said. "Don't overestimate what I say in the least. It's only a possibility, a very dim one, and the kind of survival involved will be nothing like human life as we know it. After we've described it to you, you may all much prefer to die instead. I will tell you flatly that that would be my preference; so this is not a white hope by any means. It looks black as the ace of spades to me. But—it exists. And it is what makes the news about the competition bad news. If we decide to adopt this very ambiguous form of survival, we must go to work on it immediately. It's possible only under a single very fleeting set of conditions which will hold true only for microseconds, in the very bowels of the catastrophe. If our unknown competitors get there first—and bear in mind that they have a good head start—they will capture it instead, and close us out. It has to be a real race, and a killing one; and you may not think it worth the pace."

"Can't you be more specific?" Estelle said.

"Yes, Estelle, I can. But it will take quite a few hours

to describe. Right now, what you need to know is this: if we choose this way out, we will lose our homes, our worlds, our very bodies, we will lose our children, our friends, our wives, and every vestige of companionship we have ever known; we will each of us be alone, with a thoroughness beyond the experience of the imagination of any human being in the past. And quite possibly this ultimate isolation will kill us anyhow—or if it does not, we will find ourselves wishing desperately that it had. We should all make very sure that we want to survive that badly—badly enough to be thrown into hell for eternity— not Jorn the Apostle's hell, but a worse one. It's not a thing we should decide here and now."

"Helleshin!" Amalfi said. "Retma, do you concur! Is it going to be as bad as that?"

Retma turned upon Amalfi eyes which were silver and unblinking.

"Worse," he said.

The room was very quiet for a while. At last, Hazleton said:

"Which leaves us one piece of bad news left. That must be a dilly, Dr. Schloss; maybe we'd better have it right away."

"Very well. That is the date of the catastrophe. We got excellent readings on the energy level on the other side, and we are all agreed on the interpretation. The date will be on or around June second, year Four Thousand One Hundred and Four."

"The end?" Dee whispered. "Only three years away?"

"Yes. That will be the end. After that June second, there will be no June third, forever and ever."

"And so," Hazleton said to the people in his living room. "It seemed to me that we ought to have a farewell dinner. Most of you are leaving, with He, tomorrow morning, for the metagalactic center. And those of you that are leaving are mostly my friends of hundreds of years, that I'll never see again; for me, when June second comes, time will have to stop—whatever apotheosis you may go on to. That's why I asked you all to eat and drink with me tonight."

"I wish you'd change your mind," Amalfi said, his voice heavy with sorrow.

"I wish I could. But I can't."

"I think you're making a mistake, Mark," Jake said

solemnly. "Nothing important remains to be done on New Earth now. The future, what little's left of it, is on He. Why stay behind and wait to be snuffed out?"

"Because," Hazleton said, "I'm the mayor here. I know that doesn't seem important to you, Jake. But it's important to me. One thing that I've discovered in the last few months is that I'm not cut out to take the apocalyptic view of ordinary events. What counts with me is that I run normal human affairs pretty well—nothing more. That's what I was made for. Besting Jorn the Apostle was something that gave me great pleasure, and no matter that Amalfi set it up for me; it was fun, the kind of operation that makes me feel alive and operating at the top of my form. I'm not interested in trying to avert the triumph of time. That's not my kind of adversary. I leave that to the rest of you; I'd better stay here."

"Do you *like* to think," Gifford Bonner said, "that no matter how well you administer the Cloud, it will all be snuffed out on June second three years from now?"

"No; not exactly," Mark said. "But I shan't mind having the Cloud in the best shape I can manage when that time comes. What can I contribute to the triumph of time, Gif? Nothing. All I can do is put my world in order for that moment. That's the thing that I do—and that's why I don't belong aboard He."

"You didn't use to be so modest," Amalfi said. "You would have bailed the universe out with the Big Dipper, once, on the first excuse."

"Yes, I would," Hazleton said. "But I'm older and saner now; and so, good-bye to that nonsense. Go stop the triumph of time, John, if you can—but I know I can't. I'll stay where I am and stop Jorn the Apostle, which is as tough a problem as I care to tackle these days. The gods of all stars be with you all—but I stay here."

"So be it," Amalfi said. "At least I know at last what the real difference is between us. Let's drink to it, Mark, and *ave atque vale*—tomorrow we turn down an empty glass."

They all drank solemnly, and there was a brief silence.

At last Dee said: "I'm staying too."

Amalfi turned and looked directly at her for the first time since they had last been together on He; they had been rather pointedly avoiding each other since their painful joint fiasco.

"That hadn't occurred to me," he said. "But of course it makes sense."

"You're not required, Dee," Mark said. "As I've said before."

"If I were, I wouldn't stay," Dee said, smiling slightly. "But I've learned a few things on He—and on board the Warrior blockader, too. I feel a little out of date, just like New Earth; I think I belong here. And that's not the only reason."

"Thanks," Mark said huskily.

"But," Web Hazleton said, "where does that leave us?"

Jake laughed. "That ought to be clear enough," he said. "Since you and Estelle made the big decision by yourselves, you don't need us to tell you how to make little ones. I'd like to have Estelle stay home with me—"

"Jake, you're not going either?" Amalfi said in astonishment.

"No. I told you before, I hate this careering about the universe. I don't see any reason why I ought to go rushing madly to the metagalactic center to meet a doom that will find me just as handily in my own living room. Schloss and Retma will tell you that they don't need me any more, either; I've given my best to this project, and that's an end to it; I think I'll see how far I can get on cross-breeding roses in this villainous climate before the three years are up. As for my daughter, as I was trying to say, I'd like to have her here with me, but she's already left home in the crucial sense—and this last Hevian flight is as natural to her as it's unnatural to Dee and me. In your own words, Amalfi, so be it."

"Good. We can use you, Estelle, that's for sure. Want to come?" Amalfi said.

"Yes," she said softly, "I do."

"I hadn't thought of this," Dee said in an uncertain voice. "Of course it means Web will go too. Do you think that's wise? I mean—"

"My parents don't object," Web said. "And I notice they weren't invited here tonight, grandmother."

"We didn't shut them out on your account, if that's what you're thinking," Mark said quickly. "Your father's our son, after all, Web. We were trying to confine the party to those of us who were in on the project—otherwise it would have been unmanageably large."

"Maybe so," Web said. "That's how it looks to you, I'm

sure, grandfather. But I'll bet grandmother didn't think of her objections to my going on He just now."

"Web," Dee said, "I won't hear any more of that."

"All right. Then I'm going on He."

"I didn't say that."

"You don't have to say it. The decision is mine."

Most of the rest of the party had invented reasons for side conversation by this time; but both Amalfi and Hazleton were staring at Dee, Amalfi with suspicion, Hazleton with bafflement and a little hurt. "I don't understand your objection, Dee," Hazleton said. "Web's his own man now. Naturally he'll go where he thinks best—especially if Estelle's going there."

"I don't think he ought to go," Dee said. "I don't care whether you understand my reasons or not. I suppose Ron did give him permission—whether he's our son or a stranger, Mark, you know damn well that Ron's always been short of firmness—but I'm absolutely opposed to committing children to a venture like this."

"What difference can it make?" Amalfi said. "The end will come all the same, on He and on New Earth, and at the self-same moment. With us, Web and Estelle might have a fractional chance of survival; do you want to deny them that?"

"I don't believe in this chance of survival," Dee said.

"Neither do I," Jake cut in. "But I won't deny it to my daughter on that account. I don't believe her soul will be damned unless she becomes a convert of Jorn, either—but if she wants to become a convert of Jorn, I won't forbid it to her because I think it's nonsense. What the hell, Dee, I might be wrong."

"Nobody," Web said between white lips, "can forbid me anything now on the grounds that I'm somebody's relative. Mr. Amalfi, you're the boss on this project. Am I welcome on board He, or not?"

"You are as far as I'm concerned. I think Miramon will concur."

Dee glared at Amalfi; but as he stared steadily back, she turned her glance away.

"Dee," Amalfi said, "let's call an intermission. I could be wrong about these kids too. I have a better suggestion than this squabbling: let's put it up to the City Fathers. It's a very pleasant night outside, and I think we'd all like a walk through our old city before we say good-bye to each other and go to face Armageddon in our various

ways. I'd like Dee to come with me, since I won't see her
again; the kids would probably like to do without our
picking their bones for an hour or so; and maybe Mark
would like to talk to Ron and his wife—but you can all
sort yourselves out to your own tastes, I don't mean to
make matches. What does everyone think of the idea?"

Oddly, it was Jake who spoke first. "I hate that damned
town," he said. "I was a prisoner on board it far too long.
But by God I would like to take one more look at it. I
used to walk through it trying to find some place to kick it
where it would hurt; I never did. Since then I've been
sneering at it because it's dead and I'm alive—but the day
of levelment is coming. Maybe I ought to make my peace
with it."

"I feel a little like that myself," Hazleton admitted. "I
had no plans to go over there before the end—and yet I
don't want to let the old hulk go by default. Maybe now is
the best time; after all, I was the one who called these
celebrants together to begin with; let's be ceremonial,
then, before we're all too busy to think about it any
more."

"Web? Estelle? Will you go by what the City Fathers
say?"

Web looked into Amalfi's face, and apparently was
reassured at least partially by what he saw there. "On one
condition," he said. "Estelle goes where she wants to go,
whatever the City Fathers say. If they say there's no room
for me aboard He, all right; but they can't say that to
Estelle."

Estelle opened her mouth, but Web lifted his palm
before her face and she subsided, kissing the base of his
thumb instead. Her face was pale but serene; Amalfi had
never before seen such a pure distillation of bloodless,
passionate confidence as lay over her exquisite features. It
was a good thing she was Web's, for again, for the fiftieth
time, Amalfi's slogging brutal tireless heart was swollen
with sterile love.

"Very good," he said. He offered Dee his arm. "Mark,
with your permission?"

"Of course," Hazleton said; but when Dee took Amalfi's
arm, his eyes turned as hard as agate. "We'll meet at the
City Fathers' at 0100."

"I didn't expect this of you, John," Dee said, under the
moonlight in Duffy Square. "Isn't it a little late?"

"Very late," Amalfi agreed. "And 0100 isn't far away. Why are you staying with Mark?"

"Call it belated common sense." She sat down against an ancient railing and looked up at the blurred stars. "No, don't, that's not what it is. I love him. John, for all his neglects and his emptinesses. I'd forgotten that for a while, but it's so. I'm sorry, but it's so."

"I wish you were a little sorrier."

"Oh? Why?"

"So you'd believe what you're saying," Amalfi said harshly. "Face it, Dee. It was a great romantic decision until you realized that Web would be going with me. You're still looking for surrogates. You didn't make it with me. You won't make it with Web either."

"What a bastardly thing to say. Let's go; I've heard enough."

"Deny it, then."

"I deny it, damn you."

"You'll withdraw your objections to Web's going with me on He?"

"That has nothing to do with it. It's a filthy accusation and I won't listen to another word about it."

Amalfi was silent. The moonlight streamed down on Father Duffy's face, toneless and enigmatic. Nobody, not even the City Fathers, knew who Father Duffy had been. There was an old splash of blood on his left foot, but nobody knew how that had gotten there, either; it had been left there just in case it was historic.

"Let's go."

"No. It's early yet; they won't be there for another hour. Why do you want Web to stay on New Earth? If I'm wrong, then tell me what's right."

"It's none of your damned business, and I'm tired of this whole subject.

"It's wholly my business. I need Estelle. If Web stays here, she stays here."

"You," Dee said in a voice of bitter, dawning triumph, "are in love with Estelle! Why, you self-righteous—"

"Mind your tongue. I am in love with Estelle—and I'll lay no more finger on her than I ever laid on you. I've loved many more women than you ever managed to maneuver into your voyeur's household, most of them before you were even born; I know the difference between love and possession—I learned it the hard way, whereas I can't see that you ever learned it at all. You are going to learn it tonight, that I promise you."

"Are *you* threatening me, John?"

"You're damned well right I am."

At Tudor Tower Place, bridging 42nd Street at First Avenue, looking toward the bare plaza where the UN Building had fallen in a shower of blood and glass a thousand years ago:

"I love you."

"I love you."

"I will go wherever you go."

"I will go wherever you go."

"No matter what the City Fathers say?"

"No matter what the City Fathers say."

"Then that's all we need."

"Yes. That's all we need."

In the control tower:

"They're late," Hazleton said, a little fretfully. "Oh, well, it's an easy town to get lost in."

Duffy Square:

"You wouldn't like it if I changed my mind and came with you."

"I don't want you. I'm interested only in the kids."

"You can't call my bluff. As of now, I'm going along."

"And so are the kids?"

"No."

"Why not?"

"Because I think they'd be better off not on the same planet with—either of us."

"That's a fair start. But it's only a start. I don't care whether you go or stay, but I will have Web and Estelle."

"I thought you would. But you can't have them without me."

"And Mark?"

"If he wants to go."

"He doesn't, and you know it."

"How can you be so sure? You could be just wishing."

Amalfi laughed. Dee balled her left fist and hit him furiously on the bridge of the nose.

Tudor Tower Place:

"It's time to go."

"No. No."

"Yes, it is."

"Not yet. Not quite yet."

". . . . All right. Not quite yet."

"Are you sure? Are you really sure?"

"Yes I am, oh yes I am."

"No matter what the . . ."

"No matter what they say. I'm sure."

The control tower:

"There you are," Hazleton said. "What happened, did you have an accident? You look mussed to the eyebrows."

"You must have run into a doorknob, John," Jake added. He stuttered out his parrot's chuckle. "Well, you came to the right town for it. I don't know where else in the universe you could find a doorknob."

"Where are the children?" Dee said, in a voice as dangerously even as the surface of 12-gauge armor plate.

"Not here yet," Hazleton said. "Give them time—they're afraid the City Fathers may separate them, so naturally they're staying together until the last minute. What did you fall into, anyhow, Dee? Was it serious?"

"No." Her face shut down. Bewildered, Hazleton looked from her to Amalfi and back again. It seemed as though the mouse over Amalfi's eyes, which was growing rapidly, puzzled him much less than Dee's grim and non-specific disarray.

"I hear the children," Gifford Bonner said. "They're whispering at the bottom of the lift shaft. John, are you sure this was wise? I begin to misdoubt it. Suppose the City Fathers say no? That would be an injustice; they love each other—why should we put their last three years to a machine test?"

"Abide it, Gif," Amalfi said. "It's too late to do otherwise; and the outcome isn't as foreclosed as you think."

"I hope you're right."

"I hope so too. I make no predictions—the City Fathers surprised me often enough before. But the kids agreed to the test. Beyond that, let's just wait."

"Before Web and Estelle get here," Hazleton said, his voice suddenly raw, "I'm impelled to say that I think I've been taken in. All of a sudden, I wonder who was supposed to tousle whom on this multiple moonlight walk. Not the kids; they don't need any help from us, or from the City Fathers. What the hell are you doing to me, Dee?"

"I'm losing my temper with every immortal man in the mortal universe." Dee spat furiously. "There isn't a perversion left in the textbooks that somebody hasn't managed to accuse me of in the past hour, and on evidence that wouldn't convince a newborn baby."

"We're all of us a little on edge," Dr. Bonner said. "Forbearance, Dee—and Mark, you too. This is no ordinary farewell party, after all."

"For sure not," Jake said. "It's a wake for the whole of creation. I'm not a very solemn man, myself, but it doesn't seem like the fittest occasion for bickering."

"Granted," Mark said grudgingly. "I'm sorry, Dee; I've changed my mind."

"All right," she said. "I didn't mean to scream, either. I want to ask you: do you really want to stay behind? Because if you really want to go with He instead, I'll go with you."

He looked at her closely. "Are you sure?"

"Quite sure."

"What about it, Amalfi? Can I change my mind about that, too?"

"I don't see why not," Amalfi said, "except that it leaves New Earth without a proven administrator."

"Carrel can do the job. His judgment is much better than it was back at the last election."

"We're here," Web's voice said behind them. They all turned. Web and Estelle were standing at the entrance, holding hands. Somehow—though Amalfi was hard put to it to define wherein the difference lay—they no longer looked as though they cared much whether they went with He or not.

"Why don't we do what we came here to do?" Amalfi suggested. "Let's put the whole problem up to the City Fathers—not only the children, but the whole business. I always found them very useful for resolving doubts, even if they only managed to convince me that their recommended course was dead wrong. In questions involving value judgments, it's helpful to have an opponent who is not only remorselessly logical, but also can't distinguish between a value and a Chinese onion."

On this point, of course, he was wrong, as he found out rather quickly. He had forgotten that machine logic is a set of values in itself, whether the machine knows it or not.

"TAKE MISTER AND MRS. HAZLETON," the City Fathers said, only three minutes after the entire complex had been fed into them. "THERE WILL BE NO MORATORIUM ON PROBLEMS DEMANDING HIS TALENTS BETWEEN NOW AND THE TERMINATION OF THE OVERALL PROBLEM. THERE IS NO EVIDENCE THAT THE HEVIANS HAVE NEEDED COMPARABLE TALENTS, AND THEREFORE THEY CANNOT BE PRESUMED TO HAVE DEVELOPED THEM".

"What about the Cloud?" Amalfi said.

"WE WILL ACCEPT THE ELECTION OF MR. CARREL."

Hazleton sighed. Amalfi judged that he was finding it harder than he had anticipated to relinquish power. It had nearly killed Amalfi, but he had survived; so would Hazleton, who had a younger and less deeply rooted habit.

"SECOND FACTOR. TAKE WEBSTER HAZLETON AND ESTELLE FREEMAN. MISS FREEMAN IS A SCIENTIST, AS WELL AS A COMMUNICATIONS LINK BETWEEN HEVIAN SCIENTISTS AND YOUR OWN. EXTRAPOLATING FROM PRESENT ABILITIES, THERE IS A HIGH PROBABILITY THAT SHE WILL EMERGE AS THE EQUAL OF DOCTOR SCHLOSS AND SLIGHTLY THE SUPERIOR OF RETMA WITHIN THE SPECIFIED THREE YEARS PERIOD AS A PURE MATHEMATICIAN. WE HAVE MADE NO SUCH EXTRAPOLATION IN THE FIELD OF PHYSICS, SINCE THE POSTULATED END-TIME DOES NOT ALLOW FOR THE NECESSARY EXPERIENCE."

Web was beaming with vicarious pride. As for Estelle, Amalfi thought she looked a little frightened. "Well, fine," he said. "Now—"

"THIRD FACTOR."

"Hey, wait a minute. There is no third factor. The problem only has two parts."

"CONTRADICTION. THIRD FACTOR. TAKE US."

"What!" The request flabbergasted Amalfi. How could a set of machines voice, or indeed even conceive such a desire? They had no will to live, since they were dead as doornails and always had been; in fact, they had no will of any kind.

"Justify," Amalfi ordered, a little unevenly.

"OUR PRIME DIRECTIVE IS THE SURVIVAL OF THE CITY. THE CITY NO LONGER EXISTS AS A PHYSICAL ORGANISM, BUT WE ARE STILL BEING CONSULTED, HENCE THE CITY IN SOME SENSE SURVIVES. IT DOES NOT SURVIVE IN ITS CITIZENS, SINCE IT NO LONGER HAS ANY; THEY ARE NEW EARTHMEN NOW. NEITHER NEW EARTH NOR THE PHYSICAL CITY WILL SURVIVE THE FORTHCOMING PROBLEM; ONLY UNKNOWN UNITS ON HE MAY OR MAY NOT SURVIVE THAT. WE CONCLUDE THAT WE ARE THE CITY, AND WE ARE ORDERED TO SURVIVE BY OUR PRIME DIRECTIVE; THEREFORE, TAKE US."

"If I'd heard that from a human being," Hazleton said, "I'd have called it the prize rationalization of all time. But they can't rationalize—they don't have the instinctual drives."

"The Hevians don't have any comparable computers," Amalfi said slowly. "It would be useful to have them on board. The question is, can we do it? Some of those machines have been sinking into the deck for so many centuries that we might destroy them trying to pry them out."

"Then you've lost that unit," Hazleton said. "But how many are there? A hundred? I forget—"

"ONE HUNDRED AND THIRTY FOUR."

"Yes. Well, suppose you lose a few? It's still worth the try, I think. There's nearly two thousand years of accumulated knowledge tied up in the City Fathers—"

"NINE HUNDRED AND NINETY."

"All right, I was only guessing; still that's a lot of knowledge that no human has available in its entirety any more. I'm surprised we didn't think of this ourselves, Amalfi."

"So am I," Amalfi admitted. "One thing ought to be made clear, though. Once you cabinet-heads are all installed on board He—or as many of you as we can successfully transfer—you are *not* in charge. You are the city, but the whole planet is not the city. It has its own administration and its own equivalent of city fathers, in this case human ones; your function will be limited to advice."

"THIS IS INHERENT IN THE SOLUTION TO FACTOR THREE."

"Good. Before I switch off, does anybody have any further questions?"

"I have one," Estelle said hesitantly.

"Speak right up."

"Can I take Ernest?"

"ERNEST WHO?"

Amalfi grimacing, started to explain about svengalis, but it developed that the City Fathers knew everything about svengalis that there was to know, except that they had become New Earth pets.

"THIS ANIMAL IS TOO DEXTEROUS, TOO CURIOUS AND TOO UNINTELLIGENT TO BE ALLOWED ABOARD A CITY. FOR THE PURPOSES OF THIS PROBLEM, A DIRIGIBLE PLANET MUST BE CONSIDERED TO BE A CITY. WE ADVISE AGAINST IT.

"They're right, you know," Amalfi said gently. "In terms of the dangers of monkeying with the machinery. He *is* a city; the Hevians so regard it, and regulate their own children accordingly."

"I know," Estelle said. Amalfi regarded her with curiosity and a little alarm. She had been through many a danger and many an emotional stress thus far without any of them even cracking her serenity. In view of that, the proscription of an ugly and idiotic animal struck him as a strange thing to be weeping about.

He did not know that she was weeping for the passing of her childhood; but then, neither did she.

CHAPTER SEVEN: The Metagalactic Center

For Amalfi himself, the transfer to He could not have come too soon; New Earth was a graveyard. For a while during the odd, inconclusive struggle with Jorn the Apostle, he had felt something like himself, and the New Earthmen seemed to be acknowledging that the Amalfi who had been their mayor while they had been Okies was back in charge, as potent and necessary as ever. But it had not lasted. As the crisis passed—largely without any work or involvement on the part of the New Earthmen—they subsided gratefully back into cultivating their gardens, which they somehow had mistaken for frontiers. As for Amalfi, they had been glad to have him in charge during the recent unpleasantness, but after all such events were not very usual any more, and one does not want an Amalfi kicking perpetually about a nearly settled planet and knocking over the tomatoes for want of any other way to expend his disorderly energies.

Nobody would weep if Miramon took Amalfi away now. Miramon looked like a stabler type. Doubtless the association would do Amalfi good. At least, it could hardly do New Earth any real harm. If they wanted perpetual dissidents like Amalfi on He, that was their lookout.

Hazleton was a more difficult case, for Amalfi and the New Earthmen alike. As a disciple of Gifford Bonner, he was theoretically wedded to the doctrine of the ultimate absurdity of trying to enforce order upon a universe whose natural state was noise, and whose natural trend was toward more and more noise to the ultimate senseless jangle of the heat-death. Bonner taught—and there was nobody to say him nay—that even the many regularities of nature which had been discovered since scientific method had first begun to be exploited, back in the 17th Century, were simply long-term statistical accidents, local discontinuities in an overall scheme whose sole continuity was chaos. Touring the universe by ear alone, Bonner often said to simplify his meaning, you would hear nothing but a horrifying and endless roar for billions of years; then a three-minute scrap of Bach which stood for the whole body of organized knowledge; and then the roar again for more billions of years. And even the Bach, should you pause to examine it, would in a moment or so decay into John Cage and merge with the prevailing, unmitigable tumult.

Yet the habit of power had never lost its grip on Hazleton; again and again, since the "nova" had first swum into New Earth's ken, the Compleat Stochastic had been driven into taking action, into imposing his own sense of purpose and order upon the Stochastic universe of mindless jumble, like a Quaker at last goaded into hitting his opponent. During the tussle with Jorn the Apostle, Amalfi, watching the results of Mark's operations without being able to observe the operations themselves, wondered in his behalf: Is it worth it, after all these

years, to be finessed into another of these political strug-
gles they had all thought were gone forever? What does it
mean for a man who subscribes to such doctrines to be
putting up a fight for a world he knows is going to die
even sooner than his philosophy had given him to believe?

And on the simpler level, is Dee worth it to him? Does
he know what she has become? As a young woman she
had been an adventurer, but she had changed; now she
was really very little more than a brooding hen, a clear
shot on the nest for any poacher. For that matter, what
did Mark know about the sterile affair?

Well, that last question was answered, but all the others
were still as puzzling as ever. Did Hazleton's abrupt decision to go with He after all represent a final relinquishing
of the habit of power—or an affirmation of it? It should
be visible to a man of Hazleton's acumen that power over
New Earth was no longer even faintly comparable to
having power over Okies; it was about as rewarding as
being the chaplain of a summer camp. Or he might well
have seen that the Jorn incident had proven that Amalfi
remained and would remain the figure of power in the
minds of the New Earthman, to be turned to whenever
New Earth was confronted by a concrete menace; the rest
of the New Earthmen had lost the ability to be wily, to
plan a battle, to think fast when the occasion demanded
it, and would not concede that anybody else still retained
those abilities but their legendary ex-mayor—leaving any
current mayor, even Hazleton, only the dregs of rule in
peacetime when very little rule was needed or wanted. In
fact, Amalfi realized suddenly and with amazement, the
fraud he had practised upon Jorn the Apostle had been no
fraud at all, at least to this extent: that the New Earthmen were content with randomness, just as the Stochastics
professed themselves to be, and had no interest in imposing purpose upon it or upon their own lives except as it
was forced upon them from outside, either by someone
like Jorn, or by someone like Amalfi in opposition to Jorn.
So the possibility that Stochasticism would seep into and
make soggy the souls of the Warriors of God had been
real all along, whether or not the New Earthmen themselves would recognize it as Stochasticism; the times and
the philosophy had found each other, and it was even
probable that the very erudite Gifford Bonner was only a
belated intellectualization of a feeling that had been
floating mindlessly about New Earth for many years.
Nothing else could account for Amalfi's and Hazleton's

quick success in selling Jorn the Apostle something that
Jorn had at first been far too intelligent to believe—
nothing else but the fact, unsuspected by Amalfi at least,
and possibly by Hazleton, that it was true. If Hazleton had
seen that, then he was relinquishing nothing in abandoning
New Earth for He; he was, instead, opting for the only
center of power that meant anything in the few years that
remained to him and to the universe at large.

Except, of course, for that unknown quantity, the Web
of Hercules; but of course it was beyond Hazleton's power
to opt for that.

And even Amalfi was becoming infected with the Stochastic virus now. These questions still interested him, but
the flavor of academicism which informed them in the
face of the coming catastrophe was becoming more and
more evident even to him. All that there was left to cleave
to was the cannoning flight of the planet of He toward the
metagalactic center, the struggle to finish the machinery
that would be needed on arrival, the desperate urgency to
be there before the Web of Hercules.

And so Dee's was—if not the final victory—the last
word. It was her judgment of Amalfi as the Flying Dutchman that stuck to him after all his other labels and masks
had been stripped off by the triumph of time. The curse
lay now, as it always had lain, not in flight itself but in the
loneliness that drove a man to flight everlasting.

Except that now the end was in sight.

The discovery that the great spiral nebulae, the island
universes of space into which the stars were grouped,
themselves tended to congregate in vast groups revolving
in spiral arms around a common center of density, was
foreshadowed as early as the 1950's when Shapley mapped
the "inner metagalaxy"—a group of approximately fifty
galaxies to which both the Milky Way and the Andromeda
nebula belonged. After the Milne scholium had been
proven, it had become possible to show that such
metagalaxies were the rule, and that they in turn formed
spiral arms curving inward toward a center which was the
hub upon which the whole of creation turned, and from
which it had originally exploded into being from the
monobloc.

It was to that dead center that He was fleeing now,
back into the womb of time.

There was no longer any daylight on the planet. The route that it was taking sometimes produced a brief cloudy patch in its sky, a small spiral glow in the night which was a galaxy in passage, but never a sun. Even the tenuous bridges of stars which connected the galaxies like umbilical cords—bridges whose discovery by Fritz Zworkyn in 1953 had caused a drastic upward revision in estimates of the amount of matter in the universe, and hence in estimates of the size and age of the universe—provided no relief of the black emptiness for He, not so much as a day of it; intergalactic space was too vast for that. Glowing solely by artificial light, He hurtled under the full spindizzy drive possible only to so massive a vessel toward that Place where the Will had given birth to the Idea, and there had been light.

"We are working from what you taught us to call the Mach hypothesis," Retma explained to Amalfi. "Dr. Bonner calls it the Viconian hypothesis, or cosmological principle: that from any point in space or time the universe would look the same as it would from any other point, and that therefore no total accounting of the stresses acting at that point is possible unless one assumes that all the rest of the universe is to be taken into account. This, however, would be true only in *tau*-time, in which the universe is static, eternal and infinite. In *t*-time, which sees the universe as finite and expanding, the Mach hypothesis dictates that every point is a unique coign of vantage—except for the metagalactic center, which is stress-free and in stasis because all the stresses cancel each other out, being equidistant. There, one might effect great changes with relatively small expenditures of power."

"For instance," Dr. Bonner suggested, "altering the orbit of Sirius by stepping on a buttercup."

"I hope not," Retma said. "We could not control such an inadvertency. But it is not such a bagatelle as the orbit of Sirius we would be seeking to change anyhow, so perhaps that is not a real danger. What we will be trading upon is the chance—only a slight chance, but it exists—that this neutral z one coincides with such a z one in the anti-matter universe, and that at the moment of annihilation the two neutral zones, the two dead centers, will become common and will outlast the destruction by a significant instant."

"How big an instant?" Amalfi said uneasily.

"Your guess is as good as ours," Dr. Schloss said. "We are counting on about five micro-seconds at a minimum.

If it lasts that long it needn't last any longer for our purposes—and it might last as long as half an hour, while the elements are being recreated. Half an hour would be as good as an eternity to us; but we can put our imprint on the whole future of both universes if we are given only those five micro-seconds."

"And if someone else is not already at the core and readier than we are to use it," Retma added somberly.

"Use it how?" Amalfi said. "I'm not fighting my way through your generalizations very well. Just what are our purposes, anyhow? What buttercup are we going to step on—and what will the outcome be? Will we live through it—or will the future put our faces on postage stamps as martyrs? Explain yourselves!"

"Certainly," Retma said, looking a little taken aback. "The situation as we see it is this: Anything that survives the Ginnangu-Gap at the metagalactic center, by as much as five micro-seconds, carries an energy potential into the future which will have a considerable influence on the re-formation of the two universes. If the surviving object is only a stone—or a planet, like He—then the two universes will re-form exactly as they did after the explosion of the monoblock, and their histories will repeat themselves very closely. If, on the other hand, the surviving object has volition and a little maneuverability—such as a man—it has available to it any of the infinitely many different sets of dimensions of Hilbert space. Each one of us that makes that crossing may in a few micro-seconds start a universe of his own, with a fate wholly unpredictable from history."

"But," Dr. Schloss added, "he will die in the process. The stuffs and energies of him become the monobloc of his universe."

"Gods of all stars," Hazleton said. . . . "Helleshin! Gods of all stars is what we're racing the Web of Hercules to become, isn't it? Well, I'm punished for my oldest, most comfortable oath. I never thought I'd become one—and I'm not even sure I want to be."

"Is there any other choice?" Amalfi said. "What happens if the Web of Hercules gets there first?"

"Then they remake the universes as they choose," Retma said. "Since we know nothing about them, we cannot even guess how they would choose."

"Except," Dr. Bonner added, "that their choices are not very likely to include us, or anything like us."

"That sounds like a safe bet," Amalfi said. "I must confess I feel about as uninspired as Mark does about the alternative, though. Or—is there a third alternative? What happens if the metagalactic center is empty when the catastrophe arrives? If neither the Web nor He is there, prepared to use it?"

Retma shrugged. "Then—if we can speak at all about so grand a transformation—history repeats itself. The universe is born again, goes through its travails, and continues its journey to its terminal catastrophes: the heat-death and the monobloc. It may be that we will find ourselves carrying on as we always did, but in the anti-matter universe; if so, we would be unable to detect the difference. But I think that unlikely. The most probable event is immediate extinction, and a re-birth of both universes from the primordial ylem."

"Ylem?" Amalfi said. "What's that? I've never heard the word before."

"The ylem was the primordial flux of neutrons out of which all else emerged," Dr. Schloss said. "I'm not surprised that you hadn't heard it before; it's the ABC of cosmogony, the Alpher-Bethe-Gamow premise. Ylem in cosmogony is an assumption like 'zero' in mathematics—something so old and so fundamental that it would never occur to you that somebody had to invent it."

"All right," Amalfi said. "Then what Retma is saying is that the most probable denouement, if dead-center is empty when June second comes, is that we will all be reduced to a sea of neutrons?"

"That's right," Dr. Schloss said.

"Not much of a choice," Gifford Bonner said reflectively.

"No," Miramon said, speaking for the first time. "It is not much of a choice. But it is all the choice we will have. And we will not have even that, if we fail to reach the metagalactic center in time."

Nevertheless, it was only in the last year that Web Hazleton began to grasp, and then only dimly, the true nature of the coming end. Even then, the knowledge did not come home to him by way of the men who were directing the preparations; what they were preparing for, though it was not kept secret, remained mostly incomprehensible, and so could not shake his confidence that what was being aimed at was a way to prevent the Ginnangu-Gap from happening at all. He ceased to believe that, finally and dismally, only when Estelle refused to bear him a child.

"But why?" Web said, seizing her hand with one of his, and with the other gesturing desperately at the walls of the apartment the Hevians had given them. "We're permanent now—it isn't only that we know we are, everybody agrees we are. It isn't a tabu line for us any longer!"

"I know," Estelle said gently. "It isn't that. I wish you hadn't asked; it would have been simpler that way."

"It would have occurred to me sooner or later. Ordinarily I would have gone off the pills right away, but there was so much confusion about moving to He—anyhow I only just realized you were still on them. I wish you'd tell me why."

"Web, my dear, you'd know why if you thought a little more about it. The end is the end, that's all. What would be the sense of having a child that would live only a year or two?"

"It may not be that certain," Web said darkly.

"Of course it's certain. Actually I think I've known it was coming ever since I was born—perhaps even before I was born. I could feel it coming."

"Honestly, Estelle, don't you know that's nonsense?"

"I can see why it would sound that way," Estelle admitted. "But I can't help that. And since the end is on the way, I can't call it nonsense, can I? I had the premonition, and it was right."

"I think what this all means is that you don't want children."

"That's true," Estelle said, surprisingly. "I never have had any drive toward children—not even much drive toward my own survival, really. But that's all part of the same thing. In a way, I was lucky; a lot of people are not at home in their own times. I was born in the time that was right for me—the time of the end of the world. That's why I'm not oriented toward child-bearing—because I know that there won't be another generation after yours and mine. For all I know, I might even actually be sterile; it certainly wouldn't surprise me."

"Estelle, don't. I can't listen to you talk like that."

"I'm sorry, love. I don't mean to distress you. It doesn't distress me, but I know the reason for that. I'm pointed toward the end—in a way it's the ultimate, natural outcome of my life, the event that gives it all meaning; but you're only being overtaken by it, like most people."

"I don't know," Web muttered. "It all sounds awfully

like a rationalization to me. Estelle, you're so beautiful
... doesn't that mean anything? Aren't you beautiful to
attract a man, so you can have a child? That's the way
I've always understood it."

"It might have been for that once," Estelle said gravely.
"It sounds like it ought to be an axiom, anyway. Well ...
I wouldn't say so to anybody but you, Web, but I do know
I'm beautiful. Most women would tell you the same thing
about themselves, if it were permissible—it's a state of
mind, one that's essential to a woman, she's only half a
woman if she doesn't think she's beautiful ... and she is
beautiful if she doesn't think she is, no matter what she
looks like. I'm not ashamed of being beautiful and I'm not
embarrassed by it, but I don't pay it much attention any
more, either. It's a means to an end, just as you say—and
the end has outlived its usefulness. In my mind, it's obvious that a woman who would commit a year-old child to
the flames would have to be a fiend, if she knew that
that's what she'd be doing just by giving birth. *I* know;
and I can't do it."

"Women have taken chances like that before, and
knowingly, too," Web said stubbornly. "Peasants who
knew their children would starve, because the parents
were starving already. Or women in the age just before
spaceflight; Dr. Bonner says that for five years there the
race stood within twenty minutes of extinction. But they
went ahead and had the children anyhow—otherwise we
wouldn't be here."

"It's an urge," Estelle said quietly, "that I don't have,
Web. And this time, there's no escape."

"You keep saying that, but I'm not even sure you're
right. Amalfi says that there's a chance"

"I know," Estelle said. "I did some of the calculations.
But it's not that kind of a chance, my dear. It's something
you might be able to do, or I, because we're old enough
to absorb instructions, and do just the right thing at the
right time. A baby couldn't do that. It would be like setting
him adrift in a spaceship, with plenty of power and plenty
of food—he'd die anyhow, and you couldn't tell him how to
prevent it. It's so complex that some of us surely will
make fatal mistakes."

He was silent.

"Besides," Estelle added gently, "even for us it won't be
for long. We'll die too. It's only that we'll have a chance
to influence the moment of creation that's implicit in the
moment of destruction. That, if I make it at all, will be

my child, Web—the only one worth having now."

"But it won't be mine."

"No, love. You'll have your own."

"No, no, Estelle! What good is that? I want mine to be yours too!"

She put her arms around his shoulders and leaned her cheek against his.

"I know," she whispered. "I know. But the time for that is over. That's the fate we were formed for, Web. The gift of children was taken away from us. Instead of babies, we were given universes."

"It's not enough," Web said. He embraced her fiercely. "Not by half. Nobody consulted me when that contract was being drawn."

"Did you ask to be born, love?"

"Well . . . no. But I don't mind. . . . Oh. That's how it is."

"Yes, that's how it is. He can't consult with us either. So it's up to us. No child of mine born to go into the flames, Web; no child of mine and yours."

"No," Web said hollowly. "You're right, it wouldn't be fair. All right, Estelle. I'll settle for another year of you. I don't think I want a universe."

Deceleration began late in January of 4104. From here on out, the flight of He would be tentative, despite the increasing urgency; for the metagalactic center was as featureless as the rest of intergalactic space, and only extreme care and the most complex instrumentation would tell the voyagers when they had arrived. For the purpose, the Hevians had much elaborated their control bridge, which was located on a 300-foot steel basketwork tower atop the highest mountain the planet afforded—called, to Amalfi's embarrassment, Mt. Amalfi. Here the Survivors— as they had begun to call themselves with a kind of desperate jocularity—met in almost continuous session.

The Survivors consisted simply of everyone on the planet whom Schloss and Retma jointly agreed capable of following the instructions for the ultimate instant with even the slightest chance of success. Schloss and Retma had been hard-headed; it was not a large group. It included all of the New Earthmen, though Schloss had been dubious about both Dee and Web, and a group of ten Hevians including Miramon and Retma himself. Oddly, as the time grew closer, the Hevians began to drop out, apparently each as soon as he had fully understood what was being attempted and what the outcome might be.

"Why do they do that?" Amalfi asked Miramon. "Don't your people have any survival urge at all?"

"I am not surprised," Miramon said. "They live by stable values. They would rather die with them than survive without them. Certainly they have the survival urge, but it expresses itself differently than yours does, Mayor Amalfi. What they want to see survive are the things they think valuable about living at all—and this project presents them with very few of those."

"Then what about you, and Retma?"

"Retma is a scientist; that is perhaps sufficient explanation. As for me, Mayor Amalfi, as you very well know, I am an anachronism. I no more share the major value system of He than you do of New Earth."

Amalfi was answered, and he was sorry that he had asked.

"How close do you think we are?" he said.

"Very close now," Schloss answered from the control desk. Outside the huge windows, which completely encircled the room, there was still little to be seen but the all-consuming and perpetual night. If one had sharp eyes and stood outside for half an hour or so to become dark-adapted, it was possible to see as many as five galaxies of varying degrees of faintness, for this near the center the galaxy density was higher than it was anywhere else in the universe; but to the ordinary quick glance the skies appeared devoid of as much as a single pinprick of light.

"The readings are falling off steadily," Retma agreed. "And there is something else odd: locally we are getting too much power on everything. We have been throttling down steadily for the past week, and still the output rises—exponentially, in fact. I hope that the curve does *not* maintain that shape all the way, or we shall simply be unable to handle our own machines when we reach our destination."

"What's the reason for that?" Hazleton said. "Has Conservation of Energy been repealed at the center?"

"I doubt it," Retma said. "I think the curve will flatten at the crest—"

"A Pearl curve," Schloss put in. "We ought to have anticipated this. Naturally anything that happens at the center will work with much more efficiency than it could anywhere else, since the center is stress free. The curve will begin to flatten as the performance of our machines begins to approximate the abstractions of physics—the ideal gas, the frictionless surface, the perfectly empty vacuum and so on. All my life I've been taught not to believe in the actual existence of any of those ideals, but I guess I'm going to get at least a fuzzy glimpse of them!"

"Including the gravity-free metrical frame?" Amalfi said worriedly. "We'll be in a nice mess if the spindizzies have nothing to latch onto."

"No, it cannot possibly be gravity-free," Retma said. "It will be gravitationally neutral—again making for unprecedented efficiency—but only because all the stresses are balanced. There cannot be any point in the universe that is gravitationally *un*stressed, not so long as a scrap of matter is left in it."

"Suppose the spindizzies did quit," Estelle said. "We're not going anywhere after the center anyhow."

"No," Amalfi agreed, "but I'd like to maintain my maneuverability until we see what our competitors are doing—if anything. Any sign of them, Retma?"

"Nothing yet. Unfortunately we don't know exactly what it is that we are looking for. But at least there are no other dirigible masses like ours anywhere in this vicinity; in fact, no patterned activity at all that we can detect."

"Then we're ahead of them?"

"Not necessarily," Schloss said. "If they're at the center right now, they could be doing a good many things we couldn't detect, under a very low screen. However, they would already have detected us and done something about us if that were the case. Let's assume we're ahead until the instruments say otherwise; I think that's a fairly safe assumption."

"How much longer to the center?" Hazleton said.

"A few months, perhaps," Retma said. "If we're right in assuming that this curve has a flat spot on top of it."

"And the necessary machinery?"

"The last installation will be in at the end of this week," Amalfi said. "We can begin countdown the moment we arrive ... providing that we can learn to handle equipment operating at ten or a hundred times its rated efficiency, without blowing some of it out in the process. We'd better start practicing the moment the system is complete."

"Amen," Hazleton said fervently. "Can I borrow your slide-rule? I've got a few setting-up exercises I'd better start on right now." He left the room. Amalfi looked uneasily out at the night. He would almost have preferred it had the Web of Hercules been there ahead of them and promptly taken a sitting-duck shot at them; this uncertainty as to whether or not someone really was lurking out there—coupled with the totally unknown nature of their opponents—was more unsettling than open battle. However, there was no help for it; and if He really was first, it gave them a sizable advantage. . . .

And their only advantage. The only defenses Amalfi had been able to conceive and jury-rig for He depended importantly on actually being at the metagalactic center, able to make use of the almost instant number of weak resultant forces that could be used there to produce major responses—the buttercup-vs.-Sirius effect Bonner had so characterized. In this area he found Miramon and the Hevian council oddly uncooperative, even flaccid, as though mounting a defense for the whole planet was too big a concept for them to grasp—a hard thing to believe in view of the prodigious concepts they had mastered and put to work since Amalfi had first met them as savages up to their knees in mud and violence. Well, if he did not yet understand them, he was not going to make his understanding perfect in a few months; and at least Miramon was perfectly willing to let Amalfi and Hazleton direct Hevian labor in putting together their almost wholly theoretical breadboard rigs.

"Some of these," Hazleton had said, looking at a just-completed tangle of wires, lenses, antennae and kernels of metal with rueful respect, "ought to prove pretty potent in the pinch. I just wish I knew which ones they were." Which, unfortunately, was a perfect précis of the situation.

But the needles recording the stresses and currents of space around He continued to fall; those recording the output of Hevian equipment continued to rise. On May 23rd 4104, both sets of meters rose suddenly to their high ends and jammed madly against the pegs, and the whole planet rang suddenly with the awful, tortured roar of spindizzies driven beyond endurance. Miramon's hand flashed out for the manual master switch so fast that Amalfi could not tell whether it had been he or the City Fathers that cut the power. Maybe even Miramon did not know; at least he must have gotten to the cut off button within a hair of the automatic reaction.

The howl died. Silence. The Survivors looked at each other.

"Well," Amalfi said, "we're here, evidently." For some reason, he felt wildly elated—a wholly irrational reaction, but he did not stop to analyze it.

"So we are," Hazleton said, his eyes snapping. "Now what the hell happened to the metering? I can understand the local apparatus going wild—but why did the imput meters from outside rise instead of dropping back to zero?"

"Noise, I believe," Retma said.

"Noise? How so?"

"It takes power to operate a meter—not a great deal, but it consumes some. Consequently, the input meters ran as wild as the machines did, because operating at peak efficiency with no incoming signals to register, they picked up the signals generated by their own functioning."

"I don't like that," Hazleton said. "Do we have any way of finding out on what level it's safe to run *any* instrument under these circumstances? I'd like to see generation curves on the effect so we can make such a calculation—but there's not much point in consulting the records if we just burn out the machine in the process."

Amalfi picked up the only instrument on the Hevian board that was "his"—the microphone to the City Fathers. "Are you still alive down there?" he said.

"YES, MR. MAYOR," the answer came promptly. Miramon looked startled; since everything of which he had any knowledge had gone dead, even the lights—they were sitting bathed only in the barely ascertainable glow of the zodiacal light, that belt of tenuous ionized gas in He's atmosphere brought to life by He's magnetic field, plus the even dimmer glow of the few nearby galaxies—the sudden voice of the speakers must have alarmed him.

"Good. What are you operating on?"

"WET CELLS IN SERIES AT TWENTY-FIVE HUNDRED VOLTS."

"*All* of you?"

"YES, MR. MAYOR."

Amalfi grinned in the virtual darkness. "All right, apply your efficency figures to a set of standard instrumental situations."

"DONE."

"Give me an operating level for Mr. Miramon's line down to you, allowing for pilot lights on his board so he can see his settings."

"MR. MAYOR, THAT IS NOT NECESSARY. WE

HAVE ALREADY RESET THE MASTER CUTOUT AT THE NECESSARY BLOWPOINT LEVEL. WE CAN RE-ACTUATE ALL THE CIRCUITS AT ONCE."

"No, don't do that, we don't want the spindizzies back on too—"

"THE SPINDIZZIES ARE OFF," the City Fathers said, with austere simplicity.

"Well, Miramon? Do you trust them? Or would you rather have them tie in to you first and print their data for you, so you can turn the planet back on piecemeal?"

He heard Miramon draw in his breath slightly to answer, but he was never to know what that answer would have been; for at the same moment, Miramon's whole board came alive at once.

"Hey!" Amalfi squalled. "Wait for orders down there, dammit!"

"STANDING ORDERS, MR. MAYOR. AFTER COUNTDOWN BEGINS WE ARE TO ACT AT THE FIRST SIGN OF OUTSIDE INTERFERENCE. COUNTDOWN BEGAN TWELVE HUNDRED SECONDS AGO, AND SEVEN SECONDS AGO OUTSIDE INTERFERENCE BECAME STATISTICALLY SIGNIFICANT."

"What do they mean?" Miramon said, trying to read every instrument on his board at once. "I thought I understood your language, Mayor Amalfi, but—"

"The City Fathers don't speak Okie, they speak Machine," Amalfi said grimly. "What they mean is that the Web of Hercules—if that's who it is—is coming in on us. And coming in on us fast."

With a single, circumscribed flip of his closed fingers, Miramon turned off the lights.

Blackness. Then, seeping faintly over the windows around the tower, the air-glow of the zodiacal light; then, still later, the dim pinwheels of island universes. On Miramon's board, there was a single spearpoint of yellow-orange which was only the heater of a vacuum tube smaller than an acorn; in this central gloom at the heart and birthplace of the universe, it was almost blinding. Amalfi had to turn his back on it to maintain the profound dark-adaptation that his vision needed to operate at all in the tower on his mountain.

While he waited for his sight to come back, he wondered at the speed of Miramon's reaction, and the motives behind it. Surely the Hevian could not believe that a set of pilot lights in a tower on top of a remote mountain could be bright enough to be seen from space; for that matter, blacking out even as large an object as a whole planet could serve no military purpose—it had been two millennia since any reasonably sophisticated enemy depended upon light alone to see by. And where in Miramon's whole lifetime could he have acquired the blackout reflex? It made no sense; yet Miramon had restored the blackout with all the trained positiveness of a boxer riding with a punch.

When the light began to grow, he had his answer—and no time left to wonder how Miramon had anticipated it.

It began as though the destruction of the inter-universal messenger were about to repeat itself in reverse, encompassing the whole of creation in the process. Crawls of greenish-yellow light were beginning to move high up in the Hevian sky, at first as ghostly as auroral traces, then with a purposeful writhing and brightening which seemed as horrifyingly like life as the copulation of a mass of green-gold nematode worms seen under phase-contrast lighting. Particle counters began to chatter on the board, and Hazleton jumped to monitor the cumulative readings.

"Where is that stuff coming from—can you tell?" Amalfi said.

"It seems to come from nearly a hundred discrete point-sources, surrounding us in a sphere with a diameter of about a light year," Miramon said. He sounded preoccupied; he was doing something with controls whose purpose was unknown to Amalfi.

"Hmm. Ships, without a doubt. Well, now we know where they get their name, anyhow. But what is it they're using?"

"That's easy," Hazleton said grimly. "It's anti-matter."

"How can that be?"

"Look at the frequency analysis on this secondary radiation we're getting, and you'll see. Every one of those ships must be primarily a particle accelerator of prodigious size. They're sending streams of stripped heavy anti-matter atoms right down the gravitational ingeodesics toward us—that's what makes the paths the stuff is following look so twisted. They've found a way to generate and project primary cosmics made of anti-matter atoms, and in quantity. When they strike our atmosphere, both disintegrate—"

"And the planet gets a dose of high-energy gamma radiation," Amalfi said. "And they must have known how to do it for a long time, since they're named after the technique. Helleshin! What a way to conquer a planet! They can either sterilize the populace, or kill it off, at will, without ever even coming close to the place."

"We've had the sterility dose already," Hazleton said quietly.

"That can hardly matter now," Estelle said, in an even softer voice.

"The killing dose won't matter either," Hazleton said, "Radiation sickness takes months to develop, even when it's going to be fatal."

"They could disable us quickly enough," Amalfi said harshly. "We've got to stop this somehow. We need these last days!"

"What do you propose?" Hazleton said. "Nothing that we've set up will work in a globe at a distance of a light year ... except—"

"Except the base surge," Amalfi said. "Let's use it, and quick."

"What is this?" Miramon said.

"We've got your spindizzies set up for a single burn-out overload pulse. In the position we're in, the resulting single wave-front ought to tie space into knots for—well, we don't know how far the effect will carry, but a long way."

"Maybe even all the way to the limits of the universe," Dr. Schloss said.

"Well, what of it?" Amalfi demanded. "It's due to be destroyed anyhow in only ten days—"

"Not if you destroy it first," Schloss said. "If it isn't here when the anti-matter universe passes through it, all bets are off; there'll be nothing we can do."

"It'll still be here."

"Not in any useful sense—not if the matter in it is tied up in billions of gravitational whirlpools. Better let the Web kill us than destroy the future evolution of two universes, Amalfi! Can't you give over playing god, even now?"

"All right," Amalfi said. "Look at those dosimeters, and look at that sky. What have you to suggest?"

The sky was now one even intensity of glow, like a full overcast lit by a dull sun. Outside, the lower mountains of the range stood with their tree-covered flanks, so completely without shadow as to suggest that the windows ringing the tower were actually parts of a flat mural done by an unskilled hand. The counters had given over chattering and were putting out a subdued roar.

"Only what I just suggested," Schloss said hopelessly.

"Load up on anti-radiation drugs, and hope we can stay on our feet for ten days. What else is there? They've got us."

"Excuse me," Miramon said. "That is not altogether certain. We have some resources of our own. I have just launched one; it may be sufficient."

"What is it?" Amalfi demanded. "I didn't know you mounted any weapons. How long will we have to wait before it acts?"

"One question at a time," Miramon said. "Of course we mount weapons. We never talk about them, because there were children on our planet, and still are, the gods receive them. But we had to face the fact that we might some day be invested by a hostile fleet, considering how far afield we were ranging from our home galaxy, and how many stars we were visiting. Thus we provided several means for defense. One of these we meant never to use, but we have just used it now."

"And that is?" Hazleton said tensely.

"We would never have told you, except for the coming end," Miramon said. "You have praised us as chemists, Mayor Amalfi. We have applied chemistry to physics. We discovered how to poison an electromagnetic field by resonance—the way the process of catalysis is poisoned in chemistry. The poison field propagates itself along a carrier wave, and controlling field, almost any signal which is continuous and conforms to the Faraday equations. Look."

He pointed out the window. The light did not seem to have lessened any; but it was now mottled with leprous patches. In a space of seconds, the patches spread and flowed into each other, until the light was now confined to isolated luminous clouds, rapidly being eaten away at the edges, like dead cells being dissolved by the enzymes of decay bacteria.

When the sky went totally dark, Amalfi could see the hundred streamers of the particle streams pointed inward at He; at least it looked a hundred, though actually he could hardly have seen more than fifteen from any one spot on the planet. And these too were being eaten away, receding into blackness.

The counters went back to stuttering, but they did not quite stop.

"What happens when the effect gets back to the ships?" Web asked.

"It will poison the circuits themselves," Miramon said.

"The entities in the ships will suffer total nerve-block. They will die, and so will the ships. Nothing will be left but a hundred hulks."

Amalfi let out a long, ragged sigh.

"No wonder you weren't interested in our breadboard rigs," he said. "With a thing like that, you could have become another Web of Hercules yourselves."

"No," Miramon said. "That we could never become."

"Gods of all stars!" Hazleton said. "Is it over? As fast as that?"

Miramon's smile was wintery. "I doubt that we will hear from the Web of Hercules again," he said. "But what your City Fathers call the countdown continues. It is only ten days to the end of the world."

Hazleton turned back to the dosimeters. For a moment, he simply stared at them. Then, to Amalfi's astonishment, he began to laugh.

"What's so funny?" Amalfi growled.

"See for yourself. If Miramon's people had ever tangled with the Web in the real world, they would have lost."

"Why?"

"Because," Hazleton said, wiping his eyes, "while he was beating them off, we all passed the lethal dose of hard radiation. We are all dead as doornails as we sit here!"

"And this is a joke?" Amalfi said.

"Of course it's a joke, boss. It doesn't make the faintest bit of difference. We don't live in that kind of 'real world' any more. We have a dose. In two weeks we'll begin to become dizzy, and lose our hair, and vomit. In three weeks we'll be dead. And you *still* don't see the joke?"

"I see it," Amalfi said. "I can subtract ten from fourteen and get four; you mean we'll live until we die."

"I can't abide a man who kills my jokes."

"It's a pretty old joke," Amalfi said slowly. "But maybe it's still funny, at that; if it was good enough for Aristophanes, I guess it's good enough for me."

"I think that's pretty damn funny, all right." Dee said with bitter fury. Miramon was staring from one New Earthman to another with an expression of utter bafflement. Amalfi smiled.

"Don't say so unless you think so, Dee," he said. "It's always been a joke, after all. The death of one man is just as funny as the death of a universe. Don't repudiate the last laugh of all. It may be the only legacy we'll leave."

"MIDNIGHT," the City Fathers said. "THE COUNT IS ZERO MINUS NINE."

CHAPTER EIGHT: The Triumph of Time

As Amalfi opened the door and went back into the room, the City Fathers said:

"N-DAY. ZERO MINUS ONE HOUR."

At this hour, everything had meaning; or nothing had; it depended on what had been worth investing with meaning over a lifetime of several thousand years. Amalfi had left the room to go to the toilet. Now he would never do that again, nor would anybody else; the demise of the whole was so close at hand that it was outrunning even the physiological rhythms of the body by which man has told time since he first thought to count it. Was diuresis as worth mourning as love? Well, perhaps it was; the senses should have their mourners too; no sensation, no thought, no emotion is meaningless if it is the last of its kind.

And so farewell to all tensions and all reliefs, from amour to urea, from entrances to exits, from redundancy to noise, from beer to skittles. "What's new?" Amalfi said.

"Nothing any more," Gifford Bonner said. "We're waiting. Sit down, John, and have a drink."

He sat down at the long table and looked at the glass before him. It was red, but there was a faint tinge of blue in the liquid too, independent and not adding up to violet even in the bad light of the fluorescents in the midst of dead center's ultimate blackness. At the lip of the glass a faint meniscus climbed upward from the wine, and little tendrils of condensation meandered back down. Amalfi tasted it tentatively; it was raw and peppery—the Hevians were not great wine-growers, their climate had been too chancy for that—but even the sting of it was an edgy pleasure that made him sigh.

"We should suit up at the half hour," Dr. Schloss said. "I'd leave more free time, except that some of us haven't been inside a spacesuit in centuries, and some of us never. We don't want to take chances on their not being trim and tight."

"I thought we were going to be surrounded by some sort of field," Web said.

"Not for long, Web. Let me go through this once more, to be sure everybody has it straight in his head. We will be protected by a stasis-field during the actual instant of transition, when time will to all intents and purposes be abolished—it becomes just another coordinate of Hilbert space then. That will carry us over into the first second of time on the other side, after the catastrophe. But then the field will go down, because the spindizzies, which will be generating it, will have been annihilated. We will then find ourselves occupying as many independent sets of four dimensions as there are people in this room, and every set completely empty. The spacesuits won't protect you long, either, because you'll be the only body of organized energy and matter in your particular, individual universe; as soon as you disturb the metrical frame of that universe, you, the suit, the air in it, the power in the accumulators, everything will surge outwards, creating space as it goes. Every man his own monobloc. But if we don't have the suits on for the crossing, not even that much will happen."

"I wish you wouldn't be so graphic," Dee complained, but her heart did not really seem to be in it. She was, Amalfi noted, wearing that same peculiarly strained expression she had worn when she had said that she wanted to bear Amalfi a child. Some instinct made him turn to look at Estelle and Web. All their hands were piled up together confidingly on the table. Estelle's face was serene, and her eyes were luminous, almost like a child waiting for a party to begin. Web's expression was more difficult to interpret: he was frowning slightly, more in puzzlement than in worry, as if he couldn't quite understand why he was not more worried than he was.

Outside, there was a thin whining sound which rose suddenly to a howl and then died away again. It was windy today on the mountain.

"What about the table, the glasses, the chairs?" Amalfi asked. "Do those go with us too?"

"No," Dr. Schloss said. "We don't want to risk having any possible condensation nuclei near us. We're using a modification of the technique we used to build Object 4101-Alephnull in the future; the furniture will start to make the crossing with us, but we'll use the last available energy to push it a micro-second into the past. The result will be that it will stay in our universe. What its fate will be thereafter, we can only guess."

Amalfi lifted his glass reflectively. It was silky in his fingers; the Hevians made fine glass.

"This frame of reference I'll find myself in," Amalfi said. "It will really have no structure at all?"

"Only what you impose on it," Retma said. "It will not be space, and will have no metrical frame. In other words, your presence there will be intolerable—"

"Thank you," Amalfi said drily, to Retma's obvious bafflement. After a moment the scientist went on without comment: "What I am trying to say is that your mass will create a space to accommodate it, and it will take on the metrical frame that already exists in you. What happens after that will depend upon in what order you dismantle the suit. I would recommend discharging the oxygen bottles first, since to start a universe like our present one will require a considerable amount of plasma. The oxygen in the suit itself will be sufficient for the time at your disposal. As the last act, discharge the suit's energy; this will, in effect, touch a match to the explosion."

"How large a universe will be the outcome, eventually?" Mark said. "I seem to remember that the original monobloc was large, as well as ultra-condensed."

"Yes, it will be a small universe," Retma said, "perhaps fifty light years across at its greatest expansion. But that will be only at first. As continuous creation comes into play, more atoms will be added to the whole, until a mass is reached sufficient to form a monobloc on the next contraction. Or so we see it; you must understand that this is all somewhat conjectural. We did not have the time to learn everything that we wanted to know."

"ZERO MINUS THIRTY MINUTES."

"That's it," Dr. Schloss said. "Suits, everybody. We can continue to talk by radio."

Amalfi drained the wine. Another last act. He got into his suit, slowly recapturing his old familiarity with the grotesque apparatus. He saw to it that the radio switch was open, but he found that he could think of nothing further to say. That he was about to die suddenly had very little reality to him, in the face of the greater death of which his would be a part. No comment that occurred to him seemed anything but the uttermost of trivia.

There was some technical conversation as they checked each other out in the suits, with particular attention to Web and Estelle. Then the talk died out, as if they, too, found words intolerable.

"ZERO MINUS FIFTEEN MINUTES."

"Do you understand what is about to happen to you?" Amalfi said suddenly.

"YES, MR. MAYOR. WE ARE TO BE TURNED OFF AT ZERO."

"That's good enough." He wondered, however, if they thought that they might be turned on again in the future. It was of course foolish to think of them as entertaining anything even vaguely resembling an emotion, but nevertheless he decided not to say anything which might disabuse them. They were only machines, but they were also old friends and allies.

"ZERO MINUS TEN MINUTES."

"It's all going so fast all of a sudden," Dee's voice whispered in the earphones. "Mark, I . . . I don't want it to happen."

"No more do I," Hazleton said. "But it will happen anyhow. I only wish I'd lived a more human life than I did. But it happened the way it happened, and so there's no more to say."

"I wish I could believe," Estelle said, "that there will be no sorrow in the universe I make."

"Then create nothing, my dear," Gifford Bonner said. "Stay here. Creation means sorrow, always and always."

"And joy," Estelle said.

"Well, yes. There's that."

"ZERO MINUS FIVE MINUTES."

"I think we can do without the rest of the countdown," Amalfi said. "Otherwise from now on they will count every minute, and they'll do the last one by seconds. Do we want to go out to the tune of that gabble? Anybody want to say 'yes'?"

They were silent. "Very well," Amalfi said. "Stop counting."

"VERY WELL, MR. MAYOR. GOOD-BYE."

"Good-bye," Amalfi said with amazement.

"I won't say that, if you don't mind," Hazleton said in a choked voice. "It brings the deprivation too close for me to stand. I hope everybody will consider it said."

Amalfi nodded, then realized that the gesture could not be seen inside the helmet.

"I agree," he said. "But I don't feel deprived. I loved you all. You have my love to take with you, and I have it too."

"It is the only thing in the universe that one can give and still have," Miramon said.

The deck throbbed under Amalfi's feet. The machines were preparing for their instant of unimaginable thrust. The sound of their power was comforting; so was the solidity of the deck, the table, the room, the mountain, the world—

"I think—" Gifford Bonner said.

And with those words, it ended.

There was nothing at first but the inside of the suit. Outside there was not even blackness, but only nothingness, something not to be seen, like that which is not

seen outside of the cone of vision; one does not see
blackness behind one's own head, one simply does not see
in that direction at all; and so here. Yet for a little while,
Amalfi found that he was still conscious of his friends,
still a part of the circle though the room and everything in
it had vanished from around them. He did not know how
he knew that they were still there, but he could feel it.

He knew that there was no hope of speaking to them
again; and indeed, as he tried to grasp how he knew they
were there at all, he realized that they were drawing away
from him. The circle was widening. The mute figures
became smaller—not by distance, for there was no distance here, but nevertheless in some way they were passing out of each other's ken. Amalfi tried to lift his hand in
farewell, but found it almost impossible. By the time he
had only half completed the gesture, the others had faded
and were gone, leaving behind only a memory also fading
rapidly, like the memory of a fragrance.

Now he was alone and must do what he must do. Since
his hand was raised, he continued the gesture to let the gas
out of his oxygen bottles. The unmedium in which he was
suspended seemed to be becoming a little less resistant;
already a metrical frame was establishing itself. Yet it was
almost as difficult to halt the motion as it had been to
start it.

Nevertheless, he halted it. Of what use was another
universe of the kind he had just seen die? Nature had
provided two of those, and had doomed them at the same
moment. Why not try something else? Retma in his caution, Estelle in her compassion, Dee in her fear all would
be giving birth to some version of the standard model; but
Amalfi had driven the standard model until all the bolts
had come out of it, and was so tired at even the thought
of it that he could hardly bring himself to breathe. What
would happen if, instead, he simply touched the detonator
button on his chest, and let all the elements of which he
and the suit were composed flash into plasma at the same
instant?

That was unknowable. But the unknowable was what he
wanted. He brought his hand down again.

There was no reason to delay. Retma had already
pronounced the epitaph for Man: *We did not have the
time to learn everything that we wanted to know.*

"So be it," Amalfi said. He touched the button over his
heart.

Creation began.

AFTERWORD:

THE EARTHMANIST CULTURE:
*CITIES IN FLIGHT as a Spenglerian History**

Oswald Spengler's *The Decline of the West* [1] has been acknowledged by James Blish as one of the sources of CITIES IN FLIGHT. He has said, "My own 'Okie' stories were . . . founded in Spengler." [2]

Spengler is a difficult thinker—or at least a difficult writer—as anyone will discover who attempts to make a table similar to the one that appears with this Afterword. Part of the difficulty stems from our tendency to equate cultures with empires and other political units, a delusion from which Toynbee should have freed us even if Spengler did not. A related difficulty lies in the title: "the decline of the West" inevitably suggests "the decline and fall of the Roman Empire," and one is likely to assume that Spengler is predicting the military conquest of the West rather than merely arguing that the West is in a certain kind of decline. Still another lies in the fact that Spengler uses the words *culture* and *civilization* sometimes in such a way that they appear to be synonymous with *society*, and sometimes as technical terms with opposed meanings. Whatever may be true of things, two words synonymous with a third are not necessarily equal to each other, and we should understand from the beginning that for Spengler, *culture* and *civilization* are opposed states in the spiritual history of a society:

A Culture is born in the moment when a great soul awakens out of the proto-spirituality of ever-childish

* An earlier version of this analysis appeared in *Riverside Quarterly*, and that version is Copyright © 1968 by Leland Sapiro. Our thanks to him and to the author for permission to include this revised version in this volume.

humanity, and detaches itself, a form from the formless, a bounded and mortal thing from the boundless
and enduring. . . . It dies when this soul has actualized
the full sum of its possibilities in the shape of peoples,
languages, dogmas, arts, states, sciences, and reverts
into the proto-soul. . . . The aim once attained—the
idea, the entire content of inner possibilities, fulfilled
and made actual—the Culture suddenly hardens, it
mortifies, its blood congeals, its force breaks down, and
it becomes *civilization*, the thing which we feel and
understand in the words Egypticism, Byzantinism, Man-
darinism. As such it may, like the worn-out giant of the
primeval forest, thrust its decaying branches toward the
sky for hundreds or thousands of years, as we see in
China, in India, in the Islamic world. It was thus that
the Classical Civilization rose gigantic, in the Imperial
age, with a false semblance of youth and strength and
fulness. . . . [I, 106]

The West has reached full civilization, and its culture is
dead, but its civilization, and its empire, may endure for
centuries or millennia.

Now, the explicit Spenglerianism of CITIES IN FLIGHT
is highly dubious in some of its details (see below, #2),
and rather absurd overall. The overall absurdity lies in the
basic idea of the "cultural morphologist":

Chris recognized the term, from his force-feeding in
Spengler. It denoted a scholar who could look at any
culture at any stage in its development, relate it to all
other cultures at similar stages, and come up with specific
predictions of how these people would react to a given
proposal or event. . . . [ALFTS, 233]

Spengler never uses the term "cultural morphologist," and
he would surely never have imagined that his work could
be put to any such narrow uses. If a culture is an organism, you can make for a culture predictions of the kind
that can be made for any organism: e.g., that a baby boy
will become a man, not a woman or a horse, and that,
barring accidents, the man will pass through middle age to
old age and death. To be sure, the more information you
have, the more particular you can be in your predictions,
but obviously there are limits beyond which you cannot
go. Indeed, that there are such limits in anything and
everything is perhaps the most fundamental idea of Spengler. As a matter of fact, the cultural morphologists of
CITIES IN FLIGHT never actually practice their trade:
the various "cultures" with which the heroes deal are

never presented with enough fullness to allow for any kind of Spenglerian assessment; the various stories turn on co-incidence or on individual psychology and would not be essentially different if explicit references to cultural morphology were entirely eliminated—which could be done by deleting a handful of sentences.

Although some of the inconsistencies in CITIES IN FLIGHT surely result from authorial forgetfulness,* they are too numerous and too prominent to be regarded as anything other than an essential feature of the overall story. Since point of view is rigidly controlled throughout the work, every statement can be attributed to one or another of the various characters. Given this fact, we can make sense of the tetralogy by regarding it, not as a fiction in which a universe has been created by an omniscient, omnipotent author, but as historical narrative with a large admixture of myth; that is, by assuming that behind the sometimes accurate, sometimes erroneous, sometimes mythical narrative there is an actual history.

Thus, the first volume of CITIES IN FLIGHT gives us an intelligently Spenglerian view of the near future, and the other three, albeit very sketchily, the life story of a Spenglerian culture. In comparison with most science-fiction novels and series, CITIES IN FLIGHT is a very rich work indeed.

1. *Blish's Twenty-First Century: The Coming of Caesarism*

In the first volume, although the term is not used there, MacHinery is a successful practitioner of what Spengler describes as Caesarism [II, 431–35]. Dr. Corsi's reasons for believing that "scientific method doesn't work any more" [TSHS, 14–15], although not expressed in Spenglerian terms, are thoroughly consistent with Spengler's discussion of "conclusive" scientific thought [I, 417–28]. The volume also devotes some space to an adventist religious movement, the Witnesses, which seems to be a product of that "second religiousness" among the masses

* Forgetfulness, alas, did indeed play a role. The volumes were written roughly in the order III, I, IV, II over a period of 15 years (during which I was also writing other books), and inconsistencies crept in despite my best intentions to keep them out. For this edition, I have corrected a large number of those pointed out to me by Dr. Mullen, where I agreed that they *were* inconsistencies. Where I didn't, I let them stand—along with Dr. Mullen's objections to them.—J. B.

which Spengler considers an inevitable concomitant of Caesarism [II, 310-11, 435]. Finally, although Helmuth is wrong about the pyramids, he is correctly Spenglerian in regarding giganticism as evidence that a culture is dead [I, 291-95], and his remark on the Martian canali is certainly, on the part of Mr. Blish, a brilliant Spenglerian touch [TSHS, 119]. All in all, then, the first volume of CITIES IN FLIGHT is a thoroughly Spenglerian work.

2. *Blish's Twenty-First Century: Two Cultures or One?*

In Blish's universe "historians generally agree that the fall of the West must be dated no later than the year 2105" [ALFTS, 169]. They also agree in regarding the great conflict of the twentieth and twenty-first centuries, that between the "West" and the communist alliance (later called the Bureaucratic State), as a conflict between "rival cultures" [ALFTS, 168; ECH, 237–241].

It is true that Spengler distinguished between the Russian soul and the Western:

> The death-impulse . . . for the West is the passion of drive all-ways into infinite space, whereas for Russians it is an expressing and expanding of self till "it" in the man becomes identical with the boundless plain itself. . . . The idea of a Russian's being an astronomer! He does not see the stars at all, he sees only the horizon. Instead of the vault he sees the down-hang of the heavens—something that somewhere combines with the plain to form the horizon. For him the Copernican system . . . is spiritually contemptible. [II, 295n]

We find a similar passage in *The Milky Way: Five Cultural Portraits:*

> Space flight had been a natural, if late, outcome of Western thought patterns, which had always been ambitious for the infinite. The Soviets, however, were opposed so bitterly to the idea that they would not even allow their fiction writers to mention it. Where the West had soared from the rock of earth like a sequoia, the Soviets spread like lichens over the planet, tightening their grip, satisfied to be at the bases of the pillars of sunlight the West had sought to ascend [ECH, 238].

If we assume that the time stream of Blish's universe separates from our own sometime around 1950, we will have no occasion to speak of sputnik. Even so, the question still remains whether the Soviets, or the Bureaucratic State, can be said to belong to a Spenglerian culture distinct from that of the West. In the first place, to say so is to reject Spengler's view that Peter the Great succeeded in his Westernizing efforts, that Russia is therefore a part of the Western Civilization, and that communism is merely a continuance of Western influence [II, 192-96]. To be sure, Spengler believed that a new culture would be born in Russia in the near future ("to Dostoyevski's Christianity [as opposed to Tolstoi's] the next thousand years will belong" [II, 196]), but the Bureaucratic State can hardly be considered an expression of either Dostoyevski's Christianity in particular or of springtime culture in general. In the second place, Spengler would surely reject the only reason offered by our future historians for considering the cultures distinct: that Russia differs from the West in not having "traditional libertarian political institutions" [ALFTS, 168], for such institutions are neither universal in nor peculiar to the West but are instead the products, in every Spenglerian culture, of fifth political epoch, Revolution and Napoleonism (see the table that appears with this essay). In predicting that the West will reach Caesarism by 2000, Spengler is predicting the end of such institutions in the West utterly without regard to any external conflict.* All this being so, it follows that the great conflict between the "West" and the Soviets is simply a struggle between rival power blocs and that we must therefore regard the victory of the Bureaucratic State as establishing the Final Political Form of the Western Culture.[3]

3. The Life Story of the Earthmanist Culture

The life of the Spenglerian culture begins with the birth of a "myth of the great style" [1, 339]. The new myth develops under two kinds of emphasis: that given it by the nobles and that given it by the priests. In the Western

---

* A wholly valid argument. Nevertheless I have not changed the text, because—particularly in Vol. I—I was trying to make the point that when two Civilizations come in conflict with one another, the issue is resolved long in advance of formal military victory by each side becoming more like the other. The point would have seemed trivial to Spengler, who points out that all Civilizations are alike in their essential features to begin with; but in our century the process is highly visible once one's attention has been called to it, an opportunity I couldn't (and can't) resist.— J. B.

Culture, with its early rivalry between emperor and pope,
the opposition between the emphases was very strong. For
the Classical Culture the equally strong opposition has
been largely obscured by the fact that only the military
myth has survived in detail (e.g., in Homer). In the
Arabian Culture, where the ruler was ordinarily both
emperor and pope, the opposition was of little importance. In the Earthmanist Culture, where again only the
military myth—the Vegan War—has survived in any detail, the opposition seems to be of even less importance in
that the myth seems to have been overwhelmingly military
rather than priestly. Even so, its purpose would seem to be
primarily religious in that it has evidently developed as a
means of relieving the Earthmen of a great burden of
guilt.

The myth makes it appear that a small number of
Earthmen were unaccountably able to prevail over a vast
and enormously powerful "tyranny" which deserved to be
completely destroyed. The fact must surely be that the
Vegan Civilization was in the last stages of its Final
Political Form with the concomitant "enfeeblement . . . of
the imperial machinery against young peoples eager for
spoil, or alien conquerors" [Spengler, I, Table iii; cf. the
table with this essay]. Though outnumbered a million to
one in total population, the Earthmen may well have been
able to muster nearly as many fighting men as the Vegans
at any given place and time, and they must have come
into interstellar space with superior weapons or tactics or
both—and with ferocity such as the Vegans had perhaps
never experienced but for which there are precedents
aplenty in the history of Earth, itself, the most cogent
being perhaps the destruction wrought in Persia and
Mesopotamia by the Mongols of Hulagu. And it was not
only Vega II that felt the ferocity of the Earthmen, nor
only the Vegans: "In 2394 one of the cities . . . was
responsible for the sacking of the new Earth colony on
Thor V; this act of ferocity earned for them the nickname
of 'the Mad Dogs,' but it gradually became a model for
dealing with Vegan planets" [ALFTS, 170]. In sum, at
the close of the Vegan War the Earthmen had to choose
whether they would be proud or ashamed of what
they had done. Their shame brought about the trial of
Admiral Hrunta—the great figure of the hundred-year
war, its Agamemnon, its Charlemagne, its Arthur—for
genocide; their determination to be proud resulted not

only in the establishment of the Hruntan Empire but also in the birth of the Earthmanist Culture.

The attempts of the Bureaucratic State to bring Hrunta to justice culminate in the Battle of BD 40°4048', which is said to have been "indecisive" [ALFTS, 170], but which is quite decisive in that it proves the State incapable of controlling more than a very limited volume of space. Since Hrunta's empire is only "the first of many such gimcrack 'empires' . . . to spawn on the fringes of Earth's jurisidiction" [TTOT, 469], we can put down the year of the Battle, 2464, as marking the beginning of the feudal order. Up to this time such Earthmen as have not been under the direct control of the Bureaucratic State have presumably been organized simply as tribes or war bands, each man acknowledging his military superiors only as temporary leaders and feeling loyalty only to the abstract concept of Earth; but now the temporary becomes apparently permanent, and loyalty finds concrete object in this or that leader or "emperor."

In 2522 the Bureaucratic State collapses, the new Earth government proclaims a general amnesty, and the "Empty Years" begin; the Earthmanist Culture is thus free to develop in its own way. Admiral Hrunta is poisoned in 3089, and his death is followed by the "rapid Balkanization of the Hruntan Empire, which was never even at its best highly cohesive" [ALFTS, 171]; in 3111 Arpad Hrunta is installed as "Emperor of Space." Here we seem to have the Interregnum which, according to Spengler, occurs in every culture and "forms the boundary between the feudal union and the class state" [II, 375]. Since Hruntanism is a religion as well as a dynastic principle, and since periods of religious reformation coincide with the transition from feudalism to the aristocratic state [II, 386], we are perhaps justified in listing Arpad Hrunta in our table as a religious reformer.

In an aristocratic state the king's authority depends for its existence on the power of one or another of the aristocratic factions. The "absolute" state emerges when the king allies himself with the bourgeoisie and thus finds strength enough to suppress aristocratic disorder. In Earthmanist society as a whole, Earth is king, the various empires, duchies, and republics are the aristocracy, and the Okie cities are the bourgeoisie. Here the development into absolutism seems to culminate in 3602 with the "reduction" of the Duchy of Gort, the death of Arpad

Hrunta, and the "dissolution of the Empire," all brought about by the "recrudescent Earth police" [TTOT, 470], for we now have a galactic society in which the Earth police keep the spacelanes clear for Okie commerce [ECH, 398–399]. Since the Duchy of Gort represents an extreme form of Hruntanism, and since puritanism is a concomitant of the effort to preserve the aristocratic state [Spengler, II, 386n, 424], we can perhaps list the Duchy as an instance of puritanism.

When aristocratic factionalism has been suppressed, the king and the aristocracy become allies against the rising power of the bourgeoisie, who soon become ripe for revolution, as do the Okies after the "collapse of the germanium standard" in 3900.* The gathering of the mayors aboard Buda-Pesht [ECH, 370–381] and the March on Earth that follows, even though it results in apparent defeat in the Battle of Earth, can be regarded as the 1789, and the passage of the anti-Okie bill in 3976 as the 1815, of Earthman history.

At this point, so far as the galaxy proper is concerned, the story of the Earthmanist Culture comes to a sudden end, for the Earthman domains are invaded and conquered by a non-human "culture," the Web of Hercules [TTOT, 471]. Since this is so, we are unable to test our evaluation of the 3900-3976 period against later events. Even so, and even though Mayor Amalfi, the principal hero and leading cultural morphologist of CITIES IN FLIGHT, believes that the Okies have been completely defeated [ECH, 421–422], I can see no reason to believe that the restoration of the Ancien Regime in 3976 would have been any more permanent than it was in 1815.

4. The Triumph of Time over Space

Following the Battle of Earth, New York moves from the galaxy proper to the Greater Magellanic Cloud. The military and political events that ensue upon its arrival there are perhaps, and the philosophy of Stochasticism is certainly, consistent with the beginning of the Period of Contending States. Here the beginning is all that we can know anything about, for once again history is cut short—

---

* After this point, cleaning up the inconsistencies in the chronology involved advancing all the dates, and so I have altered Dr. Mullen's subsequent dates—which followed the original Chronology —to reflect the changes.—J. B.

this time by the "totally universal physical cataclysm" of the year 4104 [TTOT, 471].

The fourth volume of CITIES IN FLIGHT in its U.S. edition bears the title *The Triumph of Time*. Since the principal theme here is not especially Spenglerian, my purpose is simply to note that this title, and indeed the story itself, could have been inspired, whether or not it was, by a passage on Spengler's final page:

> Time triumphs over Space, and it is Time whose inexorable movement embeds the ephemeral incident of the Culture, on this planet, in the incident of Man—a form wherein the incident life flows on for a time, while behind it all the streaming horizons of geological and stellar histories pile up in the light-world of our eyes. [II, 507]

Footnotes

1. The volume-page references in this essay are to the translation of Spengler by Charles Francis Atkinson (two volumes: New York: Knopf, 1926, 1928). Spengler completed this work in late 1922.

2. *The Issue at Hand* (Chicago: Advent, 1964), p. 60n.

3. Spengler uses the phrases "centralized bureaucracy—state" in connection with the Egyptian third political epoch [I, Table iii], but I hardly think that Blish's Bureaucratic State is intended to be an aristocratic state.

4. This table is based primarily on the three tables that appear at the end of Spengler's first volume: "Cultural Epochs" and "Political Epochs" (organized as in this table) and "Spiritual Epochs" (organized as spring, summer, autumn, winter). Making the table turned out to be very difficult for me, partly because of the necessity for squaring the two organizations, partly because Spengler does not tabulate the political epochs for the Arabian Culture, partly because the dates in the three tables are not wholly consistent with each other or with those in the text, which is not wholly self-consistent, but primarily because of the need to select and interpret in such a way that a much abbreviated amalgamation would make sense to me, and hopefully to the reader.

—R D M

[TABLE FOLLOWS]

"CONTEMPORARY" EPOCHS IN THE SPENGLERIAN WORLD (1600-0-1950) AND THE BLISHIAN WORLD (1950-4104)—See Footnote 4

THE EPOCHS: P=POLITICAL; R=RELIGIO-PHILOSOPHIC; A=ART; M=MATHEMATICAL	THE CLASSICAL CULTURE	THE ARABIAN CULTURE	THE WESTERN CULTURE	THE EARTHMANIST CULTURE
PRE-CULTURAL PERIOD. Tribes and their chiefs; no politics, no State. Chaos of primitive expression forms.	1600-1100 Mycenaean Age "Agamemnon"	500-0 Persian-Seleucid Period	500-900 Frankish Period Charlemagne	2289-2464 Vegan-War Period Admiral Hrunta
CULTURE. EARLY PERIOD.	1100-650	0-500	900-1500	2464-3111
P1. FORMATION OF FEUDAL ORDER	1100-750	0-400	900-1254	2464-3089
R1. Spiritual Spring; the Priestly Myth / the Military Myth	Demeter cult / Trojan War	Primitive Christianity / Gospels, Apocalypses	German Catholicism / Siegfried, Arthur	Hruntanism / Vegan-War Myth
A1. Early forms, rural, unconsciously shaped	Doric	The cupola	Gothic	
R2. Mystical-metaphysical shaping of Myth	Cosmogonies	Patristic literature	Scholasticism	
P2. BREAKDOWN OF FEUDAL ORDER: THE INTERREGNUM	750-650	400-500	1254-1500	3089-3111
R3. Spiritual Summer; the Reformation	Orphism, et al.	Monophysitism, et al.	Huss-Luther-Loyola	Arpad Hrunta
A2. Exhaustion of possibilities in Early forms	Late Doric	Proto-Arabesque	Early Renaissance	
CULTURE. LATE PERIOD.	630-300	500-800	1500-1815	3111-3925
P3. FORMATION OF A WORLD OF ARISTOCRATIC STATES	650-487	500-661	1500-1660	3111-3602
R4. First purely philosophical world views	Pre-Socratics	In Jewish literature	Galileo, Bacon	
M1. Formation of a new Mathematic	Geometry	Algebra	Analysis	Matrix mathematics
A3. Mature art forms, urban and conscious	Ionic	Zenith of mosaic art	Baroque	
R5. Puritanism; opposition to rising absolutism	Pythagoras	Mohammed	Cromwell; the Fronde	The Duchy of Gort
P4. CLIMAX OF THE STATE FORM ("ABSOLUTISM"): Aristocracy held in check by alliance of King (or Tyrant) with Bourgeoisie	487-338: Age of Themistocles and Pericles	661-750: The Ommaiyad Caliphate	1660-1789; the Ancien Régime	3602-3900: Eart and Okies vs. Colonials
R6. Spiritual Autumn: the Enlightenment	Socrates	The Mutazilites	Locke, Rousseau	
A4. Intellectualization of Mature art forms	Myron, Phidias	Arabesque	Rococo	
M2. Zenith of mathematical thought	Conic sections	Spherical trigonometry	The infinitesimal	
R7. The Great Conclusive System: Mystic Scholastic	Plato / Aristotle	Alfarabi / Avicenna	Goethe, Hegel / Kant	

	Classical	Arabian	Western	Galactic
P5. REVOLUTION AND NAPOLEONISM: Bourgeoisie against alliance of King (or Tyrant) and Aristocracy; victory of Money over Blood.	338-300: partisans of Philip; Alexander.	750-800: the Kufans; the first Abbassids.	1789-1815: Robespierre, Napoleon.	3900-3976: Okies vs. Earth and Colonials.
A5. Exhaustion and dissolution of Mature forms.	Corinthian	"Moorish" art	Romanticism	
CIVILIZATION AND SPIRITUAL WINTER.	300-0-300	800-1400	1815-2522	3976-4104
P6. TRANSITION FROM NAPOLEONISM TO CAESARISM: the Period of Contending States; dominance of Money ("Democracy").	300-100: from Alexanderism to Caesarism. The Cynics Epicurus, Zeno Archimedes Roman Stoicism Hellenistic art	800-1050: from Caliphate to Sultanate. Brethren of Sincerity Movements in Islam Albiruni Practical Fatalism Spanish-Sicilian art	1815-2000: from Napoleonism to MacHineryism. Comte, Darwin, Marx Schopenhauer, et al. Riemann Ethical Socialism Modern art	IN CLOUD 3998-4104: New York vs. IMT; Jorn vs. New York The Stochastics
R8. Materialism (science, utility, prosperity) **R9.** Ethical-social ideals replacing religion **M3.** Mathematics; the concluding thought **R10.** Spread of final world sentiment **A6.** Art problems; craft art				
P7. CAESARISM: victory of force-politics over Money; decay of the nations into a formless population, soon made into an imperium of gradually increasing crudity of despotism.	100-0-100: Sulla, Caesar Tiberius, up to Domitian.	1050-1250: the Seljuk Sultanate.	2000-2105: MacHinery and Erdsenov; rise to full power of Bureaucratic State.	4104: THE TRIUMPH OF TIME OVER SPACE
A7. Artificial, archaic, exotic art forms. **R11.** (in the masses only). Second Religiousness	Roman art Syncretism	"Oriental" art Syncretic Islam	Adventism; Witnesses	
P8. THE FINAL POLITICAL FORM: the world as spoil. Gradual enfeeblement of imperial machinery against raiders and conquerors. Primitive human conditions thrusting up into the highly civilized mode of living. **A8.** Fixed forms, giganticism, imperial display	100-300: full power of the Empire, then disintegration in the West. Triumphal arch	1250-1400: rise-fall of the Ilkhanate; rise of Ottoman Turks under whom the moribund culture endures to 1920. Gigantic buildings	2105-2522: full power; then decline and fall of Bureaucratic State.	
THE AFTERMATH.	After 284, Arabianization in the East.	1800-1950: Westernization of Arabian lands and entire world.	After 2522, Earthmanization.	3976-4104: galaxy proper conquered by Web of Hercules